North of the River

North of the River

Mark B. Higginson

Writer's Showcase
San Jose New York Lincoln Shanghai

North of the River

Writer's Showcase
an imprint of iUniverse.com, Inc.

For information address:
iUniverse.com, Inc.
5220 S 16th, Ste. 200
Lincoln, NE 68512
www.iuniverse.com

This book is a work of fiction and any resemblance to real people,
living or dead is purely coincidental.

ISBN: 0-595-14925-1

Printed in the United States of America

DEDICATION

This novel is dedicated to those soldiers who have served along the Korean DMZ, especially those killed and wounded in action during their service there. And to those few women of the American Red Cross who supported them. And to my friends of long ago. Here's to Tim, Bob, Tom, Larry, Jack, Chris, Suzanne, Art, Bill, Seth, Penny, Dave, Toni, and all the rest. To the fun times. And to George. R.I.P.

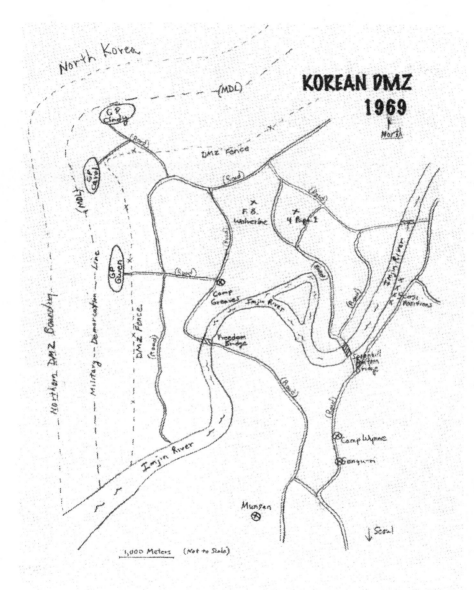

FOREWORD

The "Second Korean War" began on November 2, 1966 with the ambush and destruction of an eight man American patrol south of the DMZ by the North Koreans. Hostile action continued for the next three years, during which time 51 Americans were killed in action with an additional 111 wounded. While the DMZ was designated as a hostile fire zone, nowhere will you find the names of the dead commemorated on a wall. During this same period, total ROK casualties are estimated at almost 1,000. Approximately 715 North Korean soldiers died. The United States Army was pulled back from the DMZ proper in 1971 and replaced by ROK troops. Service in and around the DMZ by a relatively small group of American soldiers of the Second and Seventh Infantry Divisions has been generally unrecognized and unacknowledged by the American public. This novel tells the story of some of these soldiers in fictionalized form.

ACKNOWLEDGEMENTS

Thanks to Tim and Chris for their memories and assistance in the writing of this book. Thanks also to those who encouraged me throughout its writing. Thanks to Susan for putting up with me.

CHAPTER I

June 2000. Clay Holloway, Colonel, US Army (Ret.) stood casually in front of the fireplace in the new home, which he and his wife had completed only a few weeks earlier. His right foot was propped on the brick hearth and his eyes were fixed on the screen of his Panasonic wide screen television set. Outside, rain dripped from the roof and an unusually cool June wind swept across Lake Erie and through the open screen door of the Cleveland suburban home. Holloway's right hand held a frosty mug of freshly poured Heineken, which rested easily on the mantle above him. The white foam at the top of the mug had crested the rim and was almost at the point of running down the side. He ended that threat with a quick sip. Then, unexpectedly, there it was on the screen. A high chain linked fence in the foreground and a dark forbidding silhouette of a hill behind it. Twice he blinked in succession as though not believing what he was seeing. Silently he stood for a long moment, his eyes transfixed with the sight of it. His body tensed momentarily and memories began flooding his consciousness. Long ago memories of heat and dust and sweat. Memories too of cold and snow and icy Siberian wind. And yes, still the distant memories of blood and pain. Faces of young men mixed with a few young women. Often the faces were attached to names. Family names like Hardesty, Courtney, and Hackworth. And others with the nicknames by which he would always remember them; "Sweeper," "Hostileman," and, of course, "The Red Baron." Still others whose names he had forgotten long ago, but not their faces; never their faces. Some he'd seen again, but most not for almost 30 years. Well into middle age by now, he wondered how would they look, if they were even all still alive. Eventually he turned his head and directed his voice toward the other room.

"Well, Honey, it just may be the beginning of the end. After all of these years, it might be coming to a close." he called to his wife in the kitchen. The earlier object of Holloway's attention had been the CBS Nightly News, which had just taken him momentarily to Pyongyang, North Korea, where two heads of state stood shaking hands. And they were smiling!

It seemed almost impossible. Kim Jong Il, the North Korean dictator sometimes rated "most likely to start a nuclear war" and Kim Dae Jung, the South Korean

President, had met face to face for the first time ever. In fact, the first time any South Korean head of state had met with either Kim Jong Il or his deceased father, Kim Il Song.

It was a sight Holloway did not think he would ever see. The CBS commentator noted that the Korean War had begun exactly fifty years ago that month, when the North Korean Peoples Army, backed by the Soviets and Red Chinese, had attacked the South. The war had lasted three bloody years. Since that time there had been an uneasy truce, although an armistice had never been signed. The commentator closed his broadcast by stating that the fighting had ended in 1953. Holloway snickered at that remark.

The Korean Peninsula had poked its head periodically into the world news during the decade of the 90's. Seemingly on the brink of war more than once, the Communist North continued to maintain one of the world's largest standing armies, with the majority stationed within spitting distance of the DMZ. It also maintained a large arsenal of chemical and biological weapons and had been accused of secretly developing a nuclear capability. In one highly publicized incident it had, in fact, demonstratively tested its delivery system by firing a missile over Japan to land in the Pacific beyond. Over the last several years it had become the world's leader in exported rocket technology and the supplier of choice for many rogue nations. Constant threats were levied at the South. This while tens of thousands of its own people starved to death at home annually. Not many years earlier, a North Korean submarine had run aground in South Korea, its crew subsequently murdered by the commando team it carried, which in turn, was eventually hunted down and destroyed by the ROK Army. Patrol boat clashes in the Yellow Sea were not uncommon. Promises made, promises broken. The death of Kim Il Sung, the only dictator North Korea had ever known, had gained much publicity and fear of instability. The list went on and on. But it was the Korea of the 1960's, the time which later would be referred to by some as the "second Korean War," which had captured a permanent place in Clay Holloway's mind. And it was a television image of that hill called GP Cindy, which had sent his conscious brain thirty years into the past.

Holloway snorted, stared at the logs in the fireplace for a long moment and then turned and stalked out of his family room. He passed through the eating area and into the kitchen where his wife and Barbara Bennett were sitting at the ceramic tile covered island chatting and eating celery with blue cheese dip. Barbara lived three doors up the street. Both women had moved into their respective new homes only the month before, but already the two had become fast friends.

Holloway spoke excitedly. "Did you hear the TV? The North and the South are finally talking seriously about economic cooperation. They may open the borders to families. And get this. They've turned off the speakers in the DMZ."

His wife glanced at him lovingly. "Yes, I caught a little of it earlier. Do you trust them?"

"Ha! You know the answer to that one. It's hard to trust anything they do or say, but this may just be the beginning of the end. It's long overdue, that's for sure. And I must admit, this somehow seems promising, especially since it's being initiated by the North. But, did you see the pictures of the Z? They had a close-up of Cindy. It gave me a funny feeling," he admitted as he massaged his left upper arm, "and a little twinge in my shoulder."

"They showed Cindy? Really?" His wife looked at him wide-eyed.

Barbara Bennett shifted her gaze from one to the other, feeling lost in the conversation. "Who's Cindy? And what does your shoulder have to do with all this?"

"Cindy's not a person," Holloway's wife replied amusedly. "It's a hill. Guard Post Cindy. And he's talking about his wound. But don't get him started."

"Wound? From what? I thought you told me Clay hadn't been in Vietnam. And I know he wasn't wounded in Desert Storm," Barbara stated.

"He wasn't wounded in Vietnam. It was Korea. The DMZ," Mrs. Holloway clarified.

Barbara laughed mockingly. "Korea! You're not old enough for that, Clay Holloway. The Korean War happened fifty years ago. How could you be wounded in Korea?"

Holloway smiled knowingly. It wasn't the first time he'd experienced this. He'd tried to avoid explaining his wound on several occasions, but whenever he had worn his Army dress green uniform the Purple Heart was there along with several other rows of ribbons and invariably someone who didn't know him would ask how he'd been hit. It was understandable that Barbara couldn't identify with Korea. Even those Americans alive at the time of the late 60's were for the most part unaware of the happenings in that country then. That included most of the military people with whom Holloway had worked and associated for the past three decades and who had only a very sketchy knowledge of the Korean DMZ. In the late 1960's America was focused on Vietnam. That had been the big show. The only real show. The situation in Korea had gone largely ignored by the press and the American public. There had been a few headlines when the USS Pueblo was captured or that EC-121 electronic reconnaissance plane had been shot down killing all aboard. And occasionally some other happenings would find the news. Once Holloway and his then future wife had even been part of those headlines, but mostly the events had not made the papers at all or if they had, were relegated to one or two paragraphs on page ten. No, he'd never gotten to Vietnam. By the time his shoulder had mended and he had completed his next tour in Germany, the US withdrawal from Southeast Asia was in full swing. A year later the war in Vietnam ended, at least for America. A decade after that the Berlin Wall had come down and the two Germanys reunited. The once powerful Soviet Union had disintegrated. But Korea seemed to go on and on, like a 50 year bad dream that refuses to end.

In retrospect, 1969 had been a long time ago. He and his wife had been so young. The whole world it seemed had been young then. And although seeing the television pictures made it feel like yesterday, of course it wasn't. Two grown sons were testimony to that. Amazing! One was about to graduate from Ohio State and the other was parked out in the desert as a US Marine at Twenty Nine Palms. A lot had happened since Korea. Marriage, two kids, and a lot more years of serving Uncle Sam. Two tours in Europe, Ft. Sill, Ft. Knox, Panama, London, the Pentagon twice, several temporary duty assignments, and a war in the Gulf. And finally, retirement as a bird colonel with a full thirty years of service, a pension, a brand new house back in the area where he was raised, and a job with corporate America, which Holloway had begun three weeks earlier. But it was Korea where it had all really started. His first tour of duty. His first command. His first taste of violence and bloody death. His transition from college boy into what it really meant to be a soldier. Holloway looked at his wife and smiled. Their eyes locked for a brief moment.

"It wasn't during the Korean War, Barbara," she said. "It was much later. It was how we met. How we came to be together. We've been married for almost thirty years and that's where it all started. The Korean DMZ. The land that time forgot."

"You were there too? The DMZ?" Barbara asked."

"Oh, she was very much there," Holloway interceded. "And the truth of the matter is that not only was she there, but if she hadn't been, I seriously doubt that I would be standing here talking to you right now."

"Well, I was only actually inside of the DMZ once. But trust me, that was more than enough," Holloway's wife added mysteriously.

Barbara arched an eyebrow at both of them. "OK. Well, now you've really got me interested. Pour me a tall one and start talking. I've got all evening and a screwdriver would be fine, thank you very much," she announced as she slid onto one of the high-legged stools standing at the island counter in the kitchen.

"Are you sure you want to hear about all of this?" she asked Barbara skeptically.

"You're darn right I'm sure. I want to know how you met and what GP Cindy is," Barbara replied emphatically.

"Well, Bagger," his wife said looking at Clay. "It's your story more than mine and you're a better story teller. What do you say?"

"Bagger?" Barbara echoed. "I haven't heard you call him that before."

Clay Holloway showed a glimpse of a distant smile and glanced toward the logs in the other room. Outside it was unseasonably cool for a June evening and they both enjoyed the fire even though it was unnecessary. "I'll tell you what, Barb. If you're really interested and I'm going to tell this story properly it's going to take a while. Call up your husband and tell him to grab his beer and trudge on up here. I'm not going to make Ken miss his dinner and I'm not going to go through it all twice. There's shrimp in the fridge and we'll throw some steaks on the grill when the two of you are ready." He handed Barbara the cordless phone. She jerked up the rod antenna and started pushing buttons, which made little electronic beeping sounds.

Holloway walked back into the family room, glancing out of the sliding glass door at the lush green woods behind the house and then fixing his gaze on the fire in front of him. Strangely, the memories had created a sudden urge for a cigarette, although he had given up smoking almost ten years earlier. He rejected the desire and refocused his thoughts. Until recently his most vivid military recollections had centered more on the artillery battalion he had commanded with the Big Red One in Saudi Arabia and Kuwait during the Gulf War a few years earlier. Then a few months ago as some of the current happenings in Korea were beginning to receive media coverage, he'd found himself reflecting more and more on that country as events had continued to unfold there. And now the newscast displaying the area of the DMZ that he knew so well had served to stir his memories and focus his mind, but it had been the actual pictures of Cindy that had broken the dam that held the reservoir of memories. It had been right there in front of him again. From a different angle than when he'd last seen it, but there was no doubt it was the hill. The hill that used to be known as Guard Post Cindy or GP Cindy as they had all called it. It was a silhouette buried long ago in the recesses of his mind and only now had unexpectedly burst forth.

He was only vaguely aware when Ken and Barbara entered the room a few minutes later and after a brief greeting took seats on the leather sofa. In front of him the fire began crackling and popping and shooting sparks into the protective screen as the sap and moisture in the wood reached the necessary temperature, but by then Holloway was hearing nothing, even as he began to speak.

*   *   *

In the summer of 1969 twenty two year old Army second lieutenant of field artillery Clay Holloway was on his way to the Republic of Korea, the ROK. The Hermit Kingdom. Land of the morning calm. He still hadn't made up his mind as to exactly how he felt about that. He wasn't sure whether he should be grateful or angry. Most of his contemporaries were either in Vietnam, on their way to Vietnam, or heading toward a temporary assignment in the States or in Germany before getting orders to go to Vietnam. Ever since his ROTC days the Army had told him that he would be going to what the military termed as the "live fire exercise in Southeast Asia." Everyone went to Vietnam. Fully one quarter of his Army field artillery officer basic course at Ft. Sill, Oklahoma had been composed of US Marine Corps officers and all of them were already there. Holloway's gung-ho roommate in the Bachelor Officers Quarters (BOQ) at Ft. Sill had even requested that his orders be changed to Vietnam. So why in God's name was Holloway on his way to Korea, which nobody had even talked about for more than fifteen years, instead of Vietnam?

He had received his active duty orders the previous November, which had simply stated that he was assigned to Ft. Sill for completion of the officer's basic course, which would be followed by an overseas assignment to APO San Francisco 96220. That APO meant the Far East and where else in the Far East would they send a field artillery officer in 1969 but Vietnam. It wasn't until Holloway had been at Ft. Sill for almost a month that he learned that APO San Francisco 96220 was, in fact, not the Republic of Vietnam, but the Republic of Korea. The basic course, which lasted four months, would give him an elementary understanding of how artillery worked and what field artillery officers did to keep busy. It also made him understand that there is only one primary job for a second lieutenant of field artillery in a hostile fire zone and that is the job of forward observer. The forward observer, or FO as he is called, is the eyes of the artillery. It is the job of the FO to put himself in position to observe the enemy so that he can call for and adjust artillery fire on top of them. Of course, it seems only likely that if the FO can observe the enemy, the enemy can also observe the FO. That is why, Holloway kept hearing at Ft. Sill, that the FO's life expectancy is measured in seconds when engaged in heavy combat. The enemy will go to great lengths to eliminate the FO and his radio so that they can keep the rain of shrapnel off of their heads. With this thought at least partially in mind, Holloway had finally concluded that if the Army wished to assign him to the Republic of Korea rather than the Republic of Vietnam, they must have a good reason for doing so and who was he to question their judgment. If his orders assigned him to Korea that is where he would go.

Clay Holloway knew how he felt about Vietnam as a soldier. He was a good soldier and as a good soldier would do what his government asked him to do. But he had never quite made up his mind about how he felt about Vietnam as an individual. He had always supported the government and the military in the decision to fight the Communists in Vietnam, but by 1969 it was pretty obvious that something was drastically wrong. The war seemed to be dragging on forever. He simply could not see how the United States could actually defeat the Communists by continuing to fight the war the way they were doing it. If the enemy were beaten in a battle they would simply withdraw to Laos or Cambodia and regroup and resupply and come back when they were ready. More and more Americans were opposing the war for a variety of reasons and Holloway was finding it increasingly difficult to want to risk being maimed or killed for a war that few people in America seemed to care about. Many Americans, in fact, openly criticized soldiers for going there. Holloway had already had three classmates and friends killed there and several others wounded. The idea of going to Korea, however, was almost like a non-question. It was difficult to form an opinion about something of which he knew virtually nothing.

The young officer had spent four days passing time at Ft. Lewis, Washington outside of Seattle as he waited for a chartered flight to carry him overseas. While there he was housed in a World War II era wooden frame Bachelor Officers Quarters (BOQ) along with some other junior officers, some senior enlisted men, and several young warrant officers. The warrant officers were all helicopter pilots freshly graduated from helicopter school at Ft. Rucker, Alabama. The first thing that Holloway noticed about the helicopter pilots was their similarity of personality. Holloway decided that he had never seen a group of people that had more self-confidence or even cockiness. One young pilot was a Canadian who had volunteered for the US Army to fly helicopters and fight Communists. Most people thought that was rather unusual since many other Americans were crossing the Canadian border heading the other way in order to escape military service. A majority of the pilots were on their way to Vietnam, although a few, like Holloway, were headed for the ROK.

Warrant officers are not commissioned officers and they are not enlisted men. They hold a classification somewhere in between the other two. A warrant officer has a "warrant" for a particular specialty, which may be supply or personnel, or, as in this case, as a helicopter pilot. Over half of all warrant officers in the United States Army in 1969 were pilots. A commissioned officer may also be a pilot, however, a commissioned officer is assigned to a branch such as infantry or field artillery. Usually a commissioned officer who is a pilot has assignments which alternate between flying assignments and ones which utilize the qualifications of his branch, such as being a company commander or an operations officer. Helicopter warrant officers, unlike commissioned officers, do only one thing; fly helicopters. Like commissioned officers, however, warrant officers rate a salute from enlisted men and they are considered eligible members of the officers' club. Once Holloway came upon the later fact while reading his Officer's Guide in his room, he wandered down the hall of the BOQ, poked his head into one of the rooms and invited several of the warrant officer pilots to join him for drinks at the club, to be followed by a prime rib dinner that was being offered at the buffet for $2.95.

"Hey, that sounds good, Sir! This will be the first time I've ever been in an O club as anything but a student guest," replied one of the WO's. "Ft. Rucker was pretty strict about that."

"You know, you really don't have to call me sir. I mean I know I outrank you, but we're all just staying here in this Q together for few days so what's the big deal. My name's Clay Holloway. I'm from Cleveland."

"Hey, Clay. I'm Hardesty. Todd Hardesty. Chicago. How's it going?" The blond young warrant officer extended a friendly hand. "This is Mickey, Howie, and Brian," Hardesty said as he pointed around the room. There were greetings and handshakes. "Why don't you give us about fifteen minutes to change into our class A's and we'll meet you."

"Roger, that. I'll be back in one five," Holloway responded as he turned and walked back down the hall toward his room, which was part of a suite of four sleeping rooms with a common room in the middle. The common room contained a wooden table, two easy-chairs, several straight back wooden chairs, and an old white refrigerator with gouges on the door. Two weathered looking E-7's dressed in fatigues were sitting in the easy chairs holding bottles of Olympia and smoking Lucky Strikes. They looked up as Holloway entered the room.

"Hey, Lieutenant, what do think about killing some time later tonight with some poker? We're trying to get a game goin'. What do you say?" one of the E-7's asked.

"Well thanks for the offer, Sarge, but I've already got plans. They're serving prime rib at the O club buffet and some of the pilots down the hall and I are going to take them up on it. Couple of cold beers and prime rib sound like a winner. Thanks anyway. Maybe another time." Holloway wasn't sure he wanted to play even if he hadn't been leaving. The senior enlisted people that were staying there seemed pretty salty. They'd obviously been around the block a few times and Holloway didn't feel like being hustled. On the other hand, maybe it would be good spending some time with some of these more experienced people. It looked like all of them had had at least one tour in Vietnam and maybe Korea too. Maybe he could learn a few things from them in an informal atmosphere like a poker game. Maybe there would be another game tomorrow night and he could join in then. He'd think about that.

Holloway grabbed the hand engraved leather shaving kit from the top of the worn dresser and carried it into the little bath. The razor was buried near the bottom. Holloway dug it and a can of Barbosol out and hurriedly shaved, finishing with a splash of English Leather on his sun tanned neck. He was dressed in the permanent press version of the khaki short-sleeved Army summer uniform. He preferred it over the standard cotton khaki uniform which soldiers were issued and which usually looked like it had been slept in after only a couple of hours on a hot day. Holloway unzipped the front of his trousers and tucked in his shirt, aligning the shirt seam with the fly of the pants. He wiped a smudge from the glossy brass belt buckle and decided the shine on his shoes would last for at least the rest of the night. There was a knock at the door.

"Yeah?" called Holloway.

Todd Hardesty poked his head through the partially open door. "All set, Clay?"

"Sure. Let's go. Are the other guys ready?"

"Right. I told them we'd meet them on the first floor."

The two young men strode out into the hall, walked down the narrow corridor, and virtually ran down the two flights of wooden steps to the main floor. The three other warrant officers were standing on the sidewalk just outside of the door sensing the warm evening of the Pacific Northwest. The five soldiers joined together and headed in the direction of where they thought the officers' club was supposed to be located. It turned out to be less than ten minutes away and a few moments after that were seated in a cluster at the bar having been informed that it would continue to be happy hour for the next forty-five minutes. Hardesty paid for the first round of beer.

"So all of you guys are just out of flight school, is that right?" asked Holloway.

"Well, not really flight school," replied the pilot named Mickey McGinnis. "Flight school was a while back. We just got out of helicopter school. Rotary wing school. The world is full of fixed wing pilots. A monkey can fly fixed wing. Rotary is a whole different world."

"I take it that means it was tough," said Holloway.

"Yeah, it was tough. A lot of pressure. You know if you wash out it's over. You're back to being an enlisted man for the rest of your commitment. No warrant, no chopper, no nothing. Probably wind up in a rifle company in the 'Nam walking point, lookin' for booby traps. I'm just glad we all made it. I can't believe Vietnam can be any worse than chopper school. We probably lost more guys in accidents than they do in combat. One dude flew his Huey right into a high tension line a week before graduation. Bird blew up when it hit the ground."

"Is that where you're going? Vietnam?"

"That's it. Only way to fly. No pun intended. All of us are except Hardesty," replied Mickey.

Holloway looked at Todd Hardesty. "Where are you going?"

"Korea," he replied. "Second Aviation Battalion, Second Infantry Division."

"That's where I'm going too. The Second Division that is. Probably to an artillery battalion. How do you feel about that? Going to Korea instead of Vietnam."

Hardesty looked at Holloway a moment before speaking. "I'm really not sure. Sometimes I feel like I ought to be going with these guys. We've had some good times together. I'd get a lot more flight time in the 'Nam too."

Mickey spoke up. "Todd, man, you're nuts. If I had orders to Korea I'd be singing and dancing in the aisle of that Boeing 707 all the way across the Pacific. Even with the other three of us going to Vietnam we're all going to get split up once we get in country. As far as flight time, you'll get plenty and you won't have to be dodging ground fire to get it."

Thus far Mickey had done most of the talking. It seemed to be a show of bravado, as he steeled himself against the days ahead. Holloway looked at the other two pilots. Howie was the quiet one. He was of medium height with short curly blond hair and an easy grin. Brian was short and muscular. He seemed to always be nervous and his eyes darted around constantly. Holloway decided he was worried about going to Vietnam. He was right to be nervous. No one knew it, of course, but three months later Brian would be dead, a victim of an air-to-air collision over an LZ.

An hour at the bar was followed by almost two hours at the dinner table. The prime rib buffet had been a feast. An unlimited supply of rare beef, Yorkshire pudding, potatoes, gravy, and asparagus tips sautéed in butter. Cheesecake and coffee had ended the meal, followed by liqueur glasses of Drambuie. Three hours later the five men walked slowly back to the BOQ moaning with every other step, vowing to never eat that much again.

The next morning Holloway met Todd Hardesty for coffee in the officers' open mess. After a brief conversation the two men had realized that they were both assigned to the same overseas flight and both had the same in-processing schedule. They spent the next several hours together in typical military fashion, by standing in lines. But by noon, their bureaucratic tedium almost complete, the two had found that they shared many similar interests and viewpoints and their friendship had begun to grow. Hardesty had had two years of college at Illinois while Holloway had graduated from Penn State. And, in fact, both men had belonged to different chapters of the same fraternity. Both had been liberal arts majors and while Holloway had been in ROTC and graduated the year before, Todd Hardesty had dropped out of school to join the Army's warrant officer helicopter pilot program, graduating in the top ten percent of his class. Flying seemed to be his main focus in life and the fastest and least expensive way for him to accomplish that goal was to do exactly what he was doing, flying Army helicopters. He planned to fly for at least the four years of his Army enlistment commitment and then evaluate what to do next. Holloway, on the other hand, already knew what he wanted to do. He wanted a military career.

When Clay Holloway returned to the BOQ that evening and walked into the common room with the refrigerator, five of the senior NCOs were seated around the table for their nightly poker game. The air was thick with smoke and the smell of liquor was in the air.

"Hey, Lootenant. Pull up a chair. We need some fresh blood," one of the E-8's called.

"Thanks, Top. I think I'll just watch for a while," Holloway responded. He'd played his share of poker; beginning in junior high school when he'd joined in the nickel and dime games played under the streetlight at the tennis courts when he was thirteen. But he worried that maybe he was out of his league with some of these veterans who'd been around the world more times than he'd been in love. But as Holloway watched the betting it became quickly obvious to him that there was some really stupid poker being played on that table. Most of the players were drinking straight Jim Beam or Jack Daniel's; no glass, no ice. No one seemed to ever fold. Even if a player had a complete bust for a hand, he would call everyone just to see what they had. Bluffing was obviously impossible in this game. Holloway decided to give it a try. Considering his upcoming departure the next night, it didn't seem likely that he'd be needing much money for a while.

"Deal me in, Sergeant Major," Holloway said as he dragged one of the wooden straight back chairs across the worn carpeting. "Anybody here going to Korea?" he asked.

"I am," said a burly black master sergeant. "So's Mac," he noted pointing his thumb next to him.

"You ever been there before?" Holloway asked as he pulled the five cards toward him.

"Twice '52 and '63, Vietnam once already too."

Christ, thought Holloway to himself. Here I am as nervous as a whore in church about all of this, like it's the most important thing that ever happened to anybody and here's this guy acting like it's just another day at the office. "What's it like?" Clay asked.

"Depends, Sir. Where you going?"

"Second Infantry Division. That's all I know."

"Shit! Second Division. That ain't no fun at all, Lieutenant. That's the DMZ. They park you up on a frozen hilltop in the Z in January, you'll be praying to go to Vietnam. You ought to try to get your orders changed to I Corps."

"Hey I hate to interrupt this travelogue, but does anybody have jacks to open?" asked the Sergeant Major.

Holloway opened for a dollar. Within forty-five minutes the NCOs had gotten drunker and Holloway had gotten richer. He went to bed an hour later with some understanding of the DMZ and an extra hundred dollars in his wallet.

CHAPTER 2

It was 0400 hours the following night (morning) when Second Lieutenant Clay Holloway, Warrant Officer First Class Todd Hardesty, and one hundred and fifty-two other assorted military personnel exited the green military buses and stood on the tarmac, in the rain, in the dark, at McChord Air Force Base a few miles northeast of Ft. Lewis. Slowly they began boarding a red tailed Northwest Orient Boeing 707, which would carry them on their fourteen-hour journey to the Far East. Holloway, at almost six feet two inches, was able to convince his five feet ten companion of the necessity of Holloway having the aisle seat so that he could stretch his long legs occasionally. He also did not believe there would be anything worth viewing through the window during the flight. He was correct. There was a brief refueling stop at Anchorage, Alaska and a second in Tokyo, but a few scattered buildings and more rain constituted the only view.

The Asian skies were also gray and overcast when the plane touched down at midmorning on the airfield at Kimpo, just outside of Seoul, Korea. The two friends strained to peer out of the small windows. Both men were surprised by what they could see.

"Check that out, Clay!" exclaimed Hardesty excitedly pointing at a pair of camouflage painted F-4's parked on a runway nearby. "Those are Phantoms all loaded for bear. Full loads of rockets and bombs on both of them. They must be on an alert status. See how their canopies are unlocked so that the pilots can get in fast. I wonder if they keep them like that all the time?"

"Maybe because of what happened to the Pueblo," replied Holloway, referring to the American intelligence gathering ship that had been ignominiously captured by the North Koreans a year and a half earlier. "I remember at the time the North Koreans attacked the ship that somebody told me that neither the Americans nor the South Koreans had any aircraft available to scramble to help her."

"And look at all the antiaircraft weaponry," Hardesty said. "There's twin 40's and 50 caliber's all along the side of the runways. Bunkers! Man, we're sure not Stateside. I didn't know it was like this over here. I wonder if they're expecting something to happen?"

"Guess we're about to find out aren't we?" said Holloway. The door to the big silver jet was pushed outward by one of the stewardesses and a tall metal stairway was wheeled up to the open door and secured. The stewardess motioned to the men closest to the door and immediately the entire population of the aircraft stood up, clogging the aisles, and standing for several minutes before they were able to walk out of the door and into the warm muggy air with an usual odor. Carefully, the soldiers walked down the metal steps, holding onto the handrail with their right hands, carrying flight bags with their left, and feeling the stiffness in their bodies from the long flight began to slowly work its way free.

A fifty yard walk across the damp tarmac brought the men into a large reception area. Army clerks dressed in short sleeved khaki summer uniforms were trying to channel the new arrivals into various lines. Once everyone was inside the terminal, a young buck Sergeant climbed onto a chair and made an announcement.

"Give me your attention, gentlemen. I want all officers to move into the line on your far right. All NCOs E-5 and above to move into the second line on your right. Everybody else form a line on your left. Once you have arranged yourselves into the proper line, I want you all to loosen your belts and be prepared to drop your drawers. Everybody is going to be getting a gamma globulin injection. There are medical teams that are going to be giving the injections while you are filling out the currency exchange forms that are being circulated at this time.

Listen closely. I ain't gonna say this twice. Everyone has got to turn in all of his greenbacks at this time for military payment certificates, MPC. It is a federal crime and against Army regulations to bring any US greenbacks into this country if you are military personnel. This is no joke. Anyone found keeping even one dollar American will be in serious difficulty. Get out all of your dollars, count it out, put it down on the form, and get ready to turn it in at the counter." The E-5 stepped down from his chair and disappeared into the crowd.

The injection was given on the upper quarter of the right buttock. The needle penetrated deeply into the soft flesh. Holloway truly believed that it was the most painful shot he had ever received. He quickly buckled his trousers and tried to forget about the discomfort as he counted out his money, which included his poker winnings from two nights before, and entered the total on the form that he had been given.

Thirty minutes later twenty-eight soldiers, including Clay Holloway and Todd Hardesty, were on a military bus heading for someplace called Ascom City, which was supposedly not too far away. The skies had cleared, the sun was shining, and the temperature was rising dramatically. It was hot in the bus. Men were beginning to perspire and the strange odor remained in the air, smelling as though somebody's toilet had overflowed. Todd Hardesty wrinkled his nose.

"What the hell is that smell?" he asked to no one in particular.

"It usually smells like this," said a pudgy Army major with a Quartermaster Corps insignia on his collar. "You'll get used to it. The only time the smell dissipates a bit is during the winter when everything is frozen. You'll know it's spring when you can smell it again. Koreans fertilize their rice paddies with human excrement. Most of the farmers don't have indoor plumbing. They just use all the shit they accumulate in their honey pot to feed the fields. Think about that the next time you have rice in your mess kit. Say, where are you two headed anyway?"

"We're both going to the Second Infantry Division, Sir," Holloway replied formally.

The major sniffed. "Second Division, huh. That's too bad. There's not too much fun up there. Bad shit. You boys ought to find a way to stick around here and have some fun. I'll tell you what. Korea is the best kept secret in the United States Army. At least down around here or Taegu or Pusan. You can live like a king in this country. Rent yourself a yobo. She'll give you a place to stay off post. Cook your food. Booze is cheap here too. Great place. Great place. Can't beat it with a stick."

"Excuse me, Sir. What exactly is a yobo?" Holloway asked.

"I think it's Korean for wife. Fifty, maybe a hundred bucks a month max. You just rent one and she's like your wife for as long as you're here."

"You're saying that people rent wives for fifty dollars a month?" Holloway asked incredibly.

"Sure. Happens all the time. Good looking girls. Give you anything you want. Usually they have a decent hooch. Great sex. They'll cook for you. Have to give them some extra money for food if you want them to feed you though."

Holloway was taken aback. Admittedly, he had been brought up in the Midwest by middle class Presbyterian parents, but he certainly did not consider himself a prude by any stretch of the imagination. But the idea of just plopping down fifty bucks and renting a wife for a month at a time was something that was alien to his value system. Todd Hardesty, on the other hand, was fascinated by what sounded like a pretty good deal.

"Fifty bucks. That's not bad. You say some of them are pretty good lookin'."

"Hell, yes. 'Course Koreans as a people aren't as attractive as say the Vietnamese or the Thai's, but there are some good looking kimchi critters running around. A good thing about having a yobo is that you probably won't get the clap. As long as she's your yobo she won't sleep with anybody else so you're safe. Business girls sleep with anybody, so you're bound to get the clap from them sooner or later."

"What did you call them? Kimchi critters?" Todd asked.

"Yeah. Kimchi critters. Kimchi is the national food of Korea. Some of them eat it every day. They even smell like it. GI's call anything that is Korean, kimchi. A kimchi critter is a Korean girl. A kimchi cab is a Korean taxi. And so forth." the Captain said.

"Sounds good to me. Tell me about the Second Division. What did you mean before when you said it was bad shit?"

The major peered at Holloway over his glasses. "You need to understand that duty in Korea Is not bad as long as you're not up north. But the Second is in the DMZ. People get killed there. Even if nobody is shooting at you you're in the boonies all the time. Anything north of the Imjin River is the hostile fire zone, in case no one bothered to tell you. No civilians up there at all. Even south of the river there's no cities or towns to speak of. Just a few little villages scattered around. You live in the field a lot. I see you're artillery. Maybe that won't be too bad. If you were infantry I'd really feel sorry for you." There was a pause. "You're a pilot?" the major asked Todd Hardesty, looking at the wings pinned above his pocket. Hardesty nodded. "Well, that shouldn't be too bad either. At least if you're a pilot you can fly your ass out of there once in a while. Maybe even take him with you." The pudgy major snickered at what he considered a joke.

The bus stopped momentarily at the main gate at Ascom City. The driver handed his trip ticket to the gate guard who examined it momentarily and returned it. The bus pulled quickly into the interior of the huge base, then stopping outside of a transient BOQ.

The Noncommissioned Officer In Charge (NCOIC) who had been riding in the first seat stood up, turned to face his audience, and cleared his throat. "Attention, all officers. Gentlemen, this is your BOQ and final in-processing station before your unit assignments. Please disembark at this time. Sergeant Major Dawson is standing outside ready to direct you further. Please insure that the houseboys get all of your luggage out of the luggage bay." The E-5 climbed down the three steps of the bus, and out of the open door into the sunlight.

Two hours later, the newly arrived officers filed into a small briefing room, their stomachs filled by the noon meal that had just been provided for them in a conveniently located mess hall. Sergeant Major Joshua Dawson, a large black senior noncommissioned officer with the Combat Infantry Badge (CIB) pinned over the left shirt pocket of his khaki uniform stood at the front of the room waiting to begin.

"Gentlemen," the Sergeant Major began, "I know that the first thing all of you want to know is when are you going to get to your new duty station. This part is easy. Those of you going to I Corps or Eighth Army will be leaving this afternoon when the bus gets here around 1500 hours. There's no one here going to Seventh Division. Those few of you going to the Second Division are probably going to have to make yourselves comfortable. Second Division says they can't send a bus down today from Camp Howze and tomorrow is the Fourth of July and nobody is going to be working if they don't have to. So I'm afraid y'all are going to have to plan to spend the holiday here with us. I have to ask you not to leave the base, but you're welcome to use the Officer's Club, the steam bath, the PX or about anything else you'll find on this compound.

Next I'd like to talk with you about three primary areas of concern before you get any farther into your thirteen month tour of the Republic of Korea. After that I'll be more than happy to talk about anything you want to talk about.

First, MPC, military payment certificates. It is completely unauthorized for military personnel to have any American currency in their possession at any time while in the ROK. You should have turned in all of your greenbacks at Kimpo when you landed. Just in case you might have "forgotten" somehow to turn it all in for MPC I'd like to offer you one more opportunity to do so. There are strict punishments for anyone holding American money in their possession. Do not allow your friends or relatives to send you any. If you get some in the mail, turn it in to your adjutant immediately. Does anyone have any American currency with them? No? OK then.

Second thing I need to mention is venereal disease. It's everywhere over here. I strongly advise each of you to avoid having intercourse with Korean nationals. If you chose to disregard my advice, then I will strongly advise you to use prophylactics. If you do not, you will almost assuredly contract syphilis or gonorrhea. Sometimes it will be curable and sometimes it may not be. Any Korean national that will allow you to have intercourse with her should be considered a business girl. Nice Korean families don't allow their daughters to associate with American GI's. All the girls you meet will be business girls. Statistically, if you have intercourse with a business girl one time during your thirteen month tour of duty here, you have a fifty percent chance of contracting a venereal disease. Some girls will show you a health card that says they have been inspected and are clean. Don't pay any attention to them. These girls buy and sell health cards like they're baseball cards. They mean nothing. Even if the card is legitimate, it only means the girl was clean the last time she was checked, not now. Some people think prostitution is legal in Korea because it is so common. It is not. You can be arrested with for consorting with a prostitute. Any questions on that?"

"Yes, Sergeant Major. Do you know of anyone that was ever arrested for consorting with a prostitute?" asked a First Lieutenant with the crossed rifles of the infantry on his collar.

The Sergeant Major gave a little smirk. "No, Sir, I don't. I'm required to say that and I did." Most of the men in the room smiled. "But I'll tell you this, gentlemen. The clap is something you don't want to get. If you've had it once you don't ever don't want to see it again.

The third thing I want to mention is slicky boys. I don't know if any of you officers who haven't been to this lovely country before have heard of Korean slicky boys, but if you haven't I want you to know that the best thieves in the world reside in the Republic of Korea. The unqualified best. They're better than the Arabs, better than the Mexicans, better than the Vietnamese. Nobody else holds a candle to them. They'll steal anything that isn't nailed down and if it is nailed down they'll steal the nails too. Guard everything. Watch everything. They're not violent. You really don't have to fear for your personnel safety. They don't carry guns and it's never like an armed robbery. They use stealth. They're bold and they're quiet and I guarantee you they'll steal things you never thought could be stolen, like the transmission out of a two and a half ton truck while it's sitting along side of a road. There is most definitely a sophisticated black market in Korea and anytime there is a demand, somebody is going to find a supply.

Now that I have discussed what I am required to discuss, I have here some copies of maps of this compound that will assist you in finding things like the PX. Sir, if you'll just pass these around?" the Sergeant Major asked as he handed the thin stack of papers to Hardesty. "Now, are there any questions?" He paused. No one spoke. "Very well then. Gentlemen, good luck on your tours. I'll be in the orderly room across the way for the rest of today if anything comes up."

The Fourth of July passed slowly. The Army celebrated the day as a holiday. Most soldiers had left the base to find entertainment elsewhere. Clay and Todd had slept late. The flight from the States and the accompanying change in time zones with its fourteen hour difference had taken its toll on their bodies, but now after ten hours of uninterrupted sleep, both men felt ready to take on the world. Unfortunately, there was no world to take on since the base appeared to be almost deserted and they were not authorized to leave the compound. They were, however, authorized to use the Officers' Club pool which they did for the remainder of the afternoon as they read and sunned themselves.

"Do you believe this, Todd?" Clay asked, folding his hands behind his head and turned slightly to get a better look at a Korean girl who strutted by in heels and a white bikini. "It's like we're on vacation over here or something. And all this time counts on our tour. Maybe we can hang around here for the next year. This is not bad at all. Did you see the sign inside for the party tonight? There's going to be a band on the roof. This is incredible. "

"I wouldn't get used to this if I were you. You know what that major said. The Second is up north and it's not like this up there. Enjoy it while you can."

The party that evening was a pleasant nightcap to the two days of laziness. The two young men dressed in their summer khaki uniforms sat on the roof admiring the attractive Korean girlfriends of several of the other officers. Most of the women were dressed in brightly colored silk dresses of emerald green, royal blue, and bright red, with slits of varying lengths running up the sides of their thighs. Their shiny long black hair hung down the women's' backs in most cases, though occasionally Clay would notice a girl with hair piled high on her head in a more formal fashion. Unfortunately, all of the women were accompanied and they presented no opportunities for Todd or Clay to dance or even to start a conversation. Both men viewed the oriental women curiously. Neither soldier could remember ever having had even a conversation with an Asian female.

At 10:00 sharp the fireworks began. Everyone gathered at the rail surrounding the roof to watch the explosions of color as they burst high above and sent multicolored showers plummeting toward the ground. Some of the explosions reminded Holloway of the parachute flares of the illumination rounds he had adjusted during his days as an artillery student at Ft. Sill. He looked around at the cluster of supply and transportation and finance officers and wondered if any of them had ever seen an illumination round or if they ever would. It seemed so civilized here, so relaxed and easy going. He reminded himself, though, that this was not where he was assigned. He wouldn't be working in I Corps or Eighth Army. He was headed north. For the one-hundredth time he wondered what lie ahead.

*   *   *

"Lt. Holloway! Mr. Hardesty! Your ride to Second Division is here," called out the young specialist fourth class from down the hallway.

"On our way!" Holloway called back. He slung his heavy duffel over his shoulder, tucked his blue nylon flight bag under his other arm, picked up his gray hard-shelled suitcase with his still free left hand, and staggered down the hallway. Todd Hardesty was a few seconds behind. Outside was a one and a quarter ton truck with a canvas top covering the bed and the tailgate lowered. The two men set their luggage onto the truck bed. They were the only passengers and elected to ride together in the back, leaving the driver by himself.

Less than an hour later and having driven out of the populated area and into the Korean countryside, the truck pulled through the main gate of Camp Howze, headquarters of the Second Infantry Division, the Indianhead Division. A large replica of the division patch adorned the sign over the main gate. A black shield with a white star and the head of an Indian chief in the center was the symbol that had existed since its baptism of fire in World War I, where it had been one of the leaders in the November offensive in the Argonne which broke the back of the German Army. The Second had fought across Europe during World War II after landing at Omaha Beach on D plus one. During the Korean War the patch had symbolized the American Army to many Koreans. It had been thrust into the fray soon after the fighting began and had fought almost continuously until the cease-fire. Though it had come close to annihilation near Kunu-ri in the fall of 1950 when the Red Chinese had entered the war unexpectedly, it had been rebuilt and three months later would exact its revenge of the Chinese. In February 1951 it again suffered severe casualties and the loss of many of its howitzers in the area of Wonju. But in the days to follow, it initiated one of the most devastating artillery victories in the history of warfare. Catching massed formations of Chinese troops in the open, the Division artillery fired thunderous barrages for hour after hour after hour as the massed Chinese marched forward, refusing to retreat. The incredible slaughter continued until the remnants of the formations faltered at last and turned in an attempt to escape the rain of steel. When it was over, 5,000 Chinese troops lay dead with perhaps another 15,000 having suffered wounds. For the Second Division's artillery, the "Wonju shoot" was one of its finest moments. Following the cease-fire in 1953, the Division returned to the United States. But in 1965 it again was deployed to the Korean DMZ to replace the First Cavalry Division as the Cav had been recalled to be reorganized and equipped as the First Cavalry Division (Airmobile) on its way to Vietnam.

Camp Howze was clean and orderly. It had been built into the backside of a large hill. In fact, when Holloway walked from one building to another, he invariably found himself going up or down hill. Most structures on the compound were metal Quonset huts painted a light green and sometimes joined together to form T's or L's. The whole place reminded Clay Holloway of an outlaws' hideout in the old west.

"Don't bother unpacking," the assistant G-1 (adjutant) had told both men. "You're not going to be here very long. Maybe enough time for a cigarette and a cup of coffee. There are vehicles on the way for both of you. Lieutenant Holloway, you're on your way to DivArty (Division Artillery) probably to be assigned to one of the artillery battalions that are scattered around the countryside. Mr. Hardesty, you're going to Second Aviation. From there it's anybody's guess."

The assistant adjutant had been correct. No sooner than Holloway and Todd Hardesty had shaken hands and wished each other well, than a 1 ¼ ton truck stopped in front of the G-1 building. A straw haired freckle faced specialist fourth class slid out from behind the wheel.

"Lt. Holloway? I'm here to take you to DivArty. I'll put your gear in the back." The spec/4 dropped the tailgate as Clay Holloway set the gray suitcase and his blue flight bag containing his records and many of his personal effects onto the steel bed. The driver tossed the large duffel in next to the suitcase. Holloway began to climb into the back.

"Sir? Don't sit back here. It'll be a pretty rough ride and it gets real dusty where we're going. There's plenty of room up front," the spec/4 said.

"I thought I'd better keep an eye on my gear," said Holloway. "I hear the slicky boys will get anything that's not guarded."

"Well, that's true enough, but I can see the back with my mirrors and I know where they're likely to be, so it won't be a problem. You'll be a lot more comfortable up front."

Reluctantly, Holloway nodded and climbed into the passenger seat in front. Then he turned and gave a final wave to his blond warrant officer friend. "It's been nice traveling with you. We'll have to do it again some time. Maybe the Caribbean." Hardesty tossed him a mock salute as the truck started down the hill toward the gate.

Half an hour later, when the truck arrived at DivArty and Clay Holloway went to the back to retrieve his gear, the first thing he noticed was that his blue flight bag was no longer next to his duffel in the back of the truck. Quickly he dropped the tailgate and looked under the wooden seats. It was gone.

Angrily, Lt. Holloway ordered the driver to backtrack their route hoping that it had just bounced out. But inside he felt violated and naive, vowing that never again would he allow himself to be caught like this. Holloway had just learned lesson one regarding service in the ROK. Slicky boys are smarter than spec/4's. In fact, Holloway decided, never again would he listen to a spec/4. Buck sergeants OK. Maybe even corporals. But not spec/4's. There is an old saying in the Army that goes "The two most dangerous things in the Army are a spec/4 with a wrench and a second lieutenant with a map. One of them will take your ass apart and the other one will lose it."

He was sure a slicky boy had mounted the back of the truck, taken his bag, and probably at this very moment was eating kimchi and fondling his hand carved leather shaving kit from Mexico and taking pictures with his Kodak Instamatic camera which still contained undeveloped film from a friend's wedding in the States the month before. Holloway was correct. The bag had disappeared and with it all of his official records.

There was, however, one small piece of salvation. Inside of his khaki shirt pocket was a folded copy of his orders. The DivArty S-1 seemed genuinely sympathetic to Holloway's predicament once he learned what had transpired and had ordered his clerk immediately to make several copies of the orders so that Holloway could continue with his processing. Without orders Holloway shuddered to think how screwed up things might have become. The S-1 excused himself for a moment and left his office. Holloway glanced about the room. It was quite similar to every other office he'd seen since he'd been in country. The walls were painted a semi-gloss light green and all the furniture was olive drab steel. There was one different item that attracted his attention almost immediately, however. A large acetate covered chart with a blue wooden frame hung from the wall. The chart had numbers written on the acetate with a blue grease pencil. It was a record of all of the Purple Hearts awarded in the Division thus far in 1969. There were twenty-four of them. Purple Hearts are only given to two types of people; wounded people and dead people. Holloway studied the chart for a moment and then looked away. He was surprised to say the least. He could not remember once having read about a battle casualty occurring in Korea during 1969 while he had been in the States. It must have been in the papers somewhere, he thought, but if it was, he hadn't seen it. The S-1 reentered the room, interrupting his thoughts.

"Lieutenant Holloway, you're being assigned to the Eighth Battalion, Eighteenth Artillery (8/18th pronounced eighth of the eighteenth). It's a 105mm Howitzer (towed) battalion, stationed at Camp Wynne. The battalion commander is Colonel Moody. You're lucky in a way. Your whole battalion, all four batteries, is on one compound. The other battalions in the division are split up on battery sized compounds all over the place. At Camp Wynne you have a decent sized O Club because of the size of the compound. You have another bonus there too."

"What's that?" Holloway asked.

"That's where the Doughnut Dollies are stationed," the captain replied.

"What the hell are Doughnut Dollies?"

"The Red Cross girls. I think they've been called that since World War II. There's about twelve or fourteen of them. They're assigned by the American Red Cross to bring a touch of home to the troops of the Division. They visit other compounds and guys in the field and take them coffee and Kool Aid and doughnuts of course. They live in their own hooch at Camp Wynne. They use the O Club there too. They'll probably be the only round eyed girls you see for the next thirteen months.

Bill Grant is on his way up here now. He's S-1 for the 8/18th. He's only been here about a month himself. Real gung-ho. Wants combat. Applied for Vietnam. Can't believe he didn't get it. As soon as he gets here you can shove off. Good luck."

The captain stood and extended his hand. Holloway shook it, picked up the reproduced copies of his orders that the captain had brought with him, and walked outside. His stomach growled. It was almost two o'clock and he hadn't eaten since breakfast in the mess hall at Ascom City. He shook his head slowly, thinking of the bureaucracy of the Army. Why in the hell couldn't this Lieutenant Grant just have picked him up at Ascom this morning instead of him being trucked to Camp Howze, then trucked to Div Arty, and then driven to Camp Wynne? The only thing he had accomplished by this sight seeing tour of the Korean countryside was to get his bag slickied. Well, thought Holloway, he might as well get used to it. He presumed correctly that it was just the Army way.

An open topped jeep was driving up the gravel covered road, throwing a tan cloud of dust behind it. The quarter ton vehicle towed a quarter ton trailer behind it that was covered with a canvas top. The jeep slid to a stop in front of Holloway. In the passenger seat sat a second lieutenant dressed in starched olive drab (OD) fatigues and wearing aviator style sunglasses. Short blond hair showed around the edges of his fatigue cap.

"Howdy. You Lieutenant Holloway?"

"You got it."

"I'm Bill Grant, S-1 of the 8/18th." The lieutenant stepped out of the jeep and extended his hand smiling.

"Clay Holloway, Bill. How do you do."

"Annahashamika! That's Korean for hello. Is this all of your gear?" Grant asked pointing toward Holloway's duffel and suitcase.

"All that's left of it, yeah." Holloway related what had happened to the blue flight bag with his personal effects and his 201 file. Grant frowned.

"You telling me your pay records and your medical records are gone? This is not good. Not good at all. You might have to retake all of your shots. Besides that, you might not get paid for a while. Everything is going to have to be reconstructed. Damn! This is not good at all."

Grant's driver had placed the two pieces of luggage into the trailer and tied down the heavy green canvas over them. Grant tilted the jeep seat forward and pointed toward the back as Holloway stepped into the vehicle and perched himself on the canvas covered cushion. Grant returned to his seat in the front, cocked his boot on the edge of the vehicle and twisted around as the jeep headed back down the road the way it had come.

"We're really glad to see you, Holloway. Really glad. You can't believe how short we are of officers. Charlie Battery only has one officer, the BC (Battery Commander). The others have only two. I can't tell you officially, but you'll probably be going to Charlie as the XO."

"Executive Officer? I didn't know they made second lieutenants XO's. Aren't there any first lieutenants around?"

"Sure there are. But they're the Battery Commanders. All the BC's are first lieutenants."

"Wait a minute. BC's are supposed to be captains. That's what they taught us at Ft. Sill."

"You can forget that shit right now. I'm telling you we're short of officers. Vietnam has so many officers they're tripping over each other. But Korea? Shit. We get nothing. There is not one captain in the entire battalion. Not one and we're authorized ten. You've got to step right in, learn fast, take charge and get the job done. Excuses don't get it. In case you haven't noticed, I'm a second lieutenant and I'm the adjutant. That's a captain's slot too. Hell, I've only been here a month myself. I'm right out of OCS (Officers' Candidate School). That's just the way it is."

"Well, how do you know what you're doing?" Holloway asked.

"Who said I knew what I was doing? I just fumble my way along the best I can just like you will. I've got some good NCOs in my section and the Sergeant Major helps me out."

Holloway shook his head slowly. He had hoped to be able to ease into his new assignment, not get thrown into a job for which he had limited training and no experience. He felt uncomfortable with what Grant had told him. Mentally he began reviewing the things that he had learned in artillery school about what XO's did for a living.

The jeep threw a large continuous dust cloud as it drove along the narrow dirt road that was the primary route from Div Arty to Camp Wynne. Holloway noted that the rural countryside consisted mainly of hilly areas with sparse vegetation and flatlands covered with rice paddies. He peered at occasional Koreans walking along the road as the jeep passed them. The women that he saw all wore long plain cotton skirts and T-shirts. The men seemed to all wear baggy white cotton pants with some sort of waist length jacket. As the vehicle entered Munsan-ni, the only town of any size in the Second Division area of operations (AO), Holloway noticed that the surface had turned to blacktop. It remained that way as they turned left near the center of the town and headed down the two mile stretch toward Sonyu-ri, the village adjacent to Camp Wynne. As the jeep approached the built up area, Bill Grant again swiveled around in his seat.

"This up ahead on the right is Recreation Center #4, called RC#4. It's the only place close by that we have. There's a movie theater, a bowling alley, a PX, a gym, and a few other things. Just past it here is Sonyu-ri. We're just down at the other end of the ville."

The jeep driver reduced his speed to 10 mph as he entered the village. This pleased Holloway since he was able to get a better look at his new home. RC#4 was a cluster of white buildings surrounded by a wire fence. What Grant had referred to as a village surprised Holloway. He really had not had a picture in his mind of what Sonyu-ri would look like, but if he had, he would not in his wildest dreams have pictured it the way it was.

There was only the single road that ran through the center of the "ville." On either side was a ditch that ran the length of the town. On the other side of the ditch was the walking area that was composed of scattered wooden planking or pallets or sometimes just dirt. There were narrow alleys that ran between some of the one or two story buildings that lined both sides of the street. The buildings seemed to be primarily little shops of one sort or another. Outside of several of the structures sat or squatted young women who seemed to be in their teens or early 20's. Many wore garish make-up and gaudy clothing. Holloway assumed that these were the business girls he had been warned about. Grant pointed toward one of the girls who had opened her blouse to expose her breasts to the soldiers then turned and looked at Holloway, grinning silently behind his sunglasses.

As the jeep reached the end of the village, it turned right onto a gravel driveway and stopped next to a guard shack where a helmeted MP stood with his arm extended and his palm outward. Recognizing the battalion adjutant, the gate guard came to attention, saluted, and waved the jeep through the gate. Ahead was sturdy wooden bridge, which crossed a small stream fifty feet below. In the stream, three children waded naked. The jeep crossed the narrow waterway and came to a halt in front of two Quonset huts that were joined together in the middle. On the lawn stood a tall white flag pole, which held at its top the flag of the United States of America.

"This is Battalion HQ. Let's see if the old man is here. I know he's expecting you," Grant said. Then he turned toward his driver. "Ski, you take Lt. Holloway's gear over to the old BOQ and get one of the houseboys to put it in room five."

Bill Grant motioned to Holloway and the two men strode toward the HQ entrance. Once inside, Grant turned to his left and entered the battalion orderly room. Holloway noticed a gray vacant desk with a wooden nameplate on the front. The nameplate had a dragon carved on either end. In the middle the plate read "Lt. Grant—Adjutant."

"Is Colonel Moody here, Sergeant Major?" Grant asked of a tall lanky NCO who was in the process of stapling papers to a bulletin board.

"No, Sir. He had to go out for a bit. Major Posey is not here either. Is this our new lieutenant?"

"Yes. Lt. Holloway."

"How do you do, Sir!" Holloway and Battalion Sergeant Major Houston exchanged greetings. Holloway silently reflected that the Sergeant Major had the most enormous hands he had ever encountered.

"A pleasure, Sergeant Major."

"Lieutenant Holloway, let's get you started with your paperwork. There's a lot to get done to reconstruct all of your records," Grant declared, removing his sunglasses. It was the first time Holloway had actually seen his steel gray eyes. The adjutant told the Sergeant Major about the theft of Holloway's records. Another senior NCO walked over to Grant's desk and together the men decided exactly what would have to be done.

Thirty minutes later, Holloway had signed his name seventeen times and completed one hundred and twenty four blank spaces. That had apparently satisfied the NCOs.

"OK, Lieutenant. That will get it started except for your medical records. They'll have to take care of that at the dispensary," proclaimed the Sergeant Major.

"Clay, why don't you go over to the BOQ and make sure your room and your gear is squared away. I'll send someone for you when the Colonel gets here," Grant stated. "I've got some other work I need to do."

Holloway left the Headquarters and walked in the direction that Grant had pointed. He was famished. He still hadn't had anything to eat since that morning and he glanced at his watch to see if it was almost time for dinner. As he headed for the door of the BOQ he was aware of an older man wearing glasses who was walking toward him. Holloway glanced briefly at the man's camouflaged insignia of rank that adorned the front of his fatigue cap and determined that the man was a warrant officer who certainly did not rate a salute from a second lieutenant. Camouflaged rank insignias of black or dark gold had become standard since the Vietnam War had begun in order to make it more difficult for the enemy to pick out officers and NCOs. Holloway reached for the handle of the BOQ door.

"Jesus Christ, Lieutenant! Don't you know how to salute?" the man barked. Holloway looked back. He flushed. The man was not a warrant officer. The man was a lieutenant colonel. The black embroidered nametag above the right breast pocket of his fatigue shirt read "Moody." It was Holloway's new commanding officer.

"Yes, Sir! I'm sorry, Sir! I didn't see your rank," Holloway stammered. He came to attention and saluted. The colonel returned it.

"You're the new lieutenant, aren't you?" the Battalion Commander asked.

"Yes, Sir. Lieutenant Holloway, Sir."

"Well, come on over to my office. We need to talk. I didn't mean to jump down your throat. It seemed like you were intentionally ignoring me. Discipline is getting difficult to maintain with all these draftees in the ranks and we've got to make sure that we do maintain it."

"Yes, Sir. I assure you I was not ignoring you. From a distance that black oak leaf looks like a warrant officer insignia."

"OK. Let's just forget that." They reached Battalion Headquarters and the colonel entered first, nodding toward Lieutenant Grant and Sergeant Major Collins as he lead Holloway down the short hallway to his office.

"Have a seat, Lt. Holloway. Why don't you tell me a bit about yourself before I start briefing you about our situation here. Are you married?"

"No, Sir, I'm not. No kids either." he added, hoping for a laugh.

"Well, I guess that's best," replied Colonel Moody, ignoring Holloway's attempt at humor. "A tour like this is a lot tougher if there's a separation involved. How did you get your commission?"

"ROTC at Penn State. I was commissioned last summer after Advanced Camp at Indiantown Gap, Pennsylvania. I've been on active duty since January. Basic Artillery Course at Ft. Sill and then Redeye Missile School at Ft. Bliss, Texas."

"Oh, you're Redeye qualified? Well, that's good. We already have a new Redeye Platoon Leader, but it's good to have a spare around, so to speak. You don't have Survey School do you?"

"No, Sir. I'm afraid not. Just the routine survey training during the Basic Course."

"Hummpf. OK, I was just wondering. There never seem to be enough survey-qualified officers around. That or gunnery specialists. Are you a gunnery specialist?" The Colonel was peering over the tops of his gray-rimmed glasses as he posed the question to Holloway.

"I really can't say that was my strong suit, Sir. I think I was probably best at observed fire while I was at Sill."

"I see. Well, Lieutenant, we have need for Forward Observers here, although it is the least of our needs. This battalion is required to keep FO's in the DMZ with the infantry. Some of them are officers and some are NCOs. You may have an opportunity to serve in that capacity in a few weeks because one of them is almost due to rotate home and I believe it is good experience for a young artillery officer to serve as an FO in a hostile fire zone for a while. It will also help you to better understand our mission in this country. However, for the present I am assigning you as the XO (Executive Officer) of Charlie Battery. That will be your official position even if you go to the DMZ as an FO for a month or two. Eventually you will return here as the Charlie XO. Certainly that will be your position for the battery tests, which are held in November at Camp St. Barbara.

Your Battery Commander (BC) will be Tom Courtney. He's a good man. Knows what he's doing. Charlie Battery is pulling SCOSI duty this week and Lieutenant Courtney will probably be leading them into the field before long. You may not be able to meet him until tomorrow."

"Excuse me, Sir. I don't know what SCOSI duty is," noted Holloway.

"Oh, sorry. SCOSI stands for Security and Counterespionage Operations South of the Imjin River. Our batteries have to take turns acting as infantry to try to help stop North Korean commando teams from slipping into the south for their dirty work. Primarily, they occupy fixed positions on the south bank of the Imjin River and ambush anyone trying to cross. It all happens at night. That's why I said Lieutenant Courtney is probably about ready to leave. Today is their last SCOSI day for a while. The duty shifts to another battalion beginning tomorrow night. I'd send you with them, but you need some time to get settled. You probably haven't even had time to draw your field gear yet, have you?"

"No, Sir, I haven't. I'll try to do that first thing in the morning."

"Well, that's good because you're sure to need it before too long. You'll probably spend a lot of time in the field, especially if you stay with Charlie Battery for your whole tour.

This is a good battalion, Lieutenant Holloway. And Charlie Battery is a good battery. But we're short of everything over here. Short of officers, short of NCOs and enlisted men. In fact, about a fourth of each of the firing batteries is made up of Korean soldiers on loan to us. They're called KATUSA's, which stands for Korean Augmentation to the US Army. Most of them don't speak very good English, but they get along all right. They don't have any command responsibilities and can't sign for any equipment though. They're warm bodies, that's all. Besides people, we're short of vehicles and parts and gasoline and you name it. Vietnam is drowning in supply. They've got so much of everything stockpiled at Cam Rahn Bay its disgusting. And we've got nothing. We have to work long hours and endure some difficult conditions, but we have an important mission here. You'll find out more about that mission as time goes on, but very briefly the Second Infantry Division is here as a tripwire. North Korea cannot re-invade the South without attacking directly into our front. That would immediately involve the United States and the North thus far has not wanted to risk that. But they are probing constantly. Trying to stir up trouble. Trying to find a weakness and trying to set up cells of supporters here in the South. They would love to establish a Viet Cong type of front here. I don't think they can. There's too much support for the government here in the South. The South Koreans are strongly united against the Communist North. They like having the US here as their ally. They support our presence strongly. We pulled their ass out of the fire once and the Korean people trust us to keep it out of the fire now."

The Colonel paused for a long time, seemingly deep in thought. "I don't want to throw too much at you at once, Lieutenant. Go over to your room and get squared away. It's just about the end of the workday. Chow is served in the Officer's Club at 1730 hours. I think they're having pork chops tonight. If I don't see you at dinner, perhaps I'll see you in the bar later on." He paused again. "Do you have any questions?"

Holloway had at least a thousand questions, but he had no idea which one to ask first. He was struggling just to recall what SCOSI meant. "No, Sir. I'm ready to get started," Holloway replied. He stood, walked to the front of the Battalion Commander's desk, and came to attention. Colonel Moody stood and offered his hand.

"Welcome aboard, Holloway."

Chapter 3

Lieutenant Yoon Kim Lee of the 124th Army Unit of the North Korean Peoples' Army of the Democratic Peoples' Republic of Korea sat stiffly on a folding wooden stool inside of the reinforced concrete bunker on the elevated land mass the Americans called Speaker Hill. His German manufactured Zeiss binoculars traversed slowly to his left, stopping to study the sandbagged bunker on the far left flank of the American position 2000 meters away. Yoon could not detect any crew served weapons, but he was sure they were there. Machine guns in the DMZ were forbidden under the cease-fire agreement, of course, but if the Americans didn't have any heavy machine guns hidden on the hill they were even more stupid than Yoon thought they were. Not that it would matter. The Americans were going to be out gunned no matter what they had on their puny position which intelligence had reported was known by the Americans as Guard Post Cindy.

There did not appear to be more than ten to twelve men on the position. Most of them lolled around carelessly throughout the day, sometimes walking in full view of Yoon's eyes. Tomorrow all of that would change. Tomorrow the Americans would find one of their guard posts missing or at least dramatically altered. The first move would come tonight. Under cover of darkness an ambush team would be moving into position south of the MDL (Military Demarcation Line which officially separates North and South Korea) and behind the guard post The team's mission was to ambush any movement along the road leading to the hill after phase two began. Phase two would involve a surprise barrage of the hill. Three Russian-made 12.7mm Degtyarev heavy machine guns, as well as a recoilless rifle, would simultaneously begin firing late in the morning from the North Korean side of the MDL and to the right and front of the American position, thoroughly riddling the lightly defended hill. There would be a pause of a few hours to see what the Americans would do. Yoon was certain that at the very least the Americans would attempt to evacuate casualties and to reinforce the hill almost immediately. That meant the relief column would have to take the road behind the hill. If they did, the Americans were in for even more casualties. That was what the ambush team was for.

Then, tomorrow evening three separate heavy machine guns hidden in entirely different areas of the woods to the front and left of Cindy would resume the attack by raining fire upon the hill for another half hour. Their mission would be to try and eradicate the sandbagged bunkers that dotted the trench line. The North Korean gun mounts were already in position. Even in total darkness the automatic weapons fire would be exactly on target since the traverse mechanism on the mounts had been perfectly aligned. Lieutenant Yoon felt badly that he would not be personally firing any of the heavy machine guns that would be triangulating the fire on the little knob of ground. But firing heavy machine guns was not the job of a commando, especially not a commando officer. No, he was there today only as an observer, as he had been with the 215th North Vietnamese Army Division in Vietnam's Central Highlands just two months earlier. It was all part of his overall final orientation before his re-initiation into active operations against the Second Infantry Division and the stupid puppets of Park Chung Hee.

That fool! Yoon and his comrades had almost killed the South Korean President more than a year earlier. Had almost cut off his head. Thirty men! Thirty good brave men had given their lives to try and end Park's dictatorship of the Korean people. And they had almost done it. Thirty-one North Korean commando officers had penetrated the DMZ and gotten all the way to Seoul. All the way to within less than a block of the Blue House and close to the American Embassy before those stupid policeman had arrived and sounded the alarm that had brought the swarms of ROK soldiers. Even then the commandos had fought like tigers. No one would ever know exactly how many ROK soldiers the team had dispatched to see their ancestors, but Yoon felt sure it had been more than a hundred. The South Korean press had listed their dead at only thirty-eight, including two Americans, but his comrades had been too tough and too well schooled and motivated not to have taken many more with them. Lieutenant Yoon had trained months with all of them. The long runs through the mountains with packs of rocks tied to their backs. The hundreds of hours of Tae Kwon Do, which had reshaped their gnarled hands. The night operations and, of course, the weeks of weapons training with literally every individual weapon that currently existed on either end of the Korean peninsula had prepared the commandos for virtually anything. Yet in the end they had died. Died at the hands of the cowardly, yet lucky, Americans. It was the American Second Division that had stumbled upon most of the commandos as the team retreated north, trying to recross the DMZ and return to their homes. Not only had they stumbled upon them, but had done so at the worst possible time; as they were trying to cross the mighty Imjin. Most of the unit had still been alive at that point, Yoon believed. But then they were caught like rats in a trap. How could they have fought back when they were swimming in the river, many without their weapons? Yoon had been the lucky one. He had been separated earlier, so that he was not one of those massacred. Nor had he been captured like the one traitor who had surrendered rather than die a hero's death and who had given a full confession about the mission. Of the thirty-one men of the insertion team, Yoon Kim Lee alone had survived the mission and returned to the North.

But Yoon's deep-seated hatred of the Second Infantry Division had not come from that mission alone. The Second had altered his life many years before at the edge of a river other than the Imjin. That river had been the Naktong, in the south near Pusan. In the summer of 1950, Yoon's father had been serving with the North Korean Peoples Army in the war to liberate the South from the imperialists. Yoon Jong Pak had been part of the liberation forces since the fighting had begun in June and by the end of that summer he sat with his comrades ready to drive the Americans out of Pusan and into the sea. But the NKPA supply lines had become too long and the American buildup of strength had been too great. The UN forces had been reinforcing their perimeter for several weeks and finally they counterattacked. When the assault came against the NKPA, Yoon Jong Pak had bravely given his life to defend his countrymen and the Korean people against the imperialist Second Division. Yoon Kim Lee had been only five years old when his father was taken from him. But even at that early age he learned to hate. Hate for the South Korean pigs. Hate for the Americans. And especially hate for the soldiers of the Second Infantry Division. Ironically, he had even seen some of them briefly. In the fall of 1950 the Second had pushed northward with the other UN forces and passed along a road that curved next to Yoon's village. His mother had told him who they were. And even though she had warned him sternly not to say or do anything to anger them he had stood defiantly in the middle of the dirt road and thrown pebbles at the infantrymen as they walked stoically by, all but ignoring him. On the soldiers' left shoulders he saw their big black patch with the white star and the red man with feathers on his head. He stared at it and he remembered it and he despised it. The fact that by 1969 many of the soldiers of the United States' Second Division had not even been alive at the time of the death of Yoon's father was irrelevant to him.

The entire American Army was nothing but cowards. Yoon was convinced of it. They had luck. They had technology. Their manufacturing base had supplied them with excellent equipment. Those were the only reasons North Korea and his allies in North Vietnam had not yet been able to unite their respective homelands. None of had to do with bravery or dedication or devotion. Twice the American Army had inflicted heavy casualties on his friends and comrades because of its luck and its technology. First the aborted commando raid to Seoul over a year ago. Then most recently during his visit with the Peoples' Army of North Vietnam. His host unit had ambushed an American convoy near Pleiku. The attack had gone well until American helicopters of the First Cavalry had appeared without warning from the cloudless blue sky, firing their rockets and machine guns into them as they had attempted to close on the convoy and destroy it. The helicopters had devastated them. Yoon and his North

Vietnamese hosts had tried to fight, but it was hopeless. They had only their AK's and a few light machine guns. The American gunships were like angry wasps darting above them and cutting the soldiers down with their incredible firepower. Yoon had survived, but many had not. It was with a heavy heart that he returned to his Korean homeland a month later, still hearing the sounds of the helicopters in his ears and thinking of the day he could take his revenge on them. The First Cavalry was a long way from the Korean DMZ and there was realistically not much Yoon could do about them right now. But elements of the Second Division were only about two kilometers away at the moment. Their time was almost at hand.

"Well, Americans," thought Yoon, "your time of retribution is approaching. Tomorrow will only be a taste of what will follow at my hands and the hands of my men. We will avenge our commando brothers. We will avenge the death of my father. And we will avenge the deaths of our brothers in Vietnam as well. Revenge for the deaths of all Communist brothers will be forthcoming if it is left to me. That I promise." Yoon removed his cap and rubbed his hand through his short black hair that formed a vee over his forehead. His eyes narrowed as he again raised the binoculars to his raw boned face.

It had been three years earlier that the North Korean "Great Leader," President Kim Il Sung, had declared that "US imperialists should be dealt blows and their forces dispersed to the maximum in Asia." The Korean War had never officially ended. A cease-fire had been signed in 1953, which stopped most of the shooting, but Kim had never renounced his ultimate goal of reuniting the two Koreas under his domination. By 1966 the time was right to test the waters of resolve to determine if it was possible to accomplish that goal. The American military was preoccupied in Vietnam where its buildup increased monthly. At the request of the United States, the South Korean government had sent more than two divisions to Vietnam. Kim Il Sung reasoned that there might never be a better opportunity. Clearly he believed that by developing a more aggressive stance toward the South and the United States that he was helping to destabilize Asia and lessen US influence. The increased tensions on his peninsula would also keep American troops and equipment where they were in Korea rather than redeploying to the American war effort in Vietnam and may even force the South Koreans to recall their units from Vietnam.

Therefore, on November 2, 1966 North Korea unofficially reopened hostilities against the Americans by ambushing and destroying an eight man patrol south of the DMZ, while President Lyndon Johnson visited Seoul only twenty-six miles to the South. Six GI's and one KATUSA (Korean Augmentation to the US Army) were killed. The lone survivor was a seventeen-year-old soldier who was spared only because he had played dead as his wristwatch was ripped from his arm by the ambushers. From that point on, firefights became more frequent, as did the number of North Korean infiltrators slipping south for intelligence and terrorist activities. To counter those infiltrations, the DMZ barrier fence was constructed in 1967. However, it had failed to stop the raids. In 1968 Kim launched a major escalation of hostilities that included the capture of the USS Pueblo and Yoon's Blue House Raid designed to kill Park Chung Hee and to attack the American Embassy as well. It was also timed to coincide exactly with the Tet Offensive in Vietnam. The Korean escalation succeeded in diverting thousands of US troops slated for Vietnam and extending the tours of many soldiers already in the ROK. In 1968 alone, the United States and its South Korean allies recorded 700 hostile actions by the North.

*   *   *

"Vietnam. That's where the action is. That's where I should be," declared Bill Grant. "I applied for Vietnam and they send me to Korea. Do you believe that shit? And if that's not bad enough, after I get here I figure I can at least get up on the DMZ with the grunts and maybe get a little trigger time, but what happens? They make me the goddamn Adjutant. The Adjutant! Mr. Paperwork. Armed with the M1A1 pencil, yellow, lead, one each."

Holloway studied Bill Grant. He struck Holloway as the definitive gung-ho lieutenant. His heavily starched fatigue uniform had obviously been tailored to be form fitting. He wore spit shined Corcoran jump boots and all of the nametags for his fatigues were embroidered with black thread rather than stenciled. Even the back of his special order fatigue cap had his name embroidered on it. Holloway smiled. Major Matt Gentile, S-3 Operations Officer for the 8/18th smiled too. He'd heard it all before on several occasions and Grant had only been there for slightly more than a month. "Rocky" Gentile had already been to Vietnam. The itching on his left forearm that was a form of "jungle rot" that never completely went away was proof enough of that. The discomfort always seemed to be worse in hot muggy weather and the last few days had been very hot and very muggy. In some ways the Korean weather was similar to Vietnam and in other ways more like the climate in which he had grown up in the Midwest, although the summers seemed to be a bit hotter and the winters a bit colder. The last Korean winter, in fact, had seemed like something routed directly from the North Pole. Then there was the Korean rainy season that was about to start. That was the part of the weather that would remind him of Vietnam.

"You know, Bill, you ought to consider yourself lucky you didn't go to Vietnam. That live-fire exercise a couple thousand miles south of here is not really all the fun its cracked up to be. I was never so glad to get out of a place in all my life."

"Sure, Major, but the point is you went. It's in your 201 file now. Combat time. How the hell is a man supposed to get promoted a few years down the line from now without any combat time on his record? Besides that, I'd love to just get a crack at some of those little Red bastards. Show 'em who's really in charge. But now that I'm here you'd think the Colonel would at least let me get up to the Z on one of the GP's.

That's where you're supposed to go in a week or two, Holloway. But I'll be honest with you, I'm gonna try my best to change the old man's mind and send me."

"Ain't gonna happen, Bill," stated Major Gentile. "You've picked up your new duties here very well. The Colonel's real pleased with the job you're doing here. He told me so. He's not gonna send you to the DMZ and break in another adjutant."

"Well, Sir, Colonel Moody DEROS's out of here in three months. Maybe our new commander will let me go once I get him broken in."

Rocky Gentile shrugged and took a sip of his beer. The three men were seated in a corner of the Officer's Club bar following Holloway's first dinner at Camp Wynne. Clay Holloway was glad the day was officially over. It had not been one of his more impressive outings. Bouncing around the Korean countryside in a truck for half the day, having his bag with all of his personal effects and 201 file stolen by a slicky boy, failing to salute his new battalion commander, and then to top it all off throwing away a thirty dollar jackpot on the dime slot machine that sat inside the door to the bar. That had happened only twenty minutes ago. As he had walked into the room for the first time in his life he spied the four slot machines lined up in a row to his right. Fishing into the pocket of his khaki cotton pants, he came up with several coins and decided to try his luck. Clay Holloway had never operated a slot machine before, but they didn't appear to be particularly complex. With his third dime the windows had shown him three sets of three stars each and the machine had dumped a whole bunch of dimes into the tray below. Deciding that his luck had finally changed for the better, Holloway had scooped up the two fists full of dimes and proceeded to deposit another dollar back into the machine before taking his winnings and walking away. While relating his good fortune to Bill Grant ten minutes later, Grant asked him if had collected the thirty dollar jackpot from Mr. Yun behind the bar. Holloway looked at Grant blankly. Grant laid his head down on top of his hands on the bar.

"Holloway," Grant told him, "you're supposed to do two things when you hit a jackpot in here. One is to collect the jackpot from whoever is behind the bar and two is to ring that big brass bell that hangs from the ceiling. That means you're buying a round for everyone that's in the bar at that moment. It's too late for the money now. They're not going to give you a thirty dollar jackpot without verifying it. Better luck next time."

Holloway shrugged with an air of resignation and changed the subject. "Major Gentile, you're the Battalion Operations Officer. If you wouldn't mind, could you just brief me a bit on what the DMZ is like. I'm still not real clear. What is it exactly?"

"I haven't spent a lot of time there, Clay. There are no artillery units in that area. It's all infantry. In fact, there's never been an artillery battery north of the river in recent years that I know of. But I spent a day there on an orientation tour and I've visited all three guard posts where we have forward observers, so I know something about it." He paused to pack his pipe with tobacco from a leather tobacco pouch. "Anything north of the Imjin River, which is two miles north of here, is considered the hostile fire zone. About a mile north of the river is the southern boundary of the Demilitarized Zone, the DMZ. The "Z," as they call it, is 151 miles long. It runs the entire width of the country at what is basically the 38th parallel. It's pretty much the positions that were occupied when the real fighting stopped in '53. Most of it is manned by the ROK's. The US sector of the Zone is eighteen and a half miles long, which is defended by two brigades of infantry. The battalions in those brigades take turns rotating back south every three months. The Zone itself is two and a half miles across and exactly in the middle is the Military Demarcation Line called the MDL. The MDL is the actual line between them and us. The whole place up there is like a wild game preserve. Lots of wooded area. Lots of vegetation. There are no civilians north of the Imjin and the number of wild animals in the area now is just phenomenal. Beau coup deer, wild boar, cranes, and even an occasional tiger or bear. The place is eerie. Mysterious. Most of the land has been completely untouched by man for over fifteen years."

"Well, what do the troops do? Are they just all dug in waiting for the next Korean War to start?" asked Holloway.

"No. It's not really like that. Their primary mission right now is to stop commando infiltration rather than to defend against an all out attack. To do that troops are deployed in three ways." Gentile held a wooden match to the pipe bowl and puffed away as he continued speaking. "First, some occupy foxholes, bunkers, and towers behind the DMZ fence, which was built a couple of years ago. Second, we run ambush patrols in the DMZ. The third way is by occupying the Guard Posts. The GP's are simply hills where we have occupied the military crest and have built bunkers and trench lines and a command post. There are maybe ten to twenty men on each of the GP's. They're like miniature forts. The GP's are out in the Zone. Some are as close as fifty meters from North Korean territory. The three GP's that we support are named Cindy, Carol, and Gwen."

"OK, so what do the Forward Observers do? Do they ever call in artillery fire on the North Koreans?"

"They've asked for it on a couple of occasions, but it's never been fired. It would take some major action to cause us to fire artillery into North Korea. That could start a war. And quite frankly, our guns could barely reach the DMZ if we had to shoot from this compound. No, the FO's main job is to observe during daylight hours and to report anything unusual. Of course they will also be there and be ready if any large scale action does occur. Life on the Guard Post is rather Spartan. There are not many amenities up there. Usually the FO is on the hill for three to five days and then he rotates with his recon sergeant."

"What if the North Koreans do come in force some day, Sir? What do the guys on the GP's do then? Do they have a chance to get out?" Holloway asked.

Rocky Gentile smiled slightly and ran his fingers through his thinning hair. "We like to think that we would have some warning before any large scale attack could take place. But if we didn't I think the GP's would just disappear. They wouldn't have a chance against a determined assault. Anyone north of the Imjin would probably be gone if they couldn't get south before the bridges were blown. There are only two bridges in our AO; Freedom and Spoonbill. Of course, some people might be able to swim the river or walk over it if it was frozen. That would be their only chance."

Holloway sighed slowly, changing the focus of his eyes away from Rocky Gentile and toward the black swinging doors of the bar entrance. An officer Holloway had never seen before was entering. The young man was dressed in a gray rain suit, the jacket of which was unzipped in the front. Holloway could see that the suit was lined with a camouflage pattern of canvas, which he guessed meant that the rain suit was reversible. The officer was about six feet tall and his short black hair was laying flat on his head indicating that he had been wearing the steel helmet that he was now carrying in his left hand. He was wearing the standard combat web gear consisting of heavy canvas suspenders attached to a pistol belt. A black leather holster containing a .45 caliber automatic pistol hung on his right hip, while a canteen sat perched on his left. He looked toward the semicircular bar and then began to scan the other areas of the room.

Major Gentile was seated with his back to the door, but noticing Holloway looking past him, Gentile swiveled his neck to look to his rear. Seeing the man in the rain suit the major waved. "Tom! Come on over!" The young officer immediately walked toward where Gentile, Holloway, and Bill Grant were seated. Major Gentile pushed back his chair and stood up.

"Tom, I'm glad you're here. I want you to meet your new XO, Clay Holloway."

The man in the rain suit gave a crooked smile that spread over his oval shaped face and which reminded Holloway of Elvis Presley and then extended his hand. "Clay. It's a pleasure to meet you. I'm Tom Courtney, Charlie Battery Commander."

Holloway stood up quickly and reached for Courtney's hand. "It's my pleasure, Sir! How do you do. I was told you were on SCOSI duty all night."

"We are. I just dropped by to pick up the mail so I could git it up to the men before dark," Tom drawled in a deep voice laced with a very noticeable southern accent. "Where y'all from?"

"Cleveland."

"Cleveland, Tennessee?" asked Courtney, his eyes brightening.

"Ohio."

"Oh, a Yankee, huh. Well, I'll try not to hold that against you. And I'll tell you what. I can use all the help I kin git. We're awful short of officers raht now. Along with everything else."

"I was just telling Clay about the DMZ. He'll probably go up there at some point for a little while," interjected the Major.

"Not for a long while I hope. I could sure use him here." Courtney winked at Holloway and flashed him another Elvis type grin. "Well, I really need to be going if I'm gonna git back before the sun goes down. This is the last naht for SCOSI for a while. Clay, I'll see you sometime tomorrow. Probably after I wake up in the afternoon. We don't get back in until 0800."

"Sounds good. I'll wander over to the battery area and look around tomorrow after I draw my field gear. I'll try to meet some of the men," said Holloway.

"That would be fine. Take it easy. Don't let your meat loaf," he quipped. Courtney turned and walked back out of the door from where he had come. Holloway watched him walk out and felt that something good had finally happened to him. He had a sense that Tom Courtney was going to be a positive influence on him. He seemed to exude a certain self-confidence that imparted that same feeling to people around him. That deep, slow talking southern voice seemed like it was custom designed for an Army officer. Holloway wondered if the Army had ever considered voice lessons to teach other officers to talk like that.

"Tom's a good officer, Clay. I think you'll like working for him," said Major Gentile.

"I think I will too." He was sincere in his statement. "Let me get us another round of beer," Holloway offered as he scooped up the three empty bottles and carried them to the bar. He set the bottles down and held up three fingers to Mr. Buster, the head bartender. Mr. Buster walked to the other end of the bar and slid open the door of the cooler.

"Budweiser, OK?" Mr. Buster asked.

"Sure. Fine," Holloway responded. As he watched Mr. Buster dip into the cooler he realized there were two American women standing at the other end of the bar talking. They paid no attention to him and after paying for the beer he returned to his chair at the table in the corner. "Who are the round eyes?" he asked, trying to use the appropriate slang term for the women.

Grant peered over toward the bar. "Oh, that's a couple of the Doughnut Dollies. The tall one with the dark hair is Sherry Cifrianni and the blond is Beth Kisha. Sherry's been here for a while, but Beth came up from I Corps just about three weeks ago. Didn't I tell you the Doughnut Dollies were based here?"

"I heard it somewhere," Holloway replied. He gazed back toward the bar. Both young women were relatively attractive. Beth was tilting her head back in an inviting throaty laugh, which Holloway could hear from where he was sitting. He decided that all things considered, this tour could be a lot worse. Maybe a stint with the Second Division wouldn't be as bad as some people had made it out to be.

*   *   *

The next day was Saturday, which normally meant that the battalion worked until noon and then quit for the weekend. Holloway had breakfast in the Officers' Open Mess where he met a few more of the officers that he hadn't seen the night before. Most of them had been cordial to him the previous evening, welcoming him warmly. Just as Bill Grant had told him, there wasn't a captain to be found anywhere in the battalion. There were three field grade officers (major and above) and everyone else was either a second or first lieutenant. Therefore almost the entire compliment of nineteen battalion officers was virtually identical in age. The only real difference among them was how long they had been with the 8/18th. Lieutenants who had been there for five months or more were considered to be the old hands and were assumed to know everything there was to know. Ones who had been in country for one to four months were assumed to know most things and at least be competent in their respective positions. Those that were there less than one month generally had a couple of weeks to learn before being called upon to accomplish virtually anything. There were only two battalion officers in the last classification. Clay Holloway was one and the other Holloway had not met because he was currently assigned as a forward observer on one of the Guard Posts. His name was Bob Hoover, although everyone referred to him as "Sweeper." He was presently located on Guard Post Cindy.

During breakfast Bill Grant had briefed Holloway about the configuration of the compound. The battalion-sized post was divided into areas by battery. Approximately twenty percent of the compound belonged to Alpha Battery, twenty percent to Bravo Battery, twenty percent to Charlie Battery, and the remaining forty percent to Headquarters and Headquarters Battery. Holloway was told that Charlie Battery, his battery, was in the northeast quadrant. Following the morning meal he began walking in that direction.

Holloway could feel the moisture thickened air as he walked toward his destination. He sniffed the air and visually searched the skies seeing mostly heavy gray clouds. It seemed obvious that the rainy season he had heard about was close at hand. Within a few minutes he saw the sign he had been searching for: "Headquarters C Battery, 8th Bn. 18th Artillery, 1Lt. Thomas J. Courtney Commanding, 1st Sgt. Hudson St. Clair." The black lettering surrounded the battalion crest on the heavy white sign. There was a strong looking red wooden frame that held the sign by two links of chain. Holloway walked up the sidewalk and into the front door of the single story building that stood adjacent to the sign.

"'Tench hut!" called a young enlisted man seated behind the desk which faced the door.

"As you were," Holloway replied quickly. The man who had called attention sat back down. The chunky clerk on Holloway's left had not yet risen. "Is the First Sergeant in?" Holloway asked.

"No, Sir! He had to go out. Can I help you?" the young man asked.

"My name's Lt. Holloway. I'm the new XO. How about the Chief of Firing Battery? Is he around?"

"Sorry, Sir. He's still out on SCOSI with Lt. Courtney. They probably won't be back from that for another hour. If I might suggest…Umm, have you drawn your field gear yet?"

"No, I haven't had a chance," Holloway replied.

"Well let me take you over to the supply hooch. Sergeant Carlton should be there and he can take you to Camp Justice where you can draw all of your TA-50. Then when you get back we'll take you to the arms room and you can get a weapon and a gas mask assigned. By then I'm sure everyone will be here."

Holloway gazed at the man's nametape. He seemed to be on the ball. "Thanks, Corporal Gash. That sounds like a good idea."

An hour later Holloway and Carlton lifted two water proof duffel bags from a jeep with the designation C-5 stenciled in white on the bumper. The bags contained two sets of woolen fatigues, a pair of rubber boots, a pair of insulated rubber boots called "Mickey Mouse" boots, two field jackets with liners, two pairs of field pants with liners, a parka with liner, a parka hood with liner, a steel helmet with liner, reversible camouflage cover, and elastic band, two winter field caps, insulated mittens with trigger finger, a poncho, a two piece rain suit, a pistol belt, combat suspenders, a butt pack, a canteen, an aid pack, a sleeping bag with cover, an air mattress and two shelter halves with poles and stakes.

Holloway grabbed one duffel in each hand and after flicking open the screen door with his foot stepped into the hallway of the BOQ and walked across the corridor to his room. Inside was a Korean man he had not seen before. Holloway assumed it was his houseboy Skinny Yee, so named as to distinguish him from the other houseboy, Fat Yee, who resembled Buddha with a flat top haircut.

The slender man was about forty. He was wearing an undershirt, sandals, and a pair of faded American Levi's. He looked up from the bed he was making as Holloway entered.

"Ahhh! You Lieutenant Holloway? I am Yee. I am houseboy. I makee bed numba one. How you do?"

"I do good, Yee. How you do?" Holloway replied good naturedly as he set down the heavy bags.

Holloway's room was small. There was a single wooden frame bed, a wooden dresser, and a wooden desk. There was only a small area in the middle of the room that was open. The space was only six by six. Even two people standing in the room made it crowded. "Yee, why don't you give me a chance to unload this gear and sort it out. I want to pack a ready bag. You can come back in about an hour and finish up."

"I do for you. I know how," Yee responded.

"I'm sure you do, but I'd like to do it myself. I want to put my web gear together. I need to adjust the pistol belt and the suspenders and so forth. Just come back in an hour, OK?"

Yee seemed somewhat disappointed, knowing that he could do the work probably better than the young lieutenant and wanting to demonstrate his prowess. Nevertheless, his new honcho had spoken.

"OK, I come back." He slipped silently out of the door and disappeared down the hallway. Yee had four other officers and their rooms to take care of and he didn't need to waste time talking to number five. He would have plenty of opportunities to prove himself.

Holloway dumped both duffels upside-down on his freshly made bunk. Then he set aside all of the winter gear believing that it would be at least until October before he would need even the field jacket liners. He repacked one bag with everything that he thought he would need if he were told to go to the field tomorrow for an overnight. The second bag he packed with the winter gear and set it on the floor of the closet. It was then that he noticed that all of his clothes, both civilian and military that he had already unpacked and hung in the closet, had been ironed and rearranged apparently by Yee. In addition, all of his shoes and boots had been shined. Grant had told him that the houseboys would "take care of everything for ten dollars a month," but Holloway had not realized he would get this kind of treatment. He saw that Yee had also arranged the top of his dresser with many of his personal items. The arrangement wasn't bad, but he wanted to alter a few things. It was then that he heard the sharp knock on the frame of the open door behind him. Turning he recognized Major Gentile, the Operations Officer. A look of concern clouded his face.

"Lieutenant Holloway, there's trouble in the DMZ. The North Koreans are shooting up one of the guard posts. Division thinks they may try to over-run it. It sounds bad. We've heard there are one dead and two wounded already. They're getting the mechanized strike force ready to reinforce the GP, but they want artillery support up there ASAP. Charlie Battery has got the job. Right now Lieutenant Courtney is across the river with the First Sergeant reconning the position. You're going to lead the battery north. Get over to Charlie and take over. Wait for Tom Courtney's call on the radio. Don't move until you get it. Any questions?"

Holloway was dumb struck. Any questions??? Any questions??? Yeah, he had some questions. What the fuck was this guy talking about? Holloway was simply standing in his room rearranging the top of his dresser, deciding where to strategically place his aftershave, and wondering what was going to be for lunch at the Officers' Club. He had been in Korea for less than four days and this battalion less than one. He was not really sure where exactly in the country he was even located. During his entire six months of Army experience he had never even been in a regular unit. All he had ever done was be a student in Field Artillery Basic School or Redeye Missile School. And now this guy, with whom he had a couple of beers the night before, had suddenly stuck his head into Holloway's room and told him to go organize a one hundred man artillery battery, of whom about twenty-five percent were Koreans who spoke little or no English, with six howitzers, twenty five vehicles, 2,000 rounds of high explosive 105mm ammunition, and assorted small arms and lead them into a hostile environment which he had never been to and, in fact, did not even know where it was, and prepare to start blowing people up.

"Yes, Sir. I have a question," Holloway finally said tentatively. "Are you serious???"

"You're damn straight I'm serious, Lieutenant. Get moving!"

And so he did.

CHAPTER 4

The DMZ mechanized reaction force had assembled quickly once the frightened RTO on Guard Post Cindy had started screaming to the Brigade TOC that the hill was receiving automatic weapons fire late in the morning. The reaction force commander, 2nd Lieutenant Keith "Hacker" Hackworth, had been alerted by the TOC that three men on the GP had been caught in the open in the initial burst of the deadly heavy machine gun fire. At the time, the soldiers had been stringing additional concertina barbed wire between the steel stakes that surrounded the section of the hill that faced North Korea. One man had been killed instantly and a second had been seriously wounded in the thigh. The third GI had helped the wounded one crawl into the trench line. The dead soldier continued to lay in the open. His corpse had been struck numerous times by the heavy machine gun rounds over the next half hour and was now no more than a heap of bloody green rags.

Hackworth was impatiently waiting for only one thing, orders to move. The four M113 Armored Personnel Carriers (APC's) were tactically spaced behind the south barrier fence gate that was 2000 meters behind GP Cindy. Their engines idled loudly as the drivers sat with their upper bodies protruding from the open hatchways. Each APC of the reaction force held ten men in addition to the two-man crew. Besides the driver, there was a machine gunner for the .50 caliber heavy machine gun mounted on top of each track and ten infantrymen who would ride inside. Currently, the infantrymen stood or squatted outside the rear of the idling vehicles talking nervously. The perspiration on their faces came both from the heat and the tension. It was not unusual for the reaction force to be activated, but normally it was done to search for one or two UI's or to provide security. This was different. This sounded like big time. The heavy power-operated gate located on the inward sloping backside of the track lay open. The reaction force had already been at the fence for thirty minutes and Hackworth had ordered the men out of the vehicles so that they wouldn't get claustrophobic. Though heavy clouds covered the sun, it was hot and muggy inside and there was a complete lack of circulation with the vehicle standing still. It was SOP for the reaction force to be kept at a high state of readiness. It had only taken them four minutes from the time the call came until they had begun moving toward the gate. The old army tradition. Hurry up and wait. At last the radio crackled.

"Bravo 20 (two-zero), this is Bravo 6, over."

Hackworth reached through the hatch to take the mike. The caller was the Bravo Company Commander himself.

"Bravo 6, this is Bravo 20, over."

"Bravo 20, this is Bravo 6, enter the Zone and relieve Cindy. Return machine gun fire as long as enemy fire continues. Deploy your people to stand by to repel a ground assault. Keep them protected from the incoming, over."

"Bravo 6, this is Bravo 20, wilco, over."

"This is Bravo 6, good luck, out."

Hackworth zipped his flak jacket to the top. "Mount up. Let's roll. We're going to the GP. I want everyone inside the tracks except for the gunners and the squad leaders." Hackworth knew that many of the men liked to ride on top of the armored vehicles when it was hot. He climbed onto the lead APC and slipped on the tanker helmet with the headphones and the built-in microphone. Once everyone started boarding the tracks it was impossible to communicate by yelling. The rear gates were closing, the engines were revving, and men were scrambling. With his helmeted headset he could talk to the squad leaders in the other three APC's.

"Have your gunners keep their eyes peeled. Let's do it!"

Hackworth led the way through the gate, as the four tracks lurched forward forming themselves into a diamond formation once they entered the Zone. The ground to the sides of the single lane dirt road was soft from the summer rains and Hackworth worried momentarily about whether it would impede the APC's. Nevertheless, it was crucial to move toward the GP in a tactical formation, not in a single file on the road. There was no way of knowing for sure what lay between them and their destination two kilometers away. Within two minutes the formation rounded the first of three curves. Directly in front of them were several large shapes spread nonchalantly across the road and adjacent grassy area.

As the first track sped into view, the surprised heads of the herd of deer snapped up instantly. There was only the slightest of hesitation before the deer broke and ran, bounding for the safety of the woods a hundred yards away to the northwest. Directly in their path and completely undetected by either the deer or the Americans, sat the hidden force of twenty North Korean commandos which had moved silently into position an hour before day break. The commandos had been casually watching the deer for more than fifteen minutes. The soldiers were downwind from the deer and well secluded in the high grass of the field in front of the woods. It really didn't matter to the ambushers if the deer sensed their presence or not. Whether the deer stayed or ran away did not seem to be of any consequence to the North Korean soldiers who were there for the sole purpose of wrecking havoc with whatever reinforcements the

Americans attempted to send to their Guard Post. The Koreans had hoped that there would not be armored vehicles involved, although they had two teams armed with rocket-propelled grenades (RPG's) just for such an eventuality. However, when the commando leader saw that there were four APC's moving swiftly by, he silently signaled his men to hold their fire. Attacking four armored vehicles was too dangerous. He would allow the vehicles to pass. If no softer targets appeared before dark, he would withdraw the team to the woods at their rear and make their way 1500 meters directly north to their own side of the MDL.

It was then that fate intervened. The one element of the operation that could not have been foreseen happened almost without warning. Charging at full speed toward the woods to escape the terrifying armored vehicles, the small herd of six deer ran headlong into the cluster of twenty well camouflaged, highly trained and more highly disciplined North Korean commandos. Nineteen of the men were successful in burying their heads and, although two were trampled, made no noise or movement of any kind. But the remaining soldier, a young twenty-year-old private named Park Lo Chung, was kicked directly in the front of the face by one of the running deer. The sharp hoof shattered his nose and knocked out both of the young man's upper front teeth. Park rose involuntarily to his knees moaning and clutching at his face, which was already gushing blood. Fifty meters away, Corporal James Washington, machine gunner of the APC on the left flank of the formation, had been watching the deer as they ran for the woods. As Park leaped up, Washington yelled "UI's" (Unidentified Individuals) into the microphone of his helmet and instantaneously hit the trigger of the .50 caliber machine gun mounted on a ring in front of him. Firing in practiced five round bursts he swept the area near where Park tottered on his knees.

"Left! Left!" Washington screamed frantically at the driver. Instantly the left track of the APC stopped and the right one dug into the dirt, spinning the armored vehicle in a 45-degree turn toward Private Park. Within moments all four of the APC's were charging toward the aborted North Korean ambush, firing their machine guns. For the commando team, there was no choice. The Korean team leader leaped to his feet and called to his men to run for the woods only thirty yards behind them. He didn't think the vehicles could follow them there. Seventeen of the soldiers reached the tree line. Private Park was not one of them. Of the seventeen survivors, fifteen were unscathed, one had lost the index finger of his right hand as it was neatly severed by a bullet, and one had been shot through the back, with the heavy slug exiting his lower left chest leaving a gaping exit wound. Two of his comrades dragged the seriously wounded man into the woods as they ran, trying to escape the view of the Americans. Two hundred meters into the woods the team leader halted his men and spread them quickly into a defensive perimeter, waiting to see if they were being pursued. But the Americans had halted at the edge of the woods.

"Bravo 6, this is Bravo 20, over," Lieutenant Hackworth called breathlessly.

"Bravo 20, this is Bravo 6, go," shot back the Company Commander.

"This is Bravo 20, we have contact. Large body of UI's has been flushed from the undergrowth five or six hundred meters inside the fence. We've taken them under fire and they're shaggin' ass into the woods. We can't take these tracks into the trees. Do we dismount and follow them on foot or go to the Guard Post, over?"

"This is Bravo 6. Are there any casualties, over?"

"Bravo 20. That's a negative. We have zero friendly casualties. I say again, we have zero friendly casualties. I'm sure we hit some of the UI's, but I can't see the bodies because of the high grass. We'll have to search. What do you want us to do, over?"

"This is Bravo 6. Wait, over."

Hackworth didn't like sitting at the edge of the trees buttoned up in their armored coffins. He didn't like being a target. The UI's seemed to be heading for North Korea as fast as they could, but what if they doubled back? It looked as though some of them were carrying RPG's and light machine guns.

"All tracks, this is Bravo 20, dismount your troops and form a skirmish line, over."

Before the troops had cleared the rear of the APC's the Company Commander was back on the radio.

"Bravo 20, this is Bravo 6, pursue the UI's with dismounted troops. Leave two tracks in the area for support. Don't let them ambush you. The dinks have stopped firing on the hill and there's no sign that they're going to launch a ground attack. Send the other two tracks to Cindy to evacuate the casualties on the hill. We'll get you more help if you need it, over."

"Bravo 20, roger, out."

Hackworth quickly designated two of the tracks, minus their troops, to head for Cindy. The other two he directed back toward the road. Ordering his platoon to spread themselves into a tactical vee, he advanced them carefully into the woods.

The commando force, meanwhile, had taken quick stock of the situation. They had not come to engage in a relatively equal battle in the woods, but to ambush and destroy without warning. The plan had not worked, but there was nothing they could do about that now. A bloody bandage covered the hand of one of the wounded. The other wounded man lay on his back, his chest making sucking sounds as he breathed. He appeared to be near death, but they certainly were not going to leave his body for the Americans. They had already left three bodies in the high grass. That was regrettable, but there was nothing that could be done about that now either. The force commander ordered two men to carry the mortally wounded soldier. Then the entire team formed quickly into a column with point and flank security and began running for the safety of the MDL.

It was almost one hour later that Hackworth was finally satisfied that the North Koreans had departed his side of the MDL. He had taken his time in probing the woods. He had no wish to lose anyone to a sniper or an ambush team deployed to delay their advance. Once satisfied that the area was clear, he reported that fact to the battalion Tactical Operations Center (TOC) and to the Company Commander. Then he reversed his course, remounted the two APC's with half his men, and drove on to the GP. Upon arrival he sent the two tracks back to retrieve the bodies of the dead North Koreans and to pick up the remainder of his force.

The Guard Post was a shambles. The Degtyarev machine guns, apparently mixed with some recoilless rifle rounds, had done an amazing amount of damage to the overall structure of the sandbagged bunkers. Loose sand and dirt lay everywhere along with the tattered remnants of the greenish plastic material that had held it. Wooden four by fours stood splintered, their jagged edges pointing toward the sky. One bunker had been set on fire by incendiary rounds and while the flames had been extinguished, black smoke continued to drift into the air. Total casualties stood at one dead and two wounded, of which one was American and one a KATUSA. The remaining men seemed to be in shock. None of them had ever experienced real combat and it had shaken them. The firing had been relentless. The official after action report would later state that it had lasted eighteen minutes.

The Guard Post Commander, a twenty one year old infantry second lieutenant, was still shaking when Hackworth arrived over an hour after the firing had ceased. He was trying to light a cigarette when he saw someone approaching him. Hackworth flipped open his Zippo with the First Cavalry crest on the side and held it forward. Then he shook loose a Winston from his pack, and lit it for himself.

"Thanks, Hacker," said Lieutenant Bobby Reynolds nervously, gazing toward the ground. "Jesus Christ, my hands are still shaking. I ain't never seen anything like this before in my life. Hope I never do again either. It wouldn't stop. It just wouldn't. All we could do was lay on the fuckin' deck and pray." Reynolds shook his head slowly from side to side. "Kwan tried getting our .50 into action and about got his arm ripped off by a slug. It was hopeless. Nobody could even fuckin' move, man. They were using three or four machine guns that they had hidden in the woods about four or five hundred meters out. That and a mortar or rockets or something. Sergeant Jamieson thinks it was a recoilless rifle."

"Listen, Bobby, why don't you get your people rounded up and load them onto my tracks. There isn't enough room for all of us up here and we're fresh. We'll stand by for further orders." Reynolds nodded. "What were your final casualties?"

Reynolds looked at the ground. "Alesio is dead. He got it in the first burst. Never had a chance. He's all shot to shit. There was nothing left of him. I don't know how many times they hit him. We just wrapped what was left in a poncho and put it on one of your tracks. Then there was Kwan and Murdock hit in the leg. They went in on the same track. Those machine guns do some serious harm to a man's body."

"OK, hang in there for a minute, Bobby," Hackworth said. He walked to his radio, keyed the mike, and called the TOC.

"Bravo 6, this is Bravo 20, over."

"Bravo 6, over."

"Ah, this is Bravo 20, we are on the objective and are requesting instructions, over."

"Bravo 20, this is Bravo 6, meet me lima lima (land line), out."

Hackworth walked briskly into what had been the CP bunker. The upper half had partially collapsed into the lower half that had been built below ground. He reached down and pulled aside two sandbags in an area where he knew the field telephone should be. It was there, covered in dust and sand. He lifted it up, set it on a table that was still intact, and cranked the handle.

"Battalion TOC," a voice answered.

"This is Lieutenant Hackworth on GP Cindy. Is Captain Gustafson there?"

A new voice came over the phone. "Hacker? It's Captain Gustafson. Give me a SITREP (situation report)." After absorbing everything Hackworth had told him he asked a few questions. Once satisfied that he had all available information he made his decisions and relayed them to the young lieutenant. Hackworth took a few notes on the little spiral notebook that he carried in his left fatigue shirt pocket, hung up the phone, and walked back outside.

"We're set, Bobby. The whole brigade is on alert now. You and your men go back to Camp Greaves. They want to debrief all of you. I'm keeping thirty of my men here. There's no room for more. I'll keep two tracks down on the backside of the hill out of sight just in case we need them. We need to keep the artillery forward observer though. There's no replacement for him. Who is it?"

"Lieutenant Hoover. The guy they call Sweeper. I'm not sure where he is. I saw him a few minutes before you got here though." Reynolds turned his head slowly, searching for the artillery FO. "There. He's working on his bunker."

Keith Hackworth walked toward where Hoover was setting undamaged sandbags back onto the overhead cover portion of his position. "Hey, Sweeper. Looks like you could use some help," Hackworth called to the man.

"Probably won't get any from you though, will I, Hacker?" Sweeper observed with a wry smile and then spit into the dirt.

"Hell no. Not from me personally, but I've got enough people here to do that for you. Take a break," Hackworth replied.

Sweeper wiped his forehead with the sleeve of the upper part of his right arm. "You'd think I'd be used to this humidity coming from Mississippi and all, but I'm not. I don't ever get used to it. I just sweat like a dog."

"Listen, Sweeper. Reynolds and his troops are going down off the hill. I'm afraid you've got to stay here with me though. You're the only artillery FO we have available right now and its pretty damn obvious we may have some serious work for you to do if the shit hits the fan again," Hackworth said, looking him in the eye. "How'd you hold up today?"

"I'm OK. I understand that I should stay. That's no sweat," Sweeper said. Then he smiled wanly. "That's why they're paying me the extra $65. I'll tell you what, though Hacker. I know I've only been in this country a month, but I sure didn't plan on seeing something like this. This ain't supposed to be Vietnam you know."

"Yeah, well I've been there too. I've seen a lot worse than this in the 'Nam, but I didn't expect something this large scale here in Korea either," noted Hackworth. "That was a hell of an ambush team we stumbled onto on the way up here. Did you hear about that?"

"Yeah. We could hear the firing and Reynolds told me what happened, but I didn't know you were in Vietnam," Sweeper replied in a surprised voice. "How could you still be a second john if you've been in the Army that long?"

"I was enlisted for four years," Hackworth stated matter-of-factly. "Got out of Vietnam as an E-6 after most of our NCOs became casualties. They asked me if I wanted OCS after that and I said sure. I'm up for first lieutenant next month. So all told I've been soldierin' for about five and a half years."

"Damn, Hacker. No wonder you always act like you know what you're doing. Cause you do. Guess I should have noticed that Cav patch on your right shoulder didn't come from an army surplus store."

Hackworth smiled. "Let's get those troops up here to fix up your bunker. We've got to be ready for darkness in a few hours. I've requested four .50 calibers with tripods. We're going to be ready if it happens again. Is there anything you'd like sent up?"

"Yeah. A complete remote set for my radio," said the artillery officer. "My old one's all shot to shit. The radio is OK, but the remote set that was in my bunker is a write off. I'll need batteries for it too. And commo wire. I started to call for artillery right after the shooting started, but the remote set got hit and that was that. Not that it mattered. I know goddamn well that the 105's on our compound could never reach those North Korean guns from there."

"Well," said Hackworth, "help is on the way. I've heard that one of your 105 batteries from the 8/18th is supposed to be moving north of the river. I hope it gets into position before anything else happens."

*   *   *

Second Lieutenant Clay Holloway, once he was told that he was to lead Charlie Battery north of the Imjin River and set up a firing position, moved quickly. He threw some extra fatigue uniforms, a second pair of boots, and some other personal items into his empty waterproof duffel and set it and his ready bag into the hall for someone to retrieve. Then he strapped on the web gear he had assembled and adjusted only a few minutes before, put his helmet on his head and headed immediately for the battery area.

He stalked purposefully toward the area of Camp Wynne that was occupied by his new unit. Approaching the Charlie CP and seeing what was happening on the street in front of it made him feel immeasurably better. He was not going to have to start from scratch. Several vehicles were already lined up on the street indicating that the convoy was forming. Obviously this was not the first time they had gone on alert and somebody knew what the hell they were doing, even if he didn't. The battery area was a madhouse. A variety of things were happening simultaneously. Holloway stopped at the lead vehicle in the formation, a one and a quarter ton truck. A young soldier was carrying a wooden footlocker toward the truck bed which was already half full of other things. Holloway recognized the man as the corporal he had met in the CP that morning.

"Corporal Gash," Holloway called. "Where's the Chief of Smoke?" The term Chief of Smoke was common slang for the Chief of Firing Battery, the second most senior NCO in an artillery battery after the First Sergeant. Gash's eyes brightened when he saw the new Battery Executive Officer.

"He's on pass, Sir! Somewhere in the ville, but nobody's found him yet. The First Sergeant and the BC aren't here either. Are you going with us?"

"I'm leading the battery, yes," Holloway replied. "Lieutenant Courtney and the First Sergeant are reconning our firing position. They're supposed to call us when they're ready. Are you driving the lead vehicle?"

"Yes, Sir. I always do. Usually the Chief of Smoke and me."

"Fine. I'll be with you. Do you have radios mounted in the back?"

"Yes, Sir. We're in good shape. This truck has been used all week for SCOSI so the radios are all hooked up."

"Are they turned on?" Holloway asked.

Gash looked sheepish. "Uhh, I don't think so."

"Get them turned on and turn the volume up loud so we can hear them if we're away from the truck. Make sure they're on the right frequency to talk to Lieutenant Courtney and then run a radio check with Battalion. I want to look around."

Holloway began walking down the column of vehicles that had grown slightly larger even while he and Gash had been talking. Most of the vehicles were still spread around the battery area as their crews loaded them. Holloway walked slowly, taking mental note as to what was happening all around him. He was fully aware that many of the troops were observing him in return, sizing him up and wondering what kind of an officer he was going to be. Holloway wanted desperately to appear confident and knowledgeable, even though he had some uncertainty and a small amount of self-doubt as to how he was going to accomplish what he had been ordered to do. But he couldn't let that show. No way. In the last thirty minutes the seriousness of the situation had settled deeply into Holloway's mind. There were American soldiers only a few miles away whose very existence might depend on how well and how quickly he and the members of Charlie Battery did their jobs in the next few hours. The people on the Guard Post were badly in need of the potential of the six Howitzers currently lined up in front of the CP. Six Howitzers that newly arrived Second Lieutenant Clay Holloway was now charged with getting to where they were supposed to be.

Crates of ammunition and fuses were flying into the backs of the ammunition trucks. Each of the six gun trucks carried 100 rounds of howitzer ammunition as a basic load, but they might need more than that. Preparedness was essential. The commo section was loading a myriad of communications equipment as well as all the gear they would need for living in the field for an undetermined amount of time. Holloway watched Sergeant Carlton carrying a pair of folding cots toward one of the supply trucks. Hearing the chattering of a diesel engine behind him Holloway turned and saw the field kitchen truck lumbering into the motor pool area. The convoy was beginning to take shape. It was also beginning to get wet. The rain that had threatened all day had finally begun.

Holloway returned to his vehicle at the head of the convoy. "Gash, have someone drive over to the BOQ and pick up the two bags in the hall just outside of room five. I'm going to the arms room." Holloway walked to the Quonset hut adjacent to the Charlie CP and stepped inside the door. A slender red haired man wearing Army issue sunglasses was standing behind the counter loading M-14 rifle magazines with 7.62mm ammunition. He looked up as Holloway entered.

"You must be Lieutenant Holloway," the red haired man said. "I've got your .45 and a gas mask ready for you. I need you to sign this weapon card for me though please." The man pushed the card toward the new executive officer along with a black ballpoint pen marked US Government. Holloway scribbled his name and pushed the card back.

"Give me a couple of clips of ammo," Holloway ordered. The red haired man reached into a footlocker full of loaded .45 caliber magazines and set four of them on the counter. Holloway hesitated for only a moment and then retrieved all four. He immediately loaded one into the empty butt of the .45 and placed the other three into the ammo pouch attached to the pistol belt he was wearing. Finally he holstered the pistol and strode back out of the arms room door. The weight of the .45 on his hip and the ammunition in his ammo pouch gave the young officer a needed shot of confidence. Increasingly, he felt like a soldier. He had something important to accomplish and he was damn well going to do it.

A slender black NCO approached. "Sir, I'm Sergeant Jackson, the commo sergeant. I got your SOI here. You're liable to need it." The SSI/SOI was a thin book containing all of the call signs, frequencies, and authentication codes currently in use for the division. A strong cord was attached to the book. Holloway took it and put it around his neck, tucking the book itself inside of the front of his fatigue shirt.

"Good, Sarge. Thanks." Jackson flashed him a grin and walked away. Holloway noticed that Corporal Gash was in the process of loading Holloway's two duffels into the back of his truck. Walking quickly to the vehicle he climbed into the back and withdrew his rain jacket from one of the bags. It was still raining and giving no indication of stopping or even slowing down. Most of the other men were wearing either both pieces of their rain suits or at least the jacket. He climbed back outside of the truck and looked down the long column of vehicles that snaked down the street and then looped around back of the large motor pool building. It looked like everyone was in position.

"Lieutenant Holloway!"

Holloway turned at the sound of the voice. Major Gentile was walking up the street toward him carrying a plastic covered object in his hand. Holloway saluted.

Gentile was not wearing a rain jacket. "Let's go inside of your CP," he said. Reaching the cover of the building Major Gentile took off his fatigue cap and shook the loose water from it. "I brought you a map. I thought it might be a good idea to tell you where the hell you're going. The map case is mine. I had it made in the ville. It'll keep the map clean and dry for you, but I'd like to have it back when this is over." He laid the map on a vacant desk.

"Here's Sonyu-ri and our compound," he said laying his index finger on top of the transparent plastic. "Here's the road you're going to take to the river. There's a pontoon bridge there called Spoonbill. Be careful once you get to the other side. The fields on either side of the road are heavily mined. They're marked to tell you that. Follow the road about another five kilometers to this cross road. The field adjacent to it is going to be your firing position. They'll be someone waiting to lead you into position.

Now, I'm not trying to scare you, but you need to know that after the GP took the machine gun fire today, the armored reaction force that was sent to the GP to reinforce it ran into a large North Korean ambush. Our guys got the better of it, but it tells me that the machine gun fire and the ambush was a coordinated effort. In other words, the machine gunning wasn't just a spontaneous event by some trigger-happy dink like some of the others have been. My point here is that we can't rule out the possibility of anything. There is no report of any North Korean force penetrating the south fence, but somehow their people keep showing up in the south and we really don't know how they are doing it. Just be prepared for anything."

Holloway had been paying rapt attention to every word the S-3 was telling him. "I understand, Sir. I'll do my best."

"OK, Clay. Just some basics. On the radio Tom Courtney is Charlie 6 and you're Charlie 5. Battalion FDC is 33. You'll be using the standard frequency of 88.75. I see you're wearing your SOI. That's good. Your convoy looks like its ready. Keep the men near the trucks. You might not hear from Tom for a while. He'll call when he's set.

Just hang loose, OK?" He winked at Holloway. Holloway smiled for the first time in two hours.

The two men walked back outside and Major Gentile began walking back toward battalion headquarters. After a few steps he turned and called back to Holloway. "Oh, I almost forgot. Alpha Battery mess hall is fixing some sandwiches for your men. The alert came in before anyone had a chance to eat the noon meal and it's unlikely that you're going to have much of a dinner." Then he turned and shielding his face from the rain walked away.

Holloway traveled the length of the convoy on foot, stopping at each vehicle to insure that everyone had drawn a weapon and ammunition. He also asked each of the drivers to shut down his vehicle engine. There was no telling how long they would be sitting there and he didn't want to move out on alert with their fuel tanks half empty. Then he returned to his truck to wait for Tom Courtney's call. It was a long wait. More than two hours passed before the radio crackled.

"Charlie 5, Charlie 5, this is Charlie 6, Charlie 6, over."

Holloway snatched the microphone excitedly and pressed the push-to-talk button. "Charlie 6, this is Charlie 5, over."

"This is Charlie 6, are you ready to move, over?"

"Charlie 5, ah, roger that, over."

"Charlie 6, y'all know where you're going, over?"

"Charlie 5, that's affirmative, over."

"Charlie 6, roger. Move out at this time. Somebody will meet you near the crossroads, over."

"Charlie 5, roger, out."

Holloway stepped out of his vehicle and stood in the middle of the street where the convoy could see him. Staring at the string of olive drab vehicles, he twirled his index finger in the air. There was a series of deep-throated roars as twenty-five trucks started their engines. The smell of diesel filled the damp air. Next he pointed to his eye. Twenty-five pairs of headlights flickered on. Headlights were standard procedure for a convoy on the move, but their brightness made Holloway realize that dusk was approaching as well. The cloudy skies and rain seemed to be hastening the approach of night. Holloway took a deep breath and returned to his seat next to his driver. This was it.

"Well, Corporal Gash. I don't know where we're going, but we're definitely on our way. Let's hit it." Gash shifted into first and headed slowly down the street toward the main gate. Rocky Gentile was standing outside of battalion headquarters smoking his pipe as the convoy passed. Holloway tossed him a salute. Gentile returned it and then stood there in the rain with his arms folded watching Charlie Battery with its six 105mm howitzers as it rolled out of the gate, turned right, and headed north.

The route seemed simple enough. Just one left turn after leaving the main gate and then follow the road all the way to the river. Move parallel to the river for a few klicks until you see Spoonbill Bridge. Cross the bridge and follow the road to the first crossroad. Holloway looked back at the convoy, which was strung out for some distance over the winding dirt road. Twenty-five meters between vehicles is what he had been told at Ft. Sill. The drivers seemed to be doing a good job of keeping the proper spacing. A half hour passed. Holloway's truck rounded a curve and ahead he could see the Imjin. Several minutes later he spied a low profile structure that reached across it. Gash came to a stop at the edge of the bridge and then eased the truck forward. Holloway had expected to feel a sag as the truck's weight shifted onto the steel planks supported by the heavy black pontoons. It didn't happen. The construction of the bridge was strong and solid. The pontoons were so tightly anchored that there was none of the movement in the bridge that Holloway anticipated. Gash drove slowly, keeping the truck wheels in the middle of the steel paths.

Mine fields began immediately on the north side of the river. Large open areas that forced individuals to stay on the road rather than attempting to travel overland. Charlie Battery was in the hostile fire zone now. Compared to the area around Camp Wynne, it was like the difference of night and day. There were no villages, no houses, no taxicabs, and no civilians north of the river. This was Indian country. This was real. This was where soldiers didn't go without a loaded rifle and a flak jacket. Charlie Battery had never been there before. In that respect, Holloway was no less experienced than anyone else in the unit. He could see some of the mines in the field beyond the barbed wire and the small painted warning signs. Over time dirt had washed away from some of the mines, exposing their ugly rounded snouts. It gave Holloway an uneasy feeling to know that if any of his vehicles were to stray from the road disaster awaited.

"Do you want me to go to blackout lights, Lieutenant?" Gash asked, referring to the shielded low power bulbs that emit only enough light through a slit to allow the driver to see a small part of the road directly in front. They give sufficient light to travel slowly on a dark night, yet cannot be seen by others more than a few yards away.

Damn, Holloway cursed silently. Why hadn't he thought of that? "That's a good idea. Go ahead," he replied. The natural light was fading rapidly. There was no sunset, no hues of oranges or pinks or reds, but only the vanishing of light. The rain had turned to mist. The convoy continued to creep forward, winding its way slowly up a gentle slope. As the lead vehicle neared the top of the hill, Holloway was conscious of the walls of red dirt rising above them on either side where engineers had cut the road through the crest of the hill. Subconsciously he placed his hand on the checkered grips of his .45. Next to him, Gash pulled the M-79 grenade launcher lying on the front seat closer to him. He spoke first. "It looks like a hell of a good place for an ambush, doesn't it, Sir!"

"That's just what I was thinking. This area is supposed to be secure, but the DMZ strike force ran into an ambush today. I hope whoever set up this little road march knows what the hell he's doing," Holloway responded. Tactics classes had taught him that in Vietnam it was a favorite ploy of the Viet Cong to launch an attack against a position and then ambush the column sent to relieve it. It was how the battle of the Ia Drang Valley had begun in 1966. Holloway hoped fervently that the North Koreans had not attended the same school as the Viet Cong. He also realized that if there was an ambush, a .45 pistol was not going to do him a whole hell of a lot of good.

Total darkness had settled in. Gash and Holloway both struggled to see the edge of the road through the misty rain with only the soft glow of the blackout lights. Through the mist a small bridge appeared ahead. Attached to the wooden structure were two steel planks. Gash crept slowly onto the planks steering his wheels into the center. Holloway worried that some of the other vehicles might have difficulty negotiating the bridge, especially trucks towing trailers or guns. But there wasn't anything he could do about it. The bridge ended and the convoy continued. They had been traveling for slightly more than an hour since the lead truck had passed through the gate at Camp Wynne. Suddenly, out of the darkness, a figure appeared at the side of the road. He wore a field jacket and a helmet. There was a pistol strapped to his side. Gash stopped.

"It's about time. Where the hell have you guys been?" the figure inquired impatiently.

"We left as soon as we got the call. It's tough to make time driving 10 miles an hour in the dark. Who are you?" Holloway retorted.

"My name's Ruminski. I'm your Liaison Officer. I need six gun guides. Let's get moving."

Holloway dismounted his truck and started down the length of the column. Something was radically wrong. Directly behind his lead vehicle had been the six gun trucks followed by the rest of the convoy. But now there were only five. How could a gun truck be missing??? One of his gun chiefs approached out of the darkness.

"Lieutenant Holloway! We lost one of the gun trucks."

"I can see that. Where is it?" Holloway demanded.

"It was that little bridge about a klick back down the road. Sergeant Lamerieux's howitzer wheel fell into the crack between the two steel planks and they couldn't pull it out," the gun chief said.

"Then how did the rest of the convoy get here?" Holloway wanted to know.

"On account of Sergeant Steele. He was right behind Lamerieux's truck and when the gun got stuck Steele seen what happened and drove his truck down into the streambed and up the other side. The whole convoy followed him."

"Hey, Holloway, I still need the goddamn gun guides. We got to get this cluster fuck in gear." It was Ruminski. He was right. They did need to get in gear.

"Gun guides, dismount!" Holloway called. Immediately, five men appeared. "Follow Lieutenant Ruminski. He'll show you where the guns are going." Holloway and the five men followed the Liaison Officer (LNO) into the wet field. Ruminski stopped at a wooden stake and pointed.

"Number one right here." Ruminski continued to walk quickly around the field pointing to stakes and calling out numbers until all five gun positions had been given. The first guide had already returned to his truck and was leading the big deuce and a half into position in the darkness. The truck made a sweeping turn and stopped with the left tire of the howitzer almost exactly next to the stake. Instantly the gun was unhooked from the truck and the vehicle pulled ahead a few feet to give the crew room to work in spreading the howitzer trails and preparing the gun for action. The gun crew was using flashlights with red filters. The device gave enough light to enable the men to work, but was virtually invisible more than a few feet away.

Another darkened figure approached Holloway. "Clay! It's good to see y'all. How'd it go?" It was Tom Courtney, Holloway's Battery Commander that he'd met briefly the night before. Holloway was pleased to hear that at least he had remembered his first name.

"OK, Sir. But we've got a little problem. We lost the number five gun in that little bridge one or two kilometers down the road. The Howitzer wheel fell into the hole in the middle and they couldn't get it out. The rest of the convoy drove over the streambed to get here. Sergeant Lamerieux and his crew stayed with it."

"What? Shit! That's all we need. Does Ruminski know about it?" Courtney asked.

"Yes, Sir. He knows," Holloway replied. He paused for a moment. "Where should I set up my aiming circle?"

"Don't bother, Clay. The First Sergeant has already got one set up. He's starting to lay the battery now."

"I'll go over and give him a hand then, if you don't mind, Sir," Holloway said.

"I don't mind at all. Top got the aiming circle set up in the daylight and put on the night vision lights and all. We just figured it was easier that way. You haven't met him have you?" Courtney asked.

"No, I haven't, but I saw the sign back at the CP. His name's St. Clair isn't it."

"You got that raht. You want me to introduce you?"

"I'll be fine, thanks," Holloway said. He turned and walked in the direction of the First Sergeant's voice that had just called out. "Number four adjust! Aiming point this instrument!"

Holloway strode through the wet knee high weeds that succeeded in soaking his fatigue pants within the first few steps. Hearing the First Sergeant continuing his process, Holloway approached him from the side. It was difficult to discern his features in the darkness, but he appeared to be a heavy set black man.

"How's it going, Top?" he asked. All First Sergeants like to be called "Top."

"Who's that?" First Sergeant Hudson St. Clair asked, peering into the darkness toward the unfamiliar voice.

"Lieutenant Holloway. I'm your new XO."

"Oh, good, Sir. Real good. Excuse me here one minute. NUMBER ONE ADJUST! DEFLECTION 2812," he called.

"Deflection 2812" a voice replied out of the darkness.

"DEFLECTION 2812. NUMBER ONE IS LAID," Top called back. "Now where the hell is number five?"

"Number five isn't here, Top. It's stuck in the little bridge back down the road."

"Damn, Sir. How did that happen?" Holloway explained what had transpired. "Well, at least we got five guns ready to go if they need them. Did you hear any more about the situation lately, Sir? Just a minute. NUMBER TWO DEFLECTION 2818."

"Number two deflection 2818," another voice from an invisible gun chief called out.

"DEFLECTION 2818. NUMBER TWO IS LAID. BATTERY IS LAID," Top yelled. The unit was ready to fire.

"No, I haven't heard anything, but if we're ready to shoot, I'm going to check on the situation right now." Holloway turned and picked his way back through the weeds to the area where the FDC (fire direction center) truck was silhouetted against the night sky. The FDC was the nerve center of the artillery during a fire mission. It contained the radios that would be used by anyone requesting artillery fire and it was where the firing coordinates would be plotted and then passed to the guns. Holloway assumed that was where he would find both Ruminski and Courtney. He assumed correctly. Tom Courtney was walking out of the back of the FDC van as Ruminski and Holloway approached from different directions.

"Do we have an update on the situation, Lieutenant Ruminski?" Holloway asked.

"Call me Dave. Yeah. It's like this. A little before noon GP Cindy started taking heavy machine gun fire. A lot of it. They think there was some rockets or recoilless rifle fire mixed in too. It went on for almost twenty minutes. They took three casualties. The reaction force was sent to reinforce the GP, but on the way it ran into a large body of UI's, maybe twenty of them. They may have been planning to ambush the reaction force, but anyway the reaction got the best of it. Three dead UI's and the rest "cauda chogied." Since then it's been pretty quiet.

Now, the DMZ is about a half mile away in the direction your guns are pointed. You've got a full company of infantry in front of you for security, so don't worry about that. They've also got ambush patrols scattered around the area. In fact, one of them was watching as your convoy passed through and the number five gun got stuck in the bridge. The infantry's going to guard it for the night so I told them to send your crew up here. You can recover the gun in the morning. Other than that, just continue to improve your position and be ready to shoot if you have to. Now that you're in place and so is the infantry I don't think you need any more from your friendly Liaison Officer tonight. I'm gonna unass the area. I'll be back in the morning after the Brigade briefing."

"OK, Dave," drawled Tom Courtney. "Thanks for your help."

Ruminski disappeared into the darkness, heading for the jeep he had left near the edge of the field. Courtney turned toward Holloway. "Clay, I'm going to find Sergeant Carlton and tell him to get with the Mess Sergeant and break out some C rations for the men. You hang around the firing battery and get familiar with it. Did they ever find the Chief of Smoke down in the ville?"

"He never showed, Sir," Holloway said. "I didn't hear anything about him."

Courtney nodded angrily. "That goddamn drunk. Well, it's up to you to run the firing battery then if anything happens tonight." He put his hands into the pockets of his rain jacket, hunched his shoulders, and walked into the night.

Holloway could see that the position was taking shape as he made his way cautiously around the area. The gun crews had dug the spades of the Howitzers into the ground to stabilize the guns. Ammo tarps had been erected to protect the ammunition and fuses that had been unloaded from the gun trucks. Sergeant Jackson and his communications people were assisting the gun crews and the FDC in laying commo wire for the field phones at each gun, the FDC, and the XO's post. The new Executive Officer moved from gun to gun, introducing himself and talking to the gun chiefs and the crewmen.

Suddenly, the sky lighted up to the north. Tracer rounds arched through the night and searchlight beams shot into the air, illuminating the clouds. The artillerymen stopped what they were doing and stared into the distance feeling a sense of excitement and danger and wondering what it meant. The noise of automatic weapons reached Charlie Battery a few seconds after the fireworks show began. Sound does not travel nearly as quickly as light. Utilizing the "flash/bang" method of calculating range that he had learned at Ft. Sill, he counted three seconds between the time he saw the flashes and when he heard the subsequent explosion. Since sound travels at approximately one kilometer per second, it was a simple calculation to know that the firing was approximately three kilometers away. A moment late the radio in the Fire Direction Center hissed and crackled.

"Charlie 33, this is Eagle, fire mission, over."

The RTO (radio-telephone operator) in the fire direction center grabbed for the microphone hanging from a hook next to the radio. "Eagle, this Charlie 33, fire mission, out." he responded. Men were scrambling. The FDC crew was bent over their charts, instruments in hand. Gun bunnies ran for their positions at the guns. Holloway grabbed the field phone at the XO's post behind the guns. It was dead. The wire hadn't all been installed yet.

"This is Eagle, grid 048045, direction 5128, over," the forward observer called.

"Grid 048045, direction 5128, out," the FDC replied.

"North Korean machine guns firing on us. Three or four of them. Adjust fire, over."

"Machine guns, adjust fire, out," the FDC responded.

Tom Courtney was inside the fire direction center now, reaching for the radio microphone. "Eagle, this is Charlie 33 is this a live fire mission? Are you taking enemy fire, over?"

"Eagle, hell yes we're taking fire. They're shooting the shit out of this place again. We need artillery ASAP, over." Eagle's voice was two octaves higher than normal.

"This is Charlie 33, roger, but we've got to get clearance to fire. Wait, out," Courtney said.

The FDC chief spoke, "Maybe we should have them authenticate the call for fire. This is serious."

"Fuck the authentication. That's Lieutenant Hoover up there. I know his goddamn voice." Courtney switched radios, calling the Battalion FDC back at Camp Wynne.

"Ruby Bracelet 33, this is Charlie 33, we've got a live call for fire from the Gulf Papa. They're taking machine gun fire again. Request permission to shoot, over."

"Charlie 33, this is Ruby Bracelet 33, I'm monitoring your fire net. I heard the call. That's a negative at this time. We're checking with higher (DivArty headquarters). Plot your fire coordinates and have the guns set it off, but do not, I say again, do not load any rounds into the tubes. I'm not ready to start the second Korean War all by myself, over." Courtney recognized the voice of Major Gentile himself in the FDC bunker.

"33, this is Charlie 33, roger, out," Courtney replied with a noticeable tone of displeasure. He hadn't brought Charlie Battery this far north to be told he couldn't fire when his help was needed. "Sergeant Applebee, plot the mission," Courtney ordered. The chart operators were already at work. Without the field phones being completely installed, Applebee yelled the data to Lieutenant Holloway through the back door of the van.

"Battery adjust, fuse quick, Lot X-ray, Charge 5, center one round, deflection 2789, Do Not Load, quadrant 289," yelled the FDC chief. Holloway repeated the commands to the five Howitzers, insuring that the projectiles were not loaded into the breech. The gun crews were reacting well, just as they had been trained and had practiced countless times. Within seconds each gun was ready, a crewman holding the thirty-five pound projectile in his hands as he stood behind the breech waiting for the order to load. There was only silence as the entire battery waited for the clearance to shoot. A clearance that could only come from DivArty, who would get it from Division HQ. A minute went by. The machine gun fire in the distance increased in intensity. The artillerymen looked at the sky, looked at the ground, looked anywhere but in each other's faces. Their thoughts were identical. American soldiers were in deep shit only a couple of miles away. They desperately needed what Charlie Battery waited to give them, wanted to give them. Let us load the rounds. Let us pull the lanyards!

The radio in the FDC van popped squelch. The speakers were turned up and the van door was open. Everyone was listening.

"Charlie 33, this is Eagle, where the hell is the fire. We need the fire ASAP, over."

"Eagle, this is Charlie 33, sorry, no can do." Tom Courtney was almost whispering into the microphone. The very thought that he was not permitted to provide the assistance that he knew he could provide was breaking his heart. "We're waiting for clearance from higher. We're trying. There's nothing we can do. Hold on. It'll be there. We're ready to shoot the mission, over."

"I'm giving you the goddamn clearance! Pull the trigger. They're killing us. Shoot now. Shoot now!" Sweeper's voice was still high pitched and excited.

Holloway could see Courtney through the door of the FDC. His jaw was thrust forward and his teeth were clenched. But it was the eyes that transfixed Holloway. The eyes seemed to glow as they stared at the big map laid out on the chart table. His fingers were white as they gripped the microphone in his right hand, threatening to crush it like a Styrofoam cup. He grabbed for the microphone connected to the other radio; the one to the S-3 bunker at Camp Wynne.

"33, this is Charlie 6. We've got to shoot. There are Americans dying up there. We can help. We've got to help. Sir, we're going to shoot!" Courtney's southern drawl was pleading. He wanted desperately to hear Major Gentile agree with him, to tell him he was right.

"Charlie 6, this is 33. Negative. You'll do no such thing. We'll have an answer any moment. Sit tight. We're talking about a major violation here shooting artillery into North Korea. I can't make that decision and neither can you. Out!"

There was a pause of only a few seconds. The radio hissed again. "Charlie 33, this 33. Permission to shoot is denied. I just got the word. Higher has not given clearance, over."

"Bullshit. Fuck 'em all. Let's just do it anyway. We can't just sit here like this!" It was Sergeant Applebee, the normally placid FDC chief that had spoken. Momentarily everyone looked at Applebee, but then the eyes swept back to the Battery Commander to see what he would do. It was his call.

"Wait a minute!" It was Clay Holloway bounding up the stairs of the FDC. "Ask them for permission to fire illumination. We can shoot the flares right up to the North Korean border. It'll light up the machineguns and maybe scare 'em into thinking high explosive is coming right behind it. Maybe they'll bail out. See if DivArty will go for it."

Courtney focused on Holloway, but only for a moment. "33, this is Charlie 33, request permission to fire illumination rounds. We'll lay them right on the edge of the MDL. Nothing will land in North Korea. Maybe it'll help, over."

"Charlie 33, this is 33, wait, out." Major Gentile needed to check with Division.

Hang in there, Sweeper. Hang in there, baby. We're trying, man. We're trying.

"Applebee," Tom Courtney ordered. "Go ahead and plot the data. Put your pins just this side of the MDL right in between GP Cindy and those gook machine guns. How far away will that put the illumination rounds from the machine guns?"

The horizontal chart operator looked up from his table. "Only about two hundred meters short of the machine guns, Sir. It sure ought to get their attention having those big assed flares floating down right in front of them."

"Charlie 33, this is 33, permission granted. Illumination fire authorized to explode and land south of the MDL only. Is that understood, over?"

"This is Charlie 33, roger, will advise, out." Tom Courtney set down the mike. "Applebee, give me the data!"

"Correction deflection, deflection 2795, illumination, battery one round, time 23.7, correction quadrant, quadrant 292, do not load."

Courtney grinned at Holloway and pointed his index finger at him. Holloway flashed a smile, turned and jumped down the FDC steps, yelling the commands at the guns. There was initial confusion by the gun crews. They had been told to prepare HE (high explosive) rounds. Now, in the middle of the fire mission it had been changed to illumination. Section chiefs scrambled to get an illumination round out from under the ammo tarp. Then a time fuse had to be mounted and the time set with a fuse wrench. Still, in less than a minute all five guns were ready. Holloway was running from gun to gun, using his red filtered flashlight to check the rounds, confirming that illumination was going to be fired, not the forbidden high explosive. Meanwhile the FDC was calling Lieutenant Hoover.

"Eagle, this is Charlie 33, battery one round illumination in effect, over."

"What the hell are you talking about? I don't want illumination, I want HE. Give me the HE, over."

Courtney's mind raced. He motioned for the RTO to give him the microphone. What if the North Koreans were listening to his transmission? It was all being sent in the clear. Hell, maybe the enemy already knew permission to fire HE had been denied. But why take a chance.

"Eagle, this is Charlie 33, illumination will be first. HE to follow, over."

"This is Eagle, roger. Hurry it up. I don't know how much longer we can take this. They may come at us at any second. We're partially on fire again."

"Battery is ready," Holloway yelled anxiously toward the FDC.

"Go ahead," Courtney called back.

"Quadrant 292." A moment's pause to load. "Batteryeeee, FIRE!" Holloway screamed, dropping his raised hand and instantly feeling the concussion from the anticipated "WHAM" coming from the five Howitzers to his front.

*   *   *

Second Lieutenant Robert (Sweeper) Hoover was almost beside himself with frustration. The acting Guard Post Commander, Second Lieutenant Keith Hackworth, had been screaming at him off and on for the last five minutes, calling him and every other sorry son-of-a-bitch who wore the crossed cannons of the field artillery on their collars, every foul name Hoover had ever heard and several that he hadn't. Hoover had tried explaining to Hackworth that it just wasn't their fault. There wasn't a damn thing he could do, but yell and plead into his radio. Division just wasn't going to let anyone fire artillery into North Korea no matter how many machine guns were firing at them. Hackworth wasn't used to that. In Vietnam, he'd had artillery on call. When his unit needed it, it was usually there within seconds. But in Korea, that wasn't happening. The GP was returning the fire with its own .50 calibers that Hackworth had installed earlier that evening, but they had not yet been effective in knocking out any of the North Korean automatic weapons. For one thing, the Koreans were firing from an area that was much further left of the position from where they had fired earlier that day and for that reason, only two of the .50s had line of sight to the aggressors.

The only reason Hackworth had finally stopped yelling at Hoover was because one of his men in the next position had been wounded by flying wooden splinters created by the incredible volume of automatic weapons fire they were now taking on a continuous basis. Hackworth had scurried over to the position to help tend to the wounded man just as Hoover heard the Charlie Battery FDC tell him that illumination rounds were on the way.

"Hacker! Hacker! It's on its way, man. Illumination is first. We're gonna light those fuckers up, right now!" Hoover was screaming at the top of his lungs, trying to make Hackworth hear him over the din of the incoming and outgoing machine gun rounds. Hoover switched his attention back toward the flashes coming from the North Korean machine guns. At almost the same moment there it was. It was gorgeous. Just gorgeous. A string of five bright flashes high in the night sky, halfway between GP Cindy and the machine guns. Just about where the MDL should be. Momentarily Hoover wondered why there were five flares rather than the usual six, but then quickly dismissed the thought. The flashes turned to a shimmering brightness that lighted up the entire area, transforming it into an artificial daylight. The woods, the fields, their own hill, and best of all the area where the North Korean machine guns were so well hidden and protected. Virtually every soldier on GP Cindy raised up from the floors of their bunkers or the bottom of their trench lines to peek at the flares as they dangled from their parachutes and floated ever so slowly toward the earth. Hoover was back on his radio quickly.

"Charlie 33, this is Eagle. Beautiful Charlie 33, beautiful. Now I want HE in effect. Add two hundred, fire for effect, over," Hoover requested, unaware that no high explosive was authorized to be fired and that none would be coming. But even as he spoke he realized that the North Korean machine guns had paused in their murderous work.

"Eagle, this is Charlie 33, are you still receiving fire, over," the Charlie Battery FDC was asking.

"This is Eagle, uhhhh, wait, over."

A minute passed before the radio in the Charlie FDC again crackled with a message. "Charlie 33, this is Eagle. The automatic weapons fire has temporarily halted. Can we still shoot the HE, over?"

"This is Charlie 33, that's a negative. If their guns have ceased firing our rules of engagement do not allow us to fire the HE at them. Do you want a repeat of the illumination or an end of mission, over?"

"Charlie 33, repeat illumination, over."

Within sixty seconds the fading light in the target area was renewed with five more "pops" high in the sky, followed by the flares in the dangling parachutes. The silence from the woods north of the MDL continued. The enemy to the north had ended the evening's activities, unsure as to whether or not the United States was prepared to initiate artillery duels along the DMZ. To do so would have begun a major escalation in the uneasy situation that had existed since 1953 and which had been altered violently three years earlier. In 1969, the Democratic People's Republic of Korea was content with harassment, espionage, and ambush. The directive from the government of Pyongyang had not authorized anything that might initiate the beginning of the second Korean War. For the time being, at least, the machine guns would remain silent.

*   *   *

"End of mission! End of mission! They've stopped firing. The zips have quit shooting," Tom Courtney was yelling out the back of the FDC van to the men of Charlie Battery. They hadn't heard any firing off in the distance for the last minute or two, but this made it official. Shouts and cheers echoed up and down the gun positions. "Hey, Lieutenant Holloway. It worked. The illumination rounds worked. We must have worried them enough that they decided to pack it in. You sandbagged them on that call. Nice going for a rookie. A Yankee rookie besides," Courtney drawled in his deep Tennessee voice. He walked down the steps of the van and extended his hand. Holloway grabbed it and shook it warmly, smiling until his face hurt.

"Great. That's great, Sir!" Holloway exclaimed. He turned back toward the battery. "Fine job, gentlemen. Stand easy." Holloway took off his helmet and ran his fingers through his sweaty hair and gazed off into the direction of the DMZ. The feeling of success was intoxicating, exhilarating. We wanted to jump into the air and yell, but he restrained himself. Officers were supposed to be calm and composed, after all. He looked at his watch. Almost 2200 hours. Ten hours ago he'd been standing in his room at the BOQ wondering what was for lunch. Now he and Charlie Battery had successfully completed a combat mission. He looked back at Courtney.

"You get any details from the GP? How many casualties this time?" Holloway asked.

"No. We'll find out later. We don't want to be putting too much information out over the radio in the clear. Sweeper owes us a couple of beers after this. We'll get the full story then.

Tell the troops to stand down. I think its over for tonight, but I want a round of HE and a round of illum ready at each gun just in case. The NK's know there's artillery in the area now. I don't think they're going to start up again. If they were going to hit the GP with an infantry assault they'd have done it by now."

"Right, Sir! I'll have them sleep close to the guns. We're not going to put up tents tonight are we?" Holloway asked.

"Listen, Clay, calling me "Sir" in front of the troops is good, I guess, but otherwise just call me Tom. And no, we're not gonna fart around with the gol damn tents now. People will find places to sleep; they've done it before. I'm going to check on a few things and then turn in. Most of us haven't had much sleep in the last two days," he added with a amiable glare at Holloway. "We were on SCOSI last night, remember."

"OK, Tom. I'd just like to say one thing though. I like Charlie. It looks like one hell of an outfit and I'd just like to say I'm really glad I'm here. See you tomorrow." Holloway walked away.

A half hour later, after finding where Gash had parked his one and a quarter ton truck, Holloway climbed into the back, dug out his newly issued sleeping bag, and laid it out on the hard metal truck bed. He removed his web gear and took off his helmet and boots. Next he slipped off his rain jacket and shirt, took the .45 pistol out of its holster, checked to be sure the safety was on and then tucked the heavy handgun into the front of his pants. He gazed one more time out of the open back of the vehicle and looked at the night sky. He mused over what an incredible day it had been. To think that a week ago he and Todd Hardesty had been sitting at a bar in Seattle having a beer and wondering what the next thirteen months would be like. Now he was finding out. He hoped it wouldn't be like this every day. He hoped he'd still be alive when the sun came up.

CHAPTER 5

Early morning sunlight was pouring through the open back of Holloway's truck. He awoke with a start, glancing quickly at his watch. It was almost six thirty. The events of the previous night flashed quickly through his mind as he peered outside. The morning was beautiful. It smelled fresh and the dew on the grass made everything seem clean. Feeling an ache in his upper body, he thrust both arms into the air and stretched the muscles of his back and arms. Then he swung one leg over the tailgate and climbed out of the truck and looked about. Several of the troops were moving around. Everything looked much different in the daylight. The field where they were located was larger than he had realized in the darkness. It was at the intersection of the road on which he had arrived and another road that ran parallel to the DMZ, about a half-mile south of the fence. As he looked to the north he could see a hill a couple of miles away. He correctly observed that it must be Guard Post Cindy. He wondered how they were getting along this morning.

Much of the dawn's activity seemed to be centered around the mess truck that sat fifty yards away and where breakfast was being prepared. Holloway dressed himself with the few articles of clothing he had removed prior to climbing into the sleeping bag the night before and began walking toward the FDC. First Sergeant Hudson St. Clair was the first person he encountered.

"Hey, Sir! How'd you sleep?" asked the First Sergeant, his ebony face breaking into a wide smile.

"Good, Top. Little stiff though. Those truck beds aren't real soft."

"No, Sir. And it don't get no easier when you get older either." First Sergeant St. Clair looked to be about thirty-five. The patch on the right shoulder of his fatigue shirt was that of the Fourth Infantry Division, meaning he'd had at least one tour in the Delta of Vietnam. "We got a latrine dug if you need one. It's back over there. All the comforts of home. Don't have a screen for it yet, but we'll get everything all straightened out later today. Get you a cot up here too."

"Any idea how long we're gonna be up here?" Holloway asked.

"Not really. But they didn't send us up here just to turn around and go home. I'll bet we'll be here for a while. Make sure everything gets cooled down. I don't think anything else important happened last night, although I did hear some automatic weapons fire off in the distance a couple of times."

Holloway nodded and moved past the First Sergeant. He had decided that as much as he wanted to go to the FDC to see what was happening, he had first better first locate the latrine that Top had mentioned. He discovered it a moment later. It turned out to be a hole dug into the red clay with a half of a fifty-five gallon drum perched over the opening and a toilet seat bolted to the drum. A roll of toilet paper hung from a branch next to it. It was a reminder to Holloway that the normal functions of life did not cease just because the unit had gone on alert.

A few minutes later, feeling noticeably more comfortable, Holloway again began walking toward the FDC. His Battery Commander was just walking down the back steps.

"Mornin' Clay," Tom Courtney called.

"Good morning, Sir. Anything going on?"

"Let's go have breakfast over at the mess truck. We can talk there. Top will be there soon." Courtney plunged his hands deeply into his pockets and strode past Holloway. The mess crew had placed a card table and four metal folding chairs under the overhanging branches of a tree near the mess truck at the edge of the clearing. Courtney plopped himself into one of the chairs. Holloway took one of the others. One of the cooks approached immediately with a large mug of black coffee.

"Here's your coffee, Lieutenant Courtney," the cook said. "Lieutenant Holloway, how do you like your coffee?"

"Just like my women, Donofrio. Hot, sweet, and blond," Holloway replied winking at the cook.

Courtney chuckled and shook a Kool loose from his pack. He held out the package to Holloway who shook his head. Holloway rarely smoked before noon. "Well, Clay, you might have to change your taste in women 'cause most of the ones you're gonna come upon in this country are likely to be short and dark and smell like kimchi."

"Oh, I don't know. I noticed one of the girls at the bar at the Club that fits my description. Beth Kisha was her name I think. You know her?" Holloway asked.

"Well, hell yes, I know her. I know all the Doughnut Dollies. Matter of fact, they're all in love with me," Courtney retorted.

"Oh, and he's modest too," Holloway mocked. "Is she available?"

"I suppose so. Most of those girls have boyfriends scattered all over the Second Division. Don't mean nuthin'. They're always in demand 'cause there's so few round eyes over here. You like her, huh?"

"I didn't really get a chance to meet her. I just wondered," Holloway remarked. Donofrio returned with another mug of coffee, loaded with cream and sugar and set it on the table. "OK, Tom, what's the situation here? Anything else happen last night?" Holloway asked, changing the conversation to the real subject at hand.

"I haven't heard anything official, but Major Gentile just called on the radio. He and Colonel Moody will be arriving here about 0930. Ruminski will probably be here before that and we'll get all the latest news flashes from him. There's a briefing every morning at the infantry compound at Camp Greaves at 0730. Ruminski will be here directly after that." Courtney paused momentarily as the First Sergeant joined them at the table. "We need to get things onto the right track now that it's daylight. Top, make sure our outposts are looking good and the guards know what they're supposed to know. Make sure all the troops are shaved and in the proper uniform. We need to get beau coup tents set up. We're probably going to have a lot of different visitors today.

Clay, I want you to make sure the gun chiefs are working on improving their positions. Camouflage, including the netting, sandbags and so forth. Make sure all the telephone wire gets laid including a line to the infantry battalion TOC. We want to be able to patch in to Camp Wynne by telephone.

Also, we need to get that Howitzer out the bridge first thing and get it into position and laid. Get the motor sergeant to help Sergeant Lamerieux."

Donofrio returned to the table juggling three trays of breakfast. Scrambled eggs, toast, home fries, and sausage were heaped onto the tray. Holloway dug into the feast eagerly. Normally he wasn't much of a breakfast eater, but the food looked and tasted wonderfully. He believed he had a few minutes of leisure time before he attacked the day's activities.

By 0815 the battery area was already taking shape. The number five gun had been retrieved from the hole in the bridge with the help of a wrecker truck from the 1/9th, the infantry battalion that Charlie Battery was supporting. Its gun crew was working diligently to catch up to the other five sections in organizing their firing position. The commo wire had been laid internally in the battery area and a wire team was on its way to the battalion TOC three miles away, laying wire along side of the road as the wire team crept along slowly in a medium sized truck with a large spool of the thin plastic coated black wire mounted in the back.

Dave Ruminski didn't arrive until almost nine. Colonel Quinn, commanding officer of the 1/9th Infantry, was normally a stickler for keeping the morning briefings to less than thirty minutes. However, today's briefing had gone on for one hour and fifteen minutes. The events of the previous day and evening had generated an atmosphere of danger and excitement, tempered by the loss of one soldier's life and the wounding of two others. Contacts with UI's were not uncommon, but the machine gunning of Guard Post Cindy combined with the attempted ambush had set off a chain of unusual events which needed to be reviewed and discussed in some detail. Ruminski was in a good mood because the artillery had received several compliments from the infantry officers regarding how well it had accomplished its mission the night before. As the artillery Liaison Officer to the 1/9th that was his responsibility.

Courtney saw Ruminski coming and signaled to Holloway and First Sergeant St. Clair to join him at the card table near the mess truck. The CP (Command Post) tent had not yet been erected.

"Come on, Ruminski. Give us the scoop," Courtney requested as the men seated themselves.

"OK, here we go. Most of it you already know so I'll just tell you what you don't. Fortunately, there was only one American slightly wounded by wood splinters in last night's attack. Lieutenant Hackworth, the GP commander that took over after he lead his reaction force up there, had everybody prepared for the worst. So the troops were under pretty good cover when the machine guns opened up the second time and we were able to return fire in their direction. Sweeper is up there as FO and, of course, he called for the fire mission that you took on. By the way, he was really pissed when I told him over the telephone today that there wasn't gonna be any HE rounds if the illumination hadn't worked. He was all set to start blowing the shit out of North Korea.

Then later last night the guys on the fence nailed two UI's trying to cut a hole in it. They must have thought the GI's were asleep and they were working almost right in front of a two man foxhole when the one guy in the hole gave them a burst and dropped them right there. Some other positions reported their Claymores turned around backwards. One Claymore was stolen. We're not aware that any penetration of the fence was successful, but then you can never be sure. We know some of those fuckers get through. So counting the three UI's that Hacker nailed with his reaction force, that's five dead UI's in one day. That's probably some kind of record.

Now as near as I can tell, the grunts are going to want you guys to hang around here for a few days anyway. They want to make sure things are really back to normal. There hasn't been an artillery battery north of the river for as long as anyone can remember. I think it gives the grunts a good feeling to know they have six 105's on call anytime that they want them. Oh, and before I forget, the DivArty commander, will probably be showing up here at your position around lunchtime. Make sure you have enough food for him. Son of a bitch eats like a horse. And you might as well get used to the idea of having visitors for a few days."

"Why the hell does everyone and his uncle feel like he has to visit Charlie Battery on the first morning we're here?" asked Courtney.

"Hell, Tom. You know how tourists are. The infantry is used to being the whole show up here. You guys are a novelty."

Lieutenant Ruminski was correct. The Battalion Commander, Colonel Moody, Major Gentile, Bill Grant and a host of other visitors from the 8/18th all came and went during the morning. Having an artillery battery north of the river really was viewed as a special event and the battalion hierarchy was making the most of it. Grant also brought Holloway some good news. His flight bag had been found by a local papasan in a ditch where the slicky boy who had stolen it had apparently abandoned it. Holloway's personal articles were missing, of course, but his 201 file was intact. That file would allow him to be paid normally at the end of the month and keep him from mandatorily being reinoculated for a variety of diseases.

Also as predicted, the DivArty commander paid a social call, as did Lieutenant Colonel Quinn and his XO of the 1/9th Infantry. They appreciated the work Charlie Battery had done and were more than complimentary in their remarks.

By nightfall the battery position looked as though it had been there for a week. Although a unit in the field is never finished in constantly improving its position, by the time the evening meal was ready, all of the tents were up, the big 292 radio antenna was installed, the gun positions were camouflaged and things generally were in good order. The Chief of Smoke, Sergeant Thompson, had finally been located in the village. He had claimed to be completely unaware of the alert, having signed out on Friday night for a forty-eight hour pass.

Holloway used the time of the next few days to further his informal education. It was an opportunity to learn the people and the procedures of his new unit and he took advantage of it. It was the first time the young officer had ever lived with an artillery unit in the field. And it was clear that these troops were field soldiers, not garrison troops. Most had adopted an air of bravado as they walked and talked as though they had spent half their adult lives in that field parked right behind the DMZ.

Three days after the occupation of the position had been initiated, the rainy season began in earnest. Important work didn't stop, the men working in rain suits when necessary, but much of the activities was kept to a minimum. Before long, the red clay had become a quagmire, making walking difficult and driving impossible. Colonel Moody had told Courtney that the infantry had said Charlie Battery could return to Camp Wynne whenever it wanted. There had been no more action in the DMZ since the first night and the situation appeared to be stabilized. Courtney had balked at returning. The way he looked at it, the battery should be able to stay for a seventh day, thereby qualifying each of the men for hostile fire pay for the month of July. The rules for receiving that pay were different in Korea than they were in Vietnam. While in that country to the south each American serviceman qualified for hostile fire pay no matter where he was or what he did. But there wasn't supposed to be a war in Korea, so in order to draw combat pay the requirements were more stringent. In order to qualify, an individual had to be assigned to a unit stationed in the hostile fire zone north of the Imjin River, make ten trips north of the river, or spend at least seven days of a month there. Or, of course, a man could also collect if he was wounded, even if he'd only been there for five minutes. Apparently the Army felt that it was a fairly good indication that a soldier had been exposed to combat if he was wounded and therefore deserved the pay.

Courtney got his way and was able to parlay the trip into a seven-day stay, but the rest of the week was quiet. It was as though the fighting had never taken place. In the

DMZ the two sides sat on their respective hills once again just peering at one another through binoculars. In the artillery position Charlie Battery went about its field routine and waited for something to happen which never did.

Late in the afternoon on Friday, Clay Holloway and Tom Courtney sat on their respective wooden frame cots inside of the CP tent sipping Cokes. The sides of the tent had been rolled up to allow optimal air movement inside of the canvas shelter. Holloway had just lighted a Winston and was watching the smoke drift lazily across the tent and out into the rain that was cascading onto the tent top and pouring down the sides.

"So, you just have the one son, Tom?" Holloway was asking.

"That's it. He was just born last month. Tom Junior. I won't even see him until he's nine months. 'Course Elaine has sent me about two thousand pictures of him, but it's not the same. My daddy tells me he looks just like me when I was his age. How 'bout you? Anybody special back home?"

"Nobody. I went with a girl in college for a while, but it didn't work out. I wasn't ready to get serious anyway. Who wants to get serious when you plan on going overseas for a year? I have to believe its pretty tough on you being away like this," Holloway commented.

Tom Courtney took a long gulp of his Coke, crushed the can, and threw it toward a cardboard box in the corner. "Yeah, it is. I feel like I've been here half my life and its only been six months. Sometimes it's real hard remembering what it's like to be with Elaine. I can't really remember what she feels like or what she smells like. And knowing that there's this little Tom Junior alive in Tennessee that I've never even seen. Well, that's real tough too. Believe me, you're better off being single in a situation like this.

So tell me, Clay," said Courtney. "You've been with Charlie for a full week now. What do you think?"

"I like it. I really do," Holloway responded enthusiastically. I think there are some really good people in this outfit. Not a lot of experience in some of the positions, but they try hard and seem to get by all right. People have been helpful. I've learned a lot this week, I'll tell you that."

Courtney took a pull on his cigarette. "Yeah, it's been a good week up here except for all the rain. I think that's starting to wear on people right now. But Gawd, it felt good to be able to help out those boys on that GP on the night we got here. And it's good just to get off the compound for a while. Keeps your field skills sharp. Well, we're going in tomorrow. I'll leave early in the morning with Top. You bring the rest of the convoy as soon as they're ready, probably around eleven. Tell Gash to stop at one of the wash points on the river before you come back to get all this mud off the vehicles. You ought to be back to Camp Wynne by 12:30." He glanced toward the mess truck. "Hey, the rain's lettin' up and some of the troops are getting in line. Let's go see what's fer dinner."

The rain had indeed stopped and the weather remained clear throughout the night and following morning. The dry air helped immeasurably in allowing the battery to strike its tents and load its trucks, though the tents would have to be set up on the parade ground after the unit returned to Camp Wynne to ensure that they were completely dry before putting them away. Otherwise mildew would rot the canvas. The ground in the battery area, however, remained slippery and wet. The erosion that began with the rains had created large ruts. In trying to exit the field, truck after truck slid sideways and often dropped into the ruts, some of which were eighteen inches in depth. Most military vehicles are equipped with front mounted winches for that very reason. Half of Charlie Battery's vehicles were forced to use those devices, hooking onto trees or other vehicles to pull themselves forcibly through the muck. The Battery would not reach Camp Wynne until almost three o'clock in the afternoon. By that time, Clay Holloway realized he had learned more about the functioning of an artillery battery in the field in one week than he had in his entire field artillery course at Ft. Sill.

CHAPTER 6

Life at Camp Wynne had seemed rather austere to Holloway when he had arrived the previous week. Now it felt almost luxurious compared to the slippery red mud in which he had spent the last few days. Charlie Battery had returned to the compound on Friday afternoon. By midday Saturday, when duty for the weekend normally ended, all of the Battery's equipment had been cleaned and put away. The Korean houseboys had taken over the tasks of washing, laundering, and shining personal clothing and equipment. Tents had been erected on the parade ground near the CP and were drying in the warm sunshine that had begun with the pink dawn. Holloway and Tom Courtney left the CP at exactly noon and walked together along the gravel street toward the BOQ.

"Let's stop into the PX a minute, Clay. I need some smokes," mentioned Courtney. He tugged open the wooden screen door and held it for Holloway. It was the first time Holloway had been inside the little building. In fact, it was the first time he had even noticed that it was a PX. He had passed it three or four times walking from the BOQ to the Battery area, but had always been preoccupied by other things and every green Quonset hut on the compound looked pretty much like the next one. As he stepped inside it occurred to him that he needed to buy several personal items. Losing his leather shaving kit to the slicky boy had cut deeply into his supply of toiletries. Fortunately he had an extra toothbrush along with a second stick of deodorant in his suitcase, but the entire time he had been in the field he had borrowed Tom Courtney's razor and shaving cream. This was his first opportunity to buy a new shaving kit and replenish its contents. There were only a few small aisles inside the little shop, but ten minutes later when the two men departed, Holloway's arms held two bags full of items.

"So what do you have on tap for this afternoon, Tom? Anything special?" Holloway asked.

"Not a damn thing that's important. After lunch I've got an appointment with Miss Lee in the barbershop at the club. I'm lookin' forward to gettin' muh back rubbed." Courtney shrugged his shoulders a few times for emphasis.

"How do you talk Miss Lee into rubbing your back?" Holloway inquired.

"I don't talk her into it, man. I pay her. This is Korea, not Ohio. They got a whole laundry list of services on the sign on the wall. I usually go for a full ride. Haircut's a quarter. Shave is another quarter. Back and shoulder massage is thirty-five cents and so forth. You can get a mudpack facial if you want one. Even a manicure. If you get everything on the list ain't gonna total more than $2.50," Courtney related to his new XO. "Mah long range plannin' hasn't gone past the barbershop for the day."

"Do you ever go into the ville? Into Sonyu-ri?"

"There's not much reason to. Officers aren't allowed off the main street, so you really can't frequent those little comfort houses the way the EM's do. DivArty doesn't want its officers gettin' into trouble and I guess they figure the best way to do that is keep us out of the ville. All the girls down there got rotten crotches anyway. The beer tastes like water buffalo piss. And that fuckin' mockely they drink will give you the shits so bad your anus will be redder than a possum's ass at pokeberry time.

You can only buy so many brass and wooden statues to send home. I guess you can get fitted at the tailor shop for a suit if you want, but if you do you'd be wise to supply your own thread. I've heard stories about guys goin' back to the States and six months later when they're out to dinner, one of the sleeves falls off of the jacket or the pants split in half. Anyway, when all is said and done, goin' to the ville ain't all that great.

I'll tell you what. I got a football. Maybe I'll come find you about three o'clock and you can run some pass routes for me just to keep mah arm in shape in case the Tennessee Volunteers send me a TWX that says come on back."

"You played football for Tennessee?" Holloway asked dubiously.

"Only in mah dreams, Holloway. Only in mah dreams." Courtney's eyes twinkled as he gave Holloway a little wave and walked away.

Courtney lived in what was referred to as the new BOQ, which was a two-story cinder block building housing the Battalion Commander and XO, the Battery Commanders, and the primary staff officers. The old BOQ housed the remainder of the other officers, all of whom were second lieutenants and was nicknamed "The Ghetto." Composed of two metal Quonset huts running parallel to each other and joined in the middle by a third Quonset hut, the old BOQ formed the letter H. The middle of the H was the latrine which contained four sinks, four stalls with commodes, four urinals, four showers, and a utility sink. All of the rooms in the old BOQ, with the exception of the two on the tops of the H, were large enough for only one man. The larger pair could handle two men if necessary. Given the current shortage of officers in the 8/18th, however, several of the rooms were vacant.

Each room had a metal-framed single bed, a wooden dresser, and a wooden desk with chair. There was also a closet that contained, in addition to the clothes bar, a light bulb socket twelve inches above the cement floor. The heat from the bulb kept the boots and shoes from becoming covered with mildew during the rainy season. The walls were normally painted with a tan or mint green semi-gloss paint. There was no carpeting and only the flimsiest of plain colored material served as curtains to cover the single small window. Holding his two bags in one hand, Holloway unlocked the padlock that secured his room and pushed the door open with his boot. A musty smell greeted his senses.

Entering the room, he placed his purchases on the desk, flipped his fatigue cap at the top of the dresser, and propelled himself into the air, landing on his back on the bed. The metal springs supporting the mattress growled loudly. The mattress felt good. Seven nights on the canvas cot in the tent had gotten tiring. Holloway sighed deeply and stared at the ceiling. A moment later he heard laughter. A feminine giggling sound was coming from outside. Rolling quickly out of the bed he stood at the window and pulled the curtains just slightly to the right. When the BOQ had been built, the area for the cement slab foundation had been excavated so that the floor of the building was four feet below the sidewalk that ran along side of it. Holloway peered out of the window at the two pairs of nylon-clad women's legs that strutted past his room. He could see the hem of blue and white seersucker cotton uniform dresses which ended three inches above the women's knees. Twisting his neck he tried to see both a bit more thigh and the faces of the two Doughnut Dollies who were passing by. He was successful in neither endeavor, but the sexy laugh that he heard was the same as what he had heard at the Officer's Club bar the night of his arrival. He was sure the laugh belonged to Beth Kisha. There was a knock on his door.

"Hey, are you Holloway?" a stocky young man with a shiny face and wearing second lieutenant's bars asked through the partially open doorway. The shiny face showed scars of what had probably once been a severe case of acne. It also held a large grin.

"You got it. Who are you?" Holloway inquired.

"Bob Hoover. Most people around here call me Sweeper. I'm the FO on Cindy. I've heard tell you and Charlie Battery are the ones that helped pull my young ass out of the fire last week."

"You're the voice on the radio. You're 'Eagle'. I'm glad to meet you." Holloway smiled and extended his hand. "So what are you doing down here?"

"That's the way the system works. Sometimes you're on the hill and sometimes you're not. I try to get back here once every week or two. This is my battalion, you know, even if I spend most of my time with the grunts. My room's just down the hall. I like Camp Wynne on a Saturday night. As far as I can see, it's the best O Club in the Second Division.

Well, anyway I wanted to stop in and say hello and thanks for the other night. You can't know what it feels like to have those pricks just blowing the living shit out of your bunker and not being able to do anything about it but plead into the radio. I heard it was your idea about firing the illumination rounds."

Holloway shrugged.

"That was cool," Sweeper continued. "I just wish we could have been allowed to bring some steel rain down on their young slanted asses. Maybe better luck next time."

"You're going to be around all weekend?" Holloway asked.

"Right. I'm not due back onto Cindy until Monday afternoon. I'll buy you a drink tonight," Sweeper offered.

"I wouldn't miss it for the world. But I'll buy your drinks. See you later." Sweeper withdrew from the room and walked down the hall. Holloway mused briefly about Sweeper's southern accent and decided that it must be a different part of the South than where Courtney was from. Sweeper seemed to be a whole lot easier to understand.

*   *   *

"Clang!!! The big brass bell that hung from the ceiling near the black bar in the Camp Wynne Officers' Club reverberated loudly after Second Lieutenant Bob Hoover had slammed the clapper against the bell's side. The loud noise was the traditional announcement of a free round of drinks for everyone in the room, which at the moment totaled fourteen.

"Belly up, people. The drinks are on me," Sweeper cried loudly to be heard over the din of voices and the driving music of the Rolling Stones that echoed in the background of the smoky room.

"That's the kind of talk I like," said Bill Grant getting up from his chair at the table in the corner and walking toward the bar to collect. Clay Holloway slid back his chair and followed a few steps behind. He surveyed the room as he walked toward the semicircular bar with its twelve high-legged black vinyl covered bar stools. Half of the chairs were occupied, with another five or six officers standing in groups around those who were seated. In front of the bar and about fifteen feet away was an area where Holloway had been seated and which contained ten small tables, each of which had four straight back chairs. The tables were scattered about the room in no particular order. The wall behind the tables held a large stone fireplace. Along the west wall were four slot machines. The east wall was plain because it could be folded and pushed against the back to open a party room and combine it with the main room. Holloway had been told that when a Korean band was hired for some special occasion, that was the way the room would be set up. Behind the bar were the customary shelves that held the liquor, a large mirror, a stereo system, and a long shelf containing eighteen silver mugs. Each mug had inscribed upon it a name, one for each officer of the Battalion along with his arrival date, the insignia of the Second Infantry Division, and the Regimental Crest. Once each officer received his orders and learned the date of his departure from Korea, that information would also be inscribed.

Several of the other lieutenants had clustered around Sweeper patting him on the back and offering to buy him drinks. Everyone had heard about GP Cindy. Sweeper, and to the lesser extent Tom Courtney and Clay Holloway, had become celebrities of sorts, since they had participated in something that the other lieutenants had not. Most of the junior officers of the Battalion were present in the room. Holloway had at least said hello to virtually all of them by now. Eric Auslander, tall and blond, and the Battery Commander of Alpha Battery, was standing near the end of the bar talking to Tom Courtney. Near them sat "Bear" Buckner, the BC of Bravo, sitting quietly and sipping on a Jack Daniels. Buckner was a good six inches shorter than Auslander, but his broad back and shoulders combined with this muscular arms struck an imposing figure. He had dark piercing eyes that seemed to glow when he talked, although talking was not something he did frequently.

Also in the room was an officer who had arrived in the Battalion while Charlie Battery was in the field. Lester Joe Bufford was the new Battalion Communications Officer. He was a member of the Signal Corps and wore the crossed flags of that branch on the left lapel of his fatigue shirt. He was the only officer in the Battalion who was not Field Artillery, other than the Battalion Surgeon, Doc Kramer. Lester Joe was standing by himself at one end of the bar near the two swinging doors of the entranceway looking a bit lonely. Holloway collected his free bourbon and soda from Mr. Buster (pronounced Meesta Busta) and walked toward where Bufford was standing.

"How's it going?" offered Holloway. "We haven't met. My name's Clay Holloway, Charlie Battery. Where are you from?"

"Atlanta!" Bufford replied, his face transforming itself into a smile as broad as the Chattahoochee River of his hometown. I just got here Thursday."

"That's great! That is really great!" cried Holloway.

"What's great? Atlanta?"

"No, not that. I just met someone who's been here less time than I have. I'm shorter than you. That's fucking great!"

Bufford's smile lessened slightly. It didn't seem all that great to him. Counting the two days of in-processing, he'd been in Korea a grand total of four days. He had 391 left to go on his tour. "I'm happy for y'all," he said unenthusiastically.

"Hey, it's not bad here," Holloway said, not meaning to antagonize the man. "I think there are really good people in this Battalion. All the ones I've met are top shelf. Just look around in here. People are smokin' and jokin' and just having a good old time. Monday we'll hit it hard, but right now I just feel good being back here in civilization. We've been in the field all week."

"Are you married, Clay?" Bufford asked.

"No. I guess you are by the looks of that ring on your finger."

"Yeah. And that's the difference." Holloway could see the sadness in Bufford's light blue eyes. "I suppose that if you like soldiering maybe this place wouldn't be so bad. I guess it's better than going to Vietnam. But I've only been married three months and

I still haven't adjusted to the fact that I'm not even going to see Susan for another thirteen. That's going to be the hard part for me and for her."

Holloway really didn't know how to respond to that. He'd never had a relationship that he felt so deeply about that it would affect him the way it was obviously affecting Bufford. There was a short period of silence during which Holloway reached for his cigarettes as something to fill the void. Clumsily the package slipped from his fingers and fell to the floor. He stooped to retrieve it. As he began to straighten up, his backside collided unexpectedly with the soft flesh of someone else, knocking Holloway forward into Bufford's legs.

Catching himself, Holloway turned to see what in the world had happened. He hadn't realized there was anyone near him.

"Was it fun for you?" Beth Kisha inquired mischievously, rubbing her hand on her right cheek and hip.

Holloway could feel his face flushing. "Did we both bend over at the same time?" he asked, not being able to think of anything witty to say. He could see two other young women standing behind Beth laughing softly and covering their mouths.

"Are you trying to tell me that was an accident, Lieutenant? I've been around this place long enough to know when a guy is trying to rub his ass on mine," she said in mock accusation. "I hope that the next time you're a little less obvious about it, not to mention more gentle."

"No, really. It was an accident," Holloway protested. The temperature in his face was continuing to rise. The other women were laughing harder.

"I like you. You're cute," Beth announced. An impish smile had crept around the corners of her mouth. She held Holloway's face lightly with her right hand and kissed him briefly on his cheek. "Now tell me who you are."

"My name's Holloway."

"I can read that on your name tag, Lieutenant. What's your first name?"

"Clay. And you're Beth."

"And just how did you happen to know that, Clay Holloway?"

"Well, the First Sergeant announced at the morning formation that Beth Kisha going to be present here this evening. He said I'd recognize her because she had the softest buns in the ROK. I'll have to tell him he was right." Holloway retorted, having regained his sense of wit. If she was going to toy with him, he was going to toy back.

Beth Kisha tilted her head back and laughed the throaty little laugh that had intrigued Holloway the week before. He studied the dainty muscles in her neck and her soft lightly tanned skin that disappeared into the vee of the navy colored blouse that she wore tucked into a white cotton skirt. The artificial lighting from above seemed to reflect from her shiny blond hair. He did not consider her beautiful, but there was no question that Beth Kisha was a very desirable young woman. Holloway wondered fleetingly what would have driven her to give up a year of her life in order to hang around with a bunch of Korea soldiers out here in the boondocks.

"So, you admit it. You were standing there waiting to ambush me in an assault from the rear," she challenged.

"The only thing I'll admit is that we ought to change the subject before I really get myself into trouble by commenting on anyone's rear. Who are your friends?" Holloway asked, nodding to Beth's two companions.

She pressed her lips together in a pout. "OK, I'll let you off the hook. But watch your step, Clay Holloway. And now let me present Kathy Kelsey and Joan Brannigan. I'm sure you know we're all emissaries of the American Red Cross."

Holloway bowed slightly from the waist and was greeted in return by two mock curtsies. He extended his arm behind him and nodded toward his companion. "Allow me to present a man who has been one of my closest friends for at least five minutes. What did you say your name was again, Lieutenant?" The girls laughed.

"Lester Joe Bufford. Call me Lester Joe," he replied.

Beth rolled her eyes at Holloway. She had never met someone named Lester Joe before, let alone someone who wanted to be called by that name. She didn't think the name fit him. He had light brown hair, an almost a cherubic face, and a friendly grin and she wondered if she would ever be able to bring herself to call him Lester Joe. The five people all exchanged greetings. Holloway gazed for the first time at the other two women. Kathy Kelsey was an athletic looking young woman with high cheekbones, classic chiseled features, and light brown hair worn short in the back. Joan was a perky brunette with bobbed hair, dancing Irish eyes, and freckles.

"Has everyone collected on Sweeper's bell ringer yet?" Holloway asked.

"No," Kathy noted. "We must have come in right after it happened. If you're not here when the bell's rung it doesn't count."

"Well, I guess we'll have to fix that," Holloway responded. Taking three steps to reach the bell he grasped the cord hanging from the clapper and whipped it into the side of the bell. There was a cheer throughout the bar. Mr. Yun, the club manager, came out from behind his little office. The small room was almost hidden in back of the large mirror behind the bar. Yun correctly believed that Mr. Buster was going to need some assistance in keeping up with the increasing demand for drinks. Both bartenders were mixing and lining up drinks as quickly as they could, trying at the same time to remember how many had been poured. Tom Courtney approached the bell from the other direction.

"I'll be damned if I'm gonna be outdone by mah own XO," Courtney announced. "Clang!!!" The bell sounded for the third time in less than ten minutes. The drinks were beginning to stack up on the crowded bar as the bartenders continued to fill glasses with ice, mix, and liquor or pull the flip tops from the cans of beer. The volume of the stereo located behind the bar had been increased to allow the Stones album to be heard over the din of party voices. Holloway looked at Beth Kisha.

"Wow! Does it always get like this in here?"

"No," she answered in an elevated voice. "But it is Saturday night and it looks like it just might be one of those nights. Have you two gentlemen been initiated yet?"

"Initiated in what way?" Holloway asked.

"Uh oh! Bad answer. I think that means no," Beth replied with the impish look returning to her face. "Yoo-hoo! Lieutenant Courtney! We need to speak with yoouuu!"

Courtney walked slowly down the bar. "Yes, Darlin'. What can I do for y'all this evenin'?" he asked.

Beth put one hand on the bar and the other on her hip. "Well, it has come to our attention that these fine young officers who are now members of the 8/18th and this Officers' Club have yet to be properly initiated. As the commanding officer of one of them and being at least a senior officer to the other and a Club member in good standing, I propose that you undertake some action here."

"You're raht of course, Sweetheart. Mr. Yun. Mr. Yun. Over here," he said pointing to the bar where he stood. Yun held up a single finger indicating that he'd be there in a moment. He was still trying to catch up with the last two bell ringers.

Holloway leaned over to Lester Joe and spoke softly. "I'm not sure I like the looks of this, but I don't know what we ought to do about it."

Mr. Yun finished setting up the last round of drinks and scribbled some numbers on a pad of paper behind the bar indicating who owed how much money. Then he walked over to where Tom Courtney was standing. "Yes, Sir?" he asked arching his eyebrows slightly.

"Mr. Yun, we need to officially initiate these two young men. One is a true son of Dixie and the other's a damn Yankee, but he seems not to be too bad so far, so I guess we'll go ahead and initiate him anyway. Set 'em up." Many of the other people in the club had rearranged themselves to form a circle around Courtney, the two men, and the three Doughnut Dollies who had started all this. Courtney turned to the two new officers. "Y'all are going to get three free drinks. The first one's called artillery punch and it tastes gooooood." He watched as Mr. Yun poured vodka, rum, sloe gin, cranberry juice, and ice into a metal blending container and shook it fully. He added an orange slice to each of the glasses into which he poured the contents of the blender.

Holloway didn't think it looked too bad. He picked up one of the glasses. "To your health, Lester Joe." He tapped his glass against Bufford's and they each drained them. Holloway could feel the drink's potency. It did, after all, contain three jiggers of liquor.

Courtney looked at the two men approvingly. "Nice job. Now here's number two. It's a 155, named naturally after a 155mm Howitzer round. Light 'em, Mr. Yun." Courtney looked back at the bar. Mr. Yun was holding a lighter to the top of two full liqueur glasses. Soon both were ablaze. Holloway wasn't sure what to do. Should he blow out the flame, drink it on fire, or let it burn to use up more of the alcohol?

"Hurry! Blow it out before it makes the glass hot or you'll burn yourself," Kathy called out. Holloway and Bufford both grabbed their glasses and puffed out the flames. They glanced briefly at one another and threw the glasses to their mouths, dumping the liquid down their gullets. Both immediately clutched their throats. Bufford tried to talk.

"Ooohhhh!" he rasped hoarsely. He was unable to speak, his entire mouth and throat turning instantly numb. Holloway echoed Bufford.

"Whaaat in God's name is that?" Holloway croaked.

"Ahh told you," said Courtney. "It's a 155."

"It's actually Ronrico 151." added Joan. "You guys did pretty well."

"Well, you're almost home. Two thirds of the way. Mr. Yun is that French 75 ready yet?" asked Courtney.

"Yes, Sir, Lieutenant Courtney. Everything but da eggs and here dey go." Yun cracked a raw egg on the side of Holloway's glass and dumped the gooey contents into the reddish liquid that filled the glass. Then he did the same for Bufford and pushed the two glasses in front of the two new lieutenants.

Holloway peered suspiciously at the eggs. He felt like his insides were on fire. The 155 seemed to be still working its way throughout various undiscovered crevices of his body. He believed that maybe whatever the unknown reddish liquid was, it could probably help put out the fire. It looked like Kool-Aid. Besides, he really wanted to get this whole thing over. He and Bufford exchanged glances once more and tossed the egg containing liquid into their throats. As anticipated by the spectators, the eggs passing into the gullet triggered the gag reflex and almost immediately Holloway and Bufford bolted wildly for the exit, which was being held open by Eric Auslander who knew, along with everyone else in the Club, exactly what was going to happen. The two men reached the out of doors in the nick of time. Sounds of retching reached the waiting ears of the twenty or so people standing at the bar as the rum and gin and vodka and 151 and grenadine and sloe gin and cranberry juice and orange juice and raw egg reversed its earlier course. Some of the crowd stood silently smiling while others grimaced at each other. Conversations had resumed by the time Holloway and Bufford returned to the room looking somewhat queasy and shaken. Courtney held his hand out toward Lester Joe. Beth Kisha put her arm around Holloway's back. He laid his hand upon her shoulder.

"Are you OK?" she asked gazing into his face, a look of obvious concern on hers.

"I think I'll live," Holloway replied softly, a wry smile on his sweaty face as he felt her left breast pressing into his side. "But I'm not sure I want to. What I need is a drink." Beth laughed and pushed one of his two remaining bourbon and sodas toward him. Tom Courtney walked over to greet Holloway.

Courtney waved his arm musically. The music from the Beatles' White Album began pouring from the big Pioneer speakers above the back of the bar. Everyone in the room stopped speaking and began singing the catchy tune. It reminded Holloway of a scene out of a Broadway musical. Obviously, he and Bufford were not the only ones who had been asked to learn the words. It was the official Camp Wynne alma mater. Holloway smiled and shook his head slowly and looked at Beth who still had her arms around him and was still gazing at his face as she sang. What a place, he thought. Those boys down in Seoul just don't know what real fun is all about.

The party continued for some time. Colonel Moody and his Executive Officer, Major Posey, stopped by later in the evening for a few minutes. By eleven o'clock Holloway had been able to meet five more of the Doughnut Dollies and had learned how to play the dice game that he had first seen played at the bar at the Officer's Club at Ft. Sill months earlier.

Much of the crowd began filtering out by eleven thirty. Courtney, Bufford, Sweeper, and Holloway still stood in a circle at the end of the bar. Holloway lit what he decided would be his last cigarette of the night. He knew that he tended to smoke too much when he was drinking. He exhaled slowly and looked at Lester Joe. A transformation seemed to have occurred with him. Most of the evening he had appeared to have been as mild mannered as anyone Holloway had ever met. His slow speaking Georgia drawl and innocent face gave no indication of anything else. But after several drinks it had become noticeably apparent that Lester Joe's entire personality was changing. His eyes seemed to gloss over, his expression became cocky and his attitude had evolved into what might be described as friendly combative. Virtually anything that the others had said within the last hour had been challenged by Lester Joe. As his arguments and caustic comments increased, Holloway was no longer sure whether his grin meant he was amused or was ready to do verbal or physical battle. Holloway decided that he needed to watch what he said to Lester Joe when he was drinking. Holloway pulled Tom Courtney aside.

"You notice anything different about old Lester Joe Bufford, Tom?" Holloway asked.

"Well, yeah. Seems like he's gettin' meaner as the night goes on," Courtney responded. "Aah think it's the damn booze. It's makin' him hostile. Hey, Lester Joe," he called in a loud voice. "Come on over here. Clay and I are just tryin' to figure out how come you're gettin so hostile toward us."

"Me?" Lester Joe answered with his little grin. "I'm not gettin' hostile. It must be y'all's imagination."

"No, Lester Joe. It's you. You're drinking all of that hostilejuice and it's turning you into a hostile man. That's you. Hostileman," Holloway said.

Mr. Yun had heard the conversation. "What you call him? Hostileman? What that mean?"

"It means he's a bad actor, Mr. Yun. You just better watch out for Hostileman or he'll knock yer dick in the dirt. Hey, when you order Lieutenant Bufford's silver mug to put on that shelf behind the bar with everyone else's, I want you to inscribe "Hostileman" on the mug. That's his new name."

"Well, you know what," Holloway ventured. "This kind of reminds me of a story that is similar to this current situation. And I'm not allowing anybody to leave until I tell it."

Hostileman and Courtney leaned back against the bar, a slight smile upon their faces in anticipation.

"Yessir. There was this elementary school teacher near my home who one day told her class that she would like to have them relate stories of things that had happened to them that had helped them develop a philosophy for their lives. So the class sat there for a moment thinking. Finally one little boy raised his hand. The teacher calls on him and the boy says, 'I know one, teacher. I live on a farm and one day I went out to the chicken coop to collect some eggs. Well, I stepped into a hole and fell and broke all of the eggs.'"

"Well," said the teacher. "What philosophy did you develop from that?"

"Simple, teacher," said the boy. "Don't put all of your eggs in one basket!"

"Very good," said the teacher. "Does anyone else have a story?"

"I do," said a little girl. "I also live on a farm and one day I was milking our cow and she kicked back her leg and knocked over the whole pail of milk. My philosophy is that you shouldn't cry over spilled milk."

"Wonderful," said the teacher. "Anyone else?"

"Yes," said little Tommy. "It's a story about my Dad. He was in the war. And one day he was in a foxhole out in front of all of his other men. All he had was his rifle, two bullets, a bayonet, and a bottle of Scotch that he had found in a French farmhouse the day before. It was a nice sunny day and he decided he might as well drink some of the Scotch. Well, while he was sitting there sipping on the Scotch he looked outside of the foxhole and there came three Germans right at him. So Dad jumped up and shot two of the Germans and killed the other one with his bayonet."

"My," said the stunned teacher. "How horrible. But what philosophy for your life did you learn from that episode?"

"Hey," said Tommy. "Don't fuck with the old man when he's drinkin'."

Tom Courtney and Hostileman looked at each other and broke into a fit of laughter. "Hostileman, if you're not that boy's daddy, you ought to be. That story is about you," Courtney declared. Courtney swallowed the remainder of his drink, paused for a moment, and then turned away from his companions. "Good night gentlemen. I'm goin' to bed."

It was three days later that Lieutenant Courtney called his new XO into his office in the Charlie Battery CP. Courtney motioned to the worn looking small leather sofa against the wall. Holloway eased himself into the seat slowly, trying not to spill his coffee. He waited for Courtney to finish signing a small stack of forms that lay on his desk. Finally he laid down his pen and looked up.

"Clay, I was hoping I'd be able to keep you around the Battery here for at least a few weeks before they send you up to the DMZ. I know Colonel Moody has told me you'd be spending some time up there as a Forward Observer on one of the Guard Posts. I'm afraid the timetable has been moved up. Lieutenant Bledsoe's orders came in. He's the FO on GP Gwen. He's leaving two weeks earlier than anticipated so's he can attend some damn school he put in for at Ft. Benning. I think he only did it so he could get out of here early. But anyway, Colonel Moody doesn't see any reason to fuck around with somebody else for just a week or two so you're going to be his replacement starting on Monday. You'll be there at least a month, maybe longer. A lot depends on if we start gettin' some more officers around this place. Right now I'm gonna be back to being a one man show here at Charlie Battery.

Bledsoe will probably be rollin' in this afternoon cause he's gotta start his out processing and gettin' all his equipment turned in. I've heard he's throwin' a party for himself this Saturday at the club. Son-of-a-bitch has been on the goddamn hill almost his whole tour. I guess he's saved up almost $5,000. There's not much to spend money on up there. Now he's decided to throw himself a big shindig before he goes home. Fortunately, we all get to be recipients of his generosity. I heard he's having a roast pig and barbecued chicken and all kinds of good shit.

So if you get a chance it would probably be a good idea to get him aside and talk to him about the GP and the DMZ. I've never been on one of the Guard Posts, so he can tell you a lot more than I can."

"Christ, Tom. You're saying he spent his whole thirteen months over here parked up on top of a hill? Why?" Holloway asked.

Courtney leaned back on his chair, put his feet on his desk, and folded his hands over his stomach. "He fucked up. One day the first month he was here he was in Colonel Moody's office. The Colonel had just gotten here the week before. Well, ole Bledsoe decided he was gonna impress the new CO with is his knowledge and skill with firearms. He was showing the Colonel some damn thing about the .45 pistol when it went off and blew a hole in the Colonel's ceiling. Well, you know you fire a .45 in a little room like that it sounds like a goddamn cannon. Like to drove the Colonel into cardiac arrest. Colonel never forgave him; considers him a menace. Two days later he was told he was going to the DMZ for a while and he's been up there ever since. Only reason the Colonel let him come down now is so he can go home."

Holloway shook his head, silently hoping he never fucked up that bad. He didn't mind the thought of serving on the GP for a few weeks, feeling that he would probably learn quite a bit about the infantrymen with whom he would be serving, but he had absolutely no desire to spend his entire thirteen month tour on top of a little hill with ten or twenty grunts and staring at the North Koreans and wondering if they were going to shoot at him that day. Holloway decided that he would heed Courtney's advice. He would talk to Bledsoe.

Russell Bledsoe was engaging Bill Grant in a ping-pong game when Holloway first saw him at the Officers' Club that evening. He was skunking Grant thirteen to two at that moment, but the thing that immediately caught Holloway's attention was his suntan. The man looked like a California lifeguard. Holloway waited until the game was over and then introduced himself, asking Bledsoe if he could buy him a drink.

"Sure, you can buy me a drink. So you're my turtle, huh?" Bledsoe replied smiling.

"I'm your what?" Holloway asked.

"My turtle. My replacement. You ever take a look at your helmet. It looks like a turtle shell. It's just an expression," Bledsoe said.

"Well, yeah, I guess I am. I'm wondering if you could just give me a little private briefing about what to expect and how I might best prepare myself," Holloway said seriously. "Here, let's sit at the bar."

"Give me a double J&B and water, Mr. Buster," Bledsoe said as he slid onto the barstool and propped one foot onto the brass rail beneath him.

"You want bourbon soda, Lootenant Holloway?" Buster asked.

"Good, Mr. Buster." Holloway lit a Winston and turned back to Bledsoe. "Fire away."

Bledsoe clutched his right hand in his left and began cracking his knuckles as he spoke. "Well, there's three Guard Posts in First Brigade area which are manned right now by the 1/9th Infantry. They're Cindy, Carol, and Gwen. Each hill has an artillery officer as a Forward Observer. The officer alternates duty on the hill with his recon sergeant. Usually it's four days on the hill, four days off. The days you're not on the hill you're usually back at Camp Greaves, the infantry compound behind the DMZ. The days that you're down you might have to pull some extra duties. Maybe FO a shoot for some of the battery's from here. Maybe be a safety officer for a shoot. Something like that. But, most of the time if you're not on the hill you're on your own. Shit, you can go to Rec Center #1 and go shopping at the PX or get a steam bath. See a movie somewhere. Play ping-pong or read or whatever. I got real fuckin' good playin' ping pong since I've been up there. The infantry O Club at Camp Greaves has great food, nice pool table, nice ping-pong table. You'll like it there. Numba one place."

"OK, that sounds pretty good, but what about when you're not at base camp. What about when you're on the hill?" Holloway wanted to know.

"You're going to Gwen. That's a good GP as far as that goes. You'll probably rotate to the other two occasionally, but mainly Ruminski likes to keep the same FO on the same hill. Gwen has about twenty grunts including the medic and the antipersonnel radar operator. The CP is built into the back of the hill. A lot of the structure is poured and reinforced concrete including the bunkers. It's got a sleeping bunker and an ammo bunker too. Most of the time it's pretty boring. Take a lot of books with you. You'll have lots of time to read."

"You're telling me they're sending me up there to read?" Holloway asked incredulously.

"No. They're sending you there to observe and to report and to be ready to call in artillery fire if they ever need it. It's just that you can only observe so much and unless a full scale war starts you're probably not going to have to call in any artillery fire," Bledsoe replied matter-of-factly.

"Does anything ever happen?"

"Sometimes. Last week the pricks almost got me," Bledsoe said.

"What does that mean?" Holloway queried.

"Well, I was just laying out on top of my bunker, trying to catch some rays and some son-of-a-bitch started sniping at me. First round hit about a foot from my head. I rolled off the top of the bunker and into the trench. Skinned my knee all up. Second round hit the dirt next to me as I was falling into the trench. I heard the "smack," but I never saw where they came from." Bledsoe stopped talking and took a long pull on his Scotch. He pulled a fresh pack of cigarettes out of his fatigue shirt pocket and lit one with a battered gunmetal gray Ronson lighter.

"You don't know why they started shooting at you?" Holloway asked.

"I've thought about it a lot. The same thing happened in May when I was on top of the bunker. To tell you the truth I don't think they liked my red bathing suit. I think it pisses them off when I wear red." Bledsoe started blowing smoke rings at the ceiling. "The thing is, you never know what they're going to do over there. You can go for months and nothing happens whatsoever and all of a sudden, BANG! Ambush and two men dead or BANG, sniper round. Or BANG, grenade lands in your trench. My sniper fire came in the daylight, but most of the time though, everything happens at night. You learn to live with it, but you gotta understand there is a certain amount of tension that goes with this job. You're only 200 meters away from North Korea when you're on Gwen you know. There's nothing in between you and them but a couple of trees and some bushes. If they ever decide to come at you in real strength you won't have much of a chance. Thinking about that all of the time. That's the tough part." Bledsoe looked at Holloway a long time. His tour was over. Holloway's was just beginning.

CHAPTER 7

Motor stables were a daily occurrence in each of the four batteries of the 8/18th. At Charlie Battery, the activity began at 1300 hours immediately following the noon meal and lasted approximately one half hour. During motor stables the designated driver and assistant driver of each of the approximately twenty-five trucks and jeeps of each battery would listen to the inspection techniques being read aloud by the Chief of Firing Battery and check the items designated. Mechanics were available for consultation and tools were present for the repair of items that could be attended to easily. More difficult repairs were entered into the vehicle logbook to be addressed by the motor pool section personnel at a later time. The battery Motor Officer was normally present during motor stables primarily to emphasize the importance of the activity. In Charlie Battery the Motor Officer was Second Lieutenant Clay Holloway, who normally began motor stables by standing well to the rear of the Chief of Firing Battery as he read from his checklist. As the activity progressed, Holloway usually walked slowly along the front of the vehicles observing the work. Once he reached the end of the line he would walk to the rear of the last vehicle and slowly walk back up the line. On Friday afternoon, Holloway appeared to be attending to the activity in his normal fashion as Staff Sergeant Thompson read from his checklist in a loud voice.

"Awright, listen up, you mens. Check all hoses. Look for any cracks or loose clamps. Check for any signs of leakage or wear anywhere around the hoses. Look for dripping liquids anywhere on the ground beneath the engine compartment."

In truth, Holloway had heard virtually nothing of what Sergeant Thompson had just said, nor anything he had said for the previous ten minutes. His thoughts alternated between two things, wondering what his life was going to be like on GP Gwen and trying to decide how he was going to be able to see Beth Kisha occasionally while he was camped in the middle of the DMZ and she was located at Camp Wynne. He also wondered where she was and what she might be doing at this very moment. Fleetingly, he became jealous of whatever troops she might be entertaining. Holloway knew that Beth was quite good at what she did. Some of the Charlie Battery soldiers had mentioned to him that Beth was generally regarded around the Division as everyone's favorite Doughnut Dolly. She was attractive, friendly, vivacious and intelligent. Holloway was already well aware of what a brilliant conversationalist she was. He felt she could probably get a cactus to talk if she wanted to. Her games were inventive and her quick wit had more than once turned a rude comment into a joke that the entire audience enjoyed. Often if was not an easy task to hold the attention or get willing participation from a group of grumpy tired draftee soldiers.

A few minutes later motor stables ended and Holloway walked across the blacktopped area, crossed the street, and walked into the front door of the CP, still thinking more about Beth Kisha than his duty as motor officer. He had spent at least part of each evening of the last three with her. The more he was near her the more he wanted to be near her. Tom Courtney stopped by Holloway's desk, seemingly reading his mind.

"Hey, XO! How are you and that little sweetheart Beth gettin' along?"

Holloway put on his serious face. "Come on, Tom. We're just friends," he answered softly. "She's a nice girl. I like her."

"Holloway, come on into my office a minute. I got to talk to you about somethin'," Courtney replied. Clay did as he was told, following his Battery Commander obediently into his office, and assuming his usual place on the worn black leather couch. Courtney sat down slowly and stared at the desk for a moment before beginning to speak.

"Let me tell you something here, young LT. You're right. Beth Kisha is a nice girl and I like her too. And there is no doubt in my military mind that she likes you as well. But don't let yourself take this little flirtation too seriously. You need to understand that she likes to flirt. Not just with you. Not just with me. She's a lot of fun. Almost everyone likes her and she is a damn fine looking young lady. If you can get to second base with her, I say more power to ya. It's gonna be a long tough tour over here and if you can find some warm soft extracurricular activity while you're here it might help you through the cold dark winter. Have a ball." Courtney's lip curled up slightly as he showed a sly one sided grin. "But young man, I've been farther around the world than you've been around a tea cup lookin' for its handle and if there's one thing I know, it's don't take something like this too seriously. Things seem different over here. It's not like the world you left. Back there you have time to get to know people and work things out. There's no need to make quick decisions about things. But, here people come and go all the time. She'll be goin' home in four or five months. There might be a new captain that rolls in here next week that she takes a likin' to. She might meet some buck sergeant that she's handin' a doughnut to tomorrow that sets her little heart a flutter. She's havin' fun. She's livin' life. You should do the same. But don't fall in love with this girl, Holloway. Or any other girl you meet over here. The world you left three weeks ago is the real world. This place is like fantasy land. A year from now it ends and you'll probably never see any of these people again ever."

Holloway stared at Courtney trying to decide if he was psychic or if his own emotions were really that easy for others to decipher. "Why are you saying this?"

Holloway asked defensively. "I'm not in love with Beth Kisha. I only met her a few days ago."

"I know you're not in love with her yet, but you're workin' on it. Your mind is about fifty miles south of where it ought to be. You're just not with it and I figure that's gotta be the reason."

Holloway smiled at Courtney and nodded. "You're right. I won't fall in love. At least I'll try not to." He got to his feet and took two steps toward the door. "I'm going over to the Motor Pool. I want to make sure the TEAR's clerk got that starter for C-16 ordered like I told him."

"Good," said Courtney. "I'm trying to get a poker game started tonight. You want to sit in?"

"I'd love to, but I can't."

"Why the hell not?" Courtney demanded.

"Because Beth and I are walking down to RC#4 to see a movie!" Holloway grabbed for the doorknob laughing. Courtney leaped to his feet grabbing a heavy brass ashtray that sat on his desk.

"You asshole!!" Courtney roared, throwing the ashtray toward the door. Holloway ducked. It bounced harmlessly off of the doorframe and landed on the floor with a clang. Holloway laughed and ran out the door slamming it shut behind him.

At exactly 7:00 p.m. Clay Holloway appeared in the waiting lounge of the Doughnut Dolly Hooch. Like the old BOQ and many of the other buildings around Camp Wynne, Quonset huts formed the Doughnut Dolly Hooch. For this particular structure the two huts formed a T. The horizontal hut was the lounge, while the vertical leg contained the single rooms of the young women. The lounge was not as large as the living section, but it was still spacious and contained several easy chairs, two sofas, and a few wooden tables, some of which held lamps. Normally the girls greeted the visitors in the lounge in the same way that Holloway had been greeted in the women's dormitory during his college days. Men were allowed in the women's rooms if escorted there by the occupant. However, all male visitors had to vacate the premises by 11:00 on weekdays and midnight on Friday and Saturday night.

A moment after Holloway arrived, Sherri Cifrianni walked in.

"Hi, Sherri. Would you tell Beth that I'm here?" Holloway asked.

"Sure, Clay. I'll tell her. Hold on just a minute," Sherri replied.

Holloway eased his slender frame into one of the vinyl-covered chairs and reached for the only magazine on the table next to him. Quickly discovering that it was a three month old issue of McCall's he returned it to the tabletop and sat quietly. The door leading down the hallway toward the women's rooms opened a moment later. Beth's head peeked its way through the door and looked around. Spying Holloway she waved him over to her. A white terry cloth robe pulled tight at the waist covered her. She held it closed at the neck with one hand.

"Come on back, Sweetie. I'm not quite ready yet." She put her arm through his and led him quickly down the hallway and steered him into a room near the end of the corridor. "I'm sorry I'm running a little late," she whispered close to his face. Her mouth smelled clean as though she had recently brushed her teeth. Holloway caught the light scent of her perfume. She pushed the door shut behind him and looked longingly at him. He smiled in return, saying nothing. Tilting her face upwards and parting her lips slightly, she closed her eyes. Holloway kissed her softly. She tasted warm and wet and sweet, her full lips moving gently around his. They stopped for a moment, only for a moment. She kissed him again a bit harder. Her mouth opened wider, their tongues touching and caressing. Beth sighed deeply.

Holloway pulled back gently and looked questioningly at her. "I thought we were going to the flicks. We'll never make the early show at this rate."

"Do you care?" she asked.

"No. No, I don't. You caught me by surprise. I wasn't expecting this." He paused. "God, you taste good."

The next kiss lasted longer. "Mmmmmm. You taste good too." Beth whispered. "But you're right. Let's go to the movie. It's only 7:00. We'll have lots of time later." She smiled sweetly at him. "Are we going to walk or take the Staff Duty vehicle?"

"We have time to walk if you want to. Are you afraid to walk through the ville?" Holloway asked. "It'll be dark when we get out of the show."

"Not a problem with a big strong lieutenant like you with me," she teased. "Is it nice outside?"

"It's a beautiful evening. Let's go ahead and walk. I haven't seen much of Sonyu-ri except for driving through it once or twice."

"OK. Can I trust you to turn around and not to peek while I finish getting dressed?" she asked coyly.

Holloway smiled and nodded. "I'll do my best."

"Your best at what? To peek or not peek?"

"Don't you trust me by now?" Holloway asked.

"Of course, I do, Sweetie," she smiled. "Why do you think you're back here instead of sitting in the lounge?"

Ten minutes later the couple passed through the main gate and turned left, walking toward Rec Center #4 located at the other end of the village a half-mile away. The smells of the orient greeted the two Americans. Aromas of strange smelling foods drifted out of open windows. There was the scent of incense and the ever-present odor of the fertilizer in the fields and rice paddies. The air smelled warm and damp following a brief shower an hour earlier. At one shop, American rock music blared from a large loudspeaker mounted above the door.

The pair walked at a leisurely pace, picking their way around people standing on the wooden sidewalk or leaning out of doorways. The other people on the street were a mixture of Koreans and black and white American soldiers dressed mostly in civilian clothing. Fatigue uniforms were not authorized in the village unless the soldier was on duty. Only the summer khaki or dress green uniform was allowed if a uniform was going to be worn at all. Some people gazed strangely at Beth. Round-eyed women were almost never seen there. There were no female soldiers at Camp Wynne. In fact, the few in Korea were either nurses or clerks at Division headquarters. Holloway noticed several business girls sitting or squatting in groups. Often the business girls would pay particular attention to Beth who was beginning to feel exposed and uncomfortable.

"Just keep walking. Don't make eye contact with them. They're not going to do anything," Holloway advised. Before long they had reached the end of the village and moved quickly through the gate at RC #4 and into the movie theater. Two hours later they were back on the street heading home.

It was dark. The last vestiges of daylight had disappeared more than twenty minutes earlier. The atmosphere of the village grew louder. Music was blasting out of several clubs and from some of the hooches of the business girls. The number of prostitutes astounded Holloway. He had heard that the village contained over two thousand of them. His battalion compound had only five hundred soldiers. That was a ratio of four hookers for each soldier. The normal fee for the girls was five dollars for a "short timer" and ten dollars for an "overnighter." At least that was the rate at the beginning of the month. As the days after payday passed, the price sometimes declined, hitting bottom a couple of days before the next pay. Holloway had heard that one of his cooks had gotten laid for two flashlight batteries and a bar of soap. The batteries were slightly used, but the soap was not. The number of business girls actually on the street at that moment was probably close to four or five hundred if Holloway's estimate was correct. At times they actually stood in rows waiting for an opportunity for a paying customer. Most were dressed in mini skirts or hot pants. Often their make-up seemed as though it had been applied with a paintbrush and the lipstick covered only half the mouth. Holloway wondered how many of them were carrying one or more strains of venereal disease. It was professional curiosity. In addition to being his battery's motor officer, he had also been given fourteen additional duties, one of which was VD control officer.

Holloway and Beth Kisha found it more difficult to walk back through the village than it had been coming the other way. The numbers of people crowding the narrow walkway forced the couple to walk mainly in the street, dodging stagnant puddles of rainwater that remained on the dirt. Glancing to his right he saw a GI leaning against a wall in a darkened alley with a Korean girl on her knees at his feet apparently giving him, or more properly, selling him, oral sex. Embarrassed, Holloway looked quickly away. He flashed a quick look at Beth, but she seemed not to have noticed. Two thirds of the way through the village there stood a small white one story building with wooden framed sliding glass doors in the front. One door was open, yellow curtains moving slowly in and out of the opening as the air currents changed. Three business girls stood clustered in front of the open door. One of the three, seemingly older than the others, and noticeably more drunk, looked at Holloway and Beth and they approached.

"Yoboseyo! Yoboseyo! Eedywah!! What you want her for? Huh? What you want her for? How much she cost? Me only five dolla! Five dolla, good price. Me suckee suckee. She no suckee. You come here, huh?" The girl was walking toward them, talking loudly. She approached within a few feet.

"Back off, josan. Just back off!" Holloway ordered angrily, pointing his finger at the girl's face. She stopped and stared at him, momentarily startled by his tone. Holloway moved to Beth's right side, putting himself in between her and the drunken prostitute. "Stay away from my wife!"

The prostitute remained standing in the street looking at them as they continued past her, Holloway keeping his gaze fixed on her face. The other two business girls had started whispering to each other. He believed that referring to Beth as his wife had confused them, at least long enough for him and Beth to walk by without further problems. Beth squeezed his arm tenderly.

"Hey, you're pretty good at that. Do you get a lot of practice warding of hookers?" Beth whispered to him.

"First time," Holloway answered. "I think she's drunk. Something tells me I need to brush up on Korean phrases. I think I'm going to need them."

Camp Wynne's gate loomed ahead. Beth still clutched Holloway's arm, but her grip seemed tighter than it had earlier. He looked down at her face. Her mood had changed. When the evening began she had seemed happy and affectionate. Now she seemed tense and preoccupied. "Midnight Cowboy" was a depressing motion picture, with the Dustin Hoffman character, Ratzo Rizzo, dying in the end. The show, combined with the vulgarity and coarseness of the village on a Friday night, had altered her mood. She seemed quiet and subdued. He sensed that the anticipated romantic ending to the evening had been postponed.

"What do you want to do now?" Holloway asked softly as they crossed the wooden bridge into the compound. He hoped she would invite him to her room.

"Let's go to the Club and see what's going on. We'll see who's there," Beth replied in a quiet voice. The Club appeared relatively calm from the outside. Perhaps Bledsoe's party planned for the next evening had had the effect of keeping much of the normal crowd away for this night, saving themselves for Saturday. Holloway pulled open the outside door and held it for her. He repeated the motion on the swinging door into the bar area. Hostileman and Bill Grant stood closest to the door. Another ten people were scattered about the room, talking quietly. Music from the Beatles' "Rubber Soul" album floated lightly through the air, singularly setting the sedate mood of the Club.

Following a single drink and a polite discussion of the movie they had just viewed, Beth announced that she was tired and felt like calling it a night.

"Will you walk me back?" she asked looking at Clay.

"Of course I will," he answered. "What kind of a date do you take me for?"

"You're a good date, Clay Holloway. You're a good man. I just feel kind of down right now. I hope you understand. Let's get a good night's sleep and save our strength for Bledsoe's party tomorrow. That should be a blast."

"I'm looking forward to it. Only bad part is that two days after that I'm going north for a while. I think I'm going to miss you," he said in reply.

Her look grew more melancholy. "Come on." She slid off the bar stool and walked with Holloway back out the way they had come, saying good night to the others at the bar and Mr. Yun behind it. The Doughnut Dolly Hooch sat only a hundred feet from the door of the Camp Wynne Officers' Club. Within moments they reached its entrance. Beth glanced around quickly. Seeing no one, she took Holloway's face in her hands and kissed him tenderly on the lips. "Good night, sweetie. Come see me tomorrow, OK? I'm sorry if I'm confusing you. I don't mean to do that. I think you're very special. I just need to be alone now. I need to go to sleep."

"It's OK," Holloway answered. "I'll see you tomorrow." He turned and walked quickly back toward the BOQ wondering if he would ever in his entire life understand women and why they acted like they did. He rationalized that it was good that it had been an early end to the evening. After all, he did have to get up and work until noon the next day. But lying on his bunk in his room he found it hard not to think about her perfume, her hands on his face, and her full warm lips on his. Cupid had smitten him. He hadn't wanted to say good night and he hadn't wanted to sleep alone. Holloway hoped Bledsoe's party would turn out to have a more satisfying conclusion to the evening.

CHAPTER 8

Corporal Clinton Gash whipped quickly through the gears of the one-quarter ton vehicle, more commonly known throughout the world as a jeep. The vehicle, designated as C-3 and pulling behind it a quarter ton trailer, was heading north toward Camp Greaves along the Main Supply Route (MSR), having left Camp Wynne only a few minutes earlier. Gash's only passenger was Second Lieutenant Clay Holloway, who was now temporarily attached to the 1/9th Infantry as an artillery forward observer. Camp Greaves, located north of the Imjin River in the hostile fire zone, served as the headquarters compound for the 1/9th. In a few months, when the 1/38th Infantry relieved the 1/9th from its operations in and around the DMZ, Camp Greaves would become headquarters to that battalion. Holloway was to meet his Liaison Officer, First Lieutenant Dave Ruminski, at Camp Greaves. From then on he would be in Ruminski's hands.

Holloway had his fingers wrapped around the wooden fore stock of his M-14 rifle, steadying it as the butt rested on the floor of the jeep. Absentmindedly his fingers roamed softly over the smooth walnut stock. Holloway's thoughts, however, were not about the rifle. They were about Beth Kisha and the events of last night and the night before that.

Bledsoe's farewell party on Saturday had been a time he would not soon forget. The food had been sumptuous. Bledsoe had paid Mr. Yun to hire some of the local people to dig a pit and roast a whole pig. Holloway had never seem an entire roast pig before, complete with a large red apple in its mouth. It had cooked slowly for almost a day before it was served. By that time the meat was so tender that there was no need to carve the pig. The pork literally fell off of the bones onto the plate. Besides the pig, there was barbecued chicken, charcoaled steaks, and appetizers and vegetables and breads too numerous to recall. He had almost eaten too much, even after telling himself ahead of time to be sure and not stuff himself. Finally he had worn off the fullness by dancing. As he might have guessed, Beth Kisha was a marvelous dancer. Her motions were flawless, a mixture of rhythm and sexiness. He had danced with some of the other Doughnut Dollies too, Kathy and Joan, but even while he danced with them his eyes searched out Beth. More often than not she was looking back at him. By eleven o'clock they had touched and danced and teased each other long enough. Clearly her moodiness from the night before had disappeared. The vivacious woman he had met their first night together had returned. The last half hour had been filled with glances, some quick and darting and others long and silent. Holloway's senses had sharpened until he was almost breathless with anticipation. Beth had finally whispered two words into his ear as they danced. "Let's go," she'd said. That was all she had needed to say.

They had tried to slip unobtrusively through the exit, but as he reached to hold open the swinging door for her, Tom Courtney had leaned over from the bar and issued some Battery Commander advice. "Don't trip over yer tongue, Holloway," he'd said in his low deep tone. Holloway had felt his neck reddening. Were they that obvious?

They'd gone to her room in the Doughnut Dolly Hooch. The building seemed deserted as most of the other residents were still at the party. Men were allowed in the rooms until midnight so it would not have been improper even if they had been seen by another of the girls, but they weren't. Closing the door behind him, Beth had wasted no time in aggressively encircling her arms around his neck, pressing him back against the door, and kissing him fully on the mouth. Neither of them spoke. They'd stood there for several minutes kissing slowly and tenderly, enjoying the taste of one another. Beth's tongue darted about his mouth teasingly. Softly Holloway stroked her hair and then bent and began to kiss the side of her neck beneath her ear, eventually moving to her tempting soft throat as she tilted back her head and offered it to him. Moving slowly he kissed and nuzzled her throat. Momentarily he paused and drew back and looked her in the eyes. She looked back through half closed eyelids. Still a word had not been spoken, but he had no doubt about what she wanted. Quickly he unbuttoned the top three buttons of her cream colored dress. She was wearing a low cut lacy white bra and he tenderly kissed the valley between her milky breasts. There was an audible sigh. Gracefully, he bent at the knees and picked her up in his arms and carried her to her bed, gently laying her down and then lying on the bed beside her. They kissed again and again and he could hear her breathing becoming heavy, almost panting, as he reached beneath her dress and caressed the curve of her hip. She'd stood then and slipped off her dress, letting it fall to the floor in a heap at her feet. Gently she'd climbed on top of him unbuttoned his shirt and then laid on his bare chest, kissing him again and again. He'd unhooked her bra at that point and almost gasped aloud as the flimsy cotton slid down her arms and exposed her naked breasts. They'd made love hungrily, each trying to devour the other. Exhausted then, they'd laid lovingly in each other's arms, caressing and stroking, and sharing a sense of contentment.

He'd stayed all night, hoping no one would do an official bed check. He didn't think they did that. In the morning they'd made love again after she'd awakened him at five by nuzzling and kissing his stomach, bringing him to a state of readiness. Beth had sat astride him with her hands on his chest. He'd let his hands hold her hips and then move gently up her sides and lightly across her back, before caressing her breasts and watching as her eyes closed and her body shuddered. Before dawn he'd sneaked back to the BOQ, his mind spinning with the memories of her warmth and her touch. Sunday morning he'd packed his gear for the DMZ and by mid afternoon was with her again, lying in their swimming suits on a blanket behind the Doughnut Dolly Hooch and enjoying the July sun. Holloway could still smell the coconut aroma of the suntan lotion they had delighted in rubbing over each other's bodies. By that evening they were in bed, making love again and again.

Now it was over. Only the memory of her existed for him. He wondered about the way she'd talked when he'd said good-bye. He hadn't thought about it until later. Now it concerned him. She'd said, "It was wonderful." Not "this is wonderful" or "let's do it again sometime," or "I'm going to miss you and I can hardly wait until you get back," but "it was wonderful." Then she'd kissed him and let him out of the back door of the hooch and closed the door. Holloway hadn't made love for a long time, not since he had broken up with his college girl friend a month after graduation. Spending the night with Beth had been almost indescribably delicious, awakening sensations he hadn't felt for some time. He could not believe how things had worked out. He had been prepared for thirteen grueling months hunkered down in a bunker or a tent somewhere around the DMZ and instead had wound up spending the better part of two amazing nights in the rack with one of the sexiest most fascinating women he had ever known. He wondered if it was the beginning of something very long lasting. He hoped that it was. But somehow his instincts told him that was not the case. Holloway was learning to trust his instincts. The jeep came to a halt.

"You OK, Lieutenant Holloway?" Clinton Gash asked, looking at him curiously.

"Yeah, Clinton. I'm fine." Holloway looked up. The jeep was stopped behind two other vehicles which were waiting for their trip tickets to be checked by the MP's standing at the south end of Freedom Bridge, which spanned the mighty Imjin, gateway to the DMZ. Steel was the primary component of the bridge, with wooden planking laid on the bridge's floor. The structure had once been a railroad bridge that had stood adjacent to a vehicle bridge. During the Korean War, the vehicle bridge had been destroyed, the only remnants being stone columns that arose from the river like singular statues. The railroad bridge had been damaged, but repaired and converted to carry vehicles rather than rolling stock. Its steel girders still bore the numerous scars of the violence.

After crossing the bridge Gash followed a winding dirt road. Soon after rounding a curve, Holloway could see Camp Greaves located on the top of a hill to his right. The familiar shape and light green color of the single story Quonset huts made the compound appear like so many others he had seen in the Division area south of the river. The jeep was waved through the gate and Gash drove to what seemed like the highest point in the compound. He stopped next to a one level building.

"This is your BOQ, Lieutenant Holloway. All the FO's and some of the infantry officers stay here when they're not on the GP's. Lieutenant Ruminski ought to be around here somewhere. I'll carry your gear in for you."

Two duffel bags and a footlocker were brought inside. Gash pointed to the east end of the building. "Up there is where the cannon cockers hang out, Sir. The grunt officers are at the other end. That bunk used to be Lieutenant Bledsoe's so I guess it's yours now." Gash placed the footlocker at the end of the metal-framed bunk. Holloway swung the duffels onto the freshly made bunk, noting that they must have houseboys even at Camp Greaves.

The building had only one room, which contained ten single metal-framed bunks that sat on a red linoleum floor. There was ample room between the beds, but no partitions of any sort for even a hint of privacy. There was a four-drawer dresser and a large metal wall locker against the wall near the head of each bed, along with a sort of combination desk and shelving unit. Many of the desks in the room contained expensive Teac and Akai reel-to-reel tape decks, paired with Sansui or Pioneer amplifiers and a variety of speakers of different brands. There were two cold diesel-burning space heaters. One near each end of the building.

"Holloway! Good to see you." Holloway turned. It was Dave Ruminski. "I see you got the right bunk. There's a houseboy up here named Pak. He'll take care of putting your gear away. You do need to pack up whatever you want to take to the hill though. I brought you a flak jacket. We'll be going to the hill right after lunch. Did you bring your weapons?"

"Yeah. My .45 is right here and the M-14 is next to my wall locker. I brought five twenty round mags of 7.62 like you told me," Holloway replied. He knew that his M-14 would be the oddball on the Guard Post. All of the infantrymen had been issued the M-16A1 rifle the year before, but there were not yet enough of them for every soldier in Korea. Vietnam was given the first priority.

Ruminski spent the next few hours showing Holloway around the compound. Holloway visited the Tactical Operations Center (TOC), watched an ambush patrol being debriefed after returning from the Z, and met many of the junior infantry officers. He noticed that many of them appeared to be more serious than the artillerymen he had met at Camp Wynne. Smiles seemed rare, as though the business at hand was nothing to smile about. There was a small movie theater, a tiny but nicely stocked PX, and of course the Officers' Club. The PX seemed to have a good supply of cameras, watches, and electronics for such a small compound. Holloway was particularly interested in the cameras, knowing that he had to soon replace the camera that had been stolen when his flight bag had been slickied. Ruminski had saved the O Club for last.

"OK, Holloway, it's almost time for lunch. I need to stop in at the barbershop and pay Miss Lee some money I owe her. Then we'll move into the dining room and eat and then unass the area."

Opening the door to the O Club, Holloway sensed immediately that something was wrong. The voices of the few people inside were loud and excited, laced with profanity. Ruminski grabbed one of the grunt lieutenants by the shirtsleeve.

"D'Amico! What the hell's going on?" Ruminski asked.

"Patrol just went into a mine field in the Z. The point man had his foot blown off. Major Greene went in with two other guys to try to help get the patrol out and he triggered one too. His leg and groin area are all fucked up. The others finally probed their way out. They're in the process of medevacing the casualties out now." D'Amico answered, his voice angry.

"Whose patrol was it?" Ruminski asked.

"Tyler's," was the reply.

"What's his first name?" Holloway wanted to know.

"Wally."

"Damn! Goddamn it!" Holloway cried.

Ruminski looked at Holloway with surprise. "You know him?"

"Yeah. Wally Tyler and I were together at Ft. Bliss at Redeye School. He and I used to play chess together every day on the bus on the way out to the gunnery range at White Sands. We both knew we were coming here to the Second Division," Holloway answered. "How'd it happen?"

"All I know is that they were off course. Tyler's only been here a month. This was only his second or third time as the patrol leader. I don't know whose fault it is," D'Amico responded, "but I do know that we got two people hurt real bad." Everyone stopped talking for a moment and looked toward the ceiling. There was a very loud "whop, whop" sound directly above them. Every man in the room knew the sound and what it represented. It was the inbound Huey that was coming in to medevac the casualties to a medical facility to the south.

Warrant Officer Todd Hardesty gazed down from the copilot's seat of the UH-1B "Huey" adorned with the big red cross on the side that distinguished it as a medical helicopter. In the left seat was the pilot, Chief Warrant Officer Michael "Magic" Maloney. "See the green smoke?" Hardesty asked pointing ahead.

"Roger that," Magic answered over the intercom. Then he released the intercom switch and spoke over the radio. "Tango 55, this is Honey Bear. Identify green smoke. I am on my final. Be on the ground in zero two mikes, over." The aircraft continued to lose altitude. Hardesty could see the unending ribbon that was the DMZ fence about two hundred meters north of where the green smoke was billowing up. There were lots of people milling around the LZ and vehicles parked haphazardly in the area. The ground rose up. The helicopter flared as Magic pulled back on the joystick, hovering momentarily, and then settled gently to the red dirt.

Four men carrying the first casualty ran quickly to the side of the aircraft, holding the stretcher with one hand and shielding their faces from the rotor blast with the other. The crew chief inside the aluminum skinned bird secured the stretcher to the helicopter floor and waited for the second litter to arrive. IV bottles with long transparent tubes and needles connecting the bottles to the arms of the casualties accompanied both wounded men. One of the medics who had been treating the wounded climbed aboard and began yelling into the ear of the senior medic telling him about their condition.

Hardesty turned his head, looked behind him at the casualties lying on the stretchers on the floor, and grimaced. One was a white officer in his thirties with thinning sandy hair. His fatigue trousers had been cut off and his midsection was wrapped in a series of blood soaked wound bandages and additional gauze. The other soldier was a young black man probably not more than nineteen. His left foot was missing, the stump also covered with layers of bloody white bandages. He was moving his head slowly from side to side, his eyes half closed. Hardesty guessed that both men had already been sedated. The crew chief gave a thumbs-up signal and Hardesty whispered to Magic over the intercom. The helicopter shuddered for a moment, lifted into the air, banked to its left and picked up speed as it headed south.

Lunch in the Camp Greaves Officers' Club was subdued. The initial excitement that people had felt upon hearing of the mornings' events had been replaced with a sense of sadness and remorse. Their battalion Executive Officer, a man respected and liked by all of the other officers was badly hurt. The other officers would probably never see him again. They were struck by the irony of the situation. Major Greene had served in the I Corps area in Vietnam. He'd weathered countless firefighters and mortar attacks and returned home unscathed. Now, two and a half years later he lies critically wounded, his future and career uncertain, the result of a mine planted more than fifteen years earlier. It has happened during a routine ambush patrol in a situation and in a part of the world that few people in America even realized existed. The future of the young nineteen-year-old soldier who stepped on the first mine has been totally altered. Within the span of a few seconds his life has been radically transformed. One moment he was at the peak of physical condition and looking forward to going home and hanging out with the guys and looking for a job. The next moment he was scheduled for a future of months of pain and years of rehabilitation and a life of wearing a prosthesis so that he would be able to walk in a reasonably normal manner.

Ruminski and Holloway eat the noon meal in relative silence. It is disturbing way for Holloway to begin his new assignment. Silently, they finish and look at each other across the table. Ruminski slides his wooden chair back making a squeaking sound on the tile floor. It is time to meet Ruminski's driver. It is time for Holloway to begin earning his pay.

The hot July sun beat down upon the jeep as it drove down the hill and out of the Camp Greaves main gate. Holloway looked at his bare forearms, which already had little rivulets of sweat running down them. The open topped jeep was moving and Holloway was still astounded by the heat that he felt. What would happen when the jeep stopped?

Five minutes later the jeep came to a halt in the sweltering heat. It was though someone had opened the door to a furnace. A few feet ahead was the barrier fence. Holloway was impressed. The fence seemed to run on forever in either direction like a giant serpent, crossing everything in its path. It was ten feet high chain link with rolls of concertina wire at its base and its top. Steel stakes only six inches apart were driven to a depth of three feet. There was no vegetation for 100 meters on either side of the fence.

"How do they keep the vegetation trimmed like that?" Holloway asked Ruminski.

"Trees they cut down. They use Rome plows and then they spray everything else with some kind of new weed killer. I watched them they other day. They use something called Agent Orange. I've heard they use it in Vietnam a lot," Ruminski replied offhandedly.

Two GI's, one a KATUSA, manned the gate. To the left of the gate was parked an infantry jeep with an M-60 machine gun mounted on a unipod that was bolted to the jeep floor. A gunner stood nonchalantly at the machine gun. A shotgun rider sat next to the driver holding a loaded M-16. Everyone wore flak jackets and steel helmets. Both jeeps, like every other United Nations vehicle that entered the Zone, flew a white flag and bore a sign that read "DMZ Police." Each occupant of the vehicles wore a black vinyl armband that read the same in both English and Korean. Ruminski had made arrangements to have the escort jeep meet them and accompany them into the Zone. He pointed to the other jeep. The double gate was swung open and the escort jeep lead the way through the fence driving slowly, the drivers watching the road for mines that could have been laid during the night. They would automatically avoid any puddles or anything that seemed to be the least suspicious. It was unlikely that there would be a mine since the road was swept every morning and the chow truck had already been over the route once that day, but habits once learned are not easily altered.

Ruminski turned in his seat and looked at Holloway riding in the back. "Lock and load. You watch the left and rear. I've got the front and right." Holloway pulled back the bolt on his M-14 and released it, hearing the round slam into the breech. He tapped the base of the twenty round magazine, insuring it was securely locked into the rifle. Then he looked around. The terrain was mostly flat, only a few shallow streams breaking the lay of the land. High weeds were the primary vegetation, though clumps of bushes were interspersed throughout the fields. Ahead of them and to the right about two kilometers away, rose a landmass.

"Is that Gwen?" Holloway asked.

"That's it. We'll be on top in about ten minutes," Ruminski answered.

A thought flashed through Holloway's mind. "Is this the road where the reaction force ran into the ambush a couple of weeks ago?"

Ruminski looked back and smiled knowingly. Holloway believed that was the first time he had ever seen Ruminski smile. "No, Holloway. That was on the road to Cindy about two klicks that way. You get to it from the next gate to the east."

Holloway sighed and sat back. He wasn't frightened really, but he would admit later to some uneasiness. The thought that he was riding around with a loaded rifle waiting to see if anyone was planning to ambush him was a new experience, though one that would become routine in the weeks and months ahead. The jeep reached the foot of the hill. Ahead of them the dirt road wound back and forth across the backside of the hill. From the base Holloway could see no sign that the hill was even inhabited. Ruminski's driver downshifted as their ascent began. Near the top Holloway turned to look back from where they had come. It was visually captivating. A Technicolor panorama the likes of which he had never encountered. Military maps of the area stated that the crest of the hill was 167 meters above sea level, about 500 feet. It was no mystery why the land mass had been selected as a Guard Post. The visibility from this vantage point was limited only by atmospheric conditions. The driver gunned the engine hard as the jeep crested the backside of the hill, shot through an open wooden framed gate, and came to a halt on a flat area of dirt. The gate stood open because the people on the hill had been called by the people at the fence and told that visitors were on the way. Holloway climbed out of the vehicle behind Ruminski and looked about. Ahead of them were open doors leading into a bunker complex.

Holloway reached back into the jeep and grabbed his duffel bag. Carrying it and his rifle he followed Ruminski through the open doorway and into the back of the hill. Inside it was cool and dark. A second door to the left took them into the sleeping bunker. A row of double metal-framed bunks wound its way around the walls. There were two rows running laterally across the cement room. Two bare electric light bulbs shown from the ceiling, which were powered by a large field generator that Holloway had noticed on the back of the hill as he had entered the doorway. Ruminski pointed to an upper bunk.

"That's the artillery rack. The bag on it must belong to Sergeant Shavers," Ruminski stated. "Let's go find him."

Leaving his duffel next to the bunk, Holloway followed Ruminski through a second opening, up a flight of wooden stairs, and out into the sunbathed trench line. The view from the front of the hill was as breathtaking as the one from the rear. Holloway gazed in the direction of North Korea as they moved through the log lined trench, finally stopping at a small concrete position with an eight inch thick reinforced concrete roof above an eighteen inch opening for observation or firing, which wrapped its way around three sides of the bunker.

"This is position number 4, the artillery position. And that is your BC scope," said Ruminski pointing to the twin tubed optical instrument that stood on a tripod and resembled a periscope. As Holloway bent to look through it, nearby footsteps sounded on the wooden trench floor. "Here's Shavers now."

Sergeant Shavers spent the better part of an hour giving Holloway all the information he felt the new lieutenant would need to assume the duties of the Forward Observer. There was a field telephone and a radio remote set in the bunker that was connected by commo wire to the AN/PRC 25 radio housed in the Command Post. The remote set allowed Holloway to operate the radio either from the bunker or the CP. The BC scope was directionally oriented so that the operator could align it with anything he wished and read the directional azimuth on the brass scale below the eyepiece. Shavers pointed out some of the more notable spots on the landscape in front of them. Then he removed a hard covered notebook that hung around his neck from a heavy canvas cord. It was the SOI/SSI, which contained all of the radio call signs, frequencies, and codes. It was something that was never to be misplaced. If an SSI was lost it had to be reported immediately to Division who would then change every bit of information in the book and reissue it. Even if the book was not lost by anyone, the change was made routinely every few weeks as part of standard procedure.

The briefing complete, the three men walked back into the sleeping bunker. Shavers grabbed his duffel. "I guess that's about it, Lieutenant. The Sergeant Major who commands this place is back at the compound for a shower and a change of clothes. He'll be up this afternoon. Any questions you might have he can help you. I'll be back to relieve you in four days. Good luck." With that the Recon Sergeant nodded at Ruminski and headed toward the door. Ruminski gave Holloway a little grin. It was the second time he had seen Ruminski smile.

"Call in a few simulated fire missions to Battalion once in a while and be sure to do radio checks every other hour. At night the grunts may want you to call in a searchlight mission if they need some illumination. If you need to talk to me at any length, call me on the land line, not the radio," Ruminski said. I'm heading over to Cindy now and see how Sweeper's getting along. I dropped him off yesterday. I'll pick up both of you sometime on Friday."

Holloway walked out of the back of the bunker onto the flat area. Both jeeps had been turned around and were headed toward the gate, the two drivers sitting in the same jeep smoking cigarettes and talking about women. Seeing him approach, Ruminski's driver field stripped his cigarette and climbed behind the wheel of his own vehicle. One of the grunts swung open the gate and Holloway watched as the two jeeps headed back down the hill, their transmissions whining as first gear kept their speed to a minimum on the steep grade.

It was time to get acclimated. Holloway walked inside of the rear door of the main bunker and up the steps to the CP located at the top and buried inside of the hill. None of the CP was visible from the outside except for the ventilation shafts that protruded up through the ground. The Command Post was a small room where one Radio-Telephone Operator (RTO) was on duty as well as whoever was in command of the Guard Post at any given time. The GP commander had a folding cot in the room so that he was basically on duty twenty-four hours a day and could respond to any emergency instantly. At the bottom of the steps and to the left was the sleeping bunker. To the right of the steps was the ammo bunker. Holloway would learn that weapons were limited by the armistice agreement to small arms. However, in the interest of survival, the GP was, in fact, armed to the teeth. In different locations throughout the hill were to be found two .50 caliber Browning heavy machine guns, three M-60 medium machine guns, a 90mm recoilless rifle, three cases of LAW's (light antitank weapons), Claymore mines (some already in place on the slopes of the hill), M-16 rifles, M-79 grenade launchers, and an M-1G Garand sniper rifle mounted with a 20x telescopic sight zeroed for 1,000 yards. There were also several cases of hand grenades, which included smoke, fragmentation, and CS tear gas. Each evening near dusk when the infantrymen occupied their bunkers for their night vigil, they would take much of the weaponry and ammunition into their fighting positions with them, returning it to the ammo bunker when daylight came.

On the flat area behind the hill were a wooden latrine and two wooden shower stalls under a pair of 55-gallon drums. The showers were rarely used. The soldiers preferred to rotate in shifts back to Camp Greaves when the need for showers arose. On the other side of the flat area stood a metal water buffalo, which contained all of the potable water for the hill.

Surrounding the position was an irregular trench line with eight reinforced concrete fighting positions with concrete overhead cover at tactically selected points. Each position was sequentially numbered starting with number one at the west side of the rear gate. The entire trench was log lined, about six feet deep, and contained a wooden shelf that was used as a step up to observe or to shoot. Beneath the wooden trench floor was built-in drainage. There were also randomly placed heavy cardboard tubes buried half in the ground with gravel pits beneath them. The tubes had once held 105mm Howitzer shells. Now they were used to urinate into. For obvious reasons they were called piss tubes.

Military maps are divided into grid squares of 1,000 meters or one kilometer each. A kilometer is approximately three fifths of a mile. Therefore, something that is five kilometers, or klicks as they are referred to, away on the map is about three miles. Maps are essential to the workings of an artillery officer and one of the first things he is trained to do is associate the terrain around him with what is depicted on the map. Holloway spent much of the rest of the daylight hours doing things that FO's are supposed to do. He selected reference points on the landscape, measured the distance to them on his map, shot directional azimuths to them with his compass and wrote those ranges and directions down as an immediate reference in the event he would have to call for artillery fire or illumination. Because of the irregular line formed by the DMZ, Holloway's bunker, while facing North Korea, looked due west. Directly to his front and at a range of 2,000 meters, was a hill with an altitude of 57 meters that was known throughout the DMZ as "Speaker Hill." On this hill sat four of the largest loud speakers Holloway had ever seen. He was not sure of their exact height, but he could see a North Korean soldier working inside of one, the top of which towered above him. Apparently, then, the speaker was at least ten feet high. Holloway had been told that the speakers were used to play a wide variety of sounds, songs, and speeches, both during the day and the hours of darkness.

To the left of Speaker Hill and one kilometer away were the remains of a train that had been struck by an air strike during the Korean War. The locomotive and some of the cars lay on their sides. All of the other land to the front was lowland, some heavily foliated and some sparse. Beyond the northern boundary of the DMZ lay Propaganda Village, so named because it appeared to be a model of a supposedly thriving North Korean village. People bustled to and fro during the day. The village looked clean and orderly. As observers studied the village, however, they noticed that there were neither any children nor animals in the village. Most soldiers did not even believe there were any backs on the buildings, like the fantasy of a Hollywood set. To the right of Speaker Hill and a couple of kilometers to the rear lay what appeared to be cluster of government buildings. Over one of the buildings flew an enormous red North Korean flag. Sergeant Shavers had estimated the size of the flag to be at least one hundred feet in length. It dwarfed the building over which it flew. The North Koreans seemed to thoroughly enjoy making things big.

To Holloway's complete right, which was actually north from GP Gwen, and at a distance of almost twelve kilometers, lay Panmunjom. Negotiations, which began in 1952, had been ongoing at that site. Aside from the actual negotiating team, duty at Panmunjom was not considered a fun tour by any stretch of the imagination. Both sides attempted to intimidate each other on a consistent basis. DMZ soldiers stationed at Panmunjom were all volunteers. Each American had to stand at least six feet tall and be in prime physical condition. Each was well schooled in the art of self-defense, with a strong emphasis on Tae Kwon Do, the Korean form of Karate. On several occasions in the late 1960's North Korean soldiers harassed UN troops. Often this harassment evolved into fistfights or even all out brawls. At times North Koreans would swoop out of concealed positions armed with clubs and outnumbering the UN soldiers two or three to one.

Very near to the village of Panmunjom lay the Bridge of No Return. The bridge was barely visible to Holloway through the big eyes of the tripod mounted BC scope standing in his bunker. A few months earlier, the captured crew of the USS Pueblo had been finally released over that bridge after almost a year of capture, beatings, and torture. With that in mind, the bridge would have to be considered improperly named.

Many kilometers to the west and north, so far away that they were well beyond the borders of Holloway's map, lay an imposing range of mountains. The peaks were often capped with snow, even in summer. Besides the snow, the mountains also contained caves and tunnels, which began in the foothills and extended deeply into the range. In the caves lay huge stocks of weapons, ammunition, equipment, and supplies. Anyone attempting to launch a ground offensive into that area would have to be prepared for a very long and very bloody operation.

Sergeant Major Emerson McKee arrived shortly before the evening meal was served. He was an impressive individual, almost scholarly in appearance. A full growth of closely cropped white hair covered his suntanned head. He spoke with the classic drawl of a Virginia gentleman. Fifty-two years old, he was a veteran of twenty-seven years of service, had fought in three wars, and had been wounded four times. Holloway liked him immediately. Sergeant Major McKee was the Guard Post Commander. Although Holloway outranked him, as an artillery officer he was there only to observe and if necessary coordinate fire support. He had no command function and was in charge only of himself and his mission.

"Lieutenant Holloway, if there's anything you need or I can do, please let me know. My troops will be moving into their night positions in a little while. Did you wrap up your BC scope and move it out of the way?" the Sergeant Major asked politely.

"I certainly did. I was just going to open up my C-rats. Care to join me?" Holloway offered.

The Sergeant Major chuckled. "No, Sir, I don't think so. I just had myself a nice juicy steak at the NCO Club before I came back up here. I go down every few days just to get cleaned up and have a few drinks and a good meal. You just go right ahead. There are a few things I'd like to check on. Come on up to the CP later on."

"Sounds good Sergeant Major. I'll see you then."

After eating Holloway returned to his bunker. Earlier he had observed a steam shovel working about three miles away. He wasn't sure if the project was a pipeline ditch of some sort or a trench. The work had apparently stopped for the day and there appeared to be little else to capture his attention.

About an hour before dark, the infantrymen began moving into their positions in the bunkers. Two of the grunts carrying their rifles and a box of ammunition stopped outside of Holloway's position number 4 and looked at him as though asking why he was still in the bunker they were supposed to occupy.

"Evening, Sir. How's it going?" one asked.

"Goes good. You guys waiting for me to leave?"

"Yessir. Artillery is usually out of here by this time. Is this your first trip to the hill?"

"Yeah, it is."

"Well, Sir, you sleep tight now. Bravo Company, 1/9th will be on guard above you. Nothing to worry about. No, Sir!"

"What, me worry? I wouldn't think of it. You guys have a good night." Holloway winked at them and moved past them and down the trench line. He visited the CP for a while, listening to what the Sergeant Major had to say about the hill and the DMZ and what to expect both at night and during the day. Dutifully Holloway ran his radio checks and called in a practice fire mission. About ten thirty he excused himself and went to find his bunk. His job was a daylight job. The grunts had the night shift.

Holloway walked down the twenty-one wooden steps to the sleeping bunker, switched on his flashlight, and entered. In the eerie glow of the flashlight the whitish gray concrete of the walls and ceiling reminded him of a tomb. His duffel was still on the "artillery bunk" where he had left it. A dirty gray mattress with blue stripes covered the steel springs of the metal bed. He unrolled the sleeping bag and was met by a musty odor. Laying the bag open to air, he removed his pistol belt and boots. Pulling the slide back on his .45 he insured that there was a round in the chamber. After gently lowering the hammer, he replaced the pistol into the stiff black leather holster and hung the belt so the handgun was next to where his arm would lay. A bayonet hung from the same belt. Those were his security blankets. The last line of defense in case something outside went horribly wrong. He thought of the grunts in the bunkers above him and hoped they were alert. "Well, God," Holloway thought. "Here I am. What happens now?"

Sleep came quickly, although seven hours later he awakened with a start as he sensed the soft, but distinct flute music. It was pitch dark in the damp bunker and after switching on his flashlight he realized he was still alone. He glanced at his watch. At 0630 the infantrymen were in the process of coming off of their night vigil as daylight began. The flute music baffled Holloway. Where was it coming from and what did it mean? It was weird, like something out of a Bela Lugosi "Dracula" movie made in the 30's. He pulled on his boots, slipped on his web gear, picked up his helmet, and walked up the stairs and into the trench line. Suddenly he felt like he was inside of a light bulb. He was in the log-lined trench and there was light, but Holloway could see nothing. It was fog, but not like any fog he had ever experienced. It was the thickest most impenetrable fog imaginable. When he extended his arm he could not see his fingers. He touched the walls of the trench and felt his way around toward his position. Suddenly two ghostly shapes rose up out of the mist startling him as he did them. It was the two infantrymen from his bunker. They nodded in recognition.

"What's with the flute music?" Holloway asked.

"That's them dingy dingy gooks across the way. They're playing one of their golden oldies on Speaker Hill just trying to rattle us."

Holloway looked in the direction of Speaker Hill, the flute music was clearer than it had been when it was inside. Visibility was hopeless. He could barely see the two men to whom he was speaking. Footsteps were approaching down the trench line. It was an E-5 from the CP.

"Morning, Sir," he greeted. Then he turned to the two men. "Sergeant Major doesn't want to stand down from the positions yet because of the fog. Klein, you stay in the bunker and let Fortunato go eat, then switch. Won't be no chow truck this morning. Too much chance of an ambush and they can't even see the road anyway. There's a case of C-rats on the back of the hill next to the entrance. Pick out whatever strikes your fancy. Fog'll burn off before too long, but we need to stay in the positions until we can see what's out there."

The two men nodded in understanding. One went to pick his way through the C-ration crate and the other headed back toward position #4. Suddenly his voice called from the mist. "Hey Fortunato! Grab me something good. None of them fuckin' ham and lima beans. Get something with a pound cake in it."

"You'll eat what I give you and like it," the other voice chided from the unknown.

"Prick!" the first voice called resignedly.

By ten o'clock the sun had warmed the earth sufficiently to burn off enough fog that the clump of trees at the top of Speaker Hill was finally visible, though everything else below was still hidden. Holloway felt like he was in an airplane looking down at a field of clouds. It was not until almost noon that the Sergeant Major felt comfortable enough to tell everyone to stand down and go to bed. The grunts would have to be up by six to eat and prepare for the next night of vigil. At least for the evening meal the chow truck would be bringing a hot dinner carried in mermack containers.

Holloway returned to his observation bunker after his lunch of C-rations. He removed his heavy BC scope from its wooden case, extended the legs, and tightened the screw that held to periscope to the base. Then he oriented the instrument and began slowly traversing from left to right, which took almost fifteen minutes. Seeing nothing he made a radio check with the TOC and called in a practice fire mission with his Battalion fire direction center at Camp Wynne. Then he opened a package of cherry Lifesavers, lit a cigarette, and let his mind wander. At first his thoughts were of Beth. He felt strongly attracted to her. He had enjoyed her from the first night they had "bumped into each other." But now after two days of love making, he was thoroughly infatuated with her. Thinking of those nights was starting to arouse him. Holloway decided that there was no sense in making himself horny with there being nothing he could do about it, so reluctantly he forced himself to shift his thoughts to other things.

The afternoon passed slowly. There was little air movement and by mid-afternoon it had become uncomfortably hot. Holloway continued to scan the DMZ intermittently, sometimes with only his eyes, sometimes with binoculars (or binos as the troops called them), and occasionally with the BC scope. He marveled at the green lushness of the Zone and its natural beauty, but there was virtually nothing to keep or even attract his interest and he wondered how long he would actually have to stay there. How could Bledsoe have possibly spent most of his tour on that hill and not died of boredom? Holloway returned to the sleeping bunker, pulled a paperback novel out of his duffel, and carried it back to his observation post. He spent much of the rest of the afternoon intermittently reading and scanning his assigned area.

It was night again. Holloway had been asleep in the sleeping bunker for almost four hours when he felt someone or something shaking him. Someone had a flashlight turned on in the dark room.

"FO, wake up. Sergeant Major wants you. We got noises on the side of the hill," a young black soldier was telling him.

"OK, OK. I'm coming," Holloway answered, making himself come awake quickly. He slipped on his boots, grabbed his gear, and followed the PFC up the stairs and into the trench line. The Sergeant Major and the E-5 from the CP were standing in the darkness listening intently. The Sergeant Major peered at Holloway through the darkness.

"Sir," he whispered, "we have got noises down below us. Sounds like we may be getting probed. Sometimes they try to get up close and test our defenses. We haven't been able to see anything with our starlight scopes. It's just too dark. I'd like you to call in a searchlight mission and shoot the beam up into the sky. The light coming off of the clouds will help our starlights a lot."

"You got it, Sergeant Major. I'll use the phone in my bunker. Searchlight crew is probably getting bored anyway." Holloway moved silently into position #4 and cranked the field telephone to the switchboard at the TOC. "This is Lieutenant Holloway on Gwen. Give me the searchlight." There was a pause and then the searchlight crew answered. Holloway called for the light, thankful that Sweeper had told him in advance to review his procedures for that sort of mission. During Holloway's entire sixteen weeks of training in the States, no one had ever mentioned that there even was such a thing as a searchlight mission. Although, when he looked in his red forward observer's handbook, there it was. The procedures were fairly basic once he had read them over a few times.

Within seconds the big beam 2,000 meters to his rear lighted up the night sky. Holloway could hear the low hum of the starlight scope of Private Klein who, along with Fortunato, was in the bunker with him. The starlights were high tech optics which used ambient light and magnified it several times to allow the user to see clearly at night, although the world was green and black when viewed through the observation device. Klein's starlight was mounted on top of his M-16 and he panned slowly from one side to the other saying nothing. Holloway adjusted the searchlight three beams to the left to better utilize a large cloud. Then he walked back to where the Sergeant Major stood and watched quietly as the Sergeant Major panned the terrain below with his scope. Several minutes passed. Finally he turned to Holloway.

"If they were there they're gone now. Sorry to disturb your sleep, Sir. Looks like it was a false alarm," the Sergeant Major said softly. Holloway nodded, said good night, and headed back toward the sleeping bunker. It was almost four AM. He would try to grab two more hours of rack time before dawn.

Holloway's four-day tour on the hill was extended to five because of a problem with one of Ruminski's recon sergeants. All told, his stay had been hot and boring more than anything else. It had not taken him long to get into the routine of the hill and once he was used to it, it varied little. Now his time was up and Holloway sat on the side of the hill next to the entrance with his duffel bag waiting for Ruminski's jeep to come through the gate. A moment later it happened. Holloway walked over to the jeep as Sergeant Shavers got out.

"How'd it go, LT?" Shavers asked.

"Fine. No problems. Kind of boring," Holloway answered climbing into the back seat.

"Well, Holloway," Ruminski said, "you've got the weekend off, but then we've got a special assignment for you on Monday. It's an FTX (field training exercise) with the 1/38th. You're going out for two or three days as one of the FO's. Good training. You'll love it." Ruminski laughed out loud and the jeep lurched forward and headed down the hill and toward the barrier fence a mile away.

CHAPTER 9

Clay Holloway stepped out of the shower at Camp Wynne's old BOQ and began drying himself with a white cotton towel. Noting the uneven distribution of suntan that decorated his body, he shook his head disgustedly. His neck and lower face was darker than his forehead because of the cap or helmet that he constantly wore on the hill. His forearms and hands were tan, yet his chest and upper arms were almost white. Naturally his legs were white too. He was going to have to figure out a way to even things out. No wonder Bledsoe had risked sniper fire to lay on top of his bunker sunning himself. It was simply to keep himself from looking like a variation of a Panda bear.

His stomach was uneasy. There was a Saturday night poker game scheduled to begin at the club in about an hour, which in a way, he was anticipating fondly. Nevertheless, what he had really wanted to do was to see Beth Kisha and that was not going to happen. When he had arrived that morning, he had been told that she was spending the weekend visiting some friends at Yongsan in Seoul, whatever that meant. Holloway was rapidly coming to the realization that whatever their relationship was, he was not the one in charge of it. He wrapped the towel around his waist and walked down the hallway and into his room. His houseboy, Skinny Yee, had laid out a navy blue knit golf shirt, a pair of tan slacks, and his cordovan loafers. Holloway was looking forward to donning the civilian clothes. He had lived in his olive drab fatigues for the last six days.

"Hey, Holloway! You gettin' ready to get yer Yankee clock cleaned?" Bob Hoover called from the doorway.

"Uh uhh, Sweeper! You got that backwards," Holloway retorted.

"Shheeeit! I ain't never seen a Yankee yet that could match a southern gentleman at the gaming table. Here. Have a glass of this fine Kentucky bourbon while yer gettin' dressed." Sweeper held a bottle of JTS Brown in his left hand and a glass filled with ice, whiskey, and water in the right.

"I don't think so. A man's got to watch his liquor if he's going to be gambling with real money. And we are playing with real money tonight, you know. Not none of that worthless Confederate paper you Southern boys think is money. Yessir, we're going to be playing with genuine US Military Payment Certificates here tonight. Therefore, I can't be drinking none of that bourbon. It slows a man's mind."

Sweeper grinned at him from the doorway. "You're all right, Holloway. Hey, how'd your first week go on the hill?"

"Numba one. Plenty of rack time. Little hot, though," Holloway answered.

"Yeah, hotter than a cotton patch, that's for sure. Did Ruminski tell you I took some more incoming on Cindy Thursday?"

Holloway turned and looked at him. "No. What happened?"

Sweeper sat down on the edge of Holloway's bunk. "Three shots from the woods. I never saw a thing, but I heard the "pop" and then the "smack" into a sand bag about two feet away. Right in the middle of the afternoon."

"No shit! Nothing has happened at Gwen at all except some of the troops thinking they have some night movement on the side of the hill. I've about come to the conclusion that nothing is ever really going to happen."

"Don't do that, Clay. Don't get careless. Just when you're sure that nothing is ever goin' to pop, that's when it'll happen. Don't ever relax too much. Most of the time there's no warnings up there. One minute everything is fine and the next you could be in deep shit." Sweeper stood up. "Well, what do ya say? Ready to go over to the club?"

"Not quite. I've got to get dolled up a little bit just in case the girl of my dreams stops into Camp Wynne tonight."

"Yeah, fat chance of that happening. OK. I'll see you over there," Sweeper replied and disappeared down the hall.

*   *   *

The poker game was well under way when Holloway walked into the O Club a half hour later. One of the round tables had been dragged into the corner directly under the illumination of a ceiling light and Sweeper, Tom Courtney, Hostileman, Bill Grant, and Doc Kramer were concentrating on a fresh deal of seven-card stud. A cloud of smoke hovered over the table as Grant puffed away on a fat brown corona that was clenched between his teeth. Holloway dragged a chair between Sweeper and Grant, noting that Courtney seemed to be the early winner based on the seven stacks of chips in front of his person.

"What are we playing and what's the limit?" Holloway asked as he sat down and pulled out his wallet.

"Dealer's choice. Quarter ante, dollar limit," Grant answered. "You just missed your deal." Sweeper, now on Holloway's left was shuffling the cards.

"OK, gents, we're playing Texas Hold 'Em," Sweeper announced as he began the deal.

"Wait a minute, goddamnit," Grant complained. "The last time you dealt we played Criss Cross, whatever the fuck that was, the time before that you dealt Low Ball, and now you want to play Texas Hold 'Em. Where on God's green earth do you get these fucking games?"

Sweeper looked hurt. "Mah pappy taught me these games. He knows all kinds of card games."

"Well, yor pappy ain't sittin' at the table tonight," said Courtney in his low slow drawl. "How 'bout playin' somethin' we all know."

"OK. OK. How about three-card draw. I assume all of you big time gamblers know that game," Sweeper stated condescendingly, as he began to redeal.

Two and a half hours passed. Most players gained a bit and then lost a bit more. But Tom Courtney's stack had continued to grow. Holloway too had been doing well. He was thirty dollars ahead more or less. The bar area had begun to fill up and the volume of voices was increasing. Holloway turned around in his chair to survey the room. Most of the battalion officers including Colonel Moody were in the room. Several of the Doughnut Dollies were present too. Kathy Kelsey caught his eye and waved. Holloway winked at her. Tom Courtney had also been looking around the room. "What do you say we make this the last hand for a while," Courtney said. "I'm gettin' a little stiff sittin' here. Let's go dollar ante five dollar limit on the last hand. It'll give some of you boys a chance to get even."

"Sounds good to me," Grant said as he shuffled. "Dollar ante, five dollar limit. It's draw poker, jacks to open, nothin' wild but the dealer." He dealt the hand, picked up his cards, and held them close to his body.

Holloway had been studying the other players all night. Courtney was impossible to figure out, clearly a man with lots of poker savvy and experience. Doc Kramer played conservatively, never bluffing and dropping out early if he had nothing. Hostileman was easy to read. His eyes narrowed noticeably whenever he had something good. With this hand Holloway saw no such movement. Grant always grunted as soon as he saw he had nothing worth betting. This time Holloway heard no such grunt, meaning there was at least something there. However, the real key to the hand for Clay Holloway was Sweeper, who sat directly to Holloway's left. He had noticed that throughout the evening, Sweeper's hand moved immediately, though slowly, toward his chips whenever he picked up a good hand. Though Holloway had not yet looked at his own cards, he had already noticed Sweeper's hand movement in the direction of his chips, as he seemed anxious to throw money into the pot.

Clay Holloway fanned his hand slowly, spreading the cards one at a time. He made only a slight grimace to mask his elation. He was holding four natural queens. Grant to his right had dealt. It was Holloway's turn to open.

"Well, Holloway, what do you say. You have jacks or better to open?" Grant asked.

Holloway was counting heavily on Sweeper opening behind him. He decided to take a chance. He rapped his knuckles on the hard topped table. "Check!" Holloway said.

The eyes at the table shifted to Sweeper. "I open for three dollars," Sweeper said, keeping his eyes on his cards. Courtney, Kramer, Hostileman, and Grant all called the bet. After all, it was the last hand. It was Holloway's turn.

"Up five bucks!" Holloway announced in a flat tone, tossing a five dollar MPC note into the middle of the table.

"What! You checked," Sweeper cried out.

"Yeah, but then you opened. I can raise if I want to," Holloway said, holding his ground.

"Well, goddamnit! OK, fine. Here's my five," Sweeper said.

Courtney peered at Holloway trying to see what he was up to. "OK, Forward Observer. Here's my five bucks." The other three followed suit. It seemed likely that Holloway might be trying some kind of a bluff.

"How many cards, Holloway?" Grant asked.

"One," he responded.

The rest of the table mentally nodded. So that was it. Holloway had checked the open and then drawn one. He must be trying to fill a straight or a flush and betting on it ahead of time to fatten the pot. Sweeper looked at the two pair in his hand and drew one card. His heart leaped. That did it! He'd filled out his two pair. He had a full house. The rest of the table drew their cards in turn.

"Your bet, Holloway," Grant said.

"No, it's not. Sweeper opened. It's his bet," Holloway answered. He turned his eyes to the left.

"Three dollars again," Sweeper said, not wanting to scare people out of a pot he was sure his full house had won. Courtney had two pair, in which he had little confidence. But he was already into the pot for nine dollars and it was the last hand. He tossed in the three. Doc Kramer folded, seeing no sense in throwing good money after bad. Holloway considered that to be a smart move. No wonder he was a doctor. Hostileman stayed with a pair of kings just to see what people had. Grant had been dealt three sevens. He had not improved in the draw, but he felt that he had a definite chance to win. Holloway, Sweeper, and Courtney had all drawn one, indicating two pair or trying for a straight or a flush. Grant called the three dollars.

It was Holloway's turn. "Up five dollars," he said again.

The players moaned. "What!" Courtney yelled. "Jesus Christ!"

Sweeper was silent. He had a full house. Clearly Holloway had drawn his straight or flush or whatever he had and thought he was going to win. Sweeper planned to bounce his Yankee ass good. "Five dollars more," Sweeper announced. Courtney tossed in his cards. Two pair was not going to win this one. Hostileman did the same, accompanied by a notable sigh. Bill Grant was in a tough spot. Sweeper had opened and drawn one. Therefore he had to have two pair. Holloway had raised after checking and drawn one. Then he'd raised again. That meant one of two things. He had filled his straight or flush or he had failed to fill it and was now bluffing. It might be a bluff. It just might. Grant called along with Sweeper.

"Let's see the openers, Sweeper," Holloway requested. Lieutenant Hoover tossed the full house on the table and leaned back in his chair with his arms folded smirking at Holloway who had shifted his gaze to Grant. Sweeper's hand had obviously beaten the Adjutant. Grant threw his hand onto the tabletop face down and slid back his chair.

"Show 'em to me, Holloway," Sweeper asked. Holloway spread the cards with one deft movement on the table. Four queens. He'd won.

Sweeper stared incomprehensibly at the cards for a moment, then leaped to his feet, his chair falling over behind him. "What? Four queens! You drew one card. You had four queens on the deal and you checked them?" Holloway nodded, a thin grin spreading across his face.

"Why you goddamn sandbagging son-of-a-bitch. You sandbagged, checking your hand like that. How could you check four queens?" Sweeper cried.

"So. There's nothing that says I have to open if I don't want to."

"Sandbagger, hell," Courtney drawled. "He's a goddamn Yankee carpetbagger is what he is. A Yankee carpetbagger slipping in here to take all of our hard earned money." He looked at Holloway and smiled appreciatively. As one poker player to another, he admired the move. "He sandbagged us just like he sandbagged those North Koreans with that illumination mission last month. The one that saved your ass to fight another day, Sweeper." Lieutenant Hoover's face reddened slightly. Courtney was right. It was a hell of a move.

Lester Joe Bufford spoke up. "Well, sandbagger or carpetbagger, one thing's for sure. If y'all are gonna call me "Hostileman," I'm sure as hell gonna call him "Bagger." The others nodded in agreement. Holloway was already cleaning off the table. The pot had totaled ninety-six dollars by the time it was over.

"Looks like a bell ringer!" Holloway announced. "In fact, looks like a triple bell ringer." He strode to the bar, grasped the clapper in his hand, and slammed it against the brass three times quickly. The crowd cheered and clapped. Holloway stood at the bar and held up three fingers. "Bourbon and soda, Mr. Buster." Tom Courtney came up behind him and put his arm around his shoulder.

"Bagger, you might be new, but you know some shit! Glad to have you in Charlie." Holloway held his hand out, palm up. Courtney slapped it. They reversed the procedure and laughed as Buster set a row of drinks on the ebony bar in front of them.

*   *   *

It was Monday morning. Once again Clay Holloway found himself in the right seat of C-3, being driven by Clinton Gash. This time, however, he was heading toward a grid square on his map where he had been told he would find Alpha Company 1/38th Infantry, which was starting a three day battalion sized FTX (Field Training Exercise).

Holloway was to act as their artillery forward observer. He located them where they were supposed to be, dug into defensive positions on the side of a hill. Asking for the Company Commander, he was directed to an area on the backside of the hill, which had been designated as the CP.

The Company Commander, a first lieutenant about the same age as Holloway, briefed him on the situation, which at that point was to defend the hill against any aggressor forces. He said it was likely they would be told to move some time during the day and he wanted Holloway to stay close to him. In his hip pocket, was the expression he used. A red headed corporal named Tracey was assigned to him to carry his radio and act as his RTO. Holloway instructed Gash to stay with his own jeep and trailer that held all of their equipment. They would be in radio contact.

Holloway did as he was directed, finding a spot in the defensive trench system, drawing sketches of the terrain, and calling in simulated fire missions to give the FDC back at Camp Wynne some work to do. By late afternoon the word came down. They were moving.

Being part of an infantry company in the field is a unique experience. There are few jobs in the world that are tougher than being in the infantry, even when no one is shooting at them. Infantrymen are rarely comfortable. They are either bathed in sweat, soaking wet from the rain, covered in mud, or freezing cold. Within the space of a few hours, Holloway would have the opportunity to experience almost all of the above. The movement covered a period of five hours, intermittently passing through soggy rice paddies, scattered woods, fields, hills, and lush green valleys. Holloway stayed close to the CC. If he turned around and wanted simulated artillery fire or even to ask advice about fire planning, Holloway was supposed to be there. The march was slow paced and included a break for a cold meal of C-rations. Finally at almost 2100 hours Alpha Company reached its objective, a small hill eight miles from where they had begun. It was nearly dark and the NCOs and officers pushed the men hard to get the defensive perimeter established while they could still see. With positions assigned, they dug in for the night. Holloway retrieved his sleeping bag from Gash who was traveling with the infantry's vehicles, and laid it out near a depression where the CP staff had assembled. Gash would move the jeep to the company supply train and sleep in the trailer to guard the equipment against slicky boys.

Holloway was exhausted. Humping the boonies for a full day was something he had not done since ROTC advanced camp the summer before. His legs were not in the same league with his traveling companions. The infantry called themselves "ridge runners" and Holloway understood the reason. Korea is covered with hills and mountains. The grunts were used to them. Holloway was not. He stretched his slender frame, thinking that he would probably feel a lot stiffer in the morning. Looking up at the night sky he noted that he could see no stars. He was about to learn why.

As a precursor to what was about to happen, a small green and black tree frog landed on his chest, startling him. The frog looked Holloway in the eye and croaked as though announcing the beginning of a momentous occasion. A moment later the skies opened. The rain, gentle at first, soon became a drenching downpour that began soaking through his sleeping bag as he struggled to get his poncho off of his web belt and around himself and his bag. There was no cover. There was nothing to do and nowhere to go. He, like the 160 infantrymen with him, could only lay in the mud and curse silently and hope for the rain to stop as the water formed puddles in the mud around him. August nights are warm in Korea. That was the only salvation.

Someone was shaking him. He acknowledged the man's presence and looked at his watch, wiping the mud from the plastic face with his finger; 0500. He had suffered through two or possibly three hours of restless sleep since midnight. The grunts, which had to take turns on guard in the two-man holes, had probably had less. His calves ached from the activities of the day before. Rising to his feet in the drizzle he asked one of the CP people about a latrine. Five minutes later he was back.

Corporal Tracey approached him. "Company Commander was looking for you, Sir. He says we go into the attack phase at 0730. There's a chow truck set up on the other side of the hill. They're going to start serving in about ten minutes. He wants us to eat. Briefing is at 0600." Holloway grunted and wrapped up his sopping wet goose down sleeping bag. He felt utterly miserable, cold and wet and tired and stiff and hungry and the day was just beginning. It was still raining. Sliding down the hill to the mess truck, he picked up one of the heavy fiberglass trays and got into the chow line. Two servers wearing rain suits dumped scrambled eggs and toast along with some link sausages onto the tray. Holloway, along with some other troopers, moved through the line with all of the enthusiasm of condemned men and then sat on the hillside, looking at his eggs that were now floating in the water that was collecting under them. The toast was a soggy mass of dough. He took a bite and gagged.

An hour later he walked out of the briefing with a good understanding of the initial phase of the battalion-sized attack. There was a series of hills about five klicks away to the east. Between Alpha Company and the objective was mostly rice paddies with some wooded areas. And there appeared to be a stream or shallow river to cross also. First Platoon had the point. He and the Company Commander would be right behind it to direct the action and call for any artillery fire (simulated) that was required. Umpires would be observing the action and grading both the infantry and the artillery work.

At last the rain stopped and the skies cleared. It was daylight and Holloway found Gash parked only a hundred meters away from where he had spent the night. The corporal was bone dry, having slept under the wooden shell top that had been built for the trailer. Holloway reached into the trailer and grasped his duffel, pulling out a dry set of fatigues. Stripping down on the road he changed quickly. The sky had turned blue. Perhaps God did not hate him after all.

Alpha Company moved out, half walking half sliding down the slippery muddy hill to the field below. Holloway walked slightly ahead of Tracey, his RTO who was humping the PRC-25 radio on a backpack. He stayed relatively close to the Company Commander who seemed to be talking constantly to his platoons via his own radio. Ahead was a sparsely wooded area perhaps a quarter of a mile in diameter. As Holloway passed through the woods and out the other side, he realized to his amazement that the thin blue line on his map indicating a stream or small river did begin to describe the torrent that he now found in front of him. There was no way to tell exactly how wide the waterway was normally, but it was obviously several times its usual size. The brown water was rushing by, swollen by the all night rains to an alarming state. The first Alpha Company soldiers were already half way across by the time the Company Commander and Holloway exited the trees and saw the river before them. There was no turning back now. Men continued to wade into the rush of water. Here and there GI's were being knocked off of their feet, submerging and reappearing a few seconds later still carrying their weapons. Some of the shorter troops, especially the KATUSA's, were in serious difficulty. If the water was at mid-chest on the men of average height, it was almost to the mouth of the shorter ones. Holloway saw one man diving repeatedly under the brown water, finally reappearing holding his 90mm recoilless rifle. Taller troops were taking radios and backpacks from shorter ones and holding them above their heads as they waded across. Holloway was half way across when the man in front of him disappeared. He reached under the water, felt a shirt collar, and pulled. A head appeared choking and coughing. He'd stepped in a hole. Holloway held the man at arms length dodging the rifle that the soldier was waving wildly, almost hitting the lieutenant in the face.

"I can't swim! I can't swim!" the man yelled.

"Nobody can swim with all this weight! Try and stand up!" Holloway told him. Eventually the trooper's feet touched the river bottom. Holloway released the man's shirt, turned around and pointed to those behind him.

"Move that way! That way! There's a hole here!" The column shifted to its right. Holloway was nearing the far bank when the thunderclap almost blew him out of the water. No one had seen or heard the Phantoms. The two fighter jets were on top of them at an altitude of fifty feet before anyone realized they were there. Igniting their afterburners to produce the incredible bang, they pulled up quickly and turned their noses up into the sun. The banshee like screams combined with the raging torrent had produced near panic in a few of the troops. Suddenly, the second two F-4's of the flight roared lengthwise down the river, seemingly even lower than their partners. Tonight their pilots would sit around in their warm dry Officers Club in Taegu or Seoul and smoke and joke about how they had popped those poor dumb bastards in the river.

Holloway thought briefly about how easily they would have been killed if those jets had red stars painted on their wings instead of USAF.

Men were on the far side extending their rifles into the river, helping to pull their comrades up the slippery muddy bank onto dry land. The battalion moved forward. Soldiers found their squads and their platoons and their positions in the formation. Head counts were taken; no one was missing. Some helmets had been lost, that was all. Tracey pulled a black waterproof plastic cigarette case out of his shirt pocket and offered it to Holloway who accepted the smoke.

The route of march eventually had taken them into the acres of rice paddies that filled the valley. Some men were able to walk the slippery dikes, but the majority was forced to slog through the endless paddies, the mud sucking at their boots with every step. Mid way through the valley the air above them again turned hostile. The sound of helicopters echoed from the nearby hills and across the rice paddies. Suddenly two Hueys appeared over one of the hills flying close to the terrain. They dropped lower once they cleared the crest of the hill. No one seemed sure if the aircraft were to be considered friendly or hostile. The infantrymen were quickly enlightened. Door gunners in the helicopters began pouring machine gun fire with blank rounds toward the troops spread out across the valley floor. The grunts hit the deck wherever they were, meaning most of them ended up laying in the water of the paddies as they returned fire with their own blank rounds. Suddenly, the troops realized that a new element of warfare had been introduced without warning, as one man after the other choked and gagged and was forced to squeeze shut his eyes. CS tear gas being spewn from the Hueys enveloped them.

"Gas! Gas! Gas!" the troops were calling out. The men scrambled for their gas masks in the muddy water, jerking them from their canvas covers and dumping out the water before donning them. Soon the air became quiet as the helicopters disappeared up the valley behind them. Eventually the all-clear was sounded and the march across the paddies resumed. Near the end of the valley the Company Commander turned and beckoned to Holloway who slogged toward him.

"We're getting automatic weapons fire from that little saddle up there," he said pointing to an elevated area to the left front. "See what you can do about that."

Tracey handed Holloway the handset and stood facing him. "Ruby Bracelet 33, this is Buzzsaw 40, practice fire mission, do not load, over."

"Buzzsaw 40, this is Bracelet 33, send your mission, out," the call came back. Holloway gave the grid coordinates and the directional azimuth of the target to the FDC, which was plotting the data on its charts at Camp Wynne, although no gun crews were actually involved in the drill. The infantry company had halted, pending the outcome of the fire mission. Holloway simulated adjusting the fire and then firing for effect on the target. Then he gave the order "end of mission" to the FDC. He looked at the white-capped umpire who had stood nearby watching and listening. The umpire wrote something in his notebook and then looked at the Company Commander.

"The machine gun is considered neutralized, Lieutenant. You can have your men continue," the umpire said matter-of-factly.

The lead elements started up the hill that was the first objective. The formation had been brought into an assault line, with supporting fire from below. Up the hill they climbed, overcoming its steepness, finding ways of ascending and firing the blank rounds from their rifles. Finally they are at the top. Holloway has seen no "aggressors," but he hears that they have been booted off of the objective. The word comes down from higher. Consolidate the objective, dig in, and then grab some lunch of C-rats.

Two hours later, the Company is again in the assault. This time the objective is a hill almost twice as high as the first. Again the scenario is repeated. Holloway walks his make believe artillery fire around the hilltop for the umpire, giving staggering estimates of enemy casualties to his FDC over the radio. The white-capped umpire tosses smoke grenades and artillery simulators and continues to scribble in his notebook as the advance continues. The fatigue shirts of the men which had dried in the hot sun are now again soaked with perspiration.

Again the infantrymen consolidate. Holloway hopes the war game is complete. The muscles of his calves tell him it is time for a PX steam bath and massage, but it is not to be. The radio of the Company Commander crackles. There is to be one more objective, one more hill. The Company Commander points it out to his platoon leaders and his forward observer who sends the grid coordinates and initiates simulated artillery fire on top of it. Again the assault begins. The third hill is the highest. Upward climb the ridge runners. Tracey is in the lead as Holloway gasps artillery adjustments into the handset. Humidity is extreme. Temperatures are soaring. Sweat is in his eyes. The RTO is almost pulling him up the steep hillside by the radio cord. They are near the top, but Holloway sees only blackness with white spots. He drops to his knees and reaches for his canteen. There is one swallow left. He gulps the water down and his eyes clear. They have swept the crest. They've made it. Platoon leaders and NCOs sort their men and set the defensive perimeter. Entrenching tools go into action as the Company digs in to defend against a possible counterattack. No counter attack materializes. The objective is secure.

Alpha Company, 1/38th is relaxing. The word has been passed that there is to be no more simulated combat. Soldiers are told that they are now in an "administrative" mode rather than a "tactical" mode. Chow is to be served in about a half hour. The Company's mess section has pulled its mess trucks to the bottom of the hill the grunts have just climbed.

"Hey, Koval! What's for dinner," Corporal Tracey calls to one of his buddies.

"Pigs in a blanket they said," the man answers.

"Fuck me," Tracey replies.

"Pigs in a blanket?" Holloway says rhetorically. "I wouldn't walk back down this hill and up again for surf and turf, let alone pigs in a blanket. Those cooks are going to have a lot of leftovers."

"Don't worry, LT. We'll take good care of you," Tracey says. Nearby are a Korean mamasan and a boy. The mamasan is carrying a galvanized metal washtub on her head filled with goodies that she tries to sell to the troops. She had passed Holloway as he staggered up the hill and had moved right along with the soldiers in their assault. She has a babysan tied to her back with a blanket in the age-old Korean custom. Her stomach protrudes enormously. The woman looks to be at least seven months pregnant. Tracey waves and calls to the woman. "Hey, knocked up mamasan! Eedywah!"

The woman and boy walk over to the group of five men sitting together with their helmets off smoking cigarettes and sucking on Lifesavers. Tracey holds up his empty canteen to the boy. "Ca-geewah water?" he asks. The boy holds out his hand and nods. Tracey collects the canteens of the five soldiers and hands them to the boy and shows the boy a 100 won note worth about thirty cents. "Ca-geewah numba one water!" Tracey orders. The boy again nods and heads down the hill. Tracey turns to the mamasan.

"Lamyon eeso, mamasan?" he asks.

The woman sets her washtub on the ground and pulls out a plastic wrapped package of dried ramyon noodles, which comes with a little packet of spices. Tracey holds up two fingers and she withdraws a second pack. She also holds up a bottle of Pepsi-Cola and looks at the GI's. Holloway seems interested.

"Don't drink that shit, LT. It ain't real Pepsi in there. They just fill it with some kind of crap that'll give you the runs and put a cap on it and act like its Pepsi. That kid will be back in a bit with some fresh spring water that will quench your thirst. I'm going to make some stew with some of it too. You'll love it."

Tracey has gathered several small stones. By placing them in a circle, he has built an oven and he lays a blue tablet that he has taken out of a sealed aluminum foil packet in the middle of the oven. The boy returns from the bottom of the hill with five full plastic canteens. The corporal pours a little water from each of the canteens into his metal canteen cup. Then he touches a match to the blue tablet. It ignites instantly into an almost invisible white-hot flame. The water comes quickly to a boil and Tracey adds the noodles and spices. "Get your meat ready, chingos," he says and his companions pull out cans of C-ration pork that they open with the little P-38 can openers that all infantrymen carry. Holloway had decided long ago that the P-38 is probably the best invention in the history of the US military. He adds his can of pork to the stew. As a final touch, Tracey reaches into his ammo pouch and withdraws a small metal flask, which contains Louisiana cayenne pepper sauce. He adds a few drops to his concoction. "Ooouuuu whee! This is gonna be goooood!" he proclaims and after a few more moments begin to dish out the meal to his companions. As soon as the canteen cup is empty he begins a second batch. The men begin to eat with chopsticks the mamasan had provided with the noodles. Tracey is correct. The meal is wonderful. Holloway feels content with the world.

An hour before dark Alpha Company is told it is moving to another hill five klicks away, where the battalion will spend the night. Holloway is told that the artillery portion of the exercise is over. There is no reason for him to stay any longer. The Alpha Company XO tells him that Corporal Gash and his jeep have already been sent home, but that Ruminski, who has been acting as Artillery Liaison Officer for the exercise, will meet him at an intersection nearby and take him back to Camp Wynne.

The infantrymen pack up and begin to move down the hill as darkness falls. Holloway locates Lieutenant Werner, the Company XO, in the fading light and asks him to tell him when they are at the intersection where he is to meet Ruminski. A few minutes later the XO taps him on the shoulder.

"This is it, FO. Your LNO will pick you up in his jeep right here in ten or fifteen minutes," Werner says.

"Are you sure?" Holloway responds. "I'm thinking it's a bit further on."

"Negative. This is it. Trust me," Werner says in the gathering darkness.

Holloway drops out of the column and stands along side of the road as the troops file by. He has said good-bye to Tracey who is still humping the radio that Holloway has been using most of the day. His five days on GP Gwen combined with this FTX have made him feel comfortable operating with the infantry in the field. He's also been able to add a few phrases that he has learned from Tracey to his Korean vocabulary. As he watches the last of Alpha Company fade from view he realizes that is almost completely dark.

Within a few minutes another column of troops approaches the crossroads. As they draw near he asks the point man what unit it is and is answered with the title "Bravo." This is the last company of the battalion. Like Alpha, this unit too fades into the darkness and soon Holloway is alone. Time passes and Holloway cannot help but wonder why Ruminski has not yet arrived. He holds the face of his Seiko watch close to his eyes so that he can read the luminous dial. Almost forty minutes have passed. Ruminski is a half hour late for the rendezvous. Soon the forty minutes have become an hour. Now Holloway is worried. He has his maps and his compass, but no radio. It stayed with the RTO. Unfolding the waterproof map case he checks his position. He is ten miles from Camp Wynne. There is nothing nearby. Something is radically wrong. There's no way Ruminski can be this late unless something is really screwed up. He begins walking in the direction that the 1/38th had taken.

Alone with the mosquitoes and crickets and frogs in the darkness of the Korean countryside, Holloway takes stock of the situation. The mosquitoes are getting thick and he is out of bug juice. He rolls down his sleeves and turns up his collar. He has his pistol in his holster, but no live ammunition since he was engaged only in a training exercise. He has a half of canteen of water so that is not a concern and he even has two or three assorted cans of C-rats in case he needs them. He decides he will follow the dirt road until 11:30. If he finds no one he will select a place to sleep and go into hiding for the night. Midnight is the bewitching hour. There is a countrywide curfew in Korea. In order to reduce the movement of North Korean commandos in the South, no one is permitted out after midnight unless they are part of a military unit that has the proper clearance. The Korean Home Guard has night ambush patrols all over the area. Anyone violating the curfew may be shot on sight.

Holloway freezes. He hears voices ahead, Korean voices. Listening for a moment he understands nothing of what is being said. Quietly, he moves into the ditch at the side of the road and moving slowly in a crouch, advances towards the voices. Only a few feet separate him from what he now can see are six Korean civilian males clustered at a small wooden footbridge.

"Annahashamika," he says in the traditional Korean greeting as he steps boldly from the ditch. The men who are not facing him whirl around. "Does anyone speak English?"

After a moment of silence, one man steps forward. "I speakee scochie English. Who you?"

"I look for American soldiers. You see American soldiers?" Holloway asks.

"Oopso. All gone long time. Go chogi," the man says pointing down the road. The man seems to sense that Holloway is lost. "Villagee chogi. You chanda in villagee?"

"No, papasan. Kamsamnida," Holloway replies, declining the man's offer to sleep in the village. He is afraid that the Koreans may steal his weapon and his equipment and perhaps whack him over the head besides. Wanting to put some distance between himself and the Koreans he moves quickly down the road. There is only a half hour until curfew. In case he is followed, Holloway believes that the safest thing to do is to find a sturdy tree and climb it and sleep in the branches. Finally he leaves the dirt road and heads into a wooded area. It is not easy to find the sort of tree that he seeks. After searching in the darkness for several minutes his ears detect a familiar sound in the distance. A military radio is hissing and popping squelch. His heart pounds with excitement as he heads quietly for the sound.

He is almost upon the source of the noise when a voice from the darkness challenges him. "Halt!"

Momentarily he stops. Nothing further is said and he takes another step. A rifle bolt slams home. "I said halt, goddamnit!" the voice calls again. "What's the password?"

"I don't know the password. My name's Holloway, FO from the 8/18th Artillery."

"OK, come on in. We've been lookin' for you. Your LNO says you're lost," the voice in the darkness says. Holloway sighs in relief and walks slowly forward. The guard shows him to where two jeeps sit on the road a few meters away surrounded by five or six armed infantrymen. "Sir, we got that FO we've been lookin' for."

A large black major turns in his seat and looks at Holloway. "Have a seat, Lieutenant," the officer says. "I'm Major Jordan, XO of the 1/38th. We wondered what happened to you." The man picked up the microphone that was hanging from the radio next to where Holloway was now sitting. "Six, this is Five. We've got that Foxtrot Oscar you've been looking for. Tell his LNO he can pick him up at the river crossing in about zero five mikes."

Major Jordan speaks again to Holloway. "Come on, Lieutenant. We'll get you out of here. Alpha Company dropped you off at the wrong place. They must have gotten confused in the dark. Your LNO waited at the pickup point, but you never showed." Holloway closes his eyes and shakes his head slowly. He swears that if he ever again sees the Alpha Company XO who told him to drop off at the crossroads he will give him more than just a piece of his mind. A broken nose is not out of the question.

When Major Jordan's jeep comes to a halt at the edge of the river a few minutes later, Holloway can see Ruminski's vehicle waiting on the other side. He thanks the major and begins wading through the water. The river is nothing like it had been further south that morning when it had been more like a raging torrent. Now the water is calm and the level barely above his knees as he reaches the far bank.

"Where in the hell have you been, Holloway? Out at the drive-in with your girlfriend?" Ruminski asks with a smirk.

"Don't give me your shit, Ruminski! It wasn't my fault and I'm not in the mood for it," Holloway shot back. The ride back to Camp Wynne is made in silence. As the driver halts the jeep in front of the old BOQ shortly after midnight, Ruminski speaks.

"You've got tomorrow off. On Thursday though I need you back on Gwen. Meet me at Camp Greaves at 0900 Thursday morning. Can chana?"

"Can chana, Dave. Can do. I wouldn't miss it for the world."

CHAPTER 10

Skinny Yee opened the door quietly and peeked cautiously into the room. He could see Lieutenant Holloway asleep, covered by the cotton sheet. Yee had assumed Holloway must be in there when he had seen the padlock missing from the hasp on the door. He stole quietly into the room to pick up the dirty clothes and boots that had been piled in the corner. What a mess! The fatigues were caked with mud, smelled like they had been dropped into a latrine, and were still partially wet. What did Holloway do in the field? Get used as a plow for the rice paddies?

Holloway's houseboy loved his kimchi. He had a large meal of it the night before and then had eaten what was left for breakfast that morning. The odor of the pickled fermented cabbage seemed to ooze from his pores as well as gush from his mouth. It was that smell more than any noise that awakened Clay Holloway. Yee saw him stir as he was trying to slip back out of the door undetected.

"Morning, Yee," he said groggily.

The houseboy bowed quickly twice as he held the dirty clothes to his chest. "Morning, Lieutenant Holloway. Morning. I try not to wake up."

"That's OK. Did you enjoy your kimchi for breakfast?"

"How you know I have kimchi?"

"Just a wild guess. Are you going to get those cleaned up for me today?"

"Yessir. Laundry this morning," Skinny Yee replied bowing again.

"OK good. I need them before you go home today. I'm only here for today and tonight. I go back to the hill first thing tomorrow morning. See if you can get my web gear cleaned up too. It's got rice paddy dung all over it."

Holloway looked at his watch. Almost 0730. The workday started right about now in the battalion compound. Technically he was currently attached to the 1/9th, but he felt duty bound to see what he could do at the Battery as long as he was at Camp Wynne for the day. He couldn't rationalize going up to Camp Greaves when he had nothing to do there until tomorrow. Besides, there was a good chance he'd be able to see Beth tonight if he stayed around. He showered, dressed, skipped breakfast, and headed for the Charlie Battery area. He'd be able to scrounge some coffee at the CP.

When he had returned from the FTX the night before he had been vaguely aware that there seemed to be more than the usual number of little tree frogs on the compound. He had heard them croaking loudly as he had walked into the BOQ, but had not thought a great deal about it. Now as he headed for the Battery area in the rain he realized that there seemed to be frogs everywhere. They hopped away from him on the gravel street when he walked. Some of them sat on the sidewalk and watched him as he strode by. He noticed several frogs sitting and croaking inside of an open end of one of the storm drains that sat in a drainage ditch in front of the little PX. Later that morning he watched a deuce and a half truck drive into the motor pool area and listened to the crackle and crunching sounds as the truck crushed at least thirty or forty of the little amphibians as it drove toward one of the truck bays. By noon frogs had been found in the latrines, in empty boots, and on peoples' desks. At lunch the frogs had become the only real topic of conversation.

The workday passed quickly for Holloway as he spent most of it with Tom Courtney and then Sergeant Carlton, familiarizing himself with the Battery supply system. At the end of the afternoon, after stopping in his room to insure that his fatigues, boots, and web gear were ready for the next day, he walked into the dining room at the Club for dinner. Beth and Sherry were sitting at one of the four person tables. Beth waved to him.

"Hi, Clay! Come sit with us," Beth called. "Or should I call you Bagger now?"

"You heard about that, huh?" Holloway remarked as he pulled back one of the wooden straight back chairs. "After the last two days you might just want to call me 'grunt'."

"You were out playing with the infantry, eh? How'd it go?"

"Well, Ruminski was right. It was good training, I'll say that. Wasn't all fun though. So, how have you two been?"

Sherry spoke first. "OK, I guess. But I'm really getting tired of this rain, you know. It just limits what we can do with the troop visits. Can you picture trying to play the guitar and sing some folk songs in an all day monsoon? It's kind of a drag."

He waited politely for Sherry to finish. Then he looked at Beth quizzically. "What about you, Miss Kisha? What have you been up to?"

She gave one of her mysterious looks. "Oh, up to mischief, of course. What did you expect?" Beth paused. "Linda Wilson went home yesterday. You missed saying good-bye to her. I'll be getting a new partner next week. Maybe even this weekend she'll be here."

Holloway hadn't really gotten to know Linda Wilson. In fact he wasn't quite sure who she was. "I'm sorry I didn't see Linda. Is the new girl coming in from the States?"

"No. They're bring her up from I Corps. She's been there about three months. Her name is Jennifer. I met her once. She's cool. You'll like her," Beth said.

The two women had been almost finished with their meals when Holloway had sat down. Sherry took one bite of the fudge brownie that had been served for dessert and pushed back her chair. "I've got some things I need to do for tomorrow, if you'll excuse me. See you all later." She left the others alone.

There was a full minute of silence. Holloway looked directly at Beth. "How have you really been? Is everything OK?"

"Of course it is. Everything is fine."

"I had hoped to see you last weekend. I heard you'd gone to Seoul."

"I didn't know if you'd make it down here from Camp Greaves or not. But anyway, I'd made the plans a month ago. I didn't want to cancel them."

"Do you have some girl friends down there?"

She looked at him for a moment before answering. Her tone seemed serious. "I have friends there, Clay. I've gotten to know a lot of people in this country in the last several months. I like to visit people whenever I can get the transportation. I don't like to be tied to one place all the time." She paused again. "Or to just one set of friends."

Holloway felt flushed. "I'm really not very hungry at the moment and I'm not good at games. Can we just take a little walk? I'd really like to talk with you alone."

"Of course we can," Beth said agreeably. They both arose from their chairs and walked into the humid air that hung over the compound like a cloak. Frogs leaped out of their way as they exited the building. Beth squeezed his hand as they started down the sidewalk.

"OK, Bagger. You requested this meeting," she joked.

Holloway tried to smile, but it was forced. He let her hand drop and looked at the ground as they walked. "Beth, I'm just really confused. Two weekends ago you and I made love five times in two days. I've thought about it a thousand times since then. I couldn't get enough of you and you were acting the same way about me. I thought we were really clicking. Our whole relationship right from the beginning seemed perfect. Then last weekend when I got off of the hill I come down here and find that you're spending the weekend in Seoul. No note in my mailbox. Nothing at all. Do you have a guy in Seoul? Is that the problem?"

"Sweetheart, don't make this difficult. Try to understand my position. I think you're wonderful. The short time we've known each other has been absolutely grand. But I'm not going to get serious with anyone over here. Especially not someone who is supposed to spend the next two or three months on a hill in the DMZ. I wanted very much to make love to you before you went up there. I knew I would miss you and I did miss you.

I've only got three months left in country. You have twelve. As I said to you earlier, I have a lot of friends over here. Some are girl friends and some aren't. You shouldn't think that because of what happened that I'm your steady girlfriend. It's not like that. We're both single adults. We're attracted to each other and the outcome of that was not unnatural. I said it before and I'll say it again. Those two nights together were absolutely marvelous. Maybe it will happen for us again. I hope it does. If you can let me know ahead of time when you are going to be down for a couple of days, that would be great. We can plan something.

But I can't commit myself to someone who's rarely going to be here for the next few months. Just about the time you might get released from duty in the Z I'll be going home. What would happen then? Should I go Stateside and wait until you get there nine months later and then go to Ft. Sill or wherever you get assigned and camp outside the gate and see if we can get a normal relationship going. That's crazy, Clay. That's just crazy and you have to agree with me. How could we really have the time to try a long-term relationship? It will never work. Just accept it for what it is. A very strong physical, romantic attraction that someday we'll both look back on with some very fond memories." She squeezed his hand again and looked searchingly into his face. "What do you think?"

Holloway was momentarily silent. Finally he spoke. "I don't know what to think. Or to say. You make sense, I guess. I hadn't thought of it like that, but I suppose you're right. We're not going to see much of each other are we? But see, I just really fell for you. I've thought about you constantly. What can I say? I can't ask you to wait. We've only known each other three weeks and almost two of them I've been gone." He looked at her. She was smiling at him.

"Life is short, Bagger. Live it to the fullest. Don't spend your time thinking about something that isn't realistic." She stopped talking and looked into his eyes. "Please say it's OK. I don't want you to be hurt. I want to be friends. I really do. What do you say?"

He gave her a tight-lipped smile. "OK. I guess that's the way it is then. Thanks for being honest."

She looked at him a lingering moment. "Do you have a light?" Beth asked holding a cigarette to her lips with two fingers.

Holloway flipped open the top of his newly purchased Zippo with the 18th Artillery crest on the side and held the flame out to her. She held his hand softly, guiding it to her cigarette. When she was finished he lit a Winston and exhaled into the sky. They had walked all the way to the opposite end of the compound. High above them stood one of the Korean civilian guards with a shotgun cradled in his arms watching them. Beth took his arm and they walked slowly back toward the Club. An expression that had become popular in Vietnam came to mind. "Don't mean nuthin'." He tried to apply it to the situation, to push away the pain. But it did mean something. And although he wouldn't let it show, it still hurt.

He walked her to the Doughnut Dolly Hooch. She kissed him quickly, yet softly and went inside. Walking back to his BOQ he tried to put her out of his mind. She made sense. They weren't going to see much of each other. Damn! If only his emotions didn't get in the way. Maybe what he needed was a yobo. Just go to the village and pick one out for a hundred bucks. What had that captain at Ascom City told him at the bar? Good-looking girls. Give you anything you want. Great sex. They'll cook for you. Maybe that was the ticket. Forget the emotional part. Put in your field time. Come back and jump into a warm rack with your yobo and feel good. When the thirteen month tour is up you go home and that's that. No muss no fuss. He'd think about that.

Back in his room, Holloway forced himself to draft a long letter to his parents to help take his thoughts away from Beth. Once the writing juices were flowing he dashed off three postcards to other relatives and then tugged open a desk drawer to search for stamps. Instead, he encountered one of the little tree frogs that leaped out of the drawer and onto the desktop.

"Damnit!" cried Holloway aloud, startled by the sudden emergence of the green and black amphibian. He grabbed the little creature with one hand, strode to the outside door and flung it into the damp air. As he did he could hear the thousands upon thousands of the frog's relatives singing in unison as dusk approached. They sounded like huge frog choirs, their voices amplified inside of the drainpipes where many of them congregated. Holloway listened for a moment, then returned to his room where he found and applied the stamps and then left the building to walk to the Officer's Club where he would mail them. Once that chore was complete he walked down the short hallway to peek into the bar area to see who was there. Abruptly, the doors swung open as he was about to reach for them and Hostileman brushed past him, in a seemingly surely mood. Behind him Holloway could see Courtney and Bear Buckner watching Hostileman leave, amused expressions on their faces.

"What's going on?" Holloway asked innocently.

Buckner's dark eyes flashed. "Your BC has got Hostileman so worked up about those damn frogs, he's now got him convinced that he should go out and exterminate every last one of them."

"Is that where he's going? To kill the frogs?"

"Yeah!" Courtney chuckled. "With his entrenching tool."

"He wanted us to go with him, but we have better things to do than spend the night killing frogs. So finally he told us to put our heads in rectal defilade and he left to get his entrenching tool," Buckner added. "Said he's not coming back until they're all dead."

"He's serious?" asked Holloway. "Has he been drinking?"

"Hell, yeah, he's serious and off course he's been drinkin," Courtney replied. "He absolutely hates those little critters. They drive him dingy dingy. And the more he had to drink and the more they kept croaking, the more pissed off he got."

"Well, Tom, you didn't help the situation any," said Buckner. "You kept telling him if the frogs really bothered him that much he ought to do something about it and not just sit here complaining all night like an old woman."

"True enough, Bear. But an officer has to take charge of a situation. It's like that old expression 'Do something, Lieutenant. Even if it's wrong.'"

Within five minutes Hostileman reappeared at the door of the Club, clad in his steel helmet with green camouflage cover, rain poncho, and carrying his collapsible entrenching tool. "This is your last chance, you two weenies. Pick up your arms and join me."

"What's the helmet for, Hostileman? You think they're going to fight back?"

"No. It's so I can sneak up on them. With this camouflage cover and poncho they're gonna think I'm their big brother and I can walk right up to them. Then whappo."

"Well, you take care of them for us. If you get into trouble send up a flare and we'll get a medic out there for you."

"OK then. Keep the beer cold." Raising the entrenching tool above his head, Lester Joe Bufford whirled, issued a damn fine impression of a rebel yell and ran out of the back door and into the rainy darkness. Within minutes the sound of a shovel intermittently slapping the soggy ground came through the thin walls of the Club. Then slowly the sound faded into the distance.

An hour passed. Eighteen or twenty people occupied the Club in small groups, sipping drinks and chatting softly. Kathy Kelsey sat between Tom Courtney and Clay Holloway talking about how she had spent her day, when the sound of the entrenching tool became audible once again outside the window.

"What is that noise?" she asked innocently.

"Hostileman's killing frogs."

"What did you say?"

"I said Hostileman's killing frogs. That's him outside. Let's go take a look."

Failing to believe what Tom Courtney had said to her, she eyed him suspiciously. "OK."

Courtney, Holloway and Kathy Kelsey walked over to the window where Courtney pulled back a drape. Other people, having overheard the conversation walked up behind them. In the darkness outside, only a few feet away, hunched a figure in a dark poncho, slick with rain. Intermittently, a small shovel would rise and then slap at the ground. Usually a muffled grunt would accompany each slap.

"That's cruel. He's really killing frogs?" Kathy asked as she stared out of the window.

"Yep!"

"Why?"

"He hates them. They won't shut up. And besides, they're communist frogs."

"How can he tell?"

"He can tell."

"How long has he been out there?"

"Little over an hour. Says he's not coming in until they're all dead. He plans to leave the bodies where they lay. We're supposed to call Graves Registration and have them police up all of them in the morning."

"This is sick. Why don't you stop him?"

"I don't think it's a good idea to argue with Hostileman when he's been drinkin'. Especially when he has a shovel in his hand. Leave him alone. He'll get tired sooner or later."

"I'm going to turn on the flood light. Maybe he'll stop," Kathy said. She reached beside her and flipped the light switch, bathing the lawn in light.

"Turn that goddamn light out! You'll ruin my night vision!" screamed Hostileman.

Startled, she extinguished the light. "Told ya," said Courtney. "Let's go back to the bar."

It was after ten o'clock when the Staff Duty officer tapped Tom Courtney on the shoulder. "Excuse me Tom, but Colonel Moody just called from Div Arty. He's bringing a friend of his with him back here. They'll be here in about a half hour. The Colonel wonders if you would be kind enough to let his friend use your room in the new BOQ for the night. The guy is a full colonel and you're the junior battery commander."

"Well, where the hell am I supposed to sleep?" Courtney asked.

"There's a couple of empty rooms in the old BOQ. That shouldn't be a problem. Just use your sleeping bag," the SDO responded.

"The room next to me is open, Tom," Holloway said.

"Mah sleeping bag? Swell. Well, shit. OK, I guess for a bird colonel I don't have much choice. I'll go get my shaving kit and sleeping bag and move it now." He turned to the others. Don't you boys go nowhere. I'll be back for a night cap."

An hour later Clay Holloway showed his Battery Commander to the vacant room next to his in the old BOQ. "Here's one of my towels, Tom. If you need anything else I'll be right next door. Gash is picking me up at 0700. I probably won't see you for a while so take it easy." Courtney thanked him and both men retired for the night a moment later.

Holloway had been asleep for almost two hours when the crash outside his door made him sit bolt upright. He threw the sheet off and ran out of the door into the hallway. Courtney was wrestling with a Korean man on the concrete floor. Holloway circled and then moved into the fray from the man's rear grabbing him in a chokehold.

"What the hell's going on, Tom?" he grunted as he applied pressure with his left forearm to the man's throat.

"Slicky boy! Son-of-a-bitch tried to steal my wallet," Courtney panted. "I woke up and he was standing at my dresser so I tackled him," he said, pinning the man's arms. "I'll hold 'em. You get something to tie the bastard up with!"

At that moment Bill Grant ran down the hall. "What the hell is this? Two guys just ran into my room and back out again. They scared the shit out of me. I think they thought it was an exit."

"Slicky boys! Wake everyone up!" Courtney ordered. Call the SDO and tell him to call Second MP. They're just right up the road. Tell the SDO to have the batteries check their people to see if anyone is missing. These guys may be KATUSA's. Either that or they penetrated the fence perimeter."

Holloway returned with the heavy lace string from his sleeping bag and his entrenching tool. Together he and Courtney tied the slicky boy to a pipe that ran along the hall. Holloway stood in front of the man holding the little shovel. The Korean stared at the floor sullenly. Sleepy eyed lieutenants in their underwear poured down the hall as the BOQ had come suddenly alive.

"There were slicky boys in the building," Courtney announced again. "At least three of them. Everybody inventory your stuff. See what all is missing. Especially wallets, watches, and rings. Grant, go over to the new Q and make sure all of the doors are secure there. If anybody is up tell them to be on the lookout." Bill Grant nodded and left. A few minutes later, Lieutenant Benning, the Staff Duty Officer, arrived with four MP's. After a brief conversation it was agreed that Courtney would give a statement the next day at the MP station and the suspect was hauled away. The other two slicky boys had not been found. Courtney's assumption would eventually prove to be right. The slicky boys were KATUSA's from the Headquarters Battery of their own Battalion. Once the captured one revealed the names of the others, they would be turned over to the ROK Army who had rather stern methods of dealing with thieves.

Eventually, the others returned to their rooms and all of the lights were extinguished. Holloway and Courtney had talked for a few minutes about what a bizarre place Camp Wynne could be. Then Holloway started back to his own room. It was then that he heard through the open doorway to the outside the sound of rustling in the bushes nearby. Someone seemed to be grunting and there was the sound of soft thuds every so often. Another slicky boy? Holloway reached into his room in the darkness and retrieved his entrenching tool. He thought about calling Courtney, but then made the decision to investigate it himself. The noise seemed vaguely familiar, but no. It couldn't be. It was almost two o'clock in the morning. Holloway slipped soundlessly outside into the darkness.

Circling the clump of thick bushes he heard the sound again. There was a thud followed closely by another grunt. Holloway dropped to his knees and crawled forward on all fours peering under the bushes. There was a pair of feet. They were wearing combat boots. He heard another thud. "Got you, you little peckerhead." The man had not yet seen Holloway who was looking upwards at him from behind. It was Hostileman. His own entrenching tool in his hand, he was still killing frogs. Holloway shook his head slowly and crawled backwards. He crept quietly to his feet and sneaked back into the door of the BOQ smiling to himself and shaking his head. Unbelievable. Absolutely unbelievable!!

CHAPTER 11

A plume of white smoke curled lazily upward from the woods to the left and far below Holloway's bunker. He had been watching it for ten minutes trying to decide why it was there. It was on the US side of the MDL and he assumed it must be from one of the patrols. How could they be that stupid? They must know how easily it could be seen. Then it dawned on him. Perhaps it wasn't a question of stupidity. The people on the patrol had possibly made the decision to announce their presence, believing that if the North Koreans knew they were there they wouldn't blunder into the patrol and therefore no one would be forced to shoot at each other. That or maybe it was stupidity. Either way, Holloway's job was to observe and report. He called the TOC on the landline and reported the location of the smoke.

Sergeant Major McKee had left the Guard Post an hour earlier to visit Camp Greaves to catch a quick shower and get a freshly laundered set of fatigues. Holloway yawned and looked at his watch. The chow truck with the evening meal was still two hours away. The Sergeant Major would probably ride back up to the GP with it. Holloway left the bunker and walked through the trench line around to the back of the hill.

Holloway chuckled to himself as he walked, thinking of what had transpired the night before with the Sergeant Major, Doc, and Spec/4 Black, the antipersonnel radar operator. When he had returned to the hill two days earlier the Sergeant Major had told him that there had been increased UI activity on the GP. It appeared as though North Korean commandos were sneaking close to the trench line at night and tossing stones into the trenches as a harassment tactic. The Sergeant Major felt that sooner or later one of them would mix in a grenade with the stones. For increased security he had ordered extra barbed wire strung on the side of the hill and added several empty C-ration cans filled with pebbles and hung from the wire to make noise. Last night the stones started landing in the trenches again. The Sergeant Major and Holloway had gone out into the trench line from the CP to watch and to listen in the darkness. A stone had landed. Then a few minutes later another. Holloway was perplexed. He found it hard to understand why anyone would get that close and risk dying just to harass them with stones. Feeling that something was not quite right, he left the Sergeant Major in the darkness with another NCO and walked into the little tunnel that led both to the CP and the sleeping bunker. Then he exited the back of the complex and quietly crept up the reverse slope of the hill toward the crest. Ahead in the darkness was soft muffled laughter. He sneaked closer. In front of him were Doc and Spec/4 Black lying on their stomachs looking down at the trench line thirty feet below. Black raised his right hand and with a flick of his wrist let loose of another small pebble. Here were the culprits, the source of the stones that the Sergeant Major was reporting to the TOC. Reports that were going all the way to Division Intelligence.

Creeping quietly ahead, Holloway reached out and grabbed Black's wrist as it slowly raised. Frightened, Black's head swiveled around and saw Holloway's angry face right above him. Black's mouth flew open in surprise. Holloway tapped Doc on the back and he also turned. The FO put his index finger to his lips and signaled with the other hand for the two to follow him down the back of the hill to the flat area.

"What in the name of God do you two think you're doing?" Holloway demanded once they stood behind the bunker entrance.

"Oh, Lieutenant Holloway, don't be pissed off. We're just having a little fun with the Sergeant Major. He takes this shit so seriously," Black replied with a grin on his face.

"Black, this is a hostile fire zone. There are real bad guys out there. How the hell can you two dick around like this?"

"Oh, Sir. I've been on this hill for two months off and on and I ain't never seen a real live UI yet. Somebody always hears a noise or a voice or sees something, but when you check it out there's never anything there. Sometimes I pick up shapes on my radar, but I bet it's probably just deer. We're just adding a little excitement to the Sergeant Major's life. He's going to retire in another six weeks anyway. Come on. You're not gonna turn us in are you?"

Holloway's hand shot forward and grabbed Black's shirt collar. He put his face three inches from the man's. "Let me tell you this once! A month ago the reaction force ran into an ambush not too far east of here. Remember that? You think that was nothing? Now, you fuck around like this one more time and I'm court-martialing both your asses. If one more stone lands near the trenches and either of you are on this hill I'm turning you in. So if you have any buddies that want to play too, you better let them know. The next stone that land's, you're both looking at a court-martial. You get my drift?"

The smile had left Black's face. He was a fun loving intelligent young man with two years of college as an English major prior to being drafted. The entire concept of the military was something that was alien to his thinking. Spec/4 Black was long on humor and short on discipline. But, he also had no desire to see the inside of a stockade. "Yes, Sir. I understand."

"Doc?"

"Yes, Sir. I understand too."

Holloway released Black's shirt. "OK then. Don't forget. I don't consider this a joke." He left them standing in the darkness as he headed toward the CP stifling a smile. Maybe it was just a little funny. But he still couldn't allow it to go on. Sergeant Major McKee would be horribly embarrassed if it ever came out that his UI contact reports were the result of two of his own men playing tricks on him. Holloway still had a smile on his face when he realized someone was calling his name. "Lieutenant Holloway! Lieutenant Holloway!"

Holloway turned. It was PFC Fortunato. "What is it?"

"The TOC just called. There's a UI spotted. He's behind the hill. Between here and the fence. They're calling out the reaction force. They want us to see if we can spot the son-of-a-bitch and maybe get a shot at him. The Sergeant Major's not here. What should we do?" Fortunato blurted out breathlessly.

Holloway's mind raced. He was artillery and technically had no command authority over the infantry, but with the Sergeant Major gone, the highest-ranking man on the hill was a young E-5 that was still copping z's in the sleeping bunker. Somebody needed to take charge and Holloway didn't believe the E-5 was quite ready for it.

"I'll get my binos. You get the sniper rifle and ammo out of the CP. Wake up the troops and get them out into the bunkers. Tell them to look sharp, but nobody shoots without my say so. Meet me back here."

The two men ran in opposite directions. Holloway raced back to his position #4 and grabbed the standard artillery issue 10x50 binoculars. Reversing his course he returned to the flat area at the rear of the CP. His eyes scanned the backside of the hill below the gate. There was a tree twenty feet outside the fence. It would be the best position from which to observe. He looked back toward the CP as the first of the freshly awakened grunts began moving quickly out of the sleeping bunker. Fortunato came rushing out too, holding the M-1 rifle with the 20x telescopic sight and the leather sling.

"Good," said Holloway taking the rifle and three clips of ammunition. "Now get a PRC-25 out here too. We need communications. I'll be in that tree." He strode out the back gate and down the hill a short distance to the foot of the medium sized poplar. He paused to load the weapon. It took him a moment. He hadn't loaded an M-1 since his freshman year of ROTC. The venerable rifle of World War II and Korean War service had been replaced by the M-14 a decade before. Now even that rifle was being phased out by the newer M-16. He was glad he'd used an M-1 in ROTC. He thought he would have looked pretty stupid not knowing how to load the damn thing. He fed the eight round clip down into the breech from the top and released the bolt, sending a round into the chamber. The scope was zeroed for 1,000 yards. If he had to shoot, that would be approximately the range the shot would be from. Swinging the rifle over his shoulder with the leather sling, he pulled himself up to the lowest branch. From there it was not difficult to go two higher. Then he straddled the branch and lifted his binoculars.

Two APC's from the mechanized reaction force were driving up the dirt road beyond the fence heading for the access gate. They should be inside the Zone in less than two minutes. Holloway scanned the underbrush, looking for any sign of the reported UI. Nothing. Fortunato was back at the base of the tree along with the infantry E-5.

"Here's the radio, Lieutenant Holloway. What should I do with it?"

"You act as my RTO. Call the TOC and ask them if they have any more info. Sergeant, you make sure your troops are checking the front of the hill for anything out of the ordinary. Nobody shoots without my permission, understood?"

"Yessir," the E-5 barked out. He seemed perfectly willing to let the artillery officer make the decisions.

"TOC says it is a confirmed sighting. UI armed with a rifle and carrying a rucksack spotted in the patch of trees near the gate down there," Fortunato called up to Holloway in the tree.

Holloway was still scanning the area with the binoculars. The gate opened and the two APC's plowed through. Then they each spun on one track and turned sharply to their left. The APC's halted, the rear hatch was lowered and twenty infantrymen poured out. Together, the tracks and the men advanced slowly in a skirmish line, firing automatic weapons and grenades from grenade launchers ahead of them. "Reconnaissance by fire" is the term of the technique, intended to flush the target from his hiding place or at least make him reveal his position.

Second Lieutenant Keith Hackworth rode in the open hatch of one of the two tracks, manning the .50 caliber himself. He and Corporal James Washington were both methodically firing three to five round bursts ahead of them as the tracks moved slowly across the level ground. He looked behind him. The troops were starting to bunch and he pushed his hand away from his body, signaling them to keep it spread out. He brought his head back around and resumed his firing. Where the hell was this guy?

Clay Holloway was sweating profusely, a combination of tension and the blazing sun of a cloudless sky. Already his pelvic area ached from straddling the hard branch. He wiped his forehead with his sleeve and squinted again through the 10x50's. His eyes widened. There was a form lying in the weeds behind a little rise in the terrain, about a hundred yards in front of the two tracks and the moving line of men. The form was motionless, as though it were another piece of the terrain. But, of course, it wasn't. The form cradled a rifle between its arms.

Holloway was sure the reaction force did not see the man. Most of the troops were to the form's right front and were not shooting anywhere near him as they continued their advance.

"Fortunato, call the TOC. Tell them the UI is to the patrol's right front at less than a hundred meters."

"77, this is Golf Papa 1, Uniform India is approximately 100 meters in front of the reaction force and to its right front, over," Fortunato yelled into the mike.

Silence.

"Did they acknowledge?" Holloway asked.

"Negative, Sir."

"Send it again. Hurry up!"

"77, this is Golf Papa 1, I say again. UI is to the right front of the reaction force and less than 100 meters away. Do you roger, over?"

"Golf Papa 1, this is 77. You're breaking up. Say again last transmission, over."

"Jesus Christ, Fortunato. They're only fifty meters away and they're not even looking at him. They're going to pass right by him. He'll open up on their flank and waste a bunch of people!"

The rifle flew to Holloway's shoulder. Should he shoot? He'd never shot at another human being in his life. The UI hadn't hurt anyone. Maybe he wouldn't. Maybe he'd just let the reaction force go by. Maybe if Holloway didn't do anything it would turn out all right. It almost seemed like a football game. They're down there on the field playing and he was just a spectator up in the top row of the stadium. Maybe he shouldn't interfere. The thoughts flashed almost randomly through his brain. The idea of trying to kill at long range was completely alien to him. But, he knew he had to shoot. What if he didn't and the UI killed an American. Or two Americans. Or even three. How could he live with that? No, he had to try. Maybe a leg shot. Wound the man, rather than kill him. Wait, that was crazy. A shot at a thousand yards was almost impossible anyway, even if the scope was zeroed for that range. And who even knew if the zero was still good?

"Fortunato, call again. I'm going to try to shoot him!"

Ten years earlier, at age fourteen, Holloway had earned a spot on his high school rifle team as a freshman. He'd owned a rifle for as long as he could remember. The Army had rated him as an expert with both the M-14 and the .45 caliber pistol following qualification shoots at the rifle and pistol ranges the previous summer. Shooting at targets was something he had always been naturally good at. Now the target was a man, but clearly the time was ripe to put the deadly skill to use if he could. He wiped his forehead once more, trying to get the stinging salty sweat out of his eyes. Earlier he had adjusted the sling. Now he looped it around his left arm and pulled it tight. He laid forward on the big branch, steadying the barrel upon a smaller branch in front of him. The rifle was at his shoulder. He squinted through the 20X scope. Even with the high-powered optics the target was still small. He aligned the cross hairs on the man's head and took up the slack in the trigger. The target was slowly raising what appeared to be an AK-47 rifle.

The North Korean commando was in a tough spot and he knew it. He never should have allowed himself to be seen by the men manning the barrier fence. Now he was almost trapped, but not quite. If he could open up on the flank of the American skirmish line and kill a few Americans he could perhaps cause enough panic and fear to make a break for the woods 150 meters away. If he could make it to the woods anything was possible. The advancing line was now almost parallel to him. It was time to do or die. He began raising his assault rifle.

PFC Juan Martinez was on the right end of the skirmish line. Martinez was freshly graduated from infantry AIT at Ft. Benning and had been in the Republic of Korea a grand total of thirteen days. This was the first time the eighteen year old had ever been put into a hostile fire position and he was understandably nervous about it. The selector switch on his M-16 had been flipped to automatic. If there was the slightest movement around him Martinez planned to hose down everything in sight. The adrenaline pumped furiously through his body, sharpening his eyesight, and making him fully aware of the scenario unfolding around him. It was a confirmed sighting. The UI had to be close, but where?

A thousand yards away, Clay Holloway was the only person on the face of the earth that could see both Juan Martinez and the North Korean soldier who had just put the rifle to his shoulder. Quickly Holloway sucked in a breath and held it as he squeezed the trigger slowly. Deep in concentration, he didn't really hear Fortunato at the base of the tree.

"77, this is Golf Papa 1, I say again...."

"Ka-pow!" The rifle recoiled against Holloway's shoulder.

It took a full second for the report of the rifle to reach the area of the patrol. Not that it mattered. None of the soldiers, whose ears were ringing from the continuing sounds of firing their own weapons, heard it. Holloway looked through his scope. The UI hadn't moved. It was though he had never fired. Shit! The reaction force was less than forty yards. Again Holloway sighted. Squeeze slowly! Concentrate! "Ka-pow! Ka-pow!

He had aimed at the head, but suddenly, following Holloway's third shot the UI grabbed sharply at his left calf. The UI lurched violently as the .30-06 bullet tore through flesh and muscle. PFC Juan Martinez on the far right flank of the skirmish line saw the movement and reacted instantly, spinning, yelling, and firing fully automatic with his M-16 from the hip until the weapon was empty. Then he dropped to his knees to reload. It was not necessary.

"We got him! We got him! I think I hit the guy and the grunts finished him," Holloway yelled as though he was at the football game he had fantasized about. His heart was pounding. The adrenaline rush had brought him to an excitement level he had rarely experienced. Simultaneously, he felt elation and anguish. He'd done what he had to. He'd done his job. But oh God, why did that guy have to be there? What the hell was he trying to do? Why did he have to put all of them into that position in the first place? He didn't have time to ponder long.

"Lieutenant Holloway we got another UI spotted in front of the hill on the dirt road. Request permission to shoot!" the E-5 was frantically calling up to the perch in the tree.

"What! In front of the hill? Show me!" He scrambled to swing his left leg over the branch and then drop to the ground. "Are you sure it's a UI?"

"Puller says it is. He's got the guy in his sights. I told him not to shoot until you cleared it. Do we have permission to fire?" the E-5 asked again.

"Show me!"

Holloway sprinted for the trench line, wondering as he ran if he was going to have to do the whole thing over again. The young E-5 was just in front of him with Fortunato and the heavy radio a few yards further back. The E-5 led the way down to position #3, the lowest bunker on the hill. There was Puller standing on the firing platform in the trench, his M-16 to his shoulder and his right eye squinting through the open sights.

"Permission to fire, Sir!"

"Where is he?" Holloway asked as he slid to a halt.

"There! Right below me on the road. See 'em?"

The figure was carrying a rifle, walking slowly up the middle of the dirt road at the bottom of the hill as though he had not a care in the world. The silhouette looked familiar. So did the rifle. Holloway brought the binoculars to his face. Clearly the man on the road was an **American** soldier carrying an M-16! There were approximately another ten or twelve men walking almost abreast, spread wide to either side. There were ten meters of distance between each of them. The undergrowth helped to conceal much of the patrol. Only the man on the road stood out clearly.

"Permission to fire?" Puller asked again.

"Negative," hissed Holloway. "That's a GI! Can't you tell his uniform and his rifle? It's one of our patrols sweeping the area. Put that rifle down!"

Puller and the E-5 stared again at the figure, now only a hundred yards below. "Patrol! Oh, shit! I didn't even see those other guys. I was just lookin' at the one on the road. I'm sorry." Clearly the man was embarrassed. He had come within an eyelash of killing one of his own men. Possibly he came from Puller's own Company. Holloway wondered if anyone would ever tell the man on the road how close he had come to dying. There had been previous incidents of patrols shooting at each other. The week before a patrol and a Guard Post had engaged in a major fire fight until cooler heads prevailed and the shooting was halted. This time they had been lucky.

"You people stay in the trenches. Cover the patrol, just in case. I'm going back to the front of the hill." Still carrying the rifle and binoculars, Holloway trotted back to his tree. Fortunato once again followed along obediently with the radio. Holloway reestablished his former position and turned his gaze downward.

The reaction force had carried the body of the UI to one of the APC's and lifted it like a sack of corn onto the top. Apparently satisfied that there were no more UI's in the area, they climbed back into their armored vehicles and lumbered back toward the barrier fence gate. Holloway scanned the area below one last time with his binoculars and climbed down from the tree. His muscles were trembling slightly and he felt a tightness in his chest.

"Congratulations, Sir," Fortunato said.

Holloway looked at him quizzically. "What do you mean?"

"You got him. You said you got him. That was a hell of a shot, you know."

His face was expressionless. "Yeah. I guess it was, wasn't it? A hell of a shot," he replied flatly. A few seconds went by. "Fortunato, I want you to unload the M-1. Then clean it good and put it back in the rack. I need to report to the TOC on the field phone." Holloway walked slowly toward the CP.

Sergeant Major Emerson McKee arrived almost two hours later with the evening chow truck. He'd already been to the TOC and gotten all of the information he could. Holloway was in his bunker drinking warm 7-Up from a can when the Sergeant Major approached.

"Lieutenant Holloway, is it true? Did you hit that UI from here with a rifle?"

"I believe so Sergeant Major. It was my third shot and I'm pretty sure I hit him in the leg. You told me that scope was zeroed for 1,000. I guess you were right."

"I zeroed it myself about two weeks before you first got here. I knew the sight was good. Still, I must say that borders on incredible. Are you a hunter?"

"No. I've never done much hunting really. I've always like to shoot though. I've always had a knack for it. But let's be honest here. That shot was mostly luck. I was aiming for his head and if I actually did hit him it was in the lower leg, so how good of a shot was it really. It was just lucky. Good luck for the strike force and bad luck for the UI."

"Well everybody is talking about it back at Camp Greaves. They're calling the kid who actually killed him "Quick Draw McGraw." And Lieutenant Hoover over on GP Cindy told the TOC that your friends call you Bagger, so now people are going around saying Bagger bagged another one."

"Oh good Christ. I got that name in a poker game. It sounds like I'm some kind of professional assassin or something."

"Maybe you are, Lieutenant Holloway. Maybe sometimes we all are. You're just starting your military career. Mine is coming rapidly to a close. Sometimes looking back on all of it I get some very mixed feelings. Just like what I think you're going through right now. You did what you had to do today. What they pay us for. But because of the way things turned out today, there is a lot of nineteen and twenty year old kids walking around with a lot of bravado who like talking tough, telling stories, and hanging nicknames on people. It's part of soldiering. Don't bother fighting it. That's just the way it is."

Holloway nodded. He understood what the senior NCO was saying. It was true. He knew that. No Americans had died that day and that was the most satisfying aspect of the entire event for Holloway. He had concluded that he was glad he had hit the UI. But secretly, in a way that he planned to tell no one, he was even gladder that it was the young infantryman who had actually killed him.

The next morning Holloway filled his metal canteen cup almost to the brim with the steaming hot coffee that the morning chow truck had brought a half hour earlier. He added some cream and sugar and stirred the mixture with a metal spoon that he kept in his shirt pocket. Carrying the cup and sniffing the coffee's aroma, he walked carefully through the trench line to his bunker. Ten minutes earlier he had finished a large breakfast. There was plenty of coffee left over and he had decided to just fill his cup and have lots to carry him well into the morning. If it got too cold he would just light a heating tablet to quickly warm the cup and its contents.

Reaching the bunker, he set the metal cup on the concrete ledge of the observation port. He stretched leisurely and prepared to set up the BC scope, which he had gotten out of the infantry's way the night before. Once the tripod was secure on the wooden floor, he leveled the instrument's bubbles and oriented its direction. Even at that early hour, he felt sure the day would be another hot one.

In the distance came far off rumblings. The sound was of trampling, of many many footsteps moving quickly, dust swirling in the midst and behind the masses of running men and lumbering vehicles. Orders were shouted, whistles blew, columns of soldiers veered to their right and to their left, filling trenches previously leisurely dug by antique steam shovels. The men belonged to the 245th Division of the North Korean Peoples Army. They wore shiny saucer shaped helmets and carried rifles with fixed bayonets. Other small groups of men moving together bore the separate parts of a variety of crew served weapons. Machine guns with tripods and many thousand of rounds of belt-fed ammunition, rocket launchers, and mortars were moved into their pre-designated positions.

The sound waves of the massive movement crossed the 2500 meters of lush green terrain between the most forward of the trenches and the hill mass on the southern side of the MDL called GP Gwen. The twenty or so infantrymen who occupied Gwen were mostly inside of the hill in their sleeping bunker or on duty in the Command Post and were unable to hear anything out of the ordinary. Like Holloway, they too had recently finished breakfast, having been on duty all night, and were preparing to sleep in their cool dark bunker for most of the hot sunny day. The noises did reach Second Lieutenant Clay Holloway who, having just oriented his BC scope on the tree furthest to the left side of the top of Speaker Hill, was about to begin a full visual sweep of his observation area, which was his practice to do first thing in the morning.

Normally the sweep began at his far left where he could see the Imjin and the Han Rivers join and end at his far right where he could see the backside of GP Cindy and just a small sliver of terrain to its right and a glimpse of Panmunjom far in the distance. With the advent of the sound waves, however, Holloway aligned his BC scope to look straight across from his position #4 where he could see dust clouds rising from the area where he had first observed a steam shovel on the day of his arrival.

As he focused his eyepiece he squinted and blinked hard. What in the world was all of that movement and dust? There were men moving forward. Armed men. Lots of them. How many? He scanned left. More men. As far as he could see there were more men, not only to the left, but to the right as well. The trenches were being filled with armed combat troops!!! What the hell was going on??? Suddenly the heretofore quiet speakers of Speaker Hill erupted in sound. Patriotic music blared loudly over the speakers. The volume increased until Holloway could actually feel the sound waves on his face. Were they going to attack? Are they attacking right now? Holloway grabbed the field phone and called the CP.

"Sergeant Major, come out here quick. We've got problems. You've got to see this!" Holloway yelled into the mouthpiece.

He was already hanging up the phone before the initial noticeable signs of fear began gnawing at him. First appeared the tightening in the chest, making it difficult for the young officer to breathe. Next came a similar constriction in the throat, almost as though he were gagging. His palms grew instantly sweaty, yet his mouth was bone dry. His mind bordered on panic. Were they coming? Was it because they had killed one UI the day before? What should he do? Should he run? Where to? Fighting the panic he managed to regain control of his thoughts, though not necessarily of his body.

Sergeant Major McKee walked briskly down the trench line. "What is it, Sir?" he asked.

Holloway could only point and rasp "Look!"

Raising the binoculars that he often wore around his neck, the Sergeant Major pointed them in the direction where the Forward Observer had pointed. "Good Lord," he whispered softly. "I have never seen anything like this before. I've got to call the TOC. You better get your artillery ready, Lieutenant Holloway. I'll be back." He walked out of the small bunker and headed back up the trench.

Picking up the microphone of the remote set that was connected by wire to the artillery radio inside the CP, Holloway attempted to request a fire mission. He was unsuccessful. Speaking was not something that his throat was prepared to do. His hands were trembling noticeably. He could depress the push-to-talk button on the microphone but when he attempted to give the call sign the words caught in his throat. He set the microphone down and reached inside of his shirt pocket for a package of cigarettes. Taking one from the pack he aimed it in the general direction of his mouth and held it between his lips. Getting out the lighter took a moment longer. He steadied his right hand with his left as he flicked the wheel of the lighter with his thumb. He sucked the smoke deeply and let it out quickly. Another puff. "Niner Niner, this is Firebird, over," he said softly, practicing to himself. Thank God. He could talk!

"Ni Ni, Niner Niner, this if Firebird, fire mission, over!" he finally stammered into the handset.

"Firebird, this is Niner Niner, you should preface your mission with the words 'practice fire mission, do not load' over."

"Niner Niner, this is Firebird, I say again fire mission, this is not a practice fire mission, over," yelled Holloway.

The FDC crew lounging quietly in the Camp Wynne S-3 bunker sat up quickly looking at one another. "Is that Lieutenant Holloway? Is he serious? He's asking for an actual fire mission?" the horizontal chart operator asked the vertical chart operator. "Tell him to authenticate."

The fire direction center RTO pressed his push-to-talk button. "Firebird, this is Niner Niner, understand live fire mission. Request you authenticate Whiskey Zulu, over."

Opening the front of his shirt, Holloway grabbed the SOI/SSI he carried on the cord around his neck. His hands still trembled slightly as he fumbled through the pages until he found the right date. Then he searched across the matrix of letters until he found the correct response. "I authenticate November, November, over."

The RTO looked searchingly at the FDC Chief who was scanning a page identical to the one Holloway was perusing. The FDC Chief nodded in ascent.

"Firebird, this is Niner Niner, send your mission, over," the RTO called. Meanwhile the FDC chief was cranking the field phone that lead to Battalion HQ to let Major Gentile make the decision as to what to do next.

Holloway finished his call for fire. There was not much he could do now but wait. Spec/4 Klein hurried down the trench line carrying two rifles and Holloway's flak jacket. He handed the FO his M-14 and set his own rifle in the corner. Then he ran back to the ammo bunker to grab an alert box filled with ammunition and hand grenades and carry it to the position. When he returned, Sergeant Major McKee was helping to carry the heavy box, holding one of the strong rope handles that were attached to each end.

"I've called the TOC. The whole brigade is coming to a complete defensive alert. The reaction force has been activated and the entire Second and Seventh Divisions are on standby. This doesn't look good, Sir. In almost eleven months up here, I've never seen anything to compare to it. How many men do you estimate are over there?"

"Four, maybe five thousand that I can see," Holloway guessed.

"That's just the first wave. If this is for real, there's fifty thousand behind them that we can't see yet."

Son of a bitch! Holloway shook his head disbelievingly. How did he get into this predicament? Was he going to die sometime in the next few minutes on top of a hill in a country where he had just arrived, knew little about, and cared less? Was the Korean War starting all over again? Was he going to be the first American to die in it?

"What do you think, Sergeant Major?" Holloway asked nervously. "Are they going to come?"

"I don't know, Sir. I truly don't."

Holloway continued to scan the lines of North Korean troops with his binoculars. A moment later he lowered them. "You know, Sergeant Major, I don't think they are. If they were, the artillery would have started on us by now. And I don't see any armored formations over there either. They'd use armor if they were coming, don't you think?" he asked hopefully of the older warrior. Looking at his hands he realized they were shaking a lot less.

"You may be right. It's also almost nine o'clock. Countries don't normally start wars at nine o'clock. They usually attack at dawn when the opposition is still asleep and they have the whole day to push their advance. I think I agree with you. They're trying to scare us. Maybe see how we react."

Spec/4 Klein was anxiously looking back and forth at Holloway and the Sergeant Major, praying that they knew what they were talking about. He wanted them to be right awfully badly. Klein had a pregnant wife at home. The desire to see her again had never been stronger than at that moment.

A few miles south of the DMZ the Division was moving to a state of readiness. Artillery batteries were preparing to depart their compounds and journey to their designated field positions, infantry battalions were loading their vehicles as they planned to move into their prepared fortifications on the south bank of the Imjin, and armored elements were massing into units that would be set to counterattack heavily into enemy forces that breached the defenses south of the river. Fighter plane squadrons in Seoul and Pusan and Taegu were ready to take off with only a few seconds notice. Thus far no enemy aircraft had been reported airborne.

Exactly one hour after Clay Holloway had first noticed the dust and the sounds of the 245th Division moving forward, the soldiers of that unit climbed back out of their forward positions and returning to the locations from which they had come. A North Korean exercise for the purpose of intimidation. No more. No less. Immediately the messages flashed from the GP's in the DMZ to the Tactical Operations Centers, to Brigade HQ's, to Battalion HQ's to Company sized compounds as the alert ended as quickly and unexpectedly as it had begun. By noon it was business as usual, as though nothing had ever happened.

Clay Holloway reached inside of his sweaty fatigue shirt and scratched his damp chest. He felt exhilarated, as though the weight of the world had just been lifted from his shoulders. Death was not going to find him on the top of an unknown hill in the Korean DMZ that day after all. Eventually he noticed a somewhat noxious odor in his bunker. The Sergeant Major had departed a minute before and Klein was preparing to carry the ammo box back to the bunker. Klein had avoided looking at Holloway for the last several minutes. Finally Holloway noticed a large dark spot around the crotch of Klein's pants and it dawned on him what the odor was. Klein had pissed his pants.

Four of the Guard Post's compliment of troops sat in the little CP later that night reviewing the events of the last two days. Holloway was providing the Sergeant Major with the details of what had happened with the dead UI and the incident of the troops almost firing on their own men at the bottom of the hill. The RTO sat in front of his radio table listening to the conversation and the infantry E-5 added bits and pieces to the story. The conversation was interrupted by the sound of automatic weapons firing outside, but not far away. Sergeant Major McKee looked at Holloway as both men grabbed their web gear and weapons and moved toward the door. Halfway down the wooden steps they halted as the E-5 called to them.

"Sergeant Major, wait. Just got a call on the radio. There's a patrol in front of our hill. They're in trouble."

Reversing their descent the two men walked back to the CP. Whispered radio voices were coming out of the speaker. "We're split in half. There's UI's in between us. We can't move and we can't shoot without hitting each other, over."

Sergeant Oliver, the E-5, spoke. "It sounds like the patrol is right around the bottom of our hill. They split into two teams to set up a night ambush and now they think there's UI's in between them. The patrol leader's team fired at the UI's, but they're afraid they might have hit their other fire team."

"Did they radio the other fire team?" the Sergeant Major asked.

"Echo Two One, this is Golf Papa One, do you have radio contact with your other element, over?"

"This is Echo Two One, negative. They won't answer. Don't know what's wrong. Can't reach them," the voice whispered, sounding young and scared. "We need help ASAP. We can't move, over."

Holloway looked at Sergeant Major McKee. "What do you think? How about if I take two men and work my way down the hill and try to come up behind the missing element and see what's wrong. If there are UI's down there maybe we can flank 'em."

"It sounds like they can use some help. If you want to try, Lieutenant Holloway, go ahead. Take Sergeant Oliver here and pick up Coleman on the way out. He's in position #3. Take your time and be careful." He snatched a walkie-talkie from under his cot and handed it to Holloway. "Take this. Keep in contact."

The two men rolled down their sleeves and buttoned their shirt collars to hide their white skin. Oliver accepted a stick of camouflage paint from the Sergeant Major, wiped it around his face and handed it to the FO who did the same. Rifles, ammunition, grenades, and the radio were all they would take, although Holloway carried his .45 as well. Helmets were left behind. Each man would wear his olive drab baseball cap. Sergeant Major McKee accompanied them into the trench line as they stopped to pick up Coleman and explain the situation to him. Five minutes had elapsed since the request for help. Suddenly the sound of M-16's firing fully automatic below them shattered the still night air once more. They could see the gun flashes near the bottom of the hill.

"Let's go," Holloway ordered. "Single file behind me. No talking, quiet as you can be. We're going to take our time going down this hill. I'm more afraid of being shot by the good guys than anything else. Sergeant Major, call the patrol and tell them we're coming and we want to see some serious fire discipline. The last thing I need is to go home in a body bag and not even get a Purple Heart cause I got waxed by my own troops." With that the three men climbed slowly over the top of the trench and began slowly and quietly working their way through the darkness down the side of the hill toward the flatland a hundred and fifty meters below.

Much of the hillside was dirt, covered with loose stones and clumps of weeds. Holloway stayed in a narrow draw where the footing was not particularly good, but where they were shielded on both sides by the wall of the depression. He was aware that they were making some slight noises. He hoped whatever awaited them below was either friendly or did not hear them. Near the bottom he slowed the pace even more, determined not to make further noise. It had taken almost ten minutes to reach the bottom, but finally he sensed the ground below his feet was now level. The gun flashes he had seen earlier had come from an area to his right and about fifty meters away. He cupped his mouth and whispered into the walkie-talkie.

"Any word from the patrol, over."

"Negative!"

"We're down. Call them. Tell them we're near. Don't shoot, over."

"Wilco!"

The three crept quietly ahead, keeping a low profile, their senses alert. Suddenly, Holloway felt the presence of people near by. He motioned his two companions flat onto the ground and crawled forward noiselessly. There was someone close, very close. All of the shooting he had heard earlier had been M-16's, which made an entirely different sound than either the burp guns or the sharp crack that the AK-47's that most North Koreans carried. Holloway hoped he was among friends. He decided to take the chance. Seeking cover behind a tree, he cupped his hand to his mouth and whispered. "Americans!"

"Yes. Who is it?" a voice replied.

"Holloway. We're from the hill. Hold your fire. I'm coming in."

He crept forward. Fifteen feet later a hand reached out and touched his sleeve. "You're from the GP?" the voice belonging to the hand asked.

"Yeah. What's the problem? Why haven't you answered your radio? Is anybody hit?"

"We had noises close by. Somebody started shooting. Our radio got hit. It's all busted up. We got one guy hit in the arm and we don't know where anybody's at," the voice said.

"What happened to the noises?" Holloway asked.

"After we started shooting the second time, they stopped. We haven't heard a goddamn thing for fifteen minutes now, but we're not moving until daylight."

"Just sit tight a minute. I've got a walkie-talkie. I'm gonna call the GP and have them talk to your patrol." Holloway squeezed the rubber push to talk button. "Golf Papa One, this is Golf Papa One Alpha, over."

"Golf Papa One, go, over."

"One Alpha, I have contact with lost element. One slightly wounded. May have been friendly fire. Their radio is knocked out, that's the problem. Call the main element and tell them we're going to join up with them. Tell them don't shoot. Whatever else was down here seems to be gone, over."

"Golf Papa One, roger, stand by, out."

"How bad is your man's arm," Holloway asked the voice quietly.

"I think it's just a graze. He seems to be OK. It's too dark to see. Scared the shit out of him. One round hit his radio and another hit him. I don't know who the fuck was doing the shootin'. We just hit the deck and waited. Then there was some more movement out in front and that time I know it was our own patrol that fired."

Holloway's radio hissed. "One Alpha, this is Golf Papa One, over," the GP called. Holloway recognized the Sergeant Major's voice.

"One Alpha, over."

"We radioed Echo Two One and gave them the situation. They say come ahead. They'll check fire. They say move ahead on compass bearing of 285 and that should take you to them. The patrol leader wants to get things sorted out and consolidate their position, over."

"One Alpha, roger. We're moving now," Holloway replied. He turned to the soldier to whom he had been speaking in the pitch-blackness. "Sit tight. I've got two other men with me I need to get. Then we'll join up with the rest of your patrol."

Thirty minutes later Holloway and his two companions began their ascent up the steep grade of GP Gwen, moving up through the narrow draw and finally into the trench line. Sergeant Major McKee greeted them as they jumped down into the trench.

"Nice going. Come on into the CP where we can talk." He led the way inside the hill and up the few steps to the lighted room. "So what the hell happened? Did you figure it out?"

"I'll tell you what I think happened, Sergeant Major." Holloway had removed his web gear and baseball cap and was rubbing his sweaty scalp. "I think after the patrol split into two elements, they had some animals, probably those little saber toothed deer, wander right in between them. Somebody got itchy and the main part of the patrol opened up on the deer, hitting one of the men in the other element and knocking out his radio. Then everybody panicked because they couldn't talk to each other. The deer came back and the shooting started all over again. You can see how when it's that dark and you hear stuff it makes you real nervous. Especially after the UI two days ago and what looked like an all out attack yesterday. I think everybody is just real jumpy right now. They thought there were UI's all over the place, but I don't think anybody was ever there except them and some animals. Otherwise I think we'd have heard somebody shooting with something besides M-16's."

Sergeant Major McKee looked at him and nodded thoughtfully. The veteran infantryman liked Holloway. He thought the young officer probably had what it took to be a good combat leader, which was a sense of what the hell was going on and enough control over his fear to be able to take charge and do what needed to be done. The Sergeant Major knew Holloway had been scared yesterday during the alert, but hell, who wouldn't be when you're looking at five thousand armed enemy troops who look like they're about to eat you for breakfast. Even with all of his years of experience he had sucked in hard when he'd looked at all those armed North Korean soldiers across the way. Holloway had still done his job, even through all the anxiety. And he'd been outstanding the last couple of days, taking over in situations that were really the infantry's job, not that of an artillery forward observer. Those things were the key to being a soldier. McKee could see him growing and maturing right before his eyes. He hoped Holloway would stay in the Army. He was the kind of officer the Army needed. Sergeant Major McKee planned to have a long chat with Holloway before he retired, which was now less than a month away.

CHAPTER 12

Beth Kisha was smiling mischievously at Holloway as Miss Soh leaned over his shoulder and placed a frozen Daiquiri on the table in front of her. "Feefty cent, please," the waitress said, bowing slightly from the waist.

"Can we run a tab, Miss Soh?" Holloway asked politely.

"Ayeee-gooh! No tab. Meesta Yun say tab numba ten, no good. Meesta Yun say always get stuck for tab. Pay cash please!" Miss Soh replied. She was one of the smallest women Holloway had ever met. Her height could not have been more than four feet nine inches and Holloway was sure he could have touched the tips of his fingers if he had tried to put his two hands around her tiny waist. Miss Soh had incredibly beautiful long black hair, which hung straight and dangled well below her hips. She worked at the Officer's Club at Camp Wynne only on weekends.

"OK, fine. Then bring me a Miller's and keep whatever change is left." Holloway handed her a $1 MPC note. Miss Soh bowed again and walked hurriedly back toward the bar.

"So, Bagger, you're building up quite a reputation for yourself. I hear you're requesting a branch transfer to the infantry. Is that right?" Beth teased.

"Fat chance. It's too tough being a grunt," Holloway responded. "I'm just glad they let me off of that hill once in a while, so that I can take a day and come down here and visit all of you civilized people." He folded his arms and looked across the table at her. "Hey, listen, if I'm such a big celebrity, I'd think that you would consider running off with me to Bangkok or some such romantic place."

"Now, Bagger. Don't start again. I'm awfully glad to see you, but I couldn't possibly go with you because I've actually signed up for a week's trip to Singapore and Hong Kong starting next weekend. It's a great package. They offered it to all of the Doughnut Dollies and Sherry and I said yes. So once again I'm afraid I'll have to pass on your offer." She leaned forward and touched his hand. "How about a picnic tomorrow? Just you and me. I know a great spot."

"Tomorrow? No can do. I'm due back on the hill tomorrow after lunch. Shit!" He pounded the table top once with the side of his fist. "I miss you, damn it. I want to be alone with you again. How about tonight?" Holloway asked, his pulse quickening to the idea.

"Oh Sweetie, I can't. Rusty McMillan is escorting me to a party at Camp Howze tonight. I won't be back until late or I might even stay over."

"Rusty McMillan? You mean Colonel McMillan, Second Brigade Commander?" Holloway asked.

"Yes, I guess he is a Colonel. Kathy and I spent a day with some of his section on Wednesday. We had a great time and so did the troops. Rusty told us what a wonderful job we were doing over here and mentioned tonight's party and asked me to accompany him. I had no way of knowing you'd be able to slip back south for a day. See that's the whole problem. I'm not going to spend my last two months over here waiting for any one guy. I tried to tell you that."

"Yes, you did. You surely did," Holloway commented resignedly. Clearly this was the most one-sided romance he had ever attempted. If only the memory of them together wasn't so strong. He had continued to fantasize about her often. Those two nights had been magnificent. It was frustrating sitting and talking with her and smelling her perfume and wanting her and knowing that tonight she would be with "Rusty" and the next weekend she was flying to Hong Kong or some goddamn place and who knew who she'd meet there. Holloway decided that Beth Kisha was probably the most fiercely independent woman he had ever known. He had to quit torturing himself.

"Look, there's JD. Have you met yet?" Beth asked.

"Who the hell is JD?" Holloway answered, his mood turning sour. "Your date for Wednesday night?"

"No. Jennifer. She's Red Cross. I told you she was coming up from I Corps. She's wonderful. I'm going to ask her to join us." Beth waved to the tall slender brunette who had just walked through the swinging doors next to the bar. The girl smiled and waved back, her eyes sparkling. Holloway got to his feet as she approached.

"JD, this is Clay Holloway. His friends call him Bagger," Beth announced. "Clay, this is Jennifer, whose friends call her JD."

"OK," Holloway said. "I'll ask. What's JD stand for?"

"Jack Daniels, Bagger. On the rocks with a splash of coke, please."

Holloway laughed out loud. "Does that trick always work this well?"

"Only with second lieutenants," JD replied, her green eyes dancing.

"Hey, is this my imagination or does the Red Cross give all of you girls a class in self confidence, savoir faire, and how to win friends and influence people before they send you to this God forsaken place?"

"Of course they do." Beth answered. "And JD and I taught the course."

Holloway fell to his seat, his right hand holding his head in mock disgust. Now there were two of them. Both attractive, both witty, and both bubbling with self-confidence. "Well, hell. I've already bought a Daiquiri. I might as well throw in a Jack

Daniel's." Holloway raised his hand and waved to Miss Soh who walked quickly toward them. He looked at their new tablemate. "And JD is from…?"

"Near Pittsburgh. But I went to school at Kent State in Ohio, if you've ever heard of it," she responded. "I graduated in May."

"Wow. You don't let any grass grow under your feet, do you. How did you get over here so quickly?" Holloway asked.

"The Red Cross came to school recruiting. They wanted intelligent, witty, charming, attractive single young women who were interested in spending one year in helping to tame the savage beast. Oh yes, and the job candidates needed savoir faire as well." JD wrinkled her nose at Holloway. "I interviewed for the job. They offered and I said yes. That was last March. I had two weeks of orientation in DC one month after graduation. They told us how long our skirts had to be and how short our hair had to be and what to say and what not to say. Then they tested us for VD and asked if we wanted Vietnam or Korea. I said it didn't matter and the next thing I knew I was landing at Kimpo. Pretty easy, wasn't it?"

"Well, you make it sound that way. By the way, I'm from Cleveland and of course I've heard of Kent State. I grew up near there."

"Cool! Where did you go to school?"

"Whoa! Time out here you two," declared Beth giving the universal time out signal. "What is the hour?"

Holloway glanced quickly at his stainless steel Seiko with the luminous dial. "Almost six thirty, why?"

"Six thirty! Damn, Rusty is picking me up at 7:30 and I haven't even showered." She leaped to her feet, grabbing her purse from the table, and pushing away her half full Daiquiri glass.

"Well, shit! We can't be late for Rusty, now, can we?" noted Holloway cynically.

Beth arched an eyebrow at him. "Now, Bagger. Let's be nice," she cautioned pushing her vacated chair under the table.

Holloway gave Beth a tightlipped smile as she walked toward the door. Jennifer was studying him intently. Rather than meet her gaze, he looked down at the tabletop. "Do I detect a bit of jealousy here?" she asked softly.

Holloway folded his arms defensively. "It's a long story, but not a new one I suppose. Boy meets girl, boy flips over girl, and girl has twenty other guys interested in her, most of whom outrank the boy. Besides that, the girl is going home in two months and doesn't want to get serious anyway. That about summarizes it, I think." He looked up at JD, keeping his arms folded.

She reached her left hand forward, touched his bare forearm, and smiled at him. "I'm sorry. Sometimes it hurts to be in love."

"I never said I was in love with her. I've only known her a few weeks." He shook his head. "God! I can't believe I'm sitting here telling you this. I just met you. I don't even know your last name."

"It's Dodge. Jennifer Dodge. But please call me JD. All of my friends do."

Holloway gazed at her. Her hand still rested on his forearm. Emotionally, he felt immensely better than he had sixty seconds ago. Had JD accomplished that? He felt the warmth of her hand, but more than that he sensed her sincerity and realized at that instant that he had just found a new friend.

"If that's an invitation to be your friend, I accept" Holloway said honestly. He looked at her. She smiled sweetly in return.

By seven thirty Holloway was starting his third beer. He and JD had been talking steadily for the last sixty minutes. He was astounded how easily they conversed with one another. They had just met, really, and already he felt almost compelled to tell her every major event of his life. Holloway had no brothers or sisters. While not consciously choosing to do so, he had simply not shared many of the things that happened in his life with other people. He had rarely spoken to his parents about his emotions, even as a child. As an adult it was simply not something he wanted to change. But suddenly it was changing. Not intentionally, not even consciously, but it was changing. Here was someone that Clay Holloway thought he could probably sit and share thoughts with for the next solid week.

"Excuse me for just a moment, please. I've got to visit the head," Holloway said as he pushed back his chair and stood up. He walked toward the men's room located near one end of the bar. There were two men just pushing through the double doors. The men wore greenish gray flight suits and both had aviator style sun glasses perched on their noses. Holloway did a double take. The blond hair, the way he walked. It had to be.

"Todd Hardesty, as I live and breathe, what in theee hell are doing in my O Club?"

"Hey, what the fuck, over!!!" his friend greeted him.

"Hey, what the fuck, out!!!" Holloway replied in their mock radio chatter. The two men rushed toward each other grasping each other's extended hand. "What are you doing here on a Saturday night?"

"My pilot dragged me up here to see his girlfriend." Hardesty turned his head and put his arm around the other aviator. "Clay, meet Magic Maloney. I really hate to say it, but it's just barely possible that he is a slightly better pilot than I am."

Magic was tall and muscular. Holloway's initial reaction was that he looked more like an outside linebacker than a pilot. The flyer pulled off his sunglasses, shook hands with Holloway, and looked around the room as though searching for someone. Suddenly he smiled.

"Magic!"

Holloway turned at the sound of the voice behind him. JD was moving quickly toward the pilot, reaching him, and then kissing him quickly on the lips. "Hi! I was hoping you'd come."

"I said I would didn't I, Honey!"

A twinge of jealousy flashed through Holloway's body. Whoa, he thought. Get a hold of yourself here, son. This lady is clearly spoken for, you just met her, and you're already hung up on Beth, so why in God's name are you feeling jealous. Reluctantly, he repressed the feeling and looked back at his friend.

"Step up to the bar here, pal. What are you drinking?"

"Just Coke, I'm afraid. We parked our Huey out back of the barn. We can't be doing any drinking tonight. At least not until we fly back to our own field."

"Well, shit, fire, and fuck, son. What kind of a reunion is this? How long are you going to be here?"

"A couple of hours anyway. We ought to get back right around dark. So how have you been? What does Uncle Sam have you doing now?"

"I'm in the Z actually, Todd. Attached to the 1/9th. It's just luck that you ran into me here tonight. This is the first time I've been here in a week. I got off of GP Gwen two days ago and I go back up tomorrow."

"I've heard that place can get hairy once in a while. We flew a medevac mission up there three weeks ago. Took out two guys that tripped a couple of land mines."

Holloway's eyes widened. "Was that your chopper? I watched it take off after you picked up the casualties. That was my first day in the Z."

"That was us. Well, tell me about it. What's it like for you up there?"

Holloway's mouth had been primed by the beer and JD's manner. He talked easily with his friend relaying everything that had happened to him since the two had parted six weeks earlier. Todd Hardesty replied in kind. Before long Tom Courtney, who brought some interesting news, joined them.

"The Colonel told me there's another lieutenant on his way here from DivArty. Ought to get here tomorrow. They're supposed to send him right up to the Z. I guess he's going to be the FO on Carol."

"That sounds right," confirmed Holloway. They've been rotating a couple of recon sergeants and Sweeper over there off and on. We could use another guy."

Magic and JD had disappeared shortly after the helicopter pilot arrived. At nine thirty the two walked back through the door arm in arm, JD's face looking flushed.

"Todd, ole stick, unfortunately, the time has come to unass the area. I told Dad I'd have the jalopy home by ten," Magic announced.

"Well, all good things must come to an end, they say," replied Hardesty.

"That's what they say all right," added Jennifer Dodge hugging Magic. "But I wish they didn't. How about if I walk you to the helipad?"

"You'd have to walk all the way back by yourself in the dark. That's not a good idea," Magic stated emphatically.

"I'll go too. That way I can walk her back," added Holloway.

"Well, OK, then. Let's do it." The four of them walked out of the club and headed for the far south end of the compound where the helipad was located near the Charlie CP. Hardesty and Clay Holloway walked together in front, with Magic and JD walking slowly behind, their arms around each others waists.

A few minutes later Holloway and JD watched as the blinking lights of the helicopter disappeared to the south. Slowly they began strolling in the direction of the Officers' Club. Holloway broke the silence. "So why do they call him Magic?" He asked as they walked.

"As the story goes, he lost a helicopter."

"He crashed?"

"No, he didn't crash it. He just lost it. It disappeared. He's never told me the full story. I don't think he wants to spoil the legend. Anyway the story goes that he filed some incredibly creative paperwork to explain what happened. People asked him how he got out of this mess and he just shrugs his shoulders and says "magic!" And that's all he's ever said about the whole thing. Just magic! That's been his name ever since."

"And he's your steady guy?" Holloway asked, confirming the obvious.

"He sure is. We haven't known each other long, but I think he's just wonderful. He flew me from Kimpo up to I Corps on his way to Division Headquarters the day I arrived in country and that night he came back to see me and we've been seeing each other whenever we can ever since. He's going home in a couple more months though. That scares me. I don't know what will happen."

"It's not the best circumstances over here to build relationships, that's for sure," Holloway answered as the two of them turned the corner near the old BOQ heading for the club. "Hey, come on. Now that those two tea toddling chopper jocks are gone we can get down to some serious partying. You ought to be ready for another JD, JD. What do you say?"

"I say you're on, Bagger, but besides that, I feel like dancing. Do you dance?"

"Well, I've been known to on occasion. You know any Philly Dog?"

"Do I? Wait 'til I show you!" Jennifer grabbed his hand and together they ran the last fifty feet to the club door, laughing all the way.

*　　　　*　　　　*

Holloway was packing his waterproof duffel bag as it sat on his cot in the open BOQ room at Camp Greaves, north of the Imjin. Clinton Gash had deposited him two hours earlier and Holloway had the bag just about ready with fresh uniforms and underwear that his houseboy had waiting for him upon his arrival. In another five minutes he and Sweeper would go to lunch and then Ruminski was supposed to take them up to Gwen and Cindy, respectively. The sound of boot soles on the shiny red linoleum made Holloway look up.

"Hey, I've got good news and bad news, you two. We got us a new FO. He just rolled in this morning from DivArty," Ruminski announced with his usual stone like expression.

"Is that the good news or the bad news?" Holloway asked innocently.

"That's the good news. The bad news is that the son-of-a-bitch looks like a goddamn hippie."

"What's that mean? Is he droppin' acid and have hair down to his shoulders?" Sweeper wondered aloud.

Ruminski grunted. "The whole ride up here from Wynne he hardly spoke a word. I was trying to tell him what it's like on the Z and the whole time the motherfucker just sits in the back of the jeep with his shades on looking straight ahead like he's not even listening. When he's not wearing the sunglasses he wears these wire rimmed John Lennon glasses like the hippies wear. He just got here and he already needs a haircut. I'm surprised they let him on the plane with hair like that. He probably never got it cut the whole time he was on leave before he shipped out. He is one sorry assed looking officer, I'll tell you that."

The door behind Ruminski opened and a second lieutenant in rumpled fatigues walked in, a duffel bag mounted on his left shoulder and a rifle carried in his right hand. His hatless head was covered with long curly brown hair, which was accompanied by a scraggly brown mustache. His face and hands were deeply tanned. "Which bunk is mine?" the young man asked.

"Over there, butter bar," Ruminski retorted pointing to the empty bunk next to Holloway's. The man's head turned toward Ruminski, but his sunglass-shrouded eyes were unreadable. He took five steps and dropped the duffel on the bunk, watching it bounce softly on the mattress.

"How about lunch, Dave?" Sweeper asked Ruminski. "I'm starved and you know we won't be in time to eat on the GP."

"You guys go ahead. I ate at Wynne before we came up. We'll go up to the hills as soon as you finish. Bagger, I'm sending you up to GP Carol this time. I want each of you to become familiar with all of the GP's. I'm putting the FNG onto Gwen for the next four days," Ruminski announced. With that he turned on his heel and stalked out of the door.

"Was he talking about me? What's an FNG?" the new man asked.

"FNG means fucking new guy. That's you. What'd you do to piss Ruminski off this early in the day?" Holloway asked.

"I have not the vaguest idea. I've hardly said anything to him. But I'll tell you this. I have not been particularly pleased about the way I've been shuffled around this goddamn country so far and I am less than thrilled with the fact that I landed at

Kimpo yesterday morning, have had almost no sleep for three days, have not had an actual meal since I left Ft. Lewis, and am now on the way to a hill that people tell me is closer to North Korea than I think I care to be. My suitcases are down at Camp Wynne and are not even unpacked. I have been issued field gear in such a hurry that I don't even know if it fits. What the hell kind of a place is this?" Following his oration, the FNG removed his prescription sun glasses and placed them carefully into a hard shelled case after withdrawing the gold rimmed glasses that Ruminski had mentioned and placing them on the slender bridge of his nose.

"Let's start at the basics here, pal. What's your name?" Holloway asked half-heartedly. The last thing they needed was some half spoiled eastern Ivy League wise ass with a New England accent to start bitching about how things were not quite up to his standards.

"Stover. Kendall Stover. And you are...?"

"Holloway. This is Bob Hoover, but everybody calls him Sweeper."

The three men nodded, no one shaking hands. In fact, smiles had been noticeably absent since the new officer had come through the door. "Well, I believe that you'll have to wait for tonight if you want to catch up on your chanda, but we might be able to help you out on the hunger part. The infantry O Club is right next-door and we're just in time for lunch. I think the food there is pretty decent actually so I hope you enjoy it. You're welcome to join us," Holloway offered.

Stover seemed undecided. He looked at his duffel, which he had been unpacking on the bed and looked also at the door of the BOQ. Sweeper saw his dilemma and spoke first. "I can tell you real fast what to take up to the hill and what to leave," he noted. "We'll still have time to eat."

"I'm quite capable of making my own decisions here, Lieutenant Sweeper," Stover replied. "Yes, I will join you for lunch, thank you. What should I do with my weapon while we eat?"

"Ruminski's driver should be outside. We'll leave it with him. Let's go."

The three men exited the side door and after leaving Stover's M-14 with Corporal D'Antonio at the jeep, walked the short distance to the Club. The dining room was spacious and bright, with white linen table clothes covering bamboo tables for four. There were flower boxes serving as room dividers and potted flowering plants hanging from the ceiling. A Korean waiter was serving the officers seated at one of the other tables when the artillerymen entered. The three men selected a table in the corner. Soon the waiter approached.

"Annahasyeo, Lee. How about three of whatever is for lunch." Holloway requested.

"Neh!" the waiter replied, bowing and shuffling away.

"So, how did you get your commission," Sweeper asked, making another attempt at conversation.

"OCS. Graduated from Sill at month ago."

"Where'd you go to school?" Holloway further probed.

"U Conn," the officer replied.

"Damn! You went to school in Alaska?" Sweeper cried.

Stover looked at him dumbfounded for a moment. Then it dawned on him what Sweeper had heard. "Jesus Christ, no. First of all the Yukon isn't in Alaska, it's in Canada. And secondly I'm not talking about that Yukon. I'm talking about the University of Connecticut."

Sweeper's normally shiny red complexion had turned three shades darker. Holloway laughed out loud. "Damn, Sweeper. Your face is redder than a possum's ass at pokeberry time," Holloway exclaimed.

Even Kendall Stover was grinning widely. "What the hell does that mean?" he asked.

"I don't know. Tom Courtney says it all the time. Someday I'll have to ask him," Holloway laughed again. All three men were still grinning as Lee approached with three warm plates full of food. He place one in front of each of them, bowed, and walked away, returning a moment later with three glasses of iced tea.

Stover looked at his plate. "What exactly is this? It smells strange."

Holloway looked at Stover's plate. "Well, let's see. You've got strips of bulgogi, rice, and kimchi. A very traditional Korean meal."

"Look, I know I have to live in this country for the next thirteen months, but do I have to eat their food too?" Stover asked.

"No. They probably have some dried out hamburgers back there. But I think you'll like this. At least the meat and the rice. The kimchi takes some getting used to. If you like pickled fermented cabbage with a lot of spices in it you'll love it."

Holloway and Sweeper both selected chopsticks from the silverware setting next to their plates and began feeding themselves expertly. Kendall Stover watched them for a moment and then picked up his fork, determined not to embarrass himself on his first day. He found the strips of marinated meat with the sesame seeds much to his liking. He toyed with the kimchi. It most assuredly would take some getting used to, but it did have possibilities. Normally Kendall Stover liked spicy foods. Nevertheless, the kimchi was very unusual. He finished the rice and bulgogi and asked Lee for a second helping. Lee seemed rather pleased that the new officer enjoyed the special of the day. A few minutes later the door to the Club opened and Ruminski stood in the entrance looking around.

"On our way, Dave," Holloway called as he pushed back his bamboo chair. His two companions did the same. Climbing into the jeep five minutes later Holloway spoke to Stover. "Glad you liked the Korean food. It's always good to try new things."

"Except for the kimchi, I didn't consider it particularly new. Rice and beef is not all that unusual, although I must say the beef was quite tender," Stover replied.

"Well, see it really wasn't beef," Holloway noted as he squeezed into the back seat of the jeep with Stover and hung on to the sides as the vehicle headed down the hill toward the gate of the DMZ barrier fence.

"Of course it was," Stover countered. "What else could it have been?"

"Dog!" Holloway corrected.

"Oh, Jesus Christ!"

CHAPTER 13

Moving from right to left two thousand meters away, the dark gray/green Russian-made T-54 medium tank was in striking contrast to the tan dirt which covered the field over which it traveled. A long dust cloud trailed behind it, swirling and then hanging in midair. Holloway watched the action through his 10x50's as he sat cross-legged and shirtless on top of his observation bunker on GP Carol. Sweat trickled down his arms to his elbows, which rested on the insides of his knees, supporting the arms, which held his binoculars. Briefly he looked down and jotted the numbers painted on the turret into his pocket sized spiral notebook. The tank seemed to be chasing someone who had run into a copse of trees a moment earlier. There were four soldiers riding on top of the tank. As the treads of the tank suddenly stopped turning, bringing the heavy armored vehicle to an almost immediate stop, the four armed men leaped from the tank and ran into the woods where the lone individual had disappeared seconds earlier. The sound of gunfire carried over the two thousand meters of trees and brush and reached Holloway's ears seconds later. Holloway picked up the handset of his field telephone that was linked to the infantry TOC. Under the terms of the cease fire agreement tanks were not allowed near the DMZ. It was, of course, not the first time the cease-fire had been violated.

"This is Lieutenant Holloway on Carol. I'm reporting a North Korean T-54 tank north of the MDL. Grid coordinates follow: 36905780."

"Say again? You got a tank across from you?" the RTO said disbelievingly.

"Roger that."

There was a pause. "Lieutenant this is Major Sutton, the S-3. Are you telling us there is a North Korean T-54 tank two thousand meters away from your GP? Is that what you're saying?"

"That's affirmative, Sir. I just checked the manual. It is definitely a T-54. He was chasing someone and firing his machine guns. There was infantry riding on top. They just jumped off and ran after the guy they were chasing."

"Goddamnit, Lieutenant. They don't have any tanks over there. It's against the rules of the cease-fire and if they did have one we'd know about it. I think you must be lookin' at a fuckin' bulldozer or something."

Holloway held the binoculars in his left hand continuing to study the tank as he spoke calmly into the handset in his right. "Sir, I know what I see and I know what I'm talking about." It was at that moment that the tank turret swung forty-five degrees to its left and fired its cannon into a wooded area one hundred meters to the west. The flash of the gun followed by the sharp crack made Holloway jump. "Holy shit!" Holloway yelled. "Major, you know that bulldozer they got over there?"

"Yeah, what about it?"

"Well, the bulldozer just fired his main gun into the trees!"

"Shit! OK. I'll send a photo team up there as fast as I can. Standby and keep your eyes on it. If there really is a tank we need to know whatever we can find out about it. Have you seen the UI they were chasing?"

"Negative. Not since he ran into the trees. I haven't seen the other men again either. It may be someone trying to cross over to our side. We'll keep our eyes peeled," Holloway stated emphatically.

The tank had stopped moving. It sat motionless in the field for several minutes. Then it turned slightly left and began clanking ahead, in Holloway's direction. Recently promoted First Lieutenant Keith Hackworth put his hand on Holloway's shoulder.

"What do you think, Bagger? What's he up to now?"

"I'm not sure," Holloway replied evenly, his eyes not leaving the binoculars. "He's moving this way, but very slowly. Your S-3 told me he's sending up a photo team to check it out. At first he didn't believe me. He thinks I don't know a friggin' tank from a bulldozer. Hey, how are we fixed for anti-tank weapons on this place, just in case?"

"We've got about five LAW's and a 90mm. Shit, I hope it doesn't come to that. You keep your eyes on that guy. I don't like having a tank prowlin' around this close to us. We're in easy range of his main gun right now, you know."

It was Holloway's second day on GP Carol. The hill was not nearly as high as Gwen, his regular guard post, and it was decidedly closer to the MDL and the North Koreans. Holloway felt noticeably more exposed. The positive side of his new assignment was that he had developed a strong liking and a healthy respect for Hackworth, the newly appointed guard post commander. Since being promoted to first lieutenant, Hackworth was no longer in charge of the reaction force, but now alternated between GP commander and running ambush patrols in the Z.

Twenty minutes had passed since the tank had fired its main gun. Currently, the metal monster was sitting in a depression near where it had first appeared. Only the top of the turret was now visible to Holloway and if he had not seen it drive into the depression he never would have been able to determine that it was sitting there. Eventually Holloway became bored staring at the same spot and lowered his binoculars. Suddenly, he noticed movement in the trees only a couple of hundred meters from where he sat.

"Hacker, look!"

A figure glided through the sparse woods, weaving from side to side and heading directly towards Carol. Every soldier on the little GP had looked up at Holloway's alert and now watched spellbound, wondering who the man was and what in the world he was doing out there. He wore dark clothing, was bareheaded, and seemed to be carrying no weapons.

"Hold your fire, people. Keep sharp, but don't shoot. I don't know who the hell this guy is, but he sure as shit looks like he wants to pay us a social call."

"Lieutenant! They're shooting at him," one of the GI's called.

"Jesus, they are!" Hackworth muttered to no one in particular.

Other figures had appeared behind the running man and puffs of smoke were visible coming from their assault rifles. The crack of the firing was easily audible to the men on the GP.

"Let's cover him, Hacker," Holloway suggested hurriedly.

"Can't, man. He's still on their side of the line. We can't start shooting into North Korea unless they shoot at us. That's the rules of engagement. You know that. We don't even know who that cat is."

"Damn. Come on, man, run!"

The figure was closing the distance to the MDL rapidly. It was less than a hundred meters now. Then unexpectedly he went down, the GI's gasped in unison. Was he dead? No! He was back on his feet, stumbling forward, his movements wobbly.

"Is he hit, Hacker?"

"Don't know. I don't think so. Looks like he's out of gas, but he's almost to the MDL."

"Come on, man. Come on." Holloway bit his lip as he watched the drama unfolding in front of him.

"Get ready people. If he gets to that little yellow sign down there he's in our territory. If they shoot at him then, take those bastards out of the game." Hackworth picked up his M-16 and laid prone on top of the bunker, sighting toward the running man. The figure's knees began to buckle with almost every step. Seemingly he was moving sideways more than forward. His head tilted backward as he appeared to gasp for air. Then it was over. One of the pursuers had dropped to one knee, taken deliberate aim and fired a long burst at the back of the running man. The force of the slugs had virtually thrown him into a nearby sapling where the weight of his body doubled over the young tree, holding it down and surrealistically suspending his corpse above the ground. The man's arms hung vertically as he lay face down, his black hair dangling in his oriental face.

Clay Holloway studied the scene in horror through his binoculars. The man had been within fifty meters of the MDL when he died, only one hundred meters away from where Holloway and the ten man garrison of GP Carol stood watching, their faces straining and their mouths silent. Through his binoculars Holloway studied the details of the four North Korean soldiers as they moved cautiously toward the fallen man. Their faces and uniforms were sweat soaked. Chests heaved as they sucked air into their burning lungs. Cautiously, they glanced up at Carol, wondering if the men on the GP were going to begin shooting at them. Two of the armed men had lost their helmets during the chase, while the third had somehow retained his. The fourth man was an officer by the look of the insignias on his collar. He wore a soft cap with a red star centered on the front.

"Hey, yoboseyo, Joe Chink! I'm gonna make your sorry ass pay for that someday!" It was Hackworth, standing on the top of the bunker with his rifle and calling to the North Korean soldiers. "Yeah, you! Kiss my rosy red American ass, why don't ya."

Holloway watched as one of the soldiers started to unsling the rifle that he had hung over his shoulder. The officer motioned him to stop. The Koreans moved warily toward the corpse, watching the American GP. Finally they reached the dead man. Two of the soldiers took hold of his arms and tugged him off of the now broken sapling. Then they clutched his shirtsleeves and began dragging him back through the woods in the direction from which they had come. It was then that the officer turned his head back toward the GP and yelled something, then walked away.

"Someday, douche bag!" Hackworth called to him. Then he turned to his left and looked down into the trench line. "Hey, Dong," he called to the KATUSA. "What did that dip shit yell at me?"

"He say he come back tonight. Cut throat." Private Dong made a motion with one finger across the front of his neck.

"Yeah? Well I hope he tries it. I really do."

"Hacker, don't you think it was taking a chance yelling at him like that?" Holloway asked. "They might have started shooting."

Hackworth gave a tight-lipped smile and his blue eyes narrowed. "That's what I wanted them to do. I'd have dropped all four of them faster than they could blink if they'd fired one round in our direction. The officer would have been first."

The forward observer looked blankly at Hackworth for a moment realizing that he meant every word and then gazed back toward the woods. The North Koreans were out of sight now. He could see no trace that they had ever been there, though he thought there must be blood on the leaves and ground where the man had lain. Death could come so suddenly out there. One moment someone is alive and the next he is not. He wondered who the man had been. Why had he been escaping? What had he done? Was he married? How old was he? Holloway thought of the UI he had shot in the leg two weeks ago. Was the score even now? Was all of this some sort of macabre game where a superior being was casually looking down at them and jotting the score into his program? Holloway glanced upward for a long moment. Was he in the program too? Would he some day wind up in the scoring column?

*   *   *

It seemed to be half mist and half fog. Whatever it was, it made it damn hard to see anything. Clay Holloway sat inside of the sandbagged CP bunker peering out of the slit in the direction of North Korea. His eyes drooped. It was 0300. Lieutenant Hackworth had told him upon his arrival that the forward observer was expected to pull a two hour night radio watch on Carol. There were only ten infantrymen on the little hill compared to twenty on Gwen. There simply weren't enough warm bodies to do everything and even though Holloway was artillery he was needed to help out with some of the infantry chores. That had been OK. But now as he strained to see into the damp atmosphere he wished that Hackworth hadn't been so abrasive with the North Koreans that afternoon. What if they did intend to come back and slit their collective throats like they had threatened? If they could sneak noiselessly through the wire, he certainly wouldn't be able to see them until they were within twenty feet of the bunker. Holloway stared warily ahead and became aware of his own body odor for the first time. No wonder, he mused. He'd been sweating steadily for almost three days. He rubbed his hand through his closely cropped brown hair and wished he could take a shower, but that was still two days away.

At 1600 the previous afternoon the photo team had finally arrived to take pictures of the tank across the way. The turret had still been visible and the team had taken about ten shots of it through a variety of telephoto lenses. Then they had left. Holloway wondered what had happened to the tank after darkness had come. It was quite possible that the four North Koreans who had killed the running man had been the ones riding on the tank earlier. Maybe they had dragged the man all the way back to the armored vehicle and driven away. He guessed he'd never know and finally dismissed the subject from his mind.

The crickets chirped and the frogs croaked. An hour passed. His eyes felt like someone was lightly rubbing sandpaper across his eyeballs. It was time to wake up the staff sergeant huddled on the wooden cot in the corner. Holloway's shift was over. He could grab another two hours of sleep before dawn.

By 0900 the sun had burned off the remnants of the ground radiation fog. The chow truck had come and gone and Holloway took the last sip of coffee out of his canteen cup and set the cup on top of a sandbag. Reaching his arms above him he stretched and yawned and then looked toward the field in front of him. Suddenly, as if in slow motion, the ground erupted in a cloud of black smoke and dirt. A muffled "whomp" reached his ears almost immediately. The explosion had occurred less than fifty meters away to the east.

"Jesus Christ, they're shelling us," someone yelled.

"Tank! It's that tank. He's coming at us!" another soldier exclaimed loudly.

Hackworth bounded to the top of the bunker, with Holloway a step behind, his ever-present binoculars around his neck. "Where's the tank?" Hackworth yelled.

Silence.

"Did anyone see a tank? What did you see?"

"There was an explosion right over there," Holloway said pointing. "Wasn't big enough for artillery. Could have been a mortar round maybe." Sergeant Stone, the senior NCO on the hill, joined them on the bunker roof.

"Sergeant Stone, call the TOC. Tell them we think we have incoming. One round high explosive, origin unknown."

"Yes, Sir." Stone scrambled back down from the top and ducked through the opening into the CP.

Minutes passed silently. There had been one explosion and nothing more. The initial sense of alarm began to pass. Maybe it had been a stray round. Possibly even an errant round of friendly practice fire. "You know something, Hacker," Holloway said. "That had a real funny sound to it. It sure wasn't the high velocity whiz-bang sound that a tank cannon makes. It definitely was not artillery and it didn't sound like a mortar either. The sound was almost muffled. In fact, if I hadn't been looking right at the spot where it hit I'm not sure I could even have identified it as an explosion. But I know it was because of the dirt flying into the air and the black smoke."

"Well, maybe we ought to check out the shell crater. You artillery boys are supposed to know about shit like that. Sergeant Stone, you stay here, but give me three men. We're going over to where that round hit and take a look at the hole."

Clay Holloway climbed down from the bunker top and picked up his helmet and rifle. "I don't have anything to measure with. We really ought to measure the crater diameter and depth for our report." He paused. "Well, I guess I can step it off. If they want more information they'll have to send up a tape measure."

"We'll just do the best we can," Hackworth said. "Come on, let's go." The five men climbed up and over the trench wall and began walking down the little hillside and across the open field to northeast. The explosion had been about fifty meters inside the MDL as well as fifty meters to the eastern side of the GP. Cautiously they approached the disrupted earth. Hackworth was the first to reach the edge of the hole and look in.

"Son-of-a-bitch! Look how deep it is!"

"Hacker, this isn't a shell crater," Holloway cried. "Jesus Christ, look at this. It's a tunnel. The hole goes way down into a tunnel. The explosion came from inside the hole not outside!"

"Thorensen, go tell Sergeant Stone to call the TOC and tell them we got a tunnel out here. Get some flashlights and see if there's any rope and get back here ASAP." The man trotted hurriedly back toward the hill.

The smell of cordite was still strong and smoke continued to hang in the space below ground. Holloway peered into the haze. "Looks like about seven feet to the bottom. What are you planning on doing?"

"Hell, we're going to explore this thing. You can see what happened. This is the end of the tunnel. Somebody got careless and got way too close to the earth's surface and blew a hole right through the roof. Looks like they've been heading upwards on a real gentle slope for a long ways and they finally screwed up big time and broke right through. Do you believe this shit? They're making their way from North Korea right under the DMZ and supposed to come out somewhere behind the south barrier fence. No wonder these dudes keep getting south. I'll bet this isn't the only tunnel. They've probably got a couple of them already operational. This is how their agents are doing it. We're up here running patrols and guarding the fence while some of these muther hunchers are going right under us."

Thorensen returned with the rope and flashlights. "Any volunteers?" Hackworth asked. "I want someone to go down and follow it back just a little ways to see what it's like."

"Yes, Sir," said Thorensen, raising his hand. "I'll go down."

"All right then. Let's tie this rope around your waist. Take my .45 and a flashlight. I don't want you to go far. The zips have probably all run like hell, but I don't want you to take any chances."

Thorensen tied the knot and stuck the pistol into his belt. "Let's go, LT." He climbed over the edge of the hole and sunk slowly into the hazy darkness as the other two infantrymen lowered the rope. Soon he stood on a pile of loose dirt of the tunnel bottom.

"I can stand up easy, LT. Man, this is huge down here. It's probably six feet across and almost six feet high. There's a lot of footprints. They come right up to the hole. These guys must have just been here."

"Be careful, for Christ's sake. Wait a minute. We need somebody else down there. Robinson, give him cover. Take your rifle and drop down there too. Just stay right at the entrance here."

Not overly pleased with the idea, PFC Robinson nevertheless did as Hackworth had directed. Silently he dropped to the bottom to stand next to Thorensen. The first man then began moving warily ahead.

"Lieutenant, Hackworth!" It was Sergeant Stone walking hurriedly across the field. "They're sending engineers and a photo team up, but it'll probably be an hour before they get here. Battalion S-2 is leaving to come most scochie."

"That's OK. I still think we need to take a look at this thing now. Thorensen, what's going on down there?"

"I'm in about thirty feet," his voice echoed. "Just bare tunnel so far. I'm not sure...BLAM!!!" The force of the explosion ended Thorensen's words in mid sentence. PFC Robinson standing crouched at the bottom of the hole staggered backwards, but regained his footing. Smoke began pouring out of the mouth of the hole.

"Thorensen! Thorensen!" Hackworth yelled fearfully.

"I git him," cried Robinson lurching forward and grabbing the rope laying on the dirt floor. He braced his feet and began slowly pulling the rope hand over hand. Holloway was on his knees looking through the smoke and haze. He could see Robinson straining as he tugged, but clearly he was making good progress. Thorensen was being steadily dragged along the dirt floor toward the opening.

"Got him, Lieutenant," Robinson called. "Pull him up!"

The three men still above ground pulled frantically on the rope. Thorensen's limp body virtually flew through the short distance until it lay on the surface of the field. Hackworth pulled his sheath knife and sliced the rope in two. Then he dropped it back down to Robinson who was waiting with his rifle slung over his shoulder. In a moment he too was back above ground. Hackworth turned back toward Thorensen.

"He's alive," said Clay Holloway. "I've got a good pulse."

Hackworth looked at the prone figure. His face was darkened by smoke and dirt and he seemed to be coughing. There was blood trickling from both his ears. Hackworth stared at the man's unconscious face. "What happened, Bagger?" he said. "What the hell happened?"

*   *   *

The intelligence briefing had not been pleasant. Lieutenant Yoon Kim Lee of the North Korean Peoples' Army shook his head slowly as he left the little conference room one kilometer north of the DMZ. He fought back the feeling of utter exasperation that he felt. How could things have been this poorly handled? Heads were going to roll, that was for sure, but nothing was going to actually repair the damage that had occurred earlier that morning. On top of that it was the second major crisis in his sector in the last twenty-four hours. First there had been that ROK agent who had somehow penetrated security and learned not only that the tunnels existed, but the locations of two of them. He had come within a hairs breadth of escaping across the DMZ with that information. Only the determination of Lieutenant Ming and three of his men had ended that potential disaster.

But then something even worse happened. The idiocy of those cursed engineers to actually blow a hole through the earth's crust on the Number 9 tunnel was unbelievable. The tunnel had begun thirty feet underground! How in the name of his ancestors could they have possibly dug the tunnel with a vertical rise of almost twenty feet over a two thousand meter distance? Yoon's uncle had spent most of his life as a supervisor in the tungsten mines in his home province of Yanggang in the northeast part of North Korea. Yoon knew that an error of this magnitude in a tunnel like Number 9 was simply inexcusable. What was even more incredible was that the hole had actually opened up within a stone's throw of one of the American guard post hills. One of the engineers had climbed up to look out of the hole and had actually seen five American soldiers walking directly toward him. After that there had been no choice.

The tunnel had to be sealed immediately before any real investigation by the Americans or their South Korean lackeys could occur. Fortunately the idiot engineers who had blown open the hole were still in the tunnel and ready to set off another charge to seal it forever. That had been clear thinking, at least. Nevertheless, months of work had been for nothing and even worse the element of surprise was now gone forever. There was no question that the Americans and probably the ROK's would now heavily increase their patrolling and other security measures south of their barrier fence.

Of course Number 9 was not the only tunnel. There were two more under construction in his sector and others had already been finished in other parts of the 240 kilometer DMZ. But the closure of Number 9 would force him to alter his scheduled October incursion into South Korea. His routes would have to be reworked and perhaps even his objectives changed. Using tunnel Number 8 would now bring up him five kilometers east of where he had originally planned to be. That assumed that Number 8 was finished on time and that no more "accidents" interfered with the schedule. Yoon hoped not. He was getting very tired of bad luck, mistakes, and incompetence.

Suddenly Lieutenant Yoon's spirits brightened. The problem with the tunnel had done nothing to alter the plan for next week's ambush. It would be his first, though hopefully not his last. More than six weeks had passed since the machine-gunning of the American guard post. Already the Americans were becoming lazy and sloppy again. Twice in the last week individual vehicles had been observed traveling on roads without escort. Obviously it had been a mistake in July to try to ambush that American reinforcement column after the machine gunning had begun. Instead of trucks they had sent armored tracked vehicles. That was a violation of the cease-fire agreement and was not expected. The blame for the error lay in faulty intelligence. But that miscalculation would certainly not be repeated. Next week there would be no warning. Lull the Americans into a sense of complacency and then strike at them swiftly and completely without warning. That was the way to do it. That is the way he would do it.

*   *   *

"Bagger, I just heard from the TOC. Thorensen is going to be OK. Well, almost OK. He's got damage to both ear drums from the concussion and he'll probably suffer some permanent hearing loss, but they think that's the extent of it."

Holloway looked up from the canvas field cot where he was sitting. He had just completed reassembling his Model 1911 .45 caliber pistol that he had cleaned thoroughly. A thin film of gun oil had been left on the inside of the slide. Holloway worked the slide back and forth several times and began wiping off the excess oil with a rag. "That's great news, Hacker. Really great news. When he first came out of that hole I thought he was dead."

"I did too, man," Hackworth said. "He looked like a lot of guys I'd seen in Vietnam who'd been wasted. He was lucky. Maybe I shouldn't have sent him down there. I don't know. No way I saw that explosion coming that soon. I thought we'd have a little time before they did anything like that."

"Nobody's right all the time, Hacker. But the thing is, we're a lot better off now, knowing for sure that these tunnels exist."

"Yeah, I guess. It's not going to stop me from patrolling though. I know they still send people through the Zone. Did I tell you what happened last week with the dog?" Holloway shook his head. "Well," Hackworth continued, "it was my first night ambush patrol. First one in Korea, that is. I had a lot of them with the Cav. So anyway, we set up near a clearing about two hundred meters this side of the MDL. About 0300 we start getting movement sounds and I can hear the brush moving. I'm sure there's UI's close and I got my safety off and my troops are waiting for me to fire the first shot. So just as I think they're going to enter the kill zone they veer off to the side and wind up going to our rear. So nothing happens.

Two nights later I set up again in the same goddamn place. Same fuckin' thing happens. These douche bags veer away at the last minute just as I'm ready to dust 'em. But I realize this time that they got a friggin' dog with 'em. That's how they're doing it. The dog is sniffin' us out and tippin' 'em off.

Well, shit. My momma didn't raise no fools. That night I go to the mess hall and look up Sergeant Benoit, our mess sergeant. I talk him into giving me a five-pound can of pepper. So anyway, the next patrol I get permission from the S-3 to go back to exactly the same spot. He doesn't want to let me cause it's really not a good idea to keep going back to the same place, ya know, but I tell him I'll move to the other side of the clearing and finally he says OK.

So we chogi on out there and move into position like usual, only this time I got the pepper. So I move around all the likely avenues of approach just shakin' pepper all over the ground. I use up the whole five pounds. OK, so then we just sit back and wait. Sure as shit, around 0230 we hear 'em again. They're gettin' real close to the kill zone this time and all of a sudden the fuckin' dog starts sneezin'. I almost laughed. The dog sounded like he had hay fever, ya know. So this ole dog is snorting and sneezing and this time the dumb asses just keep walking. We can't see 'em clearly, but we can feel them close and so I hit my trigger. We all give them everything we got including two Claymores. There ain't anything moving, but I don't want anybody walking around until daylight. Seemed like that night was going to last forever, but anyway daylight finally comes and we move into the clearing. Blood everywhere and one body."

Holloway was wide eyed. "You got one of them?"

"Yeah, we got one of them. The goddamn dog is what we got. Poor bastard was all blown to hell. I'm pretty sure we got some of the dinks, too, but they never leave bodies if they can help it. So the only confirmed kill was 'Snoopy.'"

Holloway looked at Hackworth, his eyes searching the raw boned face. "Are you bullshitting me, Hacker?"

"Hell, no, I ain't bullshittin' you. I'll tell you what. You look me up when you're not on the GP and I'll take you out on an ambush patrol with me. What do ya say?"

"I don't know, Hacker. This GP is exciting enough for me. I don't know if I'm ready for ambush patrols."

"Come on, Bagger. They ain't bad. I'll take good care of you. What do you say? Maybe next week."

Holloway was noncommittal. "I'll let you know."

*   *   *

"I am Commander Lloyd Mark Bucher, Captain of the USS Pueblo belonging to the Pacific Fleet, US Navy, who was captured while carrying out espionage activities after intruding deep into the territorial waters of the Democratic People's Republic of Korea."

The volume was well above normal as Second Lieutenant Kendall Stover listened intently to the words blaring forth from Speaker Hill to his immediate front. It was the morning of his fourth day of his first tour on GP Gwen and he had heard the speakers twice before, but it had always been a variety of Korean music. This was the first broadcast he had heard in English. Still, with the volume at that level it tended to garble the words a bit, making it difficult to understand. Finally the confession ended and the music returned. Stover made a mental note to buy a tape recorder at the PX so that he could record some of the gibberish and send it home to Mary Lou, his wife. This current announcement was not gibberish, however. It sounded like the actual confession of the commanding officer of the ill-fated USS Pueblo that had been captured the year before by the North Koreans. After almost a year of imprisonment and torture, the commander and 82 man crew had been released nine months earlier. Sergeant Major McKee had told him that the exchange had occurred by way of the Bridge of No Return far to Stover's right in the Panmunjom area. He was aware that the House of Representatives Special Subcommittee on the USS Pueblo had begun its hearings a month earlier. Now as he listened to the confession he wondered if the voice were really that of Commander Bucher or not. Having never heard the Commander speak he had no way of knowing. But for the first time he realized that events of this sort were no longer just things that he read about or watched on network television. They were now part of his new life.

Stover wished that he had gotten off to a better start with the other officers. He sensed that they felt he was some kind of an Eastern jerk. Actually they hadn't seemed like bad guys, except maybe for that stone faced Ruminski. But goddamnit, how was he supposed to feel. In addition to the lousy way he'd been treated since he left Ft. Lewis, the worst thing was that he'd been married just before Thanksgiving, which was only a week before he started OCS. During the entire six months at Ft. Sill he had seen almost nothing of his bride. Finally, after graduation and commissioning, an all too short thirty-day leave that had been almost like heaven and now there was nothing ahead but thirteen months in this hellhole. God, the leave had been great. Most of it was spent on the beaches and bars of Cape Cod and Martha's Vineyard. His brother Bill had loaned him his twenty-four foot boat for the entire month and he and Mary Lou had made the most of it. Sometimes they'd just shut down the engine in the middle of Nantucket Sound and drift as they made love on the bow or down below, their bodies intertwined and undulating in synch with the rhythm of the gentle waves. The desperation that they both felt in knowing that he'd be leaving for more than a year had seemed to make every moment more intense and more precious. Once they'd even made love during a thunderstorm. The rain was pelting down as they headed the boat for cover at Nantucket and he had glanced over at Mary Lou. Her white tee shirt was soaked by the rain and her pink nipples seemed to be beckoning him through the transparency of the cotton. She'd pushed her wet light brown hair out of her eyes and looked back, wondering why he was leering at her like that. After only a moment's hesitation he'd turned off the key and kicked the anchor over the side as the forward momentum of the boat stopped. She stood there smiling at him as he pulled the wet shirt over her head and slid her bikini bottoms down her legs, leaving her naked in front of him. Her skin was covered with goose bumps. The line between her suntanned legs and the small white area covered by her suit made her seem even more sensual. He'd picked her up, sat her on the dash next to the wheel, spread her legs gently, and buried his face in her furry warmth. He could still recall the rolling of the thunder and the sounds of her sighs.

Slowly Kendall Stover realized the echoing of the thunder was too loud to be part of his daydream. He looked to the north. There was a solid line of blackness moving across the North Korean plains approaching from the range of mountains behind it. Stover felt the cool wind on his face and reveled in it. It was a welcome change from the heat of the last four days and it reminded him again of the storm on Nantucket. Transfixed by the black wall of water rushing towards him, he made no attempt to leave the bunker and seek cover inside the hill until it was too late. The water swept over the hill like a tidal wave, blasting through the observation slit that surrounded the bunker sides. Within moments he was drenched. It didn't matter. He stood in the bunker feeling the wind and rain continue to lash his face. He thought again of Mary Lou. He missed her so much. Thirty minutes later he turned and walked through the trench line and into the bunker complex. Water was swirling around his boots and cascading down the wooden steps like a torrent, carrying two little frogs with it. It occurred to him that whoever had designed the drainage for this place certainly had nothing to be proud of. As he reached the bottom he realized the floor of the sleeping bunker already had four inches of dirty odorous water on it and rising. He surmised that the drains must be clogged. Fortunately his duffel was on his second level bunk out of harm's way. The storm had awakened the sleeping infantrymen who were now sitting on their bunks and joking about their watery environment. Suddenly one Puerto Rican soldier on one side of the sleeping bunker called over to another.

"Hey, Rico! Raton!"

Rico rolled from his back to his side pulling his bayonet from its scabbard and spotted the big rodent swimming calmly by his ground level bunk. In one fluid motion Rico stabbed down into the rat, driving him down under the water and pinning him to the floor of the bunker. Blood swirled upward. Rico held the rat submerged for almost two minutes, the other men watching, some cheering or laughing. Two days earlier a man had awakened to find a rat chewing on his leg and since that time the rodents had been targeted for extinction. Finally Rico withdrew the blade and swirled it around in the water, cleaning it. The rat floated in front of Stover who watched the corpse impassively. Finally he turned and walked back up the steps. Being outside in the storm was not fun, but being inside with the rats, frogs, mosquitoes, dirty water, and crazy people seemed even less appealing.

Stover looked at his watch and noted the time. Thank God. Almost four o'clock. Ruminski was supposed to be there by five, right about the same time as the evening chow truck. Stover had been told that Ruminski would be picking up Holloway and Sweeper on their hills first and then coming to get him. They'd all been guaranteed at least two days off of the hills, maybe three. One of the nights they would spend down at Camp Wynne. Maybe then he would actually be able to unpack his clothes and get himself organized. In addition, he'd written three letters to Mary Lou and he wanted to get them mailed. As much as anything though he wanted to get a new start with his fellow officers. He'd heard there had been some excitement on GP Carol, something about a tunnel and a tank. Kendall Stover wanted to find out exactly what had happened and was also determined to change the image of a prick that he was sure he had unintentionally initiated.

The chow truck arrived at 1700 hours and Ruminski's element of two jeeps five minutes later. The first thing the liaison officer did when he reached to top of GP Gwen was walk over the chow truck and lay into the driver. Then he walked back to his jeep and sat in the seat with his arms folded as Stover threw his bag into the back seat and climbed in behind it.

"What'd you say to that guy, Lieutenant Ruminski?" Stover asked.

"I told him to get his shit together, that's what I told him. He knows it's SOP around here to not travel in the Z by himself. He was supposed to wait for our two jeeps at the gate. He left early. There's no reason for that bullshit. He just got in a hurry. I also told him to wait for the escort vehicle before he leaves." Ruminski turned around and looked at Stover. "How was your tour? Any problems?"

"Not really, no. It was pretty boring except for that storm we had earlier and listening to Speaker Hill. Give me the scoop on what happened on Carol with the tunnel and everything."

"We'll talk about that later," said Ruminski, dismissing the request. "I was glad to see you made all of your radio checks on time and called in some practice fire missions. You seemed to do fine. By the way, I want all three of you FO's to hang around Camp Greaves tonight, but you and Bagger can go down to Camp Wynne tomorrow night if you want to. Sweeper is going to stay up here and then he'll go down and spend Sunday night after you two get back. I don't like to let all of my officer FO's out of the area at the same time." His last few words were almost lost as D'Antonio popped the clutch and the jeep lurched forward, heading down the hill. Stover looked behind him for the first time and saw his two fellow FO's in the other jeep. He gave a cheery wave. They stood and gave stiff mock salutes in return. Yeah, Stover decided. They probably were pretty good guys.

*   *   *

"So that's about it," Clay Holloway declared to his three companions seated at the circular table in the Camp Greaves Officers' Club. "Thorensen had a concussion and a couple of ruptured ear drums. Our engineers tell us it probably happened when the zips were trying to seal the tunnel rather than it being a booby trap. He was lucky he was so far away from the explosion. But I'll tell you what. This tunnel shit is scary. I mean how many of them do you think they might have?" Clay Holloway asked of no one in particular.

"I found out one thing at Brigade this morning," said Ruminski. "The brass is going absolutely bat shit over this. It's always been a major question about how the North was getting so many commando teams into the South. Mostly Intelligence thought it was a combination of penetrating the ROK sector, boats along the coast, and an occasional one or two guys getting through or under the fence. But this puts a whole new light on everything. I mean if we assume that they have other tunnels like this they could be putting hundreds of agents into the South. If they actually want to plan a full-scale invasion they could throw a couple of battalions through tunnels that big. They'd come up behind the DMZ, behind Camp Greaves, behind everything this side of the river. Everything would be cut off. We'd go right down the fuckin' tubes along with everyone else. So you're right, Holloway. This is scary shit. And as you have already noted, the real question is, do they have more tunnels?" Ruminski surveyed the three FO's seated around the table. Each of them seemed intent on what he was saying.

"So what are they going to do about it?" Sweeper asked.

"Look for tunnels, that's what. I wouldn't be surprised to see engineers going over every square foot of this AO with sound detectors and God knows what else. I'm sure they'll tighten security. Maybe we'll set up more ambush patrols south of the fence too," Ruminski theorized. "You know, you gotta wonder where they're going to appear."

There were assorted nods of ascent. Holloway drained his beer glass, waved to the bartender, and made a circular motion with his finger indicating another round. Ruminski fired up a cigar and began blowing smoke rings at the ceiling as no one spoke. Each of them seemed lost in their individual thoughts, picturing Joe Chink popping up unexpectedly somewhere.

Suddenly Holloway's face brightened. "OK, OK, I got it." Let's see who can come up with the most bizarre place Joe Chink could come up through one of his tunnels? Winner drinks free the rest of the night."

"Holloway, you asshole. This is serious shit. This isn't a game!"

"Seems to me, Dave, that everything is a game to various degrees. Life is a game and in the end everybody loses when the clock runs out. But in the meantime, you need to lighten up. The only thing that makes this place bearable is keeping your sense of humor. Come on, let's go. What's the weirdest place anybody can picture Joe Chink coming up in one of his tunnels? Sweeper, you're first."

"Why am I first? Let Stover go first. He's the FNG."

"Now wait a minute," Stover protested. "That's why I should be last. I don't even know what's around here. The senior guy should be first."

"That's right. Dave, you're senior. You're first. You've got sixty seconds."

"Shit. OK, wait a minute."

Holloway sat there humming the theme music from the quiz show "Jeopardy" and looking at his watch. Finally Ruminski spoke.

"Behind the bar, that's it. We look over and there he is with his helmet and AK-47 standing up right next to Mr. Ling and pouring himself a draft beer."

"That's good, Dave. That's pretty good," Holloway said. "Sweeper, you're next."

Sweeper frowned and looked down at the table, furrowing his eyebrows. Then his blue eyes brightened. "At the guard shack at Freedom Bridge. We go driving up in a jeep and all of a sudden he comes up right in the guard shack on this side of the bridge and says 'hands up.'"

"Sweeper, that is disappointing. Really. I mean, I thought you could do better than that. It's OK, I guess, but that's about it," Holloway stated. "All right, it's my turn." Holloway paused briefly in thought, his forehead furrowed. "I got it. The chow line in the mess hall. Here we are walking through the chow line for breakfast with our little plastic trays and all of a sudden here's this Zip with an apron on and a spatula in his hand and covered with sod and dirt and he's got leaves falling in the home fries saying, "OK, GI, how you likee heggs. Ova easee, OK?"

Kendall Stover let out a cackle and tipped his chair backwards onto the rear two legs. Sweeper chuckled softly. "That's pretty good, Bagger. That's pretty good."

"I'm last, I guess," Kendall Stover observed. "And I am all ready to speak. No extra time is needed for "Final Jeopardy.""

"Well, go ahead then Lieutenant Stover. Give it your best shot."

"I think it's pretty obvious. Joe Chink comes up in the Officer's Latrine. It's a two hole wooden structure somewhere in the boonies and I'm sitting there with my pants down reading Sports Illustrated and all of a sudden this head pops up through the other hole right next to me. He's wearing a helmet and there's all this disgusting stuff all over it and dripping from the brim and down his nose and burning his eyes and he's having trouble breathing 'cause of the stench. So he opens his mouth to get a breath and I reach down and grab a grenade and shove it into his mouth and push him down into the muck. Then I still have my pants down to my knees, but I kind of hop outside and get far enough away so when the grenade goes off I'm OK, but the wooden latrine gets blown into little teensy tiny splinters and there's crapola flying all over the place and hanging from the trees and everything and that poor jerkoff needs a ton of dental work."

Stover paused and looked around. "OK, how was that?" He realized Sweeper was having trouble catching his breath. Picturing the revolting scene, Lieutenant Hoover had begun laughing and being unable to get the imagined scene out of his mind and having exhaled virtually all of the air in his lungs, now was unable to inhale. Finally he began to choke. Ruminski patted him on the back. Holloway had begun laughing heartily as well and looking at Hoover had made him laugh harder. Soon the group was nearing hysterics, laughing like schoolboys.

Finally Holloway was able to gasp. "I think you won, Kendall. I believe it's unanimous. That's not only the most bizarre, but also the most gross. Hey, by the way. Ruminski wants to know when you're going to get a haircut?"

Ruminski groaned and buried his head in his arms.

CHAPTER 14

"Hey, Stover. Wake your ass up. We've got things to do, people to see, and places to go."

Kendall Stover opened one lazy eye and looked up. Clay Holloway was standing over his bunk with only white towel around his waist and clogs on his feet. His chest and hair were still wet from his morning shower in the building next door. The open roomed BOQ at Camp Greaves had no toilet or shower facilities.

"What's your rush? Where are we going?"

"It's Saturday, man. First we're going over to the club for a full ride in the barbershop and then we're heading south. Maybe even a trip to the PX steambath at RC #1 near the Turkey Farm. Then we'll wind up back at Camp Wynne. You can put all your gear away in your room if one of the houseboys hasn't done it and we can get ready for the evenings activities that should consist of some good times at the bar and just maybe a little poker. So come on. Bali, bali, chop, chop."

Stover sat on the edge of his bed and yawned. "OK. Let me shit, shower, and shave and I'll be ready."

"Well, the first two are OK, but don't shave and don't shampoo your hair. That's part of the barbershop ritual. I'll go over there first and get started and make a reservation for you next. I told D'Antonio to meet us at eleven with the top down on the convertible. It's a beautiful sunny day and it's great to be alive, don't you think?" Holloway chided.

"If you say so, Bagger. If you say so. Now, get out of my way so I can get going."

An hour later Kendall Stover sat reclined in Miss Lee's barber chair with his face covered with lather and Miss Lee making swift exact strokes up his neck with an ivory handled straight razor. Stover had already reached the conclusion that at least half of all Koreans were named either Kim or Lee. Meanwhile, Clay Holloway stood nearby with his arms folded pretending to supervise the work.

"Miss Lee, make sure when you wipe off all the blood from his neck and start the haircut, that you give him whitewalls on the sides. He told me last night he doesn't want a hair on his head to be over a quarter of an inch in length. Oh yeah, and trim up that raggity assed looking mustache too."

"Aey-goo. No blood. No blood," Miss Lee said stepping back to get a more panoramic look at Stover's neck. Her voice conveyed real concern.

"Bagger, why don't you go somewhere and practice disarming booby traps or something? I'm sure Miss Lee and I are perfectly capable of accomplishing this mission ourselves."

"Very well, then. I'll leave for a little while, but I'll check back to make sure she puts enough of that green goop on your face for the mudpack facial. That's the best part. Then we shall unass the area."

Shortly after noon, the jeep carrying the two FO's passed through Munsan-ni, turned left at the first intersection, and approached Sonyru-ri. Kendall Stover reached forward from the back seat and tapped Holloway on the shoulder.

"Hey, Bagger! What do you say we get out at the edge of the ville and walk the rest of the way to Camp Wynne? I haven't had a chance to really see any of this metropolis."

"Fine idea. I haven't seen much of the ville myself. He turned to the driver. "D'Antonio, pull over after you pass RC #4 and let us out. Then drop our gear at the BOQ."

The two young men dismounted a moment later, slapped their caps against their legs to remove some of the road dust, and began walking leisurely along the dirt road in front of the buildings. A girl with heavy eye shadow and bright pink lipstick sat on a plastic covered kitchen chair with her bare legs spread widely and her wadded skirt dangling down between them.

"Yoboseyo, Lieutenant." The girl's index finger beckoned them. "I have good time for yuuu. Plenty good. Five dolla, can do."

Holloway looked at his companion. "What do you say, Stover? I think she likes you. Maybe you can get her for three bucks."

"Give me a break. That's all I need. To write home to Mary Lou and tell her, oh by the way I'm undergoing a series of penicillin injections for some unknown Asian disease."

Holloway snickered as the two continued to walk. Ahead a man came out of an alley and stopped as he spied the two officers. Holloway spoke first. "Annahashamika, Papasan."

"Annahashamika. You come. See movie. Numba one movie. Pretty girls. Numba one josans."

"You say you got a matinee for us to watch, Papasan? How about popcorn. You got any popcorn?"

"Neh! Popacorn tuuu!"

"Come on, Bagger. Let's go see it. It might give us some yucks."

"Are you serious? You want to see this old dude's movie?"

"Papasan, what kind of movie is it and where is it and how much?" Stover asked.

"Chogi," he said pointing to a nearby building. "Only 100 won. Popacorn tuuu. Numba one movie."

"Fine," Holloway answered dryly. "Let's see the movie."

The old man lead the two officers to the nearby building, up a flight of old wooden steps, and into a small room. He clapped his hands loudly and called to someone. Stover and Holloway glanced around the room growing increasingly suspicious. Maybe this wasn't such a good idea. The papasan motioned to an old couch that sat across from a second sofa in the middle of the room. He clapped his hands again. Before either of the men could seat themselves, three girls appeared. Stover looked at his companion.

"Goddamnit, Holloway. Now they're going to want us to party with these ugly looking broads."

"That's not my fault. You're the one that wanted to see the goddamned movie, not me."

The three girls were holding each other's hands and giggling shyly. They were clothed in short cotton party dresses that should have belonged to a twelve year old, though clearly they were about twice that age. One girl in yellow had large red rouge marks on her cheeks. She left the others and took Stover's hand and led him to one of the sofas.

"Bagger, help me out here. Sit next to me or something."

"What! You want me to sit next to you?"

"Yeah, so they can't flank me."

"OK, but this isn't gonna look right. What if they bring some other GI's in here and you and I are sitting next to each other on that couch. What the hell are they going to think?"

"Look, just sit here." Holloway did as he was asked. Another of the girls sat on his other side. The third tried to squeeze in between them. "Don't let her in, Holloway." Stover's voice sounded nervous.

"What's the matter, Stover? Haven't you ever been with a whore?"

"No. And I don't intend to start today either. Have you?"

"Not really, but something tells me they're going to start putting on the pressure." Holloway looked up. "Hey, Papasan. Where the hell's the movie?"

"OK. One hundred won. You pick. Have 'The Picnic.' Have 'Frenchee Farma Daughta.' And have 'Nights on a Round Table.'"

"Oh, let's see. We'll take the French Farmer's Daughter. I'm buying." He stood and handed the old man two one hundred won notes. The man scurried away. Stover looked down at the girl in the yellow dress who was peering into his open wallet. "Forget it, lady." he announced and sat back onto the couch. Immediately the girl sat back next to him and began stoking his bare forearm and making clicking sounds with her tongue. Tiring of his arm after a few moments she began to stoke his thigh. Stover had had enough. He grabbed her wrist and placed her hand onto her own lap.

"Bagger, how do you say 'no' in Korean?"

"Anneyo."

"OK. Anneyo, lady. I'm married. Anneyo," Stover said firmly.

Holloway sat watching the scene, a bemused look on his face. Newly married Lieutenant Stover was trying to be so good. Suddenly, the papasan appeared carrying a card table, which he set up near the end of the sofa. Again he left and returned a moment later with an 8mm Bell and Howell movie projector, which looked as though it had been manufactured sometime prior to the start of the Great Depression. The projector had the movie reel mounted and threaded and was ready for operation. At the other end of the small room was a white bed sheet that had been thumb tacked to the pink wall.

"Do you think this is in Cinemascope, Kendall?"

"I don't even think it's in color to tell you the truth."

It wasn't. As the black and white numbers began flickering across the screen, a woman who seemed to be the papasan's wife appeared with a large tray. On the tray was a bowl of dry looking popcorn and two Coca Colas. "Popcorn free. Cokeee 100 won."

Recalling advice he had received on the field training exercise with the 1/38th, Holloway warned Stover not to drink the Coke. The popcorn was cold and dry and stale. After stuffing some in his mouth, Holloway immediately regretted doing so and looked for a place to spit it out. Seeing none, he finally swallowed it. He looked to see if Stover had seen his reaction. He hadn't.

"Have some popcorn, Kendall. It's really good. Take a big handful," Holloway offered handing the bowl to his friend. Stover did as Holloway suggested. After a few bites he stopped chewing and looked at Holloway.

"You asshole! This is terrible." Holloway began laughing out loud. Then seeing the sickly look on Stover's face made Holloway laugh even harder. By this time the black and white porno movie had begun in earnest. The movie was quite obviously ancient. The appearance of the farmer was cause for additional laughter. His oversized overalls, straw hat, and flannel shirt were so obviously staged that they made him seem farcical. When his daughter appeared and blinked her eyes into the camera Holloway slouched on the couch in hysterics. Meanwhile, the third Korean prostitute who had not yet seemed like part of the party, spied her chance to get involved. As the girl in the black and white movie tugged off her white cotton blouse, the prostitute opened her own blouse, plopped herself clumsily onto Stover's lap, put her arm around his neck, and tried to nuzzle his ear. He'd had enough. Quickly he opened his legs, dropping the surprised girl through his lap and onto the floor with a thump. Caught completely unaware, she sat there momentarily stunned. Watching her fall to the floor, her two friends began giggling in high-pitched chortles. Holloway, already in a giddy mood, broke into a belly laugh, which he could not control. Papasan, meanwhile, was trying to figure out what had gone awry with his plan of renting at least two of the girls to the two lonely Americans. The shocked girl on the floor eventually regained her feet and rubbed her bruised derriere. Then she lifted her skirt, pointed her cheeks in Stover's face, and pulled her panties partially down to expose her reddened flesh. Stover began to laugh which seemed to anger the girl even more. She spoke rapidly to Stover in Korean and began waving her finger at him. Papasan tried to calm her. At that moment the film snapped and the bed sheet on the wall went white while the take-up spool on the projector spun wildly, flapping the broken celluloid loudly against the machine.

"That's it," Holloway announced as he stood up. "I know you want to stay for the second feature, but we're gonna blow this pop stand." Stover extricated himself from the arms of the girl seated next to him and also got to his feet. The papasan put out his hands.

"You stay. You stay. I fix. You want josan? She makee you feel numba one."

"Kamsamnida, Papasan. We cauda chogi," Holloway replied. Waving a cheery good-bye, Stover and Holloway backed out of the door, ran down the steps, and found their way back down the little alley to the street. Still chuckling, they looked at each other and laughed harder.

"Well, Stover, that had to be one of the more ridiculous things I have ever done. You have any better ideas for the afternoon?"

"Uhhh, I don't think so."

"Good."

A few minutes later, the two neared the end of the village. The gate to Camp Wynne was just beyond. At a one-story building that was the third from the last on the street, a woman worked with a homemade broom in front of her shop. Her black hair was pulled back tightly along the sides of her head and formed a bun in back. Her pockmarked face glistened with perspiration. Once a business girl, she had made the successful transition to business woman. Now she ran a sort of general store that was frequented by the men of Camp Wynne. As the two officers approached, Proud Mary looked up and smiled, showing two rows of perfect teeth.

"Annahashamika, Lieutenant Holloway."

"Annahasyeo, Mary. How are you doing?"

"Numba one. What I get for you today?"

"Well, to tell you the truth, I'd kind of like to find a black leather shoulder holster for my .45. You think you can find one of those?"

"OK, can chana. Two days I have for you."

"Two days, maybe I won't be here. If you can have it tomorrow, it would be better."

Mary shrugged. "Moola. I try."

"OK. If I don't get it tomorrow, just hold on to it when you do get it and I'll be back sometime. Hey, this is Lieutenant Stover. He just got off the plane."

"Annahashamika, Lieutenant Stover. What I get for you?"

"Oh, nothing, thanks, Mary. But I'll keep you in mind."

The soldiers said good-bye and moved away from in front of the shop. Proud Mary returned to her sweeping. "Bagger, why don't you just order the holster through the supply system?" Stover asked.

"Because I wouldn't be able to get it. I'm not really authorized to have a shoulder holster. I just want one. Even if I could order one through channels it would probably take forever for it to come into the supply room. Sergeant Carlton told me I'm a lot better off to just see Mary for something like that. He also told me I can order anything from a sleeping bag to a jeep from her. She's like the local Sears catalog store. You name it. She'll get it. Most of it is black market. The government sends it over here. The Koreans steal it and then sell it back to the GI's. That's the way the system works."

They had reached the main gate and walked over the bridge and down the other side toward the BOQ. Once inside the door the two split up and went to their separate rooms. Holloway unlocked the padlock that secured his door and walked in. The familiar musty smell greeted him. Pushing the door closed behind him, he pulled off his fatigues and clad only in his under shorts pulled out the desk chair and sat in it. He tugged open the desk drawer and searched for some stationary and a pen. Absentmindedly, he began scratching his crotch as he peered into the drawer. Scratching his pubic area was something he'd seemed to be doing a lot lately. As this occurred to him, he finally stood up, dropped his drawers, and began probing around in his crotch. Shocked, he noticed a quick flurry of movement in the mat of hair. There seemed to be some sort of parasitic guests sharing his body.

"Oh, shit," he muttered. "What the hell is that?" Resignedly he pulled his fatigues back on, left the BOQ, and headed for the dispensary.

"In the parlance of the GI, you have crabs," Doc Kramer announced fifteen minutes later. "Body lice, it is more properly termed."

"What! I've never slept with any of these business girls. How the hell could I get crabs?"

"Probably in the field or on that Guard Post resort you like to frequent. It's not uncommon. You'll probably get fleas while you're up there too. Here's some powder that will get rid of them, but first I want you to take a nice hot bath to try and drown the little bastards."

"Where am I gonna find a bathtub on this compound?"

"Go to the BOQ and walk into the latrine and look around closely. You will find what you need I assure you," Doc Kramer answered. After receiving further instructions, Holloway left the dispensary mystified and trudged back to the BOQ. He knew damn well there was no bathtub in the BOQ. Walking into the latrine, he looked about. Just as the Battalion Surgeon had stated, Holloway found what he needed. A large maintenance sink used by the houseboys to fill the mopping buckets and sometimes do laundry was mounted in the corner. It would have to do. He turned on the hot water, ran back to his room, stripped naked and ran back to the sink. It was only half full. Quickly he turned on one of the showers, jumped in, and shampooed his hair thoroughly. Leaving a ring of soapsuds around his neck, he left the shower and climbed into the now full washbasin. It was a tight fit for someone of his height, but he wedged himself in and waited.

Within a minute, Tom Courtney appeared in the latrine. "Hey, Holloway. You don't want to miss dinner tonight at the club. They're serving steamed crabs."

Holloway stared disbelievingly at his battery commander. What the hell had ever happened to the privacy of a doctor patient relationship? "Is that right, Tom? Thanks for the bulletin," he responded testily.

Eric Auslander walked in behind Courtney and joined in the fun. "What are you getting so crabby about, Holloway?"

Clay Holloway rolled his eyes. Obviously Doc Kramer had called everyone he could find. Bill Grant walked in a moment later with a Kodak Instamatic and began flashing pictures as Courtney hovered over Holloway with his arms raised and spread like a giant insect monster. Then he began making screeching sounds.

"This is great, guys. You've all had your fun. Now will someone help me out of this damned sink? I think I'm stuck." The latrine now contained almost every officer on the compound. As Courtney and Auslander pulled Holloway free and he stood up, Grant flashed one more picture of his reddened naked wet body.

Grant winked at him. "Someday when you're married, Holloway, I'm gonna send it to your bride for her scrapbook."

*   *   *

The poker game had been underway since three o'clock that afternoon. Tom Courtney snuffed out his cigarette into the overflowing ashtray and picked up the five cards that had just been dealt to him. Three queens, he mused. Ought to be able to open with that. He looked around the table and waited for his turn. The FNG was sitting right across from him fanning his cards slowly in front of his face. Kendall Stover was his name. Holloway had said he was a pretty good guy, but Courtney hadn't yet decided. Anyway, what the hell kind of a name was Kendall. Tom had called him Ken, initially, but Stover had corrected him. Well, maybe he'd just call him Stover. He sure as hell wasn't going to call him Kendall.

The table checked around to Courtney. That gave him confidence that the three queens had a good chance of winning the hand. He decided to open for the minimum so as not to scare anybody out of the pot. The strategy worked. No one folded and no one topped his hand. He'd been winning most of the day. Maybe it was time to get out before his luck changed. He reached his hands forward and raked in the pot, glancing again over at Stover who was lighting a cigarette that he had withdrawn from a silver cigarette case.

"Hey, Stover. You got a cigarette holder by any chance?"

"A cigarette holder? No. Why?"

"Well, I was just wonderin'. Tell you the truth I ain't never seen anybody else around here with a cigarette case and I just thought you might have a holder to go with it. Are you sure you're in the right army?"

"Well, yeah. The last time I checked I was," Stover replied dryly.

"No. Seriously. I'm sittin' here lookin' at you with your hair and your little brown mustache all nicely trimmed and your little round glasses with no rims and now you pull out a gol damn cigarette case. I swear you look like a Kraut officer from World War I or somethin'. Like the Red Baron or one of those guys." There were a few chuckles around the table.

"Well, Tom, why don't you push your cards over to the Red Baron so he can add them to the deck. It makes for a better game when all fifty two of them are used," said Clay Holloway pointing to the five cards buried in the middle of Courtney's latest winnings.

Courtney smiled and complied with the request. Then he announced that once more around the table was enough for him. He was going to saddle up to the bar and socialize for a while. They'd been playing cards for five hours straight.

When the game disintegrated fifteen minutes later, Clay Holloway pushed back his chair on the linoleum and looked around. The swinging doors burst open and three of the Doughnut Dollies walked briskly in. Jennifer Dodge was in the lead. Spying him in the corner she waved happily and moved quickly toward him.

"Hi, Bagger. I heard you were down from the hill. How long will you be here?" she asked, her green eyes dancing.

"Just tonight, I'm afraid. Ruminski really likes us to stay around Camp Greaves when we're not on the hill. Technically we're attached to the 1/9th and we're supposed to be with them," Holloway replied. "How have you been?"

"Great. Really wonderful. I like it here. I've gotten along well with the troops during the week and all of the girls have been great and Magic is coming in tonight. Have you seen him by any chance?" she asked raising her eyebrows.

"No, but then I haven't been looking. We just finished playing poker. By the way, do you know the Red Baron here?" Holloway asked pointing to an officer she had not seen before.

"Oh, you guys. Don't you ever just call anybody by their real name? And no, we haven't met." She smiled sweetly at Stover. "I'm JD. Jennifer that is," she added, realizing the contradiction of what she had just said. "Shall I call you Red or Baron for short?"

"Baron will do I guess," said Stover taking JD's outstretched hand.

JD looked back at Holloway. "Well, anyway, Magic is going to stay the night and he's bringing your pal Todd Hardesty. They're driving up by jeep. Can I ask you a big favor, Bagger?"

"Sure you can. What do you need?"

"Can you find them a place to stay in the BOQ? Are there any spare rooms?"

"No sweat. There's a two-man room at the end of the hall that's vacant. I'll get them a couple of sleeping bags."

"You're wonderful," JD purred. She reached over and kissed Holloway quickly on the cheek. "By the way, Beth said to say hi if I saw you. She and Sherry left early this morning on that Hong Kong/Singapore excursion. I hope they have a ball."

"Knowing Beth, I'm sure they'll have a ball," Holloway replied. "What time are Magic and Todd supposed to be here?"

"Actually they're late now."

"OK, let me go over to the Q and get a hold of a couple of sleeping bags before it gets any later and make sure that room is OK. I'll catch you later."

"Thanks again, Bagger. You're a good friend." JD turned to Stover. "A pleasure meeting you, Baron. Bye."

*   *   *

Clay Holloway was laying out Bill Grant's sleeping bag on the bare mattress when he felt the presence of someone behind him. He turned his head.

"Hey, Bagger. Thanks for the hospitality," Todd Hardesty said, walking into the room.

"Hi, brother. What's the good word? Where's your pilot?"

"Aww, he's over there with sweet pants already," Hardesty smirked.

Holloway involuntarily bristled at the remark. He really hadn't been able to exactly sort out his feelings about JD, but there was one thing that had become obvious to him. One way or another, he cared a great deal about her. One of the more confusing aspects of their relationship was the fact that at the moment he met her he was still infatuated with Beth Kisha. Yet after talking with JD for only a few minutes, he had become enchanted with her. It had crossed his mind that it might have been a sisterly sort of affection that he felt for her. Having never had a sister, he was unsure about how that was supposed to feel, but he had a strange desire to take care of her. Too watch over her, in a sense. He also had never really had a close female friend in his life. His relationships with women had always been as what he considered as a normal boyfriend/girlfriend sort of thing. This mysterious feeling about JD continued to baffle him.

"So how serious are they, Todd? Actually I'm a little surprised she asked me to fix up two bunks over here. I figured she'd just slip him in the back door of the Doughnut Dolly hooch and have him spend the night with her." Holloway commented.

Hardesty laughed. "There's no doubt in my military mind that Magic would love that. He's just dying to get inside of that girl, but so far she hasn't let him."

Holloway felt a sense of relief wash over him. "Really. I'm surprised. She gave me every impression that she's wild over his ass. What's the matter?"

"Well, from what Magic tells me, the girl is a virgin, if you can believe that. I mean here we are in the middle of 1969, the age of Aquarius and free love and make love not war and all that other shit and here we have a twenty two year old absolute doll surrounded by 12,000 hungry GI's and she's never even been laid. She went to college for Christ's sake. You'd think sometime, somehow, some fraternity stud would have gotten into her drawers, but Magic says no.

I'd be willing to bet that will change though. Magic doesn't have much time left in country and I know that one thing he definitely plans to do before he leaves here is to have carnal knowledge of that woman. One thing you have to understand about Magic. He'd fuck a snake if you held its head."

Holloway was silent. Stunned really. JD had confided to him a very strong emotional attachment for Magic. There was no question in Holloway's mind that she was falling in love with the man if, in fact, she was not already in love with him. To hear Todd Hardesty tell him that what seemed to be number one on Magic Maloney's hit parade was the simple desire to just have sex with the girl infuriated him. But what the hell could he do about it?

"Annahashamika, troops!" said Kendall Stover holding a quart of Johnny Walker in one hand and an inverted steel helmet filled to overflowing with ice in the other. "Anybody have any glasses?"

Holloway was glad to see Stover. His entrance served to cool Holloway's rising anger and redirect the subject away from JD. "I think we can find some glasses, Baron. Come on in and say hello to Todd Hardesty. He's a chopper jock."

A hour later Tom Courtney and Hostileman joined them. An hour after that three other officers stuck their heads in the door. "So this is where the party is. The club is almost like a morgue. What do you say we go over and ring the bell a few times and light things up," Eric Auslander suggested.

Holloway was tired, yet this was his only night at Camp Wynne for a week and he wanted to get the most out of it. Groaning he lifted himself off of the bunk where he had been sitting and picked up his soft cap. All of the men filed out of the room and traipsed outside of the metal Quonset hut. The night air felt clean and damp. The frog invasion had ended long ago, but there were still a few of the green and black amphibians about, croaking their nighttime melodies. The limited number of people in the club looked up as the herd of eight men charged through the door.

Tom Courtney grabbed the bell cord and clanged the clapper. Joan and Kathy had been in the ping-pong room around the corner. The bell was like the siren's song calling them home.

"We're here!" Joan called as the two girls ran into the room. "You can start the party now."

Holloway smiled and headed toward them, but stopped when he saw Magic and JD walking through the door behind them holding hands. She looked radiant. JD caught Holloway's eye and touching Magic softly on his arm, slid her hand away from his, leaving him momentarily at the bar, and walked toward Holloway, smiling broadly. As she approached him she took his upper arm and guided him a few feet away from the others. Then she placed her lips near his ear.

"Bagger, I'm so happy. I have to tell you. We're not going to announce this, at least not tonight, but I just have to tell you. Magic asked me to marry him. I accepted. We're engaged!"

*   *   *

Heading north toward the Imjin, Clay Holloway's stomach was still tied in knots and the magnificent dawn had done nothing to calm it. One of the most frustrating aspects of the situation was that he was not even sure why he was so upset. What the hell was Jennifer Dodge to him really? If he added up all the time that they had actually spent with one another thus far, he doubted if it would total up to more than several hours. It was a few hours here, a few hours there. The point was, however, it was quality time. Most assuredly quality time. Holloway could not remember ever being around another human being that he enjoyed more. She was so genuine, so open with him. He felt privileged when she shared something with him. Even the engagement. She did not plan to tell any of her girl friends, at least not for a little while. Magic didn't want her to. But she had told him. He'd tried to smile and act happy for her. She was so excited that he doubted that she had unmasked his false smiles. Magic wasn't going to give her a ring yet. He wanted to wait and get one in the States. And no official date was set. He should be getting his orders within a couple of weeks and once he was at his new assignment they could make definite plans. Holloway had considered warning her, but what right did he have to do that really. What would he say? Stay away from the guy. He doesn't love you the way you love him. She'd probably tell Holloway to go fuck himself. Although he really didn't think she would use that sort of language. So he'd tried to be diplomatic by saying little things like "You haven't known each other that long. How can you be sure he's the one" and "Are you sure you want to be married to the military?" But it hadn't helped. She seemed blindly in love with him. No. All Holloway could do was support her and be her friend and hope that somehow someway everything would work out for the best. But his stomach was still tied in knots.

The situation with JD had served to clarify and crystallize one thing for him. Clearly, his fascination with Beth Kisha had been nothing more than an outrageously torrid infatuation. That weekend they had spent together had bordered on the incredible. She was a very sexy woman. She had taught him more things than the other way around. What a wonderful lover! He would never forget her as long as he lived. But it was over. She had been right.

"Hey, Bagger," Kendall Stover called from the back seat of the jeep. "Which hill is Ruminski putting us on today?"

"I'm going back to Gwen, which is my regular Guard Post and you're going to Carol, which is going to be your regular GP. Sweeper will be going to Cindy tomorrow. I told you all this once."

"Mmmm. Just checking. That's what I thought." Stover sat back in his seat and looked down into the swiftly flowing Imjin in the early morning light as the vehicle passed over Freedom Bridge on its way to Camp Greaves.

Dave Ruminski was standing outside of the 1/9th BOQ when the jeep arrived. "Get ready as fast as you can, gentlemen. We're supposed to meet the chow truck at the barrier fence gate at 0700 and then head up to Gwen with them."

Fifteen minutes later, the jeep with the driver and three officers started down the hill and toward the DMZ barrier fence gate. When it arrived five minutes later the Bravo Company chow truck was nowhere to be found. Ruminski called to one of the men manning the gate. "Isn't the chow truck here yet?"

"It was here, Sir. They waited a couple of minutes and then they decided to go on ahead."

"Damnit, that makes me mad," Ruminski exploded. "It's only 0705. They should have waited." He called again to the man on the gate. "Did the escort vehicle go with them?"

"No, Sir. It wasn't here. In fact, it's pulling in behind you right now." Holloway turned his head to see a jeep with three armed men wearing flak jackets and helmets pull up behind them.

Ruminski got out of the jeep and walked back to the newly arrived vehicle. "Can you give us an escort? We're going up to Gwen and then on to Carol."

"Yessir, no sweat. That's what we're here for."

*　　　　　*　　　　　*

Buck Sergeant (E-5) Shavers who, as Holloway's recon sergeant, alternated with Holloway on GP Gwen was anxious to leave the hill. He was awfully glad the exchange was being made so early in the morning because he had a lot of things that needed to be taken care of. Namely his yobo.

Shavers had been told by one of the 1/9th cooks that his yobo, who went by the name of Claudia, was shacking up with some grunt from the 1/38th whenever Shavers was on the hill. Probably that meant she was double dipping by charging Shavers the standard monthly yobo fee and then getting some MPC out of this other clown as well. Well, he was going to put a stop to that today. If he could get to the village quickly enough, say by 0900, he would probably be able to still catch them in the sack in her hooch. Claudia liked to sleep in on Sundays.

Shavers walked out of the back of the bunker complex onto the flat area and looked down at the road far below. There was a vehicle coming, probably Ruminski. Shavers had already dragged his duffel outside so that he could jump right in when the jeep got there. Hopefully Lieutenant Holloway wouldn't have anything that he wanted to bullshit about. Shavers glanced down at the vehicle on the dirt road. It was perhaps four hundred yards away and close enough for Shavers to see that it was the morning chow truck, not Ruminski. Shit! Well maybe he could get a cup of coffee from them while he waited.

Wait a minute! What the hell were all those puffs of white smoke around the truck! A flash of alarm shot through Sergeant Shaver's body. The sound of automatic weapons fire was unmistakable. The truck was being attacked! It was a fucking ambush! No! No! Jesus Christ, no!

"Sergeant Major! Sergeant Major! Call the TOC. They're attacking the chow truck. Call the reaction force!" Shavers was screaming at the top of his lungs. Sergeant Major Emerson McKee was standing only thirty feet from Shavers when he began yelling. He had just finished shaving out of a kimchi pail and was beginning to wipe the lather off of his clean-shaven face with an olive drab towel. Hearing Shavers screams sent a chill through his body. He ran to where the sergeant stood pointing.

To his horror the Sergeant Major could see that Shavers was exactly correct. Already several dark figures had formed a semicircle around the vehicle, which was stopped on the road and were continuing to fire into the riddled piece of equipment. "Use your rifle, Sergeant. Open fire. Number one, get your M-60 going. Hurry it up. Shoot those motherfuckers!"

The M-60 in position number one was not ready for firing. The gun was still in the bunker from the night vigil, but the ammunition belt was secured in the ammo box. It took almost a minute to get the machine gun ready to fire. Sergeant Shavers lay on the hill firing his M-14 with rapid semiautomatic shots. At four hundred yards, however, it did not appear to be having much effect. Two men from position number two had also begun firing with their M-16's. Dust began to kick up sporadically on the road. The dark figures who had closed on the truck began moving away from the vehicle and into the nearby field from which they had come, carrying with them bloody souvenirs.

The four artillerymen in the jeep heard the firing just as they drove through the fence gate and into the DMZ. The weapons didn't sound familiar. They weren't M-16's, that was for sure. It was more of a sharp barking sound. Somebody was in deep shit.

"Speed up D'Antonio. Holloway hand me the mike," Ruminski ordered. "Golf Papa One, this is Albatross, give me a sitrep, over."

"Albatross, this is Gulf Papa One, the chow truck on the road below us is being ambushed. We're calling the reaction force, over."

"What!! Hurry up D'Antonio!" Ruminski screamed. "Floor it!" He turned to the two FO's in the back seat. "Get ready! We've got a fight on our hands." Then he stood and called to the escort vehicle behind. "Ambush! Ambush ahead!"

Corporal D'Antonio wasn't completely sure that he wanted to get to the ambush. After all, he was doing the driving and wouldn't even be able to return fire. His M-14 was carried in a canvas sheath on the side of the jeep, but how hell was he going to shoot it while he was shifting gears and steering. Holloway in the back seat looked at Kendall Stover. Neither man spoke. They both understood what was about to happen.

The jeep rounded a curve. There was a five hundred meter stretch of open road ahead leading to GP Gwen. There it was! The chow truck was halted in the road, its front wheels turned at an odd angle. There were two forms lying on the road, one on either side of the truck. Dark figures were running into the field to the left. Ruminski stood up. Crack! The M-14 recoiled into his shoulder. Holloway on the left rear tapped the bottom of the twenty round magazine and began firing, sending hot empty brass shell casings into D'Antonio's back and neck. D'Antonio crouched over the wheel, trying to keep low as well as getting away from the blast of Holloway's rifle, which was going off behind his ear as fast as Holloway could pull the trigger. Kendall Stover in the right rear scanned the right side of the road, fearful of another possible ambush. He held his fire. It would be dangerous for him to try to fire between his companions anyway. He glanced behind. The escort jeep was keeping right up with them, machinegun blazing.

D'Antonio stepped on the brakes and the jeep slid to a halt twenty feet behind the smoking chow truck, as Holloway was instantly out of the jeep and running into the field.

"Holloway, stop!" Ruminski commanded. They've got three hundred yards on you and they're already to the trees. You try to follow them they'll cut you down!"

Clay Holloway stopped and looked back at Ruminski. He was right. It was hopeless. In a final act of anger he released his empty magazine, slammed home a fresh one, and proceeded to empty it into the trees where the ambush team had disappeared.

"Golf Papa One, this is Albatross, give me a sitrep, over!" Ruminski spoke rapidly into the radio.

"Albatross, this is Golf Papa One, the TOC has radioed the patrols. They're going to try to cut the UI's off. What's it like down there. How bad is it, over."

"It couldn't be any worse," was his only reply.

Ruminski turned to survey the chow truck for the first time. Nothing was moving, though steam was pouring from its perforated radiator. The wooden struts of the truck, which formed the shell for the canvas that normally covered the truck bed, stood starkly silhouetted against the sky. The struts reminded Ruminski of a man's skeletal ribs.

Holloway and Stover walked to the rear of the chow truck and stopped. It was obvious that nothing could be done to help anyone. Two dead Americans lay on the dirt surrounded by pools of blood, which was still running and soaking into the tan dust. Their clothing was in shreds from the impact of so many bullets. Holloway recognized one of the bodies as a cook that had served him his food several times on GP Gwen. He thought his name was O'Hara. Each man had been shot in the head in addition to their numerous other wounds. They weren't wearing flak jackets, which struck Holloway as odd. Whenever he had seen the chow truck arrive at the hill the men had always worn the body armor. Holloway didn't see any weapons either. He looked in the back of the truck. No weapons there either. Only hot coffee draining out of holes in the stainless steel urn that had been struck twice by bullets.

Stover walked to the front of the 1 ¼ ton truck. A slight breeze caused the white flag that was mandatorily mounted on a steel bumper rod to flutter. Of course, the white flag was the sign for "cease fire." The inside of the truck cab was covered with blood splatters and pools, which had run across the floor and down its sides where the doors had been opened. The shotgun rider was hanging half in and half out of the rider's compartment, his blood pouring down the outside of the door over the big white star that had been stenciled onto the side. Stover shuddered. What had he gotten himself into? How could he ever tell Mary Lou about something like this?

No one was speaking in complete sentences. An occasional curse or grunt was the only sound as each man surveyed the carnage, each lost in his own thoughts. The three men from the escort jeep had joined them. They too were silent, exchanging only mournful glances.

Before long, there was the whine of the APC's. Two of the metal beasts from the reaction force rounded the curve in the road and headed toward the scene, throwing clouds of dust behind them. Close behind them was the battalion XO and not long after that came the CO. There was no reason to stay. Ruminski gave them the basics of what had happened and said he and his FO's were ready for debriefing whenever they were wanted. He pointed to his jeep where D'Antonio sat behind the wheel and Holloway and Stover climbed aboard. In a few moments the jeep began its ascent up Gwen. No one looked back.

*   *   *

Clay Holloway stood in his bunker on Gwen facing Speaker Hill, a hollow stare in his eyes. Normally good-natured, it occurred to him that he hadn't laughed since he'd arrived. The GP had been quiet. Not a damn thing had happened since the horror of four days ago. That was just as well. He and the Sergeant Major had talked the whole thing to death. The UI's had gotten cleanly away. Wally Tyler and his patrol had made contact with them near the MDL and had taken them under fire, making them drop two bloody American flak jackets that they were carrying. That explained to Holloway what had happened to the jackets and probably the Americans' rifles as well. But none of the UI's had been hit. They'd recrossed the MDL and made good their escape. At the ongoing peace talks at Panmunjom the North Koreans had expressed regret that some soldiers had died, but made the absurd claim of having no involvement in the incident.

Holloway had made one decision. He was going to take Keith Hackworth up on his offer to take him on an ambush patrol. It was personal now. Holloway hated the North Koreans, hated what they had done to the four innocent men in the truck. Apparently the commando team had moved into position in the darkness and laid hidden in the field near the road until the first vehicle came along. Unfortunately, it was the unaccompanied chow truck. It might just as well have been Clay Holloway and his companions. He'd been over the scenario a hundred times in his mind. Would the UI's have struck if his jeep had been with the truck the way it was supposed to be? Would the mess crew be alive if they had waited like Ruminski had told them? He didn't know the answer, yet he felt a sense of guilt. Why was he alive and safe and they were dead and their bodies shipped back to the world and ready to be buried? If they'd been together maybe he could have helped. Realistically though, he suspected that if his jeep had been with the chow truck he would now be as dead as the mess crew was. Something had kept him alive. Was it fate? Maybe God? That's what his mother would say. God was looking out for him. Maybe she was right. Or maybe everything was just random chance. Just luck.

When Ruminski arrived two hours later to pick him up and return him to Camp Greaves, Holloway's first reaction to seeing Ruminski was pain. Simply the sight of seeing him and D'Antonio caused the memories of four days earlier to flood back into his consciousness. Driving back down the road toward the DMZ fence and passing "the spot" on the road Holloway averted his eyes to look in the other direction. Knowing that every time for the rest of his tour that he would go to or return from GP Gwen he would, of necessity, pass that spot gave him a sense of incredible sadness.

*　　　*　　　*

It was September and things were changing. The green lushness of the DMZ didn't look dramatically different, though to the men used to the dampness of the rainy season, the atmosphere certainly felt as though a change had occurred. The rains and humidity had been replaced by the dryness and cool evenings of late summer and early fall. With the new month would come a new battalion. Within the week the men of the 1/9th Infantry would rotate south of the Imjin to be replaced by the 1/38th. Holloway had delayed talking with Keith Hackworth about accompanying him on an ambush patrol and Hackworth had not mentioned the subject to him again. However, if Holloway was going to do it, he had to act quickly. Hackworth only had one patrol left until he would join his battalion in heading south. Holloway knew one thing. He had more confidence in Keith Hackworth than any other infantry lieutenant he had ever met. If he was going to join an ambush patrol it was most assuredly going to be Hackworth's.

He found him in the arms room sharpening the heavy combat knife that Holloway had seen him use to cut the rope off of Thorensen when they had pulled him from the smoking hole. Holloway recalled that the rope had almost burst apart when Hackworth had seemed to only touch the blade to the hemp. Hackworth was using a whetstone and pulling it slowly and deliberately down the blade.

"Where'd you get that knife, Hacker?" Holloway asked. He hadn't seen any of the other troops carrying one. Most of the infantrymen carried bayonets.

"Vietnam. Take a look at it," Hackworth said handing it over.

It had a black leather wrapped handle. The words "US Utica Cut. Co." were stamped on the base of the blade at the bottom of the blood channel. The edge gleamed where the metal was raw from the sharpening. A light coat of oil covered the blade. The term "razor sharp" was not adequate to describe its cutting ability.

"So when are you going to take me on that ambush patrol, Hacker?" Clay Holloway asked as he tested the knife's edge with his thumb.

Hackworth's blond eyebrows arched. "Tomorrow's my last one before we rotate south. Want to go?"

"Sure. Why not," Holloway replied. "I figure you're the best. If I'm going to go out there it might as well be with you."

"All right, Bagger! Tell you what. We'll leave the BOQ together tomorrow morning at 0415. We'll catch somethin' to eat in the mess hall. The patrol enters the Zone at 0530 through the regular gate. We need to move across the field and into the trees before daylight. It's a twenty-four hour patrol. We'll take enough C-rats for that. Bring your poncho, two canteens of water, and your basic load for that M-14 of yours. If you want, I'll get an M-16 for you. It's lighter and so is the ammo."

"I'm comfortable with my own rifle. And to tell you the truth, I haven't fired an M-16 much. I don't think this is the time to be changing."

"OK, whatever floats your boat. Wear a soft cap. No flak jacket on this one. It's too hot humping with one of those all day. Wears you out. Oh, and make sure you tape your dog tags and your rifle slings so they don't make any noise. Once we get goin' you just stick with me. I'll show you what to do. You'll be fine. Every artilleryman ought to go on ambush patrol once in his life. We'll show you how the other half lives. In fact,

Bagger, just to show you how proud I am of you volunteering for my patrol, when it's all over I'm gonna have a little souvenir of the occasion for you."

"What's that, Hacker? Your sweaty jock strap?"

"Better than that. I'm gonna give you my combat knife."

Holloway looked at the man sincerely. "Do you mean that? You'd give me that knife? The one you got in Vietnam? I don't think I should take it."

"It's OK. To tell you the truth I've got another one stowed in the arms room and another back in the States. You're a good guy, Bagger. I'd like you to have it."

Holloway looked at Hackworth a long moment and then nodded. "I appreciate this, Hacker. I really do."

*   *   *

The night air was brisk. Holloway hoped it would warm up soon. He wasn't about to wear a field jacket that would be a burden once the sun came up, but in the meantime he was shivering. Hackworth had finished his briefing and the inspection of his men and was preparing to give the point man the sign to move out. The appearance of some of the men when Holloway had seen them in the mess hall had surprised him. It was one scary looking group. When Hackworth had told him to wear a soft cap he had brought his olive drab baseball cap assuming that is what everyone would wear. Wrong! The members of the patrol seemed to take great pride in the individualizing of their selection of headgear. No two members of the team seemed to wear the same type of hat and no one but Holloway wore anything that was Army issue, except for the two KATUSA's. The most prominent headgear was a black Clint Eastwood style cowboy hat with a long hawk feather sticking out of the band. The brim was turned down all the way around. Another wore an Australian style bush hat with one side snapped up. There was a navy blue beret, a Chicago Cubs cap, and a USMC utility cap. Hackworth wore his Vietnam boonie cap with his name sewn across the back. A dark stocking cap and what appeared to be a welder's cap dyed olive drab completed the group. Camouflage paint had been applied Indian style to many of the men's' faces to make them look more fearsome. Streaks ran down the noses and high on the cheekbones. The point man was armed with a Remington 12 gauge pump shotgun, while two other men carried M-79 grenade launchers. One soldier packed the M-60 machine gun on a heavy canvas sling while the remaining members of the patrol carried rifles. Hackworth peered at them once more in the darkness and whispered to the point man to move out. Noiselessly the gate swung open on hinges that Hackworth had said he had oiled personally. The men disappeared quietly into the blackness of the DMZ.

Moving quickly and soundlessly, the patrol covered the 500 meters of open area and blended into the woods. Holloway could feel his senses becoming more alert as he concentrated heavily on moving as quietly as the rest of the veteran patrol. Most of them were graduates of ACTA (Advanced Combat Training Academy), which had been organized for the very purpose of improving the patrolling skills of the DMZ infantrymen. A feeling of nervousness had settled in his stomach that would remain with him throughout the patrol. It reminded him of the way he felt before the kickoff of his first high school football game.

It was not long before the pink rays of dawn helped light their path. The pace of the patrol quickened slightly. The route thus far was familiar to most of them. They'd been patrolling that area for three months and were more than familiar with almost every square meter. To Holloway the woods seemed virgin. Except for the occasional patrol, no man had walked the area for over fifteen years. Only an incredible variety of wildlife roamed the area. Occasionally there was a random shell crater now overgrown with weeds. Suddenly they came upon a abandoned village, the bare remnants of the hooches still visible and pieces of earthen cooking ware or rusted pots lying scattered about. Three white cranes waded in the water collected by what had once been a rice paddy. Although the dikes were crumbled, the paddy continued to retain water. The cranes noted the patrol's presence and then returned to their feeding below the water. When the patrol took a breather a half hour after bypassing the village, Holloway sought out Keith Hackworth and spoke to him in a whisper.

"Hacker, are we going to go near that old train wreck I could see from Gwen? I wouldn't mind seeing it close up," Holloway mentioned inquisitively.

Hackworth shook his head. "Sorry, no chance. For one thing our patrol routes are planned by the S-3 and we can't alter them. If we did, patrols would be running into each other and maybe shooting it out. The other thing is I don't want to go anywhere near that train. It's covered with booby traps just for curious people like you." He winked.

The patrol resumed soon thereafter, running a zigzagged pattern through their assigned area. Just before noon Hackworth called a halt. They still had the cover of thick woods, but the nearby meadows presented them with clear fields of observation and fire to two sides. Individual patrol members melted into their surroundings. This is where they would spend the day until darkness came. Sergeant Stone religiously put out security. The others were free to eat or sleep until their shift began. Sleep did not come easily to Holloway. During the last six hours he had concentrated warily on his surroundings and sleep would have been welcome under other circumstances. But mentally acknowledging his location and reason for being there, kept him alert for an additional hour. By six, many of the soldiers had awakened and were opening C-rations and warming them with heat tablets. Holloway stirred his ham and lima beans concoction with his spoon while adding some of Hackworth's hot sauce. The extra ingredient made almost everything taste better.

A half-hour after dark, signals were passed that meant prepare to move. Silently the patrol gathered itself and changed locations. By 2230 hours the horseshoe shaped ambush was set. The position had been selected because of its proximity to a favored North Korean crossing point near the MDL. Two men were detailed for rear security. Claymores were set out, directed toward the most likely approaches far in front of the patrol. Back blast from the deadly ball bearing spewing devices could be almost as dangerous as being in front of them. Wires were laid from the mine to the patrol where they were attached to the small hand squeezed generators that would send an electrical charge through the wire and into the mine to detonate the blasting cap and in turn the mine. Something Holloway had not previously seen was a motion detector. It too had wires running out to various points located far away from the main panel. At the end of the wires were attached probes, which were inserted into the ground. Vibration caused by anyone walking near the probes would alert Hackworth at the panel.

Hackworth directed Holloway into his position and reviewed the rules of engagement for him. Then he moved to his own position nearby and waited. Holloway felt uncomfortable. Not physically uncomfortable particularly, but in a sense of being in an alien environment. He was not a stranger to night in the DMZ, yet being in his bunker or the trenches of the guard post had provided him with a feeling of security. In the woods he felt naked, exposed, and isolated. Whatever happened out here, the patrol was on its own. Never before had the groans and whispers of the DMZ seemed more ominous. He spent much of the night battling the tricks of his mind.

When dawn arrived and there had been no contact, Hackworth called the TOC to request permission to return to base and Clay Holloway let out a gigantic sigh of relief. Within a few minutes the patrol was moving quickly toward the gate at the south fence an hour away. But before the column had covered a half-mile, the rear guard passed word to Hackworth that he had detected movement behind them. The patrol continued in its assigned pattern keeping a keen ear to the rear and stopping occasionally to listen closely. The rear guard walked cautiously backwards, his ears and eyes alert. There were more movement noises, audible now to most of the patrol. Tension creased the faces of the men as the realization that they seemed to have become the hunted set upon them.

Hackworth and Stone locked eyes, each nodding toward the other. As the small unit crested a small rise in the landscape Stone tapped two men and directed them quickly into some dense brush. The remainder of the patrol continued as though nothing had changed. Holloway wiped the sweat off of his forehead with his shirtsleeve and looked to the rear for the fifth time in the last minute. There was no question someone was behind them. How many could there be? Could Stone and his two men handle them even if the pursuers walked into the hastily prepared trap? A hundred yards later Hackworth suddenly dropped to the side of the patrol and deployed the men hurriedly into a defensive line. Then they waited. There had been no noise. No firing that was for sure. What was happening with Stone? They seemed to wait forever. Finally Holloway could hear someone moving through the brush. His muscles tensed. He thumbed the safety off of his M-14 and waited, his heart beating wildly. A shape appeared. It was Stone. A big grin covered his freckled boyish face.

"It was three of them. We told them to go home and leave us alone," said the NCO mysteriously.

"UI's?" asked Hackworth wide-eyed.

"Nah! Deer. Three of those little saber-toothed bastards just out for a morning stroll."

Whew! The patrol let out a collective sigh of relief. This was the last patrol for many of them before their battalion rotated south. For some of them it was their last patrol ever. Snickers and wise cracks rippled throughout the band of soldiers. Hackworth took the radio handset from the RTO and called the TOC.

"Swamp Fox 33, this is Bravo 20. Tell the boys on the fence to put their safeties on. We're coming in. Out!"

CHAPTER 15

Bob Hoover watched the little wooden boat with a detached interest. It was in the river far below him near the north bank of the Imjin and being poled against the current by a lone papa-san with a broad brimmed straw hat. Sweeper took a sip of his rum and coke and returned to his chair under the red and white striped umbrella that covered the table on the concrete patio of the Camp Greaves Officers' Club. He pulled a second of the white metal chairs close to him, put his feet on the seat, and smiled as his two friends, Clay Holloway and Kendall Stover, pushed open the screen door and walked onto the patio carrying their own rum and cokes. A moment later Dave Ruminski joined the group. "Sweeper, I've got news for you. You're going back to the Battalion. You're going to be the XO of Bravo Battery. There's another new lieutenant on his way up from DivArty to take your place up here in the Z."

"Hey, lucky you, Sweeper!" Holloway exclaimed enthusiastically. "Now maybe you too can get in line to challenge Bear Buckner to see who's really running Bravo." The comment referred to the fact that earlier in the month Bravo Battery First Sergeant Ramon Villanueva and Buckner, the Battery Commander, had removed their rank insignias and gone one on one behind the motor pool when no one was watching. Since Villanueva's arrival an unacceptable level of friction had been allowed to develop. Bear Buckner, who was built like his nickname and just as tough, had his ideas about how the battery should be run. Villanueva, a macho Hispanic who like to roll up his sleeves an extra turn so that his biceps showed, had decided that he was the top kick and was going to do things his way whether his lieutenant liked it or not. Buckner had won the fight, which had apparently settled the question as to who was really in charge. Bear Buckner was definitely one hombre that no one wanted to mess with. Three months before the latest incident he had knocked out two infantry officers in the Camp Wynne Officers' Club who had become drunk and unruly and who had refused polite invitations to leave.

"Bear's all right. He and I get along just fine," Sweeper replied.

"The other big news is this," Ruminski continued. "Colonel Moody got his orders. He's leaving next Monday. Saturday night is the official going away party. They're hiring a band and there's gonna be a ton of food. I'll rearrange the schedule so that all three of you will be able to go down for the party. But that means you, Bagger, and you, Stover will have to go back up to the GP's tomorrow. I'll get you back down first thing next Saturday morning."

Holloway nodded thoughtfully. They'd only been down from the hill for one day, but that was OK. Half the time there wasn't anything worthwhile to do just hanging around Camp Greaves anyway. The 1/38th Infantry had taken over the DMZ the day before and the 1/9th and his friend Keith Hackworth had gone south. Sergeant Major Emerson McKee had pulled the necessary strings to get himself transferred to the 1/38th so that he could complete the remaining three weeks of his last Army tour as the commander of Guard Post Gwen. At the end of that time he would fly out of Kimpo, stop in Hawaii for a week to visit some friends, and then continue his journey to San Diego where he would be discharged after almost twenty-eight years in this man's Army. After that he had no specific plans.

Clay Holloway had learned much from the old soldier. In some respects he had been almost like a father or at the least, a favorite uncle. The two had spent countless hours philosophizing about life, love, and riches. Holloway was fully aware of how much he would miss the senior NCO. He hoped that he would be reassigned to Charlie Battery soon. Maybe with a new job assignment the Sergeant Major's departure wouldn't bother him as much. He had already been in the DMZ longer than Colonel Moody had initially told him he would be.

"Hey, Holloway," Ruminski remarked. "I heard you went on ambush patrol with Keith Hackworth, is that right?"

"Yeah. I had the day off. Why do you ask?"

"I just wondered. You picked a hell of a guy to go on patrol with, didn't you?"

"Hacker knows what he's doing, Dave. He's a good guy too. You know what he did? After we got back through the fence he took off that black handled combat knife he always carries and gave it to me for a souvenir. He got the knife in Vietnam and he turns around and gives it to me. Someday I need to find a way to pay him back."

"Well, he must like you. And you're right about him knowing what he's doing. You ever hear some of the stories about him in the 'Nam?"

"No, not really," Holloway replied. "He never actually talked much about it and I didn't ask him."

"Well, I saw him in his dress greens once, right after he got here. You have never in your life seen a second lieutenant with that much fruit salad on his chest. In fact the new battalion XO pulled him aside and asked him if he was really authorized to wear all of that," explained Ruminski.

"So what's he got?"

"Well, in addition to the regular stuff that everybody over there gets, he had two Silver Stars, two Bronze Stars, one with a "V" for valor, two Air Medals, a Vietnamese medal that I didn't know, and a Purple Heart. All together he had almost four rows of ribbons along with the Combat Infantry Badge."

Holloway whistled softly. "Are you shittin' me? Man! I knew he was good. I didn't know he was that good."

"Well, he is that good," Ruminski confirmed admiringly. "It's almost a shame they just don't leave him up here all the time instead of letting him rotate back south with the rest of his battalion. Just let him stay in the Z like Sergeant Major McKee does. Now there's another old warhorse for you. How short is he now, Holloway?"

"Just about three weeks. Then he retires. I'm going to hate to see him go too," Holloway acknowledged in a melancholy tone. "I really am."

*   *   *

Sergeant Major Emerson McKee and Second Lieutenant Clay Holloway had been watching the night firefight for over fifteen minutes through their binoculars. It was the biggest action Holloway had seen in the DMZ. Far to their left, at a range of perhaps three kilometers, the ROK 199th Regimental Combat Team had detected and engaged a North Korean platoon sized element which was apparently trying to slip through the DMZ and into the south. The ROK's had the North Koreans pinned down in a valley where they were machine gunning them. Holloway was watching the curtain of red tracer bullets arching almost lazily into the area where the North Koreans were trapped. Illumination rounds were bursting in the sky over them and floating slowly to earth. Suddenly the "crump, crump" of mortars added to the din.

When the action had begun a little before midnight in the area guarded by troops of the Republic of Korea and referred to as the ROK sector, the Sergeant Major had called one of his KATUSA's into the CP to translate the ROK radio transmissions. This is how he had come to understand exactly what was occurring far to the west. Every few minutes one of the men from the CP would walk into the trench line to update the Sergeant Major with word from the TOC. Eventually the firing lessened and then stopped completely. Sergeant Major McKee told Holloway that he would call the TOC first thing in the morning to obtain a full recapitulation of the night's battle. But when morning came and Clay Holloway questioned the Sergeant Major about it, all he got in reply was a shaking of the head.

"They're putting a cap on it, Sir!" he said resignedly. "I've seen it before."

"What do you mean, a cap on it?" Holloway asked.

"I mean nobody's talking. Somebody higher up has decided they don't want this getting into the newspapers so they're just minimizing the whole thing and acting like nothing important occurred last night. People back in the States won't ever know it happened."

"You're kidding! That was a real shoot-out last night. All that fire power going off. Probably a lot of North Korean casualties if what the ROK's were saying over the radio were true. How could it go unreported?"

"Lieutenant Holloway, the people back home are upset enough about Vietnam. Every time I read a paper I find more and more folks getting up tight about the war and our involvement. I just don't think the government wants to alarm the public any more by letting them know what the situation really is here in Korea. You think last night's action was big? They landed a 120 man North Korean commando on the east coast last year. Hell, the briefings I've been to say the US has taken close to 200 casualties along the DMZ in the last three years. The ROK's another few hundred and the North Koreans at least a thousand dead. The last number I heard on captured North Korean agents in the south was over 1200, just last year. But the people back in the States know very little about it. Everything's focused on Vietnam. This is a second front, but for whatever reason, America doesn't understand that this exists. Things have a way of just never getting reported." He let out a long sigh. "Well, Sir. Less than three weeks and this place won't exist for me either. I am so short right now I could sit on a curb and my feet would never even touch the street."

"I don't want to hear about it, Sergeant Major. I just really don't want to fucking hear about it. Although I must say I am now under 300 days, which is a hell of a lot better than the 395 I was at when I got off the plane in Kimpo three months ago."

Sergeant Major McKee smile broadly, his tanned weathered face showing its lines. "It'll happen, Sir. Nothing lasts forever."

*   *   *

It had only been dark for an hour when position #2 reported the first indication that there were intruders nearby somewhere out in the darkness. "Sergeant Major, we've got radio noises out in front of us. Sounds like they're down near the bottom of the hill."

When Sergeant Major McKee heard a message like that his reaction was always the same. "Sit tight. I'll be right there," he replied calmly. Getting up from his chair in the CP he retrieved his helmet, his M-79 grenade launcher, and a canvas bag filled with a variety of M-79 ammunition which included illumination, HE, and 00 buckshot. Being the curious young man that he was, Clay Holloway strapped on his web gear, snatched his M-14 from the weapons rack, and followed the Sergeant Major down the wooden steps and out into the trench line.

Quietly pushing aside the heavy blackout curtain, the two men slipped unobtrusively into the dark trench line and moved to the bunker at position #2. The Sergeant Major poked his head into the entrance and whispered.

"What have you got?"

"Radio noises, Sergeant Major," the young E-4 whispered in return. "Listen. You can hear them. They're talkin' Korean."

Holloway's ears strained. There it was, just as the corporal had said. The sounds of a radio popping squelch some distance away. A moment later he heard footsteps on the wooden planks behind him. Turning he saw the E-5 from the CP.

"Sergeant Major, now we're getting noises from the other side of the hill! It sounds like someone trying to get through the first string of wire."

"You check it out, Sergeant Webb. I'll be there in a moment," he directed. The NCO began to hurry away when suddenly the senior NCO grabbed his sleeve. "Wait a minute. Go to the ammo bunker first and get a case of grenades and take it with you."

The man nodded and left. "Sergeant Major, I'll go over to the other side and see what's going on," Holloway volunteered.

"Good, Sir. I'll be over in a minute. I want to go to the CP and put the word out to everyone to get alert."

Five minutes later Sergeant Webb, Holloway, and the Sergeant Major all had converged on position #7. Sergeant Major McKee relayed to the others a summary of what was happening. "It's like this. We have reports of sounds and movements from every position on the hill. I'm not sure what it means, but we are definitely being probed on a very large scale. We've got to make them back off. I've called the TOC to let them know what's going on. Lieutenant Holloway, I'd like you to put up a search light mission to give us some extra illumination for the starlight scopes. Sergeant Webb, I want you to hand out that case of grenades, two per position. Nobody throws one until I give the word. I want to do it all at one time. Make sure you tell everyone that nobody tries throws from inside the bunker. That's a sure way to commit suicide. I want them out into the trench to throw. We'll do it at my command. OK, let's go."

Webb scurried in one direction and Holloway the other. After calling the searchlight position and requesting the big light be directed into the clouds high above the hill he returned to where the Sergeant Major was standing. Webb returned with what was left of the grenades a moment later.

"Sergeant Webb, why don't you let me have one a couple of those too," Holloway requested nonchalantly. He glanced at the Sergeant Major and grinned in the darkness. "Well, hell, they won't let me get any artillery fire up here, I have to do something to keep awake." Holloway took two of the smooth heavy hunks of iron and moved alone down the trench line to an area unoccupied by anyone else. Just as he halted, he heard a noise that made his heart stop.

It was a scraping. Soft and steady and worst of all, close. Holloway understood instantly exactly where it was. He had stood in that spot of the trench a hundred times, maybe two hundred. That particular location had the best unobstructed view of GP Carol and sometimes he would study his sister Guard Post three thousand meters away with his binos just to see what they were up to. By standing in that particular spot so many times he had also become intimately familiar with the terrain below the position. There was an earthen ledge below his trench, perhaps twenty feet down. It was a wide ledge, with a shallow depression in the middle. On the other side of the ledge the hill dropped off sharply. Its surface was covered in dry dirt and small stones. As soon as Holloway heard the scraping he sensed immediately the origin of the faint noise. Someone was crawling slowly on that ledge, their belt buckle scraping on the earth and stones. He was equally sure of a second fact. The individual was not there to wish him a happy Halloween.

Quickly he considered his options. He could simply walk away and get help. Of course he had no idea what the UI was planning. If Holloway left the area the UI may slip up the hill and into the trench line. Secondly he could stay there and start yelling for help. That was certainly an option, although it would tell anyone within ear shot exactly where he was. He decided neither of those was acceptable. Instead, he quietly withdrew one of the two hand grenades he had hooked onto his belt. He peered over the top of the trench and gazed downward. He saw nothing. It was much too dark to discern shapes more than five or six feet away. Straightening the heavy cotter pin that secured the safety handle and tugging the pin loose, he cradled the handle in the webbing of his right hand between the thumb and forefinger. He extended his arm over the edge of the ditch and let the grenade roll out of his hand, listening to it bounding gently down the slope. Holloway raised his rifle and waited, hoping to catch a glimpse of his adversary in the flash of the grenade and put a bullet in him. He realized he would be close to the explosion, but failed to comprehend exactly how close.

The explosive detonated with a roar, seemingly almost in Holloway's face, pelting his helmeted head with dirt and rocks and concussion. Mercifully, shrapnel was not part of the variety of debris that flew into his head and hands. He had involuntarily buried his face when the flash lighted the area in front of him. Accordingly, he had seen nothing but the explosion itself. His ears were ringing, yet he strained to discern what sounds he could. Farther down the hill than the original scraping noise he could hear a thrashing, as though someone were rolling or sliding quickly down the hill. He primed his second grenade and threw it in the direction of the noises. Again the destructive force of an explosion shattered the stillness of the night, but as before, he was able to see nothing. Holloway heard footsteps in the trench behind him.

"Sir, are you OK?" Sergeant Major McKee inquired, a concerned look on his face.

"What? My ears are ringing. I can't hear too well," Holloway whispered. The Sergeant Major repeated his question. "Sure. I'm fine. There was a UI just below me. I couldn't wait for your signal," Holloway finally replied.

"Well, did you get him?"

"He bugged out, I know that. I threw another grenade as he was heading down the hill. I don't know if I tagged him or not."

Sergeant Major McKee turned to Webb and whispered. "Go ahead and ring up the positions. Tell them to start throwing their grenades. The UI's know that we know they're here. But let's at least kick their asses back beyond our wire."

Sergeant Webb slipped away quietly into the darkness. Forty-five seconds later the sound of the first explosion ripped through the night. Holloway counted softly to himself as all sixteen charges roared, circling the hill with flame and smoke and shrapnel. Following the last explosion, the two men stood silently in the trench listening as best they could to the sounds of silence. Finally the Sergeant Major turned to Holloway. "Let's go back to the CP and check the other positions. We need to look at your face too. I think it's bleeding."

Following some treatment for his superficial cuts by the medic, Holloway had gone to bed, leaving the infantrymen to their duties. The radio noises had ceased, as had any noises around the barbed wire perimeter. The grunts would check the hillside in the morning's light. Holloway left word to wake him if anything significant happened, but the remainder of the night was calm.

The Guard Post had a visitor the next morning, the S-2 from the 1/38th. His message was straightforward. Eighth Army Intelligence was issuing a warning to friendly forces in and around the DMZ. It was generally felt that the North Koreans would be attempting a major land action within the next few weeks. Following their conquest at sea with the capture of the Pueblo, their successful downing of an American EC-121 aircraft, and evidence from other unmentioned sources, it was believed by the American intelligence community that the next major overt act by the Communist North would be the destruction or capture of an American patrol or Guard Post. All precautions were to be taken in anticipation of that threat.

During the middle of the informal intelligence briefing, Sergeant Webb, who was directing a work party on the side of the hill, had interrupted the Sergeant Major. Webb informed him that a total of twelve strands of barbed wire had been cut since the last time the perimeter had been checked the day before. Following the departure of the S-2, Sergeant Major McKee directed Webb to further fortify the perimeter by adding several extra strands of wire, additional C-ration cans filled with pebbles, and increasing by five the number of Claymore mines positioned on the sides of the hill, including one on the earthen ledge below where Holloway had stood in the trench line the night before. The ledge had been inspected, but there were no signs that anyone had been wounded by Holloway's grenade. In addition to the improvements in the perimeter, Sergeant Major McKee ordered a supply of fresh batteries for the starlight scopes. The batteries arrived that afternoon and were distributed following the evening meal to soldiers who believed their old batteries were in need of replacement. One such soldier was Corporal Hugh McDonald.

McDonald was a twenty-one year old enlistee who had been in the United States Army for slightly over two years and in the Republic of Korea for eight months. This was his first chance to serve on a Guard Post in the DMZ and he relished the opportunity. Corporal McDonald's older brother had been killed two years earlier while fighting in Vietnam's Delta. This had much to do with Corporal McDonald's initial decision to enlist. Quite simply, he wanted revenge. Although he had applied on several occasions to serve in Vietnam, his request had never been granted. Pentagon policy at the time prevented "sole surviving sons" from serving in a hostile fire zone; however, Corporal McDonald had two other brothers and therefore was technically permitted to serve in one. Unbeknownst to the young man, however, his mother had written to their senator and pleaded that McDonald not be sent to Vietnam. The senator had granted the woman's wishes and had placed a permanent flag on his orders. It would be a cold day in hell before Corporal Hugh McDonald would ever receive orders to the Republic of Vietnam. He did, however, receive orders to the Republic of Korea and to a rifle company. As a member of the 1/38th Infantry he would rotate into the DMZ with the rest of the unit. In point of fact, his mother was entirely unaware, like most other Americans, that the Korean DMZ was designated as a hostile fire zone. Not wanting to alarm his mother, Corporal McDonald had no plans to tell her.

It was with this background that Hugh McDonald stood in the trench line right outside of position #5 on GP Gwen a half hour after darkness, the night after he and his buddies had gotten to toss all of the grenades. Throwing the grenades had been exhilarating. It was his first chance ever to seek revenge for his brother's death against the Communists. He would have preferred the Viet Cong or North Vietnamese Army, of course, but he would settle for the North Koreans. It was unlikely he had hit any of them with the hand grenades, but just throwing them had made his spirits soar. His bunker mate had asked to throw one of the two grenades, but Corporal McDonald had denied the request choosing to lob them both himself. Now McDonald was looking forward to his second night of manning his defensive position on a hill just south of the MDL.

He had installed the brand new starlight scope battery into the expensive instrument an hour earlier while it was still light. Now it was completely dark and the time had come to try it out. McDonald had mounted the starlight scope to the top of his loaded M-16A1 rifle. Looking through the scope gave him the ability to see quite clearly at night unless it was just incredibly dark. Corporal McDonald felt that he would probably be able to see fairly well that evening as he turned on the switch and heard the familiar "hum" of the scope. He took the rifle and placed the stock into his right shoulder. His right finger hovered near the trigger guard as he peered through the high priced optics. Just as he had hoped. In shades of green and black, he could see brilliantly. Then suddenly, there they were! Two of them! Two UI's right in front of him running quickly across the little finger of land that jutted out from position #5. They were less than thirty yards away!

Many men in that position would have frozen or at the very least hesitated. Corporal McDonald had never been in combat. He'd never even fired his weapon in anger, although of course, he had thrown the two grenades the night before. But Corporal Hugh McDonald never hesitated for a moment. He'd waited two years for this opportunity. The scope was pointed right at the side of the second of the two running men. McDonald pulled the trigger of the M-16 with the selector switch set at automatic. A tongue of flame licked out of the muzzle. The force of three 5.56mm bullets caught the second man in his right side, killing him instantly, and blowing him over in a heap onto his left. The lifeless corpse slid slightly in the dirt and came to a halt.

The first man, Sergeant Moon Yi Kang, had reached the safety of the edge of the finger of land and leaped over the side. Once there, however, he crawled back to see what had happened to his comrade behind him. Even in the darkness he could see the man's form lying only five feet away. The North Korean soldier felt at that moment that an incredibly lucky shot had apparently killed the other member of his two-man commando team. The American's must have fired at a noise and this was the outcome. The commando was shrouded in darkness. He had been briefed about American night vision capabilities, but as his heart pounded with the realization that his friend and companion, Park Ji Yung, had just been killed, the recollection of that briefing simply did not enter his conscious brain. The soldier knew he could not leave his friend's body. So he would simply reach out and grab it and drag it over the edge and into the little valley at the side of the finger of land and then somehow get it to the bottom of the hill. From there he would place Park Ji Yung over his shoulder and carry him back to his border of his homeland, two hundred meters away. Sergeant Moon Yi Kang crawled forward and took a hold of his friend's shirtsleeve.

Corporal McDonald's heart was pumping faster than it had ever pumped. He had seen his target go down as soon as he had hit the trigger. Not only had he just atoned for his brother's death, but a moment later there was the other UI. Through his starlight, McDonald could clearly see his head sticking up like one of the rats McDonald used to shoot at as a boy at the city junkyard. The man's face was looking around as though he were trying to locate where the recent burst of fire had come from. McDonald was astounded by his good fortune. He moved the rifle just slightly to his right, centering the reticle pattern on the man's forehead and touched the trigger again. At that instant, Sergeant Moon's head exploded.

The Guard Post Commander, Sergeant Major Emerson McKee was furious. Who the hell was out in the goddamn trench line firing his rifle? He knew the troops from the 1/38th were new and they were bound to be jumpy at first, but son-of-a-bitch, he had warned them several times not to fire their weapons at noises. Shooting a rifle at night shows the bad guys exactly where you are. If there really was a noise the man should have called the CP on the telephone. Then if it was really a firing situation he should have blown a Claymore or thrown a grenade. Firing his rifle was the last thing he should have done. The Sergeant Major fumed all the way down the trench line as he stalked toward position #5 with Clay Holloway right behind him. There was a man the Sergeant Major recognized as a corporal standing ahead of him aiming his rifle down the hill and looking through his starlight.

"Corporal McDonald, what in the fuck are you doing?"

"UI's, Sergeant Major! Right in front of me. Right there," the man said breathlessly, pointing down the hill. "I got them both."

Sergeant Major McKee peered at the young man quizzically in the darkness. Saying nothing he took the rifle and put it to his own shoulder and looked through the scope. My God! There was a body not thirty yards away, lying on its side. It was motionless. The Sergeant Major panned in both lateral directions. Nothing else. He lowered the weapon.

"There's a body there, all right. Did you say you got two of them?"

"Yes, Sergeant Major. I shot the other one right in the face and blew him backwards into that little draw behind the first guy."

The Sergeant Major again held the scope to his eye. "I can't see the other one. Have you heard any other noises or seen anything else?" McDonald shook his head and the Sergeant Major lowered the rifle. "Jesus, son, you did real well. Real well! We've never had a confirmed kill on this GP in the year I've been here. For that matter there hasn't been one on any of the GP's in this Brigade sector." He paused for a moment, then spoke again. "The body is too far down and it's just on the other side of the wire. I'm not sending anyone out that far at night. We don't know how many more UI's there are. We'll set up shifts so that someone can watch the body all night. I don't want the gooks sneaking up here and snatching it. We'll check it out at dawn and look for the other one too. Nice work, corporal. Keep a sharp eye and ring me up if there's anything else."

"It was for Hal, Sergeant Major," the young man said stoically, clutching his rifle.

"Who's Hal, son?"

"My brother. They killed him in Vietnam. This won't bring him back, but somethin' tells me he knows what happened here tonight and I'll bet he's proud of me. My other brothers will be too," he said confidently as he nodded his head.

"I think you're right," the Sergeant Major said evenly. "Nice going." The senior NCO turned and walked with Holloway back to the CP to notify the other positions and the TOC about what had happened. Feeling a sense of elation, he could hardly wait to inform the TOC. His last month in the Army before retirement and his GP had gotten at least one confirmed kill, maybe two, of those sneaking, murdering, ambushing, little bastards. What great timing! That was the way an old soldier should retire.

CHAPTER 16

Lieutenant Colonel Wilbur K. Moody, commanding officer of the 8/18th Artillery, was going home. Officially his thirteen month tour was not up until Wednesday, but his orders were in and they had assigned him to a flight out of Kimpo at 0930 Monday morning. That was fine with him. Aside from the fact that he had a somewhat secretive and very fulfilling romance with a female employee of Northwest Orient Airlines who was assigned to the Seoul office, he had no reason whatsoever to regret leaving the Republic of Korea. He was on his way to what appeared to be a fairly relaxing staff assignment at Ft. Belvoir, Virginia where he and his wife would spend the last two years of his military career before accepting retirement after thirty years of service. It was fairly obvious that he was not going to be promoted to full colonel. If that were going to happen it would have happened before now. So all Colonel Moody had to do was cruise for two years and walk away with a pension equivalent to seventy-five percent of his base pay for the rest of his life. He had not been particularly excited about having to pay for a farewell party for the officers serving under him, but it was the socially acceptable and very customary thing to do and so he had his adjutant, Lieutenant Grant, organize it for him. In Colonel Moody's opinion Grant had gone somewhat overboard. Especially with that ridiculous Korean rock and roll band that he had hired. Wilbur Moody didn't even like rock music when it was played by Americans, let alone when the Koreans tried to copy it. The music sounded like shit. He would have much preferred a polka band, but he had to admit he had never seen a polka band anywhere in the Republic of Korea and couldn't chastise Grant too severely for not finding one. Well, another hour of the rock and roll and one or two more drinks and he could say a few cheery farewells and slip out of the door and go to bed in his room. Hopefully, he wouldn't be able to hear the music from there.

In a dark corner of the Camp Wynne Officers' Club where the Korean band was just wrapping up its first set, Clay Holloway was well into his fourth Scotch. His two companions, Kendall Stover and Bob Hoover, were not far behind. None of them were particularly in the party spirit, and no one had attempted to speak once the band on the other side of the room had begun playing. Now that the group had completed its version of "House of the Rising Sun" and had announced a break, the silence was noticeable. Holloway was the first to break the silence.

"Has anyone ever heard of a more fucked up situation ever in their life?"

"Are you referring to the band?" Stover replied deadpan.

The remark brought a wisp of a smile to Holloway's lips. "No, Baron. Actually I was referring to the DMZ. The whole situation is just absolutely nuts. I mean do ever try to analyze this at all?"

"Are you talking about the ambush again or what, Bagger?" Hoover asked.

"Everything. I'm talking about everything. I mean think about it. We're all lined up on our side of the MDL along the fence. Then we've got ambush patrols out in the woods and guys up on the GP's and ninety nine percent of the time we sit on our side and Joe Chink sits on his side and we just look at each other. Everything's cool. No sweat. Then for what seems like no reason whatsofuckingever, somebody starts shooting. Usually they start it, of course, unless they sneak over to our side of the MDL and if they do that and we see them then we're supposed to shit in their mess kit.

But the weird part is that when they come over to our side of the MDL we're never sure what they're doing. Why do they come sneaking around the GP's? Most of the time they don't actually do anything. They're just seeing how tough it would be to get through our wire or where we put our Claymores. Sometimes they throw stones at us. It's like they just want to fuck with us at night. Why do they want to risk their lives just to do that? Ruminski tells me that two nights ago they got careless. This young corporal on the GP looks through his starlight and there they are right in front of him so he pops 'em. Just like that. One second they're alive and just sneaking around the hill running a little recon and the next second they're dead. Then the next day we go out and get the bodies and take them back to the TOC and everybody acts like we just won the Super Bowl for a couple of days and then everything is back to normal. We sit up on the GP and look at the North Koreans and they look at us just like nothing has happened.

And think about the ambush of the chow truck. I have never been able to get that out of my mind, by the way. I still think about it all the time. But what the hell triggered it? Nothing had happened anywhere in the brigade sector for about two weeks. Then those bastards sneak over here and murder four defenseless guys delivering food. What for?? Why do they do that??"

"Maybe it was the tunnel, Bagger," Stover said. "Maybe they were really pissed off because we found their tunnel."

Holloway was silent for a moment. "Maybe. Maybe that was it, I don't know. We'll never know the reasons for most of this and I guess that's what's so frustrating for me. I don't understand why this is happening. At least I can understand what's going on in a real war. In a real war everybody tries to kill each other every day. There's the enemy, go kill him. But here it's like some days kill the enemy, but other days don't. If they violate a rule then we're supposed to try to kill them, but otherwise just be cool. What are they accomplishing when they do this shit?"

Bob Hoover spoke. "Bagger, they're just trying to keep us off balance and put on the pressure. It's because of Vietnam. The North Koreans see this as an opportunity to do its part to help the North Vietnamese. Don't you think Ho Chi Minh and Kim Il Sung are talkin' on the phone once a week? Don't you think the Tet Offensive and the Blue House Raid and the Pueblo were all coordinated? You think it was a coincidence that they all happened within a couple days of each other? If they just keep rattlin' our chain it keeps us worried and keeps us from pulling out of Korea and sending more people to Vietnam. Besides that, the ROK's have almost three divisions in Vietnam. And they're kickin' ass and takin' names from what I hear. If the North Koreans put on enough pressure, the ROK's are going to pull those divisions out of Vietnam. That's what I think it is."

"That and the fact that they really do want to take over the South. I mean that's why they keep trying to get their commando teams into the South to try to overthrow the government," Kendall Stover added.

"OK, fine. I buy all of that. Let's assume you're both correct. My question is why do most of the time when they sneak over the line they don't actually try to kill anybody, they just recon things and go home? And then every once in a while somebody changes all the rules and they kill whoever they find that day or they shoot up a Guard Post like they did to you on Cindy, Sweeper."

"It's the level of casualties that they think we will accept without going to war, Bagger," Hoover said. "They don't want to actually start a war. They're not ready for that. If they killed a lot of Americans we wouldn't stand for that and we'd probably call in some air strikes on Pyongyang or Wonsan. They don't want that. They just want to harass and kill enough to keep us off balance and worry us, not start a full scale war."

"How do you know? Maybe they will start a full-scale war. With all of the protests back home, what do you think would happen if North Korea attacked here tomorrow? Do you think we'd be able to hold? How long would it take to get five or six divisions over here to reinforce us? Where would they come from? I think America would bail out. I don't think the country would support another war, even if we were attacked. This is not a good situation, gentlemen. Not a good situation at all."

"Room for one more?" said the sweetly feminine voice from beside the table.

"Hi, JD," said Holloway looking up. "I'm not sure that you'd really enjoy our company. We're in kind of a foul mood, but I won't stop you from sitting down."

She hesitated for a moment and then pulled back a chair and sat in it. "That's OK. They send those of us in the Red Cross over here to buoy the spirits of the troops. If you don't mind me listening, I'd like to."

"Mmmm," Hoover mumbled. No one else spoke. Finally Jennifer Dodge broke the silence. "What is it? What's wrong?"

"We're just talking about the Z, JD. Things have gotten a little bloody lately." Looking at the others, Holloway returned to the earlier conversation. "That's another unreal aspect about all of this. Five miles north of here the 1/38th is manning the DMZ, right? They're strung out along the fence and on patrol and so forth. Weapons are loaded. Anything moves shoot it. This morning we were with them and now twelve hours later hours later we're sitting in this O Club drinking Scotch and listening to a band and talking with this lovely round eyed American girl. It's like we're in San Francisco or something. How can the world be this different five miles away? Doesn't anybody else think this is bizarre?"

"Of course it's bizarre, Bagger," replied Hoover. "It's an awfully weird situation. But it's also real. That's just the way it is. Go north of the river, have your gun ready. Go south of the river, no problem, at least most of the time. But you can't even be sure of that. But look around this room. Most of the officers in this battalion have never been north of the river, except for a quick look around. To them, it's something that people talk about. They know it's up there, but it's not part of their life. But it's part of my life and now that I'm back down here I'm glad, but at the same time I think I ought to be back up there."

Holloway looked around the table. "I know exactly what you mean, man. Look, I'm going to say one more thing and then maybe we can get off of this subject. Wouldn't it be an absolute bitch getting killed in the DMZ?"

"Well, hell yeah! It'd be a bitch gettin' killed anywhere," Hoover replied.

"Sure, but I mean the reason they would kill us would be strictly as political pawns. Joe Chink kills so randomly yet selectively at the same time. He seems to just target a certain thing on one particular day that he almost picks out of the air and then tries to wipe it out. If you happen to be in a certain spot at a certain time, tough shit. Just think about how close the three of us came to getting killed in that ambush. If we'd gone into the Z five minutes earlier with the chow truck they'd have most likely killed all of us too. That's how close we came. And then none of us would be sitting here drinking Scotch and listening to the music. And why would we be dead? Just because North Korea wants to keep the US off balance, that's why. And that's why we'd all be cold and dead and buried in the ground. That's why it would be such a bitch." Holloway gazed at his two friends, his eyes moving from one to the other. Behind him the Korean band was announcing its next song.

"Dance with me!"

"What?" Holloway asked JD, having almost forgotten that she was there.

"I said dance with me. Please." It was a slow dance from the '50's with which the band had started their second set. Holloway stood up at the same time as Jennifer. He followed her across the room to the dance floor. As she reached the middle of the floor she whirled around and put her hand up. He took it and slid his right hand behind her back as she pulled him close. He had never had his arm around her before. She felt warm and he could feel wetness on her cheek as it pressed against his. Her face was buried in the crook of his neck.

"Jennifer," he asked quietly. "What's wrong? Are you crying?"

She was dancing very close, refusing to pull her face away from his. "Just hold me. I can't talk," she whispered.

"Jennifer, I don't understand. What's happening?"

"Just shut up and hold me."

They danced in silence, Holloway feeling somewhat embarrassed and wondering if people had noticed her tears and realized how close they were dancing. She was clutching at him, her fingernails almost puncturing the skin of his back through his shirt. Finally the song ended. He tried to look at her as they separated, but she lowered her face and turned quickly and walked off of the dance floor and into the women's john. It was several minutes before she left the little room and by then Holloway had returned to his chair in the corner.

A few minutes later Jennifer Dodge emerged from the ladies room showing no sign of her tears and strode confidently to her former seat and rejoined the three lieutenants. "So what's the word, guys? When are they going to get you off of the hills and bring you back down here to civilization for good?"

"Sweeper's already here. Did you know that?" Holloway said. Jennifer shook her head quickly. "He's the new Bravo XO. The change of command in the Battalion confuses the issue a bit for the rest of us, I guess. We don't know what the new commander is going to want to do, but I'm still hoping that the next new lieutenant that comes in will replace me in the Z. I know Tom wants me back here in Charlie Battery."

"We may not know what the new Battalion Commander is going to do, but I did find out his name," noted Hoover. "Lieutenant Colonel Thomas J. Nordstrum. He's due in Tuesday morning Grant says."

"Really!" Holloway exclaimed. "I didn't know that. Well, I'll probably miss his arrival. Baron and I are due back up on the GP's on Tuesday, along with that new lieutenant who's taking your place. What's his name?"

"His name is Owens, but everybody has already named him the Owl. He looks like one."

"He looks like an owl?" Jennifer asked.

"Well, he's got kind of yellow brown eyes and big black horned rimmed glasses and a little mouth," Stover said. "He's standing right over there at the bar. Take a gander," he offered looking across the room. The four of them stretched or turned in their chairs until they had an unobstructed view of the end of the mahogany bar. All nodded in unison. He did look like an owl.

The band had moved to some acid rock and then eventually reverted to a slow Righteous Brothers classic. Holloway looked over at Jennifer Dodge and pointed toward the dance floor with a questioning look in his eye. She smiled and pushed back her chair. Again they picked their way through the scattered tables and moved to the center of the dance floor. Sherry Cifrianni and Bill Grant were dancing together at one end of the space and Tom Courtney with Kathy Kelsey at the other. Kathy was laughing loudly at one of Courtney's jokes. Bear Buckner was there too, dancing with a Korean girl he had invited to the farewell party. Jennifer and Holloway moved together easily and began to sway to the rhythm.

"Talk to me now," Holloway said after a moment.

"Clay, I'm sorry. I just got very emotional very quickly a few minutes ago. It's a combination of things."

"Like what things?"

"Well, there are a lot of things. I try not to let it show, but things have just been building up inside of me."

"OK. Keep talking."

"Well, three days ago Beth and I were out in the boonies with an engineering company that was having some field exercises. We were working with a group of guys, about twenty of them. We'd passed out the doughnuts and organized a dart game for some prizes. Most of the guys were great. But this one guy with a New York or New Jersey accent kept giving us a really hard time. He just wouldn't let up. His sergeant kept telling him to knock it off, but he didn't and I started thinking, what the hell am I doing here? This jerk doesn't want me here. All he does is want to make fun of us and what we're trying to do. Magic is going home soon and I want to be with him instead of over here, anyway.

Finally, Beth basically tells him to shut up and finally he does. But a few minutes after that there's gunfire in the woods nearby. Nobody knows why. You know, we're just out there in the middle of a field exercise. But about fifteen minutes later a group of ROK Marines with rifles and everything come out of the woods. Some of them seem to be carrying something and one of the Engineer's KATUSA's goes over to see what's going on. So all of us are looking at the ROK's who are moving right in front of us toward the road. Some of the GI's went over closer and I went with them and I looked down and oh my God, what they're doing is dragging a dead man through the weeds. They're holding his ankles and just dragging him. There's a lot of blood on him and the KATUSA's says that he's a North Korean agent that the ROK's have been after for two days and they finally caught him in the woods where he was spying on us. I was so shocked! I never in the world thought there were any UI's around here."

"I can see why that would upset you. It would bother anyone," Holloway said soothingly.

"Beth and I talked about it that night and I thought I was pretty much over it, but I think maybe I wasn't and besides, I haven't seen Magic all week. He's been busy and he can't always get up here. So when I saw you guys I thought you'd buck up my spirits, but all you were talking about was death. When I heard you talking about how you almost died I just wanted to cry. And finally I did. I like you, Bagger. I don't want you to die."

"Hey, JD," he said, pulling her closer as they moved around the floor, "I'm not gonna die. No way. We had one close call, but what are the odds of me getting into something like that again. It's not like they're fighting full-scale battles up there. Most of the time nothing happens at all."

"I still wish you'd get sent back here to Camp Wynne. I miss seeing you around here. Beth misses you too. She told me so."

"Well, it's nice to be missed. But whatever there was is over between Beth and me."

"I know that, but she still likes you. She does miss you." The couple danced quietly for a moment. Then Jennifer again spoke into his ear. "Bagger, there's something else. I'm supposed to tell you something that isn't pleasant."

Holloway pulled back his head and looked at her quizzically, unable to guess as to what she could be referring. "So tell me."

"Magic told me to give you a message from Todd. There's a buddy of Todd's that you met at Ft. Lewis named Brian Bishop. He was a pilot."

"Yeah. I remember Brian. There were four or five of us that bummed around together at Ft. Lewis while we waited to ship out. Brian was going to Vietnam. He didn't talk too much. What about him?"

"Todd said he's dead."

Holloway sucked in his breath. "Oh, man. What happened?"

"Magic said he was killed in an air to air collision over a landing zone. He was with the Americal Division and they went into what Magic called a hot LZ. The fire was very heavy. Brian was flying copilot in one of the Huey slicks and they had just unloaded their troops and were starting to lift off when a VC machine gun that had been hidden in the treeline nearby opened fire and the Huey right next to Brian's was hit. They don't know if the pilot was killed or what, but it went sideways very quickly and went right into Brian's chopper and they both went down and crashed. One of the doorgunners got out. Everyone else was killed. That's all Magic told me."

Holloway was silent. The music had stopped, but he continued to stand in the middle of the small dance floor with his arm around Jennifer. Brian Bishop was not the first friend he'd lost in Vietnam. He probably wouldn't be the last either. But each one took another chip out of his soul. Finally he nodded and looked at Jennifer who was standing quietly, waiting for him to accept what had happened. She took his hand and led him from the floor. When they returned to the table Bob Hoover had already moved to the bar. Kendall Stover was in the act of getting out of his chair.

"Bagger, it looks like Colonel Moody is getting ready to leave. I don't think either of us will be around here for his bridgecrossing Monday morning. I'm going to say good-bye to him."

"OK, Baron. Let's all go," Holloway suggested. They joined the group of people gathered around the outgoing Battalion Commander. Holloway reminisced silently about his first meeting with the man almost three months earlier when he had failed to salute him. So much had happened to him since then. His environment and individual experiences had altered his life considerably in those three months. In many ways he would never again be the relatively naive young man that had been driven through the main gate of Camp Wynne only ninety some days earlier. He'd have the day off tomorrow which was Sunday. Early Monday morning he and Stover would head back to the area of the Dragon Head and Camp Greaves. Then on Tuesday, it was back to the hills that were now their second homes.

*   *   *

Kendall (Red Baron) Stover and Clay (Bagger) Holloway had been killing time outside of the Camp Greaves BOQ as they waited for Ruminski to arrive and transport them to their respective Guard Posts. Ruminski had passed out the morning mail to the two Forward Observers and then driven down to the arms room to find out why newly arrived Lieutenant Owens was having difficulty getting his M-14 away from the armorer. Stover had received several pieces of mail that morning. Not only were there three letters from Mary Lou, but a small audiotape from her as well. Once he found the tape in the padded little yellow envelope, Stover had returned to the BOQ to ask one of the infantry lieutenants if he could play it on the officer's Akai tape deck, which sat on top of a small worn wooden bookshelf. Currently, he was lying on the infantry lieutenant's bunk with a set of stereo headphones over his ears, listening to his wife's voice and wishing he were with her. He looked up as Ruminski entered the large room and looked around. Slipping the headphones off of his head he stood up.

"Five more minutes, Dave. The tape's almost over."

Ruminski grunted. "OK, don't rush. We just got a radio call that said not to leave yet. We're about to get some visitors. I don't know who."

Stover resumed listening for a few minutes, pressed the stop button, and rewound the tape. Then he picked up his helmet and walked back outside. Holloway was in the back of Ruminski's jeep with the seat next to him vacant. Sweeper's replacement, the Owl, was in the second jeep with the driver. They were both munching on Three Musketeers bars. Stover began walking over to join his friend when he heard the whine of a jeep coming up the steep hill toward the little BOQ. The jeep crested the hill and then stopped directly behind Ruminski's rear bumper. Stover recognized the driver and Adjutant from the 8/18th, but neither of the other two passengers. As soon as the vehicle halted, the large man in front jumped out agilely. A tall black man and Bill Grant, both of whom had been seated in the rear, immediately followed him. Dave Ruminski leaped out of his jeep quickly and saluted. The visitor was a lieutenant colonel.

"Lieutenant Ruminski, I'm Colonel Nordstrum," the big man said returning the salute and extending his arm.

"How do you do, Sir! We didn't even know you were in country yet."

"I was able to get my flight moved up. I got in last night. I'd like you to meet Sergeant Major Collins," the Colonel said motioning to the man behind him. The new Battalion Sergeant Major of the 8/18th stood ramrod straight. He had a pleasant looking light brown face with crinkles around the edges of his mouth, from years of either grimacing or smiling. His eyes gave the impression of calmness. The Colonel himself was also an impressive individual. He was the tallest man present standing at a bit more than 6'3". And he was big all over. Not fat, just big, with a barreled chest. His rolled up sleeves revealed thick, yet well defined muscular forearms. The hair on his arms and the closely cropped sides of his head that showed below the fatigue cap indicated that he was probably a reddish blond. His complexion was ruddy and he looked very Swedish. Kendall Stover felt like calling him Olaf.

After shaking Sergeant Major Collins' hand Ruminski turned and introduced the other three officers. Colonel Nordstrum pumped each of their hands with sincerity and chatted amiably with the men for five minutes, wanting to know the usual sorts of things like where they were from and if they were married. He also noted that he had heard several good things about the work that Ruminski and all of his FO's were doing for the infantry. Then he looked at Ruminski.

"Well, Lieutenant, I don't want to interrupt your schedule. Let's go to the GP's."

"Sir? Do you mean to say you will be accompanying us?"

"Why, yes. That's why I came up here. I want to visit each of the three Guard Posts that these officers man and see them and also meet the reconnaissance sergeants that are out there now. Is there something wrong?"

"No, Sir. It's just that Colonel Moody never went up to the GP's and I didn't expect that you would either," Ruminski blurted.

Nordstrum smiled broadly, his eyes closing so tightly Holloway wondered how he could still see. "Well, I'm not Colonel Moody, am I?"

"Obviously not, Sir. Do you have weapons, ammo, flak jackets and helmets?"

"Yes."

"Then follow me, please. I'll take the lead. Have your driver fall in behind me. Owl, you take the rear." The group disintegrated, each man moving quickly back to his seat and the little convoy moving immediately down the hill toward the DMZ.

Colonel Nordstrum was in no particular hurry. Clearly he was keenly interested in each of the GP's, spending at least an hour on each of them. GP Cindy was first. The Owl seemed nervous, intimidated by the presence of his new commanding officer that was visiting his assigned new home at the same time that the Owl was getting his orientation briefing. What seemed to unsettle the Owl was that it was his first time there too and the Colonel seemed to know more about it that he did. Obviously, Bill

Grant had given him a thorough education about what he would find. Once he began looking through the big eyes of the BC scope, the Colonel wanted to be fully briefed regarding everything within sight of the hills. Thomas J. Nordstrum had been to Korea before. Fighting there as a young artillery officer during the war eighteen years earlier, he now spoke with a melancholy tone as he reminisced about some of the areas near where they stood. In addition to the landmarks like Speaker Hill and Propaganda Village he seemed to know about all of the major happenings of the last few weeks. He wanted to see where the recently discovered tunnel was and where the ambush of the chow truck had occurred. When they visited GP Gwen he talked extensively with Sergeant Major McKee about the recent history of the DMZ.

"Yes, Sir," the Sergeant Major said. "It was last March that there was an ambush of a patrol right down there." He pointed to a lightly wooded area five hundred meters away. "The NK's attacked a work party that was replacing signs on the MDL. Took three or four casualties. Firefight went on for a couple of hours. The patrol was pinned down in snow and frozen water most of the time. Most of them had hypothermia and frostbite. Eventually the shooting stopped and Brigade made the decision to send a Huey in to pick up the casualties. It was snowing hard by that time. I was watching the whole thing with binoculars from right here. So the Huey comes in and lands OK and they load up the casualties and start to take off. She gets airborne and then nobody knows for sure what happened. Helicopter just goes over sideways and flies into the ground."

"Was anyone killed?" Colonel Nordstrum asked painfully.

"Yes, Sir. All of them were killed. The whole crew and all of the casualties they had loaded up. Seven men. No one was ever sure if they were hit by ground fire or not, but I don't think so. It was snowing so hard and the wind was gusting badly. I think the wind just caught them and the pilot got disoriented. I guess we'll never know. It's hard to believe when I look at it now and it's all green and lush. Everything was white that day."

Colonel Nordstrum nodded sadly. He'd seen enough. The party walked out of the trench line and back to their waiting jeeps parked on the flat area. The Colonel wished Holloway good luck and the Sergeant Major a happy retirement and then followed Ruminski's jeep as they drove off the back of the hill. The view was spectacular from there. He could see the Imjin River and further away the sun was glinting off of the Han. He could see colors too. The leaves were not just green any more. There were tinges of yellow and an occasional red hue. Autumn meant one thing to the firing batteries of the Second Division. The battery operational readiness tests (ORT's) at Camp St. Barbara were coming soon.

Colonel Nordstrum had already made a decision. Two of the three firing batteries of the 8/18th had only one officer in them, the Battery Commanders. The Battalion couldn't afford to leave its young lieutenants in the DMZ. It needed them as Executive

Officers for Charlie and Alpha Batteries. The battery tests were important and the battery XO's were key to the successful completion of those tests. This was Colonel Nordstrum's first battalion level command. He was not about to get a substandard OER (Officer Efficiency Report) due to his firing batteries not being at their proper state of readiness because he didn't have any XO's in them. In essence, using officers as Forward Observers was a waste of manpower when he was so short of them in the Battalion. None of the FO's had ever been authorized to actually adjust artillery fire against the North Koreans anyway. Most of the time they did very little artillery work, often only assisting the infantry in their duties. If a flock of new lieutenants arrived one day, then he would reconsider and quite possibly give them a few weeks orientation on the Guard Posts. But until then, NCOs would have to handle the forward observer duties on the Guard Posts. Colonel Nordstrum would have to clear the decision through DivArty of course, but the DivArty Commander was an old friend of his. It was an appropriate time to pay him a social visit.

CHAPTER 17

It was to be the last night of the last day on the Guard Posts for Clay Holloway and Kendall Stover. Events had evolved rapidly once Colonel Nordstrum had assumed command of the 8/18th Artillery two weeks earlier. Dave Ruminski had informed both Forward Observers the week before that they were being reassigned following the completion of the next four-day tour on their respective hills. Additional reconnaissance sergeants were undergoing training and would replace the two lieutenants. Holloway and Stover, in turn, would then report back to their batteries at Camp Wynne and assume the duties of the Executive Officers in preparation for the battery tests to be held in early November at Camp St. Barbara.

Holloway was ready to go. He did not feel as comfortable with the men of the 1/38th as he had with the 1/9th. The soldiers on his GP lacked the camaraderie of their predecessors. Poker games in the sleeping bunker were often played in an atmosphere of hostility and there seemed to be decided racial tension between the black and white soldiers from the two squads that currently occupied Gwen. The dissension had started one morning when a black GI awoke in one of the trench positions to find his bunker mate asleep. The man was supposed to have been on guard. The black soldier became so enraged that the other man had fallen asleep and left the position open to infiltrators that he awakened the sleeping man with his bayonet inserted in the man's left nostril. The sleeping man realized that he had screwed up by falling asleep, but still took offense to being awakened so rudely. As the story spread around the GP, the other soldiers seemed to take sides in accordance with who was which color. There was a measurable amount of tension attendant with serving in the DMZ to begin with. This event only served to heighten it.

The changing of the seasons from summer to fall seemed to indicate a change in Holloway's life as well. He felt certain that he would miss Sergeant Major McKee, of course, but he felt ready to rejoin his own Battalion. With the exception of the obvious anger present on the hilltop, the last two tours on the GP's of both Holloway and Stover had been exceedingly dull. To pass the time and in preparation for the battery tests, Holloway had reviewed his red Executive Officer's Handbook that he had brought from Ft. Sill so many times that he could almost recite it verbatim. He was confident there was nothing further he could do to prepare himself, beyond gaining the actual experience. In addition, he had also completed reading several paperback novels and had written letters to almost every friend and relative he had in the States. Kendall Stover, meanwhile, had written two and sometimes three letters a day to Mary Lou. He had also received a special treat from her, which consisted of a homemade Playboy calendar filled with sexy photos of his wife taken by her sister with a Polaroid camera. Stover guarded the photo album closely and usually kept it with him in his observation bunker so that he could gaze at his wife's naked body longingly whenever no one else was around. It was increasingly difficult for him to imagine being unable to be with her for the next eleven and a half months of his tour and unfortunately the photos had only served to make him hornier than he already was.

By 2100 hours of the FO's last night, the trench line of GP Gwen was cloaked in darkness. Inside the CP, Sergeant Major Emerson McKee, Clay Holloway, and newly assigned Staff Sergeant Victor Abbott were engaged in a lively discussion regarding the advantages and disadvantages of the United States Army issuing the M-16A1 rifle to all of its troops as a replacement to the older M-14. The M-16 had found its way into the conflict in Vietnam three years earlier, but had received mixed reviews. The media had given much publicity to reports of the rifle malfunctioning in critical situations in combat and supposedly costing American boys their lives. Military responses insisted that most of those reports were overblown and that whatever problems did exist had been remedied. In the jungles of Southeast Asia there clearly were advantages to using a shorter lighter weight rifle that fired fully automatic and whose ammunition weighed half that of the 7.62mm NATO round of the M-14. However, at ranges over 300 yards, the M-14 was clearly more accurate. While in Vietnam there may be limited opportunities to engage the enemy at long range, in Korea and, indeed, in Europe, the terrain was different and much more conducive to long range engagements. In addition, cold weather, like that encountered during the Korean winters, was apt to affect the accuracy of the lighter weight barrel of the M-16. But clearly, the Army intended to replace all M-14's with the M-16 as soon as there were enough of them. All of the infantrymen of the Second Infantry Division already had been issued the newer rifle. But Clay Holloway and his fellow artillerymen still carried the older weapon. After more than thirty minutes of debate, all three individuals had reached a common ground that agreed that replacement of the M-14 in Korea was not a sound move. Though they all agreed good-naturedly that in the end their opinion didn't mean a damn thing.

Staff Sergeant Abbott was a tall dark haired NCO in his late twenties who was spending his first night on GP Gwen. He had only just been assigned to the 1/38th Infantry, having begun his overseas tour in Vietnam eight months earlier where he had been wounded severely enough to require evacuation from that country, but not seriously enough to qualify for a combat exclusion. He had four months left to complete on his tour and partially because of the announced cutbacks in Vietnam, he had been sent to Korea to finish his commitment.

Holloway's field telephone, which linked him by wire to the TOC and through the TOC to the other GP's, sat on a wooden table next to him. Suddenly the telephone began chirping. The phone was designed to chirp rather than ring so that it would sound more like a cricket than a telephone. Kendall Stover had once wryly observed that when the enemy hears one of the phones chirping he won't say, "I hear an American telephone ringing," but rather, "There's one of those American field phones that's supposed to sound like a cricket." Holloway picked up the chirping phone.

"Lieutenant Holloway speaking," he answered, squeezing the rubber push to talk button with his fingers.

"Bagger, it's me." Kendall Stover was on the other end.

"Hey, what's up, chingo?"

"Are you guys getting any action over there?" Stover inquired.

"Negative. Not that I know of. Why?"

"Well, be advised we're getting probed over here on Carol. No doubt about it."

"Well, just be cool. No noise. Use your starlights."

"Yeah, OK. I just wanted to let you know."

"Thanks for the scoop. Hang tough, Baron. Call back when it's over."

"Roger that. Out here."

Holloway replaced the receiver into the base. "Carol is getting probed," he announced. At the same moment the infantry telephone chirped. The RTO picked up the handset, listened for a moment and then offered it to Sergeant Major McKee, who listened for a moment and then issued his normal directive.

"Sit tight. We'll be right out." Sergeant Major McKee looked at his two companions. "Sounds like we're being probed as well. It may be a coordinated effort. I'm going outside." He picked up his grenade launcher and bandoleer of assorted grenades and exited the little CP quickly.

Sergeant Abbott looked quizzically at Holloway and smoothed his mustache. "Does this happen often, Sir? I mean do they think it's serious?"

"Never can tell," Holloway replied. "Just be alert and be quiet. Sometimes it's UI's and sometimes it's just our own people getting jumpy. We had a little action a couple of weeks ago, but a lot of the guys on this hill are still pretty green and they may be just imagining things."

Holloway and Abbott each grabbed their rifles from the wooden rack and moved down the steps in the direction where the Sergeant Major had already disappeared. Silently they moved into the trench line and walked quickly to position #2. Ahead of them they could see the back of the Sergeant Major as he spoke softly to the men inside of the little bunker. Finally he backed out and turned around. Seeing Holloway and Abbott behind him he pointed silently to the area where the noises had been reported. It was a shallow depression that ran up the left side of the hill almost parallel to the trench line on that side. The draw ended on top of the hill twenty meters in front of position #1, which was fifty feet to the left of position #2. High grasses and weeds filled both the draw and the open area surrounding it. Also in the hollowed out area was the most notable terrain feature on the hill. It was a large brownish gray boulder measuring thirty feet in circumference and standing more than seven feet high. Months earlier Sergeant Major McKee had ordered a claymore mine to be secluded at the backside base of the huge rock to adequately cover the blind spot in the draw. Beyond the boulder the terrain sloped gradually upward until it crested slightly above the trench line fifty meters away. To the left and rear of position #1 was the flat area behind the CP and at the back edge of the flat area was the fence and gate to the Guard Post. It was this gate where all vehicles, which drove up the backside of the hill, would enter the occupied area of the hill.

In total, seven soldiers occupied the area facing the draw and the boulder. Each of their eyes and ears were alerted for the slightest sensation of sound or movement in the darkness. The GI's could see the outline of the massive rock, but little else of value. The exception, however, was Corporal Hugh McDonald, who once again was using his starlight scope to seek out the face of the enemy. Each of the seven men flinched involuntarily as the unexpected noise of something heavy crashing through the grass reached their ears. The sound was easily identifiable. A rock had been displaced and was rolling down the hill. It hadn't started moving by itself. Whoever was in the draw had been awfully careless.

Sergeant Major McKee sprang into action. "Blow the claymore in the draw! Fire in the hole! Fire in the hole!"

Click! Click! Click! Whammmm! The command detonated mine exploded with a deafening roar of flame and smoke, the little ball bearings cutting a swath through the weeds. Seven heads, which had sought cover below the edge of the trench line, popped back up as the echo of the explosion reverberated across the DMZ.

"I'm going out. Cover me," Abbott whispered as he climbed over the lip of the trench keeping his silhouette low along the ground.

"Wait a minute," ordered the Sergeant Major, grabbing Abbott's pant leg. "Come back in here!"

Abbott slid backwards into the trench. Holloway poked his head into the opening to position #1. "Ring the other positions on the phone. Tell everyone we have a man going out. In fact, make that two men," he whispered. Holloway had decided to accompany the E-6.

"OK, listen," the Sergeant Major said hurriedly, having overheard Holloway's comment. "Don't go past the boulder. When you want illumination give me a signal and I'll put up a star cluster from the grenade launcher. If you get into trouble, head back in. We'll cover you."

Abbott went out first, slithering over the top of the trench and down the slight incline toward the boulder in the draw twenty meters away. Clay Holloway waited a moment and crawled out behind him, keeping to Abbott's left rear. The two men moved silently, their eyes and ears tuned to register the slightest movement or sound. Abbott sought the man who had loosened the rock. Holloway operated as his wingman, scanning the terrain to the left and ahead of them where the ground inclined slightly upward. He gripped his rifle tightly as his thoughts raced. He hoped the rifle was all he would need, though his .45 was in his black leather holster as well. But realizing he had no grenades, he wished he had brought some. The black combat knife that Hackworth had presented to him was taped upside down to his web shoulder straps to make it easier to grab in an emergency. Fervently he prayed it wouldn't come down to a knife fight. Maybe the man was already dead, a victim of the ball bearings spewed forth by the claymore. The two Americans were approaching the draw. Abbott's eyes looked beyond it and suddenly discerned a shape hidden in the weeds.

"Give me illumination," he hissed back toward the Sergeant Major waiting in the trench watching their every move. McKee pointed the M-79 skyward and pulled the single shot trigger. Bang! Pop! The flare exploded high above the draw temporarily ruining the night vision of anyone looking at it. Abbott was not looking at the flare. His eyes sought out the shape in the weeds ahead. Suddenly he was on his knees.

"There! In the weeds," he cried as he touched the trigger of the M-16, which obediently reacted, with a finger of continuous flame bursting from the muzzle as he fired fully automatic from his hip into the form lying in the weeds. Holloway could see the form too. He began firing into the same area. Then they stopped.

"Shit! Goddamnit! It's a sandbag," Abbott yelled. A mixture of relief and fear swept over Holloway. Maybe the sandbag wasn't a man, but the sandbag hadn't dislodged the rock. His senses went to full alert. The little hairs on the back of his neck stood on end and a shiver shot through the upper portion of his spine. The flare above them had illuminated both men like Christmas trees as it floated down on top of them, suspended by its small silk parachute. They had become the targets.

"Abbott, watch out! Get down!"

The sergeant turned quickly and looked back at Holloway for only a second and then dropped flat. Simultaneously the lightning bolts erupted from the crest of the hill to their right front, the whizzing of the bullets over the two men's heads mixed with the thunder claps of the AK-47 rounds exploding in the weapons' chambers.

"Jesus Christ!" Holloway was screaming into the dirt that pressed against his lips as he tried burrowing his head into the ground where he lay. Weeds and dirt pushed into his mouth. The bullets were screaming closely over his back as he heard the friendly clatter of the M-60 from position #2 replying in kind, forcing the invaders to duck away beyond the crest.

Bang! Sergeant Major McKee was blooping grenades with his launcher over the rim of the hill from where the firing had originated. A puff of black smoke was barely visible as it arose from the backside of the crest. The men in position #1 had taken up the fight as well, blanketing the side of the hill in front of Holloway with bullets. Abbott and Holloway went into reverse gear, crawling backwards toward the relative safety of the trench. Within seconds there was a whoosh to their left, followed by a blinding light from a flare that lit up the entire area of the gate. Someone had hit the trip wire in front of it. A figure, momentarily illuminated and exposed, turned and dove from the edge of the hill as the position #1 gunners shifted their fire toward the flare. WHAM!!! Chunks of wood were propelled through the air, torn loose from the 4x4 supports of the gate frame by the claymore that had just exploded behind it. Stimulated by the increases in the noise level, Holloway spun his body around and slithered the last few meters to the trench like a snake on overdrive. A second later Abbott dropped head first into the trench on top of him. Untangling themselves, they lay there momentarily panting, then finally gathering their feet under themselves and rising to a crouch.

The first parachute star cluster had burned out and been replaced by a second, as McKee alternated his firing between the flares and the high explosive rounds. The trip flare at the gate was also burning down as shadows began to replace the brightly illuminated scene. Abbott yelled to one of his people to go to the ammo bunker and get the Sergeant Major some additional illumination rounds for the M-79.

"Hold your fire," Sergeant Major McKee finally commanded. Only McDonald in position #1 had still been shooting. He stopped instantly. Holloway's ears were ringing. As the flares burned their last bit of chemical, it became apparent that all of the soldiers had lost their night vision. Once again the hill became bathed in blackness. The quiet became deafening. Holloway moved into position #1, grabbed the field phone, and cranked the handle.

"This is Lieutenant Holloway. We're secure on this side. No casualties. Don't leave your positions. Everybody stay put. Does anyone have any other enemy movement to report? Sound off if you do." No one spoke. "OK. Stay calm. Stay alert. Report any problems, but don't start imagining things." Holloway left the bunker and rejoined Sergeant Major McKee a few feet away.

"You two aren't hurt are you?" Abbott and Holloway shook their heads. "Those guys almost ruined your whole day. I think I might have hit them though. My first round dropped right over the side of the hill where they were firing. I thought I heard a scream."

"The scream was probably me," smirked Holloway. "That scared the living crap out of me!"

"Yeah! That was semi-tense wasn't it, LT?" Abbott added. "Thanks for the warning, by the way. Those pricks almost had me. What do you think happened?"

Sergeant Major McKee spoke first. "Well, the way I look at it, there was at least one UI in the draw that dislodged that rock that rolled down the hill. We either hit him with the Claymore or had him trapped there with you guys closing in on him. His chingos saw what was happening and opened up on you to pull the attention away from whoever was in the draw. It probably worked, but I'm willing to bet we're going to find blood when daylight comes. No bodies though. I guaranfuckingtee you they won't leave any bodies if they can help it. If they've got any dead, they'll gut 'em to make them lighter to carry and then they'll take the corpses with them."

A thought flashed through Holloway's mind. A picture of his body being gutted and thrown over a faceless North Korean soldier's shoulder and being whisked away into the darkness. The vision made him shudder and turn away from his companions. Ten minutes of silence followed. The hostile action seemed to be over. "I'm going back to the CP for a bit," Holloway finally announced. He wanted to check with the Red Baron to see if everything was all right on Carol.

"OK, Sir. I'll check the other positions and make sure everything is secure. I'll see you in a bit," McKee replied and moved away into the darkness. Holloway returned to his place in the CP and rang up Kendall Stover on his hill three kilometers to the northeast. The young Easterner with the wire rimmed glasses answered on the first ring.

"Stover here!"

"Hey, Baron, what the fuck, over!"

"Hey, Bagger, what the fuck, out!"

"What's shakin' over there, chingo?"

"Nada now. Those sneaky little bastards were out there all right. We lobbed a few grenades their way and they backed off. No incoming. How about you? We heard a lot of booms going off. Somebody was popping caps."

"Yeah, we got into some shit. I'll tell you about it tomorrow. No casualties for the good guys. We'll check in the daylight for Joe Chink. We may have drawn blood."

"No shit? What happened?"

"I'll tell you later. I just wanted to make sure everything was numba one at your place. Catch you later. Out here." Holloway set down the handset. It would be good to leave his friend wondering what had happened. He'd pay more attention to the story when it was told tomorrow. Holloway opened his shirt pocket and withdrew a plastic waterproof cigarette case. As he shook out a Winston he realized his hand was shaking slightly. He placed his palm on his thigh. It was trembling too. Man! Wouldn't he ever get used to this stuff? He wondered if everyone shook like this when the action was over. It must be the adrenaline, he mused. He supposed he could ask the Sergeant Major when he returned, but he didn't think he wanted to. McKee always seemed so goddamned calm. So under control. He couldn't imagine him being nervous about anything.

The field phone linked to the positions rang in front of the RTO sitting at his table. The man picked it up immediately.

"CP," answered the RTO. He listened for a moment and then turned to Holloway. "Sir, the Sergeant Major wants you to come out to position #6 right away. He thinks there's someone down in the wire on the side of the hill. He says bring some grenades."

Holloway grunted and snuffed out his cigarette. Walking quickly, he moved into the trench line near position #6 less than a minute later. Ahead of him in the dim light he could discern the forms of Abbott and the Sergeant Major. Suddenly there was the thud of something heavy landing on the wooden planking of the trench floor. Closest to him, Abbott lurched and dove at Holloway, screaming. "Down!! Down!!" Unsure what was happening, Holloway too spun about, diving away from the direction in which he had been walking.

"BLAAMMM!"

The explosion in the confined space of the timber-lined trench deafened Holloway, stunning him momentarily. He laid there, his head spinning and his thoughts jumbled. The world seemed to be moving in slow motion. He could hear yelling and shooting. People seemed to be shooting everywhere. He could see gun flashes further down the trench. Then someone was moving near him. It was Abbott who was lurching to his feet and standing up and firing his rifle and yelling. Holloway blinked three times. He tried to rise, but couldn't quite get his balance. He tried again, holding onto one of the 6x6's that supported the trench wall. There was a form lying motionless on the floor of the trench. Staggering, he moved around the shooting sergeant and approached the form lying in the darkness. He looked down. Why was Sergeant Major McKee still lying on the trench floor? Why didn't he get up and use his M-79? Holloway knelt down and peered at his face in the darkness. The man's eyes were closed. He reached under the fallen NCO and tried to raise him to a sitting position. His back was warm and wet and sticky. Oh, sweet Jesus! This can't be happening!

"Abbott! Help me!" Holloway cried. The E-6 had stopped firing and looked down behind him.

"Oh, shit! Oh, shit! He was between me and the grenade. Hey, you in the bunker!" he called to the nearest position. "Call the CP. Get Doc out here. The Sergeant Major's hit bad."

*   *   *

A misty rain seemed to hang in the cool air. Clay Holloway wore his hooded rubber rain suit jacket over his fatigue shirt. It wasn't enough. Under the rubber shell he shivered. As he squatted on the side of the hill outside of the bunker complex he glanced over at his duffel, which was just inside the doorway out of the rain. It was still dry. He looked at his watch; 0930. Ruminski should be there soon. He was already late.

He had told Holloway he would pick him up before Stover. Maybe it was that damn morning briefing that had held him up. That wasn't all bad. He might have word of the Sergeant Major's condition.

Emerson McKee had been alive when the armored personnel carrier of the reaction force had evacuated him around midnight. Holloway had watched Doc work on the wounds in the sleeping bunker where they had carried him, assisting the medic when he could. Multiple shrapnel wounds from the North Korean hand grenade had ripped the NCOs back and legs, though none appeared to be mortal. The young medic had gotten most of the bleeding stopped and by the time the APC had arrived, Sergeant Major McKee was conscious and trying to speak, although Doc had tried to keep him quiet. He was a tough old bird, that was for sure, but still his age would work against him. As they had loaded the stretcher into the back of the armored track, Holloway had taken the older man's hand and squeezed it gently, getting a faint smile in return.

The hand grenade blast had been a single, almost random event. One grenade out of the black night had been thrown and it had found its way into the trench only a few feet from where McKee and Abbott had been standing. One little kiss from the darkness and then nothing, as though it had never happened. But it convinced Abbott that earlier the Americans had, in fact, drawn blood and this was an act of revenge. Abbott's theory had been born out after daylight when he and Holloway and two other men had searched the draw and the hill beyond. Two piles of spent brass cartridge cases of 7.62 x 39 caliber with Chinese writing had been found on the backside of the hill. Nearby, where the Sergeant Major had been blooping the HE grenades, there were red splotches with a blood trail moving down the side of the hill and undoubtedly into the woods beyond. Abbott had noted that if the TOC wanted it followed one of the patrols would have had to do it. Though once the rain began an hour later, any thought of following a blood trail vanished. There was more blood in the draw along with a trampled area where someone had either crawled or had been dragged back over the side of the hill. Holloway reflected on how brazen the UI's were to move up that close to an armed position where the men used night observation devices and Claymores ringed the perimeter. And for what? Harassment or reconnaissance? Were they really there to kill or possibly to kidnap as the battalion intelligence officer had predicted the month before? Holloway knew none of the answers and realized he never would. He looked around the hill. It had become part of his life, part of his soul. In a few minutes he would take his last jeep ride down the dirt road on the backside. He would probably never come back to the hill, but he would never forget it. He could never forget it.

Jeep engines whined. The first of the two-vehicle element crested the back of the hill. The escort jeep with its M-60 mounted on a uni-pod came first. Behind it were Ruminski, D'Antonio, and the Owl. Ruminski had told Holloway that the Owl was going to take the next four-day shift on Gwen. The vehicles made tight turns in the little area and then stopped. Ruminski was out and striding toward Holloway before the jeep engine was switched off. The two officers looked silently at each other for a moment.

"You OK?" Ruminski asked.

"You could say that. Any word on the Sergeant Major?"

"Yes. And the word is good. He's already in Seoul. They pulled out six hunks of grenade shrapnel and he is resting comfortably. They don't think they'll be any complications. No vital organs were hit. Hey tell me somethin'. How come you people don't wear your goddamn flak jackets up here? What the hell do you think they're for?"

"I can't argue with you, Dave. I wish he'd had his on, believe me. Let's make sure we tell that to the Owl."

"I will," Ruminski said as he turned and waved the Owl over to where he stood. "Go ahead and cover what happened last night and then brief the Owl on what he needs to know about the hill and we'll get this show on the road and pick up your buddy Stover. I know he's anxious to get off of Carol and talk to you too."

A half hour later the misty rained had subsided and Holloway was ready to depart. He saw Staff Sergeant Abbott squatting down on the other side of the gate. Walking over to him, he extended his hand.

"Sergeant Abbott, I'm about to unass the area. I just wanted to say good bye."

The E-6 finished arming the new trip flare that he had just mounted to replace the one triggered in the action the previous night and then arose. "I understand you're not coming back, Sir," he noted shaking the lieutenant's hand.

"Right. They're assigning me as XO of my firing battery. Lieutenant Owens will be here for the next few days as the forward observer and then either Sergeant Shavers or one of the new recon sergeants will take over."

"Well, Sir, it's been a pleasure. Take care of yourself. Hey, have you heard anything more about the Sergeant Major?'

"Yeah. Lieutenant Ruminski told me that at the morning briefing they said he's doing fine. He's in a hospital in Seoul. No vital organ damage. He should recover fully in a couple of weeks." Holloway studied the gate frame close to where he was standing. The claymore had blown huge chunks out of it the night before. "Man, this thing took a pounding didn't it?"

"It sure did. I've already ordered more wood to be sent up. Well, that's great news about the Sergeant Major. We're gonna miss him. That man's forgot more about soldiering than I'll ever learn." He paused for a moment. "I guess the Company XO is coming up here this afternoon to take over as Guard Post Commander for a few days until they get someone permanent."

"Really," Holloway commented. "What's his name?"

"Lieutenant Werner."

Holloway smiled to himself. Werner, that dumb son-of-a-bitch! That was the guy that had told Holloway two months earlier to drop out of the column in the dark and wait for Ruminski at the wrong crossroads. "Well, good luck with Lieutenant Werner." Holloway wanted to say more, but he thought the better of it. He turned and walked to the jeep where Ruminski was waiting. As he climbed into the back, the jeep lurched forward and the two vehicles headed down the hill, passing the site where the ambush of the chow truck had occurred, and finally approaching the high, rusty, chain linked barrier fence that seemed to be meander all the way to the South China Sea. Then it was down the road to the gate for GP Carol, pick up the Baron, and, after retrieving their gear from the BOQ at Camp Greaves, head south toward the village of Sonyu-ri and Camp Wynne.

Holloway rode in silence as he sat huddled with Stover in the back of Ruminski's jeep. The cool October air was chilling him to the bone now that the jeep was traveling at a constant 35 mph. The events of the previous night were gnawing at him. He had come very close to being killed and his mentor had been seriously wounded. The positive news about the Sergeant Major had helped, of course. Still he felt saddened that it had happened at all. He had planned to remember Sergeant Major McKee smiling and waving good-bye to him as he drove off of the hill for the last time. It hadn't been like that. Unfortunately he knew that the way he would remember him now was lying bleeding and unconscious on the trench floor and then being loaded into the back of an APC wrapped in a poncho that covered his blood soaked bandages. Holloway looked thoughtfully at his hands. There was still some of his blood dried in the creases of his skin and under his nails. The jeep was nearing a small cluster of hooches that sat astride a small crossroads two kilometers away from Camp Wynne. One of the buildings held a hand-lettered sign in Korean and English that read "Steambath." Holloway leaned forward in the seat.

"D'Antonio, stop here," he ordered. Ruminski turned and looked at him questioningly. "Baron, make sure all my shit gets into my room will you?" Holloway asked. "Here's the key. I'll be along in a while."

"Holloway, what the hell are you doing," Ruminski asked. "Officers aren't supposed to be in the ville, you know."

"Cover for me. I have something I want to do." Holloway walked away from the jeep and didn't look back. Ruminski watched him for a moment and then signaled D'Antonio to move out.

Holloway walked directly across the street and into the wooden structure with the steambath sign. His only experience with a steambath had been on one occasion at the steambath at RC #1 and it had been an enjoyable experience. It was run by the Army's PX system. All the attendants were Korean girls dressed in aqua colored dresses that made them look like beauticians. Five dollars had gotten him a steambath, shower, bath, and massage. It had taken two hours and he had loved it. But RC#1 was an hour away and he didn't want to take the time, nor did he feel like making the effort, to go there. He'd decided to try out this local Korean steambath. It couldn't be much different than RC #1 and he suddenly felt obsessed about getting clean as quickly as he could. It was bad enough not having a shower for five days. But on top of that, he wanted badly to get the blood off of his hands and out of his head. It would be a cleansing of both the body and the spirit.

Stepping out of the daylight and through the open doorway he was greeted by a friendly female voice. "Annahashamika, Lieutenant."

"Annahashamika. I want a steambath and a massage."

"Steambath and massageee one thousand won."

"One thousand won? Neh. OK." He fished in his pocket and came out with a wad of bills. He handed the young woman behind the counter a thousand. She noticed the extra money in his hand.

"You want special massageee? Fifteen hundred won."

"What's a special massageee? What does that do for me?"

"You like special massageee. Feel good. Feel numba one."

"Sure, why not. Fifteen hundred won. Special massageee. OK."

The woman left the room momentarily and returned with a petite girl of about twenty years who was dressed in a pair of white cotton shorts and a matching halter-top. She had an attractive oval face with high cheekbones and jet-black haircut at shoulder length. Smiling at Holloway, she took him by the hand and led him down a dimly lit hallway to one of the bathrooms. Still smiling at him she confirmed, "You want special massageee?"

"Yeah, I guess so," he replied, not actually knowing what that included. "What does that mean exactly?"

The girl shrugged her shoulders. "Moola," she answered, indicating that she didn't understand the question. Clearly her English was very limited. Holloway looked around the room as she reached up to unbutton his smelly damp fatigue shirt. The cubicle was brightly lighted with fluorescent lamps. The walls were painted yellow, with matching yellow tile covering the bottom five feet of the walls that surrounded the tub and shower area. Between them was a four-legged wooden stool standing on a wooden deck that was six inches above the rest of the floor. A white steam cabinet with a front opening door sat in one corner of the room.

Tugging off Holloway's shirt and pulling his olive drab T-shirt over his head, the girl motioned for him to sit on a low bench. Once he had complied, she straddled his left leg, untied the laces of his heavy dirty combat boots, and pulled the boot free. She peeled off his sock and repeated the procedure for the other foot. Motioning for him to stand, the girl began to unbuckle his belt. Holloway began to feel self-conscious. In the PX steambath he had undressed himself after the attendant had left the room.

Whenever she had been with him he had been submerged in a tub or when on the massage table at least been covered by a small towel over his groin.

"What's your name?" Holloway asked politely, trying to relieve some the uneasiness he was feeling.

"Miss Lu," the girl said smiling and pointing to herself.

He smiled back and focused his eyes on the ceiling as she finished with the buttons on his fly and pulled his fatigue pants and under shorts down his legs. He stepped out of them and watched as she carefully folded the filthy trousers and laid them over a railing near where his shirt was hanging. She took his hand then and led him to the steam cabinet, where he climbed in. Setting the dial for ten minutes, she stroked his hair for a moment and then left the room. He could hear her chatting with one of the other girls next door.

Perspiration began to build on his brow and he could feel a droplet of sweat running down his left cheek. Quietly Miss Lu reentered the room, picked up a washcloth, and walked to the steam cabinet. She looked quizzically into Holloway's eyes and wiped his forehead with the cloth. Holloway smiled. "I'm fine. Numba one," he said.

Miss Lu glanced at the dial and again left the room only to return three minutes later to turn off the machine and open the cabinet door. A cloud of steam billowed forth as Holloway stepped out, his naked reddened body dripping with sweat. She led him to the four-legged wooden stool and motioned for him to sit. After adjusting the temperature of a hand held shower, she began moving it around his head and body, washing him clean of the perspiration. After thoroughly drenching him, she began shampooing his head. Her fingers penetrated his hair and massaged his scalp. Over and over she washed his hair, changing the motion of her hands to create small circles. Holloway could feel the tension and the fatigue washing away from him along with the oil and grit that had accumulated in his short brown hair over five days on the GP. Eventually she rinsed the shampoo from his head and began washing him gently with a soap-covered washcloth. The girl seemed to dart around his seated body, washing his neck and shoulders and back and then moving quickly to the front and repeating the process on his chest. One at a time she placed his hands on his head and scrubbed under his arms and then down his sides. Kneeling in front of him and placing his foot on her thighs she washed the soles of his feet first, then the toes, and finally the ankle. After completing the second foot, the girl again motioned for Holloway to stand. Still kneeling in front of him, she washed both legs and hips.

Holloway was trying very hard to concentrate on things other than what Miss Lu was doing. The closeness of her face to his groin area had certainly not gone unnoticed and the soft washcloth caressing his hips and inner thighs and stomach had caused him to begin to stiffen. Petrified that he would embarrass himself by becoming fully erect during what was supposed to be only a harmless bath, he began to concentrate desperately on other things. He started thinking of Christmas, then switched to dead animals in the road. Anything to take his mind away from the sensations he was feeling. Suddenly she stopped and put down the washcloth. She arose and after rubbing the soap between her hands and coating her palms with the sudsy mixture began to again wash his chest, this time caressing it with her bare hands. Finally she slid her hands down over his stomach and began to wash his pubic area gently. Holloway breathed in sharply as his body quivered. Wow! This certainly wasn't like the PX steambath, was Holloway's first reaction. He closed his eyes and sighed. When she finished washing him a moment later, ending by tugging his manhood gently, his fear had been realized. He was hard as a rock. She looked at him and smiled sweetly.

She rinsed him with a hand held shower and placed him in a large ceramic tub. After soaking for five minutes, she beckoned Holloway then and he followed her to the other side of the room and lay naked on his back on a vinyl-covered table. Miss Lu finished drying him with a fluffy cotton towel and squeezed some lotion on her hands and began to manipulate his feet. Using her strong thumbs she worked the balls of his feet for some time, finally sliding the thumbs over the arch and then working on the heel. Each toe was manipulated and popped separately before she left the foot. Then the calves were kneaded over and over with the palms of her hands. As she moved to the thighs she began a criss crossed motion, moving one hand over the other. The other leg was done in the same manner.

Holloway's eyes were closed. He was partially relaxed, yet still semi-aroused. As Miss Lu's hands worked the inside of the thigh near his crotch she brushed lightly against his manliness. Again he tried not to allow what she was doing to physically effect him. Moving to his abdomen and stomach she continued to use her palms, occasionally adding lotion to his body. Finishing the massaging action on his upper body she began to use the tips of her fingers, running them lightly over him, stopping to occasionally play with the black curly hair of his chest. Soon she began again to lightly stroke his chest using only her fingernails and touching his nipples with them. Holloway had given up trying to concentrate on other things. Fully erect by this time, he didn't know what she had planned, but whatever it was he had no intention of interfering. Suddenly he felt her hands on his shaft, her palms covered with the creamy lotion. She began to stroke softly. Holloway's mouth opened slightly and he sighed. It didn't take long. He gripped the sides of the table as his body convulsed and he felt the fears and the angers and the tension exploding out of him. Slowly he opened his eyes. Miss Lu was smiling at him.

"You likee special massagee?"

"Yeah! You could say that," he whispered.

Gently she cleaned him with a wet washcloth and then dried him. Motioning with her finger for him to roll over onto his face, she moved to the head of the table and began to work on his neck. Holloway almost purred. He still had the whole backside left to be done. Feeling the full relaxation of the moment, he closed his eyes and allowed himself to enjoy every push and pull and knead of her hands. At some point while she manipulated his back, his concentration lessened. At some further point as she massaged his buttocks he lost concentration entirely. Twenty minutes later she was calling to him and shaking him gently.

"Yoboseyo.Yoboseyo. No chanda," she called to him. His eyes fluttered open. He realized she was finished and he peeled lifted himself off of the table to which his skin had partially become attached. Seeing that he was awake, Miss Lu left the room, returning five minutes later as Holloway was tying his bootlaces. As he finished and stood up she smiled and bowed to him. He bowed in return, thanked her, and handed her another five hundred won. Then he walked down the hallway, out of the door, and down the road. Two hours earlier he had felt like finding a hole in the earth and climbing in and pulling a lid over it forever. Now his spirits were buoyed. He walked jauntily along the dirt road heading for Camp Wynne. The only thing he would have liked to have changed at that point was that he wished he had some clean fatigues instead of putting on the damp grimy ones he had arrived in. But he'd change as soon as he got back to the compound. And then he'd charge over to Charlie Battery and start acting like the Executive Officer he now was. Damn that special massageee was great! He began to whistle.

CHAPTER 18

For planning purposes, a 105mm howitzer M101A1 (towed) is assumed to have a maximum range of 11,000 meters or slightly less than seven miles. Because it is an indirect fire weapon, which is to say that the gun crew does not normally actually see the target, there needs to be a fairly large chunk of real estate with nothing of importance between the guns and the impact area in order to practice the firing of the cannons with a significant degree of safety. In addition to having a rather large impact area, it is also desirable to have an additional safety cushion around the impact area in the event that the artillery rounds do not land where they are supposed to land. To do the required maneuvering and live shooting of the guns in preparation for the upcoming battery tests, therefore, necessitated having a lot of room to practice. In the northwest portion of the Republic of Korea, Camp St. Barbara, named for the patron saint of artillery, was such a place.

Traveling by gun convoy, Camp St. Barbara, or St. Barb as it was called, was approximately three hours away from the 8/18th's compound of Camp Wynne. Therefore, a trip to St. Barb began early in the day and always required an overnight stay in the field even if only one day of shooting was involved. On Second Lieutenant Clay Holloway's third day back from the DMZ, it was his assigned mission to lead Charlie Battery to St. Barb where he would link up with First Lieutenant Tom Courtney, his Battery Commander, and direct the operations of the firing battery in a series of live fire exercises. The troops were awakened with first call at 0530, referred to as "oh dark thirty" by many of the men, fed breakfast, and directed to form the convoy in the same fashion that it had been formed the previous July when Holloway had been ordered to lead it north to the DMZ.

After departing the Battery area by 0730 and trundling out of the main gate and down the dirt road, Holloway stood up on the seat of the 1 ¼ ton truck that lead the column and looked behind him at the eighteen vehicles and six howitzers that followed. Satisfied with their spacing and overall appearance, he returned to his seat. The convoy would travel through Pobwon-ni and then southeast toward Uijongbu and the I Corps area. Autumn was in the air. The coolness of early October combined with the smell of truck diesel and registered its imprint on Holloway's brain. The leaves of the trees in the distance were filled with brightly colored autumnal bursts. He thought briefly of football and of how he would miss the entire season, seeing only an occasional final score or perhaps a black and white television rebroadcast of a game that had been played two weeks earlier. No Ohio State versus Michigan. No Cleveland Browns versus the Dallas Cowboys. The only game he could afford to be concerned with now was the final score of Charlie Battery when the battery test results were reported three weeks hence. That would be his Super Bowl.

Tom Courtney, First Sergeant St. Clair, and the rest of the advance party had departed Camp Wynne ahead of the battery. In the field artillery, it is standard operating procedure (SOP) for the battery commander to do an RSOP (reconnaissance surveillance and occupation of position) in advance of the main party. Quite simply the advance party selects the exact site where the firing battery will be located and secures the area. Then, when the main battery arrives it can be lead into the position with a minimum of confusion and turmoil.

Once Charlie Battery arrived at the firing point at St. Barbara it was directed immediately into position with the six gun guides leading their individual truck and howitzer into place. The two and a half ton gun trucks were always pulled into position heading directly opposite of the anticipated direction of fire since the technique would place the howitzer being towed behind it almost exactly where it should be when it was unhooked from the truck. Howitzer crews theoretically are composed of seven men. Given the overall shortages in the Second Division, however, it was rare to find even five men, including the chief of section. Often the crew numbered four or even only three men. Therefore, it was not desirable to leave the gun in such a place that it would have to be muscled around the field by hand. Thus it was important to unhook the gun exactly where it was supposed to stay.

Arriving at a new position, the first job of the Executive Officer is to lead the guns into position. That being accomplished, the XO moves immediately to the magnetically oriented aiming circle, which has been readied by the advance party during the RSOP. The aiming circle is similar to the instrument used by surveyors. It is essential to an artillery battery since it is used to "lay" the battery, a term used to refer to the proper orientation of the guns by using the aiming circle and the optical sighting system. Holloway laid each of the six guns as he called out the directions measured in mils. In the field artillery a circle is divided into 6400 mils compared with the 360 degrees that most people feel comprises a circle. Degrees are simply too large to give the accuracy required for precise gunnery. Once all six guns were laid, Holloway called out "Battery is laid." Technically, Charlie Battery was ready to shoot.

While the gun section chiefs and the XO were preparing themselves, the remainder of the gun crews was also at work completing their routine tasks. Gun crewmen, often called gun bunnies, were unloading ammunition, fuses, and tools from their trucks and then pulling the vehicles a safe distance away from the guns. Artillery shells are never transported with fuses in them, but instead have a screw-in nose plug, which is removed when it is time to fuse the projectile. Without a fuse the projectile is very safe. It can be hammered, shot, or run over by a truck and the shell will remain inert. There are a variety of projectiles carried by an operational field artillery crew including high explosive (HE), white phosphorous (WP or Willie Peter), high explosive anti-tank (HEAT) which is used to defend the battery against armored vehicles, beehive, which fires thousands of miniature steel darts against an infantry attack, illumination, which are parachute flares fired to light up a large area at night, and smoke, which marks or obscures a selected target.

To detonate the projectiles, Charlie Battery had three fuses at its disposal. "Quick" is a contact fuse that explodes when the projectile (projo) strikes something, normally the ground. "Time" fuses are set with a fuse wrench to theoretically explode the projectile at a time when the projo is ideally twenty meters in the air above the target, although it could be also be set for "time delay" to explode after it has buried itself in the ground. "Variable time" or "VT" is an electronic time fuse that explodes itself when it senses that it is exactly twenty meters above the ground, which is the optimal height to have maximum effect upon ground targets. "VT" is significantly more expensive than "time" and therefore is used much more sparingly, especially in practice situations.

The ammunition for a 105mm howitzer is considered separate loading, which means that the round looks like a big bullet, but the projo is separate from the brass casing. Inside the brass casing are seven powder bags connected to one another by a string. Part of the commands to the guns from the fire direction center (FDC) tells the gun crew what charge to fire (one through seven) depending on how far the projectile must travel. If, for example, the gun crew was told "Charge 5," the powder man would take two bags out of the seven in the casing and throw them away into a powder pit to be burned later. Normally the smallest charge necessary to get the projo to the target is used due to the fact that the higher the charge, the faster the howitzer barrel wears out.

The forward observer normally adjusts a "fire mission" with HE and a quick fuse. Once the forward observer has adjusted the rounds properly onto the target by using the center two guns of the battery, he will ask to "fire for effect" which will involve the entire battery of six guns firing the designated number of shells with the correct fuse. If the FO chooses to use a time or VT fuse he will continue the adjustment phase of the mission up or down in the air until the round is exploding at the right height and then ask for "fire for effect."

Besides the gun crews, the other sections of Charlie Battery were working equally hard. The fire direction center (FDC) was orienting its charts and instruments to the new firing position. If the forward observer is the eyes of the artillery, the FDC is the brain. Normally an FDC was operated out of either its custom made wooden shell mounted on the back of a two and a half ton truck or from a tent or bunker if the battery was going to be in one place for more than a couple of hours. Inside the FDC were several radios that were in contact with the forward observers as well as with the battalion FDC. Depending on the mission, the shoot could be controlled by either the battery or battalion FDC or a combination of the two. Once the FDC receives a call for fire from the FO, it plots the target location on a map and determines what settings the guns need to use to hit the target. The FDC would then pass the commands to the XO, who would in turn give them to the guns. At the individual gun section, the gunner would set off the deflection (right or left traverse) and the assistant gunner would set off the quadrant elevation. The gun section chief would observe the operation of the crew. Other crewmen would complete the loading operation. Once the section chief determined that everything was in order and his gun was ready to shoot, he would raise his hand. The battery XO, Clay Holloway, would wait until all gun chiefs who were involved in the mission had their hand raised, lift his own arm and then yell "fire," simultaneously dropping the arm. If the battery had been instructed to fire more than one round per gun, the subsequent rounds would be loaded and fired as soon as possible by the individual gun chiefs. A good gun section could easily fire ten or twelve rounds per minute per gun at a sustained rate. The effective bursting radius of a 105 mm is considered to be 35 to 50 meters. Therefore, in one minute, a single artillery battery can saturate an area 300 meters wide and 100 meters deep with approximately seventy-five rounds of high explosive ammunition.

Throughout the bright autumn day the troops of Charlie Battery practiced the three word descriptor of their mission, "shoot, move, communicate." Bouncing into position in a field, the battery set up quickly, was laid, and fired one or two or maybe three fire missions. The radio crackled, time to move, pack it up, let's go, let's go, let's go. Defuse the projos, pack the ammo, wrap up the commo wire, secure the gun, hook it up, let's roll. Convoy! Holloway constantly checked his map to see where he had been, where he was, and where he was going. If an artilleryman didn't know his location it was going to be difficult to get steel on the target. Midway to the next firing point the radio crackled, "fire mission!" No time to get to the planned firing area. The forward observer is calling for fire. Have to give it to him. "Hip shoot!" Set the battery up at the next open spot you see. Anywhere. Set it up on the road if you have to. Holloway was out of the truck running with the aiming circle in his hand. Set it up, get it oriented, get the number three gun laid, figure some quick firing data with the plastic chart that Major Gentile had invented and that Holloway carried on his clip board. "Deflection 2788, Quadrant 358." Don't dig the howitzer trails in, there's no time! Shoot them in! Get a round in the air and let the FO adjust it. "Bang!" A dust cloud around the gun is brought from the earth by the concussion. How many minutes from the time the battery pulled into position? A minute forty-five? Good time. Real good time. Maybe they could even do better on the test. Maybe.

Over and over. Shoot, move, communicate. Rounds pounded out of the tubes all day. It was the most the battery had fired since the battalion test of the previous May. One hundred and twenty rounds of 105mm were fired by 2000 hours. Charlie had fired from four different locations. The radio call had come from Major Gentile. Shut it down. Go administrative. It's over until the next time.

Holloway was tired as well as hungry. The constant concussion from the guns had worn him down. His back and neck ached from stalking behind the guns all day wearing the steel helmet and web gear. The only times he had allowed himself to sit was during the brief convoys to a new position. His voice was virtually gone, a victim of the shouting of commands in the chilly air for nine hours. He was also cold. The sun had taken what warmth there had been when it had disappeared with a blazing orange finality behind the black hills two hours earlier. He had rotated the troops to the mess truck to eat the evening meal in shifts, but had been afraid to leave himself in fear that he might not be available if a fire mission came. A figure approached in the darkness and handed him a cold cheese sandwich. It was Clinton Gash.

"Thanks, Gash," Holloway said gratefully, removing his black leather glove and holding the sandwich in his hand.

"I didn't think you'd eaten, Sir. I tried to get you a veal chop, but they were all gone. This is all I could scrounge."

"It's fine, thanks. We're finished shooting for the night. I'm heading for the CP. I've got a couple of Cokes stored in my duffel. Coke and a cheese sandwich. How you gonna beat that?" Holloway moved away in the darkness, heading in the direction that would eventually lead him to the GP medium tent where he would sleep. As its shape loomed in front of him, he slowed his pace, weary of the tent ropes that he knew would be near. A soft glow of light escaped from the edges of the canvas tent flap. He tugged the flap open and stepped inside. A woman was sitting on his cot.

"Who are you?" Holloway asked, surprised to see a Korean civilian inside the tent.

"I look for First Sargee. He tell me to come," the woman replied in broken English. She was plain looking without a trace of make up and dressed in the layered fashion of the farmer.

"The First Sergeant asked you to come here?" Holloway asked, a puzzled look on his face.

"Neh," she nodded.

Holloway shrugged and opened his duffel, looking for one of the three cans of Coke he had packed. He couldn't imagine what the First Sergeant could want from the woman, but he also didn't think it would hurt to let her sit there for a few minutes as long as he kept his eye on her. Suddenly the tent flap was pulled open. Major Gentile stepped inside.

"Clay, what the hell is she doing in here?" he asked sternly.

"I don't know, Sir. I just walked in. She said she's waiting for the First Sergeant."

"We don't allow field whores in here, for God's sake." Turning to the woman, Major Gentile pointed to the door. "Cauda chogi. Bali, bali. Cauda chogi."

Reluctantly the women arose. Refusing to look at Major Gentile, she bowed her head, walked out of the doorway, and disappeared into the night. Gentile turned back toward Holloway.

"Look, I know you're not used to all this, but this area is covered with field whores. Don't let them inside the perimeter. We don't put up with that shit."

"I didn't know she was a whore, Sir," Holloway replied naively.

"Well, she is. Believe me. I don't know if the First Sergeant asked for her or not and I don't think I want to know, but just remember what I said. They'll steal you blind. Keep them out." He paused for a moment and then resumed speaking. "OK, enough of that. I just stopped in to tell you the battery looked really good today. Especially considering that this was the first trip over here. You'll get at least two more service practice shoots like today before the test. I think you'll do just fine when the big day comes. By the way, where's Tom Courtney. I wanted to tell him good job too."

Holloway shrugged. "I haven't seen him."

"All right. Just tell him for me. I'm heading back to Camp Wynne now. I'll see you there tomorrow."

"You're driving back tonight, Sir?"

"Sure. It may be three hours by gun convoy, but it's only an hour and a half trip by jeep. I'll be at the bar by ten. My back's getting too old to be sleeping on one of these canvas cots." He gave a cheery wave, turned, ducked his head, and stepped out of the tent.

When Tom Courtney and First Sergeant St. Clair entered the tent five minutes later, they found Clay Holloway propped up on his cot with his boots off, a warm Coke in one hand, and a freshly lit Winston in the other. He was also attempting to read an article in Stars n' Stripes in the dim light of the kerosene lantern.

"Hey, Sir. You see a little josan around here?" St. Clair asked.

"Yeah, I saw her. So did Major Gentile. He threw her out."

St. Clair's eyes widened. "What? She's gone? How long ago. Which way did she go?"

"She really was waiting for you? I got my ass reamed for it, Top. She's not supposed to be in here."

Hudson St. Clair looked at his battery commander, unsure of what to say next. A little smile was forming in the corners of Courtney's mouth. He looked at the First Sergeant and nodded his head toward the tent flap. "Why don't you check the perimeter, Top?"

The First Sergeant retreated gracefully out of the opening, hoping to find where his prearranged date for the evening had gone. Courtney turned to his new Executive Officer. "Listen, XO. That was just bad luck with Major Gentile walking in on Top's josan. I know what the brass says. And when they're around I play their game like everyone else. But once they unass the area, this is my battery and I run it the way I think is best." Courtney fired up a Kool and exhaled toward the ceiling. "Charlie Battery worked hard today. They work hard almost every day. It's a tough thirteen-month tour over here and it's not like there's a lot of recreational activities to turn to. Women are one thing that is here. World's oldest profession as they say. Mah philosophy is this. If the troops treat me right, I treat them right. If they put out and bust their ass for Charlie Battery, then I'm gonna give them what I can to make this tour a little bit more bearable. If what they want is a warm little josan to share their sleeping bag tonight, then I ain't gonna say a damn thing. 'Sides that, the field whores and their mamasans help keep the slicky boys away and that's the truth. St. Barb is famous for two things, women and slicky boys. These mamasans know Charlie Battery. They like us and trust us. They look out for us."

"So you don't care if they're inside the perimeter?"

"Well, what'd I say?" Courtney held the cigarette between his lips and squinted his eyes as he popped the top on a can of Coke. "I'm telling you, Clay. If there are any slicky boys out tonight, and St. Barb is full of them, the mamasans and the girls will be a big help. I've seen it before. Trust me."

"Well, OK, Tom. You're the boss." Holloway returned to his reading, still somewhat puzzled about what the best course of action should be. He had some misgiving about not complying with Major Gentile's directive, but at the same time it didn't seem right that he try to buck his own battery commander and first sergeant regarding an issue with which he really had no experience. Hell, he'd only been back in the unit for three days.

First Sergeant St. Clair returned to the tent a moment later, followed by two wrinkly-faced mamasans wearing scarves on their heads. "She's gone all right," Top said disgustedly. "I guess ole Major Gentile put the fear of God into her. Hey, BC, these mamasans come with me to pay their respects to you."

"Annahashamika, BC," each of the women announced as they bowed several times. Courtney stood up and gave them a sly grin.

"Hello, mamasans. How y'all been."

"What we get for you tonight, BC? Plenty numba one josan. Plenty mockely."

"No, not for me, mamasan. I'm a married man. Maybe Lootenant Holloway could use a cute little josan though," Courtney replied, his eyes twinkling. "What do you say, Bagger? Caugi wah josan?" Courtney looked at Holloway grinning from ear to ear.

Holloway looked skeptically at Tom Courtney. "I don't think I'm ready for that, thanks. After all it would only be my first date with the girl. What kind of a boy do you think I am?"

One of the mamasans took a step toward him and bowed. "Hallo, Lootenant. You Korea cherry boy? I caugi wah numba one josan for you. She cherry too. Make you feel good long time."

"Go ahead, Sir," First Sergeant St. Clair chided. "Mamasan says she's cherry. That means she hasn't been laid yet today. Or at least in the last hour." He laughed to himself.

"That's OK, Clay," Courtney added, putting his arm around Holloway's shoulder. "Stick to your guns. You got a better chance of seeing God than finding a real honest to goodness Korean cherry girl at St. Barb. 'Sides that; Miss Judy will probably be around the next time we come around here. She's not here tonight they tell me, but she's a real classy lady. I think you'll like her. She speaks four languages," he announced, exhaling smoke through his nostrils and stubbing the cigarette out on the sole of his boot.

"OK. I'll just save myself for Miss Judy then. Now if you'll excuse me," Holloway stated as he returned to his seat on the canvas cot and reacquired his place in Stars 'n Stripes.

Disappointed, the two women said their good-byes a moment later and shuffled back out of the tent, vowing to come back later and to make sure the slicky boys didn't disturb anything. When they had gone Courtney turned to Clay Holloway. "All kidding aside and before I forget, Bagger, I want to tell you that I think you did real well out there today. There's room for improvement, of course. There always is. But considering this was your first day of shootin', I think you did just fine."

"Thanks. Major Gentile said some good things too. And he told me to tell you good job."

"Rocky Gentile is a good man. He's helped me a lot and you'd do well to listen to him. Unless he's talking about not fraternizing with the locals, that is. That's not his specialty. Hey, did he tell you about pulling staff duty?"

"No. What do you mean?"

"Well, unfortunately, now that you're back from the DMZ you're on the staff duty roster for Battalion Headquarters and your name is up for tomorrow night. It's gonna make it rough because you won't get much sleep and Major Gentile told me tonight that for the next week Charlie Battery has got to pull SCOSI duty on the south bank of the Imjin. That means not much sleep again. No rest for the weary, I guess."

Holloway groaned. Since his last night on the GP when the Sergeant Major had been wounded, his sleep had been fitful and filled with dreams. He doubted if this night would be particularly comfortable and following that it was pretty damn obvious that sleep would be at a premium for the next week. "Well, OK. I guess there's not much I can do about it. I think I'll take a walk around the perimeter and then turn in." He tugged on his boots and laced them hurriedly. Walking outside he sniffed the cool air and stood motionless for a moment to let his night vision get adjusted. Eventually he began walking toward the nearest truck. All of the vehicles had been pulled into a giant circle, reminiscent of a covered wagon train in the old west. The formation allowed the guards to walk around outside of the circle to guard against slicky boys that constituted the greatest threat at St. Barbara. As he neared one of the deuce and a halves he could hear giggling coming from the back. Then he heard a man's laughter and thought momentarily about what must be going on inside of the soldier's sleeping bag. He thought briefly of Beth Kisha and how sexy she was and how much he had enjoyed that one incredible weekend. He thought of the Korean girl at the steam bath and her soapy hands on his body. But most of all he thought of Jennifer Dodge, whom he had never even kissed and probably never would because she was engaged to another man whom she loved very much.

*　　　*　　　*

Clay Holloway officially began his one night assignment as Staff Duty Officer by accepting the Battalion log from Bill Grant at 1700 hours the next evening. Grant reviewed the primary responsibilities of the position with him and after answering a few questions which he had been asked by many of the other lieutenants on their first night of Staff Duty, departed the HQ until 0800 the next day when he would return along with the rest of the Battalion staff for the regular work day. In essence, Holloway was in charge of the entire Camp Wynne compound during the hours that everyone else was officially off duty. In addition to the SDO, there was assigned a Staff Duty NCO and Staff Duty driver along with a one and a quarter ton vehicle parked in front of Battalion Headquarters which was to be used for whatever purpose it was needed.

In accordance with Grant's outline of duties, Holloway walked once around the interior side of the compound's perimeter fence during the daylight and then ate the evening meal in the Bravo Battery mess hall, which allowed him to inspect the mess hall and the quality of food being served at the same time that he filled his stomach. By 1830 hours he was back at the adjutant's desk at Battalion HQ reviewing the log and eventually beginning to leaf through a magazine. At almost exactly 2000 hours the telephone rang and was answered by Staff Sergeant Wright, the Staff Duty NCO. He listened for a moment, said a few words, and then hung up the receiver.

"Lieutenant Holloway, that was 2nd MP. They've picked up one of your men from Charlie Battery who has been AWOL for about a week and are bringing him over here in a couple of minutes. They say he's pretty messed up. His name's Whitaker."

"Did they say what they meant by 'messed up'?

"They believe that he has recently consumed two quarts of Bang Yang whiskey and popped about twenty red devils."

Holloway arched his eyebrows. He wasn't sure what that combination of alcohol and drugs would do to a man, but it probably wasn't going to be something to fondly anticipate.

"Call the Charlie Battery CP and tell them what's going on," Holloway ordered. "They should find First Sergeant St. Clair and have him make arrangements to take care of this guy until morning. I'll see if I can reach Lieutenant Courtney."

Holloway was unsuccessful in locating Tom Courtney at either the BOQ or the Officers' Club, but Staff Sergeant Wright was able to learn that Spec/4 Whitaker had been a pretty fair troop until ten days ago when he received his DEROS orders sending him back to the States following the end of his thirteen month tour. Apparently Whitaker had learned that the American authorities were aware of his orders and were planning to arrest him for some alleged crime the moment he set foot back on American soil. Once having become aware of this and being a rather short sighted planner, Spec/4 Whitaker had gone over the hill until he had been picked up by the MP's two hours earlier after passing out in the Lucky Seven Saloon in Pobwon-ni. The Charlie Battery CQ (Charge of Quarters) had informed Sergeant Wright that he would try to find First Sergeant St. Clair or some other NCO to come over the Battalion HQ and repossess Spec/4 Whitaker.

Twin headlight beams from the MP's jeep shone on the front of the HQ a few minutes later. Holloway arose as three immaculately uniformed MP's walked through the front door supporting a tall muscular young black soldier wearing dirty stained fatigues. His eyes were glassy and appeared to not only be unable to focus, but to also be looking at two different directions at the same time. His mouth was slightly open and a dribble of saliva hung out of one corner. After receiving Holloway's signature on a prisoner release form, the MP's leaned Whitaker up against a table and left hurriedly. The disoriented soldier immediately chose that opportunity to begin trying to negotiate the several desks and chairs that cluttered the cramped office. After no more than three steps Whitaker tripped over the leg of one of the chairs and fell headlong onto his face on the tile floor. Resignedly Holloway and Wright pulled the man to his feet and propped him against the nearest desk.

"Would you like some coffee, Whitaker? Somebody from Charlie Battery is on his way over here now to get you."

Spec/4 Whitaker mumbled something unintelligible.

"I said would you like some coffee?" Holloway repeated. This time the man nodded slowly.

Holloway motioned to the Staff Duty driver who poured a cup from the full pot in the corner and handed it to the young man. The cup came to within five or six inches of his mouth before he lost his grip and spilled the contents of the entire container down the front of his chest. Unfazed by the hot temperature of the liquid, Whitaker looked slowly down at his shirt, trying to determine what had happened to his coffee. Unable to solve that simple riddle, Whitaker dropped the fiberglass cup to the floor and continued to stand unsteadily at the desk.

"Cigarette?" Whitaker mumbled.

"You want a cigarette?" Holloway asked. Whitaker again nodded slowly. Holloway pulled one from his shirt pocket and lighted it. Taking a drag he handed it to the GI. Whitaker took the cigarette and after appearing to study it for a moment, promptly placed the lighted end in his mouth. Again he seemed unfazed as Holloway leaped at him, ripping the cigarette away.

"Jesus, Whitaker, I've never seen anybody as bad off as you are. Come over here." Holloway lead the man to the corner of the room where the Staff Duty driver had placed a mattress, hoping to catch a few winks during the night. "Lay down here and don't move until somebody gets here for you."

Sergeants Carlton and Steele arrived soon thereafter. "Take him over to the Battery area and keep an eye on him until morning when we figure out what to do with him. You know it's tough to imagine someone going AWOL to keep from going home from this place, but I understand that's what Whitaker is trying to do."

"Yes Sir, we've got plans for him tonight. We're gonna lock him in that little supply shed. Rumor is that he's looking at some serious jail time in the States. Armed robbery I've been told."

Holloway whistled softly. "OK, thanks. I'll see you men tomorrow." As the two NCOs escorted Whitaker out of the door and disappeared into the night, he heard the Staff Duty driver cursing softly behind him. Turning, Holloway say the man peering down at his mattress and wrinkling his nose.

"What's the matter?"

"Damn, Sir. That asshole pissed on my mattress. Now where in the hell am I going to sleep tonight?"

Shortly before midnight, Clay Holloway left Battalion HQ to take his second inspection walk around the perimeter fence. Occasional electric bulbs illuminated small sections of the chain linked protective shield, yet most of the perimeter remained shrouded in darkness. Holloway walked softly, remembering as best he could what obstacles might lie in his path. On his left upper arm he wore a large black armband with white letters, which read "SDO" in English, and underneath that in smaller print was Korean printing, which supposedly said the same thing. On his web belt he wore his loaded .45 in a black leather holster. An army flashlight was clipped to the other side of the belt.

He had completed about half of his intended route, having passed through the areas occupied by Alpha Battery and his own Charlie Battery. Entering the Bravo Battery area he could see the silhouette of the wooden guard tower that rose above him. He looked up at the tower, attempting to see the civilian Korean guard who should be manning it. Noiselessly and completely unintentionally, while he was focused on the tower he had walked to within only a few feet of another Korean guard who stood at the tower base with his back to Holloway. Seeing the man only at the last second, Holloway spoke.

"Good evening."

Startled, the man swiveled around, shotgun at the ready. "Huhhh!" the man challenged in deep-throated grunt. Holloway could see his angry features. The muzzle of the pump shotgun was pointed at Holloway's chest. The guard was not kidding.

"Staff Duty Officer," Holloway responded.

"Huuhhh!" the man grunted louder. "Click-clack." He worked the slide of the shotgun, the muzzle now at Holloway's midsection. Surprised by the sudden seriousness of the situation Holloway stopped and slowly raised his hands.

What the hell? Didn't this guy speak English? Then the awful truth dawned on him. No! He didn't speak English at all. He had no idea who Holloway was in the darkness. "SDO, Officer of the Day, OD!" Holloway said, using every phrase he could conjure up to describe his position. He pointed slowly to his armband.

"Huuhhh!" the guard cried, finally recognizing who he was. The man snapped to present arms and remained rigid. Above him, the tower guard also had come to present arms and given a similar guttural cry. Relaxing, Holloway breathed a sigh of relief, tossed the man a casual salute, and walked by. Behind him he heard the guard's palm slap the stock of the weapon as he properly returned to the "order arms" position.

"Whew!" he muttered, walking quickly away. "Nothing like a shotgun blast to the midsection to ruin my whole day!" Ten minutes later he returned to the adjutant's office. To his relief, the rest of the night was uneventful.

CHAPTER 19

The three men breast stroked silently in the late night darkness across the current of the swiftly flowing Imjin, rushing westward toward its destiny with the Yellow Sea. Only their noses and eyes broke the plane of the dark river. Already they were more than half way across the wide expanse of black water. The men swam in a vee formation with Lieutenant Yoon Kim Lee in the lead. Their faces and hands were covered with dark waterproof camouflage paint and they wore black rubber wet suits to protect themselves from the chilly October water which would be four or five degrees colder in three weeks when they were scheduled to recross the river on their way back to North Korea. Each of them carried an identical waterproof bag strapped to his body which contained dry civilian clothing, five days worth of rations, which were mostly rice and dried fruit, a Makarov 9mm pistol with three extra magazines of ammunition, a dagger, two hand grenades, and a map of the area. On the maps were marked all of the known compounds of the Second Infantry Division, as well as prepared defensive positions south of the Imjin. In addition, the three men between them carried a 35mm Nikon camera with a 90x200mm telephoto zoom lens, twenty rolls of high speed ASA 500 film, a journal, a pair of Zeiss binoculars, a pair of wire cutters, and fifty feet of thin, yet very tough nylon climbing rope along with five carabineers and a hammer. Ahead of them loomed the forty-foot bluffs of the south bank of the Imjin.

On the top of the bluffs, Charlie Battery of the 8/18th Artillery was in the fourth night of its seven-day mission of Security and Counter Espionage Operations South of the Imjin (SCOSI) duty. In theory, their job was really infantry work, but there were simply not enough of those units to fulfill all of the infantry missions that I Corps wanted completed. Therefore, to supplement the infantry, all of the Division's artillery and armor units were used to rotate the nighttime guard shift along the south bank of the river. In Charlie Battery's sector there were ten foxholes, each containing three artillerymen. Their mission was to stay in the holes all night, every night, for a full week, and stop any attempted infiltration by North Korean commandos who had penetrated the DMZ and were headed south. Each of the holes contained a sergeant and two men of lesser rank. One man was to be awake at all times. Normally the shift was one hour awake and two hours asleep. The duty began at dusk, which arrived at about 1930 hours, and continued until dawn. Each evening Battery Commander Tom Courtney and Executive Officer Clay Holloway inspected all ten of the holes before nightfall and then returned to the CP to monitor the radios until dawn. The nights themselves had been uneventful. The most interesting thing that had happened thus far during the week was Staff Sergeant Orville Thompson being attacked by a drunken mamasan who acted outraged and insulted because none of the troops were permitted to rent any of her girls and keep them in the holes with them. Much to Thompson's chagrin, the woman had raked his face with her fingernails and broken the stem of his pipe during the scuffle. Normally the duty was routine. Charlie Battery had pulled SCOSI duty intermittently for almost two years. During that time no one had ever seen a North Korean.

On the far left flank of the ten holes and next to a narrow draw that ran down to the beach was Sergeant Kelly Steele, the young blond mustachioed number five gun chief, and two of his KATUSA's. At the other end of the line near a rice paddy dike, was Staff Sergeant Thompson, the Chief of Smoke. Between them were the other five gun section chiefs, Supply Sergeant Carlton, Commo Section Sergeant Jackson, and Motor Sergeant Brookins.

About fifty meters behind the line of foxholes sat the Charlie Battery Fire Direction Center (FDC), which was mounted on the bed of a two and a half ton truck. The FDC served as a Command Post (CP) for the night vigil. Inside of the van, First Lieutenant Tom Courtney was raking in his third consecutive poker pot. Following Sergeant Appleby's DEROS to the States, Sergeant Al Lepley had been promoted to FDC Chief. Now he folded his arms and sat back in his chair in disgust.

"Lieutenant Courtney, is it somewhere in the regulations that the Battery Commander has to win every time we play poker?"

"Well, hell yes, Lep. It's in one of those damn field manuals. I distinctly remember readin' it not too long ago. FM 6-40 it might have been. What do you boys think I bring y'all out here for?" Courtney drawled as he stacked his latest winnings in front of him.

Suddenly one of the radios, which had been silent for the last two hours, crackled. "Charlie 33, this is 33, radio check, over."

"33, this is Charlie 33, I hear you Lima Charlie, over." Lepley responded. Immediately a new voice came over the speaker.

"Charlie 33, this is Pegasus 20, clear the net we've got a hot one going, over."

Tom Courtney took the microphone from Lepley. "Unknown station, this is Charlie 33, this is our tactical net, over," he responded.

"Beagle 15, this is Pegasus 20, keep the illumination coming. The dinks are in the wire. I'm going down for another rocket pass! Holy shit, look at that fireball. What the hell did they hit? Break, Break. Green Man, Green Man, what the hell blew up? Over."

The six men who clustered around the wooden poker table stiffened in their chairs and looked questioningly at each other. Who the hell was that? What was going on? It sounded like a major firefight was underway. Was it a Guard Post in the Z? Were they getting over run? Why in the world was it on the artillery tactical fire net? Clay Holloway pushed back his folding chair, switched off the overhead light, opened the door, and stepped out of the van and down the three steps into the black night. The truck was less than a mile from the southern boundary of the DMZ. He looked in its direction, searching for the telltale signs of a firefight, but neither saw nor heard anything out of the ordinary. The entire situation seemed unreal. He returned to the truck just as the radio again crackled.

"Green Man, Pegasus 20, keep your heads down. Tac Air is on the way in. You got four F-4's inbound with an ETA of three zero seconds. I'm gettin' out of their way. Break, Break, Beagle 15, Check fire! Check fire! Tac Air is in the area. I'll be back. Out."

By this time the six poker players sat motionless, transfixed by the radio, and having completely forgotten their game. They had no idea what was happening, but whatever it was, someone was in a serious bind. Courtney decided to back off and wait until things calmed down.

"Pegasus 20, this is Charlie 33, call us when you're clear, out." Courtney stated, and then placed the microphone on the table.

"Charlie 33, Pegasus 20, clear the net. Break, break. Green man, this is 20, that broke their back. Charlie's running. I'm gonna make one more pass with the mini's. That should finish them off."

Charlie's running??? Suddenly it was obvious. The crystal clear voice emitting from the radio was not coming from within the area of the Second Division. Nor was it coming from anywhere within the stated twenty mile range of the AN/PRC 46 radio mounted on the shelf of the Charlie FDC van. It was impossible, yet it was happening. Through a freak of electronics the two radios were communicating with each other over a range of almost two thousand miles. Charlie Battery was talking with a helicopter gun ship in support of Fire Base Sylvester nestled in Vietnam's Central Highlands. Both units were operating on their authorized tactical nets, which happened to be 88.75. Tom Courtney waited two more minutes. All was quiet. Finally he keyed the handset.

"Pegasus 20, this is Charlie 33. Can you talk now, over?"

"Charlie 33, this is Pegasus 20, roger that. We got 'em whupped. There's nuthin' but bodies now. They're hanging on the wire, over."

"Pegasus 20, Charlie 33," Courtney said. "Are you in the RVN (Republic of Vietnam), over?"

"Charlie 33, this is 20. That's affirmative. Where the hell else would I be, over?"

"This is Charlie 33. Well I think this little radio mix up is on account of we're in the ROK. I think we might be setting radio history with this conversation. We were starting to feel like we were in the Twilight Zone. Hey, it sounds like you did a hell of a job for Green Man. Is it finished? Over."

"20, roger that. Everything's quiet right now. I'm breaking off and going to refuel. Are you serious about being in Korea? How's the weather up there? Over."

"This is Charlie 33. I think it's a lot cooler than it sounds like it is down there. I hope it stays that way. Listen, we'll switch to our alternate frequency. You keep this one. Good luck. Over."

"This is Pegasus 20. Roger that. Tango Yankee. Out."

Courtney called the Battalion FDC to announce the change to the alternate frequency, hung the handset on the hook next to the radio, consulted his SOI, and changed his radio dial to the other station. Then he sat back and folded his arms.

"That was some strange shit, wasn't it?" Courtney said. "You know, I'll bet those radio signals were using Freedom Bridge for a big antenna and then bouncing right up the river to us."

"It sounded pretty exciting, that's for sure," Lepley replied. "I'll tell you the truth. I'm glad we're here and not there."

"I don't know," said Clinton Gash. "Sometimes I wish we could have some excitement around here. We sit out here every night and not a damn thing happens. Lieutenant Holloway here is the only one of us that's ever even seen a North Korean."

"Well, Clinton, when I was outside a few minutes ago everything seemed nice and serene," said Clay Holloway. "That's the way I like it. Hey, whose deal is it?"

*   *   *

It was 0330 hours. Five hours earlier Lieutenant Yoon and his two men had emerged from a tunnel in a wooded area a quarter of a mile behind the south barrier fence of the DMZ. Now, after swimming the river, he waved his companions ashore onto the narrow sandy beach and put his finger to his lips to insure their silence. Ahead was a small cut in the high bluff. Yoon could see what appeared to be barbed wire in the draw. Slowly he crept forward. Reaching the wire, he examined it. There was enough slack. He wouldn't even have to cut it. Yoon lifted the wire as high as he could and waved his men forward. Each laid on his back and squirmed slowly under the lowest strand. A moment later all three commandos were quietly ascending the dirt wall of the cut. Above them, near the top of the draw, was more barbed wire. Again it presented no serious problem to the men in black. Within two minutes they crawled out of the depression and scanned the area. Ten yards to the left there appeared to be a prepared defensive position. Yoon approached the sandbagged foxhole silently, his dagger held ready in his right hand. He reached the edge of the hole and looked in. There were three enemy soldiers. One was blond with a blond mustache. He wore sergeant stripes. The other two appeared to be Korean. Yoon gripped his knife tightly. Momentarily he considered slitting their throats. He wanted very much to kill them. But he couldn't. It would jeopardize his entire reconnaissance mission. Finding three dead men in the hole in the morning would be an obvious giveaway of the presence of the commandos. Thousands of soldiers and home guardsmen would be sent to scour the countryside, making movement difficult. No. Yoon would bypass them. The wire had not been cut. The soldiers would not be killed. No one would ever know the commandos were there. That was as it should be. He motioned his men forward and stole silently to the south. There was almost three hours until daylight. They could cover a lot of ground in three hours.

*   *   *

When Charlie Battery rolled through the main gate of Camp Wynne at 0715 on Saturday morning after leaving the SCOSI positions at first light, it ended the seven-day tour on the bank of the Imjin. The men would have most of the weekend off duty and then make one last trip to St. Barbara for a day of practice shooting in final preparation for the battery test to be held later in the week. Holloway grabbed some breakfast in the mess hall, took a three-hour nap, and then returned to the CP just to catch up on what was going on before knocking off for the weekend at noon. As he walked through the front door of the orderly room First Sergeant Hudson St. Clair looked up and smiled.

"Hey, Sir! Are you all recovered from your week on the graveyard shift and ready to head for St. Barb?" he asked, his ebony face beaming.

"Sure, Top. Always ready. Hey, did they ever get Whitaker on that plane back to the States after he sobered up?"

"No, Sir. Didn't you hear what happened on that? While you people were on SCOSI, Whitaker went over the hill again. We had him booked on a flight yesterday and had him locked in the tool shed to make sure he stayed put. Well, I'll be go to hell if he didn't climb out the window and cauda chogi again. But they'll pick him up. It just makes us look like we got our heads in rectal defilade, that's all."

Holloway shook his head slowly. "I just can't believe a man would fight so hard to stay in this place. I'd give my left nut to get my orders DEROSing me out of here. Hey, did I tell you I broke three hundred days a while back?"

Top chuckled. "Yes, Sir. You're a short timer that's for sure."

Holloway moved beyond the First Sergeant's desk to another area where his own desk was located. He sat down and began a final check on the monthly vehicle status report. He had been at work for a few minutes when the First Sergeant walked by with a young angry looking Black GI that Holloway had seen before, but didn't really know. The First Sergeant knocked on the Battery Commander's open door.

"Sir, Private Pritchard is here like you requested. Pritchard, report to the BC." With that, First Sergeant St. Clair showed Pritchard into Tom Courtney's office, pulled the door shut, and walked back toward his desk.

"What's going on with Pritchard?" Clay Holloway asked Top.

"The BC is probably gonna Article XV his young ass. He's got a real problem with not doing what he's told."

Private Pritchard hadn't been in Courtney's office for more than two minutes when the yelling started. Almost immediately thereafter was a loud series of noises that sounded like things hitting the floor, followed by a crash into the wall that seemed to shake the whole building. Clay Holloway leaped to the office entrance followed immediately by the First Sergeant, and flung open the door. Pritchard was sitting on the floor with the heavy wooden manning chart sitting upright behind him where it had landed when it had fallen from the wall. Pritchard was holding his face. The floor was littered with papers, an in-box, and a heavy brass ashtray.

"What the hell happened, BC?" Top exclaimed.

"Goddamn Pritchard started telling me how he was a Blackstone Ranger from Chicago and how he wasn't gonna put up with our bullshit anymore. Then he cleaned off the top of my desk for me. Just swept the whole thing clean with his hand. I figured I better make him sit down before somebody got hurt." Courtney had hit him with an uppercut, smashing him into the wall and knocking down the manning board. "Lander," Courtney called to the Battery Clerk. "Get Sergeant Weathers in here." Weathers really had been a Blackstone Ranger leader in the streets of the south side of Chicago before joining the Army and making his way to E-5 and putting his leadership abilities to legitimate use. "Top, get Weathers and Steele to take Pritchard to 2nd MP and lock him up for assaulting an officer. We'll figure up the paperwork later."

First Sergeant St. Clair took Pritchard by the arm and led him out of the CP to where Sergeant Weathers was coming up the front walk. Pritchard feared and respected Weathers and Courtney felt sure he and Steele could get him to the MP station.

Holloway joined Tom Courtney in his office where he was picking some of his papers off of the floor. Holloway bent over to help. "Tom, are there any normal people in this outfit? Ever since I got back from the Z, I just keep seeing a bunch of outlaws."

Courtney winked and gave Holloway his patented little crooked grin. "Bagger, that word probably describes it best. Outlaws. Yeah, that's right. Half of this battery is made up of outlaws, but most of them will still give you a good day's work if you treat 'em raht. Pritchard is a no good son-of-a-bitch. Probably ain't worth killin'. Whitaker wasn't half bad, but he's gone off the deep end now. Next time the MP's pick him up I goddamn guarantee you we'll get him on that plane back to the land of the big PX. Probably a third of the EM's smoke grass once in a while. Hell, my driver went over the hill three times while he was in basic training. They finally just gave up and sent him over here. Did you know that your driver Gash has done prison time?" Holloway shook his head. "Sure did. Knocked over a liquor store I think, but he's doing a hell of a job over here and that's all I care about.

The point is, the Army's got a lot of outlaws and misfits and potheads right now. Most of them are draftees and most of them don't want to be here. It's our job as leaders to get the most we can out of what they give us to work with. You know we also got some Project 100,000 in here."

"What's Project 100,000?" Holloway asked, not really sure he wanted to know the answer.

"Well, a couple of years ago ole Lyndon Johnson decided that there were too many people that didn't seem to have the minimum mental requirements to be eligible for the draft. So LBJ had the government give them some remedial education and then they declared about 100,000 of them to now be smart enough to be soldiers. I think half of them wound up here," Courtney chuckled. "But, in all seriousness, Clay, this is a good unit. You've seen them in the field. Most of them are good soldiers regardless of their backgrounds." Courtney fired up a Kool and blew a big smoke ring at the ceiling. "But I'll tell you something else. Each of them is different. A commander has got to know his men if he's goin' to get the most out of them. Each of them has to be motivated a bit differently from time to time. One needs a pat on the back, another a gentle shove. Then occasionally you find a Pritchard who needs a swift kick in the ass. Always know your men, Holloway. Always. Come on we'll take a lap around the Battery area and then knock off for the day. You know, next week we have one more shot at St. Barb before the test. I think we'll be ready, don't you?"

"Yes, Sir. We'll be ready. I guarantee it."

"I'll accept that. And are you ready for tonight?"

Holloway looked at him blankly. "What's tonight?"

"Don't tell me you forgot. Tonight is the anniversary party for the 18th Artillery. It's us and the officers from the 9/18th from I Corps. I understand it's an annual event over here."

"I guess I heard about it, but somewhere along the line I also forgot about it. There's gonna be a fall barbecue with steaks and chicken and ribs, right?"

"That's the one. Don't eat too much at lunch. You need to save up for tonight."

*   *   *

Beth Kisha was taking her first bite out of the bacon, lettuce, and tomato sandwich when Clay Holloway pulled out the chair next to her and sat down. She smiled.

"Don't try to talk. I know you're glad to see me. Just put your hand on my leg," Holloway chided.

Beth half choked on the food, put the sandwich on her plate and coughed a couple of times to clear her throat. Then she took a sip of water. Her face had reddened slightly. "Shhh! Don't talk so loud. And that wasn't fair."

"If life were fair we'd be spending the weekend in Tokyo together," he replied.

She smiled sweetly and took another bite of her sandwich. Holloway picked up the paper menu in front of him and began marking his choices. "You're a connoisseur of fine foods and wine. What do you recommend for dessert, the lime Jell-O or the orange Jell-O?"

"It's really a matter of personal preference, but I think the lime is only a day old while the orange is closer to three," she remarked slyly.

"Good intelligence information is the key to success. Thank you." Holloway checked the block next to lime and handed it to one of the passing Korean waiters. "So tell me, are you and the other girls attending the party tonight?"

"Yes. Most of us are anyway. We're not invited to the dinner, but we'll be there afterward. JD won't though. She's going to be with you know who, of course. In fact, I think they are spending the weekend in Seoul together."

Holloway felt his heart drop and sink slowly to the bottom of his stomach. With SCOSI duty all week he hadn't had a chance to see JD for several days. Beth's comment answered one question for him. Apparently now that they were engaged, she had decided to share her body with Magic as well as her love. Unconsciously he sighed aloud.

"You don't approve?" Beth asked, raising her eyebrows.

"Why would it matter to me?"

"I don't know. But from looking at you I think that it does. I've always felt that you were attracted to her. I've noticed the way you look at her sometimes and you have spent a certain amount of time together."

"She's an engaged woman, Beth. I don't have anything to say about it. She's made her choice. She's crazy about Magic, you know that." Holloway paused for a moment. "I'm attracted to you too. Don't mean nuthin'."

Beth looked questioningly at Holloway for a long time without speaking. He did not meet her gaze. "I have a funny feeling about this. You know there can't be anything lasting between you and me. We've been over that and besides I'm going home in less than a month. But you and Jennifer seem to fit together and both of you are going to be here together for another eight or nine months. Magic is going home even before I am. Anything can happen then. I wonder," she mused as her voice trailed away.

*   *   *

The beer drinking had begun with the arrival of the officers of the 9/18th by bus at 1600 hours. There was a noticeable nip in the October air, but the bright sunshine on a cloudless sky had the entire compliment of officers from the two sister battalions in high spirits. Two full kegs of Schlitz had been ordered to insure that the merrymakers didn't run dry and most of the 8/18th officers had shunned the plastic cups and had asked Mr. Yun to remove their individualized silver mugs from the shelf behind the bar and were using them for beer steins. The mugs held 20 ounces each.

Many of the lieutenants of the sister battalions knew each other from Ft. Sill. Kendall Stover had graduated from OCS with one of the 9/18th's officers named Gene Prentiss and Clay Holloway had been in the artillery basic course with two others. It hadn't taken long for the good-natured bantering and bragging and challenging to begin. The jokes had started a bit later in the outdoor food line when Stover had taken a barbecued chicken drumstick and inserted it into the right pants pocket of the unsuspecting Prentiss who was in front of him. It went unnoticed until Prentiss had begun to sit down at one of the tables and feeling a bulging in his pocket had put his hand in the pocket only to withdraw it covered with barbecue sauce. Stover, of course denied any knowledge of the chicken, but somehow had failed to convince Prentiss of his innocence, especially considering the fact that the two had played tricks on each other throughout the grueling months in OCS. Stover later told Holloway that during one OCS inspection Prentiss had removed the pins from the door of Stover's wall locker minutes before the Tac Officer walked in. When the inspector tugged at the door handle the entire locker door came off in his hand, causing the whole squad to burst into laughter.

The frivolity continued throughout dinner. Once the eating ended, the cigars came forth, causing a gray/blue haze to form in the ceiling above the bar. Before long many of the Doughnut Dollies, who had not been invited to the dinner, began to infiltrate slowly into the bar area. The girls were sober. Most of the officers, on the other hand, had a five or six beer head start on them and had reached the point where many of their various inhibitions had been already relaxed. Voice levels increased and the volume of the music of Credence Clearwater Revival seemed to rise proportionately. Before long, the semi-inebriated young men began doing what men in their early twenty's had been doing for centuries, vying for the attention of the young women. However, what eventually became the focal event of the evening began when one of the visiting officers spied a 175mm projectile, which served as a decoration. It had been covered in a high gloss brass and sported the regimental crest of the 18th artillery on its side. Sitting on a table along one wall, the projo was believed to weigh approximately 170 pounds.

Later no one could recall who exactly had issued the first challenge, but at some point the room of beer guzzling young men divided upon battalion lines and a contest had begun. The rules were simple. First an officer from the 9/18th would walk to the table, pick up the heavy projectile, carry it to the bar and set it upright. Then a volunteer from the 8/18th would walk to the bar and pick it up and return the projo to the table. The first battalion, which was unable to accomplish the task, lost its turn. If the other battalion was then able to complete the mission the first battalion had one more attempt to tie. If it failed the contest was over. The stakes were $10 MPC per man. The money was piled on the bar. Both battalions seemed evenly matched.

The contest began in earnest. Each side cheered or booed the contestant in accordance with battalion membership. Bear Buckner had been the lead off man for the 8/18th and had no problem with the big shell whatsoever. Following the 9/18th's victorious attempt, Eric Auslander had succeeded. Then Tom Courtney had gone ahead. Sweeper was also triumphant. Another lieutenant from the 9/18th struggled, but was able to complete the task. Clay Holloway had some doubts about his strength. He could not recall ever having lifted that much before, but volunteered next.

"Come on, Bagger! You can do it. Go! Go! Go!" His whole battalion was cheering as he staggered across the floor with both hands under the base of the enormous weight. He could hear Beth Kisha's throaty voice above the rest. The table was just ahead. He reached it and set down the projo with a grunt. Holloway breathed a sigh of relief. It hadn't been that hard. Beth came forward and kissed him on the cheek. He smiled at her and looked back at the bar. Again the 9/18th tied the score. The ranks of contestants were noticeably thinner. Naturally each of the two units had allowed their strongest men to go first. The ones that everyone knew could accomplish the trick had been eliminated. With each new contestant the outcome became more doubtful. Holloway looked at his own group. Baron could probably do it. He wasn't that big at five feet ten inches, but he had been a high school wrestler and had only been out of OCS for three months. Both the Owl and Rick Benning, the Survey Officer, were only five feet six and of slight build. Maybe they could do it, but maybe not. Hostileman was a definite possibility. Holloway could see him getting himself mentally ready. But the most likely next contestant had to be the tall lanky assistant S-3 who everyone called "Ranger" because of the coveted ranger patch worn on his shoulder. Everyone knew that the U. S. Army Ranger School in the swamps of Florida was about the toughest course the Army had. Any graduate of that school had to be a hard dude. What the group did not know, however, was that "Ranger" had already drunk seven beers and it was the first time in his life that he had ever had more than two. During the revelry of the event the usually reserved young man from Oklahoma had gotten into the mood of the party along with everyone else and continued to refill his mug as he puffed on a long brown panatela. During the last hour his lightly complexioned skin had taken on a reddish hue. Unbeknownst to anyone else, Ranger's vision had also started to blur. He looked up. It was time again for someone from the 8/18th. Ranger Brown started forward, but at the last moment Kendall Stover stepped in front of him.

"I got it," cried the Red Baron leaping onto the floor. He snatched the projo from the bar in a fluid motion, but then staggered as the full weight of the formidable metal object tugged at him. Baron walked forward struggling under the heavy load. Halfway across the floor, a figure appeared at his side. It was Gene Prentiss.

"Hey, Stover, I think you forgot something," Prentiss announced. As the Baron took another step, Prentiss withdrew a partially eaten chicken drumstick and jammed it into Stover's shirt pocket. The crowd roared. The veins were standing out on Stover's forehead as he grinned tightly.

"You bastard," Stover grunted, as he lurched the remaining two steps back to the table and set down the heavy object. Stover turned at looked at Prentiss and the rest of the 9/18th. The onus was on them. Finally one of their number came reluctantly forward. The man did not look particularly strong and he wasn't. As he removed the projo from the table, it took him immediately to the floor as though it weighed a thousand pounds. The 8/18th cheered heartily as the 9/18th moaned. If Holloway's battalion could get it from the table to the bar they would be ahead. Then the 9/18th would either have to tie or lose the contest. Holloway looked up as Ranger Brown strode clumsily to the table. Clutching the projectile with his long arms wrapped around it rather than placing his two big hands under it, he picked up one foot and then the other. Ranger's face was getting more crimson by the moment. Sweat had already begun forming at his hairline. Holloway sucked in air as he watched. It looked like the projo was slipping out of Ranger's arms! Ranger took another couple of steps. He was almost to the bar. The 175 round was slipping badly. Suddenly Ranger went to his knees, cradling the brass hunk horizontally in the crook of his elbows. The weight continued to pull Ranger down and forward. He was losing the battle with gravity.

At the bottom of the black bar of the Camp Wynne Officers' Club was a brass foot rail, not unlike the brass foot rail that surrounds many bars. There was a gap of perhaps six inches between the inside wall of the rail and the vinyl coated front of the bar. It was into this six-inch gap that the 170-pound shiny brass object with the regimental crest swiftly and surely pulled Ranger's head. Thunk!!! The crowd gasped in unison as it became apparent that Ranger's head was wedged solidly in that position.

But the fight was not yet over. The tall blond artilleryman with the red face and the sweat pouring down his head wasn't wearing the ranger patch on his shoulder because he was a candy ass. He was on his knees and his head was stuck between the bar rail and the bar, but the projectile had not touched the floor. It was still legal!

Mightily the Ranger groaned. He sweat rolled down his face. Lurching with all his strength his head pulled free as he continued to cradle the projo in his arms. Slowly he got one foot under him, then the other. He stood erect. He took one more step and dropped the round on the bar with a resounding thud and denting the varnished surface. The cheers erupted. Arms surrounded his body and patted him on the head and back and people slapped at his hand. His crimson face exploded into an enormous grin.

Nervously a pudgy young man from the 9/18th stepped to the bar. His mates applauded. The pudgy man rolled the round off of the bar into his arms, turned around, and immediately DROPPED THE PROJECTILE ONTO HIS FOOT!!!

"Owwwww!!!" the man screamed. Immediately he began yelling and hopping around the room on one foot, holding the injured one in his hands. Another man got him a chair and guided him to it. By this time the injured officer's yells had become low moans. All of the spectators formed a circle around the man and winced along with him. Doc Kramer stepped forward to announce his position as battalion surgeon. The Staff Duty Vehicle was summoned and before long the patient was being attended to in the infirmary. The stack of $10 MPC notes were collected from the bar and distributed to the winning 8/18th. With the advent of the injury, the contest was over and for all intent and purposes, the party atmosphere as well.

Holloway and Stover leaned against one end of the bar rehashing the evenings events. Kathy Kelsey joined them a moment later and entered the conversation. Without warning the smacking sound of a palm finding flesh resounded behind them. Holloway turned just as Beth Kisha verbally began tongue lashing one of the 9/18th lieutenants who stood in front of her at the other end of the bar holding his face.

"Who the hell do you think you are?" she demanded angrily.

One of the other officers interceded. "He didn't mean any harm, Beth. He's just drunk."

"Well, he's going to be lot more than drunk if he tries that with me again." She glared again at the man holding his face. "Buddy, you ever put your hand on my boob again and I'll knock your dick in your watch pocket and then I'll have your young ass court-martialed and don't ever think I can't do it!" During the entire affair the offending lieutenant had not spoken a word. Finally he broke his silence.

"Hey, myan humnida (sorry about that), OK. I didn't think it was that big a deal," he slurred. "I was just messin' around."

"You just remember what I said," Beth hissed, lowering her tone. Clay Holloway had walked forward and stood supportively beside her. He said nothing, but she felt his presence and it comforted her. Finally she turned and looked at him. "Will you walk me to my hooch?"

"Of course," he answered quietly. Saying nothing else she put her hand on his arm and they moved slowly toward the swinging door, leaving the silent crowd behind them. Once in the hallway he spoke softly. "I certainly am glad you didn't do that to me the first night I was here when you and I bumped butts."

Beth chuckled softly, her anger subsiding. "I hope I didn't go overboard with that, but they're all so stinko drunk and when they're like that you have to really do something to get their attention. Clay, you're not blasted are you?"

"No. I've had a few and I can feel it, but I'm functional."

"That was exactly what I was hoping for." She stopped once they were beyond the door and into the darkness of the night, put her hand behind his head, and pulled his face toward her. Softly she kissed him. Moments later their lips separated slowly.

"So that guy got you turned on, eh," Holloway deadpanned.

"No, the guy I'm kissing turns me on. Why don't you come into my room for a bit and we can talk."

Holloway hesitated. Through the haze of the beer he was torn between the physical desire he had always felt for her and the wholly irrational affection he felt for someone else who was currently shacked up in Seoul City with a helicopter pilot. "OK. I'll come in for a minute."

Beth put her arm around Holloway's waist and rested her head on his chest as they walked the last few yards to the front door of the Doughnut Dolly hooch. A few moments later she unlocked the door to her room and pulled him inside.

"Well what do you want to talk about," Holloway asked once she had closed the door.

"I'll tell you after you make love to me."

Holloway's eyes narrowed. "You are the most unpredictable woman I have ever met. It's always got to be on your terms doesn't it?"

"No, not always. I want you tonight. You're very sexy, Clay Holloway."

"Well, why wasn't I sexy last week or last month. How can you just turn me off and on like this?"

"Bagger, don't. I don't know if it's occurred to you, but this will probably be the last opportunity we'll ever have to be alone together."

"What are you talking about?"

"I'm going home in less than a month. You're going to be tied up with the battery tests at St. Barb all next week and then they're sending you up to that new fire base at the DMZ for two weeks after that. By the time you return I'll quite likely be gone and realistically we'll probably never see each other again. I want you to spend the night with me tonight. Is that so wrong?"

"What fire base? What are you talking about, Beth?"

"The one they call 4 Papa 1. Haven't they told you about it yet?"

"Beth! What are you talking about? What's 4 Papa 1?"

"I heard about it at DivArty yesterday. They're pulling the 105 batteries off of SCOSI duty from now on. It doesn't seem to do much good anyway. And now they're going to start rotating them north of the river into a fire base called 4 Papa 1. Your battery is first. Right after the tests."

"So we'll be there to give fire support in the DMZ in case someone needs it?"

"That's the way it was explained to me. I can't believe they told me all this and no one has told you."

Holloway shook his head resignedly. "I shouldn't be surprised by anything any more, I guess. It's only normal that I be given my operations orders by a Doughnut Dolly."

"That's right, Lieutenant. And here's another order," she said taking his hand. "Start with this button right here and see how quickly you can get it free."

"This one?" Holloway asked, his thumb and forefinger teaming together to slip it through the buttonhole.

"Very well done. Very well done. Now this second one here."

Holloway could feel his senses sharpening. He did the second button and the third and then the fourth. Simultaneously they loosened each other's belts. Slowly he pulled apart the two sides of the navy dress, while she unbuttoned his white shirt and tugged it down his arms. Her white bra was cut deeply, exposing a noticeable portion of her breasts. His lips sought them as his hands released the tiny hooks of the bra. Then he bent forward and gently licked one pink nipple and then the other. Instantly they became hard. Beth tilted her head backward slightly and moaned. Holloway moved his lips around her body, kissing her chest and then her shoulders and then her neck. She was naked to the waist and the warm evening was making small droplets of perspiration roll slowly down her chest, finding their way into the valley formed by her breasts. Her nipples were hard against his palms. He could hear her breathing intensify.

Quickly she reached forward and pulled his white cotton shirt free from his trousers. She caressed his bare chest lovingly as they gazed into each other's eyes. "You always get what you want don't you?" Holloway asked, not expecting an answer.

"Not always. But everyone should get what they want sometimes." She pulled him gently to her and closed her eyes. Their lips melted hotly together.

*   *   *

It was almost six AM when Holloway awoke. He looked next to him quickly to see if he was where he thought he was. Yes, she was snuggled next to him, her right breast pressed against his chest and her arm draped across him. Holloway let his fingers trip lightly across her back and over her well shaped buttocks. He adored the texture of her skin and the almost invisible light blond hair that covered parts of it. His head hurt a bit, a combination of the draft beer and that cheap cigar. He was slightly surprised that Beth had not commented on the cigar smell either on his breath or his clothes. The taste of the damn thing was still in his mouth. Last night had been one hell of a nice night with an incredible ending. He looked again at her face. What a fine looking woman! No wonder she seemed to get whatever she wanted. He wondered if she would ever marry. The subject had never come up between them. It was hard to imagine that one man would ever be enough to satisfy her for very long. Although if it was the right guy, one never knew.

His thoughts turned to JD. Somewhere twenty-five miles south of Camp Wynne she was probably sleeping in the arms of Magic Maloney, her fiancée. So why in the hell did Holloway feel a tinge of guilt because he had just spent the night with Beth Kisha? It was almost like he was cheating on JD, a point, which his intellect told him, was absolutely ridiculous, yet his conscience insisted on raising. Absentmindedly his fingers had continued to roam up and down Beth's spine. Suddenly she stirred.

"Hi," he whispered as she looked at his face.

"Hi, yourself," she answered in a throaty voice. "Have you been awake long?"

"A few minutes is all. I'm just lying here thinking."

"About last night? It was wonderful wasn't it?"

"Yes, it was," Holloway answered truthfully.

"And what else were you thinking about? I'll give you twenty won for your thoughts."

"Oh, its nothing in particular."

"Were you thinking about JD?"

"Jesus!" declared Holloway wide-eyed. "Women are scary. How did you know that? Does that bother you?"

Beth laughed and stretched, exposing her bare chest to Holloway's appreciative eyes. "No, it doesn't bother me. I told you yesterday I have a funny feeling about you two."

"But why? Don't you think she loves Magic?"

"I think she thinks she does. But quite honestly I don't think he loves her. I think he tells her that he does so she'll sleep with him, although I've never said that to her. I think he'll break up with her before he DEROS's. I also think that when that happens she'll be heartbroken and vulnerable and if you still are interested in her she'll be available for you."

"It's funny you would say that. I've sort of heard the same sort of thing about him from other people. It's pretty shitty of a guy to tell someone like JD that he loves her and wants to marry her just to get her into the rack. She's such a sincere and trusting person." Holloway paused. "Tell me something, Beth. Does it make you just a little jealous that I'm here in bed with you and talking about another woman."

She lowered her head and waited a long time before speaking. Finally she looked into his face. "Since this is quite possibly the last time you and I will ever spend an intimate moment together I will be completely honest with you. The first night we met I could feel myself falling for you, but I fought it hard. I fought it during our entire relationship. As I told you, there's no future for us. The timing is all wrong and I just don't need to be dragging my heart around. But the truth of the matter is I adore you. When I realized yesterday at lunch that you really had special feelings for JD I got jealous. I had no right to, but I did. And I decided right then and there that I was going to make love to you once more before I left. I had to." He could see a tear forming in the corner of her eye. "But now," she continued, "no more serious talk. You better get out of here before the girls start moving into the hall."

"That's not the only reason I should go. Have you heard the expression, 'piss like a race horse?'"

Beth laughed out loud. "Leave! I'll see you at lunch." Once Holloway had dressed, she moved quickly to the door, opened it a crack and checked the hall. Seeing no one she waved him forward and pointed down the corridor to the back door. As he began to open the door she stopped him and sought his lips once more. "Good bye, Sweetheart. I wish you a long and happy life."

"I wish you the same." He kissed her and touched her breast and looked admiringly for the last time at her naked body. Then he slipped silently into the hall and out the back as the first rays of the pink dawn began to light the compound.

CHAPTER 20

Charlie Battery's last practice run to St. Barbara prior to the battery test had come and gone. It was followed by two days respite and final preparation at Camp Wynne and then another early morning convoy to the big gunnery range south of Uijombu to participate in the exercise for which the unit had trained for more than a month. Test day itself dawned cold and dreary, yet it dampened none of the intenseness and enthusiasm of the officers and men of the unit. They were a proud bunch that was determined to score highly. And they were not disappointed. Aside from a slight gunnery error during the shooting of a mission when Sergeant Lamerieux's gun crew fired deflection 2919 instead of 2929 and the carelessness of the ammo sergeant who unthinkingly drove one of the ammunition trucks into the line of site from the number three gun to the XO's post just as a fire mission was beginning, the test had gone very satisfactorily. It was almost 2200 hours when the shooting ended and the exercise was declared finished. Charlie Battery was confident it had been successful.

Tom Courtney, Clay Holloway, First Sergeant St. Clair, and the recently arrived Chief of Smoke, Sergeant First Class Earl Wilson relaxed in their tent, laughing and opening cold Cokes. Sergeant Wilson was chuckling about the look on Sergeant Thompson's face when Holloway had reamed him out from fifty yards away for getting his ammo truck in the wrong place at the wrong time. Wilson's words stopped in mid-sentence as he stared at the canvas doorway behind Holloway who turned quickly to see what had distracted him.

"Miss Judy!" Tom Courtney cried, standing and opening his arms to the woman who had just entered the tent.

"Good evening, Lieutenant Courtney. How have you been? It's good to see you," she replied in flawless English, embracing him and kissing him on the cheek. Clay Holloway had never heard a Korean speak in such a formal manner. Normally the chatter with the GI's was a blend of gutter Korean, Japanese, and English. But this woman's lack of an accent was probably the last feature Holloway noticed about her. She was, quite simply, stunning. Miss Judy was dressed immaculately in a sleeveless orange cocktail dress, complete with matching pumps. The dress would not have seemed out of place in a Seoul nightclub, yet appearing from seemingly nowhere inside of a olive drab army tent in the middle of an almost frozen field in the midst of an artillery firing range seemed inexplicable. Incredibly there was not a trace of mud on her shoes. Her hair was coiffured perfectly and her make up expertly applied. Holloway continued to stare at the woman as she and Courtney chatted amicably. Finally Tom turned to him.

"Bagger, I'd like you to meet Miss Judy," Courtney said motioning to the woman. "This is Lootenant Holloway."

"Lieutenant, it's my pleasure."

Holloway had risen. "How do you do?" he responded somewhat shyly. Miss Judy extended her hand and he took it. He noted that it was soft and warm, another incongruity considering it was probably forty degrees outside of the tent. He'd been wearing a field jacket and gloves all day to keep the chill away. Tom Courtney offered the woman a Coke, which she declined, explaining that the sugar was not good for the teeth. A moment later three mamasans from the surrounding area entered the tent bowing and speaking in Pidgin English. Holloway surmised that Miss Judy had been sent ahead as a good will ambassador to pave the way for the untold numbers of field whores who were undoubtedly infiltrating the circular formation of vehicles called the "wagon train" that surrounded the CP. He also suspected that she would be happy to service any of those present if the mamasans felt it was required to gain the good graces of the battery hierarchy. Miss Judy chatted for ten or fifteen minutes with Courtney and Holloway and the others. Finding that all seemed well and receiving no requests for favors she finally seated herself on Holloway's bunk. He sat down next to her. After all, it was his bunk.

"Tell me, Lieutenant, how long have you been in Korea?"

"I'm starting my fifth month," Holloway replied.

"And are you a Korea cherry boy?" she asked, her eyes twinkling.

"Isn't that kind of a personal question?" he said, wondering if she would understand his attempt at humor. "And why is it that every time I come to St. Barb someone asks me that?"

"I just thought that if you were a Korea cherry boy, we could do something about it. You cannot possibly go back to the States without experiencing a Korean woman. Tonight might be a good time to become initiated."

"Well, Miss Judy, you have to understand that I'm tired and shy and I think I'll just take a walk around the perimeter and then hit the rack."

"What are you shy about?" Miss Judy said softly, placing her hand on his. "If you'd like to make love we'll get inside of your sleeping bag. No can will see us. Are you married, is that the problem?"

He winked. "No, but I'm saving myself. Look, why don't you stay here if you like and I'll check the wagon train and be back in a bit." Holloway could not help but be tempted by the woman, but the whole scenario seemed out of place. Prostitution was not something that he had grown up being exposed to and he was still mentally questioning the entire concept, although simultaneously recognizing that it was an everyday fact of life for many of the American GI's in the land of the morning calm. Briefly he visualized Miss Judy slipping quickly out of the orange dress and crawling naked into his sleeping bag, her warm supple body adding an entirely new and not unpleasant element to the cotton covered goose down lining. He realized that the senior NCOs were watching him out of the corner of their eyes, wondering what he was going to do. He was in a position of leadership. Maybe he and Tom Courtney did turn a blind eye to the desires of the men once the duty day had ended, but if he did ever decide to have sex with a Korean girl or even to acquire a yobo for himself, he wasn't going to allow the issue to become a spectator sport for the Charlie Battery NCOs. He arose and slipped on his jacket and web gear and walked outside. As with earlier trips to St. Barb he could hear laughter and giggles coming from around the perimeter. He lapped the circle once to insure that the guards were out and nothing was out of the ordinary and returned to the CP tent.

As he entered he realized that the mamasan population in the CP had multiplied to six. They sat in kimchi squats in one corner of the tent clucking to one another, each seemingly trying to drown out the others. Miss Judy was nowhere to be found, having apparently gone in search of greener pastures. The flame in the kerosene lantern had been lowered, casting an eerie glow inside the tent. Courtney and the NCOs were already in their sleeping bags.

"Tom, are these ladies planning on spending the night?"

"Yeah, I guess. I ain't fixin' to ask them to leave. They say beau coup slicky boys out tonight. They might hit us hard. Top told the guards, but these mamasans give us some extra help. Make sure you got yer club handy." Holloway pulled a hard wood police style baton out of his duffel and put it inside of his sleeping bag along with his wallet and .45 pistol. He and Courtney always carried the clubs at St. Barb.

It was perhaps four hours later when the mamasans high pitched yells made Holloway sit bolt upright on the canvas-covered cot. Surrounding him, at least ten other mamasans were laid out asleep on the floor or still sitting in their squats.

"First Sargee! First Sargee! Wake up! All guards asleep. Beau coup slicky boys steal everything!" the woman cried.

Instantly the soldiers evacuated their bags and jumped into their unlaced boots. First Sergeant St. Clair was first out of the tent, with Courtney, Holloway, and SFC Wilson a step behind, waving their clubs in the air and yelling battle cries at the top of their lungs. They fanned out to separate parts of the wagon train that surrounded them. Immediately, Holloway came upon a slicky boy who loomed up in front of him unexpectedly out of the darkness. The man was carrying a US Army waterproof duffel. Holloway cracked him quickly on the forearm with his club. The man screamed, dropping the duffel and bolting for the perimeter of trucks. Holloway watched him dive beneath a deuce and a half and roll out the other side before turning his attention to something else. Nearby he could hear Courtney's rebel yell piercing the night air. Top was cursing and calling to the troops to wake up and get moving. Within moments the entire battery was embroiled in a wild melee. Later estimates put the number of slicky boys inside the perimeter at thirty or more. GI's awakened to find personal belongings, tools, equipment, and even clothing in the act of being slickied. High-pitched screams added to the din as the field whores began helping their American bunkmates in chasing the thieves out of the area. Holloway and Courtney looked at each other curiously as a completely naked josan ran between them, chasing a slick with a portable radio in his hand. Courtney spied the culprit and cut the man off, laying him low with a club blow behind the knee. Dropping the radio the man looked up at Courtney and raised his arm defensively, waiting for the next stroke. Instead Courtney pointed to the perimeter.

"Cauda! Cauda chogi!" he yelled. The thief regained his feet and began limping away, leaving the radio. The naked girl snatched it from the ground, cradled it in her arms, and began walking back in the direction from which she had come. She looked back over her shoulder at Courtney and smiled. It was then that Holloway realized it was Miss Judy and that Sergeant Carlton was coming out to meet her. Looking away, Holloway sensed that the tide had turned. With the entire unit awake and in action, the outnumbered slicky boys had dropped most of their loot and beaten a hasty retreat beyond the wagon train. But the confusion continued for another thirty minutes as men searched by flashlight for missing items. A full accounting could not occur until daylight and even then some things would not be noticed missing until the battery returned to Camp Wynne the next morning.

By the time First Sergeant St. Clair finished chewing out the guards for falling asleep and posting new ones it was almost 0400. He had told them there was no excuse for falling asleep on guard duty and made dire threats to the next man who couldn't keep his eyes open. If they were in Vietnam, he told them, they'd all be dead. Two hours later the unit would be reawakened for a quick breakfast and the three-hour convoy home.

*   *   *

Prior to the battery test, Tom Courtney had been briefed by Major Gentile and Colonel Nordstrum regarding the new Second Division tactical concept of positioning a 105 mm howitzer battery north of the Imjin River in the hostile fire zone, at all times, in order to have the capability to provide instant direct artillery support to the outposts in the DMZ if it were to become necessary. While technically the guns could reach the DMZ from their positions at Camp Wynne, the reality of the situation was that they were at maximum range and severely restricted in the support they could give. True to Beth Kisha's rumor from DivArty, the first battery to occupy the new position, designated 4 Papa 1, was Charlie Battery, 8/18th Artillery. Courtney had been surprised to find that Clay Holloway already knew the name of the base before he had a chance to brief him on the operation, but all that Holloway would concede to Courtney was to give a mysterious wink and say that he had friends at DivArty.

Following its return from Camp St. Barbara, Charlie Battery was given only three days to prepare for a two week stay in the wilderness surrounding Four Papa One. The position, which was located in the forest only three miles east of Holloway's former home at Camp Greaves, had been cleared in less than a week by engineers who had poured cement pads for the CP tent, the supply tent, the giant motor pool tent and a large canvas Quonset hut, called a Jamesway. Most people referred to the latter as the sleeping hooch. The firing positions for the six individual howitzers were pre-planned by DivArty and engineers had excavated holes for the ammo bunker and personnel bunker at each position, as well as erecting the wooden framework for them and beginning the process of sandbagging the bunkers and parapets. While each battery occupied the firebase, it would spend much of its time improving the position, primarily by filling and stacking sandbags. The engineers had also trimmed branches from the trees to allow for a clear field of fire for the howitzers and had been considerate enough to have constructed a wooden three-hole latrine as well as a wooden frame shower with 55-gallon drums on a rack above the shower. Since the thermometer hovered near 40 degrees on the sunny bright October day that Charlie Battery first occupied the position, it was unlikely that the showers would ever be used, at least until the following spring.

Many of the brightly tinted fall leaves still adorned the surrounding woodlands on the initial day of occupation. During delays in the process of laying the individual guns with his aiming circle, Holloway found himself marveling at the natural beauty of the wilderness surrounding him. Since they were in the hostile fire zone, the unit was without many of the distractions or nuisances of the populated areas south of the river. At 4 Papa 1, there were no mamasans, there were no slicky boys, and there were no field whores. There was only the wilderness and the creatures that inhabited it.

One of those creatures made its presence known on the second night of the occupation. PFC Daniels of the Commo Section was finding his way to the latrine. While using a red filtered flashlight to pick his way slowly along a narrow trail on the outskirts of the battery position, he realized there was a large furry four-legged shape on the trail ahead. The movement of his flashlight froze the animal for only a fraction of a second. But during that time, PFC Daniels could recall seeing only two things, a pair of glowing eyes and an open mouth full of large sharp looking teeth. Both Daniels and the unknown creature apparently turned and ran in opposite directions at exactly the same time. The young enlisted man then jumped through the first tent flap that he came upon, which happened to be the Charlie Battery CP.

"Daniels, what in the hell do you think you're doin' flying into the CP like that?" First Sergeant Hudson St. Clair yelled as Daniels stumbled in.

"Top, there's somethin' out there. It's after me. No shit, Top. It's big! It's right out there on the trail."

"What are you talkin' about, young troop? What's after you?"

"Top, I'm telling you. There is some kinda big fuckin' animal out there on the trail. I thought it was gonna get me. All I could see was these big red eyes and teeth."

Tom Courtney got up from the folding chair at his field desk and pulled his .45 out of the holster. "Show me, Daniels," he said, picking up his flashlight with his free hand. Clay Holloway rolled off of his cot, snatched up his M-14 and followed his Battery Commander and Daniels into the night air. Daniels walked cautiously back up the trail toward the latrine. Each of the soldiers scanned the nearby vegetation and peered closely at the dirt on the path. There was no sign of any animal. Finally Daniels elected to return to his squad tent and get one of his companions. Then both men, armed with entrenching tools, made the trip up the hill to the latrine.

By morning, the story had spread to every man in the battery. Speculation ran rampant. The GI's, many of whom had never seen any wild animal more dangerous than a squirrel outside of a zoo, discussed siberian tigers, wildcats, bobcats, wolves, mountain lions, raccoons, and beavers at length. No one knew what Daniels had encountered, but at the same time, no one planned to venture out after dark by himself, especially without some sort of weapon. Tom Courtney had decreed that, with the exception of the perimeter guards, no one was to fire a rifle, nor even load his weapon unless someone's life was in direct peril. The last thing anyone needed was to have someone firing indiscriminately inside the battery position. Bullets were probably a lot more dangerous than whatever the unknown beast was. So most of the soldiers took to carrying their rifles with fixed bayonets or to packing their unfolded entrenching tools to use as clubs.

A day later, the Mess Sergeant informed Clay Holloway that some animal had gotten into the garbage the night before. He had heard it rummaging around near the mess tent, but had been unwilling to go outside to investigate it, especially since by this time Daniel's description of the animal had doubled from its original size. In the morning the garbage had been cleaned up and life in the wilderness had continued.

That evening Tom Courtney elected to participate in his favorite off duty form of recreation. He organized a poker game with Holloway, some of the FDC crew, and Corporal Clinton Gash. True to form, Courtney was the early winner. Gash had brought with him his am/fm radio that was plugged into one of the extension cords that lead into the CP from the field generator near the motor pool tent. The field generator supplied enough power to give light to most of the larger tents. Naturally, the poker players were tuned to AFKN, the only station on the dial, unless they wanted to listen to the North Korean propaganda from across the way. The AFKN disc jockey announced his next selection, which happened to be a favorite of most of the poker players. The song began as a mournful sort of ballad by Three Dog Night. It was a song about Eli.

Some people would later state that not only did the beast begin to roar during the song, but that he hit it right on cue. Immediately following the song's first line came the loudest, most blood curdling, bone chilling, roar that any of the men had ever heard in their relatively young lives. Eli the critter was announcing his arrival.

"Rrrroooowwwwlllllll!!!" The deep roaring growl seemed to be just on the other side of the thin canvas tent wall. The men sitting cross-legged on the floor each froze, their mouths open, their eyes wide. They could almost feel the creature's hot breath coming through the canvas. No one spoke for a brief moment. Then Courtney looked over at the First Sergeant who had sat bolt upright in bed.

"What in the fuck was that??"

"Eli, man! Eli's here," yelled Clay Holloway.

Clinton Gash looked at Al Lepley as if to say, "That's nice, but what in God's name is Eli??" Then, as though someone had fired a starter's pistol, everyone in the tent leaped to their feet and began searching frantically for the closest weapon, as though a battle to the death was imminent. Just as quickly Tom Courtney was outside of the tent crouching with his pistol ready and scanning the area around the canvas structure. The others poured out of the tent flap behind him a moment later. As had happened two nights earlier, there was a sign of nothing. Holloway could hear voices as other soldiers approached the CP coming from the area of the squad tents behind the howitzers. He called to them.

"Take it easy. We all heard it, but no one has seen anything. Spread out and keep your eyes open."

Twenty minutes of combing the area produced nothing. Eventually many of the men stood in small groups discussing what sort of man-eating predator was so mysteriously stalking them. Finally the soldiers began moving cautiously back to their sleeping tents, vowing to not leave them again at night no matter how badly they might have to go to the latrine. Pulling armed guard duty at the five outposts surrounding the perimeter was the exception, although many of the men were leery even of that.

"So what do you think, Bagger?" Tom Courtney asked after the two had returned to the CP tent.

"You're the hunter, Tom. I'm just a city boy. What do you think it is? I know I've never in my life heard a growl like that. It sounded like it was coming straight out of the jaws of hell."

"I'll tell you straight. I've never heard anything like that before either. I kin tell you what it's not, though. It's not a bobcat. It's not a fox or a wolf either and I don't think it's a mountain lion or a Siberian tiger. It just might be a small bear. But whatever Eli is, he ain't friendly. That's one thing I kin tell you for certain. Up here around the Z these animals ain't used to seeing people. We're probably a whole new experience for him and I don't think he knows quite what to do about us. I'm gonna talk to the kitchen papasan in the morning. He told me today he wants to put out some traps near the garbage and see if he cain't come up with somethin'. I'm gonna tell him to go ahead and see what happens."

*   *   *

Thus far Yoon Kim Lee's mission had gone exceptionally well. He and his two-man team had been moving about in the Second Division's area of operations on a nightly basis. During the day they would generally go to ground to sleep in secluded areas or sometimes forage for food. But once night fell they moved like shadows across the deserted Korean landscapes to put themselves into position to observe and record whatever information they could gain about the various units of the Division. By observing a compound through binoculars they could count vehicles. The type and number of vehicles on a compound translated easily into unit size. Twenty or thirty vehicles was a company or battery sized compound. A hundred was a battalion. The numbers stenciled on the bumpers told Yoon the unit designation. It was even easier to count APC's or tanks or howitzers, making the combat units even more open to basic intelligence gathering. In addition, Yoon and his team had taken several rolls of film, which would be analyzed by the experts once they returned home.

Another mission had been that of targeting headquarters and command centers. Yoon knew there had been talk of assassination of American officers and senior NCOs. That might be done for two potential purposes. One would be for terror tactics that would make the imperialists reconsider their position of defending their lackey South Korean puppets. Kill enough of them and they might move their Second and Seventh Divisions well to the south. But a second and more likely reason to target command centers was to be prepared for the eventuality of a resumption of full-scale war between the North and South. If that were imminent, Yoon and his contemporaries would be responsible for mass assassination of senior commanders and their primary staffs just before hostilities began. This applied not only to general officers, but brigade and possibly even battalion level commanders. In order to carry forth that order properly, the government of Kim Il Sung must be constantly aware of the location of those officers.

For the past three days the commando team had patrolled the area around Camp Howze, the headquarters for the Second Division. Twice they had infiltrated the compound itself, digging under the fence in a secluded remote area and then replacing the dirt in the hole once they had finished. Moving silently during the early morning hours they had completed their top priority mission. They had identified both the sleeping quarters and headquarters of the Commanding General, Second Infantry

Division. Yoon could hardly contain his excitement until he returned home to divulge that information to his Group Commander.

*   *   *

Sergeant Al Lepley walked out of the FDC and called to his battery commander who was standing nearby.

"Lieutenant Courtney. Headquarters just called. Major Gentile is coming up this afternoon and two of the Doughnut Dollies are coming with him. They want us to make the troops available to them from sometime between 1500 to 1600 hours for some kind of games."

"OK, Lep. Give them a roger," the BC replied. He turned to Clay Holloway. "That's nice. Most of our guys like it when the Doughnut Dollies show up. I wonder who they're sending?"

At exactly 1430 the guard at the sandbagged foxhole near the intersection of the main road and the dirt road leading to 4 Papa 1 picked up the field phone and cranked the handle. In the Charlie CP the phone at the other end of the wire chirped. Clinton Gash answered it. "Gash, tell the BC that Major Gentile is pulling into our position!" a voice said. Gash relayed the message and both Charlie Battery officers were waiting outside the CP when the jeep exited the woods and entered the clearing, which the battery occupied.

Holloway looked anxiously at the back seat of the jeep wondering who the two female figures wearing parkas, helmets, and flak jackets could be. It really wasn't parka weather, but apparently they weren't taking any chances on being underdressed. Finally recognizing Joan Brannigan and Jennifer Dodge his face broke into a broad smile. He walked quickly down the little hill to meet them.

"Good afternoon, Sir!" Holloway and Courtney greeted simultaneously as they saluted the Battalion Operations Officer. Holloway forced himself to pretend to be interested in Major Gentile, although it was the presence of Jennifer Dodge who had really captured his attention.

"Hello, Tom; Clay!" Rocky Gentile replied returning their salutes. You people are really secluded back here aren't you?" He looked around approvingly. "The battery looks good. It's really shaped up in the four days you've been here."

"Thank you, Sir. We've filled over a thousand sandbags, so far. We've been hauling sand from a stream that's back that way about two hundred meters," Courtney said pointing beyond the little rise where the CP stood.

"The word around Camp Wynne is that you're being stalked by some sort of a man-eater up here."

Courtney gave a crooked grin. "Something like that. No one's had a good enough look to see what it is, but there's some kind of critter that's been checkin' us out. His name is Eli. Son of a bitch growled the other night and liked to give me a heart attack."

"Well if that's the biggest hazard you have up here I wouldn't be too worried. At least the DMZ has been quiet for a couple of weeks now. The fence is only a mile north of here you know."

"Yes, Sir," answered Holloway. "We walked up on top of that little hill behind you on the first day. You can see the fence from there. You can see all three of our GP's too."

"Really! Perhaps you can show me. The girls might like to see it too."

The two Doughnut Dollies had been standing quietly behind Major Gentile. The S-3's statement gave Holloway the opening he'd been waiting for. He turned to the two women. "Hi, ladies. Welcome to our little woodland hideaway."

"Hi, Charlie Battery," Joan answered, flashing her Irish smile.

"Hi, Clay," JD said looking directly at Holloway. "I'd love to see the DMZ. This is the first time I've ever been north of the river. It's beautiful up here."

"Not as nice as Tennessee, but it'll have to do," said Courtney. "Y'all go ahead. I'll tell Top to have the troops ready in a half hour over on the side of that hill. What are you gonna do with 'em today?"

"We've got a little contest for them," answered Joan. "It's setting up pop bottles with bamboo fishing poles and line and a rubber doughnut on the end. After that we've got a tape recorder and we're going to try some 'Name That Tune' trivia."

"Well, OK then. I'll see you a little later," Courtney said.

"Tom, when I get back I'll want to talk with you and Lieutenant Holloway while the troops are having their entertainment," noted the Major.

"Yessir!"

"It's that way, Sir." Holloway fell in behind Major Gentile one step to the rear and to the left as military custom dictated. The two women walked near him as the party began ascending the hill where Holloway had pointed. "We're going to see a few interesting things on the way. Right up ahead is the remains of a Korean cemetery; Happy Mountain they call it. The Koreans always put the cemeteries on hills so the dead will be closer to heaven."

Two stone columns marked the beginning of the cemetery. Each served as a guard to the dead. Granite burial markers could be seen scattered about the hillside, which was overgrown with bushes and trees. No one had tended to the graves since the Korean War for which the Cease Fire had been signed sixteen years earlier. Passing the cemetery Holloway again pointed ahead. "Right up here are some old fighting positions left over from the war. Tom and I found a couple of foxholes and what used to be a bunker. We found some rusted out ammo magazines and a helmet too. It's kind of eerie walking old battlefields. Especially finding pieces of gear. We wondered about what it felt like for those guys to be setting up a perimeter in a cemetery."

Everyone grew silent. Jennifer Dodge felt slightly uncomfortable. The hillside, which had looked so beautiful painted in the colors of autumn when they had begun the climb, was a place of ghosts. It forced her to remember exactly where they were and why the troops were here in the first place. They walked in silence the rest of the way. When they reached the crest five minutes later, all of them were perspiring and breathing heavily.

Holloway stood in front of the group, raised his arm, and pointed with his left index finger. "There's the road you came in on. Look out about a mile further and you can see the fence running along the open area. Do you see it?"

"Yes, there it is," JD replied. The other two nodded eagerly.

"Now over to the far left you can see a big hill about three miles out. That's GP Gwen."

"That's the hill you were on?" JD asked.

"I've been on all three of our GP's, but Gwen is the one I was on most of the time, yes. I was on Cindy when Hackworth and I found the tunnel. Cindy is the next hill to the right. It's not as big as Gwen. Baron spent most of his time on Cindy. Now to the right is one other hill. That's GP Carol. Sweeper was up there most of his tour in the Z. I think the Owl is there now. Does everyone see the hills I'm talking about?"

"Clay, where is Panmunjom from here?" Major Gentile asked.

"It's right over there, Sir," Holloway replied pointing. "If you use your binoculars you can see it and the Bridge of No Return."

"OK, got it."

Holloway patiently answered questions for a few minutes. Finally, Joan Brannigan looked at her watch and announced that they needed to leave. The two girls were supposed to start working with the troops in only fifteen minutes. As the four people started their descent, Joan engaged Major Gentile in conversation. That allowed Holloway and JD to fall a few yards to the rear.

"Is Magic gone?" he asked, looking into her eyes.

"Yes. He left yesterday," JD responded in a low voice, the note of sadness obvious to his ears. "I miss him so much already, just knowing that he's on the other side of the world and I'm not going to see him for seven months."

"Are you thinking about just quitting the Red Cross and just going home and being with him?"

Surprised, she looked at him. "Of course not. I signed up for a year and I'm going to honor my commitment. There are a lot of people over here that have loved ones at home. They don't just quit and leave and I'm not going to do it either."

"They can't quit. They're in the Army. You're not. You could resign if you want to."

"It's out of the question, Clay. I would never do that. It's like cheating or desertion or something. No way."

"Have you two made any more definite marriage plans?"

"No. Sometimes I feel like something is wrong, but I can't put my finger on it. He acted funny whenever I'd bring it up. He didn't seem comfortable talking about it. I asked him straight out if there was a problem. I asked him, you know, if he still wanted to get married. I wanted him to tell me if he didn't, but he said yes."

"So where is he now?"

"Ft. Hood, Texas. Well, not yet. He's at home in Sacramento to visit his folks for a few days and then he was going to go to Vegas with some friends and then he reports to Ft. Hood in about two weeks."

"So you're going to move to Kileen, Texas when you get out of here and get married is that the plan?"

"Bagger, I'm not sure. He was just, you know, indefinite. He said he needed some time to work out the details and he'd be writing me every day and everything would be fine by the time I go home next spring." She was silent for a moment as the footing became more difficult on a steep part of the slope. Holloway offered his hand and she held it tightly as she turned sideways on the hill and sidestepped her way down. "God, seven months seems like a long time," she finally declared as they reached the bottom. Looking ahead she could see that some of the troops had already assembled in the area designated for them. She released her grip on Holloway's hand and trotted ahead to catch up with Joan who had already begun unloading the jeep trailer with some of their props. Holloway watched her for a moment and then turned to catch up with Major Gentile who was standing and waiting for him. Together they walked to the CP tent, which stood, on the high ground behind the gun pits.

Thirty minutes later Major Gentile emerged from the CP, having given Courtney and Holloway the latest information from Camp Wynne. Alpha Battery had passed its battery test with flying colors two days earlier. Holloway felt happy for Kendall Stover who had performed well as Alpha's XO. Bravo Battery was to test next week. Tom Courtney had asked Major Gentile informally which unit had been superior in the test thus far. Pressed for a response, Gentile said it had been close, but finally conceded that Charlie was probably a shade better. Tom Courtney, competitive in virtually everything he did, gave Holloway a wink and a thumb's up as soon as they began to follow Gentile out of the tent.

As the three officers began walking toward the seated troops fifty yards away, they noted that the two Red Cross girls were just completing the planned entertainment and had uncovered five large boxes of doughnuts. Obediently, the troops had formed a single file and were accepting the doughnuts as they voiced the usual wisecracks. Next they moved toward a table that held a large canister of coffee that the mess crew had placed nearby. Holloway stood in line behind the troops.

"Got any crumbs left?" he asked playfully when his turn finally came.

"Better than that. We've got a chocolate left for you," JD answered with a big smile. "We don't usually have chocolate doughnuts, you know."

"I'll split it with you," he offered.

"No thanks. You eat it. First rule of the Doughnut Dolly. Don't eat your own doughnuts. If we start sampling our own wares we'd each gain twenty pounds before we get out of here." She looked beyond Holloway at Major Gentile who was trying to catch her eye to tell her it was time to go. She nodded back.

Holloway helped the two women stuff their equipment into a large army duffel and lower it into the jeep trailer. All the doughnuts had been distributed and eaten.

"You two take care of yourselves," Holloway counseled as they stepped carefully into the back of Rocky Gentile's jeep.

"Thanks, Clay. Watch out for the man-eater," joked Joan.

"Hey, when is Beth leaving? She's not gone yet, is she?" Holloway asked at the last moment.

"Oohhh, I'm sorry," JD answered, her hand touching her mouth. "She asked me to say hi to you. She hasn't gone yet. About another week. When are you coming back?"

Courtney looked questioningly at Major Gentile. "It will probably be a week tomorrow. We're not quite sure yet. A Battery from the 1/15th will be replacing you. They're not sure of their schedule. I'll let you know as soon as we do."

"Yes, Sir." Courtney and Holloway both stepped back and saluted. Major Gentile nodded to his driver who released the clutch quickly, causing the tires to spin in the dirt, and began driving out of the firing position.

Jennifer Dodge turned in her seat and waved. "Good bye, guys. Be careful." The jeep left a rolling cloud of dust as it disappeared down the dirt trail and into the woods on its way to the main road.

*   *   *

Lieutenant Yoon Kim Lee had left his two men in a wooded area while he reconnoitered the south bank of the Imjin. While it was still daylight, he planned to find an easy way of descending the bluffs. An hour after dark he would return to lead his team back the same way, enter and swim the river, and make their return trip to the tunnel entrance two miles to the northeast. From there it would only be a stroll through the three-mile long tunnel to home and the congratulations of his superiors. The mission had been a complete success. It had been his first deep penetration into the South, other than the ill-fated Blue House Raid. But only the first of many, he hoped.

Sergeant Kwang, Lieutenant Yoon's second in command, sat under a medium sized fir tree updating the journal that the team had maintained since the first day of the mission. Nearby, Kwang's companion, Corporal Han slept on a bed of pine needles. It would be another hour and a half until darkness fell and Lieutenant Yoon would return. There was no sense in being unproductive during his absence. And there really wasn't much else to do. Now there was only a wait of a few hours and then the last leg of the mission.

Sergeant Kwang was completely unaware of the approach of the two teenage girls until one spoke to the other when they were within fifteen feet of the North Korean soldier. Startled, he jumped to his feet, frightening the two sisters. Most rural Koreans do not normally venture far from their village without good reason. Naturally, those living in a village are well acquainted with all of the people that dwell around them. The teenage girls had never seen the tall stranger before.

Fighting panic, Sergeant Kwang put his finger to his lips. "Don't be afraid, girls. I'm just a traveler on his way to Munsan-ni. My friend and I have stopped to rest for a while before continuing our journey. What are you doing out here?" he asked cautiously.

"Our father asked us to look for wood," replied the older of the two nervously. Her sister nodded.

"Well," smiled Kwang, "I don't think there's much wood around here. These fir trees don't make very good fires."

"Perhaps not. I guess we'll walk over to that hill."

"Fine," Kwang said. "That's a good idea. Good luck." He watched indecisively as the two teenagers turned and walked in a different direction. The NCO was unsure as to what to do. He sensed that the best thing to do was slaughter the two girls as they walked away, hide the bodies, and wait until dark. But if the girls did not return, search parties might be sent. In addition, Kwang had never actually killed anyone before, let alone two defenseless teenage girls. Besides, on this mission the commando team had orders to avoid killing if at all possible. He wished fervently that Lieutenant Yoon were there. He would know the right thing to do. But, the fact was that he wasn't there. Kwang watched the girls as they continued to walk, moving farther and farther away until his decision was made for him. Perhaps the two girls would not even mention to anyone that they had seen him. All of his gear was inside the waterproof bag. The girls had no way whatsoever of knowing who he was. Why should they? And besides, he convinced himself, even if the girls mentioned seeing them to someone, who would pay attention?

The older girl spoke to her sister when they were clearly out of earshot of the strange man in the woods. "I'm afraid of him!"

"So am I. He looks mean. Let's tell father about him."

The sisters headed directly toward the hill where they had pointed. Once reaching it, however, they skirted the base until they were sure the strange man could not see them. Then they slipped into a drainage ditch and walked quickly in the direction of their village less than a mile away on the other side of some dried up rice paddies.

"Papa!" the older girl called as she stepped inside the door to her thatched roof clay hut. "There's a strange man in the woods. He scared us."

"A Korean man or an American?" the father asked with some parental concern.

"He's Korean. There were two men. One was asleep. They were just sitting in the trees on the other side of the hill. I've never seen them before."

"Did you talk with them?"

"I talked to the one that was awake. He said they were traveling to Munsan-ni."

"Where were they coming from?" the father probed, trying to determine whether or not there was something to really be concerned about.

"He didn't say."

"That does not make sense," the father mused. "The only thing north is the Imjin River and the DMZ beyond. No one to the west or east would move parallel to the river to get to Munsan. They would head diagonally directly toward it. You're not making this up are you?"

"No, Papa," replied the younger girl. "They're in the woods. They have packs with them."

The thirty-six year old father of the teenagers had served four years as an infantryman in the ROK Army as most other male Koreans had. The last ten years he had remained active as a sergeant in the Korean Home Guard. Many times he had participated in sweeps of the area after sightings of possible infiltrators, or UI's as the Americans called them. He could not ignore a report such as this. They lived too close to the DMZ. It must be investigated.

CHAPTER 21

"Lieutenant Hackworth! Battalion says there's UI's spotted near Freedom Bridge. They want the whole Company mounted and moving in fifteen minutes," yelled the Bravo Company clerk to the newly appointed Company Commander standing at the other end of the CP. Captain Gustafson had DEROS'd to the States only the week before. First Lieutenant Hackworth was not the senior first lieutenant in the battalion, but no one doubted that he was the most qualified for the command slot. He had been given the nod.

"You heard him, Top! Let's go!" ordered Hackworth. The Bravo First Sergeant flew from his desk, knocked the screen door open and ran outside, blowing into the whistle he wore on a leather cord around his neck. Hackworth took the phone from the outstretched hand of his clerk, asked several questions in machine gun like fashion, and jotted some grid coordinates on a piece of an envelope. Many of the soldiers in the infantry company were currently in a map reading class at the time of the phone call. Most of the others were scattered about the compound on various work details, but it was Bravo's week for standby alert. Gear, vehicles, and weapons were at the ready. Eleven minutes after the initial telephone call, the company was in the vehicles and moving by truck and APC out of the Camp Pelfry main gate.

As the hastily formed convoy headed north, Hackworth continued to converse into the handset connected by the flexible cord to his jeep mounted radio. Soon he had fixed a complete picture in his mind and on his map of exactly what was happening and what was expected of him. Formulating his tactical plan instinctively he began communicating it to his four platoon leaders scattered throughout the long column. He would deploy Bobby Reynolds and his first platoon along the river north of the spotted UI's sealing off that avenue of escape. At the same time third platoon would take a dirt road to the rear of the small hills to the east and tie in with Reynolds. Second platoon would stop on the main road, deploy, and block the western escape path. Once they were in position, the Korean Home Guard that was assembling in the nearby village would form a skirmish line and sweep north into the woods, driving the UI's into the Americans. A ROK liaison officer would meet Hackworth at an intersection three kilometers south of the river to coordinate the movement.

Hackworth knew the area well. Anxiously he looked at his watch. There was just over an hour of good daylight left, but he would be in position in less than fifteen minutes.

Sergeant Kwang had watched the trucks roll north on the road one kilometer west of his location in the woods. He had been alarmed when he first saw them, but they had driven past him, undoubtedly heading for Freedom Bridge on the way to the DMZ. But suddenly the trucks left the main road! They turned right onto a small dirt path running parallel to the river. The trucks were now between Sergeant Kwang and the Imjin-Gang. Kwang awakened his sleeping partner hurriedly. Even as the man opened his eyes and looked around, Kwang could hear more trucks on the main road to the west. But these trucks didn't keep going. They stopped along the road and many armed troops began leaping out of their canvas-covered beds and deploying near the road. Lieutenant Yoon had told his two men to wait in the woods until he returned. But now they couldn't. Kwang made a command decision. He motioned to Corporal Han and they grabbed their packs and began moving through the wooded area to their east toward the small hills.

*   *   *

Hiding near the river, Lieutenant Yoon, had planned to wait until dark to fetch his men. It was safer for three men to move across the open country once visibility was restricted. But suddenly the trucks had arrived and he had to make an instant decision. He could move quickly to the south toward his men and probably be caught inside of what he could see was a rapidly forming box, or he could stay where he was and remain outside of the box. His men needed him. Besides that, they had the journal and most of the photographs, which was their purpose for coming to South Korea in the first place. But Lieutenant Yoon's instincts told him exactly what was happening. He didn't know what had gone wrong, but somehow his men had been seen and these enemy soldiers were in the act of surrounding them. Yoon decided to stay put.

*   *   *

Sergeant Kwang felt that if he moved quickly enough he and Corporal Han could escape the tightening net. He was wrong. Nearing the small hills to the east he realized that soldiers were now occupying them and the lowlands that lay between them. To the south more armed men were advancing in a skirmish line across the open rice paddies directly toward them. Kwang looked at the sky. Could they hide until dark? Once darkness arrived anything could happen. But no. The soldiers coming from the village were advancing too rapidly. They would be on top of them in ten or fifteen minutes. There was only one chance. Fight their way through the line at the river and get into the water as darkness fell. The water would hide them as they floated far downstream until it was safe to come out. Kwang and Han changed direction and headed directly for the Imjin. Maybe they would even meet up with Lieutenant Yoon.

The two North Korean commandos neared the edge of the wood line. Frantically Kwang looked for a route that would give them sufficient cover to advance toward the river without being seen. Suddenly, there it was; a gift from Buddha. It was a drainage ditch. Arguably, the ditch was less than three feet deep and with only sparse vegetation that offered little in the way of concealment. But it would have to do. The two men entered the ditch and moving in a duck walk heading directly toward the river and the waiting first platoon. After ten minutes they knew they were close. Kwang motioned to Han to drop down and low crawl the rest of the way. Silently they slithered toward the river, a combination of adrenaline and the conditioning of their finally tuned muscles allowing them to move through the ditch like serpents. Kwang lowered his eyes for a moment to release his shirt, which had caught on a small branch. When he raised them he blinked. An American was kneeling in the ditch in front of him aiming a rifle. Kwang swung his Makarov up. It was the last thing he ever did.

The explosions caught Corporal Han completely by surprise. He hadn't even seen the American, but suddenly there was the ear shattering noise and Sergeant Kwang slumped to the ground ahead of him and laid motionless. Han spun around rapidly, raised to a crouch, and ran back the way he had come. Buzzing sounds near his head told him how close the bullets were. Again he dropped to the bottom of the ditch, pistol in hand. He raised his head. Americans were advancing on either side of the ditch. He jerked a small pouch containing film out of his pack. Arming a grenade he dropped it into the pouch and threw it toward the Americans who dived to the ground. The pouch exploded in a hail of confetti. Han had one grenade left. The act of surrendering did not even occur to him. Hurriedly he armed the second grenade and curled himself around it to end his life in the same fetal position in which he had begun it twenty-three years earlier.

Hackworth watched a Korean Home Guard NCO roll the body over with his foot. Horrified, the two teenage sisters stood nearby, their hands held to their faces. The ROK liaison captain standing next to them asked the girls if it was the man they had seen in the woods. Nodding in ascent they both turned away. No one bothered to have them check the second body; the face was too badly disfigured. Proudly the girls' father lead them away, back in the direction of their village nearby. A hero's greeting awaited them, as word of the death of the two North Korean agents had already reached the village. The ROK liaison officer issued orders and two of the Home Guard soldiers began checking the pockets of the two corpses. Keith Hackworth retrieved the pack of the man who had been shot in the ditch and began examining it. Finding a notebook that was almost filled with Korean writing he handed it to the ROK officer and asked him what it was.

"It appears to be a diary. A journal of sorts, which details their mission. This is excellent. Look, it tells us exactly where they were and what they did," stated the American educated young Korean captain who had received a bachelor's degree from

Washington State and a master's from Stanford. Suddenly the man frowned deeply. "Damn it!"

"What is it? What's wrong?" asked Hackworth.

"There were three men in the team, not two. There is an officer named Yoon who was the mission commander. Obviously he is still on the loose! We must find him!"

"We can continue the sweep the way we began it, but I'm not very hopeful that we'll find him. He must have seen what's happened unless he's nowhere around here. He's probably hauling ass as fast as he can right now. Check the back of the journal. Does it say where he went?"

Captain Chung turned to the last few pages that contained writing and scanned the entries. "No. It talks about how they spent last night a few kilometers southeast of here. It appears that the man writing the journal had not yet reached the point of entering all of today's events."

Frowning, Hackworth looked at the sky. Dusk was beginning. Darkness came quickly in November. He motioned to his RTO who handed him the microphone. Establishing contact with his platoon leaders, he directed a new sweep pattern, which would not be completed until after dark. Hackworth was not fooling himself. Instinctively he knew that this Lieutenant Yoon character had unassed the area. He called his battalion TOC to report what he knew. They would issue the operation order that would call for a comprehensive sweep of the entire area beginning at dawn.

Watching the cluster of soldiers through his binoculars, Lieutenant Yoon Kim Lee felt the red-hot poker of rage. He had not seen his men go down, but he could see the two bodies lying in the field a kilometer away. He had heard the roar of the grenades across the open country and hoped his two commandos had taken some of their attackers with them. Ambulances were coming up the road to the west, but Yoon could not afford to wait any longer to see how many bodies were loaded. He had no idea whether the Americans knew of his presence, but one thing was sure. It was necessary for him to get as far away from his present position as possible. There was the obvious decision to cross the river quickly and get back to the tunnel before dawn. There was no question that by the next morning his enemy would be sweeping the area with hundreds of men in a well-prepared search plan. Crossing the river, however, was not as easy as it sounded. To attempt to swim the river while there was still light was highly dangerous. No one was around him now, but what would he do if he was half way across and suddenly soldiers appeared on either of the banks. He would be trapped. Death would find him in the same Imjin-Gang where it had found his friends in the Blue House Raid the year before. It would be best to wait ten minutes. It would be dark enough then. He could move closer to the riverbank, hide for those ten minutes, and then slip into the water.

But there was an alternative. One that his enemies would not expect. Rather than moving north, toward home, he could move south; deeper into enemy territory and back into the areas where he had already been and was familiar with. What was the sense of returning home in disgrace? His men were dead. Most of what his team had accomplished was now lost, recaptured by his enemies. He still had his map, but the pictures and the journal were gone. Of course, there was Yoon's memory, but with the journal captured, the Americans would do things to counter the important things that he had learned, such as the location of the sleeping quarters of the division commander. The painful truth was that almost everything that had been accomplished early in the mission had been for nothing. Yoon made a decision. He was not going home. Not yet. If and when he returned to the North it would be as a hero, not as a loser in disgrace. He had already returned like that once, after the Blue House Raid. Outwardly they'd called him a hero, but inside everyone knew that the primary mission of killing Park Chung Hee had failed. No! He would not go through that again. He would move south and accomplish something. What that could be was unknown. But it would be significant. It would be important. He would find something. He would salvage the mission.

*   *   *

"Papasan, you get those traps out?" Tom Courtney asked the old Korean civilian who was employed by the troops to work in the mess section; thereby eliminating most of the need for the GI's to pull KP duty.

"Yes, BC. I catchee cat tonight."

"What'd you make the traps out of?"

"Wyah. Like these ah one. Put in weeds." Papasan held up a long strip of commo wire that was formed in a noose and pointed to an open area behind the mess section.

Courtney and Clay Holloway exchanged skeptical glances and shrugged. "Well, good luck, Papasan. I hope you get him," Holloway said as the two men began walking away.

Courtney tilted his head sideways and spoke when they had gone a few feet away. "Fat chance Papasan is gonna catch anything but a cold with that contraption." Holloway smiled.

Sergeant Lesley emerged from the FDC van and spying his battery commander walking by, intercepted him. "Sir, I've got another message for you. The 1/9th just got two UI's over near Freedom Bridge. They think there's another one some where around though and they want everybody to be on the lookout for him."

"Well, I'll be damned. Things have been kinda quiet lately too. Are the UI's dead?"

"Yessir, both of them. They didn't give me any more details though."

"OK, find the First Sergeant and send him up to the CP before he puts out the guard mount. I want everybody to know about this."

By 1900, the word had been passed. Men who would serve as guards in the five separate emplacements that surrounded the battery were sternly reminded of the importance of vigilance in a hostile fire zone. Not only could the guards' lives depend on their own alertness, but the lives of the entire unit as well. The incident with the UI's served as a stark reminder that just because nothing usually happened didn't mean that it couldn't happen. With the guards in place and the evening meal served and cleaned up, most of the unit retired to their squad tents or the sleeping hooch. The relatively warm temperatures which had been with them for the first week of the occupation, were being driven south by the winds from Siberia that whistled across the North Korean mountain ranges and on into the southern part of the peninsula. The little kerosene heaters in each of the sleeping quarters were operating at their maximum output. The heaters were fed by a hose attached to an inverted five-gallon can of kerosene that was on a wooden rack outside of each tent. Clusters of men habitually formed around the heaters for conversation, or reading, or cards.

In the CP, Clay Holloway had pulled a footlocker near to one of the two heaters that served the GP medium tent so that he could use it as a desk while he wrote a letter to his parents. When he finished the letter a half hour after beginning it, he addressed and sealed the envelope and dropped into a red nylon bag hanging from one of the tent poles. In the morning, the BC's driver would take it to the post office at Camp Wynne when he dropped Lieutenant Courtney at the brigade briefing. Two days earlier the brigade commander had sent word that he would like the battery commander of whatever unit was occupying 4 Papa 1 to attend the morning briefing on a regular basis. Courtney had found the briefings interesting and useful. It gave him a chance to talk with the artillery liaison officer, Dave Ruminski, and to feel like part of what was going on around the DMZ rather than the isolated and forgotten feeling he had already begun to develop at 4 Papa 1.

After dropping the letter into the mailbag and dragging his footlocker back to his cot, Holloway opened the big wooden box and rummaged around. Dinner had been finished only two hours earlier, but already he was feeling a bit hungry. He told himself that it must be working outside in the colder weather all day that was stimulating his appetite. Finally he found what he was looking for; a can of miniature wieners packed in juice. He pulled the tab on the top and the thin aluminum seal sprung open easily. He enjoyed eating the spicy little wieners, but he knew that if he had too many he'd probably wind up with indigestion. He looked over at Tom Courtney who was lying on his bunk and lazily dripping wax from a thick candle into an empty bottle.

"Tom, you want any of these little hot-dogs?"

"No thanks, Bagger. Those things bother my stomach."

"Mine too, but I still like eatin' them. How about you, Top? Sergeant Wilson, you want some?"

The first sergeant patted his stomach with a look of contentment. "No thanks, Sir. I had more than enough at dinner. Even had some of the chocolate cake for dessert."

Before Sergeant Wilson could reply to Holloway's question the still night air was once again pierced with an agonizing, shrieking, screaming, growl. Though the animal screams of three nights earlier had been mild compared to the latest banshee like cries.

"Rrrrrrooooowwwwlll!!!"

"Got damn, it's Eli again!" Courtney cried out as he leaped from his bed and grabbed for his web gear with the attached holster.

While Eli's growl had been relatively brief on the earlier night, this time it seemed almost eternal. As soon as one wild scream would end, another began. The noise rose and fell, building to a crescendo and falling away only to begin over again. And it was close. Very close.

Courtney looked around the tent. "Everybody ready? Let's go."

As the four men piled out of the tent, Courtney took the lead, a cocked .45 in his hand. The horrible noises were to the left, down the hill, in the vicinity of the mess tent. Across from the CP, the battery commander's driver and Clinton Gash had emerged from their tent and were joining their commander who was moving down the side of the elevated ground. Men were running from all directions in various states of dress and undress. One man wore only long underwear with a helmet. Like his BC, Holloway too had drawn his pistol and was moving cautiously, unsure of exactly what was happening. Flashlights came on; some with red filters some without. Whatever the animal was, it was in the weeds at the foot of the hill. The beam of a light reflected from its eyes as it whipped back and forth in the knee-high vegetation. Courtney and Holloway closed in, their pistols ready.

"Jesus Christ, what is it?" cried Holloway.

"Don't know! I don't know, but he's caught in Papasan's trap."

Suddenly the animal locked his eyes on Courtney, crouched, and then charged. Holloway and Courtney both fired at the same time flipping the animal up into the air. Incredibly, the beast landed on his feet and charged again as the two men continued to fire their weapons. As Courtney attempted to move closer, unexpectedly his feet slid out from under him on the steep slippery slope and he fell heavily on his backside. Again the animal charged, but stopped five feet short of the now prone battery commander. The animal clawed at the ground growling and trying to get to the man. He couldn't. The simple wire trap that the old Korean had put in the weeds held his hind leg securely. Holloway aimed again at the animal and pulled the trigger, but the pistol refused to fire. The slide was only part way forward. A feeding jam! Urgently, Courtney fought to regain his feet before the animal could break loose. Suddenly First Sergeant St. Clair stepped in front of him holding his M-14 rifle. He put the muzzle in the angry face of the animal and fired. There was the roar of the explosion and an echo rolling across the open field. Then there was only silence.

Holloway stepped closer to Courtney, extended his hand, and helped the man to his feet. St. Clair, meanwhile, was gazing down at the furry shape lying silent in the weeds. The two officers walked forward to join him. Courtney cleared his jammed weapon and holstered it.

"Nice job, Top! That son-of-a-bitch was one mean animal. I still don't..." There was no growl, no noise, no warning of any kind. There was only a blur of brown-gray fur and gnashing teeth as the thirty five pound female mate of the now dead wolverine slammed into Tom Courtney's chest driving him onto his back in the weeds.

"Shoot him! Shoot him!" Courtney screamed, throwing up an arm to protect his face from the flashing teeth as he flailed in the dirt. The first sergeant quickly began to circle, hesitant to shoot at the animal as it and the battery commander rolled about in the darkness, their bodies locked together in mortal combat. St. Clair and Holloway hovered above the two forms, waiting for an opening. Finally it came as Courtney rolled to his side taking the wolverine with him. The first sergeant seized the opportunity to bring the heavy butt of the M-14 crashing down into the animal. It grunted loudly. Simultaneously Holloway jerked free from its sheath the black handled combat knife that Keith Hackworth had presented to him a month earlier and drove it into the animals exposed flank. The beast screamed and flailed and scrambled to its feet, ripping the knife out of Holloway's hand and leaving it imbedded in its side. Gash stepped up and smashed him in the head with the blade of an entrenching tool just as it lunged again at Courtney. Terrified, Courtney pushed the stunned animal away, drew, and fired the .45 at point blank range. Three times in rapid succession the heavy slugs tore into the mass of fur and muscle. His pistol stopped firing and Courtney looked at the gun. The slide was locked back. It was empty. He looked at the second wolverine. It was dead.

Holloway knelt beside his battery commander and lowered him gently back down to the ground. His woolen field shirt was ripped in several places and blood was oozing through the heavy fabric. There were deep ugly gouges on his cheek and neck and hands. Holloway turned away from his friend.

"Where's Doc?" he called.

"I'm here, Sir," the young Hispanic medic nearby answered. He moved quickly to Holloway's side and knelt beside the prostrate battery commander. "Stay still, Lieutenant Courtney. Don't try to get up." Courtney closed his eyes and grimaced in pain as the medic opened his shirt and looked at the tee shirt. It was already soaked in blood. The medic grimaced too. "Oh, shit, Sir. We got to get you to a hospital. You're going to be OK. It's not too serious, but he ripped you up some with his claws. You need a doctor." The medic turned to the circle of men that had formed. "Somebody get the stretcher in my tent over there. We better carry him up to the CP." The BC's driver moved quickly toward the medic's tent.

Holloway searched the crowd looking for Sergeant Lesley. "Lep, call the TOC. Tell them we need a field ambulance. First Sergeant, you get everybody back to their posts or their tents. Just leave four guys to help carry the BC. We'll take him up to his bed and wait for the ambulance. Oh, and be sure to call the guard position out at the road and tell whoever is on duty to be on the lookout for the ambulance. The medical people probably don't even know where we're located so he may have to flag them down." Holloway stepped aside as the stretcher arrived and was laid next to the fallen officer.

"Gotdamn it, I ain't crippled. I can get on it," Courtney said angrily as some of the men tried to lift him onto the stretcher.

"That's not the point, Tom," said Holloway. "Don't move. It'll make you bleed more. Just lie back and be still."

Courtney sighed and reclined gingerly as willing hands grabbed his clothing and lifted him gently onto the heavy canvas. Struggling on the slippery incline, they carried him up the hill to the CP and laid the stretcher on his bed. Immediately behind him came Gomez, the medic, who had gotten his medical bag from his tent. He cut away the remnants of Courtney's shirt and began attending to the wounds, applying pressure to the deepest of them, which continued to pour blood. His chest and hands and arms were covered with cuts and scratches, but Holloway was relieved to see that none of them, while painful and bloody, seemed life threatening.

It was a full thirty minutes before the field phone chirped and the guard at the road informed Clinton Gash that the ambulance was on his way in. By that time, Gomez had bandaged all of the wounds and Courtney was resting quietly. A doctor had arrived with the ambulance. He checked Courtney thoroughly and spoke with him before directing that he be carried to the waiting ambulance. Before leaving, the doctor directed one of his medics to bring the carcass of the bloody dead animal with them. Before the animal was dropped into a cloth sack, however, Clay Holloway tugged his knife loose, wiped it on the fur, and replaced it into the inverted leather sheath that was taped to the shoulder straps of his web gear. After watching the medic throw the sack onto the floor of the front seat of the ambulance, the doctor climbed into the back with his patient. Before the door could be closed, Courtney motioned to his Executive Officer.

"Clay, you know you're the acting BC for a while. I'll be back soon. Take care of the men."

"We'll be fine, Tom. You just take care of yourself." Holloway smiled. Courtney gave a weak one-sided grin in return. Then he winked. The door closed and the field ambulance moved slowly out of the battery position and was lost in the black night.

CHAPTER 22

Second Lieutenant Kendall Stover was angry. He was scheduled for Staff Duty Officer duty all night, which was normally bad enough by itself, but on top of that Colonel Nordstrum had just informed him that he'd be going up to 4 Papa 1 to act as the Charlie Battery XO for a few days. That was OK. It would be fun seeing Holloway for a while. But as soon as he finished that assignment, he'd have to go directly back to 4 Papa 1 to be XO of his own battery for a week. That wasn't bad either. What pissed him off was that Bill Grant refused to let him out of being Staff Duty Officer on his last evening on compound for quite a while. He'd much rather be over at the O Club having a Scotch instead of sitting in the Battalion Headquarters filling out the SDO log and staring at the ceiling. He looked at his watch. Almost 2000. Three more hours until he should make his last check of the perimeter fence before trying to get some sleep on the cot in the Colonel's office. Stover withdrew a Marlboro from his silver cigarette case, lit it, and blew smoke at the ceiling. Then he picked up a ballpoint pen and began to write Mary Lou a letter.

A hundred yards away from where Kendall Stover sat, was the edge of the ammunition dump which consisted of four separate ammo bunkers surrounded by rolls of concertina barbed wire and two armed and roving American guards. While the compound itself was patrolled by Korean civilian guards with shotguns, the Army considered the ammo dump to be important enough to be guarded by Americans twenty-four hours a day. Most of the guards came from the Redeye Platoon. The ammo dump contained all of the artillery ammunition for the battalion, most of the small arms ammunition, and thirty shoulder fired, heat seeking, Redeye anti-aircraft missiles. Of all the ordinance in the Army's conventional weapons inventory, the Redeye missile was one of the most sensitive. As far as the United States was aware, the Redeye was the only operational missile of its type in the world. Neither the Russians, nor the French, nor even the English had one yet. The beauty of the weapon was that it weighed less than thirty pounds and could be carried by foot almost anywhere. It was simple to operate. All the gunner had to do was insert the battery, turn it on, lock on to the heat source of any aircraft within range and pull the trigger. The missile would do the rest. Naturally the United States Army was very concerned about the possibility of one or more of the Redeyes falling into the wrong hands. If the North Vietnamese were able to acquire those missiles or copies of them, they could devastate the American helicopter fleets that were sent against them on a daily basis. Such a weapon would change the complexion of the entire war being waged in Southeast Asia. For that reason, none of the missiles were even allowed inside of South Vietnam.

On this particular night, a substitute guard had been added to the guard mount. PFC Raoul Biladeau, seventeen years old and baby faced, from Baton Rouge, Louisiana, was a member of the Communications Section in Charlie Battery. However, much to his chagrin, he had not accompanied his unit to the field at 4 Papa 1. Following some nasty publicity, which occurred when some seventeen-year-old soldiers were killed in the Republic of Vietnam, the United States military, had altered its policy to exclude seventeen year olds from serving in a hostile fire zone. Along with Vietnam, the Korean DMZ was classified as such an area. So when Charlie Battery went north of the river, PFC Biladeau was forced to remain behind. This particularly embarrassed the young man because his brother was currently engaged in combat operations in the Republic of Vietnam. Since PFC Biladeau had no real duties to perform while his unit was absent, he was assigned temporarily to the Redeye Section so that he could share in the guard duties of the ammunition dump. At 2000 hours he was one hour into his shift along with the other guard, Private Thomas Killsoldier, a full-blooded Apache Indian.

Killsoldier was already legendary within the Battalion. Two months earlier he had walked up behind a Korean girl standing outside of the Camp Wynne EM Club, reached up under her miniskirt and ripped her panties off with a single jerk of the hand. For some reason the girl became rather upset with this rude greeting and after giving him a tongue lashing, reported him to his battery CQ (Charge of Quarters), who reported him to Battalion. But when the SDO (Staff Duty Officer) came to investigate him, the man had disappeared. Two hours later the CQ walked into the Headquarters Battery day room and found Killsoldier having sex with another Korean girl on the pool table. Angry at having been disturbed, Killsoldier climbed down from the pool table and punched the CQ in the nose, breaking it in two places. Again, Killsoldier disappeared. An hour later, the SDO received a call from a Captain Smith who was at RC #4 and wanted the Staff Duty driver to drive his truck down and pick him up. Obligingly, the SDO dispatched the truck. Unbeknownst to him, however, was the fact that Killsoldier had actually made the telephone call and was hiding in the back of the truck so that he could escape from the compound. The ruse worked, but unfortunately for Killsoldier, he was seen when he leaped out of the back of the truck once it passed through the gate. Realizing that the big Indian was now outside the compound the internal search for him was called off. It was with great surprise, therefore, that when the new CQ walked into the enlisted men's sleeping hooch the next morning to wake up the troops, he found Private Killsoldier asleep in his bunk, along with another naked girl. This time he surrendered quietly, being apparently too exhausted to resist. For these offenses, he was reduced one grade in rank, fined one hundred dollars, and served one month in the guardhouse. Once he was released, he rejoined his battery and was assigned his regular duties, which included walking guard at the Camp Wynne ammunition dump.

Constantly walking the same guard route over and over and over gives a soldier plenty of time to allow his mind to wander. None of the Army psychiatrists would ever be able to fully understand what happened that night, or why it happened, but for no apparent reason, PFC Biladeau suddenly had a vision. In his vision, his brother Tyrone, serving with the Ninth Infantry Division in Vietnam was brutally killed. Not killed by the North Vietnamese Army, nor even the Viet Cong, but by an American Indian in full battle regalia. To PFC Biladeau the vision was real, very real. How could he let such a thing go unpunished? The aggressor must be adjudged. With this in mind, PFC Biladeau raised his M-14 rifle and began blazing away at Private Killsoldier who was unsuspectingly patrolling his area on the other side of the ammo dump. Fortunately, Biladeau was not a very good shot and in his anger did not hit the dumbfounded Killsoldier who immediately took cover. The Apache had not the foggiest idea of why the moron on the other side of the dump was shooting at him, but being the proud individual that he was and having long ago made the decision never to take anything from anybody, Killsoldier began firing back at Biladeau. A running gun battle ensued, with both soldiers maneuvering around the ammo dump in a live fire exercise reminiscent of the cowboys and Indians games of their youth.

The sound of gunfire instantly reached the ears of the SDO, Lieutenant Stover, who dropped his pen, strapped on his web belt with his .45 and ran outside. The shots were obviously inside of the Camp Wynne compound and not far away.

"Call Second MP. Tell them we've got shots fired inside the compound. Tell them to get somebody here ASAP," Stover called to the Staff Duty NCO who was still inside of the HQ. Then he turned and ran as fast as he could toward the sound of the firing.

Major Rocky Gentile was heading toward the O Club when he heard the shooting. Immediately he turned and ran back into the BOQ and grabbed his telephone to call the MP's. The line was busy. He decided he would wait a minute and try again. He had no way of knowing that the reason the line was busy was that the Staff Duty NCO was already talking to them.

Thomas Killsoldier had finally decided to break off the engagement. PFC Biladeau, however, had continued to fire at anything that moved. He remained in the lighted area of the ammo dump swiveling his head and searching for additional targets. Eventually he found one. Kendall Stover was still running full speed toward the sound of the shooting when PFC Biladeau first saw him. Having totally lost touch with reality by this time, Biladeau aimed and fired, the bullet striking Stover's black leather holster and spinning the young lieutenant completely around in a circle and knocking him down.

Terrified he checked himself. He didn't appear to be wounded. Stover regained his feet and immediately PFC Biladeau fired again. This time Stover took a headlong dive into the drainage ditch that lined one side of the street. Bullets continued to ricochet off of the blacktopped street and the nearby buildings. There was no way Kendall Stover was going to try to get out of that ditch. He was pinned down.

Major Gentile had finally gotten through to Second MP, only to be informed they were already on their way. Moments later he too neared the ammo dump. PFC Biladeau had identified a second target and, like the first took him under fire. Finding a convenient drainage ditch, Gentile leaped in, landing with both feet in the middle of Kendall Stover's back.

"Ooofff! Who the fuck is that?" Stover demanded angrily.

"Major Gentile. Who the fuck are you?" Gentile retorted in the darkness.

"Sorry, Sir. It's Lieutenant Stover. I'm Staff Duty Officer."

"Well, you picked a great night for it. Who the hell is doing all the shooting?"

"You got me, but whoever it is, he's in the ammo dump."

"Where are the guards?"

"I haven't seen them. Maybe they're oopso."

The sound of many running feet came from behind the two men. Six helmeted MP's carrying M-16s were running down the street. Much to their tactical discredit, they were bunched together in a column. A bullet whined off of the street in front of the sergeant leading the group. He headed for the drainage ditch too, with his five men right behind him. Now Biladeau had eight men pinned down in the ditch, with no reinforcements in sight.

"What in the hell is going on here?" asked the burly MP sergeant.

"We're not sure," Major Gentile replied dryly.

"Maybe we can work our way up this ditch and flank them," offered one of the MP's.

Suddenly a large dark shape landed next to Major Gentile. The man's eyes were wide beside his high cheekbones. "It's Biladeau. The muther fucker's gone dingy dingy. He tried to kill me!"

"Killsoldier!" said Major Gentile, recognizing the man. "Were you on guard tonight?"

"Yes, Sir. All of a sudden Biladeau just started shooting at me."

"That's Biladeau over there?"

"Yes, Sir. He's nuts."

All the while they talked, random bullets continued to fly around the compound. Most off duty soldiers had taken cover in ditches or behind buildings or vehicles throughout the base. The Korean civilian guard who normally stood in the high tower had bailed out immediately once the firing began, not bothering to use the ladder, but leaping the fifteen feet to the soft ground.

"I think we've got to shoot him, Major," the MP said.

"Negative. He's only seventeen years old for Christ's sake."

"Sir, he's going to kill someone. He may already have killed some one."

"He tried to kill me," said Stover, showing everyone the hole in the front of his holster.

"Me too," added Killsoldier.

"I said no," exclaimed Major Gentile. "There's got to be another way." No one else spoke. "Wait a minute. Let's turn out the lights in the ammo dump. The electric panel is in that building over there. Then we can move in on him once it's dark."

"I don't know," said the MP sergeant. "I think we ought to shoot him. Maybe just in the leg."

"Goddamnit, we're not going to shoot him if we don't have to. Sergeant, send one of your men over there and pull the main switch on the box. That will knock out the lights in the dump."

"Smitty. You heard the Major. Do it."

Smitty didn't speak. He tensed his muscles for a moment and then flew out of the ditch, across the road, and into the doorway of the small corrugated metal building on the other side. Within a few seconds the lights in the dump were extinguished.

"Come on," said Gentile. "Let's move in."

Crouching, the men tactically dispersed themselves and advanced toward the security area a hundred meters away. Quietly they entered the dump where Biladeau had been. He was nowhere in sight. PFC Biladeau had turned the tables on them. Now he was now loose somewhere on the compound. Confused, Major Gentile looked around the area, wondering where to go next. Two shots in quick succession ended the dilemma. The explosions had come from the area of the Charlie Battery Motor Pool. Quickly the mob of pursuers hurried in that direction.

"There he is!" called the MP Sergeant.

PFC Biladeau was standing wide eyed against the big overhead door of the truck garage entrance only fifty yards away, acting like a trapped animal. Over his head shone a security light, illuminating him in the darkness. The posse closed the distance to within forty yards and leaped into a second drainage ditch nearby as Biladeau fired two more rounds from the hip.

"Listen," Kendall Stover whispered to Major Gentile. "It looks like he's on another shooting spree. Let's wait until he's empty and then rush him before he can reload."

A bullet whined off of the sidewalk nearby. "OK, that's what we'll do. If we can't get to him we'll have to shoot him," answered Gentile. "Sergeant, designate two men as shooters. Stover, you and the rest of these MP's rush him as soon as he goes dry." Stover nodded determinedly.

"Blam! Blam! Blam!"

A long pause.

"Blam, click!"

*   *   *

Lieutenant Yoon Kim Lee was even more confused than the people inside of Camp Wynne. An hour earlier he had moved into his position in the darkness and through his binoculars had begun making a standard surveillance of the compound. Thus far he had identified the battalion headquarters, as well as the headquarters of A Battery and C Battery, although C Battery was obviously not currently there as evidenced by the empty motor pool and the lack of Howitzers in the sandbagged gun pits. He had also established where the ammunition dump was located. That was extremely simple since it was the only large area on the compound that was lighted by overhead floodlights and patrolled by two armed guards. But suddenly, and for no apparent reason the two guards had begun firing their rifles at each other. Many other soldiers had arrived and before long the lights at the ammunition dump had been extinguished. Amazed, Yoon had continued to watch as all of the action shifted to the far side of the compound. The ammunition dump was left abandoned. Even the guard in the tower had left his post. THE AMMUNITION DUMP!!! That was where the Redeye Missiles were kept! This was it! This was the opportunity he wanted so desperately and it had fallen right into his lap.

The North Korean officer understood completely the significance of the Redeye Missile. During his orientation with the PAVN (People's Army of Vietnam) he himself had come under a murderous assault by the American helicopters. If the Communist world could capture one of these weapons and decipher its technology it could help lead to the defeat of the Americans in Vietnam. With Redeyes hidden in the jungle, their heat seeking missiles would wreak havoc with the American helicopters, which would drop from the skies like autumn leaves falling from a tree. Capturing a Redeye from the Americans and getting it back home would be one of the coups of the century. Nothing within his power could damage the Americans more. He had to get one. And it had to be now.

Taking a last look and seeing no one, Yoon sprinted for the chain-linked fence that surrounded the compound. He had selected a place where a metal shed sat on the other side. The shed would block the view of anyone who might wander by in the next few seconds. Scaling the fence with ease, he paused at the top to make six quick snips of the barbed wire with his wire cutters. Then he dropped noiselessly to the ground between the fence and the shed. A quick sprint to his right took him through the opening in the rolled concertina wire that lead to the entrance to the first ammo bunker. He reached the doorway and withdrew his flashlight. Six steps lead to a palletized floor where dozens of wooden ammunition boxes lay. He scanned the letters and numbers on the boxes. Small arms ammunition. He scurried to the next bunker. Howitzer projectiles and fuses. It was the third bunker where Yoon found what he was looking for. Sixty metal containers looking like coffins were stacked neatly against the walls. The containers were painted olive drab and stenciled with yellow letters. Yoon was by no means fluent in the English language. Nevertheless, he did understand the word "Missile" that was part of the letters. He flipped open the two latches and raised the lid. Breathlessly he peered inside. Yes! The box held a fully contained missile launcher. He lifted it out of the container. It was amazingly light. Probably no more than twelve or thirteen kilograms. Smaller metal boxes were also in the room. He laid the Redeye on the floor and opened one of the smaller ones and found four cylindrical batteries. Of course! The batteries must power the missile launcher. He would take a couple of those too. Hastily he closed the open boxes and then spent a minute reshuffling some of the containers so that the now empty ones would not be on top. Maybe the missile would not even be missed for some time. Then he pulled the climbing rope from his pack and sliced off a two-meter section. Quickly tying two slip knots her fashioned a sling for the missile launcher and slipped it over his head and shoulder so that it hung from his back. He jammed two of the batteries into his pack and headed back up the stairs. Time was of the essence. He did not know what had happened to the crazy guard with the rifle. But he did know that he hadn't heard any more shooting for the last couple of minutes.

*   *   *

Biladeau looked down at the rifle, which had just failed to fire, momentarily not comprehending what had gone wrong. "That's it. Let's go," yelled Stover, leaping from the ditch and sprinting directly toward the young man who had begun fumbling with his rifle. Biladeau heard the running footsteps across the blacktop of the motor pool and released the empty magazine, which clattered to the ground. He looked up briefly. Stover was twenty yards away as Biladeau pulled a loaded twenty round magazine from the pouch and jammed it into the bottom of the rifle. Stover was ten yards away and charging full speed as Biladeau pulled back the bolt and released it, driving a 7.62 mm full metal jacket round into the chamber. The rifle started up. Stover slammed into him at full tilt, driving him backwards into the doorway and knocking the wind out of him. The MP's were right behind, piling on Biladeau and wrenching the rifle out of his hand. The young man gasped for breath as the MP's rolled him onto his stomach and handcuffed him behind his back. They searched him then. He had no other weapons or ammunition. Eighty rounds had been expended, with only the one full magazine remaining. Rough hands jerked him to his feet. Stover looked at Biladeau's face. His eyes were enormous, making him look like a frightened young rabbit.

Major Gentile and the other MP's walked up. "Nice going all of you," he declared patting Stover on the back. "Biladeau, just exactly what do you think you're doing?"

"They're here, Major. They're all over here. Didn't you see them?"

"Who's here?"

"Indians, for Christ's sake. There's Indians all over the place. Look! Look, at him," Biladeau screamed, pointing at Killsoldier.

"It's OK, Biladeau. He's on our side," said Gentile.

"Yeah, he's a scout for General Custer," remarked Stover, earning a glare from Major Gentile.

"We'll talk about it later, son," said the Major calmly. "You shouldn't have fired your rifle inside of the compound like that. You might have killed someone. You're going to have to go with these MP's now. We'll come and see you tomorrow."

"I had to fire, Major. There's Indians all over, don't ya understand?"

"I understand, Biladeau. We'll talk about it later." Turning to the MP Sergeant, Major Gentile nodded his head. "Take him for the night. We'll call DivArty and get some medical people involved. I think it's pretty obvious he needs help."

Colonel Nordstrum approached, as Biladeau was being lead away. Gentile explained in detail what had just transpired. The Colonel told Kendall Stover to get in touch with each of the batteries to have them check their areas thoroughly to insure that no one had been hit in the barrage of bullets. In the morning they would need to check for physical damage. Eighty rounds had to have landed somewhere. It was not until 0200 that Kendall Stover finally shut his eyes on the cot in the colonel's office. He needed to be back up at six and would be more than happy to turn over control of the battalion headquarters to Bill Grant at 0730. Then he would pack his field gear and drive north of the river to 4 Papa 1 to join Charlie Battery as their acting executive officer for the few days they had left in the wilderness.

*   *   *

Yoon Kim Lee needed only a moment to again scale the chain-linked fence. The dangling barbed wire at the top was a sure sign that someone had been inside, but there was nothing he could do about that now. The Americans would have no way of knowing who it had been. With any luck at all it might be days before the Redeye was even discovered as missing. Landing on the dirt outside the compound he removed the Redeye from his back and cradling it in his arms, began running in the darkness along the dry rice paddy dikes towards the grove of trees three hundred meters away.

CHAPTER 23

"Hey, Bagger. What's shakin'?, over."

"Ain't nothin' shakin' but the leaves in the trees and they ain't shakin' til they feel the breeze," Clay Holloway replied as he turned and grinned at his mustachioed friend with the round wire rimmed glasses, standing in the entrance of the CP tent. "I understand you're gonna be working for me for a few days."

"In case you haven't heard about it, I started working for you last night. One of your young troops started shooting up the compound and we had him clapped in irons and hauled away to the pokey."

Holloway frowned. "What the hell are you talking about, Baron?"

Kendall Stover relayed in detail the excitement of the previous evening at Camp Wynne, ending with PFC Biladeau being taken to the guardhouse at Second MP. Holloway shook his head sadly. "I just honestly can't believe this place sometimes. As if we don't have enough problems already, we find a way of going out and creating more. What the hell kind of lunatics do we have in this man's army?"

"Yeah. Every day is a new adventure, isn't it? So now you give me the scoop. What is all this shit about a wolverine and Courtney getting clawed and bitten up. Is this for real?"

Holloway told of the encounters with the pair of wolverines. Stover listened in silence until Holloway had finished. "So Tom's going to be all right?"

"Yeah, that's the way it looks. You should have seen that thing, Baron. I can't describe how mean it was. And the noise. Between the wolverine growling and snarling and Tom yelling and swearing and the fur flying, it was one hell of a scene. This thing took a rifle butt, a knife to the side, a crack with an entrenching tool and three .45 rounds before it gave up the ghost. It was like something out of a horror movie."

"So you think there's any more of them around here?"

"Wolverines?"

"Sure."

"I hope not. There's a hell of a lot of other game around here though. Gash and Shorty shot a deer this afternoon. Says they're going to try and get a couple more and have deerskin seat covers made for the BC's jeep as a surprise for Tom. Fresh venison will taste good too. You know, I was thinking. We could borrow Ruminski's shotgun and probably get a few pheasants. You can't drive down the road without flushing three or four of them. Then we could have the Mess Sergeant do it all up at one time and have like a wild game banquet one night."

"There you go. I can see I'm going to like this place."

"Well, hey, let's take you around and make sure all the gun chiefs know that you're the acting XO and all. I think Sergeant Wilson has told them, but I want to introduce you personally."

Three days and nights passed quickly and uneventfully as the battery worked to improve the position. Their overall mission was to be there and be ready if their guns were needed, though the troops hoped that time would never come. The evening hours were spent in ways similar to those spent by millions of troops throughout the twentieth century and in centuries before. Talking, playing cards by candlelight or lantern, though the larger tents had a few electric light sockets powered by the big field generator, writing letters to home, reading, or listening softly to music. Many of the KATUSA's socialized by themselves at night, enjoying playing a board game that some of them carried with them to the field, and which was understood by none of the GI's.

On the fourth night after Stover's arrival, the night stillness was shattered by a long machine gun burst nearby. It was close. Probably position #4 which was situated on a ledge in the trees halfway down a slope near the CP. The ledge commanded a good field of fire of the open meadow below. Holloway, St. Clair, and Stover ran to the rim of the hill and looked down into the darkness.

"Who's down there tonight, Top?"

"Should be Nichols and Reid."

"Nichols? Oh, no," Holloway muttered shaking his head. Nichols was a draftee who had been recently transferred over from Headquarters Battery. He didn't seem to have both oars in the water. A full football scholarship to the University of Texas had been lost when he was thrown out of school his freshman year for standing on the top bunk in the dormitory and urinating on the three people below. Nobody ever knew what he was going to do next.

"Nichols! Reid!" Holloway called in a loud whisper. No answer. "Stay here, Top. I'm going down."

Holloway slid over the crest of the hill and began crawling and sliding down the steep embankment toward the machine gun fifty yards away. Halfway down, the M-60 opened fire again, the long tongue of flame reaching away from Holloway toward the open meadow. Now Holloway and everyone else within view of the hill knew exactly where the gun was. He remained motionless for several seconds, waiting to see if there was any return fire. There wasn't, so he continued his downward crawl over the damp leaves that covered the hillside. Realizing that he was very close to the gun he called ahead.

"Nichols! Nichols! Don't shoot. It's Holloway."

"There's something out there. Down in the meadow. Something moved."

"Just hold your fire for a minute. Every time you shoot people can see exactly where you are." Holloway dropped into the little sandbagged position. "Where's Reid?"

"He left to go take a dump about a half hour ago and didn't come back. Sir, I know there's something out there in the meadow."

Holloway stared into the blackness for a long time. "Well, if there was he's gone now. It might have been a deer. How close was he?"

"Maybe a hundred yards. Right down there," Nichols said excitedly as he pointed to an area below.

"OK. Listen, we gotta move this gun so if there was somebody there he doesn't know where you are. Let's move it up the hill and over that way about thirty meters. There's a big tree you can use for cover."

Nichols finally picked up the heavy M-60 and carried to the position Holloway had indicated. Holloway followed with the extra ammunition and the wires and triggers for the Claymores located near the bottom of the hill. They were soon joined by another figure sliding down the slope.

"Reid, where the hell have you been?" Holloway demanded.

"I had to use the latrine, Sir."

"Listen, you don't ever leave your guard post for something like that. This is a hostile fire zone, for Christ's sake. You go over in the bushes if you have to. That's bullshit. You report to me first thing in the morning at the CP." Holloway turned away and picked his way through the trees to the crest of the hill.

"Bagger, what happened?" Stover asked.

"I think he's just jumpy. All this stuff about UI's has made a lot of these guys nervous. They're not infantry and they still haven't gotten used to being up here around the Z. You know how your eyes start playing tricks on you after dark. He thinks he saw something."

"What are you going to do to Reid, Sir," asked First Sergeant St. Clair. "You can't let him off. These guys got to learn to stop jacking around on guard."

"I told him I wanted to see him first thing in the morning. I'll read him the riot act then. We go back to Wynne in two more days. Lieutenant Courtney will have to decide if he gets and Article XV. After I talk to Reid, Top, I want to address the morning formation. We have got to get their shit straight."

"You got it, Sir."

*   *   *

"At ease!"

The one hundred and two members of Charlie Battery moved their right legs slightly to the right and folded their hands behind their backs. Acting BC Second Lieutenant Clay Holloway stood facing them.

"It has become apparent to me that there are some members of this unit who do not fully grasp the concept of guard duty, so I'm going to review some of the essentials for you. I'm not talking about guard duty in basic training around some empty warehouse. I'm talking about pulling guard at night in a hostile fire zone with a hundred men's lives at stake as well as your own. I have seen some of you people fall asleep at St. Barbara. I've seen some of you fall asleep on SCOSI. This cannot and will not continue. People on guard will be alert and awake at all times. If you are in a one-man position, you had damn well better be awake and alert. If you are in a two-man position, at least one of you, if not both, had better be awake. You will not leave your guard post for any reason. Any reason whatsoever. You will not smoke on guard duty. A man can see the glow and even smell a cigarette at a hundred yards. You will not talk unless in a low whisper. You will not fire your weapon on guard duty unless you have a clear target. You do not fire at noises or shadows. I say again. You do *not* fire at noises or shadows. If there is actually something hostile out there you are one hell of a lot better off if you wait until they're close and you can see what you're shooting at. But if you do shoot, you had better be sure something is there. Don't let your mind play tricks on you.

Now I do not intend to stand up here like this again. The next guy that violates what I have just told you is going to spend time in the stockade. We are not going to lose a man up here because someone thought it was naptime. You people are going to be checked repeatedly at night. And when someone comes out you better know the password, you better not be smoking, and you better be alert. Any questions?" There were none. "OK. Battery, 'tench hut! Dismissed!"

Holloway strode away from the formation and walked up the gentle hill to the CP. First Sergeant St. Clair and Lieutenant Stover caught up with him.

"Damn, Sir. You read them the riot act!"

"Top, this is serious. We have two more nights here. I want Lieutenant Stover, you, me, Sergeant Wilson, and whatever NCO has the guard mount at night to check these people every hour or so. I want them to positively know that someone is coming around and they better have their shit straight. You just never know what's going to happen up here."

*   *   *

Lieutenant Yoon Kim Lee had spent the better part of two nights looking for a boat. Lugging the Redeye through the darkness from Camp Wynne to the banks of the Imjin River had been relatively easy. Twice he had had to circumvent Korean Home Guard night ambush sites, but that had not been very difficult. He was astounded by the lack of noise discipline from the Home Guard units. They actually sat in the darkness carrying on a conversation as though no one would be able to hear them. But now Yoon was stymied. He hadn't found a boat anywhere and he couldn't wait much longer. It had been days since he'd had enough food, the weather was turning colder, and he wasn't accomplishing anything. Without the Redeye he could have swum the river easily. But it was inconceivable that he could do it without soaking the missile, which could easily ruin it. He couldn't take that chance. He had to get it to North Korea in perfect condition if at all possible. So with no boat and swimming eliminated that only left one alternative. He would have to cross one of the two bridges, Freedom or the pontoon bridge called Spoonbill. Both bridges had guard shacks at either end, although only two guards at each shack. It would not be difficult to eliminate the guards at the south end. But then how would he cross the long bridge without the guards at the north end being suspicious of a single man walking across the bridge and carrying a missile launcher? No. There was only way to do it. It was dangerous, but also the most logical.

It was early afternoon when Yoon selected his site only a mile south of Freedom Bridge. A sharp curve between two low hills was the perfect place. Once in position, Yoon waited more than two hours before he saw a small convoy of three vehicles approaching from the south. The first vehicle was a jeep with a driver and two men. The second was 1 ¼ ton truck with a canvas covered back and the third was a 2 ½ ton, also with the back covered by canvas. It looked exactly the one he and his men had ambushed in the DMZ almost three months earlier. Clearly, he had no idea what was in the back of the truck. If it were filled with soldiers he would be in deep trouble. But the driver appeared alone in the front seat. Certainly, if there were other men with him it would be likely that one of them would be riding in the front also. It had to be more comfortable than the wooden benches in the truck bed.

Yoon waited behind a large rock on the backside of the curve. His heart was pounding as the jeep passed him. Fifteen seconds later came the second vehicle, bouncing slowly and noisily around the curve, dust trailing behind it. He tensed his muscles. Noise from the big diesel preceded the truck. This was it. The dark green shape rolled by. Yoon hoisted the Redeye onto his back, glided swiftly to the side of the rock and sprinted down the little hill and onto the dirt road behind the truck. Glancing into the rear of the bed he saw no one. Running at full speed he reached the rear of the truck and leaped as his hands found the top of the tailgate. A moment later he was inside. Perfect! The truck was filled with supplies. Four or five folding cots. Several footlockers. And twenty or so large cardboard cartons. Concealing the Redeye in the canvas fold of one of the cots, he next slid two of the footlockers away from the side to make room for him to hide behind. Unless someone physically climbed into the back of the truck Yoon could not be seen. If anyone did climb into the back of the truck it would be the last thing the man would ever do. Yoon checked the Makarov and waited.

Five minutes later Yoon felt the truck slowing and finally reach a complete halt. He could hear nothing, but assumed the men in the jeep were speaking with one of the guards at the entrance to Freedom Bridge. After a moment, the truck began moving again. No one had even looked into the back. He could feel the vibration and hear the rattling of the wooden planking under the truck. Cautiously he peered over the footlocker and out the back of the truck. There were steel girders on either side. Yes! He was on the bridge. In only another minute the rattling stopped and the truck was again on the dirt road as evidenced by the dust trails Yoon could see billowing from behind. He knew exactly where he was. He still had both his maps and his compass. But there was one thing he could not possibly know. The truck's destination. If he waited very long he might find himself in the middle of one of the compounds like the one the American's called Camp Greaves. It wasn't very far from the bridge. Again he raised his head above the footlocker. He saw nothing. No soldiers, no vehicles, and no buildings. This was as good a time as any. He arose quickly, retrieved the Redeye, and moved swiftly to the tailgate. Again he peered out. Again nothing. Yoon swallowed hard and jumped, cradling the Redeye in his arms.

His landing was less than perfect, but neither he nor the missile was damaged. Moving quickly he scurried into a drainage ditch at the roadside and looked about. Fields to the north and a hill behind him. There was no cover at all in the fields. Certainly he couldn't stay near the road. Another vehicle could come any second. He climbed the hill behind him. The other side dropped into a gully with another hill beyond that. There were brown reeds and leaves in the gully. The depression seemed to be one of those places where the wind naturally seems to deposit leaves, at least enough of them to hide a man and a missile. Lieutenant Yoon Kim Lee burrowed in and piled more of them over himself and his package. Then he went to sleep.

*   *   *

Clay Holloway couldn't sleep. He looked at the luminous dial of the Seiko and grunted softly; 0130. His mind was whirring at about 10,000 revolutions per minute, thinking of all the things that Tom Courtney would be planning on doing for the departure of the battery the next day. But, of course, Tom wasn't there. It was a big help having Baron with him, but Holloway was afraid of forgetting something important that needed to be done. And he still hadn't been able to stop thinking about the fight with the wolverine. Everyone who witnessed the fight had been left in awe of the incredible toughness of the legendary wolverine, as well as the courage of their commander. But damn it, he wanted to sleep. In four hours he'd have to be up and getting ready for the morning briefing at Brigade. Then get back to the battery and prepare to unass the area. Maybe some fresh air would do him some good. He unzipped the heavy down sleeping bag and pulled his feet free. It was cold in the tent even with the kerosene heaters. Hurriedly he laced his boots. Everyone else was asleep. Holloway stood quietly and put on his field jacket. He buckled on his web gear and after placing his helmet on his head, stepped outside of the tent. The moon and the stars shone clearly above him, bathing the battery position in an eerie nightglow. He admired the six howitzers sitting docilely under their camouflage nets in the open area below the CP. Nearby there was a cardboard piss tube buried in the ground. He moved toward it, unbuttoned his fly, and relieved himself in silence. That sensation awakened him further. It occurred to him that perhaps the guards might appreciate someone coming around to see how they were doing. More importantly, he'd knew that around two or three in the morning, even the most well intentioned guards can get drowsy. It wouldn't hurt to check on them. He decided to head for the number two position first. It was the farthest away from where he was standing, but still only a three-minute walk. Mentally he reminded himself of the password so that he could reply as soon as he was challenged. Holloway walked quietly down the trail, which had already been worn through the scattered trees.

Yoon Kim Lee was furious. The gods were definitely not smiling upon him tonight. Under cover of darkness, he had been able to move from his position in the gully to close to his tunnel's entrance without being detected. He still had the Redeye and gleefully anticipated the adulation that would be heaped upon him when he returned home with this ultimate prize. If his countrymen could copy this missile it would mean so very much to not only his own country, but to the North Vietnamese foot soldiers who needed tactical antiaircraft defenses desperately. But now he had a significant problem. After entering Camp Wynne, stealing the missile, getting it across the Imjin, and reaching the area of the tunnel entrance now this. How could this be?? An American artillery battery was sitting within fifty meters of the carefully concealed tunnel entrance and one of their outposts was no more than forty feet away.

Well, maybe that wasn't all bad. The Americans had killed his men. Should he just ignore that? No, he would not ignore that. Tonight he would take his measure of revenge. He was fully justified in killing the guard. Although his orders had been to avoid contact, that clearly no longer applied when two of his men were dead and the only way he was going to be able to get into the tunnel and the only way he was going to get the Redeye to Pyongyang was by killing whatever Americans were occupying that outpost. But the Makarov was out of the question. He would have to use the knife. Yoon laid the Redeye on the ground and moved to a position behind the sandbagged bunker.

Ahead of him, Holloway could see the sandbagged rim of the shallow foxhole. There was a figure sitting on the bags, the glow of a cigarette noticeable in his left hand. That was so careless. He'd just warned them two days ago about smoking on guard. That was it! Whoever the guard was, he was going to lose one of his stripes for this bullshit! Holloway wondered how close he was going to get before the man heard him and turned to challenge. Then from the trees to the right there was movement. A shadow appeared in front of Holloway, moving stealthily toward the guard, his hand clenched around something. Who was that? He wasn't wearing a helmet or even an army winter cap. A chill rippled down Holloway's back. There was a sense of evil to the figure. Something was wrong! This was danger! The figure was already within five feet of the guard. Instinct prevailed. Holloway ripped off his helmet and flung it directly at the back of the figure twenty feet away as he shouted a warning.

"Look out behind you!"

The heavy steel helmet hit the man hard in the left shoulder, knocking him off balance at the same moment that the surprised guard turned. Quickly Yoon Kim Lee regained his balance and pivoting quickly with his left foot executed a perfect spinning back kick. The Tae Kwon Do movement caught PFC Willow fully on the side of the face, dropping him like a wet rag. Holloway ran quickly forward, grabbing for his .45 with his right hand and reaching with his left hand to pull back the slide that would chamber a round. But he closed on the man too quickly. The catlike figure danced forward and launched himself through the air, his feet searching another target. Holloway turned sideways, his right arm going instinctively in front of his face. The flying foot smacked the forearm sharply, numbing it and knocking the .45 from his grasp. It thudded solidly on the ground somewhere behind him. Quickly, Holloway pin wheeled left as the man landed on his feet and again turned to face him. Moonlight reflected from the blade of the knife that the figure held in his hand as he crouched. So that was the way it was! Deliberately, Holloway pulled his black handled knife from its leather sheath and imitated the UI's crouch. Both men circled silently, the dark figure edging closer. Holloway dodged behind a tree, but the figure slashed around it forcing him back away from the trunk. Holloway could clearly see that the man was Asian and dressed in some sort of black suit. The UI that had gotten away from Hackworth near Freedom Bridge! It had to be!

Holloway was using the trees like a running back uses blockers. The UI tried to close, but when he moved Holloway moved, realizing that an artillery officer trained in firing Howitzers was not an even match for a commando in a knife fight. Finally the man sprang at him with a grunt, the knife held high. Holloway slashed, pirouetted to his right, and slashed again. This time he felt his blade make contact with the man's arm, but the UI hadn't seemed to slow. Holloway needed help and he knew it.

"Somebody help now! We need help out here! UI! UI!" he called at the top of his voice.

The shouting seemed to change the rules. The UI stiffened. He recognized that he had to end it quickly now before other soldiers arrived. No more knife. He reached for the Makarov in its holster at his hip, but then suddenly he froze in mid motion. There was movement behind Holloway. It was the guard. The soldier was standing, an M-14 at his shoulder. Where's the Redeye? No time now. More voices. Men were coming. No time. Lieutenant Yoon Kim Lee ducked and ran as PFC Harold Willow pointed his rifle into the darkness and fired in the direction of the shadowy zigzagging figure that headed directly for the bushes that concealed the entrance of his tunnel to home.

Kelly Steele, First Sergeant St. Clair, and Kendall Stover were the first ones to reach Holloway and Willow.

"What the hell is going on, Sir?" cried St. Clair breathlessly.

"UI, Top! He went that way."

Sergeant Steele ran ahead toward the direction that Holloway had pointed. "I can't see anything, Sir."

All five men moved forward carefully, weapons ready. "He went into those bushes and I didn't seem him come out," Holloway stated flatly. "Hose it down!" A fusillade of fire tore into the area of the bushes. Then Holloway raised his hand. "Check it out, Willow." PFC Willow moved in cautiously and turned on his red filtered flashlight.

"Nothing here."

"OK! Spread out and search the area. Top, get everybody up and alert. Call the TOC. This guy can't have gone far. We have to get organized."

Five minutes later it was PFC Willow who actually tripped over the Redeye lying on the ground. Hurriedly he brought it over to Lieutenant Holloway. "Look, LT. What is this, an antitank rocket?"

"I can't tell in the dark. Let's take it up to the CP. Baron, you and Top keep this search going, but don't let anybody go out more than a hundred yards out. If this guy has left the area we're going to have to turn it over to the grunts. We've got to stay with our guns."

Once inside of the lighted CP. Holloway knew instantly what Willow held in his hands." Jesus Christ! That's a Redeye!" he exclaimed. "That's a top secret weapon. What the hell is it doing out here?" Then in answer to his own question, he muttered. "The UI. He must have had it with him. But how?"

*   *   *

Lieutenant Colonel Thomas J. Nordstrum and several of his staff arrived at 4 Papa 1 at mid morning the following day. Holloway had only just returned from the Brigade briefing where he had personally addressed the Brigade Commander and his staff regarding the incident the night before. The entire Second Infantry Division was in a state of alarm. An immediate inventory of the missiles had been ordered in an attempt to answer a myriad of questions. Who had lost the Redeye? Had an American sold it to someone? Were there spies in the Division? Traitors? Could a KATUSA have done it? Slicky boys? How had it gotten within a mile of the DMZ? No Redeyes were authorized to even be north of the river. Even as Nordstrum and Holloway were speaking, a full company of infantry continued to sweep the woods around Charlie Battery's position as it had been doing since dawn. Holloway pulled himself to attention and saluted his Battalion Commander with a brisk movement. A serious look clouded the colonel's face; his ruddy Swedish jaw jutted forward. He looked into Holloway's red-rimmed eyes.

"You get any sleep last night, Son?"

"Negative, Sir."

"Well, if it's any consolation I didn't either. At least not after the call. You know, you people have had one hell of a tour up here."

"Yes, Sir. I hope it's not gonna be like this every time."

Colonel Nordstrum smiled. "You think your Mess Sergeant can produce enough coffee for this gaggle I brought with me?" he said pointing at his S-2, S-3, Assistant S-3, Intelligence Sergeant, Sergeant Major, a shotgun guard, and two drivers, all of whom were clustered behind him.

"I know he can. We were waiting for you."

"Well, we've been chomping at the bit to come up here, but I knew you and Lieutenant Ruminski would be at the Brigade briefing and I wanted to give you some time before we descended on you. Let's go find that coffee and start trading stories."

Holloway silently appreciated the man's sensitivity in delaying his visit to allow him to get the unit squared away before the tourists showed up. Ten minutes later the entire entourage along with several of Holloway's NCOs clustered inside of the CP tent clutching their coffee cups. The shotgun guard had traded his pump action Remington for a ballpoint pen and tablet and was seated on a footlocker poised to begin recording the highlights of the conversation.

Colonel Nordstrum removed his helmet and sat in a folding chair offered by the acting Battery Commander. "Lieutenant Holloway, let me begin by saying that Lieutenant Courtney was returned from the 44th Surgical early yesterday morning. He seems to be in pretty stable condition, all things considered. They didn't feel there was anything else they needed to do for him and he was raising such a fuss about being there that they just decided to release him back to the Battalion, but the doctors don't want him coming to the field. Too strenuous. He'll just take it easy for a few more days at Camp Wynne and do some paperwork when he feels like it. You'll continue as acting Battery Commander on a temporary basis. After you come back to the compound tomorrow, Lieutenant Courtney will resume command as soon as he feels ready." He paused for a moment to see if Holloway had any comments or questions. There were none, so the Battalion Commander continued.

"We'd all like to hear about the wolverine in due time, of course, but first of all I need to know exactly what happened in regards to the contact with the UI. Everything. Every detail."

Holloway's eyes fixed on the floor as he breathed deeply and collected his thoughts. Still somewhat shaken by the happenings of the previous night, he began to speak haltingly, choosing his words and phrases carefully. In essence it was the same story he had told to the Brigade Commander at the briefing two hours earlier.

"Was there any chance that Willow hit him with the rifle?" the Colonel asked once Holloway stopped talking.

"It's possible, sure. But the guy was dressed in black. The more I think about it, the more I believe it was a black wet suit like Scuba divers wear. My point is that once he was twenty feet away from me and dodging through the trees we immediately lost sight of him. He blended right into the darkness. If Willow hit him it was pure luck, but who knows. He emptied the whole magazine into the trees."

The S-2 spoke for the first time. "The infantry sweep found some droplets of blood on the leaves this morning. Not a lot, but it was blood."

Holloway raised his eyebrows. "Well, I'll tell you what that might be. I thought I got him on the arm with my knife during the fight. I may have cut him. Or, as you suggest, Willow may have nicked him with a bullet."

"Is that the knife?" Colonel Nordstrum asked pointing to the suspenders of Holloway's web gear.

"Ahh, yes, Sir. I picked it up in the Z from Lieutenant Hackworth with the 1/9th. It's funny how things work out sometimes. I've needed that knife twice since we got here. If Hacker hadn't given it to me, I'd probably be as dead as that wolverine right now. Once the UI kicked the .45 out of my hand I would have been pretty defenseless." He pulled the knife out of the black leather sheath and tested the blade with his thumb. Every eye in the tent focused on it. Finally he replaced it into the sheath and snapped the strap that secured it.

"Is that the same Hackworth that lead the sweep that nailed the first two UI's?"

Holloway nodded, having gained that information at the briefing. Ruminski chimed in behind him. "Yessir. That's him. They just promoted him to Company Commander of Bravo Company. He's got quite a reputation around here."

"So I hear. OK, so what did you learn at the briefing about the UI's situation? Anything?"

Dave Ruminski gave a complete summary of the morning's discussion, including a recital of how the first two UI's had been killed earlier in the week and the fact that a journal and pictures found with the bodies showed exactly how extensive and successful the reconnaissance mission had been for the North Koreans. The journal itself was an incredible stroke of good fortune for the Americans, however. For one thing it confirmed the existence, though not the location, of another completed tunnel somewhere in the immediate area. It also described in detail how the commandos were able to live and move in the countryside for three weeks without detection. Everyone realized that it had been just dumb luck combined with some alertness on the part of the Korean civilians that allowed the mission to be interrupted in the final hours before completion. In addition, the journal mentioned that the missing UI, Lieutenant Yoon, had been carrying a map on which he had located many facilities of importance as well as entering extensive notes regarding their surveillances. Unless the unlikely happened and Lieutenant Yoon was found, the US Army had to assume that all of that information was now in the hands of North Korean intelligence.

"Well, Lieutenant Holloway, I think it's pretty obvious that keeping a battery up here is a bit more hazardous that we originally thought. So we're going to need to increase security. What is the infantry planning to do differently, Dave?"

"They're going to do their part, Sir. They'll be running sweeps around this area constantly and putting out random ambush patrols as well. Right now they're pulling out all the stops to find that tunnel. I've heard they're requesting some tunnel experts from Stateside and even Vietnam to help find this thing. They want it bad."

Colonel Nordstrum seemed pleased, but turned back to Holloway. "OK, but you must impress upon your artillerymen that this is serious business up here. The guards need to be alert at all times. You might consider putting out two man positions at night instead of one."

"Yes, Sir. I had planned on doing that. But if they don't know that its serious by now they'd have to be dumber than dirt. We'd also like your help in getting us some additional ordinance up here?" said Holloway.

"What do you need?"

"Claymores and trip flares. The grunts use them all over the DMZ, but we were told the artillery doesn't need them."

"You'll get them today." He looked at his clerk to insure the request had been recorded. "Anything else?"

"A couple of starlight scopes would be nice."

"That'll be tough, Bagger," interjected Ruminski. "They're in short supply up here. The infantry's always lookin' for more of them."

"OK. Well, whatever either of you can do."

"So much for that then, tell me about the wolverine and Tom Courtney."

Holloway, along with First Sergeant St. Clair, recounted the story of Eli as it had happened from the first night that PFC Daniels had stumbled upon him on the trail. He finished the story by adding that the biggest problem with Eli the wolverine was in never understanding until too late that there were two of them. Next St. Clair answered a few questions that were put to him. Then there was silence for a few moments. Eventually the colonel put his hands on his thighs and stood up. Everyone who was sitting got up with him.

"Lieutenant Holloway, why don't you escort me around your position. This is my first time up here and I'd like to get a better feel for it. Then show me where the action was last night."

"I'd be happy to, Sir!"

Colonel Nordstrum spied the giant Motor Pool tent and began walking toward it as Holloway fell in behind him. Several of the Battalion Commander's staff trailed to the rear. Sensing their presence, Colonel Nordstrum stopped and turned.

"Gentlemen, I'd like to spend some time with Lieutenant Holloway alone," he remarked, somewhat irritated. "Major Gentile, why don't you look in on the FDC crew.?" The others turned and walked in the direction of their parked vehicles.

The motor pool tent was a massive piece of canvas compared to the other tents in the unit. It was mounted over a poured cement pad with a five-foot deep trench in the middle that allowed the mechanics to stand upright under the vehicles for repair work. Two kerosene heaters provided heat inside of the large space. Colonel Nordstrum walked into the tent and waved to one of the mechanics that was standing in the pit and working on the transmission housing of a two and a half ton truck.

"As you were. Please carry on," the Colonel called to him.

Much of the Commander's informal inspection was done in silence or with only a minimum of small talk. Once he noted that the field generator should be grounded and that two of the squad tents seemed to be too close together, but generally he seemed pleased by what he found. Completing the inspection of the equipment he turned to Holloway.

"Things look very good, Clay. Your people seem squared away. I'd like you to show me the perimeter now. Show me where the UI was."

Holloway lead him up a small rise and back through the woods along the same trail he had taken the night before. Again he described what had happened, pointing to different areas around the position. The Colonel seemed fascinated. Holloway asked the guard to sit on the sandbags in the same way that Willow had sat the night before and then Holloway approached him just as the UI had. "And the UI disappeared over in there?" the Colonel asked pointing toward a thicket of bushes.

"Yes, Sir. With that black suit and all he just vanished."

"And where was the Redeye?"

Holloway walked thirty feet in the other direction and pointed at the ground. "Willow said it was just laying on the ground right about there."

"So it would seem that the UI laid it down so he could take out the guard and then when you came along he never had a chance to go back for it?"

"It looks that way. But why would he bother with the guard? If he had something as important as the Redeye why didn't he just bypass the guard and keep going? That's the part I can't understand."

"Yes," Colonel Nordstrum mused. "That is certainly the $64,000 question, isn't it?" He turned then and began walking back toward the CP.

"You should be proud of yourself, Clay. Proud to have survived an encounter like that. These dink commandos are tough and they're good."

"I was lucky, Sir. Lucky that I came up behind him instead of him behind me. Lucky I had this knife. Then I was lucky that Willow got himself back into the fight."

"You had another piece of luck that you don't know about yet. A little while ago, you heard about the captured journal from the UI's. The part that was not mentioned at the briefing was something the Brigade Commander called me personally about just before I left to come up here and I'm passing it along to you and Tom Courtney so that you will fully understand the ramifications of what almost happened to this unit, not only last night, but three weeks ago." Colonel Nordstrum stopped walking and turned to look Holloway directly in the eye. "What I'm about to tell you, Division Intelligence learned from that journal. On the night of October 21, the three-man commando team lead by this Lieutenant Yoon swam the Imjin at night and worked their way through a draw to the top of the bluff on the south bank. When they reached the top they found a foxhole manned by three men. All three were asleep. The commandos thought about killing them, but only because they didn't want to give away their presence, they bypassed the position and headed south. The exact location of their penetration was well documented in the journal. It was on the left flank, the west flank, of the SCOSI positions. You know what unit was on SCOSI duty in that position that night, Lt. Holloway?"

Holloway put his hand behind his neck and rubbed it nervously. "I'm afraid to guess, Sir."

"This battery. You and Tom Courtney and the rest of Charlie Battery. The commandos came right through your number one hole. Who normally occupies the number one hole?"

"That would be Sergeant Steele, Sir. Kelly Steele," answered Holloway, a giant lump forming in his throat.

"Well, I think this Battery is already spooked enough because of what happened last night. I think it has duly impressed upon them the necessity of being alert. So I don't want you to mention this to anyone quite yet. Wait until you're back at Camp Wynne and then you and Lieutenant Courtney let Sergeant Steele and his men understand exactly how close they were to never waking up. I want them to know that death looked them right in the face and then walked away. You want to talk about luck? They can count every day the rest of their lives as a bonus."

Holloway reflected on what the Colonel had said. The UI's could have done some real damage that night if they had tried. Hell, they could have walked up to the FDC van which Courtney used as a CP and blown it up with everybody in it. Sure there had been a guard outside the van, but what chance would he have stood against three well trained North Korean commandos?

"OK, enough of that, Clay. Let's change subjects. No bullshit, now. I know you haven't been over here but four months and you're only a second lieutenant. It's tough being forced into a command slot like this, especially with what's been happening up here. How are you holding up? Are you OK with all this?"

"We're fine, Sir. No cugi mah."

"Is that Korean?" the Colonel asked curiously.

"It means no bullshit. That's what you said you wanted."

The Battalion Commander nodded just as his driver approached.

"The TOC just called, Sir. They want you to call in on land line ASAP."

The big Swede strode rapidly to the CP, went directly to the field phone and cranked the handle. "TOC? This is Colonel Nordstrum. Is there a message for me? Yes, I'll wait." He stood there momentarily drumming his fingers on the collapsible wooden table that held the phone. "Yes, Sir. This is Colonel Nordstrum. What's that? You're sure it's ours? Son of a bitch! Son of a bitch!!! Yes, Sir. I'm leaving now. I'll get back to you. Out here."

Shaken, Nordstrum turned to face the small cluster of men in the CP. who were watching him intently. His jaw jutted forward more than usual. "The stolen Redeye belonged to us. The serial number says it was issued to the 8/18th and one of the containers in the ammo bunker is empty. They've also found some barbed wire that's been cut at the top of the fence. I've got to get back to Camp Wynne ASAP."

*   *   *

It was two days later and just before noon that the gun trucks of Charlie Battery lumbered through the main gate of Camp Wynne. To a man, the unit was looking forward to hot showers, a warm bed, and cold beer that night. Clay Holloway led the convoy in C-6, Tom Courtney's jeep, with the two new deerskin seat covers. Currently the deerskins were only laid across the seats. Eventually they would be taken to the village where they could be properly measured and cut to fit the seats exactly. Approaching the CP. Holloway could see a young blond woman in an army parka struggling with two large suitcases on the sidewalk. He directed the driver to pull over and waved the convoy past and into the motor pool. Holloway climbed quickly out of the jeep and approached her.

"Beth, what are you doing?"

"Oh, Bagger! I can't believe this," she exclaimed angrily. I've got a flight out of Kimpo in ninety minutes. The helicopter that I'm supposed to be on is on the pad and the goddamn driver didn't pick me up to run me over to it. It's going to leave without me. I can't carry these things, they're too heavy."

"No sweat, lady. Come with me," he declared as he tossed the two suitcases into the back seat of the jeep and held his seat forward so that she could climb into the back with the luggage. He glimpsed a long sleek nylon covered leg as she moved herself hurriedly into the jeep.

"Helipad, Shorty. ASAP!" he said to the driver.

In less than a minute the jeep rounded a corner and drove up to the concrete slab just as an olive drab Huey was beginning to lift itself into the air. Seeing the jeep and Holloway's frantic waves the pilot settled back onto the ground and waited. Above him the rotors continued to turn. The jeep braked to a halt a few yards away. Holloway leaped down and held out his hand as Beth climbed out of the back. Then he reached into the jeep and grabbed both her suitcases, carried them to the waiting helicopter, and laid them onto the steel deck. She was standing behind him watching.

"Thank you, sweetie. You're wonderful and I love you." She had to yell to make herself heard.

"Sure you do," Holloway replied with a wink. "Now get out of here. I thought you were already gone. I didn't know I'd have to deal with this. I hate good-byes."

"Me too." She looked at him for a long moment, then put her hand behind his head and pulled him toward him and kissed him long and hard. "Take care of yourself."

"You too. Write to me from the world." But even as he said he sensed that he would never hear from her again. He held out his hand and she leaned on it as she climbed into the vibrating chopper, assisted by the crew chief, who reached for her other hand. She turned and said something else. Holloway could see her lips moving, but the sound was lost in the roar of the engine as the insect-like machine lifted smoothly into the air. He waved for a moment and then she was gone. He bit his lip and walked sadly back to the idling jeep. Courtney's driver was sitting there looking at him.

"Damn, Lieutenant, a broad that looks like that and kissin' you that way. Shit, I'm surprised you didn't jump in that chopper with her. At least you coulda flown down to Kimpo and then hitchhiked back."

"What, and leave all you wonderful guys. Never happen. Let's go to the CP. We'll see how Lieutenant Courtney is getting along without us to yell at."

Holloway looked into the BC's office and knocked on the door jam. "Annahashamika. When did they let you out of the hospital?"

Tom Courtney looked up from his desk. His left hand was still heavily bandaged and his right cheek held a large gauze pad secured by adhesive tape. He ignored Holloway's question. "About time you got back. What have you been doing with my battery all this time? Going sight seeing."

"Sure. Korea's so pretty when all the leaves are down, the trees are bare, and the rice paddies are brown and frozen. I just couldn't resist." He paused. "So how are you feeling?"

"Mean as a snake."

"Oh good. Nothing's changed then."

"Well, truth is I'm sore all over. These damn gouges in my body hurt like a bitch. That critter raked me good. Doc says he got in a couple of bites on mah arm and hand that were real deep too. But I'm doing OK. Heard you had a little more action that night after I left."

Holloway related everything that had happened at 4 Papa 1 following Courtney's departure in the ambulance. The BC asked him several questions during the dissertation. He seemed pleased that Holloway had chewed the men out for their performance in the night guard positions. He also decided to give Reid an article XV for leaving his guard position. "You were right to do that, Clay. The Colonel told me how those three commandos came right over Kelly Steele's hole when we were on SCOSI. He's a good kid, but I'll tell you what. I'm gonna chew his ears off this afternoon when I get him in here and tell him what happened. Then I want to have a KATUSA translator in there to make sure Dong and Yan both understand exactly what happened too. I don't know for sure which of the three was supposed to be awake, but I'm going to try and find out and if I do he's getting' an Article XV too."

"OK, so what else has been going on around here?"

"All hell's broke loose, that's all. Well, you know about that crazy son-of-a-bitch Biladeau. That happened the night before I got out of the hospital, so I haven't seen him. They got the shrinks still talking to him. They think he might have been doing acid. You know, on account of him half the buildings around here got bullet holes in them now. Whenever the wind blows you can hear different pitched whistling' sounds. And of course the place has been crawling with CID's (Criminal Investigation Division) and MP's and G-2's and you name it."

"Have they come up with anything?"

"Well, it seems likely that somebody stole the damn Redeye during the time Biladeau was running around shootin' up the compound. That was the only time the place wasn't guarded. And the missiles hadn't been out of the ammo bunker any other time. Besides that, the Korean fence guards noticed some barbed wire cut over behind the tool shed near Alpha Battery the next day."

"Do they think Biladeau was in on it? It sounds like too much of a coincidence."

Courtney stoked his face thoughtfully. "Yeah, it does doesn't it. But I don't think he was. I think he's just messed up in the head. The Army shrinks have been all over the kid. So was the CID's. He's dingy dingy to start with and he was dropping acid besides. I think somebody just took advantage of the situation and stole the Redeye when he had the chance."

"You think that UI did that, Tom?"

"Maybe. Maybe it was a slicky boy who sold it. Well, anyway thanks to you we got it back. Losing that thing could have been an unmitigated disaster for the whole Army. You'll probably get put up for a medal for this."

"I'll believe that when I see it." Holloway sat on the old leather couch and smiled. It sounded like Courtney was just about back to normal. "Anything else happen?"

"Did you hear we got Whitaker back again?"

"No! Where'd they catch him this time?"

"Pobwon-ni, the Lucky Seven, just like before. Dumb bastard is AWOL for a month and then he goes back and pulls the same thing that got him caught the last time."

"So when is he going home?"

"With any luck at all he's gone right now. The MP's brought him in late yesterday afternoon. I had two NCOs from Headquarters Battery tie him spread-eagled to the pool table in the day room til this mornin'. I wasn't takin' any more chances with him escaping. Grant got him booked on a flight that was supposed to leave at 0930 today. I told the NCOs to take him onto the plane themselves, handcuff him to the seats, and then give the key to the stewardess and wait outside the door with their billy clubs until the plane took off. They ought to be back any time."

"Are you serious? You spread-eagled him on the pool table all night?"

"We were Christian about it. We gave him a pillow and a blanket. And we let him up to take a piss once. I just wasn't about to take any chances with that man goin' over the hill again."

Holloway shook his head and laughed out loud, "I'm going over to the Q and take a nice hot shower and change clothes if you don't mind. I haven't showered in seven days. You know I said good-by to Beth Kisha a few minutes ago. She didn't say anything, but somehow I'm afraid that for the rest of her life if she ever thinks of me she will remember the guy who smelled like a horse that had been rode hard and put away wet. So maybe I'll see you at lunch. If I don't, I'll be back over here right after I eat."

"Don't rush. Hey, by the way. I'm buying the drinks tonight."

*   *   *

"I said good-bye to Beth today, you know. I helped her get onto the chopper," Holloway explained to Jennifer Dodge as he drained his first beer of the evening.

"Really! I'm glad you got to say good-bye. She thinks a lot of you."

"I guess. She's a different kind of lady. I hope she finds whatever it is that she's looking for."

"I don't know that she's really looking for anything. I think she's just having fun. I really like Beth. We've had a lot of laughs together. But I think she's lucky she left when she did."

"How so?"

"The Red Cross likes to set all the rules for us. Beth wouldn't play by them. She has her own rules. I think the Red Cross was getting upset with her reputation. They set very high standards for us girls. They're very particular about who they hire and the way we conduct ourselves after we get over here. Beth had a reputation for being pretty wild sometimes and I'm sure a few of her actions were not well received with some people."

"Was the Army upset?"

"Heck, no. Most of the brass loved her. Every general or full colonel in the Division who was having any kind of social gathering would always ask for her personally to attend. I think that kind of upset Karen," observed JD, referring to the head Doughnut Dolly who had a reputation for being jealous, vindictive, and mean. "Beth is different, Bagger. You know that."

Holloway nodded his head silently.

"She hurt you didn't she?"

Holloway waited for a moment before answering. "For a while, yes. She was very honest, though. She came right out and told me that I was not the only guy she cared about and I shouldn't consider her my girl friend because she wasn't."

"Beth told me you slept together a couple of times," JD said.

"She doesn't hold anything back, does she?" Again he paused momentarily wondering if he should comment. "Yes. We did. I guess after the first time that I assumed that she felt the same way about me that I felt about her. But it just wasn't like that. She told me there was no way she was going to be tied down seeing just one guy, especially when I was going to spend three months north of the river. But, hey. All that's history now. She's off to the next chapter of her life and you and I are sitting here in the bar at scenic Camp Wynne enjoying each other's company. Have you heard from Magic yet?" Holloway asked changing the subject.

Jennifer grimaced noticeably and she looked down at the bar. "No," she said in a whisper. "I haven't heard anything."

"Well, hey, you know how the mail is. You can go for a week and not get any mail and then get five letters in one day. It happens all the time."

"Bagger, it's been almost three weeks. Three weeks and I haven't heard a damn thing from the man who asked me to marry him. There's something wrong. I can feel it. It's not the mail. Even if he took a week to just relax and not think about Korea, you'd think after that he'd write just to say he was fine and he loved me. Wouldn't you do that? Wouldn't you?"

"Well, yes. I guess I would. Did you ever make more definite plans about getting married? Did you pick a date or anything?"

"No, we didn't. The signs were there weren't they? I just didn't want to see them."

"JD, don't give up on the guy yet. You love Magic. You told me you love him. I'm telling you, it could be the mail. Wait for a while and if nothing happens go down to the overseas phones at RC#1 and call him at Ft. Hood. He should be there now, right?"

"How would I know what number to call?"

"Just call Ft. Hood and ask for the post locator. Then give them Magic's name. They'll know where he is."

"Maybe I'll do that," she mused. "OK. I'll try not to think about it for a while, but it's hard." JD looked at him. Her green eyes seemed misty. He laid his hand on her bare arm. She, in turn, put her hand on his. "I'm worried, you know."

"I know."

It was Thursday night. The Officers' Club bar held only six or seven people. No one was within five seats of Holloway who held up his hand to order another Miller's. Suddenly the swinging doors flew open and banged against the wall. Second Lieutenant Rick Benning stalked in, his dark eyebrows furrowed and his face set in anger.

"Goddamnit, Buster, give me a 151 straight up," he ordered, climbing onto a bar stool nearby.

"You want 151 rum?" Mr. Buster asked reluctantly.

"Well, what'd I say?"

Benning glanced over at JD and Holloway. "Hey, Holloway," he said and nodded in JD's direction.

"What's going on, Rick?"

"Horseshit, that's what's going on. A big smelly pile of Mickey Mouse incompetent horseshit."

"Am I supposed to know exactly what you're referring to?"

The twenty-one year old survey officer peered at him through squinted eyes and shot down the 151. "No, I guess not. Buster, hit me again."

"It's Meesta Busta," the burly Korean bartender said softly.

"Just give me the goddamn drink," Benning repeated. Mr. Buster poured it slowly and set the bottle on the bar. Benning threw down the second drink as quickly as the first. At the same time, Bill Grant and Hostileman had entered the bar and taken seats on the other side of Benning. "I'm just getting real fuckin' tired of getting blamed for things that I have no goddamn control over. If they send me survey instruments from I Corps with the wrong goddamn declination constant on them how the hell am I supposed to survey in the right firing points? They're supposed to set that, not me. Then they chew out my ass for not doing the survey right. That's bullshit. Buster hit me again."

"Lieutenant Benning, this 151 very powerful. You know what you do?"

"I know what I'm doing, Buster. I'm havin' a drink with my friends." Again he emptied the glass. His face was beginning to color, but at least his explosion of anger was beginning to temper itself. "Hey, JD. I'm sorry about my language. I guess that's a bell ringer, swearing in front of ladies." He stepped off of the stool, grabbed the bell cord hanging behind him, and rang the bell sharply. Mr. Buster began to line drinks along the bar.

"What you want, Lieutenant Benning?"

"Another 151, what do you think?"

"Are you all right, Rick. I've never seen anybody drink four 151's before," said Holloway, watching him pour down the one hundred and fifty one proof liquor.

"Well, you better get your camera ready then because you're about to see somebody drink five."

The swinging doors at the other end of the bar opened and Sherry Cifrianni strode into the room, a broad smile on her face. "JD, I've been looking for you," she called. Rick Benning held his fifth 151 in his hand as Sherry walked in. As she passed behind him he swiveled his stool to look at her and at the same time sucked down the liquor. Unnerved by his stare she detoured slightly around his stool and walked to where JD and Holloway were sitting. Then she glanced cautiously over her shoulder as Benning slid down from the stool and unsteadily lumbered toward her. She had planned to begin speaking to Jennifer Dodge, but seeing the reddened face of Rick Benning and demonstrating obvious concern over the look in his eyes, which seemed to be having difficulty focusing, she began backing slowly away from the threatening figure. Suddenly, Benning roared at the top of his lungs and leaped at the frightened young woman. She shrieked equally as loud, causing everyone in the bar to tighten their sphincter muscles and rise up slightly in their seats. Then she turned and fled. The crowd roared. Benning, having missed with his first rush toward her, regained his balance and pivoted, locateing her just to his right. The crowd whispered. Was he kidding? Was he playing with her? No, the crowd decided. He was most certainly not kidding. Second Lieutenant Rick Benning had just gone temporarily insane.

Benning crouched and circled his prey. Sherry Cifrianni had had enough. She had not the vaguest idea what the young man with the belly full of fire water was intending, but at the same time had absolutely no inclination to stay around to find out. She turned and ran full speed toward the swinging doors at the west side of the bar. Benning was instantly hot on her heels. The crowd could hear Sherry screaming from the hallway. Then suddenly the doors on the east flew open and Sherry sprinted through, the drunken survey officer reaching in vain for her clothing, but grabbing only a fist full of air. Again she flew past the bar and out the west doors and again reappeared seconds later through the opposite ones. Holloway was unable to decide whether the scene was more reminiscent of Wyle E. Coyote and the Roadrunner or a Marx Brothers movie. A third time the pair came through it seemed that Benning was definitely gaining.

"Five dollars MPC says Benning catches her next time around," Bill Grant ventured. There were no takers. There was also no fourth time around. As Sherry reentered the bar from the east doors she ducked into what she considered the only safe haven in the building; the ladies room. Benning, however, didn't even blink an eye. Roaring, he charged through the door immediately behind her. Her shrieks reverberated throughout the Club. Showing some concern, or at least interest in what was happening in the ladies room, some of the crowd peeked through the door. Their concern for Sherry Cifrianni was misplaced. As Benning dove for her legs, she nimbly sidestepped. In his inebriated state, he was unable to stop and plunged head first into the open toilet in the corner, bumping his head on the porcelain. Sherry seized her opportunity and ran for the door, shoving aside those of the crowd who were in her way. Within seconds she had escaped the confines of the Club, raced to the Doughnut Dolly hooch, and locked herself in her room.

Eventually Rick Benning extricated himself from the commode and wobbled back out of the ladies room, the top of his hair dripping water and a ridiculous lopsided grin on his face. The other bar customers watched him cautiously, awaiting his next move. Approaching the bar, Benning spied his empty bar stool. Suddenly he gave a war cry and ran at it, leaping high into the air just before reaching it and spinning his body in a perfect 180-degree circle. It was a perfect three-point landing for Benning as his buttocks found the vinyl-covered seat. Unfortunately the stool was in no way secured to the floor and when the young Texan's body landed on it the stool, immediately tipped over backwards, taking Benning with it.

Crack! The sound of Benning's head hitting the tiled floor made everyone cringe. The young man rolled onto his side, and then sprawled motionless on the floor. Hostileman looked down at him from his stool. A patch of blood could be seen spreading in his hair. Hostileman knelt briefly beside him and satisfied himself that the survey officer was breathing.

"Hey, Bagger," Hostileman said. "What say you help me carry Benning over to the dispensary?"

"I don't know, Hostileman. I just started another beer. Besides that it's cold outside and I think it's raining besides. Just get him another 151. He'll be fine." JD looked at him in astonishment. Holloway winked at her.

"Come on, Lester Joe. I'll help you carry him," said Bill Grant sliding off of the barstool.

Benning's head was starting to move and he was moaning softly. "I was just kidding, Hostileman. I'll help you carry him," Holloway said.

"No, it's all right. You stay here. Grant and I can get him. Just leave our drinks on the bar, Mr. Buster." Together the two men pulled Benning to his feet and supported him. He was trying to hold his head up, but he seemed unable to use his legs. Mr. Buster offered a towel across the bar which Grant took and held against the back of Benning's head to stem the flow of blood as they dragged him out of the door and into the cold rainy night. The dispensary was only about a hundred yards away.

Clay Holloway reached for the telephone on the end of the bar and dialed a three-digit number. "Hello. Doc? Yeah, it's Holloway. Listen, Rick Benning just fell and hurt his head. He's being taken over to your office. Can you meet them there? Good. Thanks a lot." He replaced the receiver in the cradle. "Doc Kramer is on his way," he announced.

Jennifer Dodge had not spoken throughout the entire incident. Finally she did. "God, Clay. What the hell happened to him?" JD asked.

"That was semi-incredible, wasn't it? You know he had five 151's in less than ten minutes. I'm surprised he's not dead. I bet he won't do that again for a while."

Mr. Buster had gotten a bucket and mop and cleaned the blood from the floor. Other people had begun to file in and were immediately told the story. Finally, Sherry

Cifrianni, having regained her courage and being accompanied by Kathy Kelsey and Joan Brannigan, peeked through the swinging doors. "Where's Benning?" she asked cautiously.

"Dispensary. He knocked himself out," Jennifer replied.

"Is he going to be OK?"

"We don't know yet. Doc Kramer is taking care of him."

Dramatically the swinging doors again burst open as Hostileman and Bill Grant returned from their mission of mercy and shook the loose rainwater from their fatigue caps. "Doc's stitching him up. He's going to be fine once the headache goes away," Grant announced. Jennifer Dodge had been genuinely concerned over Benning's injury. The news that he would be fine, combined with the memory of the hysterical chase around the bar, buoyed her spirits and she bounced down from her stool and walked to the bell. "OK, everybody! It's party time!" she cried slamming the clapper against the side. "Line them up Meesta Buster."

Holloway again grabbed the bar phone and dialed Tom Courtney in the BOQ. "Hey Tom, tighten your tourniquet and get over to the Club. We got a party brewing up. Round up anybody else you can find."

Bill Grant pointed to Mr. Yun. "Put on that Temptations album I just bought!" The Club manager ducked into his little room behind the liquor shelves and a moment later the beat and the rhythm of the Motown sounds began blaring through the bar.

"Turn it up! Turn it up!" the crowd cheered.

Joan Brannigan grabbed Hostileman and tugged him toward the dance floor. No one had ever seen Hostileman dance and the crowd applauded as Joan began swaying and moving around him, as he stood on the floor in his combat boots trying to pick up the beat of the music. Eventually he bent his knees and began raising his arms and dropping them quickly in an attempt to do the "jerk." Jennifer Dodge was next, dragging Holloway onto the floor and instantly picking up the beat.

Tom Courtney burst through the doors wearing a yellow steel safety officer's helmet. Wearing any sort of headgear inside of the Club was an automatic bell ringer. Courtney was holding a wild turkey call that he had brought from Tennessee. As he headed toward the brass bell he blew into it twice, sending the turkey gobble sounds around the room and adding to the Mardi Gras atmosphere that was seemingly developing out of no where. Then he clanged the bell, sending a round of drinks around the bar to the customers who now numbered more than twenty.

Holloway looked at JD, now standing at the end of the bar and talking to Sweeper who had just walked into the room. She seemed to have forgotten her sadness of the last hour. The party was good for her. She seemed to be her usual smiling self. It made Holloway happy and he gazed at her and smiled unconsciously.

The crescendo of the party had built quickly to a high level. Once there, it plateaued at almost a fever pitch. Colonel Nordstrum had stopped in for an hour and enjoyed himself immensely. Finally he departed, sensing that if things got really rowdy he did not want to be present. If he was present it would be his duty to calm things down. People were having too much fun to be settled down. Why throw a wet blanket on it? Thomas Nordstrum had the good sense to simply retire to his room and let the party run its course. He had been gone less than five minutes when JD grabbed his arm and yelled, "Look!"

Holloway turned to see Joan Brannigan on top of the bar holding her skirt high on her thighs and dancing around the cocktail glasses that lined the polished wood. At the same time, a girl Holloway had never seen before entered the room in her bathrobe, apparently resigned to the fact that if the music was going to keep her awake in her room, she might as well join the party. She wore no make-up and seemed rather plain, with horned rimmed glasses and brown hair, which hung straight to her shoulders.

"Who is that?" Holloway asked JD.

"Gretchen Schuster. She's Beth's replacement. She got here about three days ago. I really don't know her very well."

They watched as Gretchen studied Joan's actions on the bar, as though she were trying to comprehend what she was seeing in an Officers' Club of the United States Army. Slowly she studied the people surrounding the bar assessing their reaction to the dancing Doughnut Dolly. Finally she made a facial expression as if to say "What the hell!" and climbed onto a bar stool and from there onto the bar to dance along side Joan. The two girls smiled broadly at each other and moved in unison to the cheers of the masses. Holloway looked at Hostileman who was seated right below Gretchen, his elbow on the bar, and his hand cupping his chin. He wore the silliest expression Holloway had ever seen on him.

"Hostileman, what's that shit-eaten grin on your face for?"

"She's not wearing any panties! I can see right up her robe!" the liquored up young Georgian whispered back.

Gretchen Schuster heard exactly what Hostileman had said, along with ten or fifteen other people in the bar. Her face went from white to crimson in less than a second. Having only intended initially to stick her head in the door to see what all the noise was about and having been caught up in the moment, she had been totally oblivious to the fact that under the robe she was as naked as the day she was born. Panic stricken, she reached for JD's hand and leaped from the bar. As she flew through the air the silk robe fluttered up, exposing her white flesh to the waist. The male members of the crowd cheered and applauded. The other women shrieked and laughed. Landing on the floor and catching her balance, Gretchen ran for the door and disappeared a moment later. Sherry Cifrianni ran after her.

"I'll drink to that! This calls for a toast!" Sweeper cried.

Courtney blew on his wild turkey call. "We don't need a toast. We need a fire mission!" Tom Courtney called out. "Where's mah XO? Where's Holloway?" Spying him laughing with JD he commanded, "Battery adjust! Fire mission! Target, that fireplace." He pointed to the large stone fireplace on the back wall, which held a blazing orange fire. Holloway grabbed an empty Miller's bottle and positioned himself.

"I'm the base piece. Fall in on me."

JD stepped immediately to his side holding an empty highball glass. "Wait a minute," yelled Sweeper. "You can't have a girl on a fire mission!"

"Bullshit! She's the other half of the center platoon. We need four more guns." Quickly Kathy Kelsey, Sweeper, Grant, and Auslander stepped forward, each armed with some sort of empty glassware. Courtney called the commands.

"Battery adjust, shell HE, lot x-ray, fuse quick, battery one round, deflection 2795, quadrant 171."

Mr. Yun was panic-stricken. In his sixteen years of managing the Officers' Club at Camp Wynne he had never had a fire mission called upon his fireplace. This night was getting entirely out of hand. He raised his hands in a pleading gesture. "No, no. Please wait. Don't."

Courtney flipped a five-dollar MPC note onto the bar. "No sweat, Mr. Yun. We'll help you clean up. Here's for the glasses." raising both his voice and his hand, he gave the final command. "BATTERY, FIRE!!!!"

Two bottles, three highball glasses, and a beer mug simultaneously crashed against the sandstone, spraying glass in all directions and causing the crowd to duck as it cheered' "REPEAT!" cried Sweeper. The gun crew ran for the bar to reload and reformed quickly.

"BATTERY, FIRE!!!"

The scene repeated itself to the utter delight of everyone except Mr. Yun and Mr. Buster, both of whom felt they would be there half the night sweeping up the tiny chards of glass. Finally the laughter and loud talking began to subside. The Supremes had been singing in the background and Mr. Yun chose the moment to reduce the volume on a ballad at the same time that he turned on the lights. The spell was broken and people realized it was time to wind things down. Sherry Cifrianni came back through the doors. JD moved to her.

"How's Gretchen?"

"Utterly destroyed. She said she's never danced on a bar before in her life. She say's she is never leaving her room again. And furthermore, she wants a transfer out of the Division and she is not coming out until she gets it. She says she wants to go to Vietnam and die."

Jennifer smiled sympathetically. "That poor girl. What a way to meet the troops. Let me go talk to her. Come on." She turned then and caught Holloway's eye and waved to him. He returned the motion and continued sweeping up the glass along with Grant and Hostileman and the rest of the self-appointed clean up crew. The night was over. Tomorrow was a workday.

CHAPTER 24

The heavy wet snow had begun falling only thirty minutes earlier, but already the accumulation approached two inches. The size of the flakes seemed enormous to Tom Courtney as he cupped his hands around his coffee mug both to benefit from its warmth and to keep the hot liquid from loosing heat more rapidly than was necessary. He watched his battery of six howitzers as it continued to fire the missions as the acting forward observer, Bill Grant radioed them. Courtney nodded approvingly as he heard his XO, Clay Holloway, tell Kelly Steele, the number six gun chief, to stop trying to sight on the collimator to the left front of the gun and switch to the two aiming stakes located well to the right rear. The swirling snow was causing too much difficulty for the gunner to take his sight picture on the collimator and there was no time to reset it until the end of the current fire mission. It was only a service practice mission of course. The guns had been registered at a recently developed range area nine kilometers to the west and approximately two kilometers south of the DMZ. It was proper gunnery procedure to register the guns. If it came to pass that Charlie Battery would actually be called upon to provide artillery support to the DMZ, the registering of the guns would make the shooting more precise. In truth, however, the registration had been done in clear thirty-degree weather. With the recent advent of the storm, the prior registration would not be all that accurate. The temperature had dropped almost ten degrees and the wind had increased dramatically. The snow too would effect the registration. Courtney felt that Major Gentile, who had come up to oversee the shoot, would probably ask for a second registration mission once the current fire mission was complete. He was correct. Ten minutes later he heard Holloway relay the mission to Sergeant Rivers and the base piece. Fifteen minutes after that the shooting ended for the day. Using the data that had been developed by the registration, the guns were left set with the adjusted deflection and quadrant that would allow them to fire the final protective fires for the three guard posts of Cindy, Carol, and Gwen without working up new data. Two guns were dedicated for each of the three hills. If the word would ever come, the howitzers could have high explosive artillery rounds landing on the base of any of the three hills in less than a minute after the call for fire was received.

Courtney turned and walked into the CP tent. He removed his winter field cap, shook the snow from it, and scratched his head, noting how oily his unwashed hair was beginning to feel. Then he stretched. He still had some pain in his chest from the mauling he'd taken from Eli almost a month earlier, but overall his wounds had mended nicely. Tomorrow he and Holloway would be taking the unit back to Camp Wynne. It was December and Charlie Battery had already served two tours in the firebase at 4 Papa 1. It wouldn't be their turn to come north of the river again until at least February, maybe even later than that. It really didn't matter much to him. He was short. In fact, by the end of January he'd be back home with Elaine and Tom Junior, whom he had never seen. That would be indescribably wonderful.

The first six days of their tour had been routine. The worst thing about it had been the onset of the Korean winter and its subfreezing temperatures. During half of the nights the thermometer had dropped below twenty. Everyone had been forced to get into his down filled mountain sleeping bag fully dressed, lay a blanket on top, and cover his face with a towel, leaving only a small hole for the nose and mouth. Even with all that, Courtney had normally wakened up half way through the night with the side of his body that faced the kerosene stove reasonably warm and the other side frozen stiff. Once awake, he would roll over to thaw out the frozen half. The only thing worse than trying to sleep was going to the latrine. Men waited until the last possible second before running into the three hole wooden structure and dropping their drawers. Tom Courtney had never experienced this sort of cold in Tennessee and the feeling of having one's vital parts turned into Popsicles was one that he felt sure he could do without for the rest of his natural life.

Part of the battery commander's responsibilities is the cleanliness of troops in the field. Courtney had made arrangements for shower runs to Camp Greaves so that everyone had one or sometimes two showers during the ten day stay, but even with that, most of the men were living in clothing that had not been changed for four or five days. One of the more memorable events of the stay had been Thanksgiving. A DivArty chaplain and Colonel Nordstrum had come north to join the unit for the meal and the men had been ordered to don clean wool shirts and field pants. There had even been cardboard turkeys hung on the metal water buffalo to provide the holiday spirit. Venison and pheasant that had been shot by various members of the Battery had supplemented the standard Army master menu for Thanksgiving. It had added an air of authenticity to the Thanksgiving feast. The only real drawback had again been the cold. While the cooks kept the food warm until it was served onto the plates, once exposed to the air it cooled within a matter of seconds. It was difficult to truly enjoy mashed potatoes with puddles of frozen gravy adorning the top.

But the most important incident of the period had occurred three days earlier. Engineers had finally found the tunnel that everyone felt sure was the one used by the UI the month before. After weeks of infantry sweeps, of using geological instruments to search for changes in the soil density, and after a myriad of false alarms, the tunnel specialists had finally dug into the main tunnel shaft with a back hoe almost a quarter of a mile away from 4 Papa 1. From there a squad from the 1/38th had entered the tunnel and followed it to the end which had been only fifty feet from the outpost that PFC Willow had occupied the night of the encounter. When the squad leader reached the tunnel's end he found a wooden door. The door turned out to be a foot under the surface of the earth with a large bush planted on the other side. As the infantryman heaved the door open, it swung the bush at a 45-degree angle right in front of First Sergeant Hudson St. Clair who almost shot the first GI to come out of it. Within the hour the area was swarming with people. Engineers, photographers, intelligence officers and brass converged from all over the division. A full platoon was sent into the tunnel to head north and secure it all the way to the MDL to keep it from being blown up by the North Koreans. Charlie Battery had been ordered to keep away from the area and had complied with the instructions, but with the tunnel entrance located on the edge of their perimeter, the constant commotion had made it impossible to maintain the position as a useable firebase. Division had finally decided that because of the proximity to the entrance, the next artillery battery to take up position north of the river would not do it at 4 Papa 1. Hurriedly DivArty had selected an alternate sight about three kilometers away and dubbed it Firebase Wolverine in honor of Charlie Battery's earlier adventure. The next day a battery from the 1/15th Artillery would occupy the new position. Once Charlie Battery returned to Camp Wynne, 4 Papa 1 would be left vacant for the foreseeable future.

*   *   *

The return to Camp Wynne meant a return to comfort for Tom Courtney in his room at the new BOQ. The NCOs and enlisted men also came back to their heated hooches. But for Clay Holloway and the other junior officers of the Battalion, December brought the unpleasant surprise of a total breakdown in the oil furnace that heated the old BOQ. When Holloway walked into his room after ten days of living in a tent, he found it more reminiscent of a meat locker than a bedroom. Ice coated the inside of his window and several items, like his deodorant, were frozen solid. Disgusted, he threw his duffel onto his bunk and stalked to the O Club for something to eat. It was almost the end of the lunch hour and the only other person in the dining room was a black first lieutenant whom Holloway had never seen before who was actively attacking a piece of chocolate cake.

"Mind if I sit down?" Holloway asked.

The lieutenant gave him a friendly smile and pointed to the chair across from him. "Help yourself. I'm Ron Beals," the man said extending his hand. Holloway introduced himself. The stranger was stoutly built, with a light complexion, and had a thin mustache extending from one corner of his mouth to the other.

"Are you in this battalion?" Holloway asked as he checked off his desired lunch items on the paper menu.

"Yeah. I just got here three days ago."

"Are you in the "Ghetto?" The old BOQ, that is?"

"No. The Colonel said that a first lieutenant rated the new one."

"You're lucky. I just walked into my room after ten days in the field and there's no heat. It's like walking into an igloo. I think it's colder in my room than it is outside. What a bunch of shit!"

"Yeah, I'm sorry about that. We're working on it."

Holloway raised his eyebrows. "What do you have to do with it?"

"I'm the new S-4 (Supply Officer). The furnace has a cracked heat exchanger. There are no parts through the supply system that anyone can find, but Colonel Nordstrum told me to do whatever is necessary to get some heat into the Q. There are about twelve second lieutenants that are seriously going to consider lynching me if I can't come up with something here pretty fast. I'm going into the village this afternoon and talk to some people."

"You're going into the ville to find an oil furnace for an Army BOQ? What makes you think that'll do any good. Only thing they have in that village is business girls, drugs, and Bang Yang whiskey."

"Doesn't matter what country you're in, man. You can always find what you want if you got the right connections and the right money. My first job is to make the connections so's I can find the furnace and the second is to get it for a good price, and the third is to figure out how to pay for it. If there's no furnace in Sonyu-ri then we'll check out Munsan. I'll go all the way to Seoul if I have to. Somewhere around here is what we need and my job is to find it."

Holloway was unconvinced, yet he would be the first to acknowledge that he knew next to nothing about how the supply system worked, either officially or unofficially, especially in Korea. He was very aware that there was a sophisticated black market in the country, which fed itself from the US military. The slicky boys were at the low end of the supply spectrum for the black market, but the thievery went far above that. He had heard stories even during the short period of time when he and Todd Hardesty were at Ascom City waiting to come north about how corrupt the system was. Allegedly there had been an enormous warehouse at Ascom that housed a multitude of supplies. One Thursday it was announced that a full and complete inventory of the warehouse would begin the following Monday. On Sunday night the warehouse mysteriously burned to the ground. It was the second time it had happened in three years.

"Well, good luck, Ron. I sure hope you can pull this off, because if you can't it's going to be one hell of a long cold winter. You might want to start by talking to a kimchi critter called Proud Mary in the ville. She's down about a hundred meters on the left."

Beals slid back his chair and stood up. "Proud Mary? OK, I'll keep you posted. Take it easy."

After eating his lunch Holloway walked to Tom Courtney's room and found him just walking out of his door. "Hey, Tom. What do you say I use your shower so I can get washed up and into some clean clothes? These are about to rot off of me."

Courtney gave him a quizzical look. "So why do ya need mah room?"

"'Cause there's no heat in the "Ghetto." It's about twenty degrees and the water is shut off so the pipes don't burst. I can't even take a leak in there."

Courtney smiled and shook his head. "What a place. Yeah. Here's mah key. Get yer smelly ass cleaned up and see me over at the battery."

"Yes, Sir. Kamsamnida."

*   *   *

"So where are you going to sleep, Bagger?" Jennifer Dodge asked sympathetically.

"Tom said I could use the couch in his room for a while. Baron and Sweeper are doing the same thing with their battery commanders. It makes it awfully crowded in there though. I feel like the man without a home. When the work day is over I go straight to dinner and then I just have to hang out here at the Club until it's time to go to bed." He took a sip of his Coke.

"You could pitch a tent in the lounge of our hooch."

"Yeah, I'm sure your boss Karen would love that. We'd last about two minutes before she called DivArty." JD smiled knowingly. Everyone was terrified of Karen, the head Doughnut Dolly.

"Listen, not to change the subject, but I need a favor and whenever I need a favor I think of you," JD said sweetly.

"I'm flattered beyond words. What is it?"

"Well, there's a Christian orphanage not too far away and with it being the holiday season and all the Red Cross has arranged for a Christmas party for the kids. Three or four of the girls will be going. I'm in charge, actually. And I could use a few guys to help out too. I also need a Santa Claus. What do you think?"

"What do I think about what?"

"Will you do it?"

"Will I do what?"

"Listen, Holloway, don't give me the run around. Be Santa Claus for me."

"Ahhh, JD, I'm not good at stuff like that. I don't even have any kids. And besides that I'm not fat enough. Hostileman has a little belly on him. Ask him to be Santa."

"We have the suit. We have pads to make you fat. We have a beard. We have everything but a live man to put into the suit. I don't want Hostileman. How can we have a Santa Claus named Hostileman? I want you. Please. It'll be fun."

"I honestly and truly do not think it will be fun, but for you, OK. When is it?"

"December 19th."

"December 19th? Oh, geez, I'm really sorry. We're going back to the field on the 18th."

JD raised one eyebrow. "Don't give me your lies, Holloway. I already talked to the Colonel and Charlie Battery is not going back to the field until February. I've had enough lies from men to last me for a while."

Holloway caught her meaning and noticed that her eyes had suddenly flared. "No word yet?"

"Nothing. It's over. It was a big lie. He just used me. I called Todd Hardesty. He seemed embarrassed. Todd said he hadn't heard from Magic. I called Ft. Hood like you told me to and they gave me a number. I talked to his roommate and he said he'd deliver the message. That was five days ago. Forget it. He's a bastard. The hell with him. I wish I'd never met him."

"Did you ever tell your parents you were engaged?"

"Sure I did. I called them on the overseas phone at RC#1 because I was so excited. I wasn't going to tell the other girls here, but I told one or two and then the word just got out and so everyone knew we were engaged. Now, I'm embarrassed. You and Sherry have been the only ones that know that it's over, but a lot have people have asked where my always-present smile has gone. They know something's wrong. I'm not sure what I should do."

"I wouldn't do anything. If anyone asks about him tell him you changed your mind. You don't have to explain your personal life to them."

"No, I guess not."

The telephone at the end of the bar rang and Mr. Yun picked it up before it had a chance to ring a second time. He listened for a moment and looked around the bar. Then he spoke into the receiver. "Lieutenant Courtney is not here, but Lieutenant Holloway is. OK. One second." He held the phone out toward Holloway who reached over the bar to take it."

"Holloway." He listened quietly for a moment. "I'll be right there." JD could see the grimness in his face as he turned toward her. "There's been a fight at the EM Club. One of my men is badly hurt. I've got to go to the dispensary."

"OK. I'll be here for a while."

"I'll try to make it back. It all depends. Oh, by the way, I'll do it."

She looked puzzled. "You'll do what?"

"Play Santa Claus."

When Holloway entered the front door of the dispensary he could see Doc Kramer working on the facial area of a man lying on an examining table in the rear of the treatment area. Holloway walked past the Spec/4 at the desk and back to where the doctor was working. He looked down at the sandy haired freckle faced cook from Arkansas and repressed a grimace. The man's face had been sliced open in such a manner that Holloway could look through the outside of his right cheek and see his tongue and teeth inside of his mouth. The cut started below his right eye and continued vertically to the jawbone.

"How you feeling, Campbell?"

"I been better, Sir."

"Can you tell me what happened? Who did this?"

"I never even seen him. I was sitting at the EM Club with some of the other guys and there was a crash behind me and I stood up and started to turn and something hit me in the face. Shorty told me on the way over here that it was a broken beer bottle. Nobody seems to know who threw it."

"Have the MP's been called?"

"I think the CQ called the Staff Duty Officer."

Holloway nodded. "OK, I'll check." He stepped back as Doc Kramer politely nudged him with his hip. The Battalion Surgeon had a needle and thread in hand. Campbell had already been given a local anesthetic. As Doc Kramer indicated to the patient to open his mouth a medical specialist 5th class stepped forward to assist him. Deftly the doctor began the long process of suturing the inside of the mouth. Holloway watched for a few minutes and then stepped forward to give Campbell's shoulder a gentle squeeze. "Hang in there." The young man nodded grimly. The realization that even with plastic surgery he would be scarred for life had begun to sink into his consciousness.

Turning to leave, Holloway realized for the first time that two other Charlie Battery cooks were sitting in the reception area watching. He had no idea when they had gotten there or even if they had been there when he first arrived.

"How's he doing, Lieutenant Holloway?" one asked.

"He'll be all right. The doctor is sewing him up now. Did either of you see what happened to him?"

"Not exactly," said D'Onofrio. "But it was some of those assholes from Headquarters Battery, I know that. There was three or four of them at the table behind us. We'll find them. The guys are getting ready."

"Whoa. Wait a minute. Just be cool here. I'm going to make sure the MP's are on the way. This will be handled properly."

"No disrespect, Sir, but some things have just got to be dealt with unofficially."

"Let's go outside and talk about it," Holloway said holding open the front door. As they descended the front wooden steps a jeep stopped in front of them. Two uniformed MP's climbed out.

"Are you looking for PFC Campbell?" Holloway asked.

"Yes, Sir. Is he in there?"

"Yeah, he's there, but the doc is sewing up the inside of his mouth. You're probably going to have to wait a while to talk with him. I believe these two soldiers were seated at the table with Campbell when everything happened." The two nodded in ascent. "Maybe you can take their statements first. I'll walk over to the Battery area and see if I can find any more witnesses. You can use the Charlie CP. I'll see you there in a few minutes." The MP sergeant snapped a stiff salute as Holloway walked away and headed toward the sleeping hooches. Based on what D'Onofrio had said, he feared that a vigilante movement might be underway. An all out war between two batteries of the same battalion was the last thing anyone needed.

The night air was frigid. Holloway walked quickly toward the Charlie Battery area and into one of the sleeping hooches through the rear door. It felt warm inside. The oil space heater in the middle of the room was obviously doing its job. Six men were standing or lounging on bunks talking softly. "As you were," he called immediately to keep them from rising. "How's everything in here? Everything cool?"

There were a few mumbled responses. Holloway surveyed the room. Half the men were in their stocking feet. No one looked like he was ready to go outside. A large black soldier named Winslow smiled broadly. "Yessir. Everything's under control. There's no problem. But I tell you what. When we find out who actually did that to Campbell he's gone be a hurting' dude."

"I understand how you feel. I like Campbell too. But the MP's are here right now. We should just cooperate the best we can and let them do their jobs. Nobody needs to be going off half cocked and making things worse. Do any of you have any first hand information about what happened?" There was silence. "Nobody saw anything, is that it?"

One of gun bunnies finally spoke. It was PFC Willow. "A bunch of the Headquarters mechanics were at a table talking real loud and all. I think they'd been drinkin' pretty good. Somebody walked by and one of the mechanics tripped him is what started it. I think the guy that got tripped was from Alpha. So he got pissed and turned around and all the Headquarters dudes jumped up and when that happened I think they knocked over their own table that made a big crash. And that made everybody jump up. I really can't say who threw the bottle, though, cause I don't know."

"Does anybody else have anything to add to that?" Holloway asked. Again there was silence. "OK, Willow, I want you to go over to the CP. There should be two MP's taking statements from two other guys. Tell them what you saw. Give them some names of the mechanics and the Alpha Battery guy. Maybe they can check it all out. That's the best thing to do. Go ahead and get your boots on and I'll walk with you."

Holloway spent the better part of an hour helping the MP's in compiling a list of names of those present when the trouble had started. At last it was decided that the MP's would return in the morning when everyone from the various units would be accounted for and the investigation could be carried out in an organized manner. Stopping back at the dispensary on the way to the BOQ, he was informed by Doc

Kramer that Campbell had been sent to 44th Medical where he would be hospitalized for a few days. As Holloway began leaving, Tom Courtney was walking in.

"Hi, Tom. You hear what happened?" Courtney nodded and Holloway proceeded to summarize the night's events. Courtney seemed satisfied and together they walked back toward the Club where they stopped a few minutes later and poked their heads into the bar. It was deserted. Mr. Yun spied them and offered his services.

"What I get for you?"

"Nuthin' for me, Mr. Yun," replied Courtney. "I'm tarred. I'm goin' to bed. Holloway, you comin' up and sleep on mah couch?"

"I'll be there in a bit, Tom. Thanks. Mr. Yun did Jennifer Dodge leave?"

"Yes. She say tell you she go her hooch, maybe half hour ago."

"Let me use your phone there, please." Holloway dialed the Red Cross hooch and asked for JD. Her voice came over the wire a minute later. "Hey, are you retired for the night?"

"Yes. I'm in my robe. It's getting late and I wanted to do something to my hair."

"Like what?"

"Like highlight it. I've decided to try highlighting my hair."

"How do you do that?"

"Do you really want to know?"

"That's why I asked you."

"Well, I have to put on a rubber cap that has little holes in it and then I have a thin plastic stick sort of thing that has a little hook on the end. I have to put the stick through the hole and latch a piece of hair and pull it back through the hole. I do that all over and then I put the highlighting solution on the hair that is pulled out of the holes and on the outside of the cap."

"That sounds very entertaining. I want to watch."

"What! You can't watch."

"Why not?"

"Because I look ridiculous, that's why. Besides, I think it's going to take forever to get the hair pulled through the holes."

"Then maybe I could help. It would probably be easier for two people. Have you ever done it before?"

"No. This is the first time."

"Well, then let me help and besides I want to tell you what happened at the EM Club." She hesitated. "Bagger, I don't know. Are you sure you don't want to just laugh at me?"

"I'm not going to laugh. I promise. I'll do the best job I can."

"Well, OK, then. Come on over. I'll meet you at the door in two minutes. Is that OK?"

"That's fine. I'm on my way."

JD was peeking into the lounge from the hallway when Holloway walked in. She held open the door, which led to the rooms, and he followed her back. He had never been to her room before. He thought momentarily of Beth Kisha. Her room was the only one he had ever entered. JD pointed to a door half way down the hall on the left side.

"This is it." He walked in, feeling a slight sense of embarrassment, as though he were about to do something illegal, immoral, or both. "Are you really going to do this?" she asked, blushing slightly and grinning from ear to ear.

Holloway took off his field jacket and tossed it onto a chair. Then he rolled up the sleeves of his fatigue shirt and sat on the edge of her bed located on the left side of the room. "I'm ready when you are."

"Well, OK. First read these directions while I finish drying my hair. Just stay here while I go down the hall. I'll be right back." She grinned at him again and shook her head disbelievingly. Then she disappeared out of the door holding a blow dryer and a hair brush, only to return five minutes later.

"Your hair smells clean, JD. It smells nice."

"Not for long. I think this highlighter is going to smell bad. But that part isn't yet. Let me put on this cap." She pulled out a blue rubber cap that looked like a bathing cap with holes and pulled it tightly over her head. The cap almost matched her terry cloth robe. Holloway laughed aloud. She reacted by running at him and gently beat her fists on his chest. "You creep! You said you wouldn't laugh!"

Holloway laughed harder and held her arms. "I'm sorry. You look like you're planning to swim the English Channel."

"Look, don't mock me out. You asked to be here. Either shut up and do your job or I'm tossing you out."

"Myan humnida. I'll work. I read the directions. The first thing I found out was that you wash your hair after it's highlighted, not before. So I hope you dried it good. Now, where's my plastic fishhook?" She handed it to him. "OK. Sit down on the floor and I'll sit on the bed and we'll get started. But before that and before I tell you about what happened tonight, I have got to make one thing absolutely, positively, crystal clear."

"What's that?" she asked as she arranged herself cross-legged on the floor beneath him. The position exposed much of her bare thighs, which Holloway considered to be a very pleasant, yet unexpected bonus to the job.

He tilted his head and spoke softly into her ear. "If you ever tell one person on this entire compound that I did this, I will personally sneak over here late at night when you are asleep and shave your head. No cugi mah."

CHAPTER 25

Ninety-eight pairs of black leather combat boots crunched on the frozen dirt and gravel of the narrow road, which gently wound through the wintry Korean countryside. On a map the dirt road appeared as a large loop, which ended at the same place it had begun after traversing a peninsula of land known as the Dragonhead. On one side of the road the ground dropped steeply for almost fifty feet, giving way finally to a flat open area covered by a series of snow covered frozen rice paddies, which stretched endlessly into the distance. To the right of the road a barren hill rose sharply above the two columns of troops who covered a quarter of a mile in linear distance. The troops were dressed in winter field clothing, which included parkas with liners and field pants with huge cargo pockets. Attached to the parkas were heavy winter hoods with coyote fur edges. Full pack, web gear, and a variety of individual weapons completed the uniform of the day, except for two RTO's who also carried PRC/25 radios on back packs. One of the RTO's walked near the front of the formation with the battery commander. The other RTO, PFC Nichols, was positioned near the rear. At the top of the long antenna mounted to the PRC/25, Nichols had attached a bright red Christmas stocking that fluttered occasionally in the cold wind. The very last person in the column was the battery executive officer, Clay Holloway, who caught himself watching the fluttering stocking and smiling. Holloway had decided long ago that clearly Nichols did not have both oars in the water and the Christmas stocking incident was just another example of it. He had to admit, though, that the small Korean children in the village they had just passed through had enjoyed both the stocking and the candy that Nichols carried in his pocket. During the last tour at 4 Papa 1, Nichols insisted on trying to wear a Korean War vintage helmet he had found in the woods. There were large rust holes in the helmet that made him look ridiculous, but of course that is why he insisted on wearing it. Nichols' regulation helmet was covered with a camouflage cover, as was everyone else's. The custom of the times was to write slogans or poems or whatever on the helmet cover as a display of individuality. Naturally, Nichols had printed a large peace symbol with an arrow sticking through it. Under the peace symbol he had printed his favorite expression, "Kill for Peace."

Holloway's eyes continued to scan the backs of the men in the two columns ahead of him. After spending so much time with all of them in the field he had finally reached the point where he could easily identify each of them from the rear even when they were all bundled up in their winter gear. Each was a bit different in height or the way he walked or the way he carried a rifle. Holloway couldn't help but wonder if other units in the US Army had the same number of unusual characters. Nichols, of course, was one, but there were so many more. Holloway could see Biladeau part way up the right column. He had been returned to the unit after the Army shrinks had declared him to be perfectly sane and fit for duty, his episode in shooting up the Camp Wynne compound not withstanding. OK. Nevertheless, there was a standing order in the unit that no one was ever allowed to give Biladeau any live ammunition for any purpose ever again. He was also precluded from carrying a bayonet. Rumor had it that Biladeau had been using LSD the night he lit up the compound, but he had never admitted to it. Directly in front of Biladeau was Campbell, the right side of his face still covered by a gauze bandage a week after he had been released from the hospital. Normally cooks did not partake in road marches, but Campbell had somehow managed to contract a dose of the clap sometime between being released from the hospital and reporting to Camp Wynne and had been temporarily relieved from his cook's duties. The good news for Campbell was that the MP's had finally identified his assailant and the man had been sent to the stockade, pending his court-martial.

Near the front of the left column Holloway could make out the short stocky figure of Specialist Fourth Class Marvin Bernstein. The man had only arrived in Charlie Battery two months ago, but had become a godsend to Sergeant Lepley in the FDC. Initially he had been assigned to the number two gun section, since 13A was his MOS (military occupational specialty). A 13A was a field artillery crewman. That assignment lasted until Tom Courtney reviewed his personnel file and found that Spec/4 Bernstein had a master's degree in mathematics. Major Gentile had given draftee Bernstein a crash course in gunnery and it was now generally believed that he knew more about the subject than did his FDC Chief. The list of personalities went on and on. Draftees and "lifers," potheads and juicers, blacks and whites, Puerto Ricans and Koreans, educated and dropout, patriot and former felon. They were all brought together for a single purpose. To become part of a cohesive operational 105mm howitzer battery whose mission it was to protect the Republic of Korea from further harm from its neighbor to the north. Part of that mission was being in proper physical condition, which is why the battery found itself three quarters of the way through a seventeen mile road march through the frozen Korean countryside a week before Christmas.

Division had issued the Op Order. Each unit would conduct a series of conditioning road marches beginning with five miles and continuing through seventeen. This was to be accomplished once each quarter. In the spirit of leadership, Colonel Nordstrum had volunteered to accompany a different battery on each movement. For the seventeen-mile march he had selected Charlie Battery. In retrospect, that had been a mistake. Tom Courtney, being the competitive individual that he was, had decided to beat the fastest time in the Battalion, which had been established by Bravo Battery. Courtney had begun the march with a blistering pace and three hours later had slowed it only slightly. The trek was tough enough on the men in their teen's and twenty's, but for Colonel Nordstrum, who was forty-seven, the march was causing shooting pains up and down his lower legs and a constant aching in the hip sockets. He wanted to tell Courtney to slow down, but his pride prohibited him from doing that. It was Courtney's battery and he didn't want to interfere. Nevertheless, it would be a cold day in hell before he would ever walk anything more than the five mile marches with this unit again.

It was after dark when Charlie Battery finally reached the welcome main gate of Camp Wynne. After a brief formation in the street in front of the CP, Courtney dismissed the men and he and Holloway headed for his room in the new BOQ. Holloway was still sleeping on his couch. Lieutenant Beals, the new S-4, seemed to be trying hard, but as of yet had failed to get the oil furnace in the old BOQ either repaired or replaced. The "Ghetto" now resembled a ghost town. No one went there any more often than was absolutely necessary to retrieve some personal article. Even the houseboys found excuses to keep from venturing in there. Ice covered everything and doors blew open and shut with the wind. One spare room in the new Q had been turned into a mini-dormitory and four second lieutenants slept in a row in sleeping bags on its floor. The remainder of the junior officers had all moved in temporarily with other officers in the new building. Everyone was trying very hard to get along in less than ideal circumstances, but it was apparent that the cramped quarters and lack of privacy was starting to wear slightly on everyone. Nowhere were the suppressed emotions more ready for explosion than in the second floor room occupied by "Ranger" Brown and his temporary guest Lester Joe Bufford, a.k.a. "Hostileman."

It wasn't as though the two didn't like each other. If the truth be known, Lester Joe was intensely fond of the tall blond officer. It was simply that whenever Lester Joe had a couple of drinks of hostilejuice and was immediately transformed into Hostileman in his truest form, he developed a rather acid wit which constantly challenged Ranger and tried to draw him into a verbal battle. Ranger was normally an extremely quiet young man and whenever taunted by his new roommate, tended to withdraw even more. Rather than return the joking insults hurled by the Communications Officer, Ranger's internal thermometer had continued to rise over a period of days until it exploded a few minutes before Courtney and Holloway walked onto the floor.

Neither man was later able to recall exactly what had been said that triggered the physical contact, but it had something to do with the picture on Ranger's desk of his wife in a bikini. Following Hostileman's blatantly vulgar remark regarding the structure of her very feminine upper body and what he would like to do with it,

Ranger had reached down and grabbed the two front legs of the wooden chair where Hostileman was reclining. Ranger pulled hard and the Communications Officer was immediately dumped onto his back and head. At the sound of the crash, other officers had poured into the room and separated the two combatants before an actual blow could be struck. However, after a great deal of shouting and cursing, it was decided that the fight would, indeed, continue. After some further discussion, it was mutually agreed that no punches could be thrown. It was to be strictly a rassling match. It was at this point that Holloway and Courtney walked down the hall. Robert "Sweeper" Hoover spied them and rushed to bring them into the room.

"Come on! Y'all are going to miss the fight!"

"What fight?"

"Hostileman and Ranger. It's right now. Come on in."

"Well, tell them not to start yet. We got to get all this gear off and grab a beer. Who's got a cold one?" Holloway asked.

"I do," called out Ranger. "But you have to root for me."

"I will. I promise. Where's the brew?"

Ranger pointed to his little refrigerator. Holloway grabbed two, handed one to Courtney, and tossed his parka, web gear, and helmet into Tom's now open doorway. Quickly they joined the other seven spectators who were jammed into the smoke filled little room where all of the furniture had been pushed to the walls. Hostileman appeared to be in rare form. His usually cherubic face had been transformed. His eyes had glossed over, his expression was cocky and challenging, and his normally unassuming grin was combative. Ranger, on the other hand, was just plain pissed.

Holloway was worried. It seemed to him that there was too much anger in the air and he feared that someone's temper might get the best of him, winding up with one or more of the combatants seriously injured. He decided to stall the fight.

"Wait a minute. Wait a minute," Holloway cried, leaping into the middle of the room. "We can't start the match until I tell my wrestling joke."

The audience moaned. "Not another one of your jokes, Holloway. Get out of the way."

"No, no. This is a good joke. It's appropriate to the situation and I ain't movin' til I tell it."

"Shit! OK, Bagger. Hurry up and tell it," yelled Sweeper who had gotten a tape recorder and microphone from somewhere and was in the midst of trying to tape the entire event.

"OK. This involves a young American wrestler who was headed for the Olympics. Now this guy had trained and wrestled for hundreds of hours and his coach knew that he was ready. The Olympics began and the American won all of his matches until he reached the championship round where he would face the Russian national champion. But the night before the match the American's coach called him to his office to talk with him.

'Son,' the coach said. 'I know you're ready to face this Russian, but there's one thing you need to understand. He has a move called the "pretzel hold." He's already crippled three men with this hold and I don't want to see you become the fourth. If he gets you in the pretzel hold you won't be able to move a thing. If that happens I want you to immediately tell the referee that you give in. There's no reason for you to be crippled or maimed. Promise me that, OK?'

The young American looked at his coach and nodded. 'OK, Coach. I'll do what you say.' The next day the championship match began and the American seemed to be winning. Suddenly there was a flurry of movement and the American found himself wrapped up tight, unable to move. The coach stood on the sidelines starring and holding his face and grimacing. It looked as though the Russian had applied the pretzel hold and it was all over for the American. Then, out of nowhere, there came an incredible shriek and both wrestlers flew into the air. When the two men came down and hit the mat the American landed on top of the Russian and pinned him. The American had won. The coach ran onto the mat and embraced his athlete. "Son, that was wonderful. No one has ever broken the pretzel hold before. But how did you do it and why didn't you give in?'

'Well, Coach,' said the American. 'When I found he had me in the pretzel hold, I was being choked and I couldn't even talk. But when I looked in front of me, there was the biggest, ugliest, hairiest set of gonads I had ever seen. I was about to pass out and so I finally reached out and chomped down on those gonads as hard as I could. And you know what, Coach? A man just doesn't know how much strength he has until he bites his own balls.'

The audience roared. Even Ranger and Hostileman were laughing. When Sweeper introduced the two wrestlers and stated the wrestling rules to the two fighters, the intensity level had at least dropped a few degrees. Nevertheless, the two men came together in the middle of the room with all the power of a couple of sumo wrestlers. Each man kept his feet, using power and upper body strength to keep the other from gaining an advantage. Finally Ranger turned his body and positioned Hostileman for a hip throw, which he partially executed. But when Hostileman hit the tile floor he pulled the Ranger over on top of him. A few seconds later he rolled him over and tried to pin him. But Ranger was too strong. The bout continued over the next several minutes. One man gained an advantage one moment and lost it the next. The audience began to wonder how they were ever going to decide who won. Finally both men regained their feet. Hostileman charged and drove Ranger backwards into the wall, shaking the entire room. Ranger went down and Hostileman leaped on top of him. But as he went for the pin, two things happened almost simultaneously. First the seam in Hostileman's fatigue pants split wide open and secondly Hostileman suddenly broke wind loudly. The crowd went wild, howling in glee. Then as the noise level slowly subsided, the piercing shriek of a whistle shattered the mood. The whistle blast was followed by ugly scream.

"Attench hut!"

Thinking it was a joke Sweeper turned slowly toward the open doorway, his usual grin covering his face. "Goddamn it, Lieutenant, don't you know what attention means! "The speaker stood in the doorway, one hand on each side of the frame. His dark eyes drilled into Sweeper. On the right collar of his fatigue shirt was the golden leaf of a major. No one had ever seen him before. "I said attention. All of you. Now!"

Eleven officers came slowly to attention. "I don't know if this is standard fare for you people or if this little party has been put on just to welcome me to this unit, but this is the first and last time I plan to have to speak to any of you about proper conduct in a Bachelor Officers Quarters. This is not a fraternity house. I had planned to speak to all of you in the morning, but since you insist on raising my ire, I will inform you tonight. Number one, I am the new Battalion Executive Officer. My name is Major Karl Vogel. Number two, this BOQ is not a flop house and anyone who is not assigned a room in this building will remove himself and his belongs from the premises immediately."

"Sir, the other BOQ doesn't have any heat. That's why we're here," Sweeper offered.

"I don't give a damn about your petty problems, Lieutenant. I'm telling you and your friends to collect your gear and get your young asses out of this building and into your assigned quarters now."

Outwardly, his remarks were met by utter silence. Inwardly, there was a lot of teeth grinding and stomach churning. Who the hell was this guy and why was he here? What happened to Major Posey, the old XO? Admittedly no one ever saw him. In fact, he had the nickname of "the man who never was." He rarely seemed to leave his office and spent most of his time doing administrative work. But that was often the role of a battalion XO. And what right did this FNG have to throw them out of the BOQ anyway? Colonel Nordstrum knew they were there and had never said a word. In the end, however, discretion seemed to be the better part of valor. And besides, Vogel didn't seem to be the kind of officer you could sway by arguing. Maybe someone could talk to the Colonel in the morning. No one spoke. Finally, Major Vogel gave them all a last icy stare and turned away. A moment later a door slammed shut toward the end of the hall.

Holloway and Kendall Stover stumbled through the open door of the "Ghetto" disbelievingly. Their arms were full with sleeping bags, clothes, and shaving kits. It was no more than twenty-five degrees in their rooms. "I can't even fucking believe this! I have walked seventeen miles in this cold today and my feet and legs are killing me. All I want is a cold beer and a warm rack. Instead I get Attila the Hun chewing me a new asshole." As he spoke, puffs of condensed breath bellowed forth from his mouth.

"Yeah, this guy is a real peach, isn't he? A laugh a minute."

"I've got a bad feeling about this, Baron. I think there's going to be a lot of changes in a very short time and I don't think they're going to be positive."

"How do you mean?"

"Well, Buckner and Auslander are both DEROSing sometime after the first of the year. Tom is going a week or two later. That's all three firing battery commanders. Who's going to take over the batteries? We've apparently got a new Battalion XO and I've got to believe it has something to do with the Redeye getting stolen because I know Major Posey was catching a lot of heat for that. And what about Major Gentile and the S-3 shop? I know he's getting short. We're going to be hurtin' real bad for officers here within a very short time. Either we're going to get a flock of new second lieutenants to help. And people like you and me and Sweeper are going to take over everything. Or we're going to get a shit load of new senior officers moving in. Which do you think it will be?"

"Well, maybe some of both."

"Yeah, maybe. But based on tonight, I don't think I'm liking the direction it's going." Holloway walked into his room and dumped his gear on his bed. Then he stuck his head into Stover's room next door. "So where are you going to sleep?"

"Here I guess. Aren't you?"

"Yeah, I suppose. Hell, I might as well be north of the river. At least up there we have kerosene heaters."

"Why don't you call up your buddy Jennifer? Maybe she'll let you bunk with her at the Doughnut Dolly hooch?"

"I thought about asking her if I could sleep on her floor, actually. But if anyone found out, she could get in real trouble. I can't do that to her. I guess we'll just have to gut it out here tonight and try to figure out something else in the morning."

"You stayed in the room with Beth a couple of times didn't you? What's the difference?"

"That was a whole different kind of thing. That was sex and she asked me to. She knew what she was doing. I'm not really sure why it's different. It just is. It would be really stupid to get JD sent home for letting me sleep on her floor. I can't put her in that sort of jeopardy." He turned to leave. "I'll see you tomorrow."

The clock radio began playing on schedule at 0600. The music seemed to be coming from very far away. Holloway's first sensation was that of intense cold on his face. He hit the snooze alarm and buried his face in his sleeping bag to try to warm it. Five minutes later the music came back. Again he hit the snooze. Relentlessly, the music returned. It was no use. He unzipped the bag and climbed out. He was fully dressed except for his boots. He fumbled in the desk drawer and pulled out his electric razor. Sleepily he located the electric socket and plugged it in. Frost covered the mirror making it impossible to see into it. He spent five minutes rubbing the razor around his face. Eventually he could feel no stubble with his hand so he turned off the razor, took a slug of mouthwash, and walked outside to spit it in the snow. Then he stuck his head into his friend's room.

"Hey, Baron. What's shakin'?, over." Stover moaned in return. "OK, I'm going over to the O Club to use the john. You going to breakfast?"

"Yeah. I guess. Christ it's cold!"

"You noticed, huh. OK. I'll see you over there."

It was an hour later that Clay Holloway sat on the worn leather sofa in his BC's office where he had been summoned. He waited for Tom Courtney to speak. "OK, here's what the Colonel told me this morning. Number one, Major Vogel is the Battalion XO effective immediately. Major Posey has apparently been relieved as XO. It sounds like they're just going to squirrel Major Posey away to some desk job at Division for the last month of his tour. They want Vogel in here because he's got a reputation as an ass kicker."

"Why do they think we need our asses kicked?"

"They don't really. It's just that this whole battalion is pretty young and inexperienced and they think a hard charger like Vogel will help. He's an active guy and DivArty figures he'll ride herd on all of us young lieutenants and keep us in line and show us the true light. Somebody told the Colonel he's one of the youngest majors in the United States Army. He was with the Eighty Second Airborne in Vietnam and he is considered to be AJ squared away. OK, number two. Colonel Nordstrum told me he's planning on making you Charlie BC when I go home next month."

"Me?"

"Well, who the hell else is he gonna give it to?"

"Somebody senior. Somebody with more experience. I'm only a second john for Christ's sake."

"Holloway, there isn't anybody more qualified than you. Maybe this hasn't dawned on you, but you've been here almost six months. You're one of the senior guys now. The new lieutenants will be looking to you for leadership and know how. Besides, they need three battery commanders. Baron will probably get Alpha and Sweeper will get Bravo. The only thing that could change that is if we get in some captains from somewhere. Look, don't worry about it. I still have five weeks left. I'll teach you what you need to know. Look at the positive side. You'll get my room in the new BOQ. At least it has heat."

"Did you ask the Colonel about that? Do we have to stay in that goddamn deep freeze?"

"He said Major Vogel convinced him it was not good for discipline to have all you guys living like gypsies in there with us. He swears they're gonna have the furnace fixed most scochie. Major Vogel has been told to get on it ASAP."

"Swell."

*   *   *

It was Friday night. The music of Blood, Sweat, and Tears filled the Camp Wynne Officers' Club, although the volume had recently been reduced at Major Vogel's directive. Strangely, Vogel had left the bar two minutes after ordering the music turned down. Most of the officers viewed his action as just another example of his power ploys. The man seemed to have a genuine affection for his position of control over others and ignored no opportunity to display it. It was agreed, however, that his arrival may have had some positives, however. He had stood at dinner and announced that he and Lieutenant Beals had solved the heating problem in the Ghetto and a new furnace would be installed the next day. That had brought a resounding cheer from every second lieutenant in the room.

The patrons of the Club were entirely male and would remain that way throughout much of the evening. There was a Christmas party at Division headquarters and the Commanding General had personally requested the presence of all of the Doughnut Dollies at what he considered to be one of the most important social functions of the year. Karen had been very emphatic in her directive to the other girls, which left little room for discussion. "You will attend!" The other guests included the CG's staff as well as all brigade and battalion commanders throughout the division. Major Vogel had lobbied hard for an invitation as well, but had been unsuccessful, much to his chagrin. Holloway stood at the east end of the bar with Courtney, Baron, and Bear Buckner. Through the swinging doors at the other end walked Ron Beals with a very attractive kimchi critter in a red mini dress clinging desperately to his arm. It was unusual to see a Korean girl in the O Club. On a typical Friday night the NCO Club or EM Club would have plenty of Korean women. Some of them were girlfriends or yobos of the men. A few were strictly business girls who somehow wangled an invitation onto the compound so that they could try to score with the troops. But the O Club was different. That was partially because many of the officers were married combined with the fact that the Red Cross girls were dues paying members of the Club and they traditionally did not appreciate associating with what were typically Korean prostitutes of one form or another. Redeye Officer Lieutenant Ed O'Connell had brought his Korean girlfriend to the Club one night and had been severely chastised for doing so after some of the Red Cross girls complained. O'Connell had strongly resented the Doughnut Dollies ever since. Perhaps it was because the Doughnut Dollies were going to be gone all night that Ron Beals had decided to bring the girl. Or maybe it was the fact that he just didn't care what they or anybody else thought about him or his date.

"Baron, let's go congratulate the S-4 on his procurement of a new furnace and offer to him our heart felt thanks," declared Holloway. "Besides that we can check out the josan." The two strolled down the bar and stood next to Beals.

Beals greeted them with a smile. "Hey, guys. I'd like you to meet Marie. Her uncle is the reason I'm installing a new oil furnace in the BOQ tomorrow. He's a heating contractor of sorts, you might say." The girl smiled, showing incredibly white even teeth. She stood only about five feet and like most Korean girls had beautiful long dark hair, which hung straight, down her back.

"Well, hi there, Marie. I'm pleased to make your acquaintance and please convey to your uncle my appreciation for coming up with the furnace, where ever he got it." Holloway looked at Beals. "Major Vogel announced at dinner that you and he had found a furnace. That's really great news."

"He announced what?" Beals echoed.

"That you and he had solved the heating problem," repeated Holloway.

"Well, that's kind of a unique way of looking at it. My friend Marie here, told me about her uncle and I made contact with him and worked everything out and set up the whole thing for tomorrow morning. I told Major Vogel what I was planning to do at 4:30 this afternoon. And he announced at dinner that he and I had solved the problem, huh?" Beals turned silent, reflecting on the new Major's tactics.

Finally Baron spoke. "You know for a guy who just got here you seemed to have made some real effective contacts down in the ville."

"Yeah, well it helps to get to know people. I talked to Proud Mary like you told me and she made some arrangements for me to meet the mayor today."

"The mayor of what?"

"Of Sonyu-ri."

"I didn't know Sonyu-ri had a mayor. I guess I never really thought about it," said Stover. "Well, that sounds cool." He turned to the rest of the people standing about. "Hey listen up all you second johns. I want to propose a toast to the new S-4. He and this beautiful young woman's uncle are finally getting us some heat for our hooch. In the two weeks he's been here he's gotten to know more people in the ville than all the rest of us put together. Rumor has it that he's intending to run for city council next. So anyway, here's to the new village honcho." Stover clanged the bell loudly and held his glass in the air. "To Village Honcho!"

*   *   *

It was Christmas Eve. Moving quickly and quietly in a crouch, Jennifer Dodge slipped through the shallow blanket of fresh snow that was still falling over the DMZ. By her side shuffled two infantrymen, one holding his M-16 at the ready and the other lugging a large stainless steel container of hot coffee. With her left hand she pressed her steel helmet tightly against her head while she ran to keep it from bouncing up and down and worsening her headache. In her right hand she clutched a medium sized waterproof duffel, which held disposable, cups, packets of sugar and powdered cream, and doughnuts. The threesome moved quickly from foxhole to foxhole along a seemingly endless line of positions that sat fifty feet behind the DMZ south barrier fence. At every hole the procedure repeated itself to the astonished infantrymen who manned the positions.

"Hi, honey. I'm JD. What's your name?"

"Jack."

"Well, Merry Christmas, Jack. Here's some hot coffee and a doughnut. Do you need cream and sugar?"

"Yeah. Great. Hey, who the hell are you and what are you doing way out here?"

"I'm with the Red Cross and Santa Claus sent me to wish you a Merry Christmas." If the soldier was lucky and wasn't wearing a cold weather mask, she might add a kiss on the cheek to accompany the coffee. The GI would get a scent of femininity and he'd smile. Then she and her two companions would be moving away in the darkness, heading toward the next position. They had been doing that for almost two hours and JD was tired. The moving, the bending, the cold air, and the heavy clothing, which included a flak jacket and helmet, were all conspiring to wear her down. They had already gone through five gallons of coffee, having refilled the two and a half gallon jug once. Further up the line, Gretchen Schuster was performing similar duties and beyond her Sherry Cifrianni repeated the procedure as well. By 2130 they were out of coffee and more than ready to climb into the one and a quarter ton truck that would pick them up at prearranged points behind the fence. The three young women were cold and tired. They were also exuberant. They had done what many of them had come to Korea to do. To serve, to find adventure and to meet guys.

When Jennifer Dodge returned to her room at Camp Wynne she found a note taped to the door that told her Clay Holloway had called and asked her to come over to the Officers' Club when she got back. She wasn't sure she was up to it. She telephoned the Club instead. Mr. Yun came on the line and then called Holloway to the phone.

"Bagger, hi. I got your note."

"Good. Come on over. We've been waiting for you."

"I don't know if I can. My feet are frozen solid and they're killing me besides. My newly highlighted hair is a mess and I need a hot shower desperately. Do you have any concept about what an army helmet does to a woman's hair?"

"A Jack Daniel's and Coke will fix you right up."

"How about if you bring it to me. Give me twenty minutes to get a shower and then come over if you can stand the sight of me with wet hair and no make-up."

"Well, I'll tell you what. Tom and Baron and I have been saving our presents. If you're not coming over here, we'll go up to Tom's room and open them and then I'll stop over and see you in about a half hour. I have something I want to give you. Besides the Jack Daniel's I mean. I'll bring that too."

"What are you talking about? You mean a Christmas present? I didn't get anything for you. I didn't know you were going to do that."

"Don't worry about it. This isn't much, believe me. I'll see you in a little bit."

A few minutes later, Kendall Stover, Tom Courtney, and Clay Holloway seated themselves in Courtney's room in the new BOQ. Stover began, unwrapping a red plastic inflatable easy chair from Mary Lou. The three men alternated puffing air into it until it was fully inflated. Then they took turns sitting in it and opening their other gifts from wives and mothers and fathers and brothers and sisters. Before long the floor was piled with scarves, sweaters, paperback books, handkerchiefs, dart guns, a Monopoly game, and a plastic model of the battleship Arizona, complete with glue and paints. Eventually though, the mood changed from merriment to melancholy, especially for the two married men. Christmas was a time for family and for them, family meant their absent wives. For Tom Courtney, however, that absence was coming rapidly to an end.

"Short!" Courtney called out in a deep voice.

"I don't want to hear it," Stover replied. "I'm not even over the half way point yet."

"I'm a thirty day loss. Mah name is in red letters on Bill Grant's manning chart. Twenty-five days and a wake-up and I am gonna blow this pop stand. In fact, I'm gonna get up early on Christmas morning just so I can practice mah suitcase drill."

"This is depressing. I'm going back to my room and write a letter to Mary Lou. Bagger, you coming?"

"I'll walk with you part way. I'm going to stop at the Club and get some Jack Daniels and ice. Then I'm going to stop and wish JD a Merry Christmas."

"Hey, what's the story with you two? You sure spend a lot of time together. Is she still going to marry that chopper pilot?"

"I hope not. He doesn't deserve her."

"So are you trying to step in here or what?"

"We're still just friends right now. I'm just taking things slow, man. I adore her. I've never really met anyone like her before. I just really like being with her. Sometimes I feel like I have to be with her. Do you know what I'm talking about?"

"I know exactly what you're talking about. Why do you think I'm so damned depressed right now? Well, I'm glad someone can be with the girl they want to be with at Christmas. It sure isn't me." Stover remarked woefully. "Hey, give me your presents. I'll carry them over to the Q for you."

"Thanks, Baron."

The knock of Jennifer Dodge's door came ten minutes later. She lowered the volume of the Bing Crosby Christmas carols that played over her portable tape recorder and answered the door with a towel around her head and a long silk kimono covering her still damp body. Holloway looked at the outline of her breasts and the way that they moved and decided she was probably naked under the silk. Jennifer spied the bag of ice and liquor in his hand.

"Wow, are you a sight for sore eyes. Come on in," she cried wide-eyed. As he stepped inside she closed the door quickly behind him and narrowed her eyes at him playfully. "You know, you're beginning to be a regular over here. The girls are going to start to talk."

"Let 'em," Holloway replied stepping into her room and setting down his load. Then he removed his field jacket and withdrew a small package wrapped in Christmas paper from his pocket and handed it to her.

"I wanted to give you this, JD. Merry Christmas." Holloway bent forward and kissed her softly on her lips. She kissed him back and then looked at him for a long moment, her eyes searching his.

"You've never done that before."

He reddened slightly. "It's Christmas."

"I know. It was nice." Then she changed the subject. "Can I open my present tonight?"

"I hoped you would."

She took her time, carefully untying the green bow and unwrapping the green and gold paper. It was a small box, though noticeably heavy. Slowly she raised the lid. On a bed of cotton was a small jade carving of a papasan with a wooden fishing pole that fit into a small hole drilled through his hands. She rubbed her fingers over the smooth cool finish of the stone.

"Oh, Bagger. It's beautiful. I can't believe you did this. You're really thoughtful."

"Do you honestly like it?"

"Oh, are you kidding? I love it." She reached her neck forward and kissed him again. He reacted by pulling her toward him and holding her close. She had the fragrance of soap and it intoxicated his senses. His hands felt the warmth of her back through the thin kimono. Sensing the moment, he opened his lips and tilted his head toward her, but she stiffened slightly and offered her cheek instead.

"Bagger, wait. Don't. I'm not ready for this."

He relaxed his hands. "What's wrong, JD?"

"It's too soon. I'm just not ready."

"It was only a kiss." He paused for a moment. "You're still in love with Magic, is that it?"

"No. That's not it. You are very special to me, Clay, but I'm not ready for more romance right now. I can't just jump from one guy to another like that. I'm not Beth Kisha. I'm me. That's not me."

"I know you're not Beth. I never thought that you were. But you're saying you don't still love him. Are you telling me that if you got a letter from Magic tomorrow saying he'd been lost in the desert or something and that he still wants to marry you that you'd tell him no?"

"That's not going to happen, Clay. So what's the point of asking? Look, you don't understand. You really don't."

"Then talk to me so I will. I think you're still hurting inside. That's the problem, isn't it?"

"Well, there's a couple of things really," she said turning away. "Number one, I really am not hurting inside. Not the way you think. Yes, he hurt me, but I think I'm about over that. Right now I'm just angry. I'm angry because I let him use me. I allowed someone to use me and hurt me just so he could get what he wanted with absolutely no consideration for me. That's not going to happen to me again. I've never had someone intentionally hurt me to that degree before and I can't say I like it much."

"I'm not planning on hurting you, JD. Trust me. You can't go through the rest of your life refusing to get close to anyone just because they might hurt you."

She seated herself on a high backed bamboo chair and pulled her kimono close around her. "No, I can't. And I won't. But Beth was right when she said this isn't real over here. There's not really the time or the atmosphere to get to know anyone the way you should. The way you would if you were in a regular setting in a regular job. If you meet someone you like over here, you see them so infrequently that it makes the times you are together seem more intense and you automatically try to make the most of them. I think it makes you imagine things that aren't really there. It creates unnatural pressures. If a guy is in the field or on a different compound or if he's going home in three months it makes you feel more desperate to get together. What the hell kind of a way is that to really establish a relationship? No. I'm not going to rush into anything like that again. No way."

Holloway turned away and stared at the door.

"Oh, Bagger. Hey, look at me." Hesitantly, he turned as she walked to him and wrapped her arms around him and spoke softly in his ear. He felt the softness of her breasts pushing into his chest and her sweet warm breath against the side of his face. "You are very very important to me. I need and enjoy your friendship more than I think you will ever know. I'm so glad you came over tonight, on Christmas Eve. I think the world of you and I love you being here with me. I love my Christmas present. Please, please understand. Don't try to change our relationship right now. Let's just stay the way we are, OK? Please?"

It wasn't easy, but he smiled at her. "I'm not going to push you. Take your time. I'm not going anywhere." He turned and began fumbling with the glasses on her dresser. "How about a drink?"

"I'd love one. Pour it while I comb out my hair." She smiled broadly at him. "Thanks." She pecked him on the cheek and turned away. "You know, just in case I didn't tell you, I really appreciate the way you played Santa Claus at the orphanage on Tuesday. You were magnificent. The children adored you. Some of them never stopped looking at you the whole time you were there. Their eyes were as big as saucers."

"I never thought I'd say this, but I actually enjoyed it. Those little kids were really something, weren't they? Did you see how some of them saw the hair on my forearms and pushed up my sleeve so they could touch it? That was great. They'd never seen hairy arms before."

JD laughed aloud. "Do you think they ever wondered why you had a white beard and black hair on your forearms."

"Nah. It's just one of those magical mysteries of Christmas." Holloway reflected briefly about how magical JD had looked when she played with several of the little tikes. He had never seen her with children before. She was a natural. "Are your feet still hurting?"

"Are they? God! How can you live in those damn boots?"

He handed her the drink. She accepted it and swirled the dark liquid around in the glass watching the ice cubes move in a whirlpool pattern. "Combat boots are fairly comfortable once they're broken in," he replied. "That's the key. Listen, I'll tell you what. Just because it's Christmas, I'm going to request that you allow me to take one physical liberty with your body which will also be a special present on a one time basis only."

She looked at him suspiciously. "I thought you already gave me my present. What's this one?"

He sat on the edge of the bed. "Put your feet up here on my lap. I'll rub them for you."

"Really?" she squealed. "You're really going to rub my feet? You highlighted my hair and now you're going to massage my feet? God, what a friend you are."

"Always have been, always will be." Holloway winked at her, cracked his knuckles, and grabbed at her right foot.

CHAPTER 26

New Year's Eve promised to be decidedly livelier than Christmas Eve the week before. Christmas had been a time of reflection and memories of home and of other Christmas' of earlier times, when brightly wrapped presents were piled high under the tree, and Aunt Hilda and Uncle Bill came to visit, and the house smelled like turkey all day. Mr. Yun, the Club manager, had tried hard to make the O Club seem like home. A beautiful spruce tree stood eight feet high in the corner of the bar area, complete with strings of colored lights and ornamental balls and tinsel. He had wrapped a few empty boxes for effect and placed them on a white sheet under the tree. Wreaths hung in two or three of the windows. Kendall Stover had received a miniature Christmas tree from Mary Lou. He'd kept it in his room for a few days and finally decided to bring it to the Club. It continued to adorn the bar at the opposite end of the room from where the big tree sat.

But Christmas was over. New Year's Eve was upon the 8/18th. For many Americans, this holiday represents a time of merriment and alcoholic consumption. This was something that came naturally to the members of the Camp Wynne Officers Club anyway and the fact that it was New Year's Eve only served to heighten their natural impulses. Most of the men looked forward to the night with great anticipation. Village Honcho had been assigned the mission of providing some sort of entertainment. Having already established his reputation as a man of action in obtaining a new heating system while stationed in the middle of nowhere, he was determined to enhance his image with a successful New Year's Eve blast.

Village Honcho's first act had been to obtain the services of a Korean rock and roll band. Spreading flyers throughout the Division area, he had offered one hundred and twenty thousand won, which was top dollar, for the four or five piece group that was yet to be selected. In American money that amounted to forty bucks. Naturally he would hold tryouts in the village, selecting a wooden shack called "The 007 Lounge" for the auditions. Three bands competed for the honor. Village Honcho had given them advance notice of what songs he expected to hear, all of which had a decided Motown flair. When the day for tryouts arrived, he assumed his position at a table in a corner of the room with two reasonably attractive kimchi critters and a bottle of

Johnnie Walker Red Label. He would later admit that the Scotch and the women had probably combined to relax him sufficiently enough so that the last band sounded noticeably better than the first and perceptively better than the second. At any rate, Village Honcho was suitably impressed and awarded the verbal contract to the third group, which called themselves "The Four Kinks".

In addition to the band, Village Honcho worked with Mr. Yun to organize an unusual yet sumptuous menu, which included shrimp, crab, salmon, venison, roast beef, and a smattering of dog meat that he had mixed in with some of the other selections. Later, of course, he would steadfastly deny that he had any knowledge whatsoever about including the dog in the menu, even though he was never able to keep a straight face whenever he was approached on the subject. Additionally, he ordered a variety of cheeses, stuffed mushrooms, a selection of rolls and crackers, and an assorted relish tray. In an amazing display of resourcefulness, he was able to obtain a case of French champagne, which he somehow had flown into Kimpo through some of his contacts in the US Air Force. He ordered Mr. Yun to procure some suitable stainless steel buckets so that the champagne could be served properly chilled. To add a bit of formality to the occasion he established a dress code that mandated suits or class A's for the men and dresses for any women that might attend. Every officer on the compound had already had one or more suits tailor made in the village for twenty or twenty-five dollars each and this provided an opportunity to wear one. Always included in the price of the suit was a choice of labels to sew inside the jacket. The Korean tailor shops routinely offered names like Brooks Brothers or Sax Fifth Avenue. Naturally there was no connection whatsoever between those companies and the Korean tailors, but international business and trade restrictions being virtually nonexistent in the Korean boondocks, the tailors simply sewed in any label they selected.

The subject of women had been open. All of the Doughnut Dollies had been invited to several Division and Brigade parties. Along with the invitations came strong hints from Karen about attendance. Many of the girls, Jennifer Dodge among them, preferred to stay at Camp Wynne where they felt comfortable with the 8/18th and resisted going elsewhere. Still, as representatives of the American Red Cross, they had social obligations and in the end were ordered to attend the senior officers' parties. Colonel Nordstrum, Major Vogel, and Major Gentile would also be absent from the compound that evening. That was the best news any of the young lieutenants had heard in quite a while. Major Vogel had quickly found a variety of ways to become detested by virtually every other officer on the compound. With both the Doughnut Dollies and senior officers absent, it left the door wide open for Village Honcho to do what he and Ed O'Connell and some of the other officers preferred to do anyway, which was invite some of the better looking kimchi critter residents of Sonyu-ri to the New Year's party. At least with the business girls being present the men were assured of starting 1970 with a bang if they had five dollars in their pocket and were so disposed. With the exception of O'Connell, who had found a yobo soon after his arrival, the other officers of the Battalion had not the foggiest idea how to establish a female guest list. Officers were not permitted to go into the village, other than on the main street, and most had little actual contact with the business girls. Many of the men were married and had mixed emotions about inviting what were primarily a bunch of hookers to the Club for a party. Not surprisingly then, even the men who did want to request that some Korean girls be present were happy to turn that duty over to Village Honcho who promised to line up ten of the best looking kimchi critters he could find and have them arrive en masse shortly before nine o'clock on New Year's Eve.

Officers began filing into the O Club around eight, particularly the hungry ones or those who were fearful that all of the best food would be gone before they could get their fair share. Perhaps it was the fact that everyone was wearing suits. Perhaps it was the fact that it was New Year's Eve. Perhaps it was the fact that several unfamiliar, loose, and immoral women would be arriving a bit later in the evening. But whatever the reason, the entire compliment of officers were conducting themselves like rather nervous businessmen, standing quietly in small groups, politely sipping drinks like whiskey sours and old fashions, and eating from small plates. The band had not yet arrived. Looking harried, Village Honcho burst through the swinging doors to inspect the arrangements. Seeing the staid atmosphere he stopped short.

"What the hell is this?" he cried. "A wake? Mr. Yun, get that stereo cranked up. The girls are going to take one look at this crew, think somebody died, and go home. Somebody ring the bell. Let's get somethin' going in heah!"

The music helped. So did the three bell ringers that followed Village Honcho's outburst. If there was one thing the 8/18th knew how to do it was ring the bell. Holloway noticed the band arriving through the door into the ping-pong room and was impressed by the quality of the equipment that they began bringing onto the small stage. Slowly the atmosphere loosened and the voice level increased. A ringing of the telephone on the bar pierced the hum of voices. Mr. Buster answered it and motioned to Village Honcho who listened for a moment then replaced the phone in its cradle and turned back to the crowd. "Anybody know what KMAG stands for?"

"Sure," answered Bill Grant. "Korean Military Advisory Group."

"Wrong!" shot back Village Honcho. "It stands for Korean Mooses At the Gate. They're here. We need to go out and escort them in. Give me nine volunteers." Three men tentatively stepped forward. "Come on, you guys. What's the matter here? You asked me to get some women. I can't do everything. We're supposed to have one escort for each of these broads. You don't have to marry the girl, just bring her through the gate. Bagger, come on. Benning, you too. Hostileman, let's go."

Somewhat reluctantly several of those present moved out into the hallway, plucked their coats from the hooks on the wall, and stepped outside. It was brisk, though not as cold as it had been at Christmas and the small amount of snow that covered the ground had been packed down hard. Rick Benning, the twenty-one year old Survey Officer, walked along side of Holloway as they covered the short distance to the main gate. "What do you think, Bagger? You gonna get laid tonight?"

"Doubtful."

"How come? I mean why not. It's New Year's. You ain't even married."

"We'll see, Rick. You never now. I might find the love of my life tonight. But somehow I doubt it."

"Who the hell is talkin' about love? I'm just talking about a little pogee. Some of the things these girls do are outrageous, man. Most of 'em don't have much in the way of boobs, of course, but you never can tell. You might get lucky there too. Village Honcho knows what he's doing. I'll bet he'll have some real lookers. We might all get lucky." The clump of men crossed the wooden bridge and reached the main gate a moment later. Ahead they could see a group of girls huddling near the guard shed stamping their feet and pulling their coats tightly around their necks. They seemed excited. It was rare that any of the local business girls were invited to the Officers' Club and the lure of extra money was enticing. The Korean gate guard spoke briefly with Village Honcho and began counting the number of officers that accompanied him. It seemed close enough. He waved the girls through.

The first critter through the gate wore a camel colored wool coat with a rabbit fur collar. Her eyes locked onto Holloway immediately and she ran toward him and reached for his arm. "Hey, you numba one GI. You handsome. I think I likee you." She smiled broadly at him, blinking her mascara-shrouded eyes complete with enormous false eyelashes. Holloway could smell her breath in his face. She smelled like bubble gum.

"Hi, what's your name?"

"Cherry. I numba one girl. You likee me?"

"Sure. I'm enchanted actually. Can I escort you to the Club?" They began walking in its direction.

Cherry looked somewhat puzzled. "You likee me? We go your hoochee now?"

"Well, no. I thought perhaps we could have some hors d'oeuvres and a cocktail. You know. Just get to know one another. Are you current on the international political situation in Southeast Asia?" He could hear snickering behind him. Holloway turned and looked at Kendall Stover who was walking two feet behind with a Korean girl, who had dyed her hair blond, hanging onto his arm. "What are you laughing at, Baron?"

"You. What kind of bullshit are you trying to lay on this poor girl?"

"Hey, I'm just trying to make conversation. It is our first date, you know. Who's your buddy?"

"This is Gloria. Gloria, say hello to Bagger."

"Hallo, Bagga," she said smiling. She had a finely featured face with high cheekbones and thin lips. She batted her eyelashes at him several times and continued to look at him. Holloway felt Cherry tug hard on his arm and saw her glare sternly at Gloria. She spoke rapidly in Korean at the other girl. Then she looked at Holloway.

"Hey," Cherry said pulling his face back toward her. "You my boyfriend tonight."

"Cherry, let me be clear about something here. I'm walking you back to the Club because they needed someone to do it. I am not your boyfriend. You got a grip on that?"

"Moola." Clearly Cherry's command of the English language was limited to the vocabulary and phrases most needed in her line of work. Much of what Holloway was saying to the girl was beyond her capacity to understand, although certainly her command of the English language was far superior to Holloway's lingual abilities in Korean.

Reaching the door to the Club, Stover tugged open the main door and allowed the two young women to enter. Their hesitancy reminded Stover of Alice in Wonderland as they gazed upward toward the ceiling and peeked around corners. Their coats were hung on hooks and they were shown into the bar area where the remainder of the officers waited. As the two girls moved hesitantly into the room the two tables of hors d'oeuvres immediately caught their attention and they raced hurriedly to them, stopping then to look questioningly back at their escorts to gain permission before taking any. Holloway gestured with an open hand.

"Sure. Go ahead. Help yourself. No sweat."

By this time most of the Korean guests had lined up at the tables and were heaping the enticing looking food onto their plates. After stepping away from the table they attacked the newfound feast hungrily with their fingers.

"Baron, I can see that the S-4 appears to have had an oversight in his planning for this shindig," Holloway observed.

"What's that, Bagger?"

"There's no chopsticks on the table and quite obviously our guests are not accustomed to using forks."

"Oh, well. As long as the supply of napkins holds out I'm not concerned. What do you want to drink?"

"Why ask me? You should be asking your date."

"Hey, Bagger. I can see that she's obviously more interested in getting into your drawers rather than mine." Stover smiled as Gloria walked back toward him biting into a hunk of salmon on rye and covered with onions. "Gloria, what can I get for you to drink?"

"Huh?" Gloria replied, her mouth full of food.

"Drink? Drink eeso?"

"Ahhh. Neh. Scotchee soda."

"You're a Scotch drinker? Great. I knew we had something in common. Do you prefer Johnnie Walker or Dewar's?"

"Huh?"

"Never mind. Johnnie Walker it is. Bagger? You want bourbon and soda?" Holloway nodded. "And your fiancée?" Cherry had stood patiently bye.

"Rum and Cokee."

"Got it. Mr. Yun!" he called as he sauntered off in the direction of the bar. Holloway watched Cherry finish her plate and set it aside. He surveyed the room. Hostileman was sitting at a table in the corner grinning widely at one of the kimchi critters who was perched very close to him and whose faces were separated by less than a foot. Rick Benning was attempting to teach another of the girls to do something resembling the "frug" on the dance floor. Ruminski stood quietly by himself at the end of the bar posed in his normal stone like expression. Smiling to himself, Holloway wondered if Ruminski had ever considered part time work as a statue. O'Connell and his yobo were talking loudly, her actions animated. They seemed to be arguing over something. The doors to the west end of the bar swung open and Tom Courtney strolled in wearing his new glen plaid suit which he had picked up at the Playboy Tailor Shop three days earlier.

"Hey, Tom. Where's your date?"

"Holloway, I've been here twelve and a half months. In two weeks I'll be home. I've waited this long. I reckon I kin wait a little longer. I think I'll just be dateless tonight, though I might be tempted to dance with this little sweetheart of yours once or twice if you let me." He pinched her playfully on her cheek and walked by as she giggled. Kendall Stover returned with his hands full of drinks and passed them out.

"So, Gloria, who do you think is going to win the Super Bowl this year?"

"Huh?"

"That's what I thought. Bagger, I'm running out of things to say here. This may be a somewhat socially difficult evening."

"Well, drink up. We'll think of something." He lit a Winston and blew smoke toward the ceiling. Cherry was watching him. "Would you like a cigarette?" he said holding the pack toward her and shaking it. She took three, putting one between her lips and two down the front of her dress. "Cute," Holloway observed, holding out his lighter.

Attempts at small talk were largely ignored. "The Four Kinks" were doing a reasonably good job of providing musical entertainment and any doubt about whether their amplifiers and drums worked had been immediately erased. The Korean girls were throwing themselves around the dance floor with wild abandon, their long dark hair soaring through the air as they dipped and spun, their mini dresses riding high on fishnet clad thighs. Dancing made everyone thirsty. Liquor flowed freely, loosening the inhibitions of almost everyone. Hostileman started past Stover on his way to the john.

"Hey, Hostileman. You seem to be getting pretty close to that chick. Are you engaged yet?"

"Nah. I found out we're related. She's from the South too."

"The South? You mean like Georgia?"

"No. Like South Korea, as in south of the DMZ." Hostileman laughed and walked past. He left the men's room a minute later passed Ruminski on the way in. Once inside, Ruminski immediately assumed the position in front of the single urinal that was mounted on the wall next to the open commode. Barely had he unzipped his trousers when Gloria walked in, lifted her skirt, plopped herself on the john next to him, and began chatting. Embarrassed, Ruminski jerked up his zipper and stalked out of the room clamoring for Mr. Yun. Once outside the door he immediately saw the Club waitress, Miss Soh.

"Miss Soh, I want you to explain to these women that there are two rest rooms in this club. One for the men and one for the women. They are not interchangeable. Will you please explain that to them?"

"Yes, Lieutenant Ruminski. You see, in Korea many times we have only one. We both share. Same-o, same-o."

"Not in here we don't. Just tell them! Tell them all!"

But instead, Miss Soh put her hand in front of her mouth to unsuccessfully stifle a grin. Her short stature had placed her line of vision fairly low on Ruminski's body and she had immediately observed what Ruminski had not. From across the room, however, it had not escaped the view of Kendall Stover, who instantly saw an opportunity to embarrass his former boss in the DMZ. The timing was perfect. The band had just finished a song and the room was quiet.

"Hey, Ruminski!" Stover called loudly. "Can't you wait until a little later in the evening before you let that one eyed bearded grass snake out of your zipper? Go on. Tuck it back in for a while. You trying to impress Miss Soh or what?"

By this time the attention of everyone in the bar had been drawn to Ruminski. Miss Soh was now doubled over, laughing hysterically. Ruminski was just standing in the middle of the room still failing to comprehend what was so funny. Dismayed, he looked downward as everyone else was already doing. Protruding from the top of his fly was eight inches of white cotton material. In his haste, he had zipped his shirttail into the zipper so that much of it stuck straight out of the front of his pants. "Oh, shit!" he muttered, turning away and stepping back toward the men's room. As he reached for the door handle, the door flew open as Cherry had completed her business and was on the way out. The door struck Ruminski solidly in the chest. The crowd roared. Ruminski staggered backwards a few steps, swore softly, and then left the room.

Kendall Stover was red faced and was having trouble breathing. "Bagger," he gasped. "You gotta tip your date five bucks. I don't know what she did to him in there, but she deserves five bucks whatever it was." Holloway grinned and nodded.

The band began to play. The songs were getting slower now. Many of the kimchi critters were dragging the Americans onto the dance floor and slow dancing with them. Holloway and Cherry joined in. It became a dance unequaled in his young memory. They moved together only a moment before she somehow was able to wrap both of her slender legs around his and snuggle her crotch against his thigh. Soon she placed her open mouth against his ear and began licking it. He could smell the onions.

"We go your hoochee now?" she panted.

"Well, no. I don't think so."

She began rubbing herself up and down his leg. Harder and faster she moved, her pelvic gyrations recalling memories of an oversexed cocker spaniel his family had owned in his youth. Increasingly, Holloway had the sensation that the girl was trying to suck his upper thigh inside of her warm body. Frantically, her hands began scratching his back. She was pressing her small breasts hard into his chest. "We go your hoochee now?" she asked again. At last she had succeeded in arousing him and he didn't want to be aroused.

"No. Let's sit down and have another drink."

"You no likee me? I pretty girl. I makee you feel numba one. We go your hoochee now."

"Look, you don't understand. I'm really not into this tonight, OK? Why don't you find somebody else here? Hey, wait a minute. Where's Baron?" He spied his friend leaning against the end of the bar. Gloria appeared to be stuck to him like a snail on the glass wall of an aquarium. Her left hand was stroking his chest and her right fondled his neck and ears. Their faces were only a few inches apart. Holloway watched as they turned to leave.

"Baron! Wait up." Holloway strode quickly to his side. "What are you doing?"

Stover looked guilty. "You know. She's got me turned on."

"Listen, man. You've had a few pops here and it's New Year's and you got this critter rubbing herself all over you and I know you're just dying to find out if she's a natural blond. I understand. But I guarantee you tomorrow morning, even if you're lucky enough not to have the clap, you are gonna feel like shit about screwing this broad. You know you are."

"Yeah, I know. But goddamn it, Bagger, I'm horny. It's been five months."

"Baron, I'm telling you. I know how you feel about Mary Lou. If you do this you're gonna regret it. Now, that's all I'm gonna say. You're a big boy." He stepped back.

"Hey, Bagga!" It was Gloria. Cherry stood behind her. "What's a matta?"

"Look, Gloria. I think both of you are great girls. You're a lot of fun and really swell dancers and everything. But do me a favor. Here's five dolla MPC for each of you. You don't even have to take your clothes off, OK? Just try to find somebody else to score with tonight." He handed each of them a bill. Then he turned to his friend. "Come on, Baron. Let's step outside and get some fresh air." Stover nodded. Holloway put his hand on his shoulder and together they walked toward the doorway. The blast of cold air on their faces awakened and refreshed them. Together they stood in the darkness making small talk until finally they were uncomfortably cold. Then they returned to the bar.

The population inside had shrunken noticeably. Several of the girls and their "dates" had disappeared, among them Cherry and Gloria. It was only 10:30 and the band was taking a break. "Do you think we hurt Ruminski's feelings a little while ago, Bagger?"

"He was kind of embarrassed, but what the hell."

"He's not a bad guy. Just a little tight assed once in a while. Let's go over to the Q and drag him back here. Come on." They walked back outside and quickly covered the one hundred feet of sidewalk to the old BOQ. Ruminski hardly ever stayed over night in his room at Camp Wynne since he was attached to whatever infantry battalion was on line in the DMZ, but he had been granted permission to spend a two-day weekend at Camp Wynne because of the holiday. They walked into the hallway and toward the last room in the corridor. Ruminski's door was closed but there was no padlock in the hasp. No light shown from under the door. "Goddamn guy's asleep already. It's New Year's Eve. Let's go to his hooch and wake him up." Kendall Stover pivoted on his left foot and drove the heel of his right into the wooden door, driving it forward. Holloway charged into the room reaching for the light switch.

"Ruminski, wake your ass up and get back to the club!" clamored Holloway. He stopped abruptly; stunned by the feeling that he had just committed a major fax paux. In the harsh glare of the overhead light, Ruminski laid naked on top of his bunk, a small nude body curled face down between his legs, her dyed blond hair spread out upon his midsection. His head rested in lap of a second naked girl with large false eyelashes.

"Oooops." cried Holloway. "Sorry, Dave. Myan_humnida." He started retreating from the room until he recognized the girls. "Hey, wait a minute. You can't do this. These are our dates! Baron, he's stolen our dates."

"You assholes! Get out of my room. You guys are enough to piss off Santa Claus!"

Stumbling, laughing so hard they could hardly see, Holloway and Stover backed out of the room and out into the cold. "Bagger, I don't think he's ever going to talk to us again for as long as he lives. I'm really glad we don't work for him any more."

"Man, this is unbelievable. He's always so straight. Then he winds up not with one josan, but with two of them at the same time. I wish I had my camera." The two men glanced quickly at each other. "Nah. We couldn't. Well, anyway, you found out the answer to one of your questions."

"What's that?"

"Gloria isn't a natural blond."

"Yeah, you're right." Stover shrugged. "Somehow I didn't think she would be."

By eleven thirty the Club's population had swelled to its highest level of the evening. Even the officers who had chosen not to be present earlier had arrived to insure that they were there for the stroke of midnight. Village Honcho had ordered the champagne prepared and trays containing crystal goblets already dotted the room. Party hats and noisemakers were distributed and bowls of confetti strategically placed. Sweeper jumped onto the bar and gave the official countdown. At the stroke of midnight he leaped from the bar and while in flight grabbed the bell clapper and slammed it home before landing on the floor. Mass cheers arouse from the crowd and "The Four Kinks" began a rendition of Auld Lang Syne. Confetti hung in the air like an indoor blizzard and the noisemakers cranked and whistled. The kimchi critters went about the room offering kisses to whoever wanted them, though many of the men declined, unsure of where the girls mouths had been in the last hour or so. Suddenly a new sound reached the room. In the distance was the distinct chatter of automatic weapons fire. It was not unusual to hear something like that, but it seemed much more intense than usual. It reminded everyone of exactly where they really were.

"Somebody's catching some action," Stover observed.

"Nah," said a familiar voice behind him. "They do that every New Year's Eve. It's called a mad minute. Everybody on the DMZ fence lets go with all the firepower they have right at midnight. It's their way of celebrating."

Kendall Stover turned at the sound of the familiar voice. It was Ruminski. "Happy New Year, Dave." Stover offered his hand. Ruminski glared at him a moment and then accepted it. Then he and Kendall Stover and Clay Holloway began laughing uncontrollably.

A special Korean escort had been arranged to meet the kimchi critters at the main gate at twelve thirty and walk them into the village, since the standard curfew in the country was midnight. Neither Holloway nor Stover accompanied the small group of men that walked the girls to the gate, but instead leaned against the bar surveying the room. Many of the men seemed in no hurry to leave. It was New Year's Eve. You can't go to bed at 12:30 on New Year's Eve.

"Hey, Rick, how'd you do tonight?" asked Holloway as Lieutenant Benning walked by. "Did you find the girl of your dreams?"

"Yeah, in a sense. That little critter made some of mah dreams come true, I'll tell you that. Anything I wanted."

"You get her phone number?"

"Aw, Bagger now you know these critters don't have telephones."

"Oh, yeah. I forgot," Holloway chided. "Hey, now that we've got the mooses out of the way, let's liven things up a bit. I've got an idea. Help me see if these bar stools unscrew from the bases. Let's get a contest going. Baron, order us two pitchers of beer."

"Two pitchers of beer? Who the hell can drink two pitchers of beer at this point?"

"We're not going to drink them," grunted Holloway as he found the release for the bar stool and unscrewed the circular vinyl top. "Get everybody over here. Two teams. Tell them to take off their jackets."

Tom Courtney sauntered over followed by the Owl. "Holloway, what in the hell have you got in mind here?"

"Speedboat racing."

Courtney half closed his eyes and turned his head to look at Kendall Stover in mock disgust as Holloway succeeded in unscrewing a second bar stool. "Speedboat racing the man says. OK, we give up. How does it work?"

"Have you divided into two teams yet?" Holloway asked as he set the second seat on the floor, loosened his tie and rolled up his sleeves. The crowd around him had enlarged to about ten. He counted with his finger. "OK, we're even. Half on that side, half on this. Now watch. I'll go first." He picked up a pitcher of beer and walked across the marble floor bending at the waist and pouring beer in a straight line along the length of the floor. Then he set an empty beer can on the floor about ten feet from the wall where he had begun. "Here's the starting point. You can't run past this." The others watched him closely, still not comprehending what he was doing. "OK. Here we go." With that he hoisted one of the vinyl covered bar stool seats, put his back against the wall, sprinted forward, and dove onto the seat like a boy flopping onto his sled. The seat slid easily along the river of beer that coated the marble floor. "No hands," Holloway yelled as he laid on his stomach, placed his hands behind his back, and continued to skid along the floor's surface. Finally he came to a halt about ten feet from the wall on the other side of the room. "OK, mark it!" he called out. Sweeper stepped forward to line up a Coke can with where Holloway had stopped. "Who's next?" he called out as he looked around. He didn't have to wait long. Bear Buckner was already holding the other bar seat. The stocky dark haired Bravo Battery Commander stepped forward.

"Two more weeks and I am out of this place and you know what? I am really gonna miss it." With that he backed against the wall, took three giant strides, and dove onto the stool, sliding gleefully across the floor, coming to a halt two feet short of Holloway's mark. Behind him, neckties, and in some cases, shirts were being stripped off and sleeves were being rolled as other men surged to line up and establish wagers. Eric Auslander tossed his shirt in a corner, relieved Holloway of his bar stool, and waited his turn. Four pitchers of beer later and an hour after the speedboat race had begun, a bare-chested Rick Benning won the contest in front of five of the Doughnut Dollies who had returned from their other commitments, by sliding all of the way across the floor and with his arms at his sides, slamming his head into the wall at the other side of the room. It was the second time he had knocked himself cold that month.

*   *   *

Ten miles north of Camp Wynne in a wooden framed building with a wooden framed futon lay First Lieutenant Yoon Kim Lee. The automatic weapons firing almost an hour before had awakened him. At first he had been alarmed. Then he remembered that to the Americans it was their New Year's Eve. They always acted like children on New Year's Eve. Once awakened, however, Yoon was unable to recapture sleep. He lay on his back staring at the ceiling, yet seeing nothing. The firing had only served to remind him how much he hated the Americans on the other side of the DMZ.

Lieutenant Yoon no longer led a commando team. He had been reassigned as an assistant staff officer in the division intelligence section. Though not officially a demotion, it had been made clear to him following his return from the South, that his superiors were not at all pleased with his performance. Much to Yoon's credit, he had been completely honest in his report, leaving out not the slightest detail. That was his duty. He had not been blamed for the loss of his two men, nor the journal nor photographs they had carried. There had been a lot of questions about their deaths, but in the end it had been written off as simply bad luck. However, the questions had certainly not ended there. His theft of the Redeye was at first dismissed as impossible, but within the week agents in the South easily confirmed his claim. The story that a Redeye had been stolen and then recovered had spread like wild fire throughout the Second Division's area of operations. That made the subsequent loss of the weapon by Lieutenant Yoon a more bitter pill to swallow. If Yoon had been successful in getting the missile to the North, it would have been an astonishing coup that would have elevated the stature of the North Korean government to new heights in the Communist world. The People's Republic of Vietnam, the Soviets, and even the Chinese would have been greatly in their debt. The weapon would have also had a potentially major effect on the war in Southeast Asia. Yoon would well have become a national hero. But it had all turned to dust. Yoon's decision to attempt to knife the American guard had been viewed as astonishingly poor judgment. He was second-guessed by everyone in authority, with the conventional argument being that Yoon should simply have bypassed the guard and the tunnel entrance and traveled the additional five kilometers to tunnel number 10, the location of which he had been thoroughly briefed on prior to his departure. It was repeatedly stressed to him that nothing should have been more important than 1) returning home with the captured Redeye and 2) keeping the tunnels from being discovered. Secondarily, the intelligence information that Yoon had collected was also considered something not to be risked for the sake of killing a guard. But fairly or not, Yoon had been blamed for botching almost all of those things.

Three months earlier, tunnel number 9 had been lost in the middle of the DMZ when the engineers had come too close to the surface. That accident had alerted the Americans to the existence of the tunnels in general. While they may have suspected such a thing earlier, there had never been any evidence of their existence. But as bad as that loss had been, now tunnel number 8 was gone as well, since a month after Yoon's return the Americans had somehow found and dynamited the passage that Yoon had used both to enter and return from the South. Almost eighteen months of hard work had been destroyed. Rightly or wrongly, General Yang had blamed that discovery directly on Lieutenant Yoon, believing that his disappearance in the face of the Americans had triggered extensive searches of the immediate area. That left only one operational tunnel in the entire Group sector. The primary reason for the tunnels construction had been to give the army the capability of pouring significant numbers of men into the area behind the DMZ whenever the government determined that the appropriate time had come. That capability was now reduced by two thirds. In reply, General Yang had already ordered work to begin on three additional tunnels.

Yes, the fight with the two Americans had cost Yoon his opportunity for fame and the gateway to a truly distinguished military career. Moreover, it had come very close to costing the man his life. But worse than that, in fact dramatically worse, in the eyes of Lieutenant Yoon, last week General Yang had been overheard to say that Yoon would be an old man before he ever directed anything again, with the possible exception of the planting of the spring rice crop. But, Yoon had also heard that a new tactic was being seriously considered to be used against the Americans. Though he had not been provided any details, he knew for a fact that assassination teams were being trained with the goal of killing American officers and senior noncommissioned officers in the areas south of the Imjin, where security was lax. He wanted a chance to be part of those teams. Yoon knew how to kill. If he could join them, he felt confident that he could redeem himself. He continued to stare toward the ceiling and pray desperately that it would happen.

CHAPTER 27

"Bridgecrossings" were unique to the 8/18th Artillery. That may have been because few other compounds in the Division area had a bridge leading from the compound itself to the main gate. None of the current members of the Battalion were quite sure exactly when Bridgecrossings had begun, but over time they had become deeply mired in the Battalion's tradition. Bridgecrossings were offered as an official farewell to every officer, warrant officer, or senior noncommissioned officer (E-7 or above) on the day he left for home. Attendees were anyone who wished to say good-bye as the departing soldier walked slowly down the receiving line of individuals who had gathered on the gravel street in front of the Battalion Headquarters building. As the honoree sauntered by, the loud speakers mounted on battalion headquarters blared "Leaving On A Jet Plane" by Peter, Paul, and Mary. Once reaching the end of the line where the Battalion Commander always stood, the honoree would offer his final salute, walk deliberately to the waiting 105mm howitzer, M101A1, which stood gleaming behind him and pull the lanyard, firing a blank round of the type normally reserved for artillery salutes for visiting dignitaries. The short timer's cane was then passed to the next man scheduled to leave and the honoree would turn, climb into a waiting jeep and be driven the twenty five miles to Kimpo airport and his red tailed silver winged Northwest Orient Boeing 707. January 30th was Tom Courtney's bridgecrossing. When he landed in the United States the next day, he would be honorably discharged from the United States Army.

Clay Holloway was having a difficult time dealing with Courtney's departure and as he watched his friend slowly approach down the line of well-wishers, he could feel a tightening in his throat. He glanced above Courtney's left breast pocket at the green and white ribbon that suspended the bronze emblem of the Army Commendation Medal, which had been awarded to Courtney ten minutes earlier in a private ceremony in Colonel Nordstrum's office. Holloway felt proud of the man who had commanded him and counseled him and coached him since that first day in the unit seven months earlier. Courtney was looming closer, walking slowly and chatting with almost everyone in the line, which included a large percentage of the men of Charlie Battery, all of the staff officers, the other battery commanders (with the exception of newly appointed Kendall Stover who had Alpha Battery north of the river at Firebase Wolverine), almost all of the Doughnut Dollies, and of course Colonel Nordstrum. Major Vogel had claimed to be obligated to business elsewhere and had not attended, though his disdain for lieutenants, especially those in positions of authority, was well understood.

Courtney stopped and shook hands with Kathy Kelsey who was weeping openly, her mascara running down her cold red cheeks. She pulled him close and kissed him warmly to the delight of the troops who cheered and clapped. She had always enjoyed his humor and warmth and would miss his friendship. The lump in Holloway's throat was growing larger as Courtney stood finally in front of him.

"Take care of the men, Bagger. Always take care of the men. If you don't, nobody else will. Remember that."

"Yes, Sir. I'll remember. And you take care of yourself, Tom. Say hello to Elaine and Tom Jr. for me. Maybe I'll see you in six months or so."

"I hope so. That farm in Tennessee will always be open to you. You'll have to stop by and go wild turkey hunting with me."

"I'd like that," Holloway stammered, caught up in the emotion of the moment. It was difficult for him to talk. He looked at the gravel below his feet, blinking his eyes as his friend continued down the line. Then it was over. Courtney saluted Colonel Nordstrum for the last time, bequeathed his short timer's stick to Ranger Brown, and walked to the howitzer. Everyone present knew the explosion of the blank round was coming, but it didn't make any difference. The entire compliment of onlookers seemed to leap three inches in the air when the ear shattering noise came. Courtney turned then and walked to where Shorty sat parked with the jeep engine idling. The vehicle puttered away, up and over the wooden bridge, past the guard shack, and into the ville.

Command of Charlie Battery had been passed to Second Lieutenant Holloway three days earlier as Courtney had begun his out-processing. The Unit Fund had been signed over and the multitude of details surrounding a change of command had been accomplished with the assistance of the S-1 and S-4 sections. Courtney had subjected Holloway to a last minute flurry of guidance and training about battery administration. Clay Holloway now found himself in the same position that he had discovered Courtney seven months earlier, namely being the sole officer in the unit. There were no immediate prospects for a new XO and the idea of having an Assistant Executive Officer, which the Table of Organization and Equipment said there was supposed to be, was not even worth discussing. Colonel Nordstrum had talked with him on two occasions and expressed every confidence in Holloway's ability to run the unit. The new Charlie Battery Commander was not alone in his lack of experience and knowledge. Command of Alpha and Bravo had been turned over to Second Lieutenants Robert Hoover and Kendall Stover one and two weeks earlier respectively, after Bear Buckner and Eric Auslander had departed. Three firing batteries. Three second lieutenants. Three new commanders.

As C-6 made its left turn onto the main street of the ville, and picked up speed, Clay Holloway turned quickly away, walked directly into his room in the "Ghetto," and closed the door behind him. Laying on his back on his bunk he stared at the ceiling for a long time, feeling isolated and alone. Then slowly he regained control over his wavering emotions. After a time and fully composed he left the room and walked through the cold January air to the Charlie Battery CP, his CP, and took his seat behind the Battery Commander's desk. He'd occupied that chair for the last three days, but still had not yet gained a full sense of comfort. The worn leather sofa where he had sat so many times and talked with Tom Courtney was across from him. Holloway couldn't help but wonder if he would ever get an Executive Officer and what he would be like and whether he, Holloway, could provide the right answers to give the man when he sat on the sofa and looked at Holloway and asked him questions. He had considered rearranging the room. Many new commanders liked to do that to signify a change in leadership. Holloway decided against it. There was a knock on the doorframe.

"Yeah, Top."

"Sir, we have got a few things here that we need to talk about whenever you get a chance."

"No time like the present. Come on in. Have a seat," Holloway offered as he waved toward the sofa. "Where do you want to start?"

"Well, Sir, first off C-17 is broke down on the road half way between here and the Turkey Farm. They're going to need a tow from Battalion cause it sounds like a broken leaf spring."

"OK, so tell Sergeant Brookins to get a hold of the Battalion wrecker and get it towed in."

"Sir, that's the problem. Brookins and Sergeant Timms at Battalion have been fuedin' and so when Brookins axed him for the wrecker, Timms told him to get fucked. Maybe you could speak to Lieutenant Beals."

"Yeah, I'll call him. Christ, you'd think two NCOs could at least be professional in a matter like this. Did he really tell him to 'get fucked' in exactly that language?"

"That's what Brookins told me."

"OK, what's next?"

"Last night about 2100 Sergeant Steele was passing by that deserted building behind the CP and he smelled grass being smoked. So he went around behind the building and came in through the back door. There was four GI's inside having a pot party. When Steele went in the back, they ran out the side. Then they split up and he chased one of them and almost caught him, but then Sergeant Steele slipped on the snow and fell, so the guy got away. He thinks it was Nichols, but he said he ain't sure enough to testify to that. But anyway I'm gonna talk to Nichols and let him know we're watching him. If we can bust those guys smoking shit I want to hit them hard."

"Well if Nichols was one it's a pretty good guess that Reid was in on it too. Those two are always together. And I'll bet Daniels was there also. Let their section chiefs know to just keep their eyes open."

"Yessir. OK, we now got six men at one time on the venereal disease roster, which includes another one of the cooks which means he can't work in the kitchen for two weeks."

"Put him on guard duty on the gate. I don't want him just lying around the barracks, that's for sure. We have somehow got to convince these people that if they're gonna be dipping their wicks in these kimchi critters they have got to be using protection. Is the condom box in the CP full of free rubbers?"

"No, Sir. It's empty again. The supply system has been out for a week."

"OK. I'll stop and see Proud Mary and pick up a few boxes. Also we've got to get the handrails fixed around that urinal we make the clap infected guys use in the latrine. Somebody pulled it out of the wall again even with those lead anchors you used."

"Having the clap is real painful, Sir. Some of those guys just be screaming and pullin' on that rail with all their strength when they're pissin' cause it hurts 'em so bad."

"It's hard to figure out why after they get it once they don't learn. You know Morton in Headquarters Company?" Holloway asked.

"I know who he is, Sir."

"I was talking to him the other day and you know what he told me? He said he's had the clap six times already and the dumb ass still has six months to go in country. Do you believe that? Six times!" Holloway shook his head slowly and continued. "So I asked him why he didn't use a rubber and you know what he said?" First Sergeant St. Clair shrugged his shoulders silently. "He said he couldn't because he was Catholic. Because he was Catholic! Then he told me that besides that the girls don't like them. I said so what if the girls don't like them. You're paying them for sex not the other way around. He just gave me that silly grin of his. Well, anyway, Top, tell Evans to schedule another VD class on next month's training schedule. I'll be the instructor. I'll show them the color slides with somebody's genitals eaten away by syphilis. That always shakes them up for a little while."

St. Clair smiled and jotted something into his little notebook. Then he looked back at his new BC. "Last thing, Sir. Stuart wants to see you."

"About what?"

"About gettin' married. I don't think you ought to let him."

"Do I have a choice?"

"Oh, yes, Sir. You're the commanding officer. If you don't give your consent he can't marry a Korean national. She's supposed to be pregnant. It's an old trick. These whores just want to get some GI to sign his name so they can go Stateside and be an American citizen. They're usually back out on the street six months after they get there."

"OK, send him over. I'll be here all morning. Is there any fresh coffee out there?"

"I'll get Shorty to get some from the mess hall. Oh, you know Shorty is DEROSing out of here in about ten days?"

"I didn't realize it was that soon. Well, I've got a new BC's driver picked out unless you can change my mind."

"Who's that?"

"Clinton Gash. He's conscientious and knows the area and he's a good wheelman. Besides that we work well together and I know I can trust him."

"Yes, Sir. That's a good choice. I'll tell him to ride shotgun with you and Shorty tomorrow."

"I'm not following you. Shotgun for what?"

Top chuckled. "Oh, Sir. You can't forget that. You can't start out being the BC by forgetting about payday. You've got to go down to RC#1 and pick up about $120,000 in MPC to pay the troops. I'll have Gash draw your .45 for you first thing tomorrow."

"Good, Top. Thanks for looking out for me."

"Who's looking out for you, Sir? I got plans for that money. I need to get paid too." He laughed out loud again. "OK, if Gash is going to take driving your jeep, who'll we get for an XO driver then?"

"What the hell's the difference? We don't have an XO and I don't think we're going to get one for a while. Thank God we're not going back north of the river for at least three or four weeks. Maybe something will happen by then."

St. Clair rose slowly from the sofa. "I hope so Lieutenant Holloway. For what it's worth, I'll try to assist you in any way that I can and I know Sergeant Wilson will too. Just remember Lieutenant Courtney was new once too." He waited for a reply that never came. "And I'll send Stuart in to talk about his wedding plans whenever he shows up."

"OK, Top. Thanks for everything."

＊　　　　＊　　　　＊

Clay Holloway was perched on one of the stools in the center of the bar. He was alone, both physically and mentally. Staring straight ahead he occasionally took small sips from his bourbon and soda. Eventually, Mr. Buster broke the silence. "Your chingo go home today?"

"Yeah, he did, Meesta Busta."

"You new Charlie BC?"

"That's what they tell me," Holloway replied firing up a Winston and puffing smoke rings toward the ceiling.

"You be good BC. I know. I see a lot of officer come here. I be here five year. Some no good. Some numba fucking ten. No goddamn good. I think you good man. You be good BC. Numba one."

Holloway's mouth eased slowly into a wan smile. "Thanks for the vote of confidence, Meesta Busta. I appreciate it."

At the sound of the swinging doors opening, Mr. Buster turned to his right. "Here's your girl friend. She make everything OK."

"She's really not my girl friend."

Buster cocked one eye at Holloway. "What eva you say." Buster moved to the other end of the bar as Jennifer Dodge slid onto the stool next to Holloway.

"You look like you lost your best friend," she quipped.

"You might say that. Does it really look that obvious?"

She raised her eyes and nodded. "Yes."

Holloway snorted through his nostrils, but said nothing. Finally she took his arm. "Let's sit in front of the fire. It looks inviting." They slid from the stools and walked to the back of the room where a worn and crinkled black leather sofa almost identical to the one in Holloway's office faced the fire, flanked on either side by two matching easy chairs. "So, you miss Tom already, don't you?" she asked as soon as they had seated themselves close to one another.

"Yes. There's no question about that."

"Look at the bright side, Bagger. Now you're a BC. You can move out of the "Ghetto" and into the new BOQ. You're the man in charge now. It's quite an honor. That's got to make you feel good, doesn't it?" she exclaimed loquaciously.

"I don't know, JD. I mean, yeah, everything you say is true. It does feel good to be a commander. I feel very proud of that fact, but at the same time it's a bit disconcerting. Look, I seem to tell you everything and I'll tell you this, but it's not to be repeated." She nodded her head deliberately in ascent. "This whole thing scares me a bit," he continued. "I'm not sure I'm really ready for it. Not in ability, I don't mean. I believe in myself. It's the experience factor and the knowledge, or lack there of. I really haven't been around here that long. Not counting the three months I was in the Z, I've only actually been in the Battery four months. I worry that I just don't know enough. I'm not sure I know what I should be doing on a daily basis."

You're a smart guy, Clay. You'll do fine. Just ask questions and use your head. Sweeper and Baron are in the same position. You know as much as they do. Maybe more. You'll do fine. I know you will. And I'll tell you something else. Your men respect you. They think you're fair. I've had some of them tell me that." She squeezed his arm and he turned to look at her. She winked at him and it made him smile.

"You're pretty good at making people feel good aren't you?" he asked playfully. "Maybe you should consider joining the Red Cross." He paused momentarily. "Speaking of which, why did you ever join the Red Cross? I mean why the hell does a good-looking intelligent young college graduate sign up to come to a place like this? Is it patriotism or a sense of caring or what?"

She laid her head against the back of the couch and looked reflectively at the ceiling for a moment before speaking. "Oh, it's not really patriotism. I don't know of any of the girls who came here just for that. There are a lot of things I guess. I wanted to get away from home for one."

"You went away to college you told me. Kent State you said," Holloway recalled.

"Sure, but I was still tied to home. Still in the nest. Dad was paying my bills and I always had to come home on holidays. Even during the summer breaks my parents would still insist on me being home at a certain time at night. I was always protected. Brought up to never do this or say that. There were always prescribed tasks, so to speak. So there was that and the desire for adventure. I thought that this would be something unusual in a far away land. I hope to travel a bit in the Far East before I go home, by the way. I'm thinking about Japan later this spring. Maybe Hong Kong or Bangkok too. And, of course, there's the guys," she added playfully. "I mean really. We twelve Doughnut Dollies are surrounded by 12,000 men. Simple mathematics says that's a thousand guys for each of us. That's not bad odds."

Holloway chuckled. "OK, aside from all the guys and forgetting entirely about Magic, has it been what you anticipated?" Holloway asked searchingly.

She turned toward him and pulled one leg under herself and sat on it. "Yes and no. There's no way I could actually have pictured all this ahead of time. For example, the class structure of the military is something that is completely new to me. The differences in the way that officers are treated compared to the enlisted men, for example. And the way that senior officers feel they can do almost anything they want." She looked around to see if anyone was in earshot and seeing no one continued. "I didn't tell you this, but one time when I was still in I Corps, I went to a dinner at the general's mess. I met a lieutenant colonel during the cocktail hour, who was married by the way, and he was acting very friendly and he was sort of funny for a while, you know. Well, when no one else is listening he comes right out and propositions me. I told him I really wasn't interested. Well, I guess he thought I was being coy because a bit later we're sitting next to each other at dinner and he whispers in my ear and propositions me again. I told him no again and I thought in no uncertain terms. But the next thing I know he takes my hand under the table and puts it in his crotch."

"What! What'd you do?"

"I was revolted by it. This guy was older than my father. So I jerked my hand away and turned away from him. Then I just sat there angry for a minute and composed myself. He wasn't saying anything and finally I reached over to whisper in his ear. He sort of grinned when he saw me leaning over," Jennifer recalled smiling at Holloway.

"And what did you tell him?"

"I told him that if he ever so much as looked at me again, I was going to walk over to the commanding general, tell him graphically what had just happened at the top of my lungs, walk out of the dinner, and write a long letter to his wife telling her just exactly what kind of an asshole she was married to." She folded her arms and sat back and looked at Holloway.

He wiped his brow dramatically. "I'll have to remember not to get you mad at me."

"I don't think you'll have to worry about that." She gave him her killer smile and resumed talking. "But anyway that was very unusual. Most of the time people treat us wonderfully. It's a real kick to visit the troops in the field. They seem to enjoy us. Perhaps it's because it's just something different, I don't know. But I do know this. I enjoy being with them most of the time, although often I feel like their big sister or even their mother. I can't help but notice how young many of the EM's are. They really are young, aren't they?"

"Most of them are draftees. I think their average age is nineteen. It is pretty young."

"It bothers me when I think of how many boys just like them are dying every week in Vietnam. I think it would be much more difficult for me if I was there. It's bad enough here."

"You once told me that it didn't matter if they sent you to Vietnam or Korea. I guess you've changed your mind."

"Well, I think I said that to you the first day we met when Beth introduced us. We know each other a lot better now and I have always felt that I can be open and comfortable with you," she added laying her hand on his shoulder. "You may not agree with me, but I know that you'll respect my opinion so I'll say something to you that I usually wouldn't say in a room full of military officers because I don't want to start an argument where I'm going to be horribly outnumbered. The truth is that I would not have gone to Vietnam. I made a deliberate decision not to go there. I asked for Korea for that reason. I really am not in favor of that stupid war. It's a waste. All that killing and no good will come out of it."

"I see. You don't believe in the domino theory in southeast Asia then."

"It's a civil war, plain and simple. The United States simply cannot and should not be the world's policeman. It's not our war. Leave the Vietnamese alone to solve it themselves, that's my point." She waited for a moment and then continued. "Do you believe in it? Do you think we should be there?"

"Oh, I have mixed emotions, really. I used to believe in it, but I have to seriously question the cost. We've all lost friends there. And it's hurting the country a lot. It's hurting the Army too. A lot more than most people realize. On one hand some people say if we'd stopped Hitler early on, World War II never would have happened, so from that perspective there is definitely a reason to get involved to stop aggression early. On the other hand, I don't think America is willing to pay the price. I'm not sure I am either. If I stay in the Army I'll have maybe eighteen months after I leave Korea and then I'll probably go to Vietnam. That's what usually happens. I've heard that a team of officers is coming around the Division talking to everyone about signing up for "voluntary indefinite." I need to do some serious decision making in the next few months about my future."

"So you're still considering a military career?"

"It's what I always wanted. I've got what I asked for. Now I have to decide if I want to keep it."

"So if you sign up for the voluntary indefinite, what will that mean exactly?"

"The way I understand it right now, going "vol indef" means that I make captain after two years and I get guaranteed my next duty assignment for eighteen to twenty-four months. Anywhere I want to go. Germany, Hawaii, California, whatever. But then one year before I get out I have to go where the Army sends me. Obviously that means Vietnam, assuming the war is still going on."

"And you're considering that?" Jennifer asked quizzically.

"Yes. I think I would pick Germany for my next station."

She nodded thoughtfully, digesting what Holloway had said. "When exactly would you make captain?"

"I'm up for first lieutenant in two weeks. Assuming that comes off OK, I would make captain one year later."

JD redirected the conversation toward Germany and her desire to see that country. Their chatter continued well into the night. By eleven o'clock there were few subjects that had not at least been hinted at when Mr. Yun turned on the lights to signify the club's closing. Jennifer Dodge squinted and looked about in the glare of the harsh overhead lighting. She and Holloway were alone in the room except for the Club manager. A blanket of orange embers in the stone fireplace was all that remained of what had been a blazing torch four hours earlier. The coals had stopped emitting heat a half hour before and now presented only a dull glow, but the couple on the leather sofa had failed to notice, so engrossed were they in their discussions. It had become the type of night when neither wanted it to end.

*   *   *

As the saying goes, "the only thing constant is change." By mid-February, the look of the 8/18th had again been altered. Major Matthew "Rocky" Gentile's bridgecrossing had come and gone and the Operations Shop had received a new S-3. Captain Charles Balone, a senior captain with Vietnam experience, had arrived two days before Major Gentile's departure and had worked diligently to digest everything Gentile could teach him in the 48 hours before he boarded the plane for the "land of the big PX." Balone was clearly a dedicated, hard charging career soldier in his mid-thirty's who loved his job. But while Gentile had been a teacher who was almost fatherly in his treatment of the younger officers, Balone simply issued directives and expected everyone to immediately accept his innovative philosophies without question. Colonel Nordstrum seemed to give tacit approval to most of Balone's initiatives, playing the role of peace keeper whenever one of his three new young firing battery commanders knocked on his door to vent his frustration with whatever change in SOP had just occurred. Holloway had accepted most of the alterations without complaint, hoping that Balone knew what he was doing and trying to be open minded about the situation. But he was astonished by the bombshell that the new S-3 dropped on him when he asked Holloway to stop into his office at the end of the day.

"Lieutenant Holloway, you know you're taking Charlie Battery north of the river in two weeks. You'll be occupying Firebase Wolverine."

"Yes, Sir. Lieutenant Stover just returned from there yesterday with Alpha and he's been telling me about it. I've spent a certain amount of time north of the river already. I'm comfortable up there."

"Well, there are two things that I want to tell you about the operation. One, you will be getting someone to act as your XO so you won't have to do a solo job on this. I haven't decided who it will be yet. The Colonel and I have been discussing it. It will be someone experienced, I can tell you that."

Holloway smiled. "So far, so good. What's the other thing?"

"You'll be making the movement airmobile." He paused dramatically to let the statement sink in.

"Say again, over."

"I say again, Lieutenant Holloway. Charlie Battery will make the movement by helicopter."

"Sir, we don't have any training in that at all. No one in this battalion has moved howitzers airmobile. I don't think any artillery unit in Korea has done it. We always move by truck."

"I'm aware of all that. Actually, you will officially be the first 105 battery in the ROK to make a tactical airmobile movement. Colonel Nordstrum has OK'd the operation, Second Aviation has committed to support it with the necessary aircraft, and you'll be leading it."

"We're going to move the vehicles by air too?"

"No. You'll move the howitzers, gun crews, and a forward FDC by Chinook. The vehicles can drive up and meet you."

"Will I have a Huey to take me into the LZ with the advance party?"

"That's affirmative. How did you know that's the way it's done?"

"I participated in an airmobile movement at Ft. Sill during Basic School."

"Really? What part did you play in the overall operation?"

"Well, Sir. As luck would have it I was the battery commander."

Balone laughed. "See, I knew we had the right man for the job. It shouldn't be that difficult. I know many of your senior NCOs have gone airmobile in the 'Nam. Talk to them. See who's got experience to know how to rig the loads and the slings for the guns and ammo packs. Have them prepare some classes for the troops. If you don't have enough experienced NCOs to give the classes, we'll find some in one of the other batteries." He handed a manila colored paperback book across the desk. "Here's a field manual on airmobile artillery operations. Read it. When you're finished come to me and we'll hammer out the particulars. We'll be starting to write the Op Order tomorrow. You said you've already done this once. How did it work for you at Sill?"

"Actually, it was no sweat. I went in first in the Huey, secured the LZ, got on the horn and brought the Chinooks in one at a time. Each bird carried a 105 with a sling and an ammo pack slung under the gun. Popped smoke where we wanted each of the guns set down. Pilots were crackerjack. Everything was smooth. But the thing is, we only have two weeks. When and where do we get the equipment? Do we get any dry runs? Can we alter the training schedule to jam in all the classes?"

"Don't worry about the equipment. Lieutenant Beals is working on that. It's his problem. Submit a change to the training schedule and I'll approve whatever you need. But, no. There won't be any dry runs. The first time you hook up to a chopper will be the day of the operation."

Holloway nodded. He was excited, but found himself wishing he had more time to plan. "OK, Sir. We'll do our best. I don't even know who to ask you for to be my temporary XO. Lieutenant Stover had the Owl as acting XO the last couple of weeks, but it seems kind of unfair to send him back out with us. Besides that, I'd rather have somebody with more XO experience. This battalion is so thin right now, I can't believe it. Our TO&E says we should have thirty-three officers plus warrants. At last count we had thirteen."

Captain Balone tilted the metal-framed office chair backwards and withdrew a pack of Salem from his fatigue shirt pocket. "I can't argue with you, Bagger. I was appalled when I got here and saw the personnel situation. But we just have to work around it for a while. I can guarantee you, however, that help is on the way. Nixon has just announced a major cutback in Vietnam. There are lots of officers and EM's already in the pipeline that will have to have their orders altered. We will most assuredly get some of them. It won't happen tomorrow or even next week. But it will happen. A month, maybe two. One day we'll wake up and we'll have lieutenants and captains coming out of our ears."

"I'll believe that when I see it. Listen, Captain Balone, let me ask just one little favor," requested Holloway as he arose from his chair. "You said Second Aviation was supplying the aircraft for the airmobile operation. Tell them I want Todd Hardesty for my Huey jock. He used to be flying med choppers, but he's a command pilot now and he's flying slicks."

Bolone wrote the name on a pad of paper. "I'll ask them. See you at dinner."

The meeting between Holloway, Captain Balone, and the six aviators had lasted more than two hours. Todd Hardesty had flown all of the Second Aviation people into Camp Wynne that afternoon and the entire upcoming airmobile operation had been reviewed in detail. A large field a half-mile from Firebase Wolverine would serve as the Landing Zone. Following Holloway's arrival by Huey, he would have two CH-47 Chinooks to rotate flying in his 105's, crews, and the special FDC truck that was being outfitted for the mission. Once Holloway had the six guns and ammo packs in position they would fire a mission into an impact area five miles to the southwest, then hook up the guns to the deuce and a halves and tow them into the firebase nearby. Charlie Battery would occupy that position until relieved by another battalion in early March.

Todd Hardesty drained his second Coke and scooped up the last bit of popcorn in the bowl as the flyers slipped on their flight jackets and prepared to leave the TV lounge in the Camp Wynne Officers' Club where the meeting had been held. It was dark outside, the meeting beginning later than planned due to poor flying conditions.

"So, how have you been, Bagger? How's your sex life?"

"No complaints. How about you?"

"Great. I got the cutest little yobo you ever laid your eyes on, man. She is somethin' else. I hope you can meet her sometime. Maybe you can drive down and stay at our compound some night."

"I'd like to, but that's impossible right now. I can't leave the compound except to go to the movie at RC#4 and that's only if the SDO knows exactly where to find me. I can't be away from the Battery in case something happens," Holloway noted as he held open the door for Hardesty and followed him into the bar area. As they exited the room someone nearby sounded off.

"'Tench hut!"

The two men immediately assumed the position of attention, as did every other man in the room. Bill Grant's voice boomed out of the background.

"Attention to orders! Lieutenant Holloway, front and center."

Looking confused Holloway walked forward and stood before the giant figure of Colonel Nordstrum whose bulk occupied a space in the center of the room. Grant continued to read from the set of mimeographed orders that he held in his hand. "By direction of the President, you are promoted to the rank of First Lieutenant, United States Army." Colonel Nordstrum smiled, stepped forward, and with a penknife cut the dull gold cloth from the right collar of Holloway's fatigues. Then he turned to his left and accepted from Grant the black metal bar that was the subdued insignia of a first lieutenant, and pinned it over the now empty space on Holloway's shirt.

"Congratulations, Lieutenant Holloway. Well deserved." He returned Holloway's salute and offered his hand, which the new first lieutenant shook warmly. Jennifer Dodge appeared at his side in the bright red jacket and periwinkle skirt that was the winter uniform of the Doughnut Dolly. She kissed him briefly on the lips, much to the delight of the troops who whistled and cheered. Almost immediately then she jumped back to escape the rush of cold golden liquid as Kendall Stover poured a full mug of beer over Holloway's head and grinned right in his face.

"Ring the bell, you asshole! You're buying all the drinks tonight!"

CHAPTER 28

"Charlie, 6, this is Weathervane. I am inbound. Echo Tango Alpha is zero three mikes, over."

"Weathervane, this is Charlie 6, roger, out."

Clay Holloway returned the handset to Clinton Gash and looked skyward. No sign of the Huey yet. He smiled inwardly, having recognized Todd Hardesty's voice over the radio. It would be the first time he had actually flown with his friend. Standing on Camp Wynne's cement helipad, Holloway shivered from the cold, though the sky was clear and that was the most important thing. Nearby, the Battery's six howitzers sat bundled in their olive drab nylon slings with large ammo packs wrapped in OD tarpaulins and attached by other slings to the guns. Among the guns stood Lieutenant Robert Hoover who had volunteered to assist Holloway with the movement since the Battalion was so under strength that it was unable to provide a full time Executive Officer, even for the day. He would insure that all guns and loads got airborne and headed north. From then on they belonged to Holloway. When the last gun was gone, Hoover's job would be over.

Faintly came the unmistakable "whop, whop" sound of the Huey high above. Holloway pulled his scarf tighter around his neck and looked again at his party behind him. There were three machine gun teams for security on the LZ, SFC Wilson the Chief of Smoke, Gash and himself. Holloway turned to his driver. "Be sure and watch your antenna when we board the chopper." Gash nodded nervously. He had never been in a helicopter. The Huey was drawing closer. Finally it settled softly onto the pad a few meters away, blowing icy air into their faces. On its nose was a blue circle with a mailed fist in the center. Moving at a crouch, the way men always do when they approach a helicopter, the nine man landing party trotted toward the vibrating hunk of aluminum. Suddenly, something clanged off of Holloway's helmet. He looked disconcertingly back at Gash, who was red faced and holding the stub of his antenna, which the helicopter rotors had just sliced cleanly off three feet above his head. "You got a spare?" Holloway yelled above the sound of the engine. Embarrassed, Gash again nodded, refusing to look his BC in the eye. Reaching the open door, Holloway stood beside it and watched his team board the aircraft. Then he swung in behind them, took a headset from a hook on the padded bulkhead, and plugged in the connector. Switching the radio control knob to IC (inter-com) he spoke to Todd Hardesty who was grinning at him over the back of the pilot's chair.

"Fancy meeting you here," Holloway yelled. "Nice of you to stop by."

"Hey, Bagger. Ready for the ride of your life?"

"You know where we're going. Just get me there in one piece." Hardesty flashed him a thumb's up and turned around. A moment later Holloway felt the helicopter shudder as it left the cement pad. Turning to its left and gaining altitude and speed, Hardesty tilted the nose downward and accelerated the ship. Higher they climbed until Holloway could see the Imjin only a few kilometers ahead, with Freedom Bridge off to his far left. Observing the roads, the river, and the patchwork of rice paddies, it seemed as though he was looking at a sepia tinted map of the division area, with the winter season limiting the colors to mostly brown and white. A whole new perspective of the his area of operations was quickly gained, as the helicopter flashed over the SCOSI positions and the partially frozen river. Then over Camp Greaves and Holloway immediately picked out GP Gwen, with Carol and Cindy not far away. Then the south barrier fence, the omnipresent structure which stretched east and west for as far as the eye could see, even from a helicopter. Holloway's focus changed then from the ground to his map, as he associated his red "X" on the paper to the actual spot on the ground. Hardesty banked the ship hard, diving quickly toward the surface of the earth. Skimming the tops of the naked black trees the helicopter suddenly dove lower and covered the area of the large open field beyond. Suddenly it flared, hovered momentarily, and then touched its skids to the frozen ground.

"Let's go," Holloway cried sliding open the door and leaping to the ground. He pointed each machine gun team in a different direction, dispatching them to the far reaches of the field. In a clatter of the main rotor, the Huey lifted off the ground behind them and headed quickly skyward. SFC Wilson walked briskly to an area that would eventually be behind the guns and began the task of orienting the aiming circle, which would be used to begin laying the guns as soon as the first one was on the ground. Holloway extended his leather-gloved hand toward Gash who placed the handset into it. The RTO had replaced the damaged long antenna of the PRC/25 with his spare during the short flight.

"Dragon Fly 44, this is Charlie 6, are you airborne, over?" Holloway inquired of the Chinook that was to carry his base piece.

"Charlie 6, this is Dragon Fly, that's a roger. Echo Tango Alpha is 05 mikes, over."

"This is Charlie 6, please advise when on your final, over."

"Dragon Fly, roger that, over."

"Charlie 6, tango yankee (thank you), out."

The number three gun would be first to land. Holloway walked to an area near the center of the field, which Rick Benning's survey team had marked with a pin the week before and over which, Sergeant Wilson had set up the aiming circle. Firing from that survey point would give the best possible plot for the initial rounds out of the tubes. High above them Holloway spied the dark shape of the big cargo helicopter silhouetted against the gray winter sky, lugging its heavy load beneath its belly. He withdrew a large cylindrical object with a violet slash on its side from the cargo pocket of his bulky field pants.

"Charlie 6, this is Dragon Fly, be advised, I am on my final, over."

"This is Charlie 6, roger. I am popping smoke. Do you identify? over." With that he tugged free the pin of the smoke grenade and tossed it a few feet away. Immediately volumes of violet colored smoke spewed forth and swirled upward.

"Dragon Fly, I identify violet smoke, over."

"Charlie 6, roger, come to papa, over."

With a tremendous clatter the big twin turbo helicopter appeared overhead and slowly lowered itself until the canvas-covered package containing the ammunition and tools was on the dirt. Slipping sideways, the metal insect descended slightly until the wheels of the 105 touched the ground. Then the slings were released. Thirty meters behind Holloway the helicopter landed and the rear gate was lowered by the crew chief. From the stomach of the helicopter sprang a five-quarter ton truck, its windshield lying flat on the hood to keep the vehicle height at a minimum. Spec/4 Marvin Bernstein sat hunched over the steering wheel as he guided the vehicle down the ramps to the ground. Sergeant Lepley sat in the passenger seat studying his map, with the other two FDC crewman in the bed behind. Holloway pointed them in the area of Sergeant Wilson with his aiming circle. Within two minutes the FDC crew would have their charts ready to fire a mission. Holloway looked back to the howitzer. The gun crew had followed Bernstein and his truck out of the helicopter and were stripping off the canvas and slings from the loads. Holloway could hear the helicopter's engines whining louder as it prepared for takeoff. Soon it was up, flying to the south in the direction from which it had come. But as its sound faded into the distance it was replaced by a fresher noise that grew in intensity. A second helicopter with a second gun was inbound. Gash was already holding out the microphone. The procedure was repeated. Holloway threw a white smoke grenade, which the metal insect seemed to want to inhale as the smoke was sucked around the helicopter by its rotors, almost obscuring the ship from view. A moment later the center platoon was ready to shoot.

In less than a half hour the operation was complete. Six guns had been laid and declared safe to fire by Ed O'Connell who had been assigned as the Safety Officer for the day. In an tactical firing situation, Safety Officers are not used. However, in a training shoot, one must be always be present. The Safety Officer works in conjunction with the XO and the FDC to insure that all rounds land within a prescribed safe zone of the impact area. The shooting continued for two hours and was monitored by Captain Balone and Colonel Nordstrum who had driven up to observe the entire operation. Both seemed more than pleased by the success of the event and told Holloway about it. Then they departed as Charlie Battery moved its gun trucks into the field, hooked up the howitzers, and trundled two kilometers away to Firebase Wolverine where it would spend the next two weeks camped one kilometer behind the south barrier fence.

*   *   *

The blizzard began on the afternoon of the third day. Charlie Battery had been scheduled for a practice shoot at 1400 and the FDC was monitoring a meteorological channel as it routinely did on the day of a shoot. Before noon the radio announced that the storm had first been sighted early that morning over the mountains of the northern part of the Korean peninsula and was moving due south at a relatively high rate of speed. Almost immediately Holloway had called Captain Balone at Camp Wynne who had actually been in the process of climbing into his jeep to head north when the call came. Balone checked with his Battalion FDC and got the same report. Immediately, he canceled the shoot and ordered his vehicle returned to the motor pool.

At Firebase Wolverine, even as the winds began to howl, parka clad work parties were hurriedly formed to drive tent stakes even deeper into the frozen ground and to cover and tie down anything that was not already in that configuration. Batteries were removed from the vehicles and taken inside the tents to prevent them from freezing solid. The men in the outposts were warned as well and it was determined to change the guards every two hours instead of four. They changed their footwear from combat boots with rubber boots over them to the insulated Mickey Mouse boots guaranteed to keep the feet warm, though difficult to walk in. Fresh cans of diesel were mounted on the wooden racks that fed the little stoves, and C-rations were distributed to everyone to keep the mess crew from having to try to prepare a meal in the middle of what was about to happen and simultaneously keep the bellies of the men from being empty. First Sergeant St. Clair insured that the CP tent had a few extra boxes of C's just in case. He was a big eater.

Shortly after the winds began, the first snow squall sliced into the camp like a solid wall of cotton, layering the dry white stuff immediately on the bare frozen dirt. By darkness, which seemed to come an hour earlier than usual, there were large drifts scattered about the position. By ten o'clock the thermometer had dropped steadily, finally leveling off at five degrees Fahrenheit later in the evening, according to the met station. Holloway compared the temperature to the estimated wind velocity on a card he carried. According to his calculation the wind chill reading was forty degrees below zero.

"It sounds pretty brutal out there, Top. I think we need to think about changing the outposts every hour," Holloway stated to his First Sergeant.

"People won't get much sleep if we change every hour, Sir."

"I know that, but I think they'll trade a little sleep to keep from freezing to death. Get your parka on and let's take a stroll. I want to see how bad it really is." Holloway jerked open the heavy canvas tent flap. A wall of snow met him. "Wow! Where did this come from? Grab your entrenching tool." Together the two men attacked the snowdrift, finally clearing a path wide enough to walk through in the six-foot drift. They ventured out into the battery area. Immediately their eyes sensed an unusual orange glow in the sky.

"What the hell is that, Sir?"

"I was just wondering the same thing. Oh, goddamnit! One of tents is on fire! Come on!" They wanted to run. Tried to run. It was impossible. The snowfall stood at eighteen inches and still falling rapidly. "Fire! Fire!" Holloway called out. But the sound of his voice perished in the howling of the Siberian wind biting into their faces. Frustration turning to panic overtook them as they struggled through the snow to the burning squad tent still fifty meters away. The entire roof was in flames, turning the area around it into daylight. Where the hell were the men? It seemed like an eternity, but finally the two men reached the tent and yanked open the flap."

"Get out of there! Wake up! Get out! The tent's on fire."

Falling hunks of burning canvas were landing on the floor inside where four exhausted sleeping men were finally awakening to the danger. Panic stricken, one man scrambled to his feet and tried to run, tripping immediately onto his face by the constrictions of his sleeping bag. First Sergeant St. Clair bent and grabbed the mass of man and material and literally flung the soldier and his bag out of the entranceway and into the snow. The other three men scrambled out behind him as the structurally weakened tent sank slowly into a burning heap of canvas.

Behind them a large piece of flaming cloth had been carried by the wind and blown directly into the side of the Jamesway, which served as the supply hooch. Unseen by the soldiers, the force of the gale held the burning hunk against the canvas wall for almost a minute, providing more than enough time to ignite the material surrounding it. Fanned by the winds, the flames spread rapidly, eating a hole through the wall and moving progressively in all directions. Inside the Jamesway, Motor Sergeant Brookins, who had been reading fully dressed under the glow of a Coleman lantern, saw the flames on the wall and rushed to try to beat them out. Motor Sergeant Brookins had spent much of the previous day and part of the morning helping one of his mechanics pull out, rebuild, and install a pair of carburetors. By the time that job had been complete, he had slopped a measurable amount of gasoline of his field jacket, which already contained a variety of motor pool lubricants that had accumulated over the weeks. Sergeant Brookins had learned long ago that a Motor

Sergeant needs to keep two entirely separate field jackets; one to work in, which is always going to be dirty, and one for everything else. When the fire began, he was still clothed in the one he wore for work.

"Fire!" Brookins called to the other eight men in the supply hooch. Grabbing a blanket, he aggressively attacked the flames, giving not the slightest thought to the flammable materials, which had dried, into his clothing. As he drew back the blanket to begin his assault, the intense heat of the fire ignited the front of his own jacket in his face.

"Ahhhhh!" Brookins screamed as he staggered backward slapping wildly at his chest and falling onto his back on the poured concrete floor. Simultaneously, Holloway and St. Clair burst through the flimsy wooden front door and seeing the human torch moved quickly toward him. Corporal Sohn was quicker. The wiry little KATUSA who had been sleeping near the stove had grasped the situation instantly and snatched a CO_2 fire extinguisher from the corner. Alertly, he began spraying it into Sergeant Brookins' face and body, smothering the flames. Suddenly Brookins leaped to his feet, bolted to the door, and dove headlong into the nearest snowdrift. A perceptible cloud of steam arose from his body. Meanwhile, Sohn had turned his extinguisher on the Jamesway, knocking out the flames as they tried to spread. Soon the fire was gone, replaced by black smoking tatters of cloth. There was now a four by five opening in the tent wall that had not been there two minutes earlier.

Each of the men glanced wildly around the inside of the structure searching for more danger. There was none. Sohn ran outside and circled the Jamesway. Holloway followed him out and looked about the area. There was no more fire, but the commotion had alerted everyone. Soldiers were pouring out of their tents, yelling questions back and forth through the blustery night. Spec/4 Winslow had been one of the men in the squad tent that had caught fire and burned almost to the ground. He and another man were still throwing snow onto the smoking ruins, putting out the last of the embers. Finally, they began dragging objects out of the rubble, seeing what of their belongings they could salvage. Sergeant Brookins was standing in the night looking down at his barely smoldering field jacket that lay in the snow pile where he had discarded it.

"You OK, Sergeant Brookins?" Holloway asked.

"I think so, Suh. My face may have got a little singed" He looked down at his chest "All these layers of clothes I got on musta protected me. Man, one minute I be freezin' and the next I felt like a marshmallow on a stick," he chuckled. "Where's Sohn at? That boy saved my life. Sohn! Sohn!" Sergeant Brookins yelled. The KATUSA walked out of the supply hooch, still carrying the fire extinguisher. Brookins walked to him and hugged him. "You numba one dude, man!" Brookins exclaimed. Sohn was smiling broadly. He bowed his head several times, understanding the emotion more than the words. Holloway grasped his hand.

"Kamsamnida, Sohn! You numba one GI! You saved the whole damn supply hooch."

Two hours later order had been restored to the unit. A temporary patch had been made on the Jamesway and the number two gun crew whose tent was destroyed had split up and moved in with two other crews temporarily. Earlier, Holloway had tried to establish communication with the Battalion TOC via his field phone, but had been unable to make contact. There appeared to be a break somewhere in the lines, which certainly would not be investigated tonight. It would be a difficult assignment finding the break under all of the snow even tomorrow, assuming the storm was over. In fact, Holloway was considering telling Sergeant Jackson to just lay new lines rather that wasting time trying to find the break in the old one. Besides that, the 292 antenna that had been erected next to the FDC van had been blown over and damaged in the storm. It could be repaired tomorrow, of course, but in the meantime was almost useless. Combined with the poor atmospheric conditions caused by the storm, the net effect of these incidents was that Charlie Battery was almost completely cut off from outside communication. Almost completely, but not quite.

As Holloway began crawling into his musty smelling sleeping bag the radio crackled. "Pssst, psssst, Char pssst, shhhhh, 33, over."

He lifted the handset and keyed it. "Unknown Station, this is Charlie 6, over."

"Charlie shhhhhh, psst, 33, message follows, shhhhh, shhhhh, battery commander killed, over."

Alarmed, Holloway turned to St. Clair. "What'd he say, Top? Somebody's dead?"

"Yes, Sir. It sounded that way. Something about a battery commander."

"33, this is Charlie 6, say again, over."

"Charlie 6, this shhhhhhhh. I say pstttt, shhhh, battery commander is dead. I have no pssstttt. Shhhhhhhh. out."

"Goddamnit! Who's dead? What is he talking about?" Holloway keyed the mike again. "33, this is Charlie 6, say again last transmission. Who is dead? over."

"Sssshhhhhhhhhhh. Pssssttttttt."

Again he tried. No response. Again. Followed by an unintelligible garble of static. Frustrated he flung the handset into the canvas side of the tent. "Son-of-a-bitch! Who's dead?" he screamed. The NCOs in the tent looked at him passively. Finally Sergeant Wilson spoke.

"Sir, I believe he said a battery commander is dead, but I never caught a name. I think we're just going to have to wait until morning and the weather clears."

Holloway glared at Wilson. He was right, of course, but that didn't help. Was it Baron or Sweeper? Holloway let out a long slow breath and walked to where the microphone had slid down the tent side and lay on the ground. He picked it up almost apologetically and pressed the rubber button once more. There was no reply.

By morning the snowfall had ended, though more than twenty inches had fallen and even the main roads were still blocked by the effects of the blizzard. It would be some time before any snow removal vehicles could get to Firebase Wolverine. Telephone communications were still out, but the 292 antenna was back up and Holloway called the Battalion TOC. The young RTO he spoke with had come on duty at 0800. He didn't know anything about any radio transmissions last night dealing with any dead people and was not aware of any deaths in the Battalion. Finally he said he'd try to find out from someone if anyone came by.

It was mid morning, when a single jeep was spotted driving toward the firebase. By this time Holloway was as nervous as a cat wondering what the radio message of the previous evening had meant. As the jeep drew closer the sound of tire chains could be heard singing in the crisp air and snow was being tossed in an arching pattern behind the tires as they dug into the pristine covering. Through his binoculars Holloway identified the driver as Corporal D'Antonio. Beside him, his expressionless face partially hidden by sunglasses, sat a parka covered Dave Ruminski. It took the jeep almost ten minutes to creep its way to where Holloway stood. Finally it came to a halt in front of the CP. Ruminski climbed out.

"You get the message last night, Bagger?"

"I got a partial message. What happened? Who's dead?"

"Bear Buckner."

Holloway was silent for a moment. He had assumed the message had referred to a current BC, not a former one. "Bear? He's in the States. I thought he was going to Ft. Sill."

"He did. He had a battery there. They were just doing a routine service practice shoot and Bear was down next to one of the guns observing. It was 155's. Separate loading ammo. The gun exploded. Breech blew out, although nobody knows why yet. There was three dead. Bear was one of them."

Holloway looked silently, unintentionally, skyward. It was so blue. The clouds were so white. He wanted to cry, but battery commanders don't do that. "I guess it's good that he's single."

"Yeah, I guess."

Scenes flashed randomly through Holloway's mind. Bear taunting Hostileman into beginning the great frog hunt. Bear sitting at the end of the bar, chomping down on that big cigar he liked to chew on more than smoke. Those powerful shoulders and arms that had knocked out his own first sergeant when they had duked it out behind the motor pool to see who was really going to run the battery. The tight grin on his face when he'd slid down the river of beer on the bar stool on New Year's Eve two short months ago. Holloway wondered how Sweeper was taking it. Bear had been Sweeper's BC since his first day in country. He could picture Sweeper crying out "that's not fair." Sweeper always thought things had to be fair. But, of course, they didn't. Not really.

*   *   *

March soon displayed its legendary unpredictable weather patterns. Two days after the onset of the blizzard, the temperature climbed above forty and the blanket of snow became a quagmire of sticky brown mud. Movement around the battery area became laborious, either by foot or vehicle, but the service practice shoot that had been scheduled three days earlier was reset for the next afternoon.

"Top, you remember that creek bed over at 4 Papa 1 near where Shorty got that one deer," Clay Holloway asked his First Sergeant.

"Yes, Sir. I know where you mean."

"Why don't we send a work party over there in a deuce and a half and fill it up with sand from that one area. I think if we spread it around here it will help the footing and get rid of some of this muck."

Holloway looked past First Sergeant St. Clair at the shape of a vehicle, which had just turned off of the main road, and was churning through the soft dirt and heading straight for their position. "I wonder who that is? I didn't know we were getting visitors today." His answer was quick in coming. The jeep slid to a halt in a rut five feet in front of Holloway and Major Karl Vogel climbed quickly out. Holloway saluted.

"Morning, Sir,." greeted Holloway.

Vogel touched his fingers to his helmet. "Lieutenant Holloway. I thought I'd stop by and see what this gaggle you call a battery was doing today." He swiveled his head quickly. "What a mess this place is and I don't see a great deal being accomplished at the moment, do you?"

"Most of the gun bunnies are in a training class on fuses right now, Sir. The various other sections are working in their respective areas. We're going to start spreading sand around the area today and there's a work party trying to repair a section of the Jamesway."

"What did you do to the Jamesway?"

"There was a fire the night of the blizzard. We almost lost the whole thing," Holloway said defensively. "I reported it to Battalion."

"Show me!"

Holloway began to lead the way through the ankle deep mud. Taking note of the footing, Major Vogel climbed back into his jeep, nodded to his driver, and called to Holloway. "Go ahead and take the point, Lieutenant. We'll follow you."

Arriving at the front of the canvas structure, Vogel exited the vehicle and strutted inside of the little building. Sergeant Jack Carlton and three men were in the process of holding a large piece of canvas in place while another man stitched diligently with a curved needle and heavy thread. Major Vogel glared at Holloway. "Isn't anyone going to call attention!"

"'Tench hut," Holloway stated, a dismayed tone to his voice. Grudgingly, the work party dropped the canvas and moved to the position of attention.

"That's better!" Vogel moved to within a foot of Carlton. "Who did this?" he demanded angrily.

"There was a fire, Sir," Carlton responded.

"Who started the fire?"

Holloway moved to the Major's side. "Sir, we believe during the snow storm the canvas flap on the top of one of the tents was blown against the hot flue pipe of the space heater and it caught fire. We think that part of the burning canvas blew into the Jamesway and caught it on fire."

Vogel sneered. "Jesus Christ, Lieutenant. What a cluster fuck this unit is. When are you people going to get your heads out of rectal defilade and get your shit together? What happened to the other tent?" Of course he already knew the answer.

"It was destroyed by fire, Sir," Holloway said.

"Who's paying for it?"

"Sir, I do think given the circumstances that anyone should have to pay for it."

"Well, I think differently. I'm appointing an investigating officer to review the entire case. Someone is going to be signing a statement of charges. And this Jamesway isn't even ours. It belongs to DivArty. What the hell am I going to tell them?"

Clearly there was nothing Holloway could say that would improve the situation. He remained silent. Major Vogel continued to glare at them for several seconds. Then, without another word he spun on his heel, strode to his jeep, and unassed the area. Embarrassed more for his Battalion Executive Officer than himself a chagrined Clay Holloway finally turned to his men. "Let's get back to work, Sergeant Carlton."

"Yes, Sir. Short, Sir."

Holloway looked at him questioningly. "Short?"

"Yes, Sir. Six days and a wake up."

He smiled at the NCO knowingly. "Good for you, Jack."

*   *   *

Jennifer Dodge and Gretchen Schuster had become fast friends, working together almost every day and spending many evenings in each other's rooms. JD had found her new partner intelligent, good natured, and devilish, with an incredibly dry sense of humor that was often lost on the dull witted. Gretchen had eventually outgrown her embarrassment of dancing on the bar sans underwear and, in fact, had decided to log it into her repertoire of stories with which she would one day entertain her grandchildren. Although in true conservative tradition she had never mentioned figures, from their many conversations, JD was sure that Gretchen came from money. Old money. Eastern money. Lots of it. Paupers rarely graduated summa cum laude from Smith. Gretchen and Kendall Stover had taken an immediate liking to one another as well, their almost identical eastern accents and aristocratic air providing an initial sense of camaraderie that had grown over the past few weeks.

The jeep in which the two young women were riding had passed through Pobwon-ni and was headed toward a small compound occupied by the 4//th Cavalry where they were supposed to participate in some sort of "dating game" with the troops. It was not the sort of activity that either woman enjoyed, but Karen had directed that they do so and finding it normally unproductive to argue with their boss had finally accepted the assignment. Ahead of the jeep, the road was congested, forcing the vehicle to slow perceptively. The cause of the slowdown turned out to be a funeral procession. In the Division area there was rarely a traffic problem caused by civilian motor vehicles on the two lane dirt and gravel roads. The only vehicles operated by Korean nationals were either the reckless darting little Toyota's that functioned as taxi cabs, or kimchi cabs as the troops called them, or an occasional bus or truck. Most civilians traveled by foot or bicycle. Often the bicycles carried enormous loads of wood or crops or anything else needing transportation. Loads were often stacked as high as seven or eight feet in the air.

Jennifer Dodge peered ahead through the windshield. The problem seemed to be two bicycles riding abreast not far ahead and traveling in the same direction as their jeep. The other lane was occupied by a line of carts and a group of well-dressed civilians who were apparently involved in a funeral procession. On the back of each bicycle was a large sow, weighing in excess of two hundred pounds. The pigs were securely strapped to the bicycles and because they gave no sign of movement she thought they must be dead. Approaching closer, however, she realized their eyes were open and though not appearing to focus were showing noticeable signs of movement. The long pink tongue of each pig hung straight out of the mouth, coming within six inches of dragging on the ground below. JD turned to the red haired freckle faced lad that was their assigned driver.

"Jason, how do they keep the pigs so quiet on those bicycles?"

"They're drunk."

"Drunk!"

"Sure. When they need to transport one of them the Koreans just load them up on that mockely stuff and let 'em drink their fill until they pass out. Then they pack 'em on the back of the bike and drive 'em somewhere."

JD looked at Gretchen and the two laughed heartily. The funeral procession had passed and Jason saw his opportunity to get around the two bicycles, downshifted the transmission, and moved the jeep to the left. As he passed the two cyclists a blue kimchi cab bounced wildly from the area in front of a little store onto the road ahead of them. Jason whipped right and slammed on the brakes, narrowly missing both the bicycles he had just passed and the blue cab ahead. But as the vehicle slid to a stop, it tipped forward precariously. Climbing out of the jeep, Jason realized the right front tire was suspended in mid air over the deep drainage ditch on the side of the road bordering a field of rice paddies. In tilting wildly to its right front, the left rear wheel was raised six inches off of the ground. Jason tried reverse, but the jeep wouldn't move. It was grounded.

"I think we're stuck, JD," the driver reported after looking under the vehicle. "Part of the frame is resting on the dirt and the goddamn right front wheel's hanging in mid air. We might have to get a tow."

Jennifer Dodge and Gretchen Schuster climbed out of the jeep and peered underneath. "How about if we pull down hard on the left rear," JD suggested. "That will take some of the pressure off of the front. You put it in four wheel and give it steady gas. You might be able to get enough traction to move it backwards."

Jason looked at the two women blankly. He couldn't believe that one of them could possibly know what she was talking about, but what the hell. He hated to admit it, but it actually might work. He climbed behind the wheel and shifted into four-wheel drive. The two Doughnut Dollies stood at the side of the left rear and pulled down hard on the jeep body, shifting its weight. There was a scraping sound as the vehicle moved slightly and then broke free. Jason backed a few feet and left the jeep idle as he got out and tilted his head under the body inspecting for damage to the undercarriage. So pleased with themselves were they, that none of the three Americans was remotely aware of the approach of the water buffalo which had broken free of its tether a few minutes earlier and, in an ornery mood, decided that it strongly resented the intrusion of an unknown object and three round eyed strangers into the edge of his rice paddy. Jason's attention was still under the jeep when the water buffalo trotted up behind and butted him, driving his head solidly into the metal frame. Clutching at his skull in pain, the young man collapsed onto the road in a state of semi-consciousness.

Gretchen Schuster whirled around at the noise and flurry of movement. Pawing the ground behind her, the water buffalo snorted and tossed his head toward her menacingly. Hot bursts of air from his nostrils hung in the cool atmosphere and she could smell his odor. The woman froze, awaiting the animal's next move. She didn't wait long. Lowering his head, the water buffalo smashed into the fender of the jeep next to her, moving it six inches sideways with the muscular power of his body. Gretchen glanced down at Jason's prone figure. His legs were moving slightly and he was moaning. She cowered against the fender and mouthed a quick prayer. The huge animal lowered its head and prepared a third charge.

"Thwang!" the metal shovel that had been strapped to the side of the jeep reverberated from the water buffalo's thick snout, surprising him as much as his charge had surprised Gretchen. Trumpeting in shock and pain the animal took two steps backwards and shook its head. Jennifer Dodge approached menacingly, her eyes narrowed and her arms cocked back like a baseball player awaiting the next pitch.

"Cauda chogi! Cauda chogi! Get away from my friends," she screamed at him, advancing another step forward. The animal shook its head and pawed the mud again, holding its ground. Big mistake. JD went for the homerun, clanging the shovel off of the side of the muscular animal's head and driving him to his right. She stooped and followed with a quick blow to its knee. Stunned and surprised by the force of the strikes, the black hided creature retreated slightly, finally concluding that discretion was the better part of valor. Backing a few more steps he bowed his head, blinked his eyes, and turned and trotted back to his home, sorely regretting his initial decision to venture forth. JD turned to help the young driver to his feet. A trickle of blood ran down his forehead and he was obviously disoriented.

"Jason, sit in the jeep. We're going to find a doctor," JD said steadying him. She tugged open the door to the canvas topped vehicle and helped him in. "Gretchen, get in the back." The other Doughnut Dolly blinked rapidly at Jennifer, then did as she was told as JD ran to the other side of the vehicle and slid behind the wheel. She'd never driven a jeep before, but how much different could the shift pattern be from the MG she'd owned the last two years of college? Slamming the gear shift into first she released the clutch and the quarter ton lurched ahead throwing mud behind it and accelerating past the two men on the bicycles who were now a quarter of a mile ahead.

"God, Jenn!" It was the first words Gretchen Schuster had spoken. "How did you do that? I never could have done that. I never pictured you as a violent person."

"I'm not a violent person, but what the hell would you have had me do, sit down and discuss the situation with him?"

"No, no! You did the right thing. God, I thought I was going to faint I was so scared," she whispered. "I'm starting to quiver right now."

JD was hunched grimly behind the wheel, her eyes focused on the road ahead. "I was scared too Gretchen, but sometimes you have to fight back. Sometimes you just have to."

CHAPTER 29

First Lieutenant Robert Hoover flung one leg over the open side of the vehicle and stepped out. The jeep's numerical designation was B-6, the assigned vehicle of the Bravo Battery Commander. Clay Holloway spied his friend and walked toward him from the CP tent as the man unloaded his duffel from the back seat. Once Hoover was clear, the vehicle lurched away.

"Sweeper, what the hell are you doing up here and where's your driver going? Are you planning to stay for a while?" Holloway asked, pointing at the duffel.

"Ya might say that, Bagger. I'm your new XO for a few days until you head south," Hoover replied with his usual grin.

"My XO? What the hell are you talking about? Who's gonna run Bravo Battery?"

"Haven't you heard? A new captain came in two nights ago, along with a pair of new lieutenants. Colonel Nordstrum gave Bravo to the captain and asked me to help you out up here until the 1/15th relieves you next week."

"What! We got some replacement officers? You're really not Bravo BC any more?"

"Nope. I'll go back to being its XO once we get back, but for the next few days my ass belongs to you," Hoover declared.

"Damn, Sweeper. I don't know what to say. Why didn't they send me one of the new guys?"

"They haven't even drawn their field gear yet. Besides, Captain Balone said you guys are supposed to do a practice shoot tomorrow and he didn't want to send anybody just fresh out of school. These new boys look awful young."

Holloway extended his hand. "Well, its good to have you. How do you feel about having to give up command?"

"Ah, there's kind of a hole in my stomach right now, but I'll get used to it. We all knew that someday we'd start getting in some senior officers. This Captain Sanders that took over seems like an all right guy. He's got kind of a quiet confidence. He had a battery in Vietnam. Definitely knows what he's doing. There shouldn't be any problem."

"Well, that's good. If you have to get in a new BC, you gotta hope it's a good one." Holloway looked into his friend's face. "I heard about Bear. That's a bitch."

Hoover nodded glumly. "Yeah. It's hard to understand. You put in your tour over here and spend half your time thinking about going home and as soon as you get there you get wasted in a freak accident. He and I were planning to get together when I DEROS in July." The words seemed to catch in his throat. He stopped talking for a moment and then changed the subject. "So, how's it been up here? Fought off any wolverines lately?"

"Negative, but we'd be in good shape if we had to. They sent up our Christmas presents two days ago."

"The M-16's?" Hoover asked, his eyebrows raised.

"Yeah. All shiny and new, right out of the box. Some of these guys seemed happier than a pig in a mud puddle. I've never seen these troops pay more attention in a class than they did in the assembly and disassembly of the M-16 rifle. They were fascinated. Then we spent the rest of the day taking them out on the other side of that hill and let them put two or three twenty round mags through them to try to get a decent battle zero on the sights. Now they all walk around gung ho like they're waiting for a North Korean patrol to come around just so they can zap 'em."

Hoover laughed. "OK. How's the Z been? Any action?"

"Quiet. We got alerted that we may have to fire an illumination mission for the grunts once in a while, but nothing's happened so far. Seems like ever since you and I left the GP's things have settled down a lot."

"Yeah. That must tell us somethin', but I'm not sure what. When's the shoot tomorrow?"

"0900. Come on. We'll get you settled in and then introduce you to the gun chiefs." Holloway lead the way into the CP.

The two service practice shoots extending over the following three days consumed one hundred and twenty-four rounds of 105mm ammunition. As the first round was fired on the first day, the gun crews realized the obvious. They were far better off to don their rain suits before pulling the lanyard a second time. Each 105 round that pounded out of the barrel of a howitzer drove the trails into the soggy mud, creating a spray of brown water that blanketed everything within a fifty-foot radius. Besides the existing mud, a gentle rain began midway through the second day of shooting, adding unneeded moisture to the already saturated ground. During a lull in the firing and in an attempt to create a reasonably dry working environment for himself and his temporary XO, Clinton Gash, who functioned as battery recorder during fire missions, constructed a kimchi rig XO's post behind the guns from sandbags, heavy gauge plastic, and some extra timber. Once complete it allowed him to sit on a sandbag in the mud to record the gun commands on his clipboard without the paper being soaked by the rain. It also kept Lieutenant Hoover's field phone dry. By the time the firing was complete the rain had stopped.

"That was a nice idea, Gash," said Hoover referring to the XO's post. "I hope the 1/15th appreciates the work you did for them. Too bad you guys are pulling out tomorrow. You won't get any more use out of it."

"Aren't you going with us, Sir?"

"No. I'm leaving today. They just wanted me up here to help with the shooting. I'm going to get picked up in a few minutes, assuming my vehicle can get through this quagmire. If not, we may all be mudded in here until June."

"Well, good luck, Sir. I heard Lieutenant Holloway tell Top to get some more sand in here to try to help with the mud. We'll get out OK."

Three officers from the 1/15th arrived late in the afternoon for an advanced reconnaissance of the position. They were ushered into the CP where Holloway sat reviewing the monthly vehicle status report. After exchanging greetings and taking a brief look about the area the battery commander of the unit scheduled to replace Charlie Battery the next day made a startling announcement.

"Lieutenant Holloway, I know that we usually replace one gun at a time when we make this switch, but we're going to have to alter that a bit tomorrow. See, we're coming in here airmobile," the officer declared puffing out his chest.

"That's no big deal. We came in airmobile too."

"Not like this. We're not going into a field and get towed over here. We're coming straight in here."

Holloway looked at the man strangely. "You mean that field over there?"

"No, I don't mean any field. We're dropping our guns straight into the gun pits! So therefore you people need get your guns and your vehicles out of here before we start so we don't get in each other's way."

"You mean to tell me you're going to have the Chinooks lower the 105's straight down inside those sandbagged gun pits?"

"That's what I said. It shouldn't be that tough."

"Captain, I certainly am not going to sit here and tell you how to run your battery, but quite frankly I think that's a really bad idea. There's no room inside the pits. There are all kinds of trees and obstacles around here. It could get really hairy."

"You let me worry about that, Lieutenant. Just have the area clear of your vehicles by 1000 hours."

*   *   *

Lazily the red-tailed hawk circled, as though simply enjoying the cool wind currents of Siberian air. He had been soaring for more than fifteen minutes, watching as the last of Charlie Battery's vehicles exited the firebase and formed up on the main road a quarter of a mile away. The hawk hoped that some scraps might be left behind in the area formerly occupied by the field kitchen trucks. Swooping lower he searched painstakingly for a sign of food. But unexpectedly something startled the hawk. The airwaves under his wings were changing, becoming a steady pounding as giant rotors buffeted the air. Looking to the south the hawk spied the dark shape of a small helicopter, followed a mile behind by a bigger one with a large shape under its belly. The hawk didn't like the looks of those machines and didn't like the feel of the air any longer. It banked to its right and dove sharply away.

Holloway sat in the passenger seat of C-6 enjoying the warmth pouring from the vehicle's heater. Beside him Clinton Gash sang softly in his marvelous soprano voice in conjunction with the ballad playing from his portable tape recorder. Together they watched the hawk as it dove and rose and soared away to the east. Far behind the hawk to the south they too could see the shapes of the aircraft drawing closer.

"I don't like this, Clinton. It gives me bad vibes. I'm glad we've gotten all of our people out of here." Gash nodded silently. The Huey moved closer, suddenly hovering just above the surface of the earth at the edge of the battery position as the advance party exited the aircraft. A senior NCO oriented the aiming circle as the battery commander set up with his RTO near the gun pits. Quickly he tossed a smoke grenade into one of the pits and yellow smoke hissed forth. Soon the Chinook hovered overhead, carrying the howitzer beneath it. Apparently the 1/15th had discarded the idea of carrying an ammo pack under the gun. The Chinook came lower. Suddenly the ground around the pit began to feel the beating of the two big rotors. The surface of the earth began to quiver and then move. A composite soil combination of water and mud and sand began to simultaneously be blown and sucked indiscriminately around the battery position, gaining in speed and power. The CH-47 dropped lower. The rotor blast became a wind of hurricane proportion. Suddenly the plastic and timber of Gash's newly constructed XO's post disappeared as the plastic sheeting was driven toward an open field. Holloway nudged Gash as he saw the Jamesway that Charlie had used as a supply hooch began to shake violently. By this time the helicopter had the howitzer close to the ground, but suddenly the chopper slipped slightly sideways causing the gun to slam violently into the sandbagged wall of the pit, knocking down several of the sandbags. Two of the bags were torn open, the sand being sucked instantly into the air. Rebounding from the collision, the howitzer began to spin and sway, changing the stability of the aircraft. Finally the helicopter backed off. Holloway turned to Clinton Gash.

"They're wrecking the whole firebase!"

They were also determined. The helicopter returned. Again the wheel of the gun struck the sandbagged wall, knocking an even larger hole in it. The wind whipped the sand into a sandstorm, which found the side of Holloway's jeep parked fifty meters away. Gash was furious. He'd paid his own money to have the jeep painted in the village only three weeks earlier. Angrily slamming the vehicle into reverse he backed quickly another thirty meters to the rear. Pandemonium continued. A truck from the 1/15th drove rapidly into the position. A dozen troops exited the rear and ran toward the gun pit. Halfway there they were beaten back by the sandstorm that hit them head on. Confusion reigned. The troops attempted to move forward, but each time they tried they were forced to shield their faces and were eventually driven back by the sand. Finally, an inventive E-6 pulled his gas mask from of its case, pulled it over his head and tied the hood. The others followed suit. Their faces now protected, they advanced under the hovering helicopter. Again it dropped lower. Hands reached for the gun that hung suspended in mid-air, guiding it into the pit. Suddenly the helicopter, and with it the gun, moved sideways, momentarily pinning one of the soldiers against the sandbagged wall. Behind them, the Jamesway finally collapsed in a heap from the force of the winds, its wooden struts snapping like toothpicks. Eventually though, the gun was successfully lowered into position. The soldier who was pinned earlier appeared not to be seriously injured. Releasing its sling the CH-47 lifted higher, eventually flying off in the direction in which it had come. The men on the ground wheeled the gun around into the approximate direction of fire. The section of the pit containing the ammo bunker had been partially collapsed and the sandbags had to be cleared away before the gun could be properly set. Finally the trails were spread and locked. An NCO began to lay the gun with the aiming circle standing nearby. Above him came a crescendo of noise and wind as the second gun-carrying helicopter approached and began to hover. The NCO was still trying to lay the first gun. It was hopeless. As he temporarily shielded his face, the expensive optical instrument was blown over in a heap. Nearby the heavy plastic sheeting that covered the motor pool lubricants was blown away causing many of the 55-gallon drums to tumble over and roll away haphazardly. Holloway shook his head sadly. The position was being methodically ruined.

Suddenly the big chopper began to make strange sounds. Holloway had not spent a great deal of time around helicopters, but one didn't have to be a mechanic to know the engine was malfunctioning badly.

"What's that noise with his engine, Lieutenant Holloway?" Gash asked.

"I hate to say this, but I think he's sucked too much sand into his air intake. He's in trouble." The two men watched apprehensively as the insect like machine lurched and flew backwards toward an open area, released the gun at the last moment, and slammed abruptly to the ground. A moment later the engines shut down and the two big rotors slowly ground to a halt. "What a cluster fuck! I've seen enough. Let's get the hell out of here before we get caught up in this shit storm and Major Vogel tries to blame all of this on us too."

*   *   *

Holloway pushed open the half open door of Kendall Stover's room in the new BOQ. Since their promotions to the position of battery commander, each of them now resided in the relative luxury of the second floor of that building, and were, in fact, next-door neighbors. Holloway had not seen Stover since he and Charlie Battery had returned from Fire Base Wolverine five hours earlier and had not spoken with him for the last two weeks.

"Hey, Baron, what's shakin?" Holloway greeted in their normal fashion.

"Bagger! Annahashamika! Can I pour you a cocktail?"

"Got any bourbon?"

"Hell, no. Want some Johnnie Walker?"

"You know I don't drink Scotch."

"Well, then it's time you learned. Tom Courtney's gone. You don't have to be drinking any Tennessee kimchi mash whiskey. A little Scotch and water will fix what ails you. You really could use some culture, you know. Scotch is a more refined drink. If you'd gone to school in the East you'd know that." Stover wiggled over to the dresser where he kept his mini bar and poured two fingers of Scotch into an old fashioned glass. His steel helmet, minus the liner, lay on the floor of the room filled with ice cubes. He dipped into the helmet, filled the glass and poured in a splash of water from the canteen on the dresser. Holloway snickered and accepted the glass.

"So, how's Mary Lou doing while I've been gone?"

Stover avoided Holloway's eyes. "I don't know, Bagger. The mail's been kind of sparse lately."

"What's that mean?" asked Holloway sitting on the desk chair.

"It means I'm getting one, maybe two letters a week instead of one a day, that's what it means," Stover fired back.

"What's she say in the letters? Is everything OK?"

"Hey, if you're so determined to know, the answer is no." He paused. "I'm starting to worry. She's gotten wrapped up in the antiwar movement. She goes to their meetings. She's participating in demonstrations. She keeps telling me I have to quit the Army. Can you believe that? Like I work for IBM or someone and have a choice in the matter. I told her I'm not going to re-up, but that doesn't seem to help. She says the fact that I'm in the Army and that I'm an officer makes her an outcast with her friends. It embarrasses her she says."

"We're not even in Vietnam. What the hell does she want from you?"

"I told you, goddamnit. She wants me to quit and come home," Stover snapped. "I go through all that shit in OCS to be an officer to make her proud of me and now I find it embarrasses her. I'm a Battery Commander and she says I have to quit and come home." Stover finished his drink and moved to refill the glass. "I don't know, man. It's kind of frustrating being stuck over here. I'm not sure I know how to handle this. I still have five months left in country."

"Have you talked to her on the phone?"

"I've been to RC#1 twice to use the overseas phone. She hasn't been home either time. I told her in a letter exactly what time I'd call her and she still wasn't there." Stover turned and stared out the window.

Eventually Holloway moved toward the Scotch on the dresser. "Baron," he said, trying to change the subject of the discussion and regretting that he had ever started it. "I have to give you some credit here."

"What do you mean?" Stover said looking back over his shoulder.

"This Scotch is damn good, man. Damn good," Holloway said, emphasizing the damn and taking another sip.

*   *   *

Gretchen Schuster sat at the bar two stools away from Sherry Cifrianni leaning her back on the ebony counter. Between the two women sat Kendall Stover with a frown on his face and his arms folded. He had once remarked to Clay Holloway that he believed that God had put singer Johnny Mathis on the earth for the sole purpose of allowing men and women to hold each other intimately in public without suffering chastisement. The scene before him confirmed his earlier observation. Every few seconds Gretchen would lean across Stover and make a brief remark to her tall slender friend concerning the couple on the dance floor, which the three of them were watching intently.

"Do you think they're still breathing?" Gretchen asked, reaching her body across Stover for the fourth time.

Thirty seconds passed. She leaned over for the fifth time. "Were they were born as Siamese twins or did they grow together later in life?"

Twenty additional seconds passed. "Perhaps they were exposed to a nuclear weapon and they fused together." This time Sherry giggled. Stover snorted.

Mr. Buster poked his head over the bar and pointed in the direction of the couple. "Month ago I tell Lieutenant Holloway that Jennifer Dodge his girlfriend. He say no. What chu call dat, uhh?"

On the dance floor the pair was wrapped in a deliciously close embrace. In the months ahead, neither would ever be able to determine exactly how it had happened, but their two week separation had apparently created a volcano of unplanned and consciously undetected emotion, which had begun venting itself once his arm had encircled her slender body on the dance floor and pulled her tightly to him. She had responded instantly, in a way she had never responded to anyone. It was though their bodies had melted together and there was now nothing else in the world but the two of them. Jennifer Dodge had resisted her feelings for Holloway as long as she could. All the while convinced that becoming romantically involved with him or any one else at that place and at that time was simply not the smart thing to do. But when the dam cracked, it broke completely. The intensity level of their affection had continued to escalate throughout the dance and was now on the verge of being completely out of control. Softly the music faded into the background.

"Clay," she whispered in the man's ear.

"Mmmmm?"

"Clay," she whispered again.

"Mmmmmm?" he replied.

"I think I missed you."

"I think I missed you too, JD."

"Clay," she said softly.

"Mmmmm."

"This wasn't supposed to happen."

"What wasn't supposed to happen?"

"Don't jerk me around," she whispered as she pinched his back playfully. "You know what I'm talking about. I just wanted to stay friends. We weren't going to get romantically involved. Remember? We don't want to get romantically involved over here."

"I never said that. You did. And besides," he whispered back, "who's getting romantically involved?" An unexplainable sense of electricity continued to supercharge the air. Neither had anticipated it and neither was ready to even try to talk about it. Yet both of them felt the intensity and the desire for intimacy. Inside, Holloway felt a hunger like nothing he had ever tasted, the fires burning deeply, exciting his senses and his body. She snuggled closer and nuzzled his neck.

"Clay?"

"What?"

"I think people are watching us and there's something else."

"What?"

"The music isn't playing any more."

"Does that mean I have to stop holding you?"

"No," she sighed contentedly. "I just thought I'd mention it."

Holloway took a step backwards and placed the palms of his hands lightly on the curve of her slender hips. He smiled at her and she gave him a sleepy eyed look and her killer grin in return. "Shall we join our friends at the bar?" he asked.

"If you insist. Let's sit with the others for a while to be polite. Then we'll decide what to do. We need to talk, I think. I'm not sure I understand what's going on here." She held his arm as they strolled slowly across the floor toward the bar where their friends sat watching. In less than an hour the couple left the bar, trying to be discrete. Their friends politely looked the other way. They had stayed as long as they could, playing mixed doubles ping pong against Stover and Gretchen for most of the time, trying to burn off some of the energy that had accumulated inside. But now, by an unspoken mutual understanding, they departed the Club together. Passing through the doorway and into the black night, she squeezed his arm tightly and laid her head on his shoulder.

"Would you like to come over to my room now?" she asked softly.

"You don't have to ask me twice, Sweetheart."

She really had wanted to talk, to tell him why all this wouldn't work. He hadn't let her. Once inside of the confines of the room neither had said a word. JD had bent to lighten two candles in brass candlesticks. As she straightened, Holloway had touched her face and kissed her warmly. Then they embraced each other and kissed longingly until she had sat on the bed and looked into his eyes and held his hand. Then together they lay on her bed in the candle lighted room, their lips and tongues slowly and tantalizingly exploring each other. Some kisses came deeply, others quickly, yet always with a sense of intimacy and unmistakable desire. Holloway opened his eyes and realized she was looking back at him, a sense of wild surprise etched on her face, as though she were unable to comprehend what she was feeling. He stroked her face softly with his hand, sensing and absorbing the smoothness of her skin. His fingers roamed casually backwards over her ear and through her silky thick dark hair, finally lingering along the nape of her long graceful neck.

"Undress me, Clay," she asked in a husky excited voice.

He found the zipper behind her neck and pulled it down slowly. Sliding her arms free, he tugged the dress down her body and tossed it casually in the general direction of the desk chair. Reaching around behind her back he tried to unhook the bra with his left hand. It wouldn't cooperate.

"Does this thing have a combination?"

She giggled delicately, a hint of nervousness in her voice. Sitting up quickly she reached behind herself and deftly released the two tiny fasteners, then looked at him longingly as he slid the straps down her arms and lifted the silky garment free. Unconsciously, Holloway blinked slowly as his eyes engulfed her bare supple chest. As he licked and nuzzled and kissed her, she began to tug at his belt. He rolled onto his back to make it easier for her. Her dark hair partially covered her face as she straddled him. Flashes of milky white and taut pink swayed before his eyes, hypnotizing him, while she unbuttoned his slacks and pulled them down his legs. Reaching for her, he drew his fingernails across her nipples and laughed when it made her shiver involuntarily. They became erect almost instantly and he licked them slowly, switching from one to the other as she cupped the back of his head in her hands. She began moaning softly. Then it was her turn. Starting at the bottom she slowly began to unbutton his white cotton shirt, her speed increasing as she neared the top. Finally she pulled the two sides apart and placed both of her hands on his chest and bent forward and kissed him there. "Clay, you feel so warm. You feel so good." He closed his eyes and sighed softly as she stroked him. Pulling her face toward him, he kissed her fully on the mouth and drew his fingernails gently down her bare back. What had begun slowly a few minutes earlier now increased its intensity, becoming ultimately a flurry of passion, as each tore at the other's remaining pieces of clothing, flinging them into scattered heaps across the floor. Jennifer tugged back the bed sheets and Holloway slid his now naked body between them as she crawled on top of him. Holloway wrapped himself around her, engulfing her and trying to simultaneously touch every inch of her smooth lithe body. His wide eyes locked onto hers.

"Hi, sweetheart. I've waited for this for so long," he whispered.

"Oh, Clay. God, I think I'm falling in love with you. I told you this wasn't supposed to happen. I fought this so long. I didn't want this to happen."

"Well, that's the difference between you and me," he replied as he looked into her eyes and lovingly caressed the firm mounds of her buttocks.

"What?" she sighed between the kisses that he softly began to place lightly on her neck. Without waiting for a reply, she wiggled her hips and guided him easily inside of her now wet body. Clutching her derrière he pulled her closer, filling her and making her gasp softly as he began to move slowly.

"I don't think I'm falling in love with you, JD. I know I'm falling in love with you. And I most definitely wanted it to happen!" He pushed harder and slid deeper. She gasped again and then began to push back. Intertwined, they began a dance of rhythmic love that grew with ecstasy and animal like intensity until they both cried out simultaneously and clutched at each other as they collapsed in exhaustion.

Outside, the early spring rains began in earnest, beating a rapid tattoo on the corrugated metal roof. Quickly, small rivers formed in the channels of the roof and rushed toward the edge where the water plummeted like miniature waterfalls to the ground, forming dark pools on the soil. From the sky above, the rhythm of the rain and the rustling of the soft winds absorbed the sounds of passion, which echoed long into the night from the darkened little room.

*   *   *

March completed itself, the last vestiges of winter disappearing as the rice paddies thawed and the air became odoriferous once again. Three more lieutenants had found their way to the 8/18th as replacements, so that each battery again had two officers to its compliment. Holloway was assigned a fresh-faced young man named Bobby Bottles, while Kendall Stover's new XO was a homely Irishman named Jack O'Malley, who swore like a trooper and drank like a fish. He fit right in. The other was a nondescript young man named Jed White, to whom Major Vogel took an immediate disliking and convinced Colonel Nordstrum to send to one of GP's in the DMZ just to get rid of him.

Both Clay Holloway and Kendall Stover had continued to learn and mature as battery commanders. Fights, drugs, racial tension, differences between the draftees and the "lifers," and learning to survive Major Vogel's unpredictable tirades, became part of the accustomed routine. Eventually, all became simply routine problems to be dealt with and solved one day at a time. The annual Command Maintenance Management Inspections (CMMI's) had struck unannounced from Division soon after Charlie Battery's return from Firebase Wolverine. Each battery in turn had failed the initial inspection, though after a comprehensive remedial maintenance program initiated by Colonel Nordstrum and with substantial assistance by the Battalion staff, each unit satisfactorily passed the follow-up inspection, as was normally the case for regular Army units. The month became April, which brought forth preparation for the Battalion tests at St. Barbara, similar to the Battery tests the previous autumn. The primary difference between the two being that the Battalion and its staff was judged as a unit, rather than each Battery as a separate entity. By the second week of the month, each firing battery had already made two trips to St. Barbara to sharpen its shooting skills. Lieutenants Bottles and O'Malley were making strong strides towards learning the job of directing the gun sections in the field. Lieutenant Hoover, already at the top of his game, simply used the time to refine his professional skills.

Two weeks before the battalion test, Holloway and Bobby Bottles worked late, talking about the nuances of doing a hip shoot during the test and how the umpires scored it. It was after ten o'clock when the two officers left the CP and strolled toward their respective BOQ's. Tired, neither felt like stopping at the Club. Arriving on the second floor of the new Q Holloway slowly opened the door of Kendall Stover's room. It was dark inside. Sounds of heavy breathing told Holloway his friend was asleep and he pulled the door quietly closed and retired for the evening. He had no way of knowing that the next morning his world would be significantly different.

He arose later than usual the next morning, decided to skip breakfast, and walked directly to the CP. As he approached the front door he noted that the sign announcing the unit and his name and that of First Sergeant Hudson St. Clair, was missing. That seemed strange. He opened the door and walked into his CP. Top was sitting behind his desk, writing.

"Morning, Top"

"Good morning, Sir," the First Sergeant replied, his ebony face strained. "The new BC's in your office. Or his office I should say."

"The new what?"

"The new Battery Commander. Don't you know about it?"

"Hell, no I don't know about it. Under whose authorization?"

"Major Vogel called over here a half hour ago and asked for you. I told him you weren't here yet. He said Captain Fontaine was on his way over here and he was the new BC effective immediately. I tried to get you at your hooch a few minutes ago, but no one answered."

"I see," Holloway muttered, his face tense. He walked around Top's desk and straight back toward the end of the Quonset hut where the BC's office was located. He passed the XO's desk. Bobby Bottles wasn't there yet. He poked his head into the office and rapped sharply on the doorframe.

"Good morning, Captain. I'm Lieutenant Holloway."

The man stood. He was in early middle age and paunchy, with slicked backed black hair and wire-rimmed glasses. The patch of the Ninth Division adorned his right shoulder, the combat shoulder. He'd been around. No one smiled.

"Come in, Lieutenant. I got in early this morning so I could get started in shaping this place up. I cleaned out the desk first. Your personal items are over there. I hope you don't mind."

"Sir, with all due respect here, I don't have a clue as to what the fuck is going on. I walked out of here late last night as the Battery Commander of this unit as I have been for the last three months. I walk in this morning to find you sitting in my chair, behind my desk, telling me my personal items are on the fucking sofa. My fucking sofa. Perhaps you would be kind enough to enlighten me on exactly why you are here." Holloway's voice had continued to rise throughout his dissertation.

While the Captain had only arrived the evening before, he certainly was no stranger to the United States Army or some of the situations one encountered in it. He was also smart enough to understand that he was seeing a controlled rage from someone who, quite understandably may have had a legitimate reason for being upset.

"Take it easy, Lieutenant Holloway. Have a seat. Want some coffee?"

"Gash!" Holloway called out.

"Yes, Sir!"

"Bring me and this gentleman some coffee, ASAP." He continued to stand and face the desk.

The Captain shifted slightly in his chair. "OK, it's like this. Last night another captain named Robbins, two second lieutenants, and myself got shipped in here from DivArty. We met briefly with Colonel Nordstrum who stated he had two young lieutenants running Alpha and Charlie Batteries. Since this is obviously a captain's slot, he said he wanted Captain Robbins and myself to assume command today after he had a chance to talk with you and the other BC. We said fine and bunked down in the BOQ for the night. Then about two hours later the Battalion XO showed up."

"Major Vogel?"

"That's right. He said things had changed and he wanted us to be over at out new batteries at 0700 to get off on the right foot. I assumed he or the Colonel had told you about what was happening. You're saying no one told you?"

"That's affirm. I'm hearing it for the first time right now."

"Well, for what it's worth, Lieutenant, I'm sorry. That's not the way it should be done."

"It fits. When Major Vogel is involved, it just fits." Holloway's anger toward the captain had subsided noticeably. It wasn't his fault. Gash handed him his coffee. Hot, sweet, and blond, just like he liked it. He swallowed a gulp and exhaled forcefully through his mouth. Feeling more composed, he sat down on the sofa. "Well, Sir. Am I your XO now?"

"I get the feeling that you're not, although I'm really not sure. I believe Colonel Nordstrum wants to talk with you about it."

Holloway found his Battalion Commander soon after he returned from a briefing at DivArty. He acted surprised when Holloway informed him that Captain Fontaine had showed up that morning.

"I can't understand why Major Vogel told him that. I specifically told Captain Fontaine to wait until the afternoon. I wanted to talk with you and Lieutenant Stover first to let you understand what was happening and I knew I wouldn't be able to do that first thing today. Listen, Clay, you've done a good job. You shouldn't take this the wrong way. You knew the job could be temporary. It's a captain's slot. I can't get two captains in here and assign them as your XO's. I've got to give them the commands. You were aware that would happen if we started getting in some captains. We've talked about it before."

"Yes, Sir. I guess I knew it would happen some day. I just would have liked a bit more warning and I would have liked to hear it from you."

Colonel Nordstrum seemed to wince. Holloway had struck a nerve. "Their arrival was unexpected. I didn't see you to tell you. All four of those officers that came in here late last night were on their way to Vietnam. They were so far along in their processing they had already been issued jungle fatigues at Ft. Lewis. At the absolute last minute they got their orders changed to Korea. It's part of the cut back in Vietnam. We'll probably be getting more officers and men any day. Pretty soon we're going to look like a real field artillery battalion again."

"So what happens to me now? Do I stay in Charlie as the XO? That's been my outfit since the first day I got here almost ten months ago."

"You can if you want to, Clay. But Captain Balone has asked for you in the S-3 shop. He needs an assistant Operations Officer. Actually you would be a combination of Assistant S-3 and a Liaison Officer whenever we need one to operate with one of the maneuver battalions. Either that or you can have Ruminski's job as Liaison Officer north of the river. He's going home in another week."

Holloway reflected briefly. There was a lot of freedom north of the river. Taking care of the FO's in the Z and being with the grunts was tempting. Spring was coming. That wouldn't be bad. But there was one major negative. He'd almost never get to see Jennifer Dodge. There was no way he wanted that to happen. "I don't know, Sir. I feel that Charlie is my home."

"Listen. Go talk to Captain Balone. He says you've got all the field experience anyone could hope for over here. You carried off that airmobile operation easily. You know the division area like the back of your hand. You're perfect for this for the S-3 assignment. Captain Balone really wants you there."

"Where's Lieutenant Stover going?"

"I've already talked with him. He's staying with Alpha. He likes it there and I don't think Jack O'Malley is ready for the XO's job yet anyway. It's better if Lieutenant Stover stays."

"OK, Sir. I'll do as you suggest. I'll at least talk to the S-3."

CHAPTER 30

There were noises outside. Loud frightening noises. The sounds of men running on the wooden planks and shouting in the corridor. Then the gunfire and the screams. Someone was falling down the heavy wooden steps, rolling and then stopping in a heap at the bottom. Holloway sat up quickly on the metal-framed cot and grabbed wildly for the .45 that always hung by his side as he slept. They were pouring through the door of the bunker now, evil looking men with high cheekbones, dressed in dark clothing with shiny saucer like helmets and carrying Kalashnikovs with bayonets. Holloway began to cut them down. One shot-one man. He aimed deliberately and squeezed the trigger the way he had been taught. They were piling up in the doorway, but still they came. He was close to panic. Where was help? Where were the other men? Was he alone on the hill? Now they poured through the doorway in an avalanche, spreading out to the sides, shooting and screaming and ignoring Holloway. That was good because the .45 was empty.

"Ammo! Ammo! Somebody give me some ammo!" he screamed.

He whirled, looking for the black knife, which was his only hope. Where the hell was it? He patted the green wool blanket and the sheet looking for it. There it was along with another magazine of ammunition! Just in time! But the .45 magazine was slippery with oil. Repeatedly he dropped it. One of the enemy, an evil looking man in a black wet suit with narrow slanted eyes and his hair forming a vee onto his forehead, had seen him and was coming straight on, bayonet fixed, his face contorted and menacing. Holloway was terrified. As he fumbled in vain to load the pistol, he recognized the face of the man who climbed deliberately over the huge stack of his dead comrades, focusing on nothing but his potential victim.

"Here he comes! Here he comes! I need more ammo!"

"Bagger!"

"Give me some fucking ammo!"

"Bagger!"

"What!"

"Wake up!"

"What??"

"I said wake up!"

Holloway sat bolt upright in bed. He and his bedclothes were drenched in sweat, though the room itself was relatively cool. It was the large two-man room located at the end of the hall in the old BOQ, the place they all called the "Ghetto." The two men had decided to share the room two weeks earlier when the change of commands in their batteries had forced them out of their quarters in the new Q and back to the low rent area. Kendall Stover turned on the light on the other side of the room and placed his wire rimmed glasses on his nose and sat there looking at him. Holloway stared back for a moment and blinked rapidly, trying to comprehend the recent transition from certain violent death to the calm serenity of his friend's face.

"What happened?"

"You were having a nightmare. You kept yelling for ammo."

"Oh, shit! Yeah. We were getting over run. I was back on the GP. Back on Gwen." He put his head in his hands and held it there for a few seconds. He began to speak again, but his hands partially muffled the words. "I've had the dream before." He paused again and then resumed speaking. "That was always my biggest fear up there. Getting over run at night while I was asleep and couldn't fight back."

"Yeah. I thought about it too. I would not consider it an unnatural fear."

"What time is it?"

"A little after five."

Holloway shook his head and exhaled to clear the last vestiges of the dream from his head. "You gonna go back to sleep?"

"Nah! We've both got a big day ahead. St. Barb, here we come. Battalion tests coming up."

"Right. It kind of loses something for me now, though. I don't think the Assistant S-3 is going to play all that big a role."

"What are they going to have you doing there exactly?" Stover asked as he grabbed a towel and looked around for his shaving kit.

"Well, this morning I'm leading a ten vehicle element from Headquarters Battery over there and then help get the S-3 operation organized. During the actual test I'll just be helping plan the operations of you guys. Some of the times I'll probably be a safety officer or maybe do some FO work."

"How's it going for you with Captain Balone now? Do you wish you'd stayed in Charlie?"

Holloway wiped the sleep out of his eyes. "No. I don't think so. Looking back on it, maybe it was time to leave, although I would have liked to stay on as the BC just through the test. The battery has really changed. All my favorite people, the ones I really liked as individuals, have gone home. Kelly Steele and Carlton. Top's leaving in another three weeks. Even Gash is short. Morale seems to be dropping like a stone. And there are so many drugs everywhere now. You just look at some of these guys in the middle of the afternoon and their eyes are as big as silver dollars. Maybe everything happened for the best. But I just wish all those captains hadn't come in for another month and I could have taken Charlie Battery through this last test. After that it wouldn't have mattered to me."

"Well, look at the bright side. That Captain Fontaine at least seems like a competent officer. The douche bag that took over Alpha is a flaming idiot. This guy is absolutely driving me nuts. He is worthless. He knows less than nothing."

"Nothing about what?"

"Nothing about anything. I've never seen a captain this incompetent. Someday when I'm completely under control and maybe have had just a few drinks, I'm going to ask him just exactly what he has been doing for the seven years that he's been in the Army. I'm telling you, Bagger, this guy doesn't know a 105 round from an ostrich egg. And he issues the most inane orders. It's scary. It really is."

"Seven years and he hasn't been to Vietnam yet?"

"No. I think the Pentagon must figure the war's going bad enough without sending him over there. That fucking guy could get a lot of people killed really easily. They might start a special body count column in Stars 'n Stripes just for him. I can see it now. 'Captain Charles W. Robbins kills five this week, all of them in his own battery. Year-to-date, this gives Captain Robbins twenty-three confirmed kills of friendly troops which includes nine South Vietnamese and four US Marines.'"

Holloway chuckled, wrapped a towel around his waist, and moved toward the door. Five minutes later, he stood alone in the moldy smelling shower stall with his face pointing into the weak stream of hot water, trying to divest himself of the effect of the dream, which had unnerved and frightened him more severely than he had let Stover know. It was the face. The evil face of the commando in the woods. It was the face of impending death.

*   *   *

Alpha Battery was immersed in the second day of the last full practice before the battalion test. The unit had fired three missions that morning, had been directed to pack up and move, and were now ready to fire from its new location whenever somebody sent them a mission. The officer in charge of the gun sections was Kendall Stover. The Assistant Executive Officer (AXO) in charge of the Fire Direction Center was newly arrived Jack O'Malley. O'Malley had taken an immediate liking to Stover and appeared to be noticeably more upset than Stover was when Captain Robbins assumed command of Alpha. The man assigned as Safety Officer for the day was Clay Holloway.

Shortly after the noon meal was fed, the radios in the FDC crackled, "fire mission!" Holloway picked up his steel helmet from the hood of his truck where he was leaning. He had just finished computing his cardboard safety diagram, which he would use to insure that the deflection and quadrant elevation that was issued to the guns was within the specified safety parameters. Hurriedly, he rechecked his numbers and satisfied that they were correct, placed the piece of cardboard into his fatigue shirt pocket. Already he could hear O'Malley yelling the data to Stover who would issue it to the two guns in the center platoon. They would fire the adjustment stage of the mission. The Battalion FDC, under the control of Captain Balone and his FDC Chief, SFC Johns, was actually providing the data to the Battery FDC, who was acting simply as a check for the coordinates.

"Deflection 2678!" Stover relayed to the guns.

Holloway quickly checked his safety diagram. 2678? That couldn't be right. It was thirty mils outside of the left safety limit! "Check fire! Check fire!" Holloway called loudly. "We can't shoot that!"

Jack O'Malley stuck his head out of the FDC tent. "Something's wrong. Battalion gave us 2678. We think its 2834. We're not even close." O'Malley picked up the handset. "Three three, this is Alpha 33, say again deflection, over."

"Deflection 2678, over."

"Request you recheck deflection. We compute deflection 2834, over."

There was a pause. Finally Battalion FDC came back over the radio. "Alpha 33, this is 33, meet me lima lima, over." Stover shrugged and picked up the field phone and rang battalion. Captain Balone answered at the other end. "Baron, what's the problem up there?"

"Sir, that deflection is not even close to being right. We can't shoot that."

"Trust me, Baron. The computer says it's right and our charts say it's right. Go ahead and shoot it."

"Wait, out." Stover set down the handset. "Let's take a new look at this, Jack. Plot the whole thing from the beginning." The FDC crew bent over their charts and began anew, starting with the pins that represented their battery location and the location of the target. Nothing changed. They were sure they were right. Stover picked up the field phone again and cranked the handle. "Captain Balone, we rechecked everything and still come up with the same numbers."

"Who's the Safety Officer down there? Holloway?"

"Yes, Sir."

"Put him on the horn."

Holloway took the handset from Stover's outstretched hand. "Yes, Sir?"

"Bagger, what is wrong down there? Just tell them to shoot the mission as long as it's within safety. We know we're right."

"That's why we can't shoot it, Sir. It's not within safety."

"You're saying 2678 is outside of the safety limit? That's impossible!" Holloway could hear the exasperation in Balone's voice.

"Sir, let me check one more thing." He released the push-to-talk switch and turned to O'Malley. "Jack, plot the deflection they gave us and see where that would put the rounds."

Again the FDC crew turned to their tables, as the horizontal chart operator calculated deflection 2678. He put a pin into the map and looked alarmingly at Holloway. The pin had been placed in the middle of a group of small black squares and rectangles on the map. The black marks represented buildings. If they fired the mission as ordered by Battalion, the center platoon would drop two 105mm projectiles into the middle of a populated South Korean village.

The horizontal chart operator looked at Holloway, who looked at Stover, who looked at O'Malley. Suddenly, the new Battery Commander, Captain Charles W. Robbins, ripped open the tent flap and walked in. He pushed his Army issued gray plastic framed glasses up on his nose and put his hands on his wide hips. "What's the problem here? Why aren't we shooting?" The problem was explained to him in detail. He seemed unable to grasp the problem. "Listen, you people. Battalion says shoot the mission, that means shoot the mission!"

Holloway turned away from him and again keyed the handset to the field phone. "Captain Balone, I am the safety officer. We can't shoot the mission. It is definitely out of safety."

An angry new voice came over the loudspeaker of the radio. It was the commanding voice of Major Karl Vogel. "Alpha 33, this is 5. I don't know what your problem is up there, but I am giving you a direct order. Shoot the damn mission as three three has given it to you. Do you copy, over?"

Holloway could feel the anger rising in his face. Droplets of perspiration were beginning to collect under his nose. "5, this is the Sierra Oscar. I copy, but be advised we cannot shoot the mission. The data is out of safety. We can shoot the data that Alpha 33 has computed, but not the data that Battalion 33 has computed, over."

"Don't you tell me what you will or will not do, you simple shit! I'll have your ass. You're looking at a court-martial right now!" screamed Major Vogel, entirely disregarding radio procedure and directing his tirade over the radio rather than the field phone and allowing half the people in the Battalion to hear him. Embarrassed, Holloway simply dropped the microphone and walked outside of the tent. Behind him he could hear the radio crackle again. "Alpha 6, this is 5. Robbins, take charge down there. Tell these people to get their heads out of their ass and fire the mission as it has been given to you. Do it now!"

Captain Robbins turned to face his officers. "Lieutenant Stover. Lieutenant O'Malley. Fire the mission. That's an order!"

Kendall Stover spoke softly. "With all due respect, Sir. The Safety Officer will not OK the mission and I won't either. I've explained the situation to you."

"Goddamn you, Stover! Battalion knows what it's doing. Fire the mission! If you won't I will!" Stover stared at him silently, his stomach churning. "What is the deflection Battalion gave us?" Robbins ordered.

"It's 2678, Sir," the chart operator replied.

Robbins stalked outside, past Holloway who stood outside the tent opening with his arms folded breathing deeply. Robbins cupped his hand to his mouth and called loudly. "Number 3 and number 4. Deflection 2678. Let's shoot!" Holloway ran past him at full speed. He ran all the way to the right side of the howitzer. To the place where the assistant gunner stood with the lanyard in his hand.

"Rear of the piece, fall in!" Holloway ordered. "Stand away from the gun." Reluctantly the assistant gunner stepped aside. He'd had confusing days before, but nothing like this. Holloway opened the breech and ejected the round.

"Goddamn you, Holloway. You've lost your mind," muttered Robbins glaring at the Safety Officer. It was a Mexican standoff and it was growing rapidly out of hand. Finally it was broken by Captain Balone's voice over the radio. Mercifully, it had a reassuring tone of calmness to it.

"Alpha 33, this is 33. We're going administrative. Let's take it from the top and get this resolved. What is the grid of your location?"

O'Malley took the mike. "Our grid is 74323881, over."

There was a pregnant pause. "Say again your location."

O'Malley repeated it. Captain Balone came back on the radio. "How do you get that? We have your location in the computer as 74983755, over."

The men in the FDC tent exchanged knowing glances. That was the error. Stover took the mike. "That was our location this morning. We moved three hours ago at your direction, over."

There was another pause. "Ah, roger. Wait, out." Two minutes later Captain Balone was back. "Alpha 33, this is 33. Our mistake. No one entered your new location in the computer or changed the charts. We were figuring your firing data from your old location to the target. Your data is correct. Go ahead and shoot the mission, out."

Stover winked at Holloway, who winked at O'Malley, who smiled at the horizontal chart operator. Then Holloway walked outside to safety the guns. He wondered how Major Vogel was reacting to this turn of events. But more importantly, he considered the village five kilometers away that was represented by the cluster of black squares and rectangles on the FDC chart. Those men and women and children and pigs and chickens would never know how close they had come to having their peaceful sunny routine day turned into a nightmare of flame and smoke and shrapnel and death. But Holloway knew and he felt good that it hadn't happened.

*   *   *

Stover drained the can of warm 7Up and put his cigarette out in the empty container. "So who do you think is more pissed off? Major Vogel or Captain Robbins?"

"It's got to be Vogel. The way I heard it from some of the people that were there, he had steam coming out of his ears. He was really planning to court-martial you and me for refusing a direct order. He wants to make an example out of someone so everyone else will be more scared of him than they are already." Holloway leaned back on his elbows on the canvas field cot. "When he found out we were right and the Battalion FDC was wrong, he went absolutely ape shit. He'd look like an even bigger idiot than he does already if he tried to discipline us now. He could have gotten a lot of innocent people killed yesterday. Range Control monitored the whole conversation and reported it to DivArty and they are very upset with him. The Colonel is upset with him too. So what's he do? Now he's going after Captain Balone and Sergeant Johns for issuing the wrong data in the first place. He's trying to talk the Colonel into relieving Balone as the S-3 and busting Johns back to E-6."

"Do you think he will?" Stover asked.

"I think Colonel Nordstrum would like the whole incident to go away and I think he'll tell Vogel to drop it. Tomorrow we start the Battalion test. We can't afford this distraction. We need to be able to function and focus on what we're doing. Let's just concentrate on doing well and if we do, maybe all this will be forgotten."

Stover nodded in agreement. "That would be nice. But I'll tell you, Bagger. It won't be forgotten around here very soon. Captain Robbins saw that as his first opportunity to show Alpha Battery that I'm not in charge any more. He is. And when he tried to exercise his authority, you stopped him, so right there he lost face. Then on top of that, he finds that if he had gotten the mission fired he could have killed some people. So now he's really up the creek without a paddle."

"You know the thing is, so many of these newer officers just automatically think they know everything there is to know. They get off the plane and just because they outrank us, its like they know everything and we don't know jack shit. Why is that? We've been here for nine or ten months. We've been around the block a few times too. Why can't they just listen once in a while?"

Stover shook his head sadly. "Moola, chingo. I don't know. Hey, listen. What did you ever do about re-upping? You were talking about going 'vol indef.' Are you still going to do it?"

"I did do it. I signed up at DivArty a week before all those new captains came in. Now, I'm not sure I should have, but it's too late."

"What did you ask for?"

"Germany. I'll have eighteen months in Germany and then probably Vietnam. If the war is still going on, that is. I'm hoping they can do something at the peace talks. We're just not getting anywhere over there."

"Why didn't you tell me you went 'vol-indef?'"

"I don't know, man. I wasn't sure how things were going with you and Mary Lou and I didn't want what I was doing to play with your mind at all. Are you definitely getting out when your time is up?"

"Yeah. I promised Mary Lou for one thing. Besides that, I can't believe how fucked up the Army is right now. Most of these guys don't want to be here and they act like it. It's all draftees now. Sometimes it looks like the whole disciplinary system is breaking down. I keep reading about fraggings in Vietnam. Such things used to be inconceivable. Killing your own people? That's nuts. And even over here. Did you hear about what happened at Seventh Division near Tongduchon last week?"

"I don't think so."

"One of the patrols comes in out of the Z after being out on a night ambush. There's a black dude there who's got an Afro pick sticking out of his pocket. The First Sergeant, who is also black by the way, sees this guy and tells him he can't have the Afro pick sticking out like that. Tells him to put it away. Well, I guess this guy is really steamed. Seems like he and the First Sergeant have had words before. So about five minutes later, this guy, who still has his M-16 from the patrol, jumps up and says 'I'm gonna kill that muther fucker right now,' and he starts walking toward the CP. Somebody else gets to the CP first and runs in and tells everybody that this guy is on his way with a loaded weapon."

"Jesus. What happened then?"

"Well, the Company Commander, a first lieutenant, tells the First Sergeant to get into his office and the lieutenant meets the guy with the rifle at the door. Guy says, 'Get out of my way. I'm gonna kill the First Sergeant.' The Company Commander says, 'No. I can't let you do that.' So again the guy says 'Get out of my way, Lieutenant.' Company Commander says 'I'm not moving. You'll have to kill me first.' So he does. He wastes him right there."

"What!"

"You heard me. This guy just blows the Company Commander away. Then he looks down at the guy and there's blood everywhere and he says 'Oh, shit!' Then he flips the rifle around and shoots himself in the head."

"Oh, Jesus Christ! Is all this true?"

"Every word. They were trying to keep it quiet, you know. But you can't keep something like that under wraps. What a mess."

"I don't know, Baron. Maybe I made a big mistake re-upping. I always wanted to see Germany and travel around Europe and all. But things are really getting bad. I don't know. I think one reason I did it was the fact that somebody has got to try to clean this mess up. The Army is going to need some good officers to try and counteract some of the bad ones. Vietnam isn't going to last forever. Things will get better some day if we work at it."

"I don't know if you did the right thing or not. But I do know this. Mary Lou absolutely hates the Army. And it's getting to the point that she almost hates me. All she talks about in the one letter a week I now get, is the peace movement and how she can't stand Nixon or the government or the Army. And she keeps mentioning some guy she met."

"What guy? What do you mean?"

"She calls him 'Dusty.' He's big in the peace movement. She talks about him a lot. Dusty this and Dusty that. I don't like it. I don't like it at all. It's really changing her. I get these letters and I don't even know who she is anymore."

Holloway was silent. He felt badly for his friend. How could his wife be doing this? The isolation, the loneliness, the deprivation of many of life's amenities. Then the addition of the morale problems and people like Major Vogel... This was not an easy tour. It was tough enough when the people at home were behind you. Nobody needed this on top of everything else.

"So tell me, Bagger. How are you and JD getting along?" said Kendall Stover, shifting the topic of conversation away from himself, as he often did at times like this.

"It's good. It's very very good. I will say to you that I have never in my life felt like this about a woman. We just fit, you know? We're always in tune, always on the same page. I can't imagine that other people feel the same way about each other as she and I do. It's just outrageous. I love being with her. Even while we're here in St. Barb it's driving me crazy missing her. I can't even think about what it's like for people like you with wives and girl friends at home."

"Come on. You cugi mah. Eight months ago you were hung up on Beth Kisha. Six months from now it'll be some other broad."

"No, man. You don't understand. Beth turned me on. She was great. But that was just physical. JD is a whole other dimension. Believe me. This is like another galaxy for me. There is no one else in my life that has effected me even remotely the way she effects me. I'm not used to talking like this and I doubt if I can ever adequately describe the thing, but just take me word for it. She's special. There is no doubt in my military mind. She is very, very special."

"Well, what are you going to do about it? She's getting pretty short isn't she?"

"You're damn right she's short. Five weeks and she's out of her. I have over three months and then I head for Germany. I've got to act fast."

"So, what's the plan?"

"Well, this is obviously classified information here, chingo, but I put in for five days of R&R in Tokyo under that new plan they just announced. Free flights, Seoul to Tokyo and back."

"Yeah, I heard about that. You're going with JD?" Stover asked wide-eyed.

"Not technically. The Red Cross would pack her up and ship her home if they heard about such a thing. She signed up for a package that's three days in Hong Kong and four days in Tokyo. She's going with Gretchen. As luck would have it, the four days in Tokyo are at exactly the same time as when I'll be there. What a coincidence, huh?"

"So you and her and Gretchen together in Tokyo. That should be fun."

"Well, there's a little more to it than that. Gretchen's old boyfriend is in Thailand. Air Force. He wangled a leave too and he's going to meet her in Tokyo at the same time. New Otani Hotel in downtown Tokyo, ten days from today. We'll see how everything goes and if it goes like I think it will, I'm going to pop the question."

"You're going to ask her to marry you?"

"You got that right!"

"Oh, Bagger. Wait a minute. Are you sure you're not rushing into this?"

"Hey, times running out. In five weeks she flies out of here. I've got to make a decision. And I have. She's the one. She's the love of my life and I'm not letting her go."

*   *   *

Captain Balone ran excitedly into the S-3 tent where Holloway was finishing writing an operations order for the final Battalion movement. It was the last day of the Battalion test. The first two days had gone remarkably well. Colonel Nordstrum had stepped forward to exert his leadership and calm some ruffled feathers. Inexplicably everything had fallen into place at exactly the right time. Even with the problems and distractions that had occurred earlier, the synergy of the unit seemed to expand as the umpires watched and evaluated.

"Bagger, they threw us a new wrinkle."

"What's up, Sir?"

"The umpires just told me we have to shoot the next mission with a forward observer from the air."

"They just told us that now?"

"Yeah. They always like to throw in something unexpected to see how we react to it. They know we haven't had anyone practice this before."

"So, who's going to shoot the mission?"

"You."

"Me?"

"Yes, you. You're a good FO and you're available. Besides, we don't want to drop this on any of the new guys."

"OK. What's the scoop?"

"There's an H-23 Raven that will pick you up in thirty minutes outside. You have to take your own radio. The chopper doesn't have an extra one for you to use. Here's the frequency both for the helicopter and for the fire mission," Balone said handing Holloway a piece of paper. "Do a radio check before you take off and after you get airborne."

Thirty minutes later Clay Holloway stood in an open field far enough away from the tents that the prop wash wouldn't cause any problems. It was a beautiful sunny April day. Far in the distance he could see a speck. Bringing the handset to his mouth, he established contact, then took a smoke grenade from the suspender of his web gear and flipped it in front of him, watching the yellow smoke drift upwards. The speck grew larger and eventually settled gently onto the ground in front of him. The Raven was a small observation helicopter with a Plexiglas bubble on the front. There was plenty of room for the pilot and an observer. If necessary, three men could fit on the bench type canvas covered seat. Holloway ducked into the open doorway and took his seat, setting his PRC/25 on the floor between his legs. He slipped on his headset and buckled the heavy clasp of the seat belt. Turning to the pilot he grinned and gave a thumbs up. Ten seconds later they were airborne.

Holloway had never adjusted artillery fire from the air. But it didn't take him long to realize that it was incredibly easy. Instead of trying to gauge distance over fields and hills and valleys as he did when he was on the ground, he could look directly down on both the firing battery and the target and see exactly how things fit together. There were enough key terrain features, which included a river, to allow him to easily identify the range from the battery to the target. Then he could adjust right or left along the gun target line. He called the FDC and established contact. They told him to go ahead with a mission. He picked out what appeared to be an old rusted hulk of a truck in the impact area and gave a grid location. A minute later the FDC called.

"Shot, over," indicating that the rounds had left the tubes.

"Shot, out," Holloway acknowledged. Hearing the words, the pilot banked the aircraft slightly to the right to allow his observer an open line of sight to the target. Clearly, the pilot had been through this before. Two geysers of gray smoke erupted on the ground just to the right and slightly short of the target. Those were the adjustment rounds. Normally observers are taught to establish a bracket: one group short and one group over. But the adjusting rounds had been amazingly close to the target. It was a snap.

"Left 50, add 50, fire for effect," Holloway announced calmly, indicating that the entire six gun battery should fire.

Forty seconds later the radio crackled. "Shot, over."

"Shot, out."

Again the pilot orbited the aircraft and banked slightly so that Holloway had a perfect view of the target. Feeling the tilting motion, Holloway initially braced himself, then relaxed as the wide seatbelt pressed against his midsection, holding him firmly. Suddenly, the truck that served as the aiming point flew upwards, driven into the air by the force of the explosion that had detonated only a few feet in front of it. Around the truck, five other rounds exploded simultaneously. The pilot grinned at Holloway.

"Nice shooting, FO."

Holloway pushed the button on his mike. "Convoy dispersed. End of mission, over."

"End of mission, out. Stand by for another mission, over."

"Roger, out."

The helicopter orbited lazily. Back and forth over the impact area it flew, waiting for its next assignment. Finally the call came and Holloway gave a new set of grid coordinates. Soon the first rounds were launched from the tubes and Holloway made his first correction. It was less than a minute before the entire procedure was repeated. Again he asked for "fire for effect." Then he waited. The pilot flew his pattern slowly, but finally he had reached the edge of his assigned area and the howitzers had not yet fired. The battery must be having a problem. There was no choice. It was unthinkable to leave his assigned air space. There were howitzer shells from other batteries that may fly through the air at any moment and he had to stay clear of them. The pilot was compelled to turn and fly the original route, but in reverse, trying to regain an acceptable position to observe. At a critical time, the call came.

"Shot, over."

"Shot, out," Holloway acknowledged. Damn it! They were in the worst possible position to observe the rounds.

The warrant officer at the controls fully understood the implication of being where he needed to be. He jerked the joystick and the helicopter heeled heavily to its right. Holloway felt himself sliding across the canvas seat. There were the explosions directly below him, visible through the open doorway. So intent was he on the position of the rounds that he failed to understand that he had not stopped sliding. The helicopter was still in a steep right bank. Suddenly the alarm bell went off inside of his head. It was almost too late! He had already exited the aircraft!

Both arms flailed backwards wildly. The left one missed entirely, but the right hand caught the edge of the open doorway, spinning him around and driving him face first into the Plexiglas side of the bubble. Stunned by the force of the blow, Holloway hung grimly to his one handed hold as the weight of his body tugged mightily against his hand and shoulder. Below him dangled his heavy radio, attached to him by the flexible cord to the handset that was clipped to his web gear. A half-mile beneath the radio lay the brown earth of the Korean countryside. Frantically he secured another hold with his left hand, then raised his leg and pawed the air feeling for the skid under the sole of his boot.

Within seconds the horrified pilot corrected the situation, banking the aircraft to the left and flinging Holloway back inside, almost without any conscious effort on his part. He landed in a heap on the seat and immediately proceeded to reel in his radio by the cord.

"What the hell happened to you? Did you decide to get out and walk? Hey, your head is bleeding," the pilot yelled over the noise of the engine.

Shaken, Holloway looked at the seatbelt clasp. Son-of-a-bitch! Apparently defective, the metal pin that held one end of the clasp to the other had snapped, allowing the seatbelt to break free at the worst possible moment. He put his hand to his head. It came away bloody. Subconsciously he was aware of the sound of voices on his radio.

"Do we have an end of mission, over?"

"That's affirmative. End of mission. We're coming in. Out."

The warrant officer landed the aircraft on a helipad near the post infirmary, the one where he had brought injured soldiers before, and pointed toward a building. "Just go in that door, Lieutenant. They'll be someone on duty to take care of your head."

"Thanks, pal. And thanks for flipping me back into your jalopy too. That would have been a hell of a free fall and an even worse stop at the bottom!" Holloway gave the pilot a little wave and stepped back. The helicopter lifted into the air as Holloway set the heavy radio on the ground, keyed his handset, and told Captain Balone briefly what had happened and where he was. The Battalion test was on the verge of being complete and Balone would send a jeep to pick him up. Feeling wobbly, he took hold of the radio and carried it with him inside of the doorway where the pilot had pointed. It was the back door to the dispensary.

Walking down a short hallway and turning left at the end, Holloway came upon a man seated behind a desk. His chair tilted backwards and his black combat boots were crossed on the desktop. The man wore a navy blue turtle necked sweater and fatigue pants. He was reading a Superman comic book and blowing pink bubbles from an enormous wad of bubble gum that filled his mouth.

"Can I help you?" asked the man, his eyes not leaving the comic book.

"I'd like to get some medical attention," Holloway responded flatly. "Is there a doctor here?"

Insulted, the man looked over the top of his horn-rimmed glasses. "I'm the doctor," he replied defensively. Finally noticing Holloway's forehead, he withdrew his feet from the desk and stood up. "Let me take a look. Come over here." The doctor lead him to an adjacent examining room where he flicked on a goose necked lamp and examined the gash. "Uh huh. Uh huh. I'm going to need to suture that. Probably still have a scar though. Go lie down on the table." Holloway complied. The doctor examined him further, apparently confirming his earlier diagnosis. "Yep. Go ahead and take off your jacket and make yourself comfortable. I'm going to give you a local and then clean up the cut and suture it." The doctor administered the anesthetic and returned to his Superman comic and bubble gum while it took effect. A few minutes later he returned, still blowing bubbles. He cleaned the wound and went to work with his needle. Holloway laid still, staring up at the man and wondering if the next bubble was going to entrap his nose and trying to determine whether or not this individual really was a doctor or whether this entire affair was an elaborate hoax.

"Oh, shit!" the man exclaimed suddenly.

"What do you mean, oh shit?" asked Holloway apprehensively.

"All the sutures just ripped out. I have to start over again. I guess your skin isn't as tough as I thought it was."

Holloway was silently appalled. Just when he'd thought he had encountered just about everything there was to encounter in this tour, something like this happened. The doctor blew another bubble and rethreaded his needle. Holloway was a captive patient.

"Are you the only doctor, here?"

"What's that supposed to mean, Lieutenant? We'll get this fixed right up. No sweatee da. Just hang tough here for a minute."

A few minutes later the doctor stopped working and stepped back. "That should do just fine. How do you feel?"

"Swell, Doc. I'll see you around." Holloway turned to see Clinton Gash standing in the doorway. "What the hell are you doing here?"

"They sent me to pick you up," Gash replied, a smirk on his face. "Look what happens to you when I'm not around to take care of you. Sir," he added.

"Why would they send someone from Charlie Battery to pick me up?" Holloway inquired.

"Because I'm not in Charlie Battery any more. I think the new BC felt that I resented him, and just before we came to St. Barb, Captain Fontaine told me he wanted to select his own driver and then he found out I only have five weeks to go and asked me what I wanted to do until I went home. I said work in the S-3 shop with you. I think that pissed him off, but anyway he plans to transfer me as soon as we get back to Camp Wynne just to get rid of me. I just happened to be up a headquarters today when you called and asked for a ride and so I volunteered to come get you."

"Well, thanks, Clinton. It's good to see you. Where's the jeep?"

"Sorry, Sir. No jeep. I'm driving a deuce and a half today. I'm afraid you're going to have to rough it."

Holloway laughed. "I'd love a ride in a deuce and a half. Anything that doesn't fly. Those goddamn helicopters are dangerous."

CHAPTER 31

"Nice head," remarked Jennifer Dodge mockingly as her fingers lightly traced the injured area of Clay Holloway's forehead. Stubby black pieces of suture material protruded from the freshly closed wound. Glancing cautiously about and seeing no one in the bar within hearing distance other than Kendall Stover, she continued. It didn't matter if the Baron overheard her remarks, he already knew of their plans. "Now I have to vacation in Japan with a damaged retard?"

"I cannot believe how much crap I have taken over this! Here I am almost meeting my death while simply trying to do my duty and now even the woman I love is giving me garbage about it." In fact, Holloway had taken an inordinate amount of good-natured ridicule, finding himself the butt of every second joke he had heard in the last two days. The story that he had actually fallen out of a helicopter and lived to tell about it had spread like wildfire, especially once the Battalion ORT had been declared officially completed at approximately the same time as he had returned to the Operations tent from the dispensary.

"Hey, Bagger, you have to admit that there really aren't too many other people around here who have had an accident that even remotely resembles this." A pause. "Wait, I have an idea! Why don't you tell us again in great detail exactly how this mishap occurred?" Kendall Stover baited him.

"Hey, Baron. Wait, I have an idea too! Why don't you kiss my ass?"

Jennifer Dodge laughed heartily at the good-natured banter. "Seriously, Bagger. Are you going to have the stitches out before you meet me in Tokyo? I would really prefer not being seen with you looking like that."

"Good. That means we'll have to stay in the room all the time." He flicked his eyebrows up and down several times like Groucho Marx, causing her to shield her face with her hand and grimace toward the bar. "No. Doc Kramer told me he'd take them out when I get back in on Friday afternoon."

"Back in from where?"

"Oh, sorry. I guess I didn't tell you yet. The 2/23rd is having a three day ORT and they want an artillery liaison officer and three FO's to go out with them. Looks like the old 8/18th is elected. Captain Balone is sending me out with them as the LNO. Three of the new guys are going as the FO's, including O'Malley, White, and someone else."

"So when are you leaving for that?" asked JD.

"Wednesday morning."

"Oh, great! You're leaving Wednesday and Gretchen and I are leaving for Hong Kong on Friday morning before you get back. So I guess I won't see you after next Tuesday at all until we meet in Tokyo the following week," she noted with a hint of disappointment in her voice.

"Sorry, Sweetheart. There's nothing I can do about it. The ORT won't interfere with the R&R though. I'll be at the New Otani, downtown Tokyo, a week from Monday waiting with open arms. All you have to do is find the place."

*   *   *

Gretchen Schuster and Jennifer Dodge had spent the previous hour and a half helping each other in their final packing. Each was limited to one suitcase for their vacation trip along with a carry on bag and JD felt thankful for the full sized American Tourister suitcase that had been a graduation present from her parents. Both women packed conservatively, knowing that they were sure to return from both Hong Kong and Tokyo with a lot more than they had brought with them. Finally the packing was complete. It was almost ten P.M., but their flight out of Kimpo wasn't until 11:00 the next morning. A driver from DivArty was scheduled to pick them up at 9:00 and drive them to the airport. That meant they could sleep in until a reasonable time.

"What say we catch a night cap at the Club?" Gretchen asked her friend. "It will probably help us sleep better. I don't know about you, but I am really keyed up."

"I'm pretty psyched myself. I could handle a JD and Coke. Let's do it." Jennifer shut the lid to the hard shell suitcase and secured the latches. Brushing her hands together she tugged open her bedroom door and held it open for Gretchen. A minute later they sauntered slowly through the black swinging doors of the Camp Wynne Officers' Club and surveyed the room. It was not particularly crowded. Charlie Battery was north of the river, Clay Holloway and three second lieutenants were on an ORT with the 2/23rd, and Alpha Battery was working overtime to get ready to move to Firebase Wolverine as the replacement unit for Charlie in another two days. These deployments seriously limited the available customers for the O Club on a Thursday night, though there were about eight people present. Two new staff officers sat in a table in the corner smoking cigars and trading war stories. Hostileman, Bill Grant, and Rick Benning, along with Kathy Kelsey had formed a circle at the far end of the bar and were deep in discussion about the subject of racial integration in the State of Georgia.

"How about two Jack Daniel's and Cokes, Meesta Busta," Jennifer ordered. Buster nodded silently and reached for a pair of highball glasses from under the bar. "So, Gretchen, what's the first thing you want to do when we get to Hong Kong?"

"Take a ride in a rickshaw."

"Seriously? Why?"

She wrinkled her nose. "I just think it would give me such a feeling of power and control over a man. To see him sweating and toiling in front of me like that. I wonder if I can carry a whip?"

"Gretchen! I'm shocked!" JD laughed at her.

"Well, OK. Maybe not a whip. But I definitely want a young strong looking rickshaw guy. I'm just going to have him pull me all over the city while I yell orders at him. But then I'll give him a really big tip, so he'll love it."

Jennifer laughed again. Buster put the two drinks on the bar at the same time that a five-dollar MPC note landed next to them.

"I've got the drinks, ladies." Major Karl Vogel stood between them. "How's everyone doing tonight?"

"Thanks, Major. We're doing just fine, thank you."

"It seems a bit dead here tonight compared to some of the nights I've heard about. But I guess that's a good sign. It means people are off working somewhere. What brings you two over here this late? I didn't see you here earlier when I peeked in."

"We just felt like a nightcap. We'll be leaving after this drink."

"In that case, how about having this dance with me?" he asked Jennifer. "That's my kind of music they're playing."

It was the Johnnie Mathis album that was playing on the stereo. The one to which she and Clay Holloway loved to dance. "No thanks, Major," she replied politely. "I'm too tired to feel like dancing this evening."

"It's Karl. And I really don't feel like being shot down for just one dance. Please?"

JD waited a moment before responding. "Well, all right then," she replied reluctantly. Taking a sip of her drink she slid from the stool and walked toward the dance floor feeling Major Vogel's hand on her back. Turning to face him, she took his left hand in her right and placed her other hand formally on his shoulder.

"Have you heard about Colonel Nordstrum?" Vogel asked.

JD looked puzzled. "What about him?"

"He went home today. I'm running the Battalion for the next couple of weeks."

"He went home? Why?"

"Emergency leave. His mother passed away. Even after the funeral is over, he needs to stay around to settle her estate and so forth.

"Oh. I'm sorry to hear that. Was it sudden?"

"I think she'd been sick for some time. Cancer."

"What a shame."

"Yeah. Just goes to show you how short life can be. You got to live it to the fullest every day, because you just never know." He had been lightly stroking her back since the dance had begun, sketching little circles with his fingertips. Now, encircling her fully with his arm, he attempted to draw her closer to him, though she resisted his strength. He relaxed for a moment and then tried again.

"Major, please don't do that," JD requested with just a hint of sternness.

"What's the matter, little lady? Don't you like the feel of a real man? And I asked you to call me Karl." He winked at her.

"Karl, I actually don't know you all that well and I'm really not comfortable dancing that closely with you, if you don't mind."

"Well, this is your big chance to get to know me better. Besides, you dance close with Holloway. I've seen you. You think he's better than I am? What's the problem here?"

"Major Vogel, the way I dance with Clay Holloway is my personal business and has absolutely nothing to do with you."

"Is that right? Well, let me remind you of something here, Jennifer Dodge." Contemptuously, he almost spit out the words. "You and the other Doughnut Dollies live on this compound at the pleasure of the compound commander, which at the moment happens to be me. And as you well know, improprieties of one sort or another are frowned upon, both by the military hierarchy and the Red Cross. Misconduct, sexual and otherwise, is reason for more than a reprimand over here. I would certainly hope that none of you young ladies would be guilty of anything even remotely resembling sexual misconduct with any officer or other soldier on this compound. But rest assured that if it comes to my attention while I am acting Battalion Commander that there are improprieties occurring, I will be forced to recommend the removal of whatever females may be inappropriately engaged with any of my officers. Do I make myself clear?"

The song was not ended, but the dance was. Jennifer stepped back. "I have always understood the rules under which we voluntarily serve, Major Vogel. And I would certainly hope that they apply equally to the officers of the United States Army as well as the women of the American Red Cross."

"Well, see that's not really the way things work, sweetheart. We're not going to start sending soldiers home for getting laid. If we did there wouldn't be many of them left over here. But you ladies are a different story. You step out of line and I find out about it and you'll be out of here so fast you'll think you got caught in a typhoon. So I'd think about it long and hard before you decide to get on my bad side." Major Vogel did a parade ground about face movement and stalked off of the floor leaving JD standing there alone. Abruptly, she looked away from the retreating figure and returned to her seat next to Gretchen.

"What the hell was going on out there? It didn't look like you two were having much fun."

"He came on to me. I asked him to back off and he got sort of ugly. Actually he said a few things about Clay and me and made some rather threatening remarks."

"Are you going to tell Clay about it?"

"Lord, no. He can't stand Major Vogel now. If I tell him about this he'll pop a cork and probably get himself into trouble. No. I can handle the Major. We're leaving for a week in the morning. After we get back there's only a few weeks left before I finish my tour anyway. It'll be all right. We just have to make damn sure we never breathe a word about meeting Clay or your boy friend Rob in Tokyo. Or we could both be in deep kimchi."

*   *   *

Clay Holloway and Clinton Gash were headed for home. Holloway's entire body because of the pounding he had been forced to take while bouncing around the Korean countryside in the back of his truck. Gash had done an admirable job of keeping up with the infantry battalion staff which used their APC's and jeeps as though they were cavalry horses, climbing hills, driving through forests, and zooming through valleys. But the truck itself had undergone incredible punishment. As the artillery liaison officer, Holloway was required to maintain radio contact with the TOC and his three FO's. That required that he ride in the back of the truck with the two bench mounted radios. It had been out of the question to even attempt to sit, given the sort of bumps that the truck was hitting. In fact the only legitimate chance Holloway had of even surviving the rides was to stand on the truck bed with his legs spread, hold onto the overhead wooden struts with one hand, hold the radio microphone with the other, and use his knees as shock absorbers.

The ORT for the 2/23rd had been declared complete the hour before, and while the results of it would not be known for a few days, Holloway had overheard enough conversations to know that clearly the Battalion Commander was in professional difficulty. On the final day of the exercise he had clearly waited too long to withdraw his headquarters from the hill that had served as his CP. Holloway and Gash had been only two of the people trapped on the hill by aggressor armor. The Battalion Commander and his entire staff had been declared captured, leaving the battalion effectively leaderless. Even worse in Holloway's mind, he and Gash had been ruled by the umpires as being killed when they came face to face with an enemy tank while trying to escape. As Holloway had expressed it to Gash, "I hate it when I get killed. It ruins my whole day." Because of the Colonel's poor decision, it was rumored that he may be relieved of command. If that happened it would effectively end the officer's career. It saddened Holloway to hear that, but there was certainly nothing he could do about it. He had given his best during the exercise and now looked forward to a hot shower and getting his suitcase packed for his upcoming R&R.

Ahead he could see his home village of Sonyu-ri. Squinting his eyes he peered ahead intently. Something was going on in the ville. It looked like a roadblock was ahead and there didn't seem to be the normal civilian traffic on the streets. Gash took his foot away from the accelerator and braked to a halt in front of the wooden barrier, which was manned by four soldiers with flak jackets and loaded rifles. An E-5, his M-16 slung over his field jacket, approached the truck and saluted when he saw Holloway's rank.

"What's going on, Sergeant?" Holloway inquired.

"UI's, Sir. We're sweeping the village. We got word there are North Korean assassination teams in the south. G-2 says they're looking for officers and senior NCOs to hit."

"And you think there's some around here?"

"We got a tip that there was three male strangers seen around here an hour ago. We're almost finished with the sweep, but I'm going to have to keep you here until it's complete."

"We're just going to Camp Wynne on the other side of the ville."

"Yessir. I figured that from your bumper number, but I still can't let you into the ville until it's secure. How about just pulling over to the side over there?"

Holloway grunted and nodded. It had been a tiring three days. He wanted that shower. Once Gash had pulled the vehicle to the roadside, Holloway opened the door and got out. Reaching back into the truck's riders' compartment he pulled his binocular case toward him, opened the top and withdrew his 10x50's. Leaning forward he propped his elbows on the hood and put the binos to his eyes, cupping his thumbs around the corners to block out unwanted light. Two hundred yards away he could see an armed squad of soldiers exiting the alley next to Proud Mary's shop. They were moving cautiously, swiveling their bodies and heads and covering each other's backs. The grunts were moving away from Holloway and they were almost to the other end of the village. It shouldn't take much longer. It didn't. Ten minutes later the all clear was flashed to the Sergeant and a moment after that he and his three men had taken down the wooden barrier, placed it in the back of their jeep trailer, and driven away with a wave.

Five minutes after that, Holloway walked down the dimly lighted corridor of the Ghetto, heading for the room at the end of the hall that he and Stover shared. Vaguely he became aware of the sounds of organ music. Then he recognized an acoustical guitar and a harmonica accompanied by a nasally, raspy, off key voice. Subconsciously he identified it. It was Bob Dylan trying to sing. He kicked open the wooden door of his room.

"Hey, Baron! What's shakin, over?"

"Hey, Bagger! What the hell are you doing here?"

"I live here, remember?"

"Yeah, but I didn't expect you until later. I'm just getting ready to go back over to the Battery."

Holloway pointed to the large Teac tape deck where the reels revolved slowly. "Hey, how can you listen to that guy? Why don't you put on a decent tape. How about Judy Collins?"

"I like Dylan. How can you not like Dylan?"

"I can sing better than he can. Anybody can sing better than he can."

"Maybe. But it's the lyrics. You gotta love the lyrics. Anyway, you can put on whatever you want. I've got to run."

Holloway bounced his duffel onto his bed. As he did so he glanced at Stover's hip. There was a web belt from which was suspended a black leather holster with a .45 automatic pistol in it. The butt, which was normally empty in garrison, contained a magazine.

"Why are you wearing a sidearm? Is it loaded?"

"Damn straight. Haven't you gotten the word?"

"What word?"

"About the assassination teams."

"Well, the 1/38th was sweeping the ville as we came in. But, they do that every once in a while."

"It's more than that, Bagger. G-2 is serious about this. They seem sure there are suicide assassination teams in the south to kill American officers. Nobody goes anywhere now without being armed. I've been sleeping with my M-16 in here the past two nights."

"Are you shitting me?"

"Hell, no. I'm telling you they're taking this seriously. We're not even supposed to go into the village unless it's really necessary."

"Well, hell. I'm leaving for Japan tomorrow. They better not screw that up for me."

"Yeah, well I'm glad to see you got your priorities straight. Adios." Stover pulled the door closed and walked down the hall as Bob Dylan began a new refrain.

An hour later, Holloway left the dispensary where Doc Kramer had just finished removing his stitches and headed for the Headquarters Battery motor pool where he knew Clinton Gash would be waiting to off-load their vehicle. Together they drove to the Battalion Communications hooch, disconnected their two borrowed radios with accessories, and carried them inside. Lieutenant Lester Joe Bufford, a.k.a. Hostileman, stood behind the counter with a smirk on his face.

"How'd they work, Bagger?"

"The radios were fine, Hostileman. Problem was the length of the mike cords. I have to ride in the back of the truck all the time to monitor them. That's no fun at all. Gash here aims to hit every bump he can find."

Gash grinned. "That's not true, Lieutenant Holloway. I really try to take it easy on you back there."

"Well, you don't succeed very well, I'll tell you that. Anyway, Hostileman, the next time we go out I need extra long cords so that I can sit in the front seat and run the mikes up to the cab."

"OK, we'll work out some kind of kimchi rig setup for you," Hostileman replied as he watched one of his commo men slide one of the heavy radios off of the counter and carry it to a nearby shelf. "You all set for the stripper tonight?"

"What stripper is that?"

"At the Club. Didn't you hear about it?"

"That's a negative."

"Well, Colonel Nordstrum had to fly home. His mother went to Happy Mountain. Funeral's tomorrow I think, but I guess he'll be gone about two weeks."

"That's too bad."

"Yeah, it is, but the good part is that Major Vogel has to go to DivArty tonight to represent the Battalion at some kind of hail and farewell for the commander of the 1/15th. So the point is there won't be a field grade officer left on the compound and so Village Honcho being the wise and alert individual that he is went down to the ville and booked us a stripper for tonight." He rested both elbows on the metal counter and leaned forward. "Eight o'clock sharp," he stated with a mischievous grin.

Holloway gave him a tight-lipped smile in return. "Well, I'm glad she's on early cause I can't sleep in tomorrow. I start my R&R to Japan first thing in the morning. Guess I better get back to the Q and pack right now. Something tells me by the time we get finished at the Club tonight I won't feel like packing suitcases." He turned to his driver. "Gash, you have that jeep all set for the morning don't you?"

"Yes, Sir. No sweat. Pick you up at 0830."

"Roger that. After this little fashion show at the Club tonight, just pour me into the back seat if you have to, but by all means get me onto that plane for Japan."

CHAPTER 32

The lights had been dimmed in anticipation. Her act was scheduled to begin at 8:00 pm, but it was already 8:10 and there was no sign of the sexy young entertainer. Impatient, Village Honcho had left the bar a few minutes earlier and walked toward the main gate, finding the warm May weather in stark contrast to the time he had walked toward that same gate over four months earlier to escort some of the local business girls into the compound for the Officers' Club New Years' Eve party. Inside the Club the jovial crowd was beginning to show signs of restlessness in the smoke filled room. High above them three ceiling fans fought doggedly to draw the smoke in lazy spirals toward the ceiling. The vast majority of the people in attendance were male, though three of the bolder and more veteran Doughnut Dollies had elected to watch the entertainment as well. Half of those in attendance clustered at the bar, with the remainder seated at small round tables scattered about the dance floor. Many of those present had PX purchased 35mm Japanese cameras dangling from their necks. At a little after 8:15 someone finally began a chant which started with only a few voices and quickly increased in number until the entire compliment of over twenty-five men was clapping and stomping and chanting "we want the stripper." The three American women remained silently amused during this phase of the evening. Holloway perused the room swiftly. So many new faces. So many FNG's. If the truth be known, there were a couple of those present whose names he could not even recall at the moment, although he had met and talked with all of them before. It seemed that every time he turned around another old face was gone and another new one had taken its place. Holloway had not really attempted to make friends with the newer people, not that he had anything against them. But he was short; well under 90 days. There wasn't much sense in making new friends. It would just make it more difficult to say good-by when it was time to go. Holloway hated good-byes. He found it emotionally draining to attend the Bridgecrossings anymore, though he could not insult the honoree by not attending. So he was stuck with going through the mental trauma of publicly saying farewell to people to whom he felt closer than to any others that he could recall in his life time and whom in all likelihood he would never see again. He made a quick mental calculation. Of all the officers in the Battalion, only Bill Grant and Sweeper had more time in country than he did. The times, they were a changin'.

Village Honcho strode back into the room and stood in front of the slightly elevated wooden platform that served as a bandstand. He pointed his arms out the crowd with his palms facing them. The chanting ceased and the murmuring quieted.

"OK, listen up. Miss Chong is here. She's backstage getting ready and she'll be out in less than five minutes. You're going to love her. She's a real doll and I know she wants you guys as much as y'all want her."

Whoops and cheers echoed about the room. Clay Holloway turned to the Kendall Stover and Hostileman. "I didn't know we had a backstage."

"I didn't even know we had a stage," Stover replied dryly.

"Ah think that means she's gettin' dressed in the TV lounge," remarked Hostileman.

"That's OK. As long as she's getting undressed out here," quipped Stover.

Holloway looked back toward the small groups of men seated at the tables. The Owl was at the front table along with Rick Benning and Bobby Bottles. Owl withdrew a long black cylindrical object from his shirt pocket, pulled the cellophane away from it, and held it forward toward the lighter offered by Benning. Holloway had never seen the Owl smoke anything before, let alone a big black stogie. He wondered idly how his system was going to tolerate it. The Owl had always been a curiosity to Holloway. He was a pleasant intelligent young man, studious in appearance. Smooth faced, no one had actually ever seen him shave, although he claimed that he did every morning and he did have a rechargeable electric razor plugged into the outlet in his room. He was unmarried and apparently had no love interest waiting faithfully at home. Frequently he wrote and received letters to and from his mother who also routinely mailed him packages containing cookies, canned meats, miniature cans of premixed cocktails, and assorted specialty articles of clothing.

The Owl seemed primed for a big evening. Along with the cigar, he had a double Drambuie on the rocks, and a 35mm Nikon with an expensive zoom lens in a leather case hanging from his neck. Attached to the camera straps were two leather cylinders that contained extra rolls of Kodacolor film, ASA 64. The Nikon had a large flash attachment mounted on the top of the camera and next to the Drambuie were two fresh packages of flashbulbs. Many of the others present had purchased the newer style of electronic flash units at one of the PX's, but the Owl thus far had elected to stick with his tried and true method, possibly because his mother had recently sent him another case of flash bulbs to ensure that he took plenty of pictures to display to the family when he triumphantly returned home. Somehow Holloway didn't believe that the pictures the Owl was planning to take tonight would ever find their way into mom's living room.

Suddenly the lights dimmed further and a portable spotlight being operated by a Korean civilian flicked on. Illuminated in its beam was a beautiful young oriental woman with long black hair piled high upon her head. A full length silver sequined gown adorned her body, white elbow length gloves covered her hands and forearms, and a white boa surrounded her neck. She stood on the wooden platform at the front of the dance area with her arms extended sideways and one long leg slightly in front of the other, as her body formed a T. It was unusual to describe a Korean woman's legs as being long, since as a people they were normally five or six inches shorter than American women, but Miss Chong's legs were long. She was almost statuesque, standing five feet seven with broad shoulders and a narrow waist. Her face was unusually attractive, with almond shaped eyes, high cheekbones, and full red colored lips. From the speakers in the corner emanated sultry stripper-like music featuring an alto saxophone. Cheers, howls, and an occasional rebel yell filled the room.

"Man, that is one good lookin' kimchi critter," Hostileman whispered as the girl slinked from the platform to the dance floor. Already flashbulbs and electronic lightning were doting the room. The girl's eyes flashed as she fixed her gaze on one officer and then another. She stopped at a table and motioned for Captain Balone to tug off a glove. Captain Sanders removed the other. Stooping, she aimed her back at Bobby Bottles and placed his hand on the zipper high on the back of the silver dress. Once he had it started she pulled away teasingly. She winked over her shoulder at him and walked quickly back to the front of the room and stepped up onto the six inch high bandstand that served as a stage. Some of the audience began to clap and cheer as she moved the zipper further and further down her back. Finally the motion was complete. She wriggled her body twice and pointed her arms downward. The gown fell away. Ooohh's and ahhhh's filled the room. There were no pasties, no panties, nothing under the dress but creamy soft tan skin with a tuft of dark hair at the apex of her thighs. Tiny brown nipples sat centered in the middle of her beautifully formed breasts. Many oriental women are traditionally small breasted, but this girl, while not being considered large, was quite exceptionally endowed. The troops clapped appreciatively. Sherry Cifrianni, standing at the bar, covered her eyes theatrically with one hand.

Miss Chong began to vibrate her body in perfect synchronization with the changing rhythm of the music, demonstrating her hours of preparation for the show. Drifting slowly among the tables, the woman suddenly parked herself on Grant's lap, looping her arm around his neck and pulling his head downward. Lifting her left breast, she began to touch it to Grant's face, tracing lines around his forehead and nose with her nipple. The crowd was going berserk, flashes going off in volleys. As he reached for her other breast the girl leaped from his lap and slinked toward the next table to stroke a face or touch a hand. She asked Bob Hoover to place his hand on her smooth derriere and then slapped it when he did so. Those that had stood at the bar now filled the edges of the dance floor jostling for a better view.

Suddenly she spied the Owl seated behind her firing off pictures as fast as he could pop out the old flashbulb, insert a fresh one, and cock the shutter. Quickly she dropped to all fours and began crawling and slinking across the wooden floor toward him. The Owl stood, pointed his camera at her, and popped the shutter. The flash was no more than five feet away when it fired and it seemed to blind and irritate her, but she shrugged the sensation aside and continued to crawl. Owl ejected the spent bulb, dropped into his shirt pocket, and reloaded. The naked girl climbed upon his little table and stood up. Nimbly then, she turned her back to the young man, spread her legs and bent forward at the waist. She began moving her shoulders, causing her breasts to sway sensuously with them and began rotating her hips no more than a foot in front of the Owl's face and providing a view that he had never ever encountered before. The cheers turned lustier as the girl brought the audience to a fever pitch. Owl was in shock. This was truly one of the more incredible sights he had ever seen, especially this close up. Transfixed by her smooth buttocks and adjacent attractions, his first impulse was to reach out and touch her, but feared that might be forbidden. But a picture certainly wasn't forbidden. He and everyone else had been taking photographs all night and she hadn't said a word. There they were, those beautiful smooth buns undulating in his face. He would capture them forever. Up close and personal. Up came the camera. At a range of no more than eighteen inches the flashbulb exploded.

"Aaaaahhhhhhiii!" Her scream reverberated through the room as the wounded girl clutched her freshly singed buttocks with both hands and leaped from the table onto the floor. Furiously she spun around to see what moron had just given her second-degree burns on her cheeks. The Owl leaped from his chair and stood there gaping, holding his camera against his chest, and trying to comprehend what he had just done. Her eyes blazed fire. A string of Korean obscenities shot from her mouth as she took off one high-heeled black shoe and threw it at him. The shoe missed as Owl ducked away, further infuriating her. Tugging off the other shoe she grabbed it by the toe and charged. Scrambling to get out of her way, the others at the table retreated leaving the floor cluttered with overturned chairs and the Owl standing alone and isolated. As she closed upon her target, he suddenly turned and fled seeking the door out of the Club. No such luck. Miss Chong was close on his heels as the other officers formed a semicircle around him, effectively blocking his avenue of retreat. Owl was trapped by the spotlight, which illuminated him in its glare.

The woman pressed her attack with the heel of the shoe. Her prey turned his back and covered his head as the first blow descended. The heel struck home, finding the muscles of the upper back. Another blow and then another in rapid succession. The Owl turned to run again. Flashbulbs exploded everywhere as the crowd was driven to a frenzy. Then there was a crack as the high heel met the Owl's skull. "Ooohhhhh!" went the crowd. "Ooowwwwww!" cried the Owl. The wounding of the Owl seemed to lessen her anger and momentarily quell her need for revenge. She paused in her torrent of Korean obscenities and stood there with her arms at her sides, her naked body heaving and sweating. Then she reached back and lightly stoked her painful reddened flesh. Spying the ladies room, she spun on one bare foot, strode to it, pushed open the door and disappeared inside. A second later people heard the water running.

"Damn, Owl. You sure know how to liven up an evening," cried Sweeper. "I thought we were just going to see a naked josan, not have display in sadomasochism. What a great show!"

Owl clamped his hand to the back of his head and withheld comment, since, in actuality, the young man had been rendered utterly speechless. Nothing in his entire life had remotely resembled what had just happened to him. Normally Owl was shy and reserved, choosing to stick to the background of a crowd. But now, instantly and totally without his choosing, he had been thrust literally into the spotlight in front of virtually every officer in the Battalion, not to mention three of the Doughnut Dollies. He felt terribly embarrassed. Looking at his hand as he removed it from the back of his head, and found a spot of blood that had been drawn by the heel of the shoe.

"Owl's wounded!" cried Hostileman. "That calls for a bell ringer." Hostileman moved to the young artilleryman, put his arm around his shoulder and reached over and clanged the bell. Slowly a grin spread across Owl's face. The crowd saw it and cheered. The smile grew wider. Instantly his psyche healed itself as the impact of what had happened to him struck home. He was a hero! The crowd was cheering for him! What a great night!

"Give me a Drambuie!" Owl yelled to Meesta Busta who was waiting for his order.

"Fuck the Drambuie! Give him a 151!" yelled Rick Benning. Cascades of laughter echoed about the room as the party shifted into high gear.

By midnight, the alcohol had taken its toll. It had been a long time since most of those present had let it all hang out. The battalion tests were over. And there were no senior officers on the compound. All of the Doughnut Dollies had departed the area and only a dozen lieutenants remained at the bar. Later, no one could remember who exactly had first come up with the idea, but someone suggested making a night assault on the Doughnut Dolly hooch.

"Wait a minute. I know. Let's do a fire mission on them," cried Sweeper. "Just like we did with the fireplace. Come on everybody get a couple of bottles!"

"Yeah. A battery two rounds ought to get their attention," added Bill Grant.

"I don't know about this, guys. That goddamn Karen is probably going to report us to the Colonel. Maybe even to DivArty," cautioned Holloway.

"Ah, Holloway. Just because your girlfriend lives there. Come on. Have some balls."

"Hey, JD's not even there. She's in Hong Kong. I'm just saying there's gonna be bad kimchi over this, I'm telling you."

"Piss on it. Let's go. There's a lot of FNG's here that ain't even seen one of these fire missions before. We've got to get them initiated," cried Grant. "Who's coming?"

"I am," cried Jack O'Malley, two empty Budweiser bottles in his hand.

"Me too." It was the Owl. Once he got cranked up he was hard to stop. Several others leaped forward.

"All right," said Sweeper. "Everybody shut up and listen up. Y'all move out onto the lawn and form up in a star formation. I'll give the commands. We'll fire high angle to put the first rounds in the air. Before they hit we'll repeat, but at low angle. That way we'll get twelve rounds on the target at one time."

"Kind of a time-on-target mission," Kendall Stover observed dryly.

"Exactly. Then we run a ground assault."

"A ground assault? We're going to over-run the Doughnut Dolly hooch?" O'Malley asked naively.

"You got that raht!" Sweeper stated emphatically and sounding like Tom Courtney in the process. "It looks entirely too peaceful over there." He put his finger to his lips and pointed to the doorway. A gaggle of semi-inebriated men tiptoed out into the hallway and out the back door and onto the lawn. Quietly and with a minimum of arguing, six men formed themselves in a lopsided star with Sweeper as the XO, Bill Grant as the FDC, O'Malley, Stover, Holloway, Owl, Hostileman, and Benning as the firing battery. Behind them stood five or six others watching in amusement.

Surveying the salty crew and finding them ready, Grant began the sequence that was relayed by Sweeper.

"Battery adjust, shell HE, fuse quick, lot X-ray, battery two rounds in effect, first round high angle, deflection 2809, quadrant 346."

Sweeper scanned the battery calmly. Arms were poised with beer bottles held by their skinny necks. It was time.

"FIRE!!!!"

Up into the black night arched six instruments of minimal destructive force. As they looped high, the gunners fired off the second round directly at the corrugated metal roof. All twelve projectiles landed within a second of one another, crashing and breaking in a random burst pattern all about the roof area, followed immediately by yells and shrieks and cries of dismay and alarm. Lights came on in two of the rooms.

Sweeper stepped in front of the battery. "This is it. Out of the trenches! Over the top! Attack!!!!"

Amid shrieks and hollers and rebel yells the entire twelve-man force launched themselves toward the doorway of the Doughnut Dolly hooch, illuminated by a single bulb over the doorframe. Hostileman was in the lead. Lowering his shoulder he let out a heart stopping scream and smashed full tilt into the wooden door, blasting it open and tearing it partially away from the hinges. It was fortunate for him that the door had opened. If not, the eleven men behind him would, in all probability, have crushed him against it, so close were they on his heels. Through the small lounge area the raiders poured, ripping open the door on the other side. Inside stood a bewildered Sherry Cifrianni, clad in a bathrobe, her hair rolled tightly in pink curlers. Wide eyed, she clutched the neck of her robe and stepped nimbly back into her open doorway as the raiders poured by yelling and laughing.

"Panty raid!" someone hollered.

One or two adventuresome heads poked out of doorways, only to be jerked back inside once the human wave assault was spotted. Kendall Stover grabbed a doorknob and turned it. The door opened. "Panty raid!" Stover yelled. It was Karen's room. There seemed to be someone in the room with her. A man dressed in a short-sleeved white shirt. A string of profanity came back at Stover. "Oooppps!" Stover closed the door in a hurry and followed his mates down the hall, hoping that Karen hadn't recognized him. Suddenly at the end of the hallway, Joan Brannigan stepped out, a can of deodorant in one hand and a Zippo in the other.

"Got you, you bastards!" Joan yelled, an evil grin across her face. Pointing the can of deodorant at Hostileman she flicked the lighter and depressed the button on top of the can. A five-foot tongue of flame shot down the hall as the propellant ignited like a mini flamethrower.

"Gawd!" yelled Hostileman, throwing an arm in front of his face and turning away from the fire. "Go back. Back." Turning he pushed the man behind him the other way. Joan advanced, giving more bursts from the can. The whole column had stopped in confusion. Finally it turned, running back toward the entrance from where it had come. More of the women were coming out of the rooms now, spraying and throwing things, and swinging pillows. Kathy Kelsey jerked a fire extinguisher from its rack on the wall. Aiming the nozzle at the clump of drunken soldiers she engulfed them in a cloud of CO_2.

"Counter attack! They're counter attacking! Pull back. We need air support."

Laughing and yelling the rag tag assault broke, as each man ran headlong for the front doorway amid jeers and insults and laughter which cascaded from behind them. Sides hurting from laughter, the group sprinted away from the structure and reformed on the O Club lawn. For several minutes they laid there, catching their breath and chortling like schoolboys.

"Oh, that was great. But, I've had enough," proclaimed the Owl panting heavily. "It's late. I'm gonna rack."

"Me too. I have to work in the morning."

All told, six of the people slipped away, leaving Grant, Stover, Hoover, Benning, Hostileman, and Holloway sitting or standing on the lawn.

"Let's go in for a nightcap," proclaimed Hostileman.

"Why not. Let's go," replied O'Malley, getting up from his seat on the grass and lurching unsteadily toward the rear door of the club.

Once inside, the group found that Mr. Yun had attempted to outsmart them. While they had been attacking the Doughnut Dolly hooch, he had been locking the bar and slipping out the front door to head for his home in the village.

"Hey, what the hell's this? Mr. Yun's gone and he locked up the bar," cried Rick Benning in a dismayed voice.

"Never fear, chingo. Village Honcho showed me where he keeps a key." With that Bill Grant climbed over the bar and reached his hand up under the counter. It took him a few moments, but finally he located a spare key taped to the underside of the counter. Holding his trophy high, he bowed from the waist and then proceeded to unlock the metal covers that secured both the beer coolers and the liquor. Within seconds Bill Grant began taking orders and pouring drinks. Holloway switched to Coke, thinking about his early morning ride to Kimpo. After filling everyone's request, he noted that at the north side of the bar a tight circle had formed. Kendall Stover seemed to be at the center. Feeling a bit surely, which was due in no small part to the continuing mental strain he felt from the deteriorating relationship with his wife, he had decided that it just seemed to be a good night to push Hostileman's buttons a little harder than usual.

"So, Lester Joe, how's things in the old Battalion Commo shop these days? Pretty damn exciting, I'd say. Pretty damn exciting. Sitting there all day winding your commo wire up and letting it out. Winding it up and letting it out. And then shining up those big spools so when you have to go out to the field where the tough work gets done you'll have shiny spools to play out all that pretty nicely wound black wire. Pretty damn exciting those field phones are too, I might add. Turn that little crank and make it sound just like a cricket. Yessir. Pretty damn exciting. Tell me, Lester Joe. Is there any possibility at all, I mean just the slightest possibility that I could get a branch transfer out of the Field Artillery and into the Signal Corps. That would be the cat's meow, wouldn't it, chingos. A branch transfer to the Signal Corps. God, think of it!"

Hostileman was standing placidly, listening to the Baron's sarcasm. Taking it in and waiting for a pause in the monologue. Finally it came.

"You know, Baron. Y'all have really kind hair. Did I ever tell you that?"

"Kind hair?" Stover replied suspiciously. "What the hell is kind hair?"

"You know, kind hair. The kind of hair you find on a dog's ass."

The other bystanders snickered. Baron was motionless for a moment, a thin grin slowly spreading across his face. Around him there was silence. Slowly his right arm reached behind him onto the bar at the same time as he began replying to Hostileman.

"Hummmmpf. Kind hair, you say. That's pretty interesting, Lester Joe. Is that the kind of thing you learn in the Signal Corps?" accentuating the "p" and the "s" in Corps. At the same time he brought his right arm back from the bar. In the hand was a red plastic squeeze container of ketchup. Calmly he pointed the nozzle at Hostileman who looked back at it without flinching, daring Stover to do it. Baron squeezed and a thin stream of thick red liquid shot forth from the open nozzle. Slowly Baron ran it around the top of Hostileman's fatigue shirt, finally working it down one side and up the other. Then he stopped and placed the container deliberately back onto the bar. "Well, Lester Joe. It would appear than you have a stain on the front of your shirt," Stover smirked.

Hostileman looked him directly in the eye as the others watched in eager anticipation. "You know, Baron, you're a good man. Good for shit!" As he spoke, Hostileman also leaned over to the bar and grasped a second plastic squeeze bottle. It was colored bright yellow and was the companion of the first. He aimed the bottle at the base of Stover's neck and returned the favor with a thick stream of mustard. "Well, Lieutenant Stover. It would seem that you too have a slight stain on your uniform."

At this point Jack O'Malley joined the frolic. "Don't worry, Baron. I'm sure I can get that stain out." Baron saw it coming, but again refused to flinch. A yellow cascade of beer sloshed out of O'Malley's mug, soaking the front of Stover's olive drab shirt. Baron immediately replied in kind.

Lester Joe Bufford watched the action calmly and took note of it. Then, looking at Clay Holloway, he spoke again. "Lieutenant Bagger, it would appear that you are out of uniform, what with everyone else having one or more stains on the front of their shirts." With that he dumped his beer on Holloway, who up until that point had remained unscathed. Within minutes all six of the club occupants and been soaked by each other and stood in pools of beer which flooded the floor. Finally, Bill Grant removed his shirt and threw it in the corner. Theatrically, five others followed it immediately. It was at that moment that the swinging doors burst open and Joan Brannigan and Kathy Kelsey strolled in. Unable to sleep after defending against the attack on their hooch they had decided to join the party. But observing both the appearance and the condition of the six shitfaced and semi-naked lieutenants they stopped.

"What the hell are you guys doing?" Kathy cried in astonishment.

"Step up to the bar, my sweets!" invited O'Malley leering at them through a drunken smile.

"Oh, no. My momma warned me about boys like you and I'm sure not coming into a room with six of you." O'Malley started toward them waving a bottle of Jim Beam, as they simultaneously turned and fled in the direction from which they had come. But as quickly as they had left, a new figure appeared in the doorway. The man was not from the 8/18th. He was dressed in a short-sleeved white shirt and black cotton slacks. He was a stranger.

"Who the hell are you," Bill Grant asked the stranger.

"I'm Captain Crawford from DivArty," the man slurred. "Who the hell are you and what's going on in here?" Crawford started forward, stumbled momentarily, then regained his balance by grabbing the bar. He too had obviously been drinking somewhere. "Why do you people have your shirts off? Don't you know this is an Officers' Club?"

"We know what it is. It's our Club. When did you get here?" Holloway asked.

"I was here before, don't you remember? I was here for the strip show. Then I was with one of your fair ladies in her abode. In fact, I was there when you people so unceremoniously ruined the atmosphere by running down the hall and yelling and making asses out of yourselfs," he slurred. He was as more inebriated than the rest of the people.

"Which fair lady were you with?" Benning asked him,

"Uh uh. Can't tell that. Wouldn't be chivalrous, would it?"

"I think it was Karen," Stover whispered to Holloway. "I saw him there."

"Well, OK, Captain Crawford step up to the bar here and join the party. Somebody get this officer a drink," Holloway ordered.

"I'll just help myself, if you don't mind," countered Crawford as he placed his right hand onto the bar and attempted unsuccessfully to vault over it. He failed. Neither the right nor the left foot cleared the top and he fell heavily onto the marble floor. Undeterred, he picked himself up and tried to brush off some of the beer that lay in a puddle on the floor and was now soaking into his pants. Then he climbed slowly onto the bar, slid over to the other side, and began pawing through the liquor bottles.

Ignoring Crawford, Holloway turned back to Stover and began explaining to him that it was getting fairly late and he needed to get a reasonable amount of sleep before his trip to Japan the next day. Neither of them heard exactly what Captain Crawford and Hostileman began arguing about and neither would ever have the vaguest idea what precipitated what was about to happen. They would remember that the clamor of the voices behind them rose sharply and sort of remembered Hostileman pointing his finger at Captain Crawford and warning something to the effect that, "If you say that again I'll knock your dick in the dirt." But Holloway again turned his back and returned to his conversation just as the blur of Hostileman's forearm blow to the jaw made the captain's body crumple and disappear wordlessly behind the bar.

"Smack!"

Other voices ceased as those gathered turned and stared at the young naked to the waist Georgian with an amiable smile still pasted to his face. Bill Grant climbed onto the bar and peered behind it. The newcomer captain in the short-sleeved white shirt was sprawled behind it.

"Hostileman! What the hell did you do that for?"

"Cause he's a no good son-of-a-bitch, that's why."

"Good enough reason, I guess," observed the Baron, also climbing onto the bar. Bill Grant was bending over the fallen man and checking his pulse and eyes.

"I think he's OK, but he's out cold. What the hell should we do with him?"

"Just leave him there. We'll turn out the lights and see if he can figure out where the hell he is when he wakes up," Stover suggested.

"Nah, let's carry him into the other room and lay him on the pool table," Grant suggested. "Come on somebody, help me drag him out from behind the bar. A moment later the officer was carried bodily through the swinging doors and laid peacefully on his back on top of the pool table. Ceremoniously, they folded his hands and covered him with the green canvas table cover. Then the stretcher-bearers tiptoed carefully away. Moments later they returned to the bar.

"I'll bet he won't even know what happened when he wakes up," noted Holloway.

"For Hostileman's sake, I hope not," replied Stover. Then he swiveled his head. "Hey, where'd O'Malley go?"

"Didn't he help carry that guy into the pool room?"

"I don't think so. He just kind of disappeared. Well, come on, you guys. Let's turn out the lights and get out of here. O'Malley's probably back in his hooch." Walking to the corner of the room the group reclaimed their wet shirts and filed out of the club. Outside it was raining steadily, yet no one seemed to care or even notice.

As the group covered the short distance to the BOQ, Stover suddenly pointed to a form laying on the sidewalk ahead. Drawing nearer they recognized the missing Jack O'Malley. He was laying on his back on the concrete looking up into the downpour. Under his head was a combat helmet, which he apparently was using as a pillow. The fly of his trousers was open and as the crowd gathered around him, they could see that he was urinating up into the air and watching his stream as it landed next to him. At least some of it was landing next to him.

"Hey, Jack. What the hell are you doing, over?" asked Stover caustically.

"I'm pissing, Baron. What about it?"

"It's a hell of place you picked for it. Are you aware that there is a latrine inside of this building next to you?"

"I thought there was, but I couldn't find it. I think I made a wrong turn somewhere," O'Malley responded, squinting his eyes against the rain that was driving down into his face. Finally he finished urinating and unsuccessfully began trying to button the fly of his fatigue pants.

Holloway looked at Stover. "Come on. Let's drag him." Stover nodded and each grabbed an arm and roughly dragged the man through the door and onto the cement floor of the hallway. Stover reached inside of O'Malley's room and retrieved his blanket and pillow. Then he spread the blanket over the prostrate figure and lifted his head and stuffed the pillow under it. They turned to leave.

"Wait. Don't go," O'Malley pleaded.

"What?"

"Bagger, you've got to promise me something?"

"I said what?"

"Promise me you'll never tell my wife how much I drink over here."

"I can do that, Jack."

"Thanks, Bagger. You're a good friend."

"Good night, Jack."

*   *   *

Clay Holloway awoke with a slight hangover and a stale taste in his mouth. His clock radio was playing softly and Skinny Yee was moving quietly around the bedroom, picking up clothing that he had scattered thoughtlessly as he had headed for his bed late the night before. Stover's empty bed sat against the other wall. He had already left for work. But Holloway wasn't going to work today. He was going to Japan. Suddenly he glanced again at the clock radio next to the bed. 0730. That was OK. His suitcase was packed. All he had to do was get showered and shaved and dressed. Then if there was enough time he'd grab a cup of coffee at the Officers' Open Mess and wait for Gash who was coming at 0830. But first a couple of aspirins. If only he hadn't had the last two beers and gone to bed before things had really gone crazy. Even if he'd gone to bed only an hour earlier, he would have been in great shape. But what the hell. Last night had been one hell of a lot of fun and he could sleep on the plane. He threw the covers aside, grabbed his shaving kit, and headed for the latrine. On the way he noted that O'Malley was no longer sleeping in the hall.

Outside of the BOQ the sun shone brightly from a cloudless sky. The recent stint of warm weather that had followed a rather wet April had done wonders for the fresh buds that had become blossoms and the leaves that now covered the trees and bushes. Spring had burst forth, filling the country with a fresh renewal of green vegetation. Chirping filled the air from countless birds that sat perched in the trees like spectators to some unfolding drama.

Battalion Sergeant Major Jethro Collins stood with his arms folded in front of the Headquarters of the 8/18th Artillery and gazed directly ahead toward the area of the main gate, which was seventy-five yards away on the other side of the wooden bridge. Impatiently he cast an eye at his watch. Where in the hell were those gardeners? They were supposed to be here no later than 0730 and it was now 0747. Goddamn Koreans. Couldn't count on them for anything. Sergeant Major Collins had spent several hours developing a landscaping design for the lawn and side yards surrounding the Headquarters. No one had ordered him to do that, of course. He did it because he loved landscaping. In fact, once he completed his thirty years with Uncle Sam he had every intention of starting his own landscaping business when he retired to California. There was so much new construction out there already. He just hoped the boom didn't end in the next two years before he could get his fair share of the business.

But now where the hell were the Koreans? Four men and a truck full of mulch would get the planned beds started in the front lawn. They'd probably need a second truck load of mulch to complete all of the beds, but if those people would just get here on time they could at least put a serious dent in the day's work schedule. Later in the morning a truck from a nursery near Seoul was scheduled to deliver six Japanese cherry trees, twenty evergreen shrubs, and hundreds of flowers, all to be planted in the front. More would come later. Sergeant Major Collins also planned to add four or five large decorative rocks, which were readily available from a local streambed. Looking once more at the gate and seeing nothing he let out an audible sigh and walked disgustedly back inside the building and returned to his desk.

By 0820 Holloway had dressed in his summer khaki uniform, gone to the Club and slurped down a cup of coffee. Then he had innocently peered into the poolroom. Good! No corpse on the pool table. Certainly he was not going to ask any questions about what had happened to Captain Crawford. The less said the better. Then he headed toward the BOQ to wait for Gash. When he arrived, Gash was already sitting in the open topped jeep and Holloway's gray suitcase was in the back seat. Disappearing into his room to retrieve his recently purchased flight bag, he reappeared a moment later and jumped into the front seat next to his driver.

"I am ready," Holloway announced. "In fact, if I was any more ready I'd have to get unready. Too bad you're not going with me Clinton."

"Doesn't bother me, Lieutenant Holloway. I'll be back in the world before you get back from Japan. Checkin' out the honeys, drinking beer. I'm ready too."

"You're that short?" Holloway asked surprised.

"Yes, Sir. Four days and a wake-up. I told you I was short."

"I didn't realize. Well, I guess this is our last ride together then, isn't it?"

Corporal Clinton Gash nodded and smiled.

*   *   *

Looking out of his window, Sergeant Major Collins saw the truck stop next to the guard shack at the main gate. About time. He looked at his watch again. It was almost 0830. Collins moved to the doorway and waited. It seemed to be taking a hell of a long time for the guard shack to pass them through. What could be taking so long? The shack was always manned by both a Korean civilian guard and a GI to insure there were no linguistic problems. Collins knew the guards were expecting the truck. He had told them about it personally early this morning. Finally the truck began to pull away from the gate, cross the bridge, and head toward him.

Behind the truck, Chin Kim Dae, the Korean gate guard, was cranking furiously on his field phone that was connected to the guard towers and posts inside the compound. Within seconds he was yelling words that were unintelligible to his baffled American counterpart who was trying to determine exactly what was happening. Not wanting to interrupt, he allowed Chin to continue yelling into the phone. Finally Chin threw down the handset and motioned to his partner to stay put. Then he picked up his shotgun and headed out of the door.

The truck full of mulch drove slowly over the bridge and pulled to a halt in front of the lawn at Battalion Headquarters. Sergeant Major Collins stood in the doorway with one leg crossed over the other and leaning against the doorjamb. He was angry. There was no way that they were going to get away with being an hour late and not get their asses chewed out for it. Besides that, there were only three men getting out of the vehicle instead of the expected four. What the hell was the matter with these people? He watched silently as the three workers looked about, saw the Sergeant Major, and then began moving away from the truck and up the sidewalk.

"Chong ji!!!" The cry to halt came from the side of the Headquarters building around the corner from the Sergeant Major. He couldn't see the man who had screamed the command. But he heard the action of the Remington pump shotgun as it fed a round into the chamber.

"Chong ji! Sonulturo!" The command came again.

The three men on the sidewalk hesitated for less than a second, then dove desperately in different directions and at the same time reached frantically into the folds of their cotton clothing. The boom of the first Remington seemed to explode right next to Sergeant Major Collins ear. The second and third booms were to Collins other side. Someone was killing the gardeners! Two of them lay thrashing on the ground. More booms. The third man had regained his feet, pointed a handgun at whoever was firing one of the shotguns, snapped off two quick shots, and then spun around. As he completed his pivot, he found himself face to face with the same guard that had waved him suspiciously through the gate only moments earlier. Chin Kim Dae fired the shotgun from the hip. The blast caught the Korean gardener fully in the chest and face, lifting him bodily into the air and blowing him backwards toward the Sergeant Major who stood dumb struck in the doorway. The bloody remains of a man lay crumpled on the sidewalk. None of the three gardeners were now moving. The entire affair had taken less than five seconds.

Clay Holloway's jeep had just begun to make the turn onto the gravel road leading from the old BOQ to the main gate when the first blast went off. Both men flinched from the noise and looked wildly at each other. Neither was armed.

"Get out! Out of the jeep!" Holloway screamed, leaping out of the open side of the vehicle and jumping into the drainage ditch than ran along the road throughout the compound. To the left of the vehicle, Clinton Gash executed a similar maneuver as the vehicle rolled to a stop with the engine stalled. Two more shotgun blasts went off. Holloway peeked his head up barely above the lip of the ditch in time to see a Korean national fire a handgun at something, turn to run, and then be blown instantly backwards by a shotgun blast from one of the uniformed civilian Korean guards.

Quickly then the guard wheeled around and searched the now empty truck. Finding no one he returned to the sidewalk where three dead men now lay.

"What in the hell is going on?" roared Sergeant Major Jethro Collins, who had continued to stand in the doorway throughout the brief shooting spree. No one replied. Behind the Sergeant Major everyone in the building was running for the front door to see what the shooting was about. Bill Grant ran up behind the Sergeant Major, a cocked .45 in his hand.

"Sergeant Major, what the fuck is this?"

"I don't know. I don't understand," the E-9 replied with a dazed confused look on his face. Finally he stepped out of the doorway and walked down the front walk to where the motionless bodies lay in a bloody heap. Behind him a large crowd of officers and NCOs was forming. In front of him seven Korean guards who had converged from their posts all over the compound had gathered. Quickly the senior guard ordered several of them back to their posts with advice to keep a sharp look out for more trouble. Then the man spoke quickly and quietly to another guard who stood nearby clutching at his side. Blood was seeping through the material of his shirt and between the cracks of his fingers. He was the only friendly casualty of the brief, but very deadly exchange of fire.

From the side of the building Clay Holloway and Clinton Gash walked cautiously forward, being vaguely aware that dozens of people from all over the compound were converging on the same spot. Major Vogel exited Battalion Headquarters and pushed his way through the gathering of excited people. He peered downward at the carnage and then looked up at the tense face of Chin Kim Dae.

"Who are they? Did you shoot them?"

"Yes, Sir. I kill." He pointed to the other guards. "We all kill," he said with a circling motion of the arm not holding the shotgun.

Major Vogel turned and looked back at the Headquarters. "Where's Corporal Lee?" A young KATUSA came forward. Corporal Lee was one of the few KATUSA's who was fluent in English, a product of eight years of formal study and three years in the Second Division. The KATUSA stepped forward out of the crowd.

"Lee, ask this guard exactly what the hell happened. What is going on here?"

Corporal Lee spoke excitedly to the senior guard. The guard digested the question and then began a flurry of excited gestures as he talked loudly and rapidly. Major Vogel waited impatiently. Finally Chin stopped speaking and Corporal Lee turned back to the Major.

"He says he thinks they are North Koreans. He believes they are part of the assassination teams we have been warned about. They were challenged to halt by one of the other guards and to put up their hands, but they went for their guns and so the guards shot them all."

"Why does he think they're North Koreans," asked Vogel, wide eyed.

Corporal Lee put the question to the guard who walked over to the corpses and began pulling off their clothing. Under the first man's shirt and belted to his chest were four Chinese Communist hand grenades. Chin pulled off the web belt and held it out to Major Vogel, who received it gingerly. "But why did he think they were North Koreans in the first place?"

After a further exchange with the guard, Corporal Lee again translated. "He says they just acted suspicious, and because he had never seen them before and that they spoke as though they were better educated than gardeners. He feel something was wrong and rang up the other guard posts after he let them through the gate and told them to challenge and search them after they got out of the truck."

Suitably impressed, Major Vogel reached forward and shook the guards hand. Chin smiled broadly and then saluted. "OK. Sergeant Major, get this area cordoned off with rope and get all of these people out of here except those that were actually involved. Call the MP's, DivArty, and Division G-2. Let's search the rest of the bodies and the vehicle. I don't know how they got this truck or where the real gardeners are, so we've got a lot of work to do."

Clay Holloway and Clinton Gash remained in the background, watching impassively. Suddenly Holloway looked at Gash and flicked his head. "Let's get out of here. I think it's all over and there's sure nothing we can do. I'm afraid they might seal off the compound. I've still got a plane to catch and I'm not missing it for anything. We can find out the details of all this later."

*   *   *

The pilot of the Japan Air Lines Boeing 707 Flight 7860 released the brakes and gave full throttle, hurtling the silver aircraft down the runway. Moments later it was airborne, the jet engines clawing at the sky. Far below the green Korean peninsula sat serenely, basking in the May sun. One hundred and seventy-five air miles later the eastern Korean coastline appeared and then disappeared from view, replaced by the seemingly endless Sea of Japan. The waters appeared gray and murky as the ceiling above them turned cloudy. In less than an hour from the takeoff at Kimpo, the coastline of Honshu, largest of the four major Japanese islands appeared. Much of the land mass was obscured by clouds, though occasionally holes appeared that allowed Holloway to take note of how mountainous the country was. His attention was captured only partially by the view, while on his lap a blue paper backed guide to Japanese travel conversation that had been provided by the airline lay unopened.

His mood had been somber throughout the flight, far different from the way he had anticipated the trip. The reality of what had happened to the three North Koreans had surfaced in his consciousness only once Gash had departed after the two had said what would be their final good-byes. Most of the jeep trip from Sonyu-ri to Kimpo had been consumed by discussion and speculation about what had just happened at

Camp Wynne. At first their conversation had been excited and exaggerated, like a couple of college boys talking about a sports event. Phrases like "wasted those dudes" and "waxed those bastards" and "capped those fuckers" were in heavy usage. Then there had been a period of quiet. Gash was going home in four days and Holloway was looking forward to a week's R&R. Sudden violent death should have had no part in their scenarios, no place in their lives that day. Yet it had happened right in front of them, almost including and engulfing them in the cloak of the grim reaper. It had been the second time for Holloway. The second time he had been moments behind an unexpected burst of deadly violence. First the ambush of the cooks in the DMZ and now this. A few more seconds and he and Gash would have been in the middle of the shoot-out and who knows what would have happened then. Holloway felt a shiver and tried to put it aside, but was only partially successful as the wheels of the chartered aircraft squeaked onto the wet tarmac at Yakota Air Force Base outside of Tokyo.

A blue Air Force bus provided transportation to Tachikowa Air Force Base, on the other side of the city some distance away. Tachikowa had more amenities and a transient BOQ where Holloway would stay for only a dollar a night until Monday when JD would join him at the Hotel New Otani. He had decided to conserve his money until she was with him. What good was there in spending a significant sum to stay at a luxury hotel by himself?

Subconsciously, Holloway braced himself as the bus hugged the left lane and curb of the road. Then he remembered. Like the English, the Japanese drove on the left side. He was sure that he would have considerable difficulty trying to drive in this country. Not that he planned to drive. There was a train station very close to the base that could take him to downtown Tokyo. Once there he would hail taxis if he felt the need, although he was confident that his legs and feet would probably take him anywhere he needed to go.

A misty rain hung in the air as he left the bus in front of the BOQ, his suitcase in one hand and flight bag in the other. Five minutes later he was unpacking the bag and hanging his clothing neatly in the closet. Then he returned to the front desk and looked around. There were several signs telling visitors pieces of useful information as well as pamphlets and brochures about local attractions.

It was early afternoon. His only food of the day, other than his breakfast coffee, had been two bags of peanuts and a Coke during the flight. Yet food was not first on his list of priorities. Almost with a sense of desperation he wanted to get downtown. To see what the city, any city, looked like. He wanted to feel civilization again. To smell and hear the traffic and feel the pulse of the giant metropolis. Other than a jeep drive through the outskirts of Seoul to get to Kimpo, he had not experienced a city for over ten months. Not since Seattle the previous June. He had not stepped from a curb nor watched the flashing of a neon sign, nor heard the sound of an automobile horn. He had already decided that jeep horns and those of the tiny darting kimchi cabs didn't count as real automobiles.

Checking with the affable NCO at the desk of the BOQ he confirmed both his plan and directions as to how to arrive at his destination. The E-6 provided him with a map from one of the display racks, which Holloway accepted gratefully and tucked into his pocket. Returning to his room he changed clothes quickly, dressing in a bush jacket, navy blue slacks, and a light blue shirt, all of which he had had custom made at the Playboy Tailors outside of the Camp Wynne gate. Tugging on his buckeye colored boots he looked out of the window. Gratefully, he realized that the rain appeared to have stopped. He hadn't brought any sort of rain gear. Somehow an army poncho or rain jacket didn't mesh with the way he pictured downtown Tokyo.

He walked briskly from the BOQ, covering the two blocks to the main gate quickly. Turning right he reached the train station a few minutes later, just as the E-6 had told him he would. Most of the dozen or so people who stood silently nearby were Japanese. One American airman was at the far end of the platform, but Holloway saw no reason to attempt conversation. He knew where he was going. Tokyo Station, downtown. He found the train ride most enjoyable. The gentle clackety clack of the slightly swaying railroad car seemed serene. It was not rush hour and the train was barely a quarter full. He noted the difference in the traditional dress of the Japanese women compared with the Koreans. The Japanese kimonos worn by the women were noticeably different from what Holloway was used to, both in style and design, though both cultures chose to wear white socks with sandals on their dainty feet. Thirty minutes after boarding, the train halted inside of the massive main station downtown and Holloway followed both the crowd and the white signs with black letters proclaiming "exit" in both the Japanese and English alphabets. After a few minutes he exited into the daylight and looked around.

Excitement bombarded his senses, filling him with a sense of awe. Shiny sedans and taxicabs were everywhere, honking and jockeying for position in the six lanes of traffic. Above the broad sidewalks towered giant buildings, many of which were taller than what he had ever seen. People bustled to and fro, many dressed in gray and navy blue business suits with leather attaché cases and in some cases folded umbrellas. He walked purposefully, heading in the direction of the shopping area. Eventually he came upon a department store and ventured inside. Spying an escalator, he walked directly to it and surveyed the ground floor in detail as the moving stairway ascended. He spent over an hour in the store, impressed with both the quality and variety of merchandise. He was surprised to recall how many aspects there were to life, which had completely escaped him over the last ten months. Simple things like poking around the men's department at a department store or riding an escalator between floors. In fact, he could not remember the last time he had been inside of a building that had more than one floor other than the new BOQ. Finally he exited the store, realizing that he had enjoyed himself immensely, but being unable to continue disregarding the pangs of hunger that radiated through his stomach. He checked his Seiko, 3:35. It had been almost twenty-four hours since he had eaten.

Strolling outside, he came almost immediately to a moderately sized cafeteria-style restaurant. He found only a few people inside as he entered and surveyed the room quickly. Beginning at the front of the line, he selected a tray and began walking slowly through the food lane. He chose not to speak, but instead pointed politely to a brothy looking soup, a spring roll, and some rice, as a plump middle-aged Japanese woman in a hair net retrieved his selections. Feeling that he deserved a big dinner later in the evening, he didn't want to overeat this late in the afternoon. He paid for the meal and then followed a hostess to a small table where he sat quietly, eating with his chopsticks, drinking the soup from the bowl in the oriental custom, and thinking longingly about Jennifer Dodge and what she might me doing at this very moment.

*   *   *

"Three dolla! Only three dolla! Ten dolla too much!"

"No three dolla. Special price for you. Eight dolla each dressee."

Gretchen Schuster turned to Jennifer Dodge with an exasperated look on her face. "I don't know, Jenn, maybe that's as low as he's going to go on these. I do like the dresses though. The material is great."

"You don't even know if they'll fit, Gretchen." She surveyed the open air Hong Kong market place. "It's not like there's a dressing room nearby to try them on."

Gretchen raised her left eyebrow. "That's an idea."

"What's an idea?"

Gretchen looked back toward the Chinese merchant. "OK, last offer. I don't know if these fit me. Understand? I need to try these on."

The merchant shrugged his shoulders and presented her with a blank expression.

"I'm going over there and try these on," Gretchen continued, pointing to an area two stalls away where slabs of beef hung suspended on hooks attached to heavy cables. "If they fit, I'll pay you five dolla each. Deal?"

"OK. Five dolla. Best price. Five dolla OK."

Gretchen picked up her three selections and strolled casually toward the beef, leaving Jennifer holding her purse and standing with the Chinese merchant as a human security deposit. The man seemed perplexed by what was happening.

"What she do?"

"I believe she's going to try on your dresses." The merchant still looked puzzled until Gretchen stepped between the big sides of meat and a moment later her flimsy cotton sun dress fell to the ground at her feet. The shopkeeper's eyes shot open wide as he clutched his face with both hands and his wife grabbed a hold of his arm and whispered something into his ear. A moment later a freshly attired Gretchen stepped into the open, arms spread wide and flicking her head like a New York model.

"It's you, Gretchen. It looks great. Don't you agree?" JD asked the merchant who, along with his wife, remained silently astounded by the young woman's audacity. Around him other shoppers had gathered to marvel at what was happening.

"OK, one down, two to go," Gretchen called as she retreated between the two beef sides and repeated her quick change, ignoring a wolf whistle from two passing American sailors. Five minutes later, the two women walked away from the still stunned merchant, fifteen dollars poorer, but three dresses richer. "What's the matter, Jenn? Not interested in trying on any clothes today?"

"Gretchen, you're one in a million. Anything I would now do in the way of trying on clothes would be strictly anticlimactic."

CHAPTER 33

Holloway had mentally feasted on the coming of night in the city. Fascinated, he had watched the rush hour crowds pouring out of stores and offices and moving rapidly toward their varied destinations. Lines formed at bus stops, while throngs of workers walked briskly toward the central train station, which Holloway had left hours earlier. Taxi's and buses clogged the wide streets, braking abruptly for lights changing from green to red, another phenomena Holloway had not seen for an eternity. And although he enjoyed watching and listening to the traffic, it unnerved him to some degree. Twice he had stepped carelessly into the street forgetting that cars drove on the left side and that he needed to check to his right as he left the curb.

He had feasted physically as well. After the rush hour crowds had thinned, he had found a large warmly lighted restaurant tastefully decorated with large amounts of oak. Attracting him from the front window were ceramic models of many of the eatery's entrees. A hostess had seated him alone at a table set for four. After realizing that neither she nor his waiter spoke any English, he ordered a Sapporo beer by pointing at a poster of a distinguished looking Japanese man with a mustache who was sedately drinking one. The beer was delicious. Served in a frosted mug, he let some of the foam run slowly down the outside of the chilled glass. He studied his Seiko for the one hundredth time that day and mentally calculated how many hours it would be until JD arrived and he could at last be totally and completely relaxed in her arms. No curfew at the Doughnut Dolly hooch. No fear of being caught in JD's room by Major Vogel or Karen. He anxiously wanted to tell her about the stripper and the Owl and the shocking events that had occurred at Camp Wynne with the three North Koreans. In his wildest dreams he was unable to think of what else he wanted more than for Monday to arrive.

*   *   *

Holloway's arms encircled Jennifer Dodge's naked body in the hot soapy water of the oversized tub in their suite at the Hotel New Otani. He added more soap to the palms of his hands and massaged it into her neck and bare shoulders and back. They were sitting in the tub in tandem, she between his legs. Finally he reached around her and began to caress her breasts as he nuzzled her right ear. They had finished making love only twenty minutes earlier.

"Mmmmm. You never get enough, do you?" she whispered.

"Not enough of you."

She sighed and pressed back against him, allowing her eyes to glance lazily out of the window and toward the acres of ancient gardens that were part of the hotel grounds. The Hotel New Otani had been completed in time for the 1964 Olympics and was one of the largest in the capital. Located near many of the more scenic attractions of the metropolis, it was almost a small city, containing a myriad of bars and restaurants and adjacent shopping.

It was early Monday afternoon. Jennifer Dodge and Gretchen Schuster had arrived at Haneda International Airport at 1100 that morning, had cleared customs, claimed their baggage, and taken a taxi directly to the hotel. JD had gone immediately to the registration desk in the giant lobby and leaving Gretchen to fend for herself in locating her boyfriend Rob, had ordered her bags taken to Clay Holloway's room. Five minutes later, only seconds after the bellboy had left the room, they were making love.

"Are you hungry, Honey?" Holloway asked as JD continued to scan the gardens contentedly through the window.

"Well, now that you mention it, I guess I am. We had a little breakfast on the plane, but I'm ready for lunch."

"How about room service? We'll eat in the tub."

"Clay! That sounds terrible. No one eats in a bath tub."

"If you'd spent as much time in the field as I have you'd learn to eat anywhere."

"Well, we're not in the field. We're in one of the world's largest most exciting cities. And as much as I like being in this hotel room with you I'm not going to spend the entire week here. Let's get dressed and go out."

"Are you going to call Gretchen?"

"No. We've been together constantly for the last four days and she and Rob haven't seen each other for months. We'll just leave them alone." She reached under the water and took hold of both of Holloway's legs. "OK, soldier. Where are you taking me today?"

"Well, the two closest tourist attractions are the Mejii Shrine and the Imperial Palace. I'd like to see both of those. Or we can just wander around and find something to eat. Tomorrow I thought we could take the train down the coast."

"What's down the coast?"

"There's a town called Atami that is supposed to be rather quaint and very attractive. And I thought it would just be nice to sight see from the train. We'll be able to see the ocean and Mt. Fuji."

"Wow. It seems like you've really given some thought to this. I'm impressed."

"Just stick with me, Baby, and I'll show you the world," Holloway chided.

"That sounds like an awfully nice offer." She turned to face him in the large circular tub. "Let's get started." She kissed him softly. He returned the kiss longingly, exploring her mouth. Eventually he pulled away and gazed at her questioningly as though it was her turn. She responded by kissing him deeply.

"Clay," she whispered between kisses, "I changed my mind. Let's make love again before we go."

"I don't know if I can already."

"Well, let me see if I can get you up for it," she teased kissing him again and sliding her hand mysteriously under the water.

He jerked involuntarily at her touch. "OK," he panted. "You win." Holloway stood then and with an admiring eye helped JD step out of the tub. Bending quickly, he scooped her into his arms and holding her close to him carried her dripping to the already rumpled double bed.

*   *   *

Then train moved swiftly over gleaming steel rails, passing close to the blue Pacific that lay at the bottom of the ninety-foot bluffs. Earlier Holloway and Jennifer Dodge had passed through Kawasaki and Yokohama, which, along with Tokyo, comprised the great urban sprawl known as the Greater Keihin Metropolitan Area. It seemed the perfect day for an outing. Blue cloudless skies had replaced the gray overcast weather of the previous day. And although the earlier poor visibility had restricted the couple's view of Tokyo Bay from the gigantic Tokyo Tower, it had not restricted them in the least from patrolling arm in arm the area around the moat, which surrounds the Imperial Palace and its adjacent grounds. And it had certainly not restricted in the least the smiles and laughter from a group of yellow capped school children which had been posing for a professional photographer in front of the moat when Holloway had leaped in front of the cameraman and had taken his own 35mm picture of the group, much to the surprise and delight of the students, teachers, and photographer. Then he and Jennifer Dodge had waved and smiled and walked away. By late afternoon they had accomplished their last major objective for the day by visiting the shrine built to honor the emperor Mutsuhito, who had regained power following the resignation of the last shogun in 1867. Subsequently, Mutsuhito had taken the name Meiji, meaning enlightened government, and had succeeded in setting forth to make Japan a world power by modernizing its army, navy, penal code, political system, and methods of construction. Ultimately, the Meiji Shrine had become one of the most revered in the country.

The train slowed and finally halted in the small station in the coastal town of Atami. Strolling casually down broad cobblestone streets the two Americans commented on the black granular beaches and rolling surf, then paused for several minutes to watch as fishermen mended their nets and used fresh paint to touch up a few worn spots on their open boat. By late afternoon they had spent over four hours in the little town and after each had made a purchase in the quaint shops they returned reluctantly to the train station. Jennifer's item, a beautiful string of Mikimoto pearls, had fit easily into her purse, while Holloway's purchase was somewhat more difficult to conceal. It was a full-scale replica of a Samurai sword in a wooden scabbard.

"Do you really think they're going to let you on the plane with that?" JD smirked.

"Well, yes. I'll get it back one way or another."

"I don't know, Bagger. I remember that group of Japanese students that hijacked an airplane a while back that was inbound for Seoul and tried to force it to fly toward North Korea. I don't think the authorities have forgotten about that."

"I guess you have a point, but I'll find a way. Maybe you can carry it for me. They wouldn't worry about a woman."

"Ha! Fat chance you'll get me to carry that. You bought it, you carry it. Besides that, what do you plan to do with it? Lead your troops into battle?"

"Hey, you better be nice to me or I'll hack up your chop sticks at dinner tonight."

Smiling, she clutched his upper arm with both her hands and laid her head on his shoulder. "Sweetheart, I will always be nice to you. But anyone who goes to Japan and whose sole souvenir purchase of the trip is a sword, deserves to take a little grief over it."

*   *   *

Holloway had made his decision. It was time. He reached over and tenderly stroked Jennifer's soft dark hair, enjoying its texture and shine. She purred contentedly and snuggled closer.

"JD?"

"Hai?" she replied in Japanese.

"JD, there's something I'd like to talk about," Holloway continued with a hint of nervousness in his voice.

"Go ahead," she replied keeping her eyes closed.

Holloway sat up in the roomy double bed. "Come on. Open your eyes. This is important."

Lazily, she rolled back her lids and focused her green eyes on him. Seeing the uneasy expression on his face she sat up slowly and modestly pulled up the sheet to cover her nakedness. "What is it? Is something wrong?"

Gently, he looked into her face. "You know I love you, right?"

"Yes," she smiled. "You've told me that on several occasions."

"And you've said that you love me too."

"I do love you, Clay. Very much."

"Then I guess what I'm trying to say here is that, well, let's get married. I mean, will you marry me, Jennifer?"

"Clay!"

"Is that a yes? Does that mean affirmative?"

She took his face in her hands and blinked at him several times as though trying to cut through the fog of a trance. "Honey, I don't know what to say. God, Clay. I didn't expect this."

"JD, I adore you. I want you to be my wife."

"This is really sudden. I mean two months ago you and I were still just friends. Maybe we should just wait a bit."

It was not the response he had hoped for. "I don't understand. What's wrong?"

She wrapped her arms around him and buried her face in the crook of his neck as he stoked her bare back gently. "Oh, Baby, you know what it is. It wasn't that long ago I was engaged to someone else. This scares me a bit, I think."

"Magic didn't love you, JD. Not really. Not like I do. You and I are good for each other. We're a lot alike in a lot of ways. We'll always be good together. I know we will."

"What if it isn't really love, Clay? What if its just infatuation or just passion? What if it goes away next month? What if I go home like I'm supposed to in a couple of weeks and decide this wasn't really real?"

"Why are you talking like that? It's real. We both know its real. And it's not just passion. I loved you long before we ever touched each other. I loved you when you still loved him."

"How many American girls have you seen in the last ten or eleven months? What happens we you get back to the world and go down to the beach and you see five thousand sun tanned little California girls in skimpy bikinis. Are you still going to want me then?"

"Damn it, JD. Why are you talking like this?"

"Clay, it's just so fast. Why can't we take our time? Let's just wait until we get back to the world."

"Baby, we can't. Don't you see? We'll only have a month in the States. Less actually. Then I've got to report to Germany. I want you with me. We can't wait. I can't go off to Germany by myself. When would I see you again? There's no time. We've got to decide before you leave Korea."

She hesitated before speaking. "I'm not sure I want to be married to a career Army officer. Do you have to go to Germany? Can you get your orders changed to somewhere in the States?" she asked hopefully. "Then we could be together for a while before we decide for sure."

Holloway rolled out of bed and slipped on a white silk kimono supplied by the hotel. Perplexed he ran his hand through his hair. "JD, you know that's impossible. I'm already on orders. I committed to vol indef. I can't get out of it now. I'm not saying I'm going to stay in the Army forever. I'm not even sure I did the right thing by re-upping. But I already did that. I have to go to Germany. I want you to come with me as my wife."

Jennifer Dodge had pulled her legs closer to her under the sheets, her knees pointed toward the ceiling. "Clay, I do love you. I really do. I think I'm sort of stunned. I honestly didn't see this coming. Let me think for a couple of days, OK?"

"OK," he finally replied, trying to hide his disappointment. "We'll talk about it later. Kiss?" he asked her gently as he sat on the edge of the bed.

"Oh, yes. I never have to think about that." She held out her arms to him as the sheet dropped indiscreetly away. They kissed tenderly for a moment, until Holloway pulled back and looked lovingly at her.

"How about a back rub before we go out?"

"Oh, I'd love one."

"I meant me, wise one."

"But, Honey, you're so good at it. You do me first."

"OK, fine. I'll do you first as long as you don't fall asleep because you have to do me before we leave the room."

Jennifer Dodge flashed her smile, nodded rapidly, and flipped onto her stomach. Holloway climbed upon the shapely mounds of her derriere and bent his legs under him, placing most of his weight onto his knees. Firmly he pressed his thumbs upon either side of her spine at the very bottom of her tailbone and began walking them slowly up her back. She moaned almost inaudibly, delighting in the relaxing sensation.

"God, you're good at this. You could make a million dollars with those hands if you wanted."

"I don't want a million dollars. I just want you to do my back after I finish with you."

"And you shall have your wish my dear lieutenant," she grunted as Holloway applied pressure with his palms to her middle back. "But in the meantime, you still have a while to go."

*   *   *

"Hey, what you looking for? You want nightclub? American nightclub? Everybody speak English. Nice place. Classy. You like." The Japanese street hawker had an engaging smile and a hustler's manner. He walked sideways along with JD and Holloway, gesturing with his hands as he talked the practiced chatter of his trade. Paying only slight attention to him they strolled casually along the wide sidewalks of the Ginza, marveling once again at the miles of neon lights and sheer cliff fronts of the skyscrapers above them, bathed in the light of dusk.

"What makes you think we're looking for anything?" replied Holloway with a grin.

"Hey, everybody looking for something. Come on with me. I show you nice club. Relaxed. Classy. They speak English. Good prices. Come on, what you say?"

"How far is it?"

"Just down the street. Real close."

"Any cover charge?" The man shook his head sideways. Holloway looked at his companion. "What do you think, Jenn? You want to check this place out?"

"Sure. My feet are starting to hurt. A couple of JD and Cokes before dinner is music to my ears."

Flashing a toothy grin the young man lead the couple down a nearby alley, stopping near the end to tug open a door. Just inside, another man with a white cotton shirt and black formal trousers stood at a small desk writing. He looked up as the door opened.

"Good evening, Sir. Welcome to the Smiling Tiger." The man waved to the street hawker who bowed quickly and stepped back into the alley. According to their agreement, he would get ten percent of whatever money JD and Holloway spent while in the club, including tips. The man lofted his hand and snapped his fingers. Immediately a smiling hostess in a tight red dress slit to the waist approached. "A table for our guests, please."

The hostess looked directly at Clay Holloway. "Follow me please." Without waiting for a reply she spun neatly on her heel and strode confidently away. Holloway allowed JD to step in front of him and follow the woman who led them to a candle lit corner table. The decor of the club was similar to the woman's dress. Much of the room was in shades of red, coupled with black vinyl furniture. A candle in a glass jar adorned each tabletop and American jazz played softly in the background. JD seated herself in the booth seat rather than one of the table's two chairs. Holloway perched next to her as the hostess hovered nearby and waited for them to arrange themselves.

"Would you like something to drink?" she finally asked when they were ready.

"Sure. How about a pair of Jack Daniel's and Cokes?"

"Of course." She bowed politely and turned away.

JD turned to Holloway. "Any ideas for dinner?"

"I wouldn't mind having a steak. It seems like forever since I've had a really good steak. Japanese food is good, but I'm ready for a change."

"Steak is really expensive in Tokyo, you know."

"Sure it is, but I'll tell you what. The Officers' Club at Tachikowa is gorgeous. White linen, cherry wood. And I've heard the food is fantastic and cheap."

"I don't know if I want to take a train all that way. Besides we'll be back to the military in two days anyway. I'd rather stay in the Ginza. There are lots of places we haven't been yet. Maybe we can find a good steak here in town."

Holloway looked up as the hostess approached with a small tray holding two drinks. She set them carefully on the table in front of them. "You're Americans?"

"Yes."

"What part of the States are you from?"

"I'm from Ohio if you've ever heard of it," Holloway responded.

"Ohio? Of course I have. What do you think of Kent State?"

Puzzled, Holloway looked at the hostess strangely. "Kent State? It's OK I guess. I grew up near there. Jennifer here went to school there in fact. How do you know about Kent State?" he asked the hostess questioningly.

"I mean about the shootings. What do you think about all those students being shot at Kent State?"

Jennifer Dodge's eyes flew open wide and she touched her hand to her mouth. "Shootings? What do you mean? What are you talking about?"

"Haven't you heard about it? It's all over the television and in the papers. There were many students shot to death by soldiers in a big riot at Kent State. Many more were wounded."

Jennifer Dodge was stunned. "What! I can't believe this! At Kent State in Ohio?"

"Oh, yes. It's true."

"Do you have the newspaper?" Holloway asked incredulously.

"Moment, please." She returned within seconds, a copy of the afternoon paper in her hand. The text was written in Japanese, but there in the middle of the front page was a picture of a female student with long straight hair bending over a body of another student lying face down on the ground. Her anguished face tilted upward and her mouth was open in a wail. The hostess began to read the paper to them, simultaneously translating from Japanese to English. Silently, the couple listened, shocked and hanging on every word as it was spoken. Finally the hostess finished and looked up. Only then did Holloway speak.

"Four dead. That's incredible. How can things like this be happening?"

"A year ago I would have been walking across that campus," JD burst out angrily. "Maybe now I'd be lying in a pool of blood on the street. Goddamnit! How could the United States Army do that?"

"It wasn't the Army, JD. It was the National Guard."

"What's the difference?"

"There's a big difference. These guys are weekend warriors. They're not disciplined. They're not ready for this stuff. It sounds like they were just scared. I'd like to know why the hell the rifles were locked and loaded. And why did they even have live ammo?"

Realizing the turmoil she had helped create, the hostess slipped silently away, leaving the two Americans to talk privately in hushed and worried tones about their country and what the impact of such a tragedy would eventually be. Forgotten temporarily was the talk of dinner or the Ginza. The happy glow of the day had been shattered, lost in the sadness of the newspaper's proclamations about an incident on the other side of the world geographically, but only next door in their minds and in their memories. A half hour later they left the club. It was almost dark. Silently they walked back to the New Otani and ate simply in one of the many restaurants that filled the giant hotel. Following the quiet dinner they retired early, falling asleep without making love for the first time since they had arrived.

CHAPTER 34

Faintly the mixture of familiar guitar and oboe and harmonica sounds reached Holloway's ears as he struggled toward his BOQ room weighted down with his suitcase, flight bag, and Samurai sword. A kimchi cab had dropped him at the Camp Wynne main gate five minutes earlier, fresh from his leave in Japan. The commercial flight carrying Jennifer Dodge and Gretchen Schuster had departed Haneda Airport four hours before his military charter had left Yakota. He was sure she was already in her hooch. He missed her already.

It was Saturday afternoon. Nudging open the unlatched door, he expected to see the Baron smiling at him with his smirky little self confident grin. It was not that way. The two six inch reels of the Teac tape deck were slowly revolving as anticipated with the Dylan sounds, but Kendall Stover lay on his bunk clad only in his boxer shorts, his back propped against the wall with a pillow. A half empty bottle of Johnnie Walker tilted against his thigh, held upright by a curved right hand. The right hand also held a Marlboro, from which the smoke drifted aimlessly upward and out of the open window above him. Nearby were a nearly empty silver cigarette case and an almost full ashtray. His left hand held an old fashioned glass of amber liquid with the crest of Second Infantry Division painted on its side, while on the cement floor beside the bunk was an inverted steel combat helmet with the liner removed. Inside, mostly melted ice floated in a chilled pool of water. A crumpled piece of pink stationary lay on the bunk next to his bare foot. His eyes seemed dull and unfocused, while the skin surrounding them appeared reddened. He did not acknowledge Holloway's presence.

"Hey, what's shakin', over?"

Baron finally looked at him idly. Holloway glanced again at the crumpled pink paper. It looked like a letter. A light bulb blinked on in Holloway's head and he set down his luggage.

"What is it, man? Mary Lou?"

He nodded slowly. "She left me, Bagger."

"What! Just like that? She left?"

"Yep! Just doesn't want to be tied to me anymore she says. Wants to be with someone like Dusty the hippie asshole, who really understands who she is and what she wants. Says I'm out of touch with what is going on in the world."

"Where'd she go?"

"Oh, she's going to live out in the country with Dusty and four other people that are part of their "family." She stored all my stuff at some kind of a rental storage place. Even sent me the key to it. That was considerate, don't you think?"

"I don't believe this. Look, why don't you request an emergency leave. They'll give it to you. Go find her and talk to her."

"Screw it. I don't really think I can relate to who she is now. No. It's over. It's hard to believe, but it really is over. I think I'm gonna just extend my tour here for a while and get past the whole thing. Maybe go down to the ville and fuck my brains out."

"And catch the clap and keep working for Captain Robbins and Major Vogel? Shit! You don't want to do that, man. Don't extend over here. This place sucks. Take your DEROS in three months and go somewhere else. Anywhere else."

"Hmmpf!" Stover reached into the helmet and plucked a few of the floating ice cubes from the water. Then he filled the glass with Scotch. "Want a drink?"

"Sure." Holloway sat on the edge of his bed and unlaced his black dress shoes. Then he filled his glass and leaned against the wall that bordered his bed, looking at Stover and waiting for him to talk.

"So, how about you, Bagger?" He seemed to be slurring his words slightly. "How's things with the fair Jennifer? Are you gonna get married?"

"I don't know. We had a great time in Japan. At least up until we heard about that Kent State thing. That's where she went to school, you know, and it really bothered her and it didn't help our situation either. So yeah, I asked her to marry me, but she wouldn't give me a firm answer. I think she's gun shy after what happened to her with Magic. She says she wants to go home first and take some time and think the whole thing through. Then she'll meet my plane in two months when I get home and we'll decide."

"Is that OK with you?"

"It's not the way I want it. I want her to go home and start planning the wedding so we can have a nice church ceremony a week or two after I get there. That way our friends can come and I can notify the Army that I'm getting married and they can cut travel orders for her to Germany as my wife."

"Do you really think she wants to marry you?"

"Yes. I do. I hope she does, anyway." He paused for a long moment. "Baron, I feel really shitty sitting here telling you about how I want to get married and you're sitting there telling me that you're splitting up. This is really fucked up, isn't it?"

Stover sang in tune with the next Bob Dylan selection that had come up on the tape and looked off in the distance. There seemed to be a tear forming in the corner of one eye, nearest his nose. "Sometimes I don't even think I know what's fucked up and what's normal anymore. This place gives one a jaundiced view of life, I think."

"Yeah. It's a bummer." Holloway paused momentarily, studying his friend. "Do you want to talk about Mary Lou any more?"

"Not really."

"OK." Holloway unzipped his flight bag and began nonchalantly unpacking it, feeling awkward and wondering what to say next. "Hey," he finally ventured, "let me ask you a question. Did they ever find out any more about those three North Koreans? Has anything else happened?"

"Nothing new has happened around here. Seventh Division got two more UI's south of Tongduchon. Oh yeah, and Jack O'Malley got sent up to GP Cindy. He called down yesterday and told me a patrol from the 1/9th got a kill in the Z two days ago."

"What happened?"

"Jack says the point man from our patrol came over a little rise and looked straight ahead and there's a North Korean patrol coming right at him, but their point man is looking off to the side and doesn't see him. So our guy goes down on one knee and aims and dusts him. The rest of their patrol took off north."

"All right! And nothing on the assassination team that got nailed in front of Battalion the day I left?"

"I was getting to that." Stover paused for a long pull at the Scotch. Then he fired up a Marlboro, lighting it from the still glowing butt of the old one. "The day after you left and the guards killed those three guys, some farmers found the four gardeners that were supposed to have shown up here. They were all dead. Shot and their throats cut. G-2 thinks they must have gotten into a conversation with the North Koreans who found out their destination and decided to use their truck as a way to penetrate the compound and try to kill as many of us as they could. There were satchel charges hidden in the truck, by the way. You don't know how lucky we all were. Oh, and also, all the officers chipped in and bought the Korean guards two cases of booze and a pair of Levi's each."

"Levi's?"

"Yeah. Somebody asked them what they'd really like to have and that's what they wanted, so Village Honcho ordered them out of the Sears catalog. Ought to be here any time now." He took a long drag on the cigarette and blew a smoke ring that floated lazily toward the ceiling.

Holloway finished unpacking the flight bag and tossed his heavy suitcase onto the bed. Then he flipped the twin catches on it and raised the lid. Digging down through some dirty clothes he came upon a plastic wrapped piece of silk clothing. He tugged it free and sailed it over to land on Stover's bed. "Got a present for you."

"What is it?"

"Kimono. See the writing on the back?"

"Yeah."

"It means 'I have an ace in the hole.' At least that's what the girl that sold it to me told me."

"Yeah, fat chance. It probably means 'I'm an American asshole.'" He laughed. Holloway laughed with him. Stove pulled the ivory colored kimono from the bag and slipped his arms into it. The garment hung nearly to the floor. Tying it in front he walked to where Holloway stood watching him and shook his hand. "Thanks, Bagger. It's good to see you back." They smiled at each other. Things could be worse.

*   *   *

He stood on a bare sandy colored bluff overlooking a meadow covered with low vegetation. Strapped to his back was a PRC-25 radio with a similar second unit sitting in the dust at his feet. He was in full battle gear. Near him were six other soldiers including the battalion commander of the 1/9th Infantry. The rest of the group was comprised of their S-3, three RTO's, and an umpire. It was the final day of their ORT and again Clay Holloway found himself assigned as the artillery liaison officer for the test. Each of the RTO's was in radio contact with one of the infantry companies under the battalion commander's control. All of the men gazed toward the lush green field and the azure sky beyond.

Faintly the sound of Huey's rose from the distance, their familiar "whop whop" growing louder each second. The seven men watched as the dark aluminum skinned dragonflies headed straight toward them. Four of the aircraft flew in a diamond formation, coming in low over the meadow. Suddenly, all four flared in unison. The noses came up as the tails dropped down and the tall grass around them was beaten flat by the large rotor blades that continued to whip the air. Except for the seven men on the bluff there had been no sign of other human activity. But as the diamond of helicopters touched their skids to the ground, out of the wood line fifty meters to each side of the meadow, poured columns of well organized armed men dressed in olive drab and running across the field and heading for the helicopters. Within seconds, the four helicopters were filled with the grunts, ten to a ship, a full platoon in the diamond. The helicopters lifted away from the LZ. The noses tilted toward the ground and the diamond charged ahead, gaining altitude as it flew. Already the sound of more birds filled the air even as the noise of the departing ones faded into the distance. Another diamond landed, swirling the violet smoke from the smoke grenade that marked the spot in the meadow. More troops came out of hiding, running to the ships, and taking off as before. In less than five minutes, Bravo Company, Keith Hackworth's Company, had boarded the four platoon sized diamonds and were flying toward their airmobile assault objective. Meanwhile, the other two companies of the 1/9th were making their movements in the more conventional overland assault formation.

Next it was the turn of the command party. A lone helicopter was inbound. This was the Command and Control helicopter, the C&C, the Charlie Charlie. This was the method of control on the modern American battlefield, where the battalion commander and his staff would orbit slowly over the battle area, observing the action and directing his troops as they maneuvered and fought, or in this case, simulated fighting. It was not a new concept. Generals from the beginning of time had attempted to put themselves into position to observe the battle, often from a hill or mountain nearby. The advantage to having a front row seat to a battle cannot be overstated. Rather than being in a tent or bunker on the ground and relying on sometimes unreliable radio reports to guide his actions, the battalion commander could watch the action unfold. In conjunction with his S-3, he makes adjustments as needed, changing a route of march, taking advantage of a gap in the enemy's defenses, or sweeping friendly troops to plug a hole that the enemy is about to attack. From the airborne vantage point, the battlefield becomes a giant chessboard, seen completely by the unit commander. By his side is his friendly artillery liaison officer, directing the necessary fire support through his FO's or coordinating helicopter or TAC air strikes in support of the ground action.

Soon the Huey settled to the earth and the team boarded the ship instantly. Holloway was the last man on and took the seat reserved for him near the open sliding door. From there he, with the battalion commander across from him, could observe the action and assist his three FO's on the job in coordinating the simulated artillery fires. He looked over at the three RTO's. Each of them was talking into their handsets, insuring that they still maintained radio contact now that they were inside the airborne helicopter.

Within moments they were over the objective, a partially bald, boulder-strewn hill that dominated the landscape. It was called the Cue Ball, a name ordained long before and the genesis of which had disappeared over the years. On top of the hill a company of aggressor forces were dug in. In close proximity to Cue Ball stood a smaller hill called simply Hill 177 and which was held by a reinforced platoon of the aggressors. It was the mission of the 1/9th to assault and secure Cue Ball, which was tactically impossible without first neutralizing Hill 177 and its crew served weapons. Holloway listened as his FO's simulated pounding Hill 177 with a barrage of artillery fire. At the last moment the fires shifted and the helicopters swept in landing the assault troops who quickly over ran the small hill. Next came the main assault. Alpha and Charlie Companies launched themselves against Cue Ball while Bravo supported them from the smaller hill, which they now held.

The C&C orbited slowly over the battle area as the Battalion Commander and his S-3 watched, and listened, and gave orders when necessary. Holloway, meanwhile, monitored the radio traffic of his FO's as they executed the fire plan Holloway had prepared and distributed to them the night before. He was glad that they were the ones working their way up the piece of steep terrain while he sat in the bleachers high above. Once he assisted in the call for fire when Bobby Bottles was not in a position to see the target, but otherwise things ran smoothly. He hoped the umpire was pleased with their performance. Two thousand feet below the helicopter the grunts of the 1/9th pressed home their attack, ultimately sweeping the aggressors from the top and consolidating the objective. Across from him he heard the Colonel speak into his radio and then order the pilot to land the aircraft first on Hill 177.

The Huey dropped lower, swooping around the hill mass and finally settling over a bare piece of terrain near the plume of a violet smoke grenade. The LZ was not particularly large, with heavy bushes nearly surrounding it. Tentatively, the pilot hovered, unsure as to whether he could land successfully.

Holloway could see the Battalion Commander's lips moving. "Set it down," the Colonel was saying. "Just set it down."

Finally, the pilot grimaced and shoved the joystick forward, dropping the aircraft to the earth. The skids were farther away from the ground than the young pilot realized and the shock to the passengers and crew was unusually severe. Frowning, the Battalion Commander stared accusingly at the back of the pilot's head. Finally he climbed out of the door. Holloway was right behind as he saw the infantry Company Commander approach and render a casual salute.

"Lieutenant Hackworth, a fine job on the air assault. Couldn't have been better. Let's take a fast walk around the objective." Holloway and the infantry S-3 stayed well to the rear as the Battalion Commander strode quickly about the area with Hackworth pointing and making occasional remarks about one thing or another. Five minutes later he was ready to go. He wanted to fly to the top of Cue Ball, a quarter of a mile away and above them. It was then that Holloway caught Hackworth's eye.

"Hey, Bagger. How you been?"

"Good Hacker. Real good. You people looked great. Nice job."

"Thanks, man. Piece of cake when the bullets are make believe."

Holloway smiled. "How long have you got to go now? I'd think you'd be pretty short."

"I am. This is my last overnight in the field. I'm so short I could sleep in a matchbox. Twelve days and a wake up. Bravo goes back into the DMZ next week, but I'm turning over the Company as soon as this ORT is complete. Then I'm out of here. Ft. Carson, Colorado. How about you?"

"I'm pretty short too. Sixty-three days. Hey, I've got to run. I think your Colonel wants to get airborne. Good luck. Sayonara." Holloway waved and ran the thirty yards to where the Huey sat with its rotor turning. The pilot had already gotten out to check his skids, but finding no damage from the rather jolting landing had returned to his seat.

Holloway climbed nimbly through the open doorway. "You two know each other?" the Colonel asked.

"Yes, Sir. We were on GP Cindy together. He took me out on an ambush patrol with him too."

"He's my best company commander. I hate to lose him," the Colonel yelled as the pilot applied power and the Huey rose briskly into the blue sky. "They don't come any better than him."

*   *   *

It was the day Holloway had dreaded. Jennifer Dodge was scheduled to leave in less than twenty-four hours. Homeward bound. Back to the world. And things were still not settled between them. Not that there had been much time to discuss them. Following his three days with the 1/9th he'd been surprised to find that he had been assigned temporary duty (TDY) to Division Headquarters at Camp Howze to begin work on the artillery fire support plan that was part of the Division contingency plan for the defense of South Korea in the event of a second full scale invasion from the north. That had continued for close to a week and had involved long hours away from Camp Wynne. He'd gotten back on Saturday night and they had spent the one day and two nights quietly at the Club or in her room. They had had serious discussions about their futures and what each wanted from life and from each other. Holloway was positive that she loved him, but he was still unable to convince her to commit to an August wedding and assignment to Germany. The following day he'd gone back to the field for another ORT with the 1/72nd Armor and after knocking about for three days in a tank had returned late in the afternoon. He'd gone immediately to the Doughnut Dolly hooch, but had found no one. The other Red Cross girls were undoubtedly still doing their programs in the field and JD's door was locked even though he didn't think she'd still be working when she was leaving for home the next day. Disappointed, he'd returned to his hooch to get out of his smelly dirty fatigues and take a shower.

Half an hour later and feeling refreshed he was standing naked in his room drying his hair with an olive drab towel when he heard a tapping at his window. Startled, he wrapped the towel around his mid section, walked to the window, and pulled aside the flimsy red curtain.

"Hi, handsome. That was quite a show," the smiling face of Jennifer Dodge remarked appreciatively.

"Could you see in here?" Holloway retorted embarrassed.

"Only if I bent down and looked through that gap in the curtains. I just wanted to see if you were back."

He felt his face flushing even though it certainly was not the first time he had been naked in front of her. "Well, I guess you got your answer. Where were you? I checked your room."

"I went back over to the office to just wrap things up. Besides, I couldn't leave without saying good-bye to the doughnut machine. We've become such close friends, you know."

Holloway snickered. JD had once told him that she had reached the point in her life that if she ever again smelled fresh doughnuts being made in the morning she would retch. "Just give me a few minutes. I'll be right out."

"That's all right. I need to get a few more things together in my room. Dinner is in forty minutes. I'll meet you at 5:30, OK?"

"Great!" He moved closer to the window and looked into her eyes. "JD?"

"Yes, Sweetie?"

"Can we spend some time alone tonight? I know you want to say good-bye to your friends and all, but I'd really like some time alone with you."

"Of course we're going to spend time alone! God, I'm not going to see you for almost two months. I'm just going to love you to death tonight."

Smiling a satisfied smile he winked at her and closed the curtain. Two minutes later someone rapped sharply on the doorframe of his room. Major Karl Vogel stood stiffly in the entrance.

"Yes, Sir?"

"Sorry to bother you in your room, Lieutenant, but I needed to find you as early as possible. I'm going north of the river tomorrow to recon some alternate firing positions for the batteries. Colonel Nordstrum has suggested I take you with me. For some reason he seems to feel that you know the area up there better than most and I guess since you are the Assistant S-3 for Operations it is appropriate. I've requested a chopper for 0630. I want to get an early start and I told Captain Sanders that we'd join him and Bravo Battery in the field for breakfast. They're at Wolverine now, you know."

"Ah, yes, Sir. Charlie is supposed to trade places with them tomorrow."

"Exactly. We'll have breakfast, watch the switch of the two batteries, and then do our recon both by air and on the ground. Meet me at the helipad at 0630." Without waiting for a reply he departed as abruptly as he had arrived.

*   *   *

She'd said her good-byes and there had been a last few drinks at the bar. Then they'd slipped off quietly and made love hungrily, knowing it would seem like forever before they were together again. But more than that and as hard as he'd tried to get it out of his mind, Clay Holloway had a nagging fear that this might be the last time ever. Close to midnight, he knew he had to leave soon. He had to get some sleep. Tomorrow would be a tough day.

"Baby, we have to get this settled," Holloway stated sincerely as he gazed into her face. "Please say you'll marry me."

The tips of her fingers touched his cheek and she looked at him longingly. She did not reply.

"Come on, just say yes," he cajoled with a wispy smile.

"Clay, I have thought so hard about this. I really have. Why is it so important to you that I say yes now? Why can't I just go home and let reality settle in for a bit and sort out all of what's happened to me."

"JD, you didn't say that to Magic, did you? He asked you and you just said yes. Just like that, you said yes. What you are telling me here is that you loved him more than you love me. I think that's pretty clear, isn't it?"

"That's not true. That's not even close to being true. I love you desperately, Clay Holloway. You know I do. And part of all this is because of Magic. I think I may have been pretty naïve with him. I didn't look deeply into the whole situation at all. He said he loved me, I thought I loved him, and that was all that was important. So when he asked me, I said yes. That's the way it is in the storybooks, isn't it? But the truth of the matter is, that was a mistake."

"OK, so that was a mistake, but this isn't. How can you say you love me and then in the next breath say 'but I can't say I'll marry you.' I know you're not opposed to marriage."

"Clay, please try to understand my feelings. Let me say it again. Number one, I love you. I love you more than anyone else I have ever known. That's the way I feel right now, right here, today. But I need to be sure this time. I need to be sure that you are really the one for me and I am the one for you. No mistakes. No leaping into something because of your military time constraints. No pressured decision making because I have to go home tomorrow or because you have to go to Germany in three months. I can only make this decision when I am ready to make it."

Holloway felt exasperated. "Damn it, JD. Why are you so stubborn?"

"Stubborn? Who says I'm stubborn? Why aren't you the one who's being stubborn? Just because I won't do what you want me to do, then I'm the one who's wrong? Why aren't you the one who's stubborn because you can't accept my decision?" she retorted hotly.

Holloway opened his mouth, thought better of it, and closed it again. Silently they glared across the room at each other, wondering if it was all falling apart in front of their eyes. Then without a word, he walked to her and touched her face and she touched him back. "Hold me, Clay." He wrapped his arms around her and held her lovingly, still afraid to speak, not really knowing what he wanted to say, but realizing that he did not want their last words of the night to be angry ones.

"Clay, Honey, I'll meet your plane in August. It's only seven weeks. We can make it. I'll know for sure some time between now and then. I want to go back to Pennsylvania. I want to go back to Kent State and find out what happened there too. I want to think and to talk to people and to put the world into prospective again, because sometimes

I'm just not sure what the hell is going on anymore. If I tell you I'll marry you, and I do think that's what I'll tell you, then you will know that it will be for forever and I will never look back, never think I made up my mind too quickly."

"OK, then. I accept that. I guess I have to accept that," Holloway said at last. "Write me as soon as you get home and tell me where you are and what you're doing."

"Thank you. I know this is hard on you, Honey. It's hard on both of us, I can assure you." She smiled at him and he felt better. "Will you walk me to the helipad in the morning? Todd Hardesty called to tell me he volunteered to fly up and take me to Kimpo. Maybe you can even fly down to the airport with me."

"Myan humnida, Baby. I'd love to, but Major Vogel told me I'm flying north of the river tomorrow to recon some firing points with him. I'm leaving at 0630. I don't have a choice. There is no sense in trying to argue with him. I'll ask Baron to help you with your bags and walk over to the pad with you tomorrow."

"Damn. I won't see you tomorrow? Then this is it for seven weeks, huh?"

"I'm afraid that it is. Always know how much I love you." They held each other tightly and kissed again and again, interspersed with their final good byes. Then he slipped out of her room and down the hall and out of the back door, fighting to control his emotions and wondering if he would ever see her again.

Jennifer Dodge waited for almost five minutes before starting to sob uncontrollably. It was not long before there was a knock on the thin wooden door.

"Who is it?" she blurted out angrily.

"It's Gretchen. Open up."

"Not now, Gretchen. Please not now."

"Jenn, come on. Open the door. Let's talk."

Jennifer Dodge snatched a tissue from the box on the dresser and blew her nose loudly. Grabbing a second tissue she dabbed her eyes, blew her nose again, and turned the doorknob. "Come in if you want to."

The knob turned and a pixie like head poked its way inside. "Is this because of Clay?"

"Yes. How did you know something was wrong?" she stammered.

"Are you kidding? The walls are pretty thin and I live next door. Although actually I think I would have heard you howling all the way out in the lounge." Gretchen entered the room and pushed the door closed behind her.

"Oh, my God!" Jennifer shook her head back and forth embarrassed.

Gretchen smiled weakly. "Come on. Talk to me. Is it just because you're leaving? Did you have a fight or what?"

"Oh, Gretchen! Goddamnit! I don't know what to do. I told you before that he asked me to marry him. He really loves me. I know he does."

"Then what's the problem?"

"I'm afraid. I'm just so afraid that I'm making a mistake and that one of us will change our mind."

"Why?"

"I don't know why. That's part of the problem."

"Jenn, I have always tried to make it a point to not point out the obvious, but in this case I'm going to make an exception." Gretchen settled herself in the room's only chair and drew her legs up under her. "Now listen, closely. Everyone on this compound knows how much Clay Holloway loves you. It's not like he's tried to hide it from anyone. And he's a great guy. At the same time, it is also totally obvious that you are completely utterly in love with him. These things are a given. The only sticking point is that for some reason you refuse to just let yourself go and do what every other girl in this building knows you should do. Quit screwing around and marry the guy, Jennifer. Tell him you'll marry him!"

"Gretchen, I was engaged to marry someone else five months ago."

"Oh, will you get off that! Why are you so hung up on the fact that you were once engaged to a jerk. That's history. For God's sake, Jenn, strike when the iron is hot. Tell Clay now."

"Do you really think so, Gretchen?"

"Of course I think so. It's as plain as day to everyone else."

"Damn!"

"What does that mean?"

JD sighed heavily. "It means I think you're right. I'm not sure why I needed you to tell me that, but you are right!"

"Good. Then it's settled. Are you going to go wake him up and tell him?"

"No. I want to sleep on it. I just want to sleep on it. Just to be 100 percent sure. Thanks, Gretchen. Thanks a lot."

Chapter 35

Noise and vibrations from the H-23 Raven flashing over the hooch awakened Jennifer Dodge with a start. Instantly she looked at her clock and then grabbed at it in horror. It was 0635 and she'd set the alarm for 0530! What the hell had happened? Had she turned it off and then not wakened up? Tossing and turning, she had not slept much of the night, failing to fall into a true slumber until almost three o'clock. Anxious to tell Clay of her decision, she had planned to see him before he flew north. The sound of the helicopter told her it was too late. He was already gone.

Disgusted, she climbed out of her single bed in the Doughnut Dolly hooch for the last time in her life, slipped on her robe, and headed for the shower. Her mind raced. Todd Hardesty was due into the helipad at 0930 to pick her up and fly her to Kimpo. Maybe Clay would be back by then. She wasn't sure of his schedule, but somehow she had to see him before she said good-bye to the Republic of Korea. He wanted to marry her. She had to tell him face to face. She wanted to see the look in his eyes when she told him yes.

It was just after seven when she walked into the Officers' Open Mess and spotted Kendall Stover eating breakfast in the corner with the Owl. Briskly she strode toward the table with the red and white-checkered plastic tablecloth and pulled out a chair.

"Hi, Baron. How's it going?"

"Hi, JD," Stover replied, forcing a preoccupied smile. She understood. His mind was elsewhere. Owl nodded at her and continued diving into his scrambled eggs. "Bagger asked me to help you with your luggage and make sure you got onto the chopper all right. Are you ready now?"

"No. The truth is I screwed up. I needed to talk to Clay this morning and somehow I didn't wake up in time. Do you know when he'll be back?"

"Negative. They'll probably be gone most of the morning. He and Major Vogel are going to watch Bravo and Charlie switch places and then do some recon work. Maybe they'll be back by eleven. It's hard to tell." He sipped his coffee and looked at her. "Your chopper's due at 0930 right?"

"Yes. But my flight out of Kimpo is not until noon."

"Well, you might as well have some chow then. You've got one hell of a long boring day ahead of you. Fourteen hours in the air after you leave Kimpo. I'll come over to your hooch about nine fifteen to give you a hand."

"OK. I guess you're right about the food," she sighed as she waved toward the waiter to attract his attention.

*   *   *

First Lieutenant Keith Hackworth, outgoing company commander for Bravo Company, 1/9th, was going home the next day. But prior to his departure, he wanted to pay one last visit to some of his men who were dutifully manning their sector of the DMZ. First platoon had fence duty, second platoon had the ambush patrol and GP Cindy, and third platoon was designated as the mechanized reaction force. Hackworth had been up early and listened to the patrol leader giving a final briefing to the ambush patrol in the pre-dawn hours. Then he'd watched longingly as the patrol moved quietly through the gate and into the wilderness of the Zone. He turned away only after they had finally disappeared into the mist and the darkness. He had also decided he would tour all three GP's that morning after he stopped and visited with some of the boys on the fence. Then in the afternoon he would do his final packing, park himself at the bar by 1600 and buy drinks for anyone who came through the door until 2300. Then he would go to bed. But for now he would head for the enlisted men's chow hall for breakfast.

*   *   *

The flight from Camp Wynne to Firebase Wolverine had taken only five minutes. It never ceased to amaze Holloway how close everything seemed to be to one another when one was in a helicopter. Trips that wound around hills and took a half hour by jeep took only three or four minutes by chopper. The journey from Camp Wynne to Wolverine by convoy would have been at least forty-five minutes. In fact, forty-five minutes was exactly the amount of time allotted by Captain Fontaine for Charlie Battery to leave the compound, drive north along the MSR, cross Freedom Bridge, and move parallel to the DMZ until reaching Firebase Wolverine.

After circling the position a couple of times, Major Vogel pointed to the bare area to the west of the gun pits and the young warrant officer guided the observation helicopter to a perfect landing as the Raven settled onto the fertile black soil. Bob Hoover strode out to greet them.

"Good morning, Sir. Captain Sanders is meeting with the NCOs. They should be finished in a few minutes. Would you like some breakfast?"

"That's affirmative, Lieutenant Hoover," replied Major Vogel returning Hoover's salute. "We'll eat quickly so as not to get in your way. I'm sure the mess crew wants to get packed up ASAP. What time do you plan to be ready to pull out of position?"

"0900 hours, Sir. We'll start striking the tents as soon as people finish eating."

*　　　*　　　*

Lieutenant Yoon Kim Lee was sweating profusely. It was a good kind of sweat, the kind initiated by hard work and exercise. He had led the weapons platoon in a half-hour of calisthenics, followed by a five kilometer run in formation. It was Yoon's first chance at command since his last return from the south when he had stolen a Redeye missile, only to lose it at the last minute. Since that time he had volunteered repeatedly for dangerous missions, including assassination teams that were generally considered to be on suicide missions, but his pleas had always been rejected. Officially, this weapons platoon was not Yoon's. He was serving only as a temporary platoon leader until Wong Dae Chung returned from Pyongyang where he was visiting his very pregnant wife. The baby, their first, was already overdue and Wong had been fortunate enough to have been given leave to be with her during the birth which should happen any day. Lieutenant Yoon had been in temporary command of the weapons platoon for three days and already, he believed, he had made a marked improvement in the quality of the platoon. He had revised their training schedule to allow him to personally influence many of their skills. Experience that he had obtained through months of difficult commando training and forays south of the MDL could and should be imparted throughout the North Korean Army. Lack of initiative had never been one of Yoon's failings and since he hoped to continue this assignment for another week, it was not impossible to believe that perhaps in that time he could persuade his superiors to give him a second opportunity at a regular command.

As usual, Yoon's day was fully and precisely planned. With his morning exercise routine complete, he would have a meager breakfast of kimchi and rice and then travel into the DMZ to visit three observation posts where his heavy machine gun teams were assigned. A trip into the DMZ always excited him to some degree, even though this particular inspection would undoubtedly be rather mundane. He returned to his hut, stripped naked, and wrapping a towel around his waist walked in his sandals the fifty meters to the wooden shower facility.

*　　　*　　　*

"Are you ready, JD?" called Kendall Stover as he knocked on the partially open door of Jennifer Dodge's room. She tugged it open and smiled at him.

"Hi, Baron. Thanks for coming over. There's a truck parked behind the hooch. I told the driver we'd be out as soon as you arrived. The bags are already in the back except for this little one." She picked up the navy flight bag and her purse and slipped one strap over each shoulder. "I can carry it," she stated simply, reading his mind. She glanced around the now bare room for the last time, thinking wistfully of all that had happened to her inside of its four walls. Memories of Gretchen and Joan and Sherry and Kathy and Beth. Memories of Mrs. Kim, her house girl. Then the thoughts of Clay Holloway and briefly too of Magic Maloney. Abruptly she turned and pulled the door shut and bounced confidently down the hall knowing exactly what she needed to do.

JD climbed into the cab of the 1¼ ton truck. Baron slid in beside her and nodded to the driver who ground the gearshift into first and let the clutch out slowly. Three minutes later he braked to a halt thirty feet away from the concrete circle that was the Camp Wynne helipad. Sitting on the concrete was an olive drab UH-1B Iroquois, known throughout the United States Army as a Huey. The sliding door on the side of the Huey was open and sitting on the deck with their legs dangling below them were two warrant officers clad in gray flight suits. One pilot was blond, the other a handsome looking black man with his hair cut in a short Afro. Gold-rimmed sunglasses hid both pairs of eyes, but not their smiles.

"Hi ya, JD. How ya been?" called Todd Hardesty as the pretty slender brunette sauntered forward, her own sun glasses shielding her eyes from the bright sun. Stover walked slightly behind her carrying the flight bag, while the driver lowered the tailgate and dragged her two suitcases out of the back of the vehicle.

"I'm good, Todd. How have you been?" she replied pleasantly.

Hardesty slid out of the doorway of the aircraft onto his feet and motioned to the other WO who rose as well. "This is KC Pruitt, my new copilot. KC this is Jennifer Dodge."

"Hi!" smiled Jennifer. "Thanks for coming to give me a lift, guys. How's your flight schedule look for today?"

"Open," replied KC. "This is the only flight we have booked. Why do you ask?"

"I'm glad to hear that, because we can't leave for a while," answered Jennifer.

"What's that supposed to mean?" queried Todd.

"It means I'm not going anywhere until Clay gets back."

"What are you talking about? Where is he?"

"North of the river with Major Vogel."

"Well, when's he due back?" asked Todd Hardesty in a confused voice.

"I don't know."

"What do you mean you don't know? I thought you had a flight out of Kimpo?"

"I do, but I'm not leaving here until I see Clay. I have to talk to him."

"Well, leave him a note. You have to go."

"No, I don't. I'm not leaving until he gets back. If I miss my flight so what. They'll be another one eventually."

Bewildered, Hardesty scratched his head nervously. "What am I going to tell my operations officer?"

"Tell him I'm late. Tell him I'm throwing up in the john. Tell him I sprained my ankle. I don't care what you tell him. I'm just saying to you that I'm not leaving until Clay gets back."

"Jesus Christ, JD. What the hell can be that important?"

She plucked her sunglasses from her face. "He asked me to marry him, Todd. I have to tell him yes."

*   *   *

The exchange between the outgoing Bravo Battery and the incoming Charlie Battery had gone without incident. Bravo had departed the area and all six Charlie Battery guns were laid and ready to fire. The field phones had been connected to the existing wire and squad tents were springing up around the perimeter of the position. Major Vogel seemed satisfied. Waving a farewell to Captain Fontaine, he strode confidently toward the Raven, with Clay Holloway one step to his left and a step behind, in correct military tradition. Vogel was always a stickler for military custom with junior officers. The pilot sat slouched in his seat, his feet on the control panel and his cap pulled over his eyes. Vogel rapped sharply on the Plexiglas bubble that surrounded the three-person seat and glared at the pilot as the warrant officer looked up.

"OK, young WO. Take a look at this map. We'll fly this area here at about a thousand feet," he noted pointing to the 1 to 25,000 ratio topographical military map. I'll tell you what I want to do once we get up."

WO Drew Valentine glanced perfunctorily at the map, removed his soft cap, and pulled on his flight helmet. Then he pushed the starter and the engine whined and coughed and caught with a roar. A minute later they were airborne in the warm June air.

*   *   *

The two vehicle element had left GP Gwen a half hour earlier, driven back through the gate at the barrier fence, down the road that paralleled the fence, and then back into the Zone through another gate farther east. Ten minutes later the escort jeep with a M-60 mounted on a uni-pod crested the low hill of GP Cindy. Immediately behind it, the second vehicle carrying Keith Hackworth slid to a halt in the dirt. Butch Lincoln, the GP Commander, was a young second lieutenant freshly graduated from the infantry school at Ft. Benning. Crisply he walked out of the sandbagged trench line, approached the jeeps, and saluted his outgoing company commander. Immediately to his rear stood Jack O'Malley, the artillery officer from the 8/18th who had arrived the week before to spend some time as a forward observer and to become oriented to the situation in the DMZ. Both officers had become fairly bored with the duty already. Neither O'Malley nor the GP commander had seen a single thing to justify the $65 a month hostile fire pay that they were now drawing for the month of June.

"How's Cindy treating you, Butch?" Hackworth asked warmly.

"Good, Sir. No problems. Nothing much going on at all."

"You know a year ago I was in your boots. I had the reaction force for a while and spent a lot of time on this GP." He turned to O'Malley. "You're with the 8/18th?"

"Yes, Sir. Alpha Battery."

"Oh yeah? You know Stover then."

"Sure, he's my XO."

"And Bagger and Sweeper?"

"Yes, Sir. We're all chingos."

"Those are numba one GI's. I worked with all of them up here one time or another. Sweeper was up here the day this place got shot up so bad. You hear about that?"

"A little. Sweeper never gave me much detail."

Hackworth nodded. "Yeah, I suppose. It was a day just like this one. Sunny. Hot. Dull. Nothing going on at all. There were three guys stringing barbed wire right over there. Then all of a sudden the shit hit the fan," he mused, staring silently into the distance for a long moment. "One guy was killed instantly and then two others got hit. I was leading the reaction force that day. After the initial shooting stopped they sent my platoon up here to help. Well, the NK's were waiting for us and we ran into an ambush not too far inside of the fence. A big ambush, but we kicked their ass. Killed a couple of them. Then we evacuated the casualties, set up here on the GP, and waited. They shot us up again that night, but by that time your battalion had Charlie Battery set up a little south of here. They finally got permission to fire an illumination mission at the dinks and it scared them enough to make 'em back off. The next morning everything was back to normal, but that was one halacious day and night, I'll tell you that," he reflected, staring directly at Jack O'Malley's eyes and then shifting his gaze to the GP Commander. He waggled his index finger at them threateningly. "And don't think it won't happen again, gentlemen. Just because nothing has happened up here for the last few months, don't ever stop being ready. You're only fifty meters from North Korea. There's not another Guard Post closer to the MDL than this one and never forget that. If they want to, they can be across the line and butt fuckin' your sweet asses in thirty seconds."

*   *   *

Fifteen hundred meters to the northeast and north of the MDL, Yoon Kim Lee was also visiting a hill occupied by soldiers, though they wore saucer shaped helmets and carried Kalashnikov rifles slung over their shoulders rather than M-16's. Yoon was inspecting the readiness of the defensive positions, which included two Degtyarev heavy machine guns, which sat mounted on their tripods and glistening in the sun from a fresh coat of gun oil. Nearby their crews stood proudly at attention. Yoon squatted and worked the operating handle of one of the machine guns, feeling satisfied with the smooth feel of the well-oiled parts. It was then that he first heard the sound of the helicopter.

*   *   *

"I think that last position will do quite well for us, Holloway. It's got the terrain, the natural camouflage, and the access from the road that we need. Any comments?" Major Karl Vogel spoke quickly into the microphone attached to his flight helmet.

"No, Sir. I like it too. I think all the BC's will be pleased. It's the best of the bunch."

"OK then. That's finally something you and I agree on." He smirked quickly at Holloway who continued to ride in the middle of the seat between the pilot and his Battalion Executive Officer. The selection of the new firing position completed, Karl Vogel's mind clicked over to something, which he had been secretly considering for some time. Something that might provide him with a little excitement for the day. He depressed the intercom button.

"Valentine, give us a right turn. I want to get up closer to the DMZ fence. I've never flown over it before."

"We're really not supposed to fly over it, Sir." WO Valentine replied. "It could be dangerous and they're very strict about getting too close."

"Valentine, I am not in the habit of having my orders questioned, as Lieutenant Holloway here can attest. I flew more helicopter missions against more bad actors in Vietnam than you could even dream about. When I said turn right I meant turn right. I'm running this show. You are just the driver, understand?"

"Yes, Sir," Valentine replied reluctantly. Slowly he pushed on the joystick and the light helicopter tilted to its right and changed directions. "To tell you the truth I always had a little urge to fly over the DMZ just to rattle Joe Chink's chain a little."

Valentine adjusted his course to fly east to west, a thousand feet above the barrier fence and just behind it. Clay Holloway looked at Vogel uneasily, but kept his mouth shut. Protest to Major Karl Vogel would be useless. Things had been quiet in their sector of the DMZ for some time, but no one knew better than he how quickly things could change. It wasn't as though the North Koreans weren't watching them. For the first time, Holloway realized he was slouching lower in his seat, as though somehow he would be harder for the North Koreans to see. He felt for the bulk of his .45 in its holster, wondering what help it could possibly be in a situation like this. Five minutes later, as the Han River estuary in the distance grew larger, the pilot pressed his intercom switch. "Major, we're nearing the Division boundary. We're almost to the ROK sector."

"Give us another right turn then."

"That will put us over the DMZ."

"Whose side?"

"We'll still be south of the MDL."

"Then do it."

Valentine grinned a cocky sort of grin and the helicopter heeled to its right and dove down and away as it executed a one hundred and eighty degree turn and began its return trip to the east, flying over a heavily wooded section of DMZ terrain. Holloway was unable to be still any longer.

"Sir, we can't be in here! No aircraft is ever allowed over the DMZ even if we are south of the MDL. This is major violation of the cease fire and dangerous as hell!"

"At ease, Lieutenant. If I had wanted your opinion I would have asked for it. Somebody once told me you had balls. Guess they were wrong."

"My courage is not the issue. The North Koreans are completely unpredictable. Nobody knows what he or she'll do. I don't even think they know what they're going to do half the time. With all due respect, Sir, this is insane flying this close to the MDL. What are we doing it for? We're liable to really piss them off. We need to get back south of the fence."

"Lieutenant, I'm going to make this real easy for you to understand. Shut your goddamn mouth!" Vogel barked. Turning his head toward Valentine he issued another directive. "Put us right on the MDL and drop it down a little lower. I want to see the expression on Joe Chink's face when I piss on his head."

A mile to the east of the low flying aircraft, Keith Hackworth paused in his conversation to look skyward. What the hell was that helicopter doing? It was even closer to the MDL than GP Cindy was. They were just asking for trouble.

"Butch, get one of your people to put up a flare. We've got to warn that chopper off. He must be lost."

"Yes, Sir. Murphy! Get me an M-79 with some star burst rounds."

*   *   *

Yoon Kim Lee had been observing the helicopter for five minutes. It was drawing closer and cruising lower than it had been when it was flying the opposite direction a bit earlier. Arrogant American bastard!

"Sergeant Cho. Prepare those two machine guns for firing! Now!"

The little helicopter was coming even nearer. Yoon speculated on its exact position. It may be just south of the MDL and it may not. It was entirely possible, in fact, that it was slightly north of it, a clear violation of North Korean air space. But regardless of whether he was north or south, being over the DMZ itself was a genuine violation of the cease-fire agreement. If Yoon were to shoot it down there would be no way for anyone to actually prove which side of the line it had been on anyway. There were standing orders to deal with situations like this. Any incursion into North Korea whether by land, sea, or air was to be considered an act of war and immediate retaliation against the aggressor was fully authorized. With a violation of this clarity, there was not even a need to contact headquarters.

"The guns are ready, Sir."

"When he gets a little closer, shoot him down. I will give the order."

The enlisted men under Yoon's command exchanged wide-eyed glances. Excitement and anticipation filled the air. It was a direct order from their superior officer. It would be executed gleefully and without question. One minute later, with the H-23 Raven at a range of three hundred meters, the two Degtyarev machine guns opened fire, their green tracers etching lines in the sky and enabling the gunners to direct their fire precisely into their intended target.

Riding inside of small helicopters is incredibly noisy. Which is why anyone who needs to talk with each other during the flight wears headsets and uses the intercom. With the sound of the engine above their heads and the ear phones covering their ears, none of the three Americans in the helicopter heard the firing and were completely oblivious to any danger until two rounds of metal jacketed 12.7mm fire ripped through the left side of the Plexiglas bubble above Valentine's head, spraying tiny particles of glass around the cockpit. Valentine reacted immediately, pushing the stick hard right at the same moment as another of the slugs separated the tail rotor from the fuselage of the aircraft, throwing the Raven completely out of the control. Minus the rotor, the Raven began its death dance through the azure sky, pirouetting and darting, oscillating and dipping. Inside, the hopelessly disoriented Americans grabbed in vain for something to steady them. Valiantly, the pilot struggled with the controls, trying to regain some measure of guidance over the faltering aircraft. It was useless.

"Mayday, mayday, this is Wicked Witch 49, hit by enemy ground fire over the DMZ. We're going in," Valentine cried into the radio as the aircraft continued its wild dance through the air. The ship had been just south of the MDL at an altitude of under a thousand feet when it had been struck. One minute later as the ground rose up to meet it, the helicopter was a quarter of a mile inside of North Korean territory. Suddenly, its unrestrained roller coaster ride through the sky came to an instantaneous halt as the main rotor slammed full force into a tall pine tree only a half mile from the hill where Lieutenant Yoon Kim Lee stood watching it through his binoculars and laughing uproariously at the sight.

Yoon turned and motioned to his driver. "Let's go. You two men, get in the back. Sergeant Cho, report to headquarters. Tell them to get some troops out here and some senior officers. Tell them we have downed an American helicopter on our side of the MDL. Some of the crew may still be alive." Yoon leaped gleefully into the front passenger seat and tugged his pistol from its holster as the vehicle leaped forward.

*   *   *

Kendall Stover was sitting in the doorway of the Huey and pointing to the Bravo Battery convoy, which was driving slowly up the gravel street toward its motor pool. Forty-five minutes earlier it had left its firing position at Firebase Wolverine. Suddenly the helicopter's radio crackled and a clear call for help broke through the soft static rushing sound. "Mayday, mayday, this is Wicked Witch 49. Hit by enemy ground fire over the DMZ. We're going in!" As the radio's words hung in the air, there was a disbelieving silence for a few seconds. It was Todd Hardesty who spoke first.

"Jesus Christ, that's Valentine flying that chopper. Holloway and your major must be with him!"

Jennifer Dodge stared incomprehensibly at Todd Hardesty. What was he talking about? That couldn't be right. Clay Holloway would be back any minute now. She glanced toward the sky. He had to be back soon.

Hardesty climbed between the seats and grabbed for his mike. "Wicked Witch 49 this is Green House, what is your location, over?"

Silence.

"Wicked Witch 49, this is Green House, I say again what is your location, over?"

Nothing but empty air.

"Todd, what did you say about Clay?" Jennifer Dodge finally pleaded.

"He's with Valentine. He's in that helicopter, JD," he said sadly, not meeting her gaze.

"How do you know?"

"It's the only other bird up today and you told me they were heading north of the river. It can't be anyone else!"

"Oh, dear God!" She turned violently away and buried her face in her hands.

This time it was Kendall Stover who broke the stunned silence that now permeated the little group. "Todd, get 99.65 on your radio. Hurry up!"

Hardesty did as he was told and handed the microphone toward Stover who waited impatiently. Snatching the mike from his hand, Stover pushed the rubber covered button and spoke quickly into the mouthpiece.

*　　　　*　　　　*

Jack O'Malley was looking at the wreckage of the helicopter through his binoculars when the radio crackled with the voice of his battery executive officer. Bedside him on the top of the sandbagged CP at GP Cindy was the GP Commander Butch Lincoln and Keith Hackworth. "Alpha 18, this is Alpha 5, over."

O'Malley snatched the handset which lay at his feet. "This is Alpha 18, over."

"Alpha 5, have you any sighting of a helicopter, over?" Kendall Stover demanded.

"Alpha 18, roger that!" O'Malley cried excitely. "It's down in the DMZ. It's north of the MDL about a half a klick in front of us."

"Alpha 5, did it explode, over?"

"Alpha 18, negative. In fact, there's people moving around. Somebody's alive, over."

"Alpha 5, roger. Keep us updated on anything that happens out there, out." Stover turned anxiously to Todd Hardesty. "We're going after them. Get this son-of-a-bitch fired up."

Hardesty's hand was already on the starter and the turbine engine began to whine. He turned behind him. "JD, get out of the aircraft. We'll get him for you." He addressed his copilot. "KC, it's your call. We're going to North Korea. This is not an authorized flight. Are you in or out?"

"Shit, man. I'm in. We can't leave those cats out there."

"I'm in too, Todd." It was JD.

"What? Bullshit, JD! Get out of the helicopter now. That's an order. I don't have time for this."

"No, goddamnit! I'm going with you! Take off!" Her eyes blazed with determination and her jaw jutted forward defiantly.

"That's impossible. Get out, now!"

"No way. I'm staying. Now take off!"

Hardesty shrugged resignedly and turned back to scan his instrument panel. "OK, lady. I haven't got time to argue. It's your funeral."

"Wait one!" cried Stover over the roar of the engine. "You got any weapons on this thing?"

"Negative. We were only planning to fly down to Kimpo."

Suddenly, Stover was out of the door and running across the open field toward the lead vehicle of the Bravo gun convoy that had continued its journey up the street. He waved his hands wildly and yelled as he narrowed the gap to the truck.

"Sweeper, give me your M-16!"

"My M-16? What's going on? You mad at Captain Robbins again?" smiled Robert Hoover, failing to grasp the gravity of the situation.

"Bagger's down in the DMZ. Helicopter crash. Give me your weapon and some ammo. We're going after him!"

Hoover's smile vanished. "Jesus! Are you serious?" But the look on Stover's face told him that he was. "Here. I only have two twenty round mags."

"OK. How about your driver here?"

"Sorry, Sir. I've got my M-79, but the ammo is locked up in the arms room truck."

Without another word Stover snatched the two magazines from Hoover's hand and carrying the rifle in the other, turned and sprinted back to the waiting helicopter which now hovered only fifty feet behind him. Hurriedly, he climbed through the open door as the ship rose like an angry bumblebee and roared full throttle into the cloudless blue sky.

*   *   *

When the rotor struck the pine, the force of the turning blade drove the fuselage and its Plexiglas bubble into the tree trunk as well. Then, after crashing into the tree, the light helicopter separated itself from the wood and plummeted the remaining fifteen feet to the ground, smashing onto its left side and creating a light cloud of dust from the dry earth. High above, the rotor remained embedded in the tree trunk, having been ripped completely free of its housing in the aircraft. Clay Holloway was stunned. Hanging sideways on the tilted seat, his left shoulder rested against the still form of Warrant Officer Drew Valentine. Groggily, he looked down at Valentine. The young man was clearly dead. The tree trunk into which the Plexiglas had smashed had been directly in front of the pilot and had obviously crushed him as well. What had once been his face was now completely unrecognizable, appearing only as a mass of bloody flesh and exposed bone. To Holloway's right there was movement. Major Vogel was already releasing his seat belt and attempting to crawl up and out of the open side door, which was now above them. He placed his boot on Holloway's hip as a foothold and pushed himself upwards and out into the open air.

Holloway waited for Vogel to clear the opening. Then he released the clasp of the heavy leather seat belt and slowly began to extricate himself from the wreckage. As he cleared the opening, he noticed that Major Vogel was already about fifteen yards away, staggering and wandering as though he were dazed. Holloway's side hurt terribly and he was having some difficulty breathing. Clutching his ribs, he slid off of the aircraft, staggered behind a large gray boulder and sank slowly to a sitting position on the ground. A few moments later he heard the loud cracks nearby.

Yoon Kim Lee had dismounted his vehicle forty meters away and walked slowly through the heavy brush along with his two escorts toward the wreckage of the helicopter. As they entered a small clearing where the downed helicopter now lay, a dazed American officer came stumbling toward him, apparently oblivious to their presence. Yoon smiled gleefully at the American as the man lurched again drunkenly and without the slightest hesitation shot him twice in the head with his pistol. The man sank to his knees and fell forward onto his face without a word. Yoon approached the still form and fired once more into the back of the man's head.

The gunshots focused Holloway's mind instantly. Lying on the ground and grasping his ribs, he peered cautiously around the side of the big rock. There were three armed soldiers standing nearby. At their feet lay the still body of Major Karl Vogel. Holloway had never seen a North Korean uniform up close, but he knew damn well that they weren't Americans and they weren't ROK's. That only left one possibility.

Quietly, he opened the leather flap of the black military holster, withdrew his .45, and waited, hoping that his labored breathing and pounding heart would not give away his presence. He did not have to wait long. Yoon rolled the body of Karl Vogel over with his foot and satisfied that the man was dead, approached the wreckage of the aircraft. Holloway was in a dilemma. After seeing what the North Koreans had just done to Major Vogel, the idea of surrender was out of the question. But Holloway realized that he had no bullet in the chamber of his pistol. If he racked the slide to chamber a round, the noise would immediately alert the three soldiers. If he didn't rack the slide, he couldn't fire the gun. Breathlessly, he continued to wait.

Yoon Kim Lee and the two soldiers circled the right side of the gray boulder as Holloway crawled slowly to the opposite side, keeping the granite between him and his enemies. He watched as they peered cautiously into the helicopter. It was now or never. His heart was pounding as he pulled back and then released the slide of the .45, feeding the first of his seven rounds into the chamber. At the first indication of the metal on metal sound, the three men turned as one. Later Holloway would reflect that one wore a soft cap and appeared to be an officer and for some reason there seemed to be something vaguely familiar about his face. But at that moment there was only time for reaction. Holding the pistol at arm's length he squeezed the trigger and pumped a heavy grain bullet into the chest of Yoon Kim Lee, driving him backwards into the smashed Plexiglas canopy. Swinging his arm slightly to the right he aimed at the center of mass of his next target. The pistol jumped a second and a third time as the next startled North Korean soldier attempted to bring his AK-47 into firing position. But he too was caught by the force of the heavy slugs and spun into the dirt. The remaining soldier danced quickly to his right and found cover behind the helicopter. With the element of surprise gone, Holloway now found himself heavily outgunned by the AK, which began to spit bullets like a hose. It was time to make his break. Moving in a crouch, he sprinted from behind the rock and into the trees nearby as he heard another long burst of automatic weapons fire behind him. Wildly he looked around. Where in the hell was he headed? He had to get oriented. An attempt to surrender was not even an option. He had just killed two North Korean soldiers. He had to get south and quickly.

Frantically, his eyes scanned the distance, focusing suddenly on a familiar shape. Wait! That hill! It used to be his hill! He'd seen it countless times, though never from precisely this angle. But there was no doubt about it. He could see the bunkers. It was GP Cindy. It was safety. It was his only chance. And it wasn't that far away. Weaving a zig zagged course he held his injured ribs and began running as fast as his legs could carry him toward the elevated land mass five hundred meters away.

*　　　　*　　　　*

"Holy shit, did you see that?" Jack O'Malley yelled after watching the brief, but violent gunfight through his binoculars.

"I saw it. There's one friendly left alive and he's heading this way. Murphy, get me the sniper rifle! He's going to need some cover."

"Sir, they're still in North Korea. We really shouldn't be shooting across the MDL. You could get in deep shit for this," noted Butch Lincoln. It was a valid point.

"Fuck the MDL! I went through this last summer. I've already watched one man die trying to reach safety out there and I'm not going to watch another. Especially when he's one of our guys. Get me the rifle and ammo!"

Through the binoculars, Jack O'Malley continued to focus on the running figure as he weaved through the trees. Wait a minute! Was that possible? "Hacker, you said you know Clay Holloway?"

"Yeah. Why?"

"Because I think that's him."

Hackworth grabbed the binoculars from O'Malley's hand and snapped them to his eyes. "Son-of-a-bitch! Call your XO back."

O'Malley reached for his radio. "Alpha 5, this is Alpha 18, over."

"Alpha 5, go."

"Alpha 18, is there any chance one of the people in the chopper is Bagger, over."

"Alpha 5, that's affirm, over."

"Alpha 18, be advised he is alive and headed our way with two dinks on his tail. No other survivors visible, over."

"Alpha 5, roger. You be advised that we are in-bound with an ETA of zero two mikes. We're going to try and pick him up, over."

Jennifer Dodge listened in silence to the broadcast, mouthed a quick prayer and dug her fingernails into her palms until they brought blood.

*   *   *

Joined by Lieutenant Yoon's driver, the third North Korean soldier was now in hot pursuit of Holloway. Running in a straight line, they were rapidly closing the gap on the American who was still weaving through the trees in an attempt to dodge the occasional bursts of fire. Behind them, near the site of the downed helicopter, a truck with a reinforced squad of infantrymen arrived and discharged its cargo of soldiers who were now also in pursuit of the fleeing figure who continued to clutch his damaged ribs as he ran. Even as the soldiers came closer, however, Clay Holloway was faced with another obstacle. He had just run out of trees to use for concealment. Now there was only open meadow with waist high weeds between him and GP Cindy, which was still three hundred meters away. Holloway glanced desperately at the hill, sucked in a painful deep breath, and began to run across the open area.

Behind Holloway the two North Korean soldiers also reached the edge of the woods. Yoon's driver pointed ahead. "Look! There he is. This is our last chance." Both of the men dropped to one knee, took careful aim, and opened fire. A hundred meters ahead the running figure spun around and fell heavily into the high weeds.

Clay Holloway felt as though he had been hit in the shoulder with a sledgehammer. The force of the blow had driven him face first into the weeds and dry ground. He lay there panting and wondering what the hell had happened. One minute he was running and the next it felt as though someone must have come up behind him and hit him with something. Gingerly, he placed his right hand onto the front of his numb left shoulder. Something was radically wrong. It didn't feel like his shoulder at all. Perhaps there was mud all over it. It felt warm and mushy. He looked strangely at it and felt a wave of nausea sweep over him. Oh, God! The shirt was covered in blood, which poured out of round little hole in the cloth. He tried to raise the arm. Nothing happened. It was useless. Turning his head away, he forced himself to not look at the wound. It wouldn't do any good. The most important thing now was to keep going. He looked up at Cindy. It was his only hope. Focusing his mind, he tried to get up. He couldn't.

Behind him the two North Korean soldiers jogged through the weeds looking for the spot where the body had fallen. They were intent on following the matted down trail that the man had trampled in the weeds only moments earlier. Knowing that the American must be within ten or twenty meters, they raised their weapons in anticipation.

"Kapow! Kapow! Kapow! Kapow!" Four times the M-1 with the 20x scope jumped in the expert hands of Keith Hackworth less than 300 yards away. Four times the 30.06 caliber bullets struck home. The first two rounds had taken the soldiers down. He added the other two for insurance as the bodies lay in the weeds. Hackworth moved the rifle slowly to his right and used the sight as a telescope. He could see Holloway struggling to rise and then falling over. The olive drab shirt was dark at the shoulder. It could be sweat, but Hackworth knew that it wasn't. Suddenly he spied of a new danger. Two hundred yards behind Holloway more armed men were approaching. At least twelve or fifteen. They were closing fast. He started to tell Murphy to get him more ammo. But the roar of the olive drab machine that suddenly appeared only a few feet above his head drowned his words.

*   *   *

"There's the wrecked chopper! Wait, look. Down there. There's bodies in the weeds," cried Kendall Stover.

"Alpha 5, this is Alpha 18," called Jack O'Malley over his radio on Cindy. "Bagger is right below you in the weeds. I think he's the only one alive. You see him?"

"Roger that," acknowledged Hardesty who was already dropping the aircraft rapidly toward the meadow. Seconds later its skids settled onto the ground. Simultaneously a burst of automatic weapons fire struck the side of the helicopter, rocking the ship and blowing gapping holes in both the Plexiglas and the aluminum fuselage.

"Son-of-bitch, we're taking hits!" cried KC Pruitt who was closest to the fire. "Where'd that come from?"

Kendall Stover was already standing in the doorway, his M-16 at his shoulder firing measured three round bursts at the enemy soldiers who were engaging them from the tree line two hundred meters away.

"Where's Bagger? We can't stay here long!"

"I'll get him. Wait for me!" And before anyone could say a word, it was Jennifer Dodge who was leaping out of the door in a flash of blue cotton and long nylon covered legs. Running low against the buzzing of the incoming bullets, she dashed into the weeds toward the spot where she had seen the motionless form only seconds before. Where was he? Fighting a rising sense of panic of what she might find, she screamed his name above the roar of the helicopter. "Clay! Clay! Where are you?" A second later she tripped over his prone body.

He was lying on his back, his face ashen. Already in shock and nearing unconsciousness, he looked at her stupidly. "JD! How did you get here?"

"Come on, Baby. Get up! We have to cauda chogi now."

" I can't get up. You've got to get out of here!"

"Not without you. Come on. It's not far."

"I don't know if I can," he gasped. "JD, please get out of here."

She struggled to her feet and pulled on his good arm. "Come on! Try! I can't carry you!" The numbness in his shoulder had given way to a searing pain, but along with that a sense that this was his last chance at life. A life with her. Reaching deep inside himself, he found one last pocket of strength. One last-ditch adrenaline assisted effort that took him unsteadily to his feet. She wrapped her arm around his back and with his good arm draped over her shoulder, guided and dragged and cajoled him toward the vibrating hunk of machinery only yards away. The whine of bullets came close by their heads. It was the voice of violent death seeking them as they struggled slowly toward the waiting ship. In front of them, Kendall Stover fired off his last rounds and threw the rifle down in frustration. Their only cover fire now was coming from Cindy to their rear, and Stover realized gratefully that from the hill an M-60 had joined the fray, pouring volumes of machine gun bullets toward the cluster of North Korean troops secluded in the wood line. But incoming fire was still ricocheting around the thin skin of the Huey as Jennifer Dodge wobbled and tugged and pushed the last few steps and finally helped Holloway fall onto the steel deck of the chopper. Stover seemed to falter momentarily, then reached forward and dragged him inside as JD grabbed the door and stepped onto the skid.

Hardesty was watching them over his shoulder. "Come on! Come on!" Todd Hardesty screamed as another bullet ripped through the windshield. Then the young pilot jerked the ship into the air as Stover pulled JD quickly inside and then lost his balance and sat down hard. Hardesty kept it low for a moment then screamed skyward as the helicopter maneuvered around the hill, flashed over the DMZ fence and headed south toward the river.

Jennifer Dodge sat cross-legged on the deck holding Holloway's head in her lap, stroking his hair wildly and trying to convince herself that he was going to be all right. The pain was obvious in his face. He fumbled for the aid pack on the shoulder strap of his web gear. JD tore open the paper for him, reached inside of his shirt, and pressed the giant bandage hard against the wound trying to stem the flow of blood.

"JD," he stammered weakly. "How did you do this? Where did you guys come from?"

"Don't try to talk, Sweetheart," she yelled above the noisy whine of the turbine engine. "You're going to be OK. I love you. I couldn't let my future husband get away from me this easily now could I?" She smiled sweetly at him, letting the words sink in. "Besides, it was Baron's idea. What do you think, Baron? Would I do anything to marry this guy or what?"

Stover didn't respond. Still smiling, JD turned to address the silent lieutenant. Her smile was short lived as her last few words caught in her throat. Kendall Stover sat on the floor with his back propped against the other bulkhead. His mouth was open and his eyes were closed. The front of his shirt was drenched in blood.

*   *   *

Barbara Bennett returned her coffee cup to its saucer and stared silently at Clay Holloway. What had been a dancing fire hours earlier, had become only a glowing bed of orange embers. His story had continued through dinner and well into the night. When he finally stopped talking, Barbara was at a loss for words. A tale like this was so far removed from the life that she had led that she had no frame of reference even for comment. When other couples had explained how they had met, it had usually centered around college or a party or a meeting in a bar after work. Looking at Jennifer Holloway relaxing here in her family room with one long leg crossed over the other, it was hard, no, impossible to imagine her jumping out of a helicopter, dodging machine gun fire, and dragging her future husband to safety. She just looked so.... normal. But behind those green flashing eyes and friendly smile of hers was a women of incredible strength and determination; that was obvious. Maybe those were the qualities that had drawn Barbara to her from the first moment they met.

"So what happened to the others? And how bad was the shoulder?" Ken Bennett asked finally.

"Bad enough," Holloway replied. "Fortunately the bullet itself missed the socket but the shock broke the bone and there was a lot of tissue damage. So that ended my tour in Korea. Two weeks in a hospital in Sasebo, Japan. Another three weeks in Walter Reed. Then two months convalescent leave. At least it gave us time to plan the wedding."

"Which was beautiful, I might add," interjected Jennifer Holloway. "And we even showed up in Germany right on schedule."

"Regarding the aftermath, "Holloway continued, "North Korea charged us with espionage operations against them, over flying their air space, and murder. They pounded the table at Panmunjom for a while and it made all of the papers for a few days. We counter-charged them with murder and shooting down an unarmed aircraft over UN territory. It was a couple of months before they returned the bodies of Valentine and Major Vogel. I had to answer a lot of questions about where we really were when we were hit and why we were there at all. And the truth of the matter is that I will never know if we were actually over North Korea when they shot us down, but I don't think so.

As far as the others, Hostileman eventually went on to law school and the last time I heard was practicing in Atlanta. Courtney still lives in Tennessee and still hunts a lot of turkeys. After Keith Hackworth finished his next assignment, the Army sent him off to college where he eventually earned both a bachelor's and a master's degree and is currently Brigadier General Hackworth, who was involved in Grenada, Panama, and the Gulf War. So I guess popping those guys in North Korea didn't hurt his career all that much. Todd Hardesty is presently an overseas pilot for Northwest and making the big bucks. He flies into Tokyo and Seoul all the time, but something tells me he stays well clear of the DMZ." His last comment drew a momentary chuckle from his two guests. Following an awkward pause, Ken Bennett posed a final question.

"Clay, I hate to ask this, but I guess I have to," Ken Bennett whispered. "What happened to Kendall Stover? Was he killed too?"

The ringing of the telephone at Jennifer Holloway's side interrupted the question. She snatched it up before the first ring had finished. "Hello?" she asked. Then she giggled. "What?" She listened for a few seconds and then spoke again. "Well, just a minute and I'll let you ask him yourself." She offered the telephone to her husband. "Bagger, it's that guy who was best man at our wedding. You know, the one with the funny Eastern accent and the wire rimmed glasses. He's calling from Colorado, wanting to know if we're going to come out to Aspen and visit and go skiing with him again this year."

Holloway smiled warmly and took the cordless phone from his wife. "Hey, Baron! What's shakin'?, over"

ABOUT THE AUTHOR

Mark Higginson is a graduate of Bowling Green University and also attended Youngstown State University. He is a recently retired safety manager of a large Midwestern utility. During 1969-70, he served as a field artillery officer in and around the Korean DMZ. He is a member of the Veterans of Foreign Wars and is affiliated with the USO of Northern Ohio. Currently he resides with his wife Susan, near Cleveland, Ohio.

GLOSSARY

AO—Area of Operations. The area in which a given unit operates as officially assigned by headquarters.

APC—Armored Personnel Carrier. An armored tracked vehicle that carries ten infantrymen inside. It is generally armed with an M-60 machine gun and often a .50 cal. machine gun.

BC—Battery Commander. The commanding officer of an artillery battery. It is the equivalent of a Company Commander in the infantry. The size of batteries varies, but in this novel are between 80 and 100 men, which is understrength due to manpower shortages in Korea.

BOQ—Bachelor Officers' Quarters. Often referred to as the "Q." At Camp Wynne, the new BOQ houses the senior officers and the old BOQ at Camp Wynne houses the junior lieutenants and is referred to as the "Ghetto."

CP—Command Post. The headquarters of a unit in a field situation.

DMZ—Demilitarized Zone. Often referred to as the "Z" or the "Zone." It is the divider between North Korea and South Korea and was established at the end of the Korean War in 1953. It is 151 miles long and two and a half miles wide. The military presence in the Zone is limited by agreement. For example, there should be no aircraft, tracked vehicles, or automatic weapons and only a limited number of troops with small arms. However, violations are common. It is a no man's land covered with natural vegetation and filled with wild life. It is heavily mined. On the southern edge of the Zone stands the DMZ fence, a ten feet high chain linked fence erected in the mid 60's to inhibit North Korean infiltration. The area behind the fence is heavily guarded with foxholes, bunkers, and towers.

E-4, E-5, E-6, etc.—The pay grades of enlisted men starting at Private E-1 and rising to Sergeant Major E-9.

FO—Forward Observer. He is the eyes of the artillery. The FO is an artillery observer who is assigned to company sized maneuver elements of the infantry or armor units for the purpose of observing enemy forces and requesting and adjusting artillery fire.

FDC—Fire Direction Center. This is the brain center of the artillery battery or battalion. The FDC receives the call for fire from the FO and plots the target on its charts. It then determines what settings should be placed on the Howitzers in order to hit the target. It communicates those settings to the firing battery.

FTX—Field Training Exercise. Exercises simulating combat situations in the field.

GP—Guard Post. A GP is a hill located inside of the DMZ fence and close to the military demarcation line (MDL) dividing North and South Korea. It is manned by 10 to 20 men whose mission is to observe North Korean movement and to stop attempted infiltration. The GP is a fortified position with trench lines, sandbags, and bunkers. It is armed with machine guns and antitank weapons as well as assorted small arms. The GP's in this novel are called Cindy, Carol, and Gwen.

HHB—Headquarters and Headquarters Battery. This unit contains the battalion headquarters staff as well as the support units of an artillery battalion. This battery has no Howitzers.

KATUSA—Korean Augmentation To the US Army. Approximately twenty-five percent of the artillery and infantry units in the US Second and Seventh Infantry Divisions were composed of Korean soldiers who served a three year tour in the US Army.

Klick—slang for kilometer.

Korean Phrases—Common phrases used by GI's to communicate with Korean nationals. They may be grammatically incorrect or a slang variation, sometimes mixed with Japanese phrases left over from the Japanese occupation.

Annahaseyo—A common greeting.
Annahashamika—Literally, "Is peace with you?" Another common greeting.
Anneyo—No
Can chana—Can do

Cugi mah—Bullshit

Chanda—Sleep

Cauda Chogi—Go there (or) get out of here

Caugi wah—Go get....

Chingo—Friend

Chogi—There

Bali bali—Hurry up.

Eedywah—Come here.

Eeso—Do you have...?

Josan—Girl.

Kamsamnida or Kumopsabnida—Thank you

Moola—I don't know.

Mamasan—A mature Asian woman.

Myan humnida—Sorry (or) sorry about that.

Neh—Yes.

Oopso—All gone

Papasan—A mature Asian man

Yoboseyo—Hey or hello

Yobo—slang for steady girlfriend or wife. Comes from greeting "yoboseyo."

Yogi—Here

LTC—Lieutenant Colonel. A battalion sized unit is commanded by an LTC.

LNO—Liaison Officer. A captain or senior first lieutenant who coordinates artillery fire support with a maneuver (infantry or armor) battalion. The LNO also directs the FO's assigned to the companies in that battalion. The LNO is under the control of the artillery battalion S-3 (Operations Officer) and works in the field with the supported battalion's commander and his S-3.

MSR—Main Supply Route. The primary paved road in the Second Division area of operations. It runs north and south from Seoul to the Imjin River.

MDL—Military Demarcation Line. The actual border between North Korea and South Korea, it runs down the middle of the DMZ. The MDL is marked by small yellow metal signs every 50 or 100 meters and has a few strands of barbed wire along the line.

MPC—Military Payment Certificate. Paper money printed for use by military personnel within Korea. All monetary transactions within the military in Korea are in MPC. Korean nationals are not supposed to have MPC.

M-1—The standard US rifle of World War II and the Korean War (1950-1953). It is a 30.06 caliber weapon that holds an eight shot clip. M-1's were fitted with telescopic sights and issued to the Guard Posts as sniper rifles.

M-14—The standard US rifle of the early and mid '60's. It fires the 7.62mm NATO round. It was replaced by the M-16 rifle in Vietnam beginning in 1966 and in Korea beginning in 1968.

M-16—The standard US rifle from the mid '60's through the present day. The first M-16 was the M16A1, which was replaced by the superior heavy barreled M-16A2 in the early '80's. The weapon fires the high velocity 5.56mm round. Both the rifle itself and the ammunition are lighter than the M-14.

M-60—The standard medium machine gun of the 60's. It is air cooled, belt fed, and also fires the 7.62mm NATO round. It can be carried by mobile infantry or mounted on a tripod or vehicle.

M-79—A single shot grenade launcher. It is a short-barreled shoulder weapon which fires a 40mm grenade which is loaded into the breach like a shotgun. The M-79 rounds include fragmentation, tear gas, buckshot, and illumination.

NCO—Noncommissioned Officer. Any enlisted man from Corporal (E-4) through the various grades of sergeant.

NK—North Korean.

NOD—Night Observation Device. Any optical device used by the army to allow troops to see better at night. Starlight scopes are NODs.

O Club—Officers' Club. The center of social life for the officers and Doughnut Dollies at Camp Wynne. It contains a dining room for meals, a pool table, a ping pong table, a TV lounge, a bar area, and an entertainment area. It is air-conditioned and has a large stone fireplace. There is also an EM (Enlisted Man's) Club and an NCO (Noncommissioned Officers) Club at Camp Wynne.

ORT—Operational Readiness Test. Similar to a FTX, although an ORT is officially graded by a higher authority and a unit is awarded a passing or failing grade. ORT's were usually administered annually for separate batteries as well as the battalion as a unit. Referred to as the battery or battalion tests. Sometimes referred to as a "three day war."

SFC—Sergeant First Class. An E-7.

Spec/4, (Spec/5, etc.)—Specialist Fourth Class, etc. Enlisted man in the pay grade of E-4, E-5, etc. This soldier is a specialist in some function, but is not considered a noncommissioned officer and is not expected to direct other troops.

RC#1, (RC#4, etc.)—Recreation Center. Large compounds used by troops for off duty recreation. They often contain a PX, bowling alley, photo shop, steam bath, barbershop, athletic field, and movie theater.

ROK—Republic of Korea (South Korea). ROK's refers to troops of the Republic of Korea.

RTO—Radio Telephone Operator. An enlisted man who operates a radio or field telephone. In the infantry, the RTO carries the radio on his back.

SCOSI—Security and Counter-Intelligence Operations South of the Imjin (River). A continuous operation of using armor and artillery troops as infantrymen to man defensive positions on the south bank of the Imjin River to stop North Korean commando infiltrations.

S-1, (S-2, etc.)—Staff Officers. S-1 is the Adjutant or personnel officer for battalion or brigade, S-2 in Intelligence, S-3 is Operations and Training, and S-4 is Supply. At division level and higher the letter G designates these positions.

TOC—Tactical Operations Center. The twenty-four hour a day operational command post of a battalion, brigade, or division engaged in a tactical situation.

UI—Unidentified Individual. This was the official designation of individuals encountered in the DMZ area of which their identity was not immediately known.

WO—Warrant Officer. A grade between the enlisted ranks and the officer corps. WO's have a certain specialty and each of their assignments is for that specialty whether it be as a helicopter pilot or supply specialist.

XO—Executive Officer. The second in command of a battery or company sized unit or higher.

Z—Slang for DMZ.

CPSIA information can be obtained
at www.ICGtesting.com
Printed in the USA
FSOW01n0846210218
44861FS